This Witch For Hire

This Witch For Hire

Dead Witch Walking
The Good, the Bad, and the Undead

Kim Harrison

SFBC FANTASY

Published by arrangement with
HarperTorch
an imprint of HarperCollins Publishers
10 East 53rd Street
New York, NY 10022-5299

ISBN 978-0-7394-6380-2

Visit our website at www.sfbc.com
Visit the HarperCollins website at www.harpercollins.com

Printed in the United States of America

This Witch For Hire

Contents

DEAD WITCH WALKING

To the man who said he liked my hat.

Acknowledgments

I'd like to thank the people who suffered through me during the rewrites. You know who you are, and I salute you. But I'd especially like to thank my editor, Diana Gill, for her wonderful suggestions that opened up delightful avenues of thought, and my agent, Richard Curtis.

One

I stood in the shadows of a deserted shop front across from The Blood and Brew Pub, trying not to be obvious as I tugged my black leather pants back up where they belonged. *This is pathetic,* I thought, eyeing the rain-emptied street. I was way too good for this.

Apprehending unlicensed and black-art witches was my usual line of work, as it takes a witch to catch a witch. But the streets were quieter than usual this week. Everyone who could make it was at the West Coast for our yearly convention, leaving me with this gem of a run. A simple snag and drag. It was just the luck of the Turn that had put me here in the dark and rain.

"Who am I kidding?" I whispered, pulling the strap of my bag farther up my shoulder. I hadn't been sent to tag a witch in a month: unlicensed, white, dark, or otherwise. Bringing the mayor's son in for Wereing outside of a full moon probably hadn't been the best idea.

A sleek car turned the corner, looking black in the buzz of the mercury street lamp. This was its third time around the block. A grimace tightened my face as it approached, slowing. "Damn it," I whispered. "I need a darker door front."

"He thinks you're a hooker, Rachel," my backup snickered into my ear. "I told you the red halter was slutty."

"Anyone ever tell you that you smell like a drunk bat, Jenks?" I muttered, my lips barely moving. Backup was unsettlingly close tonight, having perched himself on my earring. Big dangling thing—the earring, not the pixy. I'd found Jenks to be a pretentious snot with a bad attitude and a temper to match. But he knew what side of the garden his nectar came from. And apparently pixies were the best they'd let me take out since the frog incident. I would have sworn fairies were too big to fit into a frog's mouth.

I eased forward to the curb as the car squished to a wet-asphalt halt. There was the whine of an automatic window as the tinted glass dropped. I leaned down, smiling my prettiest as I flashed my work ID. Mr. One Eyebrow's leer vanished and his face went ashen. The car lurched into motion with a tiny squeak of tires. "Daytripper," I said in disdain. *No,* I thought in a flash of chastisement. He was a norm, a human. Even if they were accurate, the terms daytripper, domestic, squish, off-the-rack, and my personal favorite, snack, were politically frowned upon. But if he was picking strays up off the sidewalk in the Hollows, one might call him dead.

The car never slowed as it went through a red light, and I turned at the catcalls from the hookers I had displaced about sunset. They weren't happy, standing brazenly on the corner across from me. I gave them a little wave, and the tallest flipped me off before spinning to show me her tiny, spell-enhanced rear. The hooker and her distinctly husky-looking "friend" talked loudly as they tried to hide the cigarette they were passing between each other. It didn't smell like your usual tobacco. *Not my problem, tonight,* I thought, moving back into my shadow.

I leaned against the cold stone of the building, my gaze lingering on the red taillights of the car as it braked. Brow furrowed, I glanced at myself. I was tall for a woman—about five-eight—but not nearly as leggy as the hooker in the next puddle of light over. I wasn't wearing as much makeup as she was, either. Narrow hips and a chest that was almost flat didn't exactly make me streetwalker material. Before I found the leprechaun outlets, I had shopped in the "your first bra" aisle. It's hard finding something without hearts and unicorns on it there.

My ancestors had immigrated to the good old U.S. of A. in the 1800s. Somehow through the generations, the women all managed to retain the distinct red hair and green eyes of our Irish homeland. My freckles, though, are hidden under a spell my dad bought me for my thirteenth birthday. He had the tiny amulet put into a pinky ring. I never leave home without it.

A sigh slipped from me as I tugged my bag back up onto my shoulder. The leather pants, red ankle boots, and the spaghetti strap halter weren't too far from what I usually wore on casual Fridays to tick off my boss, but put them on a street corner at night . . . "Crap," I muttered to Jenks. "I look like a hooker."

His only response was a snort. I forced myself not to react as I turned back to the bar. It was too rainy for the early crowd, and apart from my backup and the "ladies" down the way, the street was empty. I'd been standing out here nearly an hour with no sign of my mark. I might as well go in and wait. Besides, if I were inside, I might look like a solicitee rather than a solicitor.

Taking a resolute breath, I pulled a few strands of my shoulder-length curls from my topknot, took a moment to arrange it artfully to fall about my face, and finally spit out my gum. The click of my boots made a snappy counterpoint to the jangling of the handcuffs pinned to my hip as I strode across the wet street and into the bar. The steel rings looked like a tawdry prop, but they were real and very well-used. I winced. No wonder Mr. One Eyebrow had stopped. Used for *work*, thank you, and not the kind you're thinking of.

Still, I'd been sent to the Hollows in the rain to collar a leprechaun for tax evasion. How much lower, I wondered, could I sink? It must have been from tagging that Seeing Eye dog last week. How was I supposed to know it wasn't a werewolf? It matched the description I'd been given.

As I stood in the narrow foyer shaking off the damp, I ran my gaze over the typical Irish bar crap: long-stemmed pipes stuck to the walls, green-beer signs, black vinyl seats, and a tiny stage where a wannabe-star was setting up his dulcimers and bagpipes amid a tower of amps. There was a whiff of contraband Brimstone. My predatory instincts stirred. It smelled three days old, not strong enough to track. If I could nail the supplier, I'd be off my boss's hit list. He might even give me something worth my talents.

"Hey," grunted a low voice. "You Tobby's replacement?"

Brimstone dismissed, I batted my eyes and turned, coming eye-to-chest with a bright green T-shirt. My eyes traveled up a huge bear of a man. Bouncer material. The name on the shirt said CLIFF. It fit. "Who?" I purred, blotting the rain from what I generously call my cleavage with the hem of his shirt. He was completely unaffected; it was depressing.

"Tobby. State-assigned hooker? She ever gonna show up again?"

From my earring came a tiny singsong voice. "I told you so."

My smile grew forced. "I don't know," I said through my teeth. "I'm not a hooker."

He grunted again, eyeing my outfit. I pawed through my bag and handed him my work ID. Anyone watching would assume he was carding me. With readily available age-disguising spells, it was mandatory—as was the spell-check amulet he had around his neck. It glowed a faint red in response to my pinky ring. He wouldn't do a full check on me for that, which was why all the charms in my bag were currently uninvoked. Not that I'd need them tonight.

"Inderland Security," I said as he took the card. "I'm on a run to find someone, not harass your regular clientele. That's why the—uh—disguise."

"Rachel Morgan," he read aloud, his thick fingers almost enveloping the laminated card. "Inderland Security runner. You're an I.S. runner?" He looked from my card to me and back, his fat lips splitting in a grin. "What happened to your hair? Run into a blowtorch?"

My lips pressed together. The picture was three years old. It hadn't been a blowtorch, it had been a practical joke, an informal initiation into my full runner status. Real funny.

The pixy darted from my earring, setting it swinging with his momentum. "I'd watch your mouth," he said, tilting his head as he looked at my ID. "The last lunker who laughed at her picture spent the night in the emergency room with a drink umbrella jammed up his nose."

I warmed. "You know about that?" I said, snatching my card and shoving it away.

"Everybody in appropriations knows about that." The pixy laughed merrily. "And trying to tag that Were with an itch spell and losing him in the john."

"You try bringing in a Were that close to a full moon without getting bit," I said defensively. "It's not as easy as it sounds. I had to use a potion. Those things are expensive."

"And then Nairing an entire bus of people?" His dragonfly wings turned red as he laughed and his circulation increased. Dressed in black silk with a red bandanna, he looked like a miniature Peter Pan posing as an inner city gang member. Four inches of blond bothersome annoyance and quick temper.

"That wasn't my fault," I said. "The driver hit a bump." I frowned. Someone had switched my spells, too. I had been trying to tangle his feet, and ended up removing the hair from the driver and everyone in the first three rows. At least I had gotten my mark, though I wasted an entire paycheck on cabs the next three weeks, until the bus would pick me up again.

"And the frog?" Jenks darted away and back as the bouncer

flicked a finger at him. "I'm the only one who'd go out with you tonight. I'm getting hazard pay." The pixy rose several inches, in what had to be pride.

Cliff seemed unimpressed. I was appalled. "Look," I said. "All I want is to sit over there and have a drink, nice and quietlike." I nodded to the stage where the postadolescent was tangling the lines from his amps. "When does that start?"

The bouncer shrugged. "He's new. Looks like about an hour." There was a crash followed by cheers as an amp fell off the stage. "Maybe two."

"Thanks." Ignoring Jenks's chiming laughter, I wove my way through the empty tables to a bank of darker booths. I chose the one under a moose head, sinking three inches more than I should have in the flaccid cushion. Soon as I found the little perp, I was out of there. This was insulting. I had been with the I.S. for three years—seven if you counted my four years of clinicals—and here I was, doing intern work.

It was the interns that did the nitty-gritty day-to-day policing of Cincinnati and its largest suburb across the river, affectionately known as the Hollows. We picked up the supernatural stuff that the human-run FIB—short for the Federal Inderland Bureau— couldn't handle. Minor spell disturbances and rescuing familiars out of trees were in the realm of an I.S. intern. But I was a full runner, damn it. I was better than this. I *had done* better than this.

It had been I who single-handedly tracked down and apprehended the circle of dark witches who were circumventing the Cincinnati Zoo's security spells to steal the monkeys, selling them to an underground biolab. But did I get any recognition for that? No.

It had been I who realized that the loon digging up bodies in one of the churchyards was linked to the spate of deaths in the organ replacement wing in one of the human-run hospitals. Everyone assumed he was gathering materials to make illegal spells, not charming the organs into temporary health, then selling them on the black market.

And the ATM thefts that plagued the city last Christmas? It had taken me six simultaneous charms to look like a man, but I nailed the witch. She had been using a love charm/forget spell combo to rob naive humans. That had been an especially satisfying tag. I'd chased her for three streets, and there had been no time for spell casting when she turned to hit me with what could have been a lethal charm, so I was completely justified in knocking her out cold with a roundhouse kick. Even better, the FIB had been after her for three months, and tagging her took me two days. I made them look like fools, but did I get a "Good job, Rachel?" Did I even get a ride back to the I.S. tower with my swollen foot? No.

And lately I was getting even less: sorority kids using charms to steal cable, familiar theft, prank spells, and I couldn't forget my favorite—chasing trolls out from under bridges and culverts before they ate all the mortar. A sigh shifted me as I glanced over the bar. Pathetic.

Jenks dodged my apathetic attempts to swat him as he resettled himself on my earring. That they had to pay him triple to go out with me did not bode well.

A green-clad waitress bounced over, frighteningly perky for this early. "Hi!" she said, showing teeth and dimples. "My name is Dottie. I'll be your server tonight." All smiles, she set three drinks before me: a Bloody Mary, an old-fashioned, and a Shirley Temple. How sweet.

"Thanks, hon," I said with a jaded sigh. "Who they from?"

She rolled her eyes toward the bar, trying to portray bored sophistication but coming off like a high schooler at the big dance. Peering around her thin, apron-tied waist, I glanced over the three stiffs, lust in their eyes, horses in their pockets. It was an old tradition. Accepting a drink meant I accepted the invitation behind it. One more thing for Ms. Rachel to take care of. They looked like norms, but one never knew.

Sensing no more conversation forthcoming, Dottie skipped away to do barmaid things. "Check them out, Jenks," I whispered, and the pixy flitted away, his wings pale pink in his excitement. No one saw him go. Pixy surveillance at its finest.

The pub was quiet, but as there were two tenders behind the bar, an old man and a young woman, I guessed it would pick up soon. The Blood and Brew was a known hot spot where norms went to mix with Inderlanders before driving back across the river with their doors locked and the windows up tight, titillated and thinking they were hot stuff. And though a lone human sticks out among Inderlanders like a zit on a prom queen's face, an Inderlander can easily blend into humanity. It's a survival trait honed since before Pasteur. That's why the pixy. Fairies and pixies can literally sniff an Inderlander out quicker than I can say "Spit."

I halfheartedly scanned the nearly empty bar, my sour mood evaporating into a smile when I found a familiar face from the office. Ivy.

Ivy was a vamp, the star of the I.S. runner lineup. We had met several years ago during my last year of internship, paired up for a year of semi-independent runs. She had just hired on as a full runner, having taken six years of university credit instead of opting for the two years of college and four years of internship that I had. I think assigning us to each other had been someone's idea of a joke.

Working with a vampire—living or not—had scared the peas out of me until I found out she wasn't a practicing vamp and had sworn off blood. We were as unalike as two people could be, but her strengths were my weakness. I wish I could say her weaknesses were my strengths, but Ivy didn't have any weaknesses—other than the tendency to plan the joy out of everything.

We hadn't worked together for years, and despite my grudgingly given promotion, Ivy still outranked me. She knew all the right things to say to all the right people at all the right times. It helped that she belonged to the Tamwood family, a name as old as Cincinnati itself. She was its last living member, in possession of a soul and as alive as me, having been infected with the vamp virus through her then still-living mother. The virus had molded Ivy even as she grew in her mother's womb, giving Ivy a little of both worlds, the living and the dead.

At my nod, she sauntered over. The men at the bar jostled elbows, all three turning to watch her in appreciation. She flicked them a dismissing glance, and I swear I heard one sigh. "How's it going, Ivy?" I said as she eased onto the bench opposite me.

Vinyl seat squeaking, she reclined in the booth with her back against the wall, the heels of her tall boots on the long bench, and her knees showing over the edge of the table. She stood half a head over me, but where I just looked tall, she pulled off a svelte elegance. Her slightly Oriental cast gave her an enigmatic look, upholding my belief that most models had to be vamps. She dressed like a model, too: modest leather skirt and silk blouse, top-of-the-line, all-vamp construction; black, of course. Her hair was a smooth dark wave, accenting her pale skin and oval-shaped face. No matter what she did with her hair, it made her look exotic. I could spend hours with mine and it always came out red and frizzy. Mr. One Eyebrow wouldn't have stopped for her; she was too classy.

"Hey, Rachel," Ivy said. "Whatcha doing down in the Hollows?" Her voice was melodious and low, flowing with all the subtleties of gray silk. "I thought you'd be catching some skin cancer on the coast this week," she added. "Is Denon still ticked about the dog?"

I shrugged sheepishly. "Nah." Actually, the boss nearly blew a vein. I had been a step away from being promoted to office broom pusher.

"It was an honest mistake." Ivy let her head fall back in a languorous motion to expose the long length of her neck. There wasn't a scar on it. "Anyone could have made it."

Anyone but you, I thought sourly. "Yeah?" I said aloud, pushing the Bloody Mary toward her. "Well, let me know if you spot my take." I jingled the charms on my cuffs, touching the clover carved from olive wood.

Her thin fingers curved around the glass as if they were caressing it. Those same fingers could break my wrist if she put some effort into it. She'd have to wait until she was dead before she had enough strength to snap it without a thought, but she was still stronger than me. Half the red drink disappeared down her throat. "Since when is the I.S. interested in leprechauns?" she asked, eyeing the rest of the charms.

"Since the boss's last rainy day."

She shrugged, pulling her crucifix out from behind her shirt to run the metal loop through her teeth provocatively. Her canines were sharp, like a cat's, but no bigger than mine. She'd get the extended versions after she died. I forced my eyes from them, watching the metal cross instead. It was as long as my hand and made of a beautifully tooled silver. She had begun wearing it lately to irritate her mother. They weren't on the best of terms.

I fingered the tiny cross on my cuffs, thinking it must be difficult having your mother be undead. I had met only a handful of dead vampires. The really old ones kept to themselves, and the new ones tended to get staked unless they learned to keep to themselves.

Dead vamps were utterly without conscience, ruthless instinct incarnate. The only reason they followed society's rules was because it was a game to them. And dead vampires knew about rules. Their continued existence depended upon rules which, if challenged, meant death or pain, the biggest rule of course being no sun. They needed blood daily to keep sane. Anyone's would do, and taking it from the living was the only joy they found. And they were powerful, having incredible strength and endurance, and the ability to heal with an unearthly quickness. It was hard to destroy them except for the traditional beheading and staking through the heart.

In exchange for their soul, they had the chance for immortality. It came with a loss of conscience. The oldest vampires claimed that was the best part: the ability to fulfill every carnal need without guilt when someone died to give you pleasure and keep you sane one more day.

Ivy possessed both the vamp virus and a soul, caught in the middle ground until she died and became a true undead. Though not as powerful or dangerous as a dead vamp, the ability to walk under the sun and worship without pain made her envied by her dead brethren.

The metal rings of Ivy's necklace clicked rhythmically against her pearly whites, and I ignored her sensuality with a practiced restraint. I liked her better when the sun was up and she had more control over her mien of sexual predator.

My pixy returned to land on the fake flowers in their vase full of cigarette butts. "Good God," Ivy said, dropping her cross. "A pixy? Denon must be pissed."

Jenks's wings froze for an instant before returning to a blur of motion. "Go Turn yourself, Tamwood!" he said shrilly. "You think fairies are the only ones who have a nose?"

I winced as Jenks landed heavily upon my earring. "Nothing but the best for Ms. Rachel," I said dryly. Ivy laughed, and the hair on the back of my neck prickled. I missed the prestige of working with Ivy, but she still set me on edge. "I can come back if you think I'll mess up your take," I added.

"No," she said. "You're stat. I've got a pair of needles cornered in the bathroom. I caught them soliciting out-of-season game." Drink in hand, she slid to the end of the bench and stood with a sensual stretch, an almost unheard moan slipping from her. "They look too cheap to have a shift spell," she said when she finished. "But I've got my big owl outside just in case. If they try to bat their way out a broken window, they're bird chow. I'm just waiting them out." She took a sip, her brown eyes watching me over the rim of her glass. "If you make your tag early enough, maybe we can share a cab uptown?"

The soft hint of danger in her voice made me nod noncommittally as she left. Fingers nervously playing with a drooping curl of my red hair, I decided I'd see what she looked like before getting in a cab with her this late at night. Ivy might not need blood to survive, but it was obvious she still craved it, her public vow to abstain aside.

Condolences were made at the bar as only two drinks remained at my elbow. Jenks was still fussing in a high-pitched tantrum. "Relax, Jenks," I said, trying to keep him from ripping my earring out. "I like having a pixy backup. Fairies don't do squat unless their union clears it."

"You've noticed?" he all but snarled, tickling my ear with the wind from his fitfully moving wings. "Just because of some maggoty-jack, pre-Turn poem written by a drunk lard-butt, they think they're better than us. Publicity, Rachel. That's all it is. Good old-fashioned greasy palms. Did you know fairies get paid more than pixies for the same work?"

"Jenks?" I interrupted, fluffing my hair from my shoulder. "What's going on at the bar?"

"And that picture!" he continued, my earring quivering. "You've seen it? The one of that human brat crashing the frat party? Those fairies were so drunk, they didn't even know they were dancing with a human. And they're still getting the royalties."

"Hose yourself off, Jenks," I said tightly. "What's up at the bar?"

There was a tiny huff, and my earring twisted. "Contestant number one is a personal athletic trainer," he grumbled. "Contestant number two fixes air conditioners, and contestant number three is a newspaper reporter. Day-trippers. All of them."

"What about the guy on stage?" I whispered, making sure I didn't look that way. "The I.S. gave me only a sketch description, since our take is probably under a disguise spell."

"*Our* take?" Jenks said. The wind from his wings ceased, and his voice lost its anger.

I fastened on that. Maybe all he needed was to be included. "Why not check him out?" I asked instead of demanding. "He doesn't seem to know which end of his bagpipes to blow into."

Jenks made a short bark of laughter and buzzed off in a better mood. Fraternization between runner and backup was discouraged, but what the heck. Jenks felt better, and perhaps my ear would still be in one piece when the sun came up.

The bar jocks jostled elbows as I ran an index finger around the rim of the old-fashioned to make it sing while I waited. I was bored, and a little flirtation was good for the soul.

A group came in, their loud chatter telling me the rain had

picked up. They clustered at the far end of the bar, all talking at once, their arms stretching for their drinks as they demanded attention. I looked them over, a faint tightening of my gut telling me that at least one in their party was a dead vamp. It was hard to tell whom under the goth paraphernalia.

My guess was the quiet young man in the back. He was the most normal looking in the tattooed, body-pierced group, wearing jeans and a button shirt instead of rain-spotted leather. He must have been doing well to have such a bevy of humans with him, their necks scarred and their bodies thin and anemic. But they seemed happy enough, content in their close-knit, almost family-like group. They were being especially nice to a pretty blonde, supporting her and working together to coax her to eat some peanuts. She looked tired as she smiled. Must have been his breakfast.

As if pulled by my thoughts, the attractive man turned. He shifted his sunglasses down, and my face went slack as he met my eyes over them. I took a breath, seeing from across the room the rain on his eyelashes. A sudden need to brush them free filled me. I could almost feel the dampness of the rain on my fingers, how soft it would feel. His lips moved as he whispered, and it seemed I could hear but not understand his words swirling behind me to push me forward.

Heart pounding, I gave him a knowing look and shook my head. A faint, charming smile tugged the corners of his mouth, and he looked away.

My held breath slipped from me as I forced my eyes away. Yeah. He was a dead vamp. A living vamp couldn't have bespelled me even that little bit. If he had been really trying, I wouldn't have had a chance. But that's what the laws were for, right? Dead vamps were only supposed to take willing initiates, and only after release papers were signed, but who was to say if the papers were signed before or after? Witches, Weres, and other Inderlanders were immune to turning vampire. Small comfort if the vamp lost control and you died from having your throat torn out. 'Course, there were laws against that, too.

Still uneasy, I looked up to find the musician making a beeline for me, his eyes alight with a fevered itch. Stupid pixy. He had gotten himself caught.

"Come to hear me play, beautiful?" the kid said as he stopped at my table, clearly struggling to make his voice low.

"My name is Sue, not Beautiful," I lied, staring past him toward Ivy. She was laughing at me. Swell. This was going to look just fantastic in our office newsletter.

"You sent your fairy friend to *check—me—out*," he said, half singing the words.

"He's a pixy not a fairy," I said. The guy was either a stupid norm or a smart Inderlander pretending to be a stupid norm. I was betting on the former.

He opened his fist and Jenks flew a wobbly trail to my earring. One of his wings was bent, and pixy dust sifted from him to make brief sunbeams on the table and my shoulder. My eyes closed in a strength-gathering blink. I was going to get blamed for this. I knew it.

Jenks's irate snarling filled my ear, and I frowned in thought. I didn't think any of his suggestions were anatomically possible—but at least I knew the kid was a norm.

"Come and see my big pipe in the van," the kid said. "Bet you could make it sing-g-g-g."

I looked up at him, the dead vamp's proposition making me jittery. "Go away."

"I'm gonna make it big, Suzy-Q," he boasted, taking my hostile stare as an invitation to sit. "I'm going to the coast, soon as I get enough money. Got a friend in the music biz. He knows this guy who knows this guy who cleans Janice Joplin's pool."

"Go away," I repeated, but he only leaned back and screwed his face up, singing "Sue-sue-sussudio" in a high falsetto, pounding on the table in a broken rhythm.

This was embarrassing. Surely I would be forgiven for nacking him? But no, I was a good little soldier in the fight for crimes against norms, even if no one but I thought so. Smiling, I leaned forward until my cleavage showed. That always gets their attention, even if there isn't much of it. Reaching across the table, I grabbed the short hairs on his chest and twisted. That gets their attention, too, and it's far more satisfying.

The yelp as his singing cut off was like icing, it was so sweet. "Leave," I whispered. I pushed the old-fashioned into his hand and curled his slack fingers around it. "And get rid of this for me." His eyes grew wider as I gave a little tug. My fingers reluctantly loosened, and he beat a tactful retreat, sloshing half the drink as he went.

There was a cheer from the bar. I looked to see the old bartender grinning. He touched the side of his nose, and I inclined my head. "Dumb kid," I muttered. He had no business being in the Hollows. Someone ought to sling his butt back across the river before he got hurt.

One glass remained before me, and bets were probably being made as to whether I would drink or not. "You all right, Jenks?" I asked, already guessing the answer.

"The sawed-off lunker nearly pulps me, and you ask if I'm *all right*?" he snarled. His tiny voice was hilarious, and my eyebrows rose. "Nearly cracked my ribs. Slime stink all over me. *Great God almighty*, I reek of it. And look what he did to *my clothes*. Do you know how hard it is to get stink out of silk! My wife is gonna make me sleep in the flower boxes if I come home smelling like this. You can shove the triple pay, Rache. You aren't worth it!"

Jenks never noticed when I quit listening. He hadn't said a thing about his wing, so I knew he'd be okay. I slumped into the back of the booth and stewed, dead in the water with Jenks leaking dust as he was. I was royally Turned. If I came in empty-handed, I'd get nothing but full moon disturbances and bad charm complaints until next spring. It wasn't my fault.

With Jenks unable to fly unnoticed, I knew I might as well go home. If I bought him some Maitake mushrooms, he might not tell the guy in appropriations how his wing got bent. *What the heck,* I thought. *Why not make a party of it?* Sort of a last fling before the boss nailed my broom to a tree, so to speak. I could stop at the mall for some bubble bath and a new disc of slow jazz. My career was taking a nosedive, but there was no reason I couldn't enjoy the ride.

With a perverse glow of anticipation, I took my bag and the Shirley Temple, rising to make my way to the bar. Not my style to leave things hanging. Contestant number three stood with a grin and a shake of his leg to adjust himself. God, help me. Men can be so disgusting. I was tired, ticked-off, and grossly unappreciated. Knowing he would take anything I said as playing hard to get and follow me out, I tipped the ginger pop down his front and kept walking.

I smirked at his cry of outrage, then frowned at his heavy hand on my shoulder. Turning into a crouch, I sent my leg in a stiff half spin to trip him onto the floor. He hit the wood planking with a loud thump. The bar went silent after a momentary gasp. I was sitting on him, straddling his chest, before he even realized he had gone down.

My bloodred manicure stood out sharply as I gripped his neck, flicking the bristles under his chin. His eyes were wide. Cliff stood at the door with his arms crossed, content to watch.

"Damn, Rache," Jenks said, swinging wildly from my earring. "Who taught you that?"

"My dad," I answered, then leaned until I was in his face. "So sorry," I breathed in a thick Hollows accent. "You want to play, cookie?" His eyes went frightened as he realized I was an Inderlander and not a bit of fluff out looking for a wild night of pretend. He was a cookie, all right. A little treat to be enjoyed and forgotten. I wouldn't hurt him, but he didn't know that.

"Sweet mother of Tinker Bell!" Jenks exclaimed, jerking my attention from the sniveling human. "Smell that? Clover."

My fingers loosened, and the man scrabbled out from under me. He awkwardly gained his feet, dragging his two cohorts to the shadows with a whispered muttering of face-saving insults. "One of the bartenders?" I breathed as I rose.

"It's the woman," he said, sending a wash of excitement through me.

My eyes rose, taking her in. She filled out her tight, high-contrast uniform of black and green admirably, giving the impression of bored competence as she moved confidently behind the counter. "You flaking out, Jenks?" I murmured as I tried to surreptitiously pull my leather pants out from where they had ridden up. "It can't be her."

"Right!" he snapped. "Like *you* could tell. *Ignore* the pixy. I could be home right now in front of my TV. But no-o-o-o-o. I'm stuck spending the night with some beanpole of backward feminine intuition who thinks she can do my job better than me. I'm cold, hungry, and my wing is bent nearly in two. If that main vein snaps, I'll have to regrow the entire wing. Do you have any idea how long that takes?"

I glanced over the bar, relieved to see that everyone had returned to their conversations. Ivy was gone and had probably missed the entire thing. Just as well. "Shut up, Jenks," I muttered. "Pretend you're a decoration."

I sidled to the old man. He grinned a gap-toothed smile as I leaned forward. Wrinkles creased his leathered face in appreciation as his eyes rove everywhere but my face. "Gimme something," I breathed. "Something sweet. Something that will make me feel good. Something rich and creamy and oh-so-bad for me."

"I'll be needing to see yer ID, lassie," the old man said in a thick Irish accent. "Ye dunna look old enough to be out from under yer mum's shadow."

His accent was faked, but my smile at his compliment wasn't. "Why, sure thing, hon." I dug in my bag for my driver's license, willing to play the game, since we both obviously enjoyed it. "Oops!" I giggled as the card slipped to fall behind the counter. "Silly little me!"

With the help of the bar stool, I leaned halfway across the counter to get a good peek behind it. Having my rear in the air not only distracted the menfolk admirably but afforded me an excellent look. Yes, it was degrading if you thought about it too long, but it worked. I looked up to find the old man grinning, thinking I was checking him out, but it was the woman I was interested in now. She was standing on a box.

She was nearly the right height, in the right place, and Jenks had marked her. She looked younger than I would have expected, but if you're a hundred fifty years old, you're bound to pick up a few beauty secrets. Jenks snorted in my ear, sounding like a smug mosquito. "Told you."

I settled back on the stool, and the bartender handed me my license along with a dead man's float and a spoon: a dollop of ice cream in a short glass of Bailey's. Yum. Tucking the card away, I gave him a saucy wink. I left the glass where it was, turning as if scoping out the patrons that had just come in. My pulse increased and my fingertips tingled. Time to go to work.

A quick look around to make sure no one was watching, and I tipped my glass. I gasped as it spilled, and my distress wasn't entirely faked as I lurched to catch it, trying to save at least the ice cream.

The kick of adrenaline shook me as the woman bartender met my apologetic smile with her patronizing one. The jolt was worth more to me than the check I found shoved into my desk every week. But I knew the feeling would wane as fast as it had come. My talents were being wasted. I didn't even need a spell for this one.

If this was all the I.S. would give me, I thought, *maybe I should blow off the steady pay and go out on my own.* Not many left the I.S., but there was precedence. Leon Bairn was a living legend before he went independent—then promptly got wasted by a misaligned spell. Rumor had it the I.S. had been the one to put the price on his head for breaking his thirty-year contract. But that was over a decade ago. Runners went missing all the time, taken out by prey more clever or luckier than them. Blaming it on the I.S.'s own assassin corps was just spiteful. No one left the I.S. because the money was good and the hours were easy, that's all.

Yeah, I thought, ignoring the whisper of warning that took me. Leon Bairn's death was exaggerated. Nothing was ever proven. And the only reason I still had a job was because they couldn't legally fire me. Maybe I should go out on my own. It couldn't be any worse than what I was doing now. They would be glad to see me leave. *Sure,* I thought, smiling. Rachel Morgan, private runner for hire. All rights earnestly upheld. All wrongs sincerely avenged.

I knew my smile was misty as the woman obligingly swiped her towel between my elbows to mop up the spill. My breath came in a quick sound. Left hand dropping, I snatched the cloth, tangling her in it. My right swung back, then forward with my cuffs, clicking them about her wrists. In an instant it was done. She blinked, shocked. Damn, I'm good.

The woman's eyes widened as she realized what had happened. "Blazes and condemnation!" she cried, sounding elegant with her Irish accent. Hers wasn't faked. "What the 'ell do you think you're doin'?"

The jolt flared to ash, and a sigh slipped from me as I eyed the lone scoop of ice cream that was left of my drink. "Inderland Security," I said, slapping my I.S. identification down. The rush was gone already. "You stand accused of fabricating a rainbow for the purpose of misrepresenting the income generated from said rainbow, failure to file the appropriate requisition forms for said rainbow, failure to notify Rainbow Authority of said rainbow's end—"

"It's a lie!" the woman shouted, contorting in the cuffs. Her eyes darted wildly about the bar as all attention focused on her. "All a lie! I found that pot legally."

"You retain the right to keep your mouth shut," I ad-libbed, digging out a spoonful of ice cream. It was cold in my mouth, and the hint of alcohol was a poor replacement for the waning warmth of adrenaline. "If you forego your right to keep your mouth shut, I will shut it for you."

The bartender slammed the flat of his hand on the counter. "Cliff!" he bellowed, his Irish accent gone. "Put the Help Wanted sign in the window. Then get back here and help me."

"Yeah, boss," came Cliff's distant, I-couldn't-care-less shout.

Setting my spoon aside, I reached across the bar and yanked the leprechaun over the counter and onto the floor before she got much smaller. She was shrinking as the charms on my cuffs slowly overpowered her weaker size spell. "You have a right to a lawyer," I said, tucking my ID away. "If you can't afford one, you're toast."

"You canna catch me!" the leprechaun threatened, struggling as the crowd's shouts became enthusiastic. "Rings of steel alone canna hold me. I've escaped from kings, and sultans, and nasty little children with nets!"

I tried to finger-curl my rain-damp hair as she fought and wrestled, slowly coming to grips that she was caught. The cuffs shrank with her, keeping her confined. "I'll be out of this—in— just a moment," she panted, slowing enough to look at her wrists. "Aw, for the love of St. Pete." She slumped, sending her eyes over the yellow moon, green clover, pink heart, and orange star that decorated my cuffs. "May the devil's own dog hump your leg. Who squealed about the charms?" Then she looked closer. "You caught me with four? *Four?* I didn't think the old ones still worked."

"Call me old-fashioned," I said to my glass, "but when something works, I stick with it."

Ivy walked past, her two black-cloaked vamps before her, elegant in their dark misery. One had a bruise developing under his eye; the other was limping. Ivy wasn't gentle with vamps preying on the underage. Remembering the pull from the dead vamp at the end of the bar, I understood why. A sixteen-year-old couldn't fight that. Wouldn't *want* to fight that.

"Hey, Rachel," Ivy said brightly, looking almost human now that she wasn't actively working. "I'm heading uptown. Want to split the fare?"

My thoughts went back to the I.S. as I weighed the risk of being a starving entrepreneur to a lifetime of running for shoplifters and illegal-charm sellers. It wasn't as if the I.S. would put a price on my head. No, Denon would be thrilled to tear up my contract. I couldn't afford an office in Cincinnati, but maybe in the Hollows. Ivy spent a lot of time down here. She'd know where I could find something cheap. "Yeah," I said, noting her eyes were a nice, steady brown. "I want to ask you something."

She nodded and pushed her two takes forward. The crowd pressed back, the sea of black clothing seeming to soak up the light. The dead vamp at the outskirts gave me a respectful nod, as if to say "Good tag," and with a pulse of emotion giving me a false high, I nodded back.

"Way to go, Rachel," Jenks chimed up, and I smiled. It had been a long time since I'd heard that.

"Thanks," I said, catching sight of him on my earring in the bar's mirror. Pushing my glass aside, I reached for my bag, my smile widening when the bartender gestured it was on the house. Feeling warm from more than the alcohol, I slipped from my stool and pulled the leprechaun stumbling to her feet. Thoughts of a door with my name painted on it in gold letters swirled through me. It was freedom.

"No! Wait!" the leprechaun shouted as I grabbed my bag and hauled her butt to the door. "Wishes! Three wishes. Right? You let me go, and you get three wishes."

I pushed her into the warm rain ahead of me. Ivy had a cab already, her catch stashed in the trunk so there would be more room for the rest of us. Accepting wishes from a felon was a sure way to find yourself on the wrong end of a broomstick, but only if you got caught.

"Wishes?" I said, helping the leprechaun into the backseat. "Let's talk."

Two

"What did you say?" I asked as I half turned in the front seat to see Ivy. She gestured helplessly from the back. The rhythm of bad wipers and good music fought to outdo each other in a bizarre mix of whining guitars and hiccuping plastic against glass. "Rebel Yell" screamed from the speakers. I couldn't compete. Jenks's credible imitation of Billy Idol gyrating with the Hawaiian dancer stuck to the dash didn't help. "Can I turn it down?" I asked the cabbie.

"No touch! No touch!" he cried in an odd accent. The forests of Europe, maybe? His faint musky scent put him as a Were. I reached for the volume knob, and he took his fur-backed hand from the wheel and slapped at me.

The cab swerved into the next lane. His charms, all gone bad by the look of them, slid across the dash to spill onto my lap and the floor. The chain of garlic swinging from the rearview mirror hit me square in the eye. I gagged as the stench fought with the odor of the tree-shaped cardboard, also swinging from the mirror.

"Bad girl," he accused, veering back into his lane and throwing me into him.

"If I good girl," I snarled as I slid back into my seat, "you let me turn music down?"

The driver grinned. He was missing a tooth. He would be missing another one if I had my way. "Yah," he said. "They talking now." The music fell to nothing, replaced by a fast-talking announcer shouting louder than the music had been.

"Good Lord," I muttered, turning the radio down. My lips curled at the smear of grease on the knob. I stared at my fingers, then wiped them off on the amulets still in my lap. They weren't good for anything else. The salt from the driver's too-frequent handlings had ruined them. Giving him a pained look, I dumped the charms into the chipped cup holder.

I turned to Ivy, sprawled in the back. One hand was up to keep her owl from falling out of the rear window as we bounced along, the other was propped behind her neck. Passing cars and the occasional functioning streetlight briefly illuminated her black silhouette. Dark and unblinking, her eyes met mine, then returned to the window and the night. My skin prickled at the air of ancient tragedy about her. She wasn't pulling an aura—she was just Ivy—but it gave me the willies. Didn't the woman ever smile?

My take had pressed herself into the other corner, as far from Ivy as she could get. The leprechaun's green boots just reached the end of the seat, and she looked like one of those dolls they sell on TV. *Three easy payments of $49.95 for this highly detailed rendition of Becky the Barmaid. Similar dolls have tripled, even quadrupled, in value!* This doll, though, had a sneaky glint in her eye. I gave her a sly nod, and Ivy's gaze flicked suspiciously to mine.

The owl gave a pained hoot as we hit a nasty bump, opening its wings to keep its balance. But it was the last. We had crossed the river and were back in Ohio. The ride now was smooth as glass, and the cabbie's pace slowed as he seemed to remember what traffic signs were for.

Ivy removed her hand from her owl and ran her fingers through her long hair. "I said, 'You never took me up on a ride before.' What's up?"

"Oh, yeah." I draped an arm over the seat. "Do you know where I can rent a cheap flat? In the Hollows, maybe?"

Ivy faced me squarely, the perfect oval of her face looking pale in the streetlights. There were lights now at every corner, making it nearly bright as day. Paranoid norms. Not that I blamed them. "You moving into the Hollows?" she asked, her expression quizzical.

I couldn't help my smile at that. "No. I'm quitting the I.S."

That got her attention. I could tell by the way she blinked. Jenks stopped trying to dance with the tiny figure on the dash and stared at me. "You can't break your I.S. contract," Ivy said. She glanced at the leprechaun, who beamed at her. "You're not thinking of . . ."

"Me? Break the law?" I said lightly. "I'm too good to have to break the law. I can't help it if she's the wrong leprechaun, though," I added, not feeling a bit guilty. The I.S. had made it abundantly clear they didn't want my services anymore. What was I supposed to do? Roll on my back with my belly in the air and lick someone's, er, muzzle?

"Paperwork," the cabbie interjected, his accent abruptly as smooth as the road as he switched to the voice and manners needed to get and keep fares on this side of the river. "Lose the paperwork. Happens all the time. I think I've Rynn Cormel's confession in here somewhere from when my father shuttled lawyers from quarantine to the courts during the Turn."

"Yeah." I gave him a nod and smile. "Wrong name on the wrong paper. Q.E.D."

Ivy's eyes were unblinking. "Leon Bairn didn't just spontaneously explode, Rachel."

My breath puffed out. I wouldn't believe the stories. They were just that, stories to keep the I.S.'s flock of runners from wanting to break their contracts once they learned all the I.S. had to teach them. "That was over ten years ago," I said. "And the I.S. had nothing to do with it. They aren't going to kill me for breaking my contract; they want me to leave." I frowned. "Besides, being turned inside out would be more fun than what I'm doing now."

Ivy leaned forward, and I refused to back away. "They say it took three days to find enough of him to fit in a shoe box," she said. "Scraped the last off the ceiling of his porch."

"What am I supposed to do?" I said, pulling my arm back. "I haven't had a decent run in months. Look at this." I gestured to my take. "A tax-evading leprechaun. It's an insult."

The little woman stiffened. "Well, excu-u-u-use me."

Jenks abandoned his new girlfriend to sit on the back rim of the cabbie's hat. "Yeah," he said. "Rachel's gonna be pushing a broom if I have to take time off for workman's comp."

He fitfully moved his damaged wing, and I gave him a pained smile. "Maitake?" I said.

"Quarter pound," he countered, and I mentally upped it to a half. He was okay, for a pixy.

Ivy frowned, fingering her crucifix chain. "There's a reason no one breaks their contract. The last person to try was sucked through a turbine."

Jaw clenched, I turned to look out the front window. I remembered. It was almost a year ago. It would have killed him if he hadn't been dead already. The vamp was due back in the office any day now. "I'm not asking for your permission," I said. "I'm asking you if you know anyone with a cheap place to rent." Ivy was silent, and I shifted to see her. "I have a little something tucked away. I can put up a shingle, help people that need it—"

"Oh, for the love of blood," Ivy interrupted. "Leaving to open up a charm shop, maybe. But your own agency?" She shook her head, her black hair swinging. "I'm not your mother, but if you do this, you're dead. Jenks? Tell her she's dead."

Jenks nodded solemnly, and I flopped around to stare out the window. I felt stupid for having asked for her help. The cabbie was nodding. "Dead," he said. "Dead, dead, dead."

This was better and better. Between Jenks and the cab driver, the entire city would know I quit before I gave notice. "Never mind. I don't want to talk about it anymore," I muttered.

Ivy draped an arm over the seat. "Did it occur to you someone may be setting you up? Everyone knows leprechauns try to buy their way out. If you get caught, your butt is buttered."

"Yeah," I said. "I thought of that." I hadn't, but I wasn't going to tell her. "My first wish will be to not get caught."

"Always is," the leprechaun said slyly. "That your first wish?" In a flash of anger, I nodded, and the leprechaun grinned, dimples showing. She was halfway home.

"Look," I said to Ivy. "I don't need your help. Thanks for nothing." I shuffled in my bag for my wallet. "Drop me here," I said to the cabbie. "I want a coffee. Jenks? Ivy will get you back to the I.S. Can you do that for me, Ivy? For old times' sake?"

"Rachel," she protested, "you're not listening to me."

The cabbie carefully signaled, then pulled over. "Watch your back, Hot Stuff."

I got out, yanked open the rear door, and grabbed my leprechaun by her uniform. My cuffs had completely masked her size spell. She was about the size of a chunky two-year-old. "Here," I said, tossing a twenty onto the seat. "That should cover my share."

"It's still raining!" the leprechaun wailed.

"Shut up." Drops pattered against me, ruining my topknot and sticking the trailing strands to my neck. I slammed the door as Ivy leaned to say something. I had nothing left to lose. My life was a pile of magic manure, and I couldn't even make compost out of it.

"But I'm getting wet," the leprechaun complained.

"You want back in the car?" I asked. My voice was calm, but inside I was seething. "We can forget the whole thing if you want.

I'm sure Ivy will take care of your paperwork. Two jobs in one night. She'll get a bonus."

"No," came her meek, tiny voice.

Ticked, I looked across the street to the Starbucks catering to uptown snits who needed sixty different ways to brew a bean in order to not be happy with any of them. Being on this side of the river, the coffeehouse would likely be empty at this hour. It was the perfect place to sulk and regroup. I half dragged the leprechaun to the door, trying to guess the cost of a cup of coffee by the number of pre-Turn doodads in the front window.

"Rachel, wait." Ivy had rolled down her window, and I could hear the cabbie's music cranked again. Sting's "A Thousand Years." I could almost get back in the car.

I yanked the door of the café open, sneering at the chimes' merry jingle. "Coffee. Black. And a booster seat," I shouted to the kid behind the counter as I strode to the darkest corner, my leprechaun in tow. Tear it all. The kid was a vision of upright character in his red-and-white-striped apron and perfect hair. Probably a university student. I could have gone to the university instead of the community college. At least for a semester or two. I'd been accepted and everything.

The booth, though, was cushy and soft. There was a real tablecloth. And my feet didn't stick to the floor, a definite plus. The kid was eyeing me with a superior look, so I pulled off my boots and sat cross-legged to harass him. I was still dressed like a hooker. I think he was trying to decide whether he should call the I.S. or its human counterpart, the FIB. That'd be a laugh.

My ticket out of the I.S. stood on the seat across from me and fidgeted. "Can I have a latte?" she whined.

"No."

The door chimed, and I looked to see Ivy stride in with her owl on her arm, its talons pinching the thick armband she had. Jenks was perched on her shoulder, as far from the owl as he could get. I stiffened, turning to the picture above the table of babies dressed up as a fruit salad. I think it was supposed to be cute, but it only made me hungry.

"Rachel. I have to talk to you."

This was apparently too much for Junior. "Excuse me, ma'am," he said in his perfect voice. "No pets allowed. The owl must remain outside."

Ma'am? I thought, trying to keep the hysterical laughter from bubbling up.

He went pale as Ivy glanced at him. Staggering, he almost fell as he sightlessly backed up. She was pulling an aura on him. Not good.

Ivy turned her gaze to me. My air whooshed out as I hit the back of the booth. Black, predator eyes nailed me to the vinyl seat. Raw hunger clutched at my stomach. My fingers convulsed.

Her bound tension was intoxicating. I couldn't look away. It was nothing like the gentle question the dead vamp had poised to me in The Blood and Brew. This was anger, domination. Thank God she wasn't angry with me, but at Junior behind the counter.

Sure enough, as soon as she saw the look on my face, the anger in her eyes flickered and went out. Her pupils contracted, setting her eyes back to their usual brown. In a clock-tick the shroud of power had slipped from her, easing back into the depths of hell that it came from. It had to be hell. Such raw domination couldn't come from an enchantment. My anger flowed back. If I was angry, I couldn't be afraid, right?

It had been years since Ivy pulled an aura on me. The last time, we had been arguing over how to tag a low-blood vamp under suspicion of enticing underage girls with some asinine, role-playing card game. I had dropped her with a sleep charm, then painted the word "idiot" on her fingernails in red nail polish before tying her in a chair and waking her up. She had been the model friend since then, if a bit cool at times. I think she appreciated that I hadn't told anyone.

Junior cleared his throat. "You—ah—can't stay unless you order something, ma'am?" he offered weakly.

Gutsy, I thought. *Must be an Inderlander.*

"Orange juice," Ivy said loudly, standing before me. "No pulp."

Surprise made me look up. "Orange juice?" Then I frowned. "Look," I said, unclenching my hands and roughly pulling my bag of charms onto my lap. "I don't care if Leon Bairn did end up as a film on the sidewalk. I'm quitting. And nothing you say is going to change my mind."

Ivy shifted from foot to foot. It was her disquiet that cooled the last of my anger. Ivy was worried? I'd never seen that.

"I want to go with you," she finally said.

For a moment, I could only stare. "What?" I finally managed.

She sat down across from me with an affected air of nonchalance, putting her owl to watch the leprechaun. The tearing sound as she undid the fasteners of her armband sounded loud, and she set it on the bench beside her. Jenks half hopped to the table, his eyes wide and his mouth shut for a change. Junior showed up with the booster chair and our drinks. We silently waited as he placed everything with shaking hands and went to hide in the back room.

My mug was chipped and only half full. I toyed with the idea of coming back to stick a charm under the table that would sour any cream that got within four feet of it, but decided I had more important things to contend with. Like why Ivy was going to flush her illustrious career down the proverbial toilet.

"Why?" I asked, floored. "The boss loves you. You get to pick your assignments. You got a paid vacation last year."

Ivy was studying the picture, avoiding me. "So?"

"It was for four weeks! You went to Alaska for the midnight sun!"

Her thin black eyebrows bunched, and she reached to arrange her owl's feathers. "Half the rent, half the utilities, half of every-thing is my responsibility, half is yours. I bring in and do my busi-ness, you bring in and handle yours. If need be, we work together. Like before."

I settled back, my huff not as obvious as I wanted it to be, since there was only the cushy upholstery to fall into. "Why?" I asked again.

Her fingers dropped from her owl. "I'm very good at what I do," she said, not answering me. A hint of vulnerability had crept into her voice. "I won't drag you down, Rachel. No vamp will dare move against me. I can extend that to you. I'll keep the vamp assassins off of you until you come up with the money to pay off your contract. With my connections and your spells, we can stay alive long enough to get the I.S. to drop the price on our heads. But I want a wish."

"There's no price on our heads," I said quickly.

"Rachel . . ." she cajoled. Her brown eyes were soft in worry, alarming me. "Rachel, there will be." She leaned forward until I fought not to retreat. I took a shallow breath to look for the smell of blood on her, smelling only the tang of juice. She was wrong. The I.S. wouldn't put a price on my head. They wanted me to leave. She was the one who should be worried.

"Me, too," Jenks said suddenly. He vaulted to the rim of my mug. Iridescent dust sifted from his bent wing to make an oily film on my coffee. "I want in. I want a wish. I'll ditch the I.S. and be both your backups. You're gonna need one. Rache, you get the four hours before midnight, Ivy the four after, or whatever schedule you want. I get every fourth day off, seven paid holidays, and a wish. You let me and my family live in the office, real quietlike in the walls. Pay me what I'm making now, biweekly."

Ivy nodded and took a sip of her juice. "Sounds good to me. What do you think?"

My jaw dropped. I couldn't believe what I was hearing. "I can't give you my wishes."

The leprechaun bobbed her head. "Yes, you can."

"No," I said impatiently. "I mean, I need them." A pang of worry had settled into my gut at the thought that maybe Ivy was right. "I already used one to not get caught letting her go," I said. "I have to wish to get out of my contract, for starters."

"Uh," the leprechaun stammered. "I can't do anything about that if it's in writing."

Jenks gave a snort of derision. "Not that good, eh?"

"Shut your mouth—bug!" she snapped, color showing on her cheeks.

"Shut your own, moss wipe!" he snarled back.

This can't be happening, I thought. All I wanted was out, not to lead a revolt. "You're not serious," I said. "Ivy, tell me this is your twisted sense of humor finally showing itself."

She met my gaze squarely. I never could tell what was going on behind a vamp's eyes. "For the first time in my career," she said, "I'm going back empty-handed. I let my take go." She waved a hand in the air. "Opened the trunk and let them run. I broke regulations." A closed-lipped smile flickered over her and was gone. "Is that serious enough for you?"

"Go find your own leprechaun," I said, catching myself as I reached for my cup. Jenks was still sitting on the handle.

She laughed. It was cold, and this time I did shiver. "I pick my runs," she said. "What do you think would happen if I went after a leprechaun, muffed it, then tried to leave the I.S.?"

Across from me, the leprechaun sighed. "No amount of wishing could make that look good," she piped up. "It's going to be hard enough making this look like a coincidence."

"And you, Jenks?" I said, my voice cracking.

Jenks shrugged. "I want a wish. It can give me something the I.S. can't. I want sterility so my wife won't leave me." He flew a ragged path to the leprechaun. "Or is that too hard for you, greenie weenie?" he mocked, standing with his feet spread wide and his hands on his hips.

"Bug," she muttered, my charms jingling as she threatened to squish him. Jenks's wings went red in anger, and I wondered if the dust sifting from him could catch fire.

"Sterility?" I questioned, struggling to keep to the topic at hand.

He flipped the leprechaun off and strutted across the table to me. "Yeah. You know how many brats I've got?"

Even Ivy looked surprised. "You'd risk your life over that?" she asked.

Jenks made a tinkling laugh. "Who said I'm risking my life? The I.S. couldn't care less if I leave. Pixies don't sign contracts. They go through us too fast. I'm a free agent. I always have been." He grinned, looking far too sly for so small a person. "I always will be. I figure my life span will be marginally longer with only you two lunkers to watch out for."

I turned to Ivy. "I know you signed a contract. They love you. If anyone should be worried about a death threat, it's you, not me. Why would you risk that for—for—" I hesitated. "For nothing? What wish could be worth that?"

Ivy's face went still. A hint of black shadow drifted over her. "I don't have to tell you."

"I'm not stupid," I said, trying to hide my disquiet. "How do I know you aren't going to start practicing again?"

Clearly insulted, Ivy stared at me until I dropped my gaze, chilled to the bone. *This,* I thought, *is definitely not a good idea.* "I'm not a practicing vamp," she finally said. "Not anymore. Not ever again."

I forced my hand down, realizing I was playing with my damp hair. Her words were only slightly reassuring. Her glass was half empty, and I only remembered her taking the one sip.

"Partners?" Ivy said, extending her hand across the table.

Partners with Ivy? With Jenks? Ivy was the best runner the I.S. had. It was more than a little flattering that she wanted to work with me on a permanent basis, if also a bit worrisome. But it wasn't as if I had to live with her. Slowly I stretched my hand to meet hers. My perfectly shaped red nails looked garish next to her unpolished ones. All my wishes—gone. But I would've probably wasted them anyway. "Partners," I said, shivering at the coldness of Ivy's hand as I took it.

"All right!" Jenks crowed, flitting to land on top of our hand-shake. The dust sifting from him seemed to warm Ivy's touch. "Partners!"

Three

    "Dear God," I moaned under my breath. "Don't let me be sick. Not here." I shut my eyes in a long blink, hoping the light wouldn't hurt so much when I opened them. I was in my cubicle, twenty-fifth floor of the I.S. tower. The afternoon sun slanted in, but it would never reach me, my desk being toward the middle of the maze. Someone had brought in doughnuts, and the smell of the frosting made my stomach roil. All I wanted was to go back home and sleep.

Tugging open my top drawer, I fumbled for a pain amulet, groaning when I found I'd used them all. My forehead hit the edge of the metal desk, and I stared past my frizzy length of hair to my ankle boots peeping past the hem of my jeans. I had worn something conservative in deference to my quitting: a tuck-in red linen shirt and pants. No more tight leather for a while.

Last night had been a mistake. It had taken far too many drinks for me to get stupid enough to officially give my remaining wishes to Ivy and Jenks. I had really been counting on the last two. Anyone who knows anything about wishes knows you can't wish for more. The same goes for wishing for wealth. Money doesn't just appear. It has to come from somewhere, and unless you wish not to get caught, they always get you for theft.

Wishes are tricky things, which was why most Inderlanders had lobbied to get a minimum of three-per-go. In hindsight, I hadn't done too badly. Having wished to not get caught letting the leprechaun go would at least allow me to leave the I.S. with a clear record. If Ivy was right and they were going to nack me for breaking my contract, they would have to make it look like an accident.

But why would they bother? Death threats were expensive, and they wanted me gone.

Ivy had gotten a marker to call her wish in later. It looked like an old coin with a hole in it, and she had laced it on a purple cord and hung it about her neck. Jenks, though, spent his wish right in the bar, buzzing off to give the news to his wife. I should have left when Jenks had, but Ivy didn't seem to want to leave. It had been a long time since I'd had a girls' night out, and I thought I might find the courage at the bottom of a glass to tell the boss I was leaving. I hadn't.

Five seconds into my rehearsed speech, Denon flipped open a manila envelope, pulled out my contract, and tore it up, telling me to be out of the building in half an hour. My badge and I.S.-issue cuffs were in his desk; the charms that had decorated them were in my pocket.

My seven years with the I.S. had left me with an accumulated clutter of knickknacks and outdated memos. Fingers trembling, I reached for a cheap, thick-walled vase that hadn't seen a flower for months. It went into the trash, just like the cretin who had given it to me. My dissolution bowl went into the box at my feet. The salt-encrusted blue ceramic grated harshly on the cardboard. It had gone dry last week, and the rime of salt left from evaporation was dusty.

A wooden dowel of redwood clattered in next to it. It was too thick to make a wand out of, but I wasn't good enough to make a wand anyway. I had bought the dowel to make a set of lie-detecting amulets and never got around to it. It was easier to buy them. Stretching, I grabbed my phone list of past contacts. A quick look to be sure no one was watching, and I shoved it out of sight next to my dissolution bowl, sliding my disc player and headphones to cover it.

I had a few reference books to go back to Joyce across the aisle, but the container of salt propping them up had been my dad's. I set it in the box, wondering what Dad would think of me leaving. "He would be pleased as punch," I whispered, gritting my teeth against my hangover.

I glanced up, sending my gaze over the ugly yellow partitions. My eyes narrowed as my coworkers looked the other way. They were standing in huddled groups as they gossiped, pretending to be busy. Their hushed whispers grated on me. Taking a slow breath, I reached for my black-and-white picture of Watson, Crick, and the woman behind it all, Rosalind Franklin. They were standing before their model of DNA, and Rosalind's smile had the same hidden humor of Mona Lisa. One might think she knew what was going to happen. I wondered if she had been an Inderlander. Lots of people did. I kept the picture to remind myself how the world turns on details others miss.

It had been almost forty years since a quarter of humanity died from a mutated virus, the T4 Angel. And despite the frequent TV evangelists' claim otherwise, it wasn't our fault. It started and ended with good old-fashioned human paranoia.

Back in the fifties, Watson, Crick, and Franklin had put their heads together and solved the DNA riddle in six months. Things might have stopped there, but the then-Soviets grabbed the technology. Spurred by a fear of war, money flowed into the developing science. By the early sixties we had bacteria-produced insulin. A wealth of bioengineered drugs followed, flooding the market with offshoots of the U.S.'s darker search for bioengineered weapons. We never made it to the moon, turning science inward instead of outward to kill ourselves.

And then, toward the end of the decade, someone made a mistake. The debate as to whether it was the U.S. or the Soviets is moot. Somewhere up in the cold Arctic labs, a lethal chain of DNA escaped. It left a modest trail of death to Rio that was identified and dealt with, the majority of the public unaware and ignorant. But even as the scientists wrote their conclusionary notes in their lab books and shelved them, the virus mutated.

It attached itself to a bioengineered tomato through a weak spot in its modified DNA that the researchers thought too minuscule to worry about, the tomato was officially known as the T4 Angel tomato—its lab identification—and from there came the virus's name, Angel.

Unaware that the virus was using the Angel tomato as an intermediate host. The airlines transported it. Sixteen hours later it was too late. The third world countries were decimated in a frightening three weeks, and the U.S. shut down in four. Borders were militarized, and a governmental policy of "Sorry, we can't help you" was instituted. The U.S. suffered and people died, but compared to the charnel pit the rest of the world became, it was a cakewalk.

But the largest reason civilization remained intact was that most Inderland species were resistant to the Angel virus. Witches, the undead, and the smaller species like trolls, pixies, and fairies were completely unaffected. Weres, living vamps, and leprechauns got the flu. The elves, though, died out completely. It was believed their practice of hybridizing with humans to bolster their numbers backfired, making them susceptible to the Angel virus.

When the dust settled and the Angel virus was eradicated, the combined numbers of our various species had neared that of humanity. It was a chance we quickly seized. The Turn, as it came to be called, began at noon with a single pixy. It ended at midnight with humanity huddling under the table, trying to come to grips with the fact that they'd been living beside witches, vampires, and Weres since before the pyramids.

Humanity's first gut reaction to wipe us off the face of the earth petered out pretty fast when it was shoved under their noses that we had kept the structure of civilization up and running while the world fell apart. If not for us, the death rate would have been far higher.

Even so, the first years after the Turn were a madhouse. Afraid to strike out at us, humanity outlawed medical research as the demon behind their woes. Biolabs were leveled, and the bioengineers who escaped the plague stood trial and died in little more than legalized murder. There was a second, subtler wave of death when the sources of the new medicines were inadvertently destroyed along with the biotechnology.

It was only a matter of time before humanity insisted on a purely human institution to monitor Inderlander activities. The Federal Inderland Bureau arose, dissolving and replacing local law enforcement throughout the U.S. The out-of-work Inderlander police and federal agents formed their own police force, the I.S. Rivalry between the two remains high even today, serving to keep a tight lid on the more aggressive Inderlanders.

Four floors of Cincinnati's main FIB building are devoted to finding the remaining illegal biolabs where, for a price, one can still get clean insulin and something to stave off leukemia. The human-run FIB is as obsessed with finding banned technology as the I.S. is with getting the mind-altering drug Brimstone off the streets.

And it all started when Rosalind Franklin noticed her pencil had been moved, and someone was where they ought not be, I thought, rubbing my fingertips into my aching head. Small clues. Little hints. That's what makes the world turn. That's what made me such a good runner. Smiling back at Rosalind, I wiped the fingerprints off the frame and put it in my keep box.

There was a burst of nervous laughter behind me, and I yanked open the next drawer, shuffling through the dirty self-stick notes and paper clips. My brush was right where I always left it, and a knot of worry loosened as I tossed it into the box. Hair could be used to make spells target specific. If Denon was going to slap a death threat on me, he would have taken it.

My fingers found the heavy smoothness of my dad's pocket watch. Nothing else was mine, and I slammed the drawer shut, stiffening as my head seemed to nearly explode. The watch's hands were frozen at seven to midnight. He used to tease me that it had stopped the night I was conceived. Slouching in my chair, I wedged it into my front pocket. I could almost see him standing in the doorframe of the kitchen, looking from his watch to the clock over the sink, a smile curving over his long face as he pondered where the missing moments had gone.

I set Mr. Fish—the Beta-in-bowl I had gotten at last year's office Christmas party—into my dissolution basin, trusting chance would keep both the water and the fish from sloshing out. I tossed the canister of fish flakes after him. A muffled thump from the far end of the room pulled my attention beyond the partitions and to Denon's closed door.

"You won't get three feet out that door, Tamwood," came his muffled shout, silencing the buzz of conversations. Apparently, Ivy had just resigned. "I've got a contract. You work for me, not the other way around! You leave and—" There was a clatter behind the closed door. "Holy shit . . ." he continued softly. "How much is that?"

"Enough to pay off my contract," Ivy said, her voice cold. "Enough for you and the stiffs in the basement. Do we have an understanding?"

"Yeah," he said in what sounded like greedy awe. "Yeah. You're fired."

My head felt as if it was stuffed with tissue, and I rested it in my cupped hands. Ivy had money? Why hadn't she said anything last night?

"Go Turn yourself, Denon," Ivy said, clear in the absolute hush. "I quit. You didn't fire me. You may have my money, but you can't buy into high-blood. You're second-rate, and no amount of money can change that. If I have to live in the gutters off rats, I'll still be better than you, and it's killing you I won't have to take your orders anymore."

"Don't think this makes you safe," the boss raved. I could almost see that vein popping on his neck. "Accidents happen around her. Get too close, and you might wake up dead."

Denon's door swung open and Ivy stormed out, slamming his door so hard the lights flickered. Her face was tight, and I don't think she even saw me as she whipped past my cubicle. Somewhere between having left me and now, she had donned a calf-length silk duster. I was secure enough in my own gender preference to admit she made it look very good. The hem billowed as she crossed the floor with murderous strides. Spots of anger showed on her pale face. Tension flowed from her, almost visible it was so strong.

She wasn't going vampy; she was just mad as all get-out. Even so, she left a cold wake behind her that the sunlight streaming in couldn't touch. An empty canvas bag hung over her shoulder, and her wish was still about her neck. *Smart girl,* I thought. *Save it for a rainy day.* Ivy took the stairs, and I closed my eyes in misery as the metal fire door slammed into the wall.

Jenks zipped into my cubicle, buzzing about my head like a deranged moth as he showed off the patch job on his wing. "Hi, Rache," he said, obnoxiously cheerful. "What's cooking?"

"Not so loud," I whispered. I would have given anything for a cup of coffee but wasn't sure it was worth the twenty steps to the coffeepot. Jenks was dressed in his civvies, the colors loud and clashing. Purple doesn't go well with yellow. It never has; it never will. God help me, his wing tape was purple, too. "Don't you get hung over?" I breathed.

He grinned, settling himself on my pencil cup. "Nope. Pixy metabolisms are too high. The alcohol turns to sugar too fast. Ain't that fine!"

"Swell." I carefully wrapped a picture of Mom and me up in a wad of tissue and set it next to Rosalind. I briefly entertained the idea of telling my mom I didn't have a job, deciding not to for obvious reasons. I'd wait until I found a new one. "Is Ivy okay?" I asked.

"Yeah. She'll be all right." Jenks flitted to the top of my pot of laurel. "She's just ticked it took everything she had to buy her way out of her contract and cover her butt."

I nodded, glad they wanted me gone. Things would be a lot easier if neither of us had a price on our head. "Did you know she had money?"

Jenks dusted off a leaf and sat down. He adopted a superior look, which is hard to manage when you're only four inches tall and dressed like a rabid butterfly. "Well, duh . . . She's the last living blood-member of her house. I'd give her some space for a few days. She's as mad as a wet wasp. Lost her house in the country, the land, stocks, everything. All that's left is the city manor on the river, and her mother has that."

I eased back into my chair, unwrapped my last piece of cinnamon gum, and stuck it in my mouth. There was a clatter as Jenks landed in my cardboard box and began poking about. "Oh, yeah," he muttered. "Ivy said she has a spot rented already. I've got the address."

"Get out of my stuff." I flicked a finger at him, and he flew back to the laurel, standing atop the highest branch to watch everyone gossip. My temple pounded as I bent to clean out my bottom drawer. *Why had Ivy given Denon everything she had? Why not use her wish?*

"Heads up," Jenks said, slithering down the plant to hide in the leaves. "Here he comes."

I straightened to find Denon halfway to my desk. Francis, the bootlicking, butt-kissing office snitch, pulled away from a cluster of people, following. My ex-boss's eyes fastened on me over the walls of my cubicle. Choking, I accidentally swallowed my gum.

Put simply, the boss looked like a pro wrestler with a doctorate in suave: big man, hard muscles, perfect mahogany skin. I think he was a boulder in a previous life. Like Ivy, Denon was a living vamp. Unlike Ivy, he had been born human and turned. It made him low-blood, a distant second-class in the vamp world.

Even so, Denon was a force to reckon with, having worked hard to overcome his ignoble start. His overabundance of muscles were more than just pretty; they kept him alive while with his stronger, adopted kin. He possessed that ageless look of someone who fed regularly on a true undead. Only the undead could turn humans into a vampire, and by his healthy appearance, Denon was a clearly a favorite. Half the floor wanted to be his sex toy. The other half he scared the crap out of. I was proud to be a card-carrying member of the latter.

My hands shook as I took up my coffee cup from the day before and pretended to take a sip. His arms swung like pistons as he moved, his yellow polo shirt contrasting with his black pants. They were neatly creased, showing off his muscular legs and trim waist. People were getting out of his way. A few left the floor. God help me if I'd muffed my only wish and was going to get caught.

There was a creak of plastic as he leaned against the top of my four-foot walls. I didn't look, concentrating instead upon the holes my thumbtacks had made in the burlap-textured partitions. The skin on my arms tingled as if Denon were touching me. His presence seemed to swirl and eddy around me, backwashing against the partitions of my cubicle and rising until it seemed he was behind me, too. My pulse quickened, and I focused on Francis.

The snot had settled himself on Joyce's desk and was unfastening the button on his blue polyester jacket. He was grinning to show his perfect, clearly capped teeth. As I watched, he pushed the sleeves of his jacket back up to show his skinny arms. His triangular face was framed by ear-length hair, which he was constantly flipping out of his eyes. He thought it made him look boyishly charming. I thought it made him look like he had just woken up.

Though it was only three in the afternoon, a thick stubble shadowed his face. The collar of his Hawaiian shirt was intentionally flipped up around his neck. The joke around the office was he was trying to look like Sonny Crockett, but his narrow eyes squinted and his nose was too long and thin to pull it off. Pathetic.

"I know what's going on, Morgan," Denon said, jerking my attention to him. He had that throaty low voice only black men and vampires were allowed to have. It's a rule somewhere. Low and sweet. Coaxing. The promise in it pulled my skin tight, and fear washed through me.

"Beg pardon?" I said, pleased my voice didn't crack. Emboldened, I met his eyes. My breath came quick, and I tensed. He was trying to pull an aura at three in the afternoon. *Damn.*

Denon leaned over the partition to rest his arms on the top. His biceps bunched, making the veins swell. The hair on the back of my neck prickled, and I fought the urge to look behind me. "Everyone thinks you're leaving because of the piss-poor assignments I've been giving you," he said, his soothing voice caressing the words as they passed his lips. "They'd be right."

He straightened, and I jerked as the plastic creaked. The brown of his eyes had entirely vanished behind his widening pupils. *Double damn.*

"I've been trying to get rid of you for the last two years," he said. "You don't have bad luck." He smiled, showing me his human teeth. "You have me. Shoddy backup, garbled messages, leaks to your takes. But when I finally get you to leave, you take my best runner with you." His eyes grew intense. I forced my hands to unclench, and his attention flicked to them. "Not good, Morgan."

It hadn't been me, I thought, my alarm hesitating in the sudden realization. It wasn't me. All those mistakes *weren't* me. But then Denon moved to the gap in the walls that was my door.

In a sliding rattle of metal and plastic, I found myself on my feet and pressed up against my desk. Papers scrunched and the mouse fell off the desk, swinging. Denon's eyes were pupil-black. My pulse hammered.

"I don't like you, Morgan," he said, his breath washing over me with a clammy feel. "I never have. Your methods are loose and sloppy, just like your father's. Unable to tag that leprechaun is beyond belief." His gaze went distant, and I found I was holding my breath as they glazed over and understanding seemed to dance just out of reach.

Please work, I thought desperately. *Could my wish please work?* Denon leaned close, and I stabbed my nails into my palm to keep from shrinking. I forced myself to breathe. "Beyond belief," he said again, as if trying to figure it out. But then he shook his head in mock dismay.

My breath slipped out as he drew back. He broke eye contact, putting his gaze on my neck, where I knew my pulse hammered. My hand crept up to cover it, and he smiled like a lover to his one and only. He had only one scar on his beautiful neck. I wondered where the rest were. "When you hit the street," he whispered, "you're fair game."

Shock mixed with my alarm in a nauseating mix. He was going to put a price on my head. "You can't . . ." I stammered. "You wanted me to leave."

He never moved, but just his stillness made my fear tighten. My eyes went wide at his slow intake of breath and his lips going full and red. "Someone's going to die for this, Rachel," he whispered, the way he said my name making my face go cold. "I can't kill Tamwood. So you're going to be her whipping girl." He eyed me from under his brow. "Congratulations."

My hand dropped from my neck as he eased out of my office. He wasn't as smooth as Ivy. It was the difference between high- and low-blood; those born a vamp and those born human and turned. Once in the aisle, the heavy threat in his eyes dissipated. Denon pulled an envelope from his back pocket and tossed it to my desk. "Enjoy your last paycheck, Morgan," he said loudly, more to everyone else than me. He turned and walked away.

"But you wanted me to quit. . . ." I whispered as he disappeared into the elevator. The doors closed; the little red arrow pointing down turned bright. He had his own boss to tell. Denon had to be joking. He wouldn't put a price on my head for something as stupid as Ivy leaving with me. Would he?

"Good going, Rachel."

My head jerked up at the nasal voice. I had forgotten Francis. He slid from Joyce's desk and leaned up against my wall. After seeing Denon do the same thing, the effect was laughable. Slowly, I slipped back into my swivel chair.

"I've been waiting six months for you to get steamed up enough to leave," Francis said. "I should've known all you needed was to get drunk."

A surge of anger burned away the last of my fear, and I returned to my packing. My fingers were cold, and I tried to rub some warmth back into them. Jenks came out of hiding and silently flitted to the top of my plant.

Francis pushed the sleeves of his jacket back to his elbows. Nudging my check out of the way with a single finger, he sat on my desk with one foot on the floor. "It took a lot longer than I thought," he mocked. "Either you're really stubborn or really stupid. Either way, you're really dead." He sniffed, making a rasping noise through his thin nose.

I slammed a desk drawer shut, nearly catching his fingers. "Is there a point you're trying to make, *Francis*?"

"It's Frank," he said, trying to look superior but coming off as if he had a cold. "Don't bother dumping your computer files. There're mine, along with your desk."

I glanced at my monitor with its screen saver of a big, bug-eyed frog. Every so often it ate a fly with Francis's face on it. "Since when are the stiffs downstairs letting a *warlock* run a case?" I asked, hammering at his classification. Francis wasn't good enough to rank witch. He could invoke a spell, but didn't have the know-how to stir one. I did, though I usually bought my amulets. It was easier, and probably safer for me and my mark. It wasn't my fault thousands of years of stereotyping had put females as witches and males as warlocks.

Apparently it was just what he wanted me to ask. "You're not the only one who can cook, Rachel-me-gal. I got my license last week." Leaning, he picked a pen out of my box and set it back in the pencil cup. "I'd have made witch a long time ago. I just didn't want to dirty my hands learning how to stir a spell. I shouldn't have waited so long. It's too easy."

I plucked the pen back out and tucked it in my back pocket. "Well, goody for you." *Francis made the jump to witch?* I thought. *They must have lowered the standards.*

"Yup," Francis said, cleaning under his fingernails with one of my silver daggers. "Got your desk, your caseload, even your company car."

Snatching my knife out of his hand, I tossed it in the box. "I don't have a company car."

"I do." He flicked the collar of his shirt covered with palm trees as if very pleased with himself. I made a vow to keep my mouth shut lest I give him another chance to brag. "Yeah," he said with an overdone sigh. "I'll be needing it. Denon has me going out to interview Councilman Trenton Kalamack on Monday." Francis snickered. "While you were out flubbing your measly snag and drag, I led the run that landed two kilos of Brimstone."

"Big freaking deal," I said, ready to strangle him.

"It's not the amount." He tossed his hair out of his eyes. "It was who was carrying it."

That got my interest. Trent's name in connection with Brimstone? "Who?" I said.

Francis slid off my desk. He stumbled over my fuzzy pink office slippers, nearly falling. Catching himself, he sighted down his finger as if it were a pistol. "Watch your back, Morgan."

That was my limit. Face twisting, I lashed my foot out, tucking it neatly under his. He went down with a gratifying yelp. I had my knee on the back of his nasty polyester coat as he hit the floor. My hand slapped my hip for my missing cuffs. Jenks cheered, flitting overhead. The office went quiet after a gasp of alarm. No one would interfere. They wouldn't even look at me.

"I've got nothing to lose, cookie," I snarled, leaning down until I could smell his sweat. "Like you said, I'm already dead, so the only thing keeping me from ripping your eyelids off right now is simple curiosity. I'm going to ask you again. Who did you tag with Brimstone?"

"Rachel," he cried, able to knock me on my butt but afraid to try. "You're in deep—Ow! Ow!" he exclaimed as my nails dug into the top of his right eyelid. "Yolin. Yolin Bates!"

"Trent Kalamack's secretary?" Jenks said, hovering over my shoulder.

"Yeah," Francis said, his face scraping the carpeting as he turned his head to see me. "Or rather, his late secretary. Damn it, Rachel. Get off me!"

"He's dead?" I dusted off my jeans as I got to my feet.

Francis was sullen as he stood, but he was getting some joy out of telling me this or he would have already walked. "She, not he," he said as he adjusted his collar to stand upright. "They found her stone-dead in I.S. lockup yesterday. Literally. She was a warlock."

He said the last with a condescending tone, and I gave him a sour smile. How easy it is to find contempt for something you were only a week ago. *Trent,* I thought, feeling my gaze go distant. If I could prove Trent dealt in Brimstone and give him to the I.S. on a silver platter, Denon would be forced to get off my back. The I.S. had been after him for years as the Brimstone web continued to grow. No one even knew if he was human or Inderlander.

"Jeez, Rachel," Francis whined, dabbing at his face. "You gave me a bloody nose."

My thoughts cleared, and I turned a mocking eye on him. "You're a witch. Go stir a spell." I knew he couldn't be that good yet. He would have to borrow one like the warlock he used to be, and I could tell it irritated him. I beamed as he opened his mouth to say something. Thinking better of it, he pinched his nose shut and spun away.

There was a tug as Jenks landed on my earring. Francis was making his hurried way down the aisle, his head tilted at an awkward angle. The hem of his sport coat swayed with his stilted gate, and I couldn't help my snicker as Jenks hummed the theme for *Miami Vice.*

"What a moss wipe," the pixy said as I turned back to my desk.

My frown returned as I wedged my pot of laurel into my box of stuff. My head hurt, and I wanted to go home and take a nap. A last look at my desk, and I scooped up my slippers, dropping them in the box. Joyce's books went on her chair with a note saying I'd call her later. *Take my computer, eh?* I thought, pausing to open a file. Three clicks and I made it all but impossible to change the screen saver without trashing the entire system.

"I'm going home, Jenks," I whispered, glancing at the wall clock. It was three-thirty. I'd been at work only half an hour. It felt like ages. A last look about the floor showed only downward-turned heads and backs. It was as if I didn't exist. "Who needs them," I muttered, snatching up my jacket from the back of my chair and reaching for my check.

"Hey!" I yelped as Jenks pinched my ear. "Cripes, Jenks. Knock it off!"

"It's the check," he exclaimed. "Damn it, woman. He's cursed the check!"

I froze. Dropping my jacket into the box, I leaned over the

innocent-seeming envelope. Eyes closed, I breathed deeply, looking for the scent of redwood. Then I tasted against the back of my throat for the scent of sulfur that lingered over black magic. "I can't smell anything."

Jenks gave a short bark of laughter. "I can. It's got to be the check. It's the only thing Denon gave you. And watch it, Rachel. It's black."

A sick feeling drifted through me. Denon couldn't be serious. He couldn't.

I glanced over the room, finding no help. Worried, I pulled my vase out of the trash. Some of Mr. Fish's water went into it. I leveled a portion of salt into the vase, dipped my finger to taste it, then added a bit more. Satisfied the salinity was equal to that of the ocean, I upended the mix over the check. If it had been spelled, the salt would break it.

A whisper of yellow smoke hovered over the envelope. "Aw shhhhoot," I whispered, suddenly frightened. "Watch your nose, Jenks," I said, ducking below my desk.

With an abrupt fizz, the black spell dissolutioned. Yellow, sulfuric smoke billowed up to be sucked into the vents. Cries of dismay and disgust rose with it. There was a small stampede as everyone surged for the doors. Even prepared, the stench of rotten eggs stung at my eyes. The spell had been a nasty one, tailored to me since both Denon and Francis had touched the envelope. It hadn't come cheap.

Shaken, I came out from under my desk and glanced over the deserted floor. "Is it okay now?" I said around a cough. My earring shifted as Jenks nodded. "Thanks, Jenks."

Stomach churning, I tossed my dripping check into the box and stalked past the empty cubicles. It looked like Denon was serious about his death threat. Absolutely swell.

Four

_____

"**R**a-a-a-achel-l-l-l," sang a tiny, irritating voice. It cut clearly through the shifting gears and choking gurgle of the bus's diesel engine. Jenks's voice grated on my inner ear worse than chalk on a blackboard, and my hand trembled in the effort to not make a grab for him. I'd never touch him. The little twit was too fast.

"I'm not asleep," I said before he could do it again. "I'm resting my eyes."

"You're going to rest your eyes right past your stop—*Hot Stuff.*" He nailed the nickname last night's cabbie had given me hard, and I slit an eyelid.

"Don't call me that." The bus went around a corner, and my grip tightened on the box balanced on my lap. "I've got two more blocks," I said through gritted teeth. I'd kicked the nausea, but the headache lingered. And I knew it was two blocks because of the sound of Little League practice in the park just down from my apartment. There'd be another after the sun went down for the nightwalkers.

There was a thrum of wings as Jenks dropped from my earring and into the box. "Sweet mother of Tink! Is that all they pay you?" he exclaimed.

My eyes flashed open. "Get out of my stuff!" I snatched my damp check and crammed it into a jacket pocket. Jenks made a mocking face, and I rubbed my thumb and finger together as if squishing something. He got the idea and moved his purple and yellow silk pantaloons out of my reach, settling on the top of the seat in front of me. "Don't you have somewhere to be?" I asked. "Like helping your family move?"

Jenks gave a yelp of laughter. "Help them move? No freaking way." His wings quivered. "Besides, I should sniff around your place and make sure everything is okay before you blow yourself up when you try to use the john." He laughed hysterically, and several people looked at me. I shrugged as if to say, "Pixies."

"Thanks," I said sourly. A pixy bodyguard. Denon would laugh himself to death. I was indebted to Jenks for finding the spell on my check, but the I.S. hadn't time to rig anything else. I figured I had a few days if he was really serious about this. More likely it was a "don't let the spell kill you on the way out" kind of a thing.

I stood as the bus came to a halt. Struggling down the steps, I landed in the late afternoon sun. Jenks made more annoying circles around me. He was worse than a mosquito. "Nice place," he said sarcastically as I waited for traffic to clear before crossing the street to my apartment house. I silently agreed. I lived uptown in Cincinnati in what was a good neighborhood twenty years ago. The building was a four-story brick, originally built for university upperclassmen. It had seen its last finals party years ago and was now reduced to this.

The black letterboxes attached to the porch were dented and ugly, some having obviously been broken into. I got my mail from the landlady. I had a suspicion she was the one who broke the boxes so she could sort through her tenants' mail at her leisure. There was a thin strip of lawn and two bedraggled shrubs to either side of the wide steps. Last year, I had planted the yarrow seeds I had gotten in a *Spell Weekly* mail promotion, but Mr. Dinky, the landlady's Chihuahua, had dug them up—along with most of the yard. Little divots were everywhere, making it look like a fairy battlefield.

"And I thought my place was bad," Jenks whispered as I skipped the step with dry rot.

My keys jingled as I balanced the box and unlocked the door at the same time. A little voice in my head had been saying the same thing for years. The odor of fried food assaulted me as I entered the foyer, and my nose wrinkled. Green indoor/outdoor carpet ran up the stairs, threadbare and fraying. Mrs. Baker had unscrewed the lightbulb in the stairway again, but the sun spilling in the landing window to fall on the rosebud wallpaper was enough to find my way.

"Hey," Jenks said as I went upstairs. "That stain on the ceiling is in the shape of a pizza."

I glanced up. He was right. Funny, I never noticed it before.

"And that dent in the wall?" he said as we reached the first floor. "It's just the right size for someone's head. Man . . . if these walls could talk . . ."

I found I could still smile. Wait until he got to my apartment. There was a dip in the living room floor where someone had burned out a hearth.

My smile faded as I rounded the second landing. All my things were in the hall.

"What the devil?" I whispered. Shocked, I set my box on the floor and looked down the hall to Mrs. Talbu's door. "I paid my rent!"

"Hey, Rache?" Jenks said from the ceiling. "Where's your cat?"

Anger growing, I stared at my furniture. It seemed to take up a lot more space when it was jammed into a hallway on her lousy plastic carpeting. "Where does she get off—"

"Rachel!" Jenks shouted. "Where's your cat?"

"I don't have a cat," I all but snarled. It was a sore spot with me. "I thought all witches had a cat."

Lips pursed, I strode down the hall. "Cats make Mr. Dinky sneeze."

Jenks flew alongside my ear. "Who is Mr. Dinky?"

"Him," I said, pointing to the framed, oversized picture of a white Chihuahua hanging across from my landlady's door. The butt-ugly, bug-eyed dog wore one of those bows parents put on a baby so you know it's a girl. I pounded on the door. "Mrs. Talbu? Mrs. Talbu!"

There were the muffled yaps of Mr. Dinky and the sound of nails on the backside of the door, shortly followed by my landlady screeching to try and get the thing to shut up. Mr. Dinky redoubled his noise, scrabbling at the floor to dig his way to me.

"Mrs. Talbu!" I shouted. "Why is my stuff in the hall?"

"Word's out on you, Hot Stuff," Jenks said from the ceiling. "You're damaged goods."

"I told you not to call me *that!*" I shouted, hitting her door with my last word.

I heard the slamming of a door from inside, and Mr. Dinky's barking grew muffled and more frenzied. "Go away," came a thin, reedy voice. "You can't live here anymore."

The flat of my hand hurt, and I massaged it. "You think I can't pay my rent?" I said, not caring that the entire floor could hear me. "I've got money, Mrs. Talbu. You can't kick me out. I've got next month's rent right here." I pulled out my soggy check and waved it at the door.

"I changed your lock," Mrs. Talbu quavered. "Go away before you get killed."

I stared at the door in disbelief. She had found out about the I.S.'s threat? And the old lady act was a sham. She shouted clear enough through my wall when she thought I played my music too loud. "You can't evict me!" I said desperately. "I've got rights."

"Dead witches have no rights," Jenks said from the light fixture.

"Damn it, Mrs. Talbu!" I shouted at the door. "I'm not dead yet!"

There was no answer. I stood there, thinking. I didn't have much recourse, and she knew it. I supposed I could stay at my new office until I found something. Moving back in with my mother was not an option, and I hadn't talked to my brother since I joined the I.S.

"What about my security deposit?" I asked, and the door remained silent. My temper shifted to a slow, steady burn, one that could last for days. "Mrs. Talbu," I said quietly. "If you don't give me the balance of this month's rent and my security deposit, I'm going to sit right in front of your door." I paused, listening. "I'm going to sit here until they spell me. I'll probably explode right here. Make a big bloody stain on your carpet that won't come out. And you're going to have to look at that big bloody stain every day. Hear me, Mrs. Talbu?" I quietly threatened. "Pieces of me will be on your hall ceiling."

There was a gasp. "Oh my, Dinky," Mrs. Talbu quavered. "Where's my checkbook?"

I looked at Jenks and smiled bitterly. He gave me a thumbs-up.

There was a rustle, followed by a moment of silence and the distinctive sound of paper tearing. I wondered why she bothered with the old lady act. Everyone knew she was tougher than petrified dinosaur dung and would probably outlive us all. Even Death didn't want her.

"I'm putting the word out on you, hussy," Mrs. Talbu shouted through the door. "You won't find a place to rent in the entire city."

Jenks darted down as a slip of white was shoved under the door. After hovering over it for a moment, he nodded it was okay. I picked it up and read the amount. "What about my security deposit?" I asked. "You want to come with me to my apartment and look it over? Make sure there're no nail holes in the walls or runes under the carpet?"

There was a muffled curse, shortly followed by more scratching, and another white slip appeared. "Get out of my building," Mrs. Talbu yelled, "before I set Mr. Dinky on you!"

"I love you, too, old bat." I took my key from my key ring and dropped it. Angry but satisfied, I snatched up the second check.

I went back to my things, slowing at the telltale scent of sulfur emanating from them. My shoulders tightened in worry as I stared at my life heaped against the walls. Everything was spelled. I could touch nothing. God help me. I was under an I.S. death threat.

"I can't douse everything in salt," I said as there was a click of a closing door.

"I know this guy who has storage." Jenks sounded unusually sympathetic, and I looked up as I gripped my elbows. "If I ask him, he'll come get it, put everything away for you. You can dissolution the spells later." He hesitated, looking over my music discs carelessly dumped into my largest copper spell bowl.

I nodded, slumping against the wall and sliding down until my rear hit the floor. My clothes, my shoes, my music, my books . . . *my life*?

"Oh no," Jenks said softly. "They spelled your disc of *The Best of Takata*."

"It's autographed," I whispered, and the hum from his wings dropped in pitch. The plastic would survive a dip in saltwater, but the paper folder would be ruined. I wondered if I wrote to Takata if he would send me another. He might remember me. We did spend a wild night chasing shadows over the ruins of Cincinnati's old biolabs. I think he made a song about it. "New moon rising, sight unseen, / Shadows of faith make a risky vaccine." It hit the top twenty for sixteen weeks straight. My brow furrowed. "Is there anything they didn't spell?" I asked.

Jenks landed on the phone book and shrugged. It had been left open to coroners.

"Swell." Stomach knotting, I got to my feet. My thoughts swung to what Ivy had said last night about Leon Bairn. Little bits of witch splattered all over his porch. I swallowed hard. I couldn't go home. *How the hell was I going to pay Denon off?*

My head started hurting again. Jenks alighted on my earring, keeping his big mouth shut as I picked up my cardboard box and went downstairs. First things first. "What's the name of that guy you know?" I asked when I reached the foyer. "The one with storage? If I give him something extra, will he dissolution my things?"

"If you tell him how. He's not a witch."

I thought, struggling to regroup. My cell phone was in my bag, but the battery was dead. The charger was somewhere in my spelled stuff. "I can call him from the office," I said.

"He doesn't have a phone." Jenks slipped off my earring, flying backward at eye level. His wing tape had frayed, and I wondered if I should offer to fix it. "He lives in the Hollows," Jenks added. "I'll ask him for you. He's shy."

I reached for the doorknob, then hesitated. Putting my back to the wall, I pushed aside the sun-faded, yellow curtain to peek out the window. The tatty yard lay quiet in the afternoon sun, empty and still. The drone of a lawn mower and the whoosh from passing cars was muffled through the glass. Lips pressed tight, I decided I'd wait there until I heard the bus coming.

"He likes cash," Jenks said, dropping down to stand on the sill. "I'll bring him by the office after he's locked up your stuff."

"You mean everything that hasn't walked off by itself in the meantime," I said, but knew everything was reasonably safe. Spells, especially black ones, were supposed to be target specific, but you never know. No one would risk extinction for my cheap stuff. "Thanks, Jenks." That was twice now he had saved my butt. It made me uneasy. And a little bit guilty.

"Hey, that's what partners do," he said, not helping at all.

Smiling thinly at his enthusiasm, I set my box down to wait.

Five

The bus was quiet; as most traffic was coming out of the Hollows this time of day. Jenks had left via the window shortly after we crossed the river into Kentucky. It was his opinion the I.S. wouldn't tag me on a bus with witnesses. I wasn't ready to believe it, but I wasn't going to ask him to stay with me, either.

I had told the driver the address, and he agreed to tell me when we were there. The human was skinny, his faded blue uniform hanging loose on him despite the vanilla wafers he was cramming into his mouth like jelly beans.

Most of Cincinnati's mass-transit drivers were comfortable with Inderlanders, but not all. Humanity's reactions to us varied widely. Some were afraid, some weren't. Some wanted to be us, some wanted to kill us. A few took advantage of the lower tax rate and lived in the Hollows, but most didn't.

Shortly after the Turn, an unexpected migration occurred when almost every human who could afford it moved deep into the cities. The psychologists of the day had called it a "nesting syndrome," and in hindsight the countrywide phenomenon was understandable. Inderlanders were more than eager to snap up the properties on the outskirts, lured by the prospect of a little more earth to call their own, not to mention the drastically falling home prices.

The population demographics have only recently started to even out, as well-to-do Inderlanders move back into the city and the less fortunate, more informed humans decide they would rather live in a nice Inderland neighborhood than a trashy human one. Generally, though, apart from a small section around the university, humans lived in Cincinnati and Inderlanders lived across the river in the Hollows. We don't care that most humans shun our neighborhoods like pre-Turn ghettoes.

The Hollows have become a bastion of Inderland life, comfortable and casual on the surface, with its potential problems carefully hidden. Most humans are surprised at how normal the Hollows appear, which, when you stop to think about it, makes sense. Our history is that of humanity's. We didn't just drop out of the sky in '66; we emigrated in through Ellis Island. We fought in the Civil War, World War One, and World War Two—some of us in all three. We suffered in the Depression, and we waited like everyone else to find out who shot JR.

But dangerous differences exist, and any Inderlander over the age of fifty spent the earliest part of his or her life disguising them, a tradition that holds true even to this day.

The homes are modest, painted white, yellow, and occasionally pink. There are no haunted houses except for Loveland Castle in October, when they turn it into the baddest haunted house on either side of the river. There are swing sets, aboveground pools, bikes on the lawns, and cars parked on the curb. It takes a sharp eye to notice that the flowers are arranged in antiblack magic hexes and the basement windows are often cemented over. The savage, dangerous reality blooms only in the depths of the city, where people gather and emotions run rampant: amusement parks, dance clubs, bars, churches. *Never* our homes.

And it's quiet—even at night when all its denizens are up. It was always the stillness that a human noticed first, setting them on edge and sending their instincts into full swing.

I found my tension easing as I stared out the window and counted the black, light-proof blinds. The quiet of the neighborhood seemed to soak into the bus. Even the few people riding had grown still. There was just something about the Hollows that said "Home."

My hair swung forward as the bus stopped. On edge, I jerked when the guy behind me bumped my shoulder as he got up. Boots clattering, he hastened down the steps and into the sun. The driver told me my stop was next, and I stood as the nice man trundled down a side street to give me curb service. I stepped down into the patchy shade, standing with my arms wrapped around the box and trying not to breathe the fumes as the bus drove away. It disappeared around a corner, taking its noise and the last vestiges of humanity with it.

Slowly it grew quiet. The sound of birds drifted into existence. Somewhere close there were kids calling—no, kids screaming—and the barking of a dog. Multicolored chalk runes decorated the cracked sidewalk, and a forgotten doll with fangs painted on it smiled blankly at me. There was a small stone church across the street, its steeple rising far above the trees.

I turned on a heel, eyeing what Ivy had rented for us: a one-story house that could easily be converted to an office. The roof looked new, but the chimney mortar was crumbling. There was grass out front, looking like it should have been cut last week. It even had a garage, the door gaping open to show a rusting mower.

It will do, I thought as I opened the gate to the chain-link fence enclosing the yard. An old black man sat on the porch, rocking the afternoon away. *Landlord?* I mused, smiling. I wondered if he was a vamp, since he wore dark glasses against the late afternoon sun. He was scruffy looking despite being clean-shaven, his tightly curled hair going gray around the temples. There was mud on his shoes and a hint of it on the knees of his blue jeans. He looked worn-out and tired—put away like an unwanted plow horse who was still eager for one more season.

He set a tall glass on the porch railing as I came up the walk. "Don't want it," he said as he took off his glasses and tucked them in a shirt pocket. His voice was raspy.

Hesitating, I peered up at him from the bottom of the stairs. "Beg pardon?"

He coughed, clearing his throat. "Whatever you're selling out of that box. Don't want it. I've got enough curse candles, candy, and magazines. And I don't have the money for new siding, water purifier, or a sunroom."

"I'm not selling anything," I said. "I'm your new tenant."

He sat up straighter, somehow making himself look even more unkempt. "Tenant? Oh, you mean across the street."

Confused, I shifted my box to my other hip. "This isn't 1597 Oakstaff, is it?"

He chuckled. "That's across the street."

"Sorry to have bothered you." I turned to leave, hoisting the box higher.

"Yep," the man said, and I paused, not wanting to be rude. "The numbers are backward on this street. Odd numbers on the wrong side of the road." He smiled, creasing the wrinkles around his eyes. "But they didn't ask me when they put the numbers up."

He extended his hand. "I'm Keasley," he said, waiting for me to climb the stairs and take his hand.

Neighbors, I thought, rolling my eyes as I went up the stairs. *Best to be nice.* "Rachel Morgan," I said, pumping his arm once. He beamed, patting my shoulder in a fatherly fashion. The strength of his grip was surprising, as was the scent of redwood coming from him. He was a witch, or at the very least a warlock. Not comfortable with his show of familiarity, I took a step back as he released me. It was cooler on his porch, and I felt tall under the low ceiling.

"Are you friends with the vamp?" he said, gesturing across the street with his chin.

"Ivy? Yeah."

He nodded slowly, as if it were important. "Both of you quit together?"

I blinked. "News travels fast."

He laughed. "Yup. It does at that."

"Aren't you afraid I'm going to get spelled on your front porch and take you with me?"

"No." He leaned back in his rocker and picked up his glass. "I took that one off you." He held up a tiny self-stick amulet between his finger and thumb. As my lips parted, he dropped it into his glass. What I thought had been lemonade foamed as the spell dissolutioned. Yellow smoke billowed, and he waved his hand dramatically. "Oooh doggies, that's a nasty one."

Saltwater? He grinned at my obvious shock. "That guy on the bus . . ." I stammered as I backed off the porch. The yellow sulfur eddied down the stairs as if trying to find me.

"Nice meeting you, Ms. Morgan," the man said I stumbled onto the walk and into the sun. "A vamp and pixy might keep you alive a few days, but not if you aren't more careful."

My eyes turned to look down the street at the long gone bus. "The guy on the bus . . ."

Keasley nodded. "You're right in that they won't try anything when there's a witness, leastwise, not at first, but you have to watch for the amulets that won't trigger till you're alone."

I had forgotten about delayed spells. And were was Denon getting the money? My face scrunched up as I figured it out; Ivy's bribe money was paying for my death threat. Swell.

"I'm home all day," Keasley was saying. "Come on over if you want to talk. I don't get out much anymore. Arthritis." He slapped his knee.

"Thanks," I said. "For—finding that charm."

"My pleasure," he said, his gaze on the ceiling of the porch and the lazily spinning fan.

My stomach was knotting as I made my way back to the sidewalk. Was the entire city aware I had quit? Maybe Ivy had talked to him.

I felt vulnerable in the empty street. Edgy, I crossed the road looking for house numbers. "Fifteen ninety-three," I muttered, glancing at the small yellow house with two bikes tangled on the lawn. "Sixteen hundred and one," I said, looking the other way to the well-kept brick home. My lips pursed. The only thing between them was that stone church. I froze. A church?

A harsh buzzing zipped past my ears, and I instinctively ducked.

"Hi, Rache!" Jenks came to a hovering halt just out of my reach.

"Damn it, Jenks!" I shouted, warming as I heard the old man laugh. "Don't do that!"

"Got your stuff set," Jenks said. "I made him put everything up on blocks."

"It's a church," I said.

"No shit, Sherlock. Wait until you see the garden."

I stood unmoving. "It's a *church*."

Jenks hovered, waiting for me. "There's a huge yard in back. Great for parties."

"Jenks," I said through gritted teeth. "It's a church. The backyard is a *graveyard*."

"Not all of it." He began weaving impatiently. "And it's not a church anymore. It's been a day care for the last two years. No one's been buried there since the Turn."

I stood, staring at him. "Did they move the bodies out?"

His darting ceased and he hung motionless. "'Course they moved the bodies out. You think I'm *stupid*? You think I'd live where there were dead *humans*? God help me. The bugs coming off 'em, diseases, viruses, and crap soaking into the soil and getting into everything!"

I adjusted my grip on my stuff, striding across the shady street and up the wide steps of the church. Jenks didn't have a clue as to whether the bodies had been moved out. The gray stone steps were bowed in the middle from decades of use, and they were slippery. There were twin doors taller than I, made of a reddish wood and bound with metal. One had a plaque screwed into it.

"Donna's Daycare," I muttered, reading the inscription. I tugged a door open, surprised at the strength needed to shift it. There wasn't even a lock on it, just a sliding bolt on the inside.

"Of course they moved the bodies out," Jenks said, then flitted over the church. I'd put a hundred on it that he was going out to the backyard to investigate.

"Ivy?" I shouted, trying to slam the door behind me. "Ivy, are you here?" The echo of my voice came back from the yet unseen sanctuary, a thick, stained-glassed quiet hush of sound. The closest I'd been to a church since my dad died was reading the cutesy catch phrases off those backlit signs they all put on their front lawns. The foyer was dark, having no windows and black wooden panels. It was warm and still, thick with the presence of past liturgy. I set the box on the wooden floor and listened to the green and amber hush slipping in from the sanctuary.

"Be right down!" came Ivy's distant shout. She sounded almost cheerful, but where on earth was she? Her voice was coming from everywhere and nowhere at all.

There was the soft click of a latch, and Ivy slipped from behind a panel. A narrow spiral stairway went up behind her. "I've got my owls up in the belfry," she said. Her brown eyes were more alive than I'd ever seen them. "It's perfect for storage. Lots of shelves and drying racks. Someone left their stuff up there, though. Want to go through it with me later?"

"It's a church, Ivy."

Ivy stopped. Her arms crossed and she looked at me, her face abruptly empty.

"There are dead people in the backyard," I added, and she levered herself up and went into the sanctuary. "You can see the tombstones from the road," I continued as I followed her in.

The pews were gone, as was the altar, leaving only an empty room and a slightly raised stage. That same black wood made a wainscot that ran below the tall stained-glassed windows that wouldn't open. A faded shadow on the wall remained where an enormous cross once hung over the altar. The ceiling was three stories up, and I sent my gaze to the open woodwork, thinking it would be hard to keep this room warm in winter. It was nothing but a stripped down open space . . . but the stark emptiness seemed to add to the feeling of peace.

"How much is this going to cost?" I asked, remembering I was supposed to be angry.

"Seven hundred a month, utilities—ah—included," Ivy said quietly.

"Seven hundred?" I hesitated, surprised. That would be three fifty for my share. I was paying four fifty uptown for my one-room castle. That wasn't bad. Not bad at all. Especially if it had a yard. *No,* I thought, my bad mood returning. *It was a graveyard.*

"Where are you going?" I said as Ivy walked away. "I'm talking to you."

"To get a cup of coffee. You want one?" She disappeared through the door at the back of the raised stage.

"Okay, so the rent is cheap," I said. "That's what I said I wanted, but it's a church! You can't run a business from a church!" Fuming, I followed her past the opposing his-and-her bathrooms. Farther down was a door on the right. I peeked past it to find a nice-sized empty room, the floor and smooth walls giving back an echo of my breathing. A stained-glass window of saints was propped open with a stick to air the place out, and I could hear the sparrows arguing outside. The room looked as if it had once been an office, having since been modified for toddlers' nap cots. The floor was dusty, but the wood was sound under the light scratches.

Satisfied, I peeked around the door across the hall. There was a made-up bed and open boxes. Before I could see more, Ivy reached in front of me and pulled the door shut.

"That's your stuff," I said, staring at her.

Ivy's face was empty, chilling me more than if she had been pulling an aura. "I'm going to have to stay here until I can rent a room somewhere." She hesitated, tucking her black hair behind an ear. "Got a problem with that?"

"No," I said softly, closing my eyes in a long blink. For the love of St. Philomena. I was going to have to live at the office until I got myself set. My eyes opened, and I was startled by the odd look Ivy had, a mix of fear and—anticipation?

"I'm going to have to crash here, too," I said, not liking this at all but seeing no other option. "My landlady evicted me. The box by the front door is all I've got until I can get my stuff despelled. The I.S. black-charmed everything in my apartment, almost nailed me on the bus. And thanks to my landlady, no one within the city limits will rent to me. Denon put a contract out on me, just like you said." I tried to keep the whine out of my voice, but it was there.

That odd light was still in Ivy's eyes, and I wondered if she had told me the truth about being a nonpracticing vamp. "You can have the empty room," she said, her voice carefully flat.

I gave her a terse nod. *Okay,* I thought, taking a deep breath. I was living in a church—with bodies in the backyard—an I.S. death threat on me—and a vamp across the hall. I wondered if she would notice if I put a lock on the inside of my door. I wondered if it would matter.

"The kitchen's back here," she said, and I followed her and the smell of coffee. My mouth fell open as I rounded the open archway, and I forgot to be angry again.

The kitchen was half the size of the sanctuary, as fully equipped and modern as the sanctuary was barren and medieval. There was gleaming metal, shiny chrome, and bright, fluorescent lights. The refrigerator was enormous. A gas stove and oven sat at one end of the room; an electric range and stovetop took up the other. Centered in the middle of it all was a stainless steel island with empty shelves beneath. The rack above it was festooned with metal utensils, pans, and bowls. It was a witch's dream kitchen; I wouldn't have to stir my spells and dinner on the same stove.

Apart from the beat-up wooden table and chairs in the corner, the kitchen looked like one you might see on a cooking show. One end of the table was set up like a computer desk, the wide-screen monitor blinking furiously to itself as it cycled through the open lines to find and claim the best continuous link to the net. It was an expensive program, and my eyebrows rose.

Ivy cleared her throat as she opened a cupboard beside the sink. There were three mismatched mugs on the bottom shelf; other than that, it was empty. "They put in the new kitchen five years ago for the health department," she said, jerking my attention back to her. "The congregation wasn't very big, so when all was said and done, they couldn't afford it. That's why they're renting it out. To try and pay off the bank."

The sound of coffee being poured filled the room as I ran my finger over the unblemished metal on the island counter. It had never seen a single apple pie or Sunday school cookie.

"They want their church back," Ivy said, looking thin as she leaned against the counter with her mug cradled in her pale hands. "But they're dying. The church, I mean," she added as I met her eyes. "No new members. It's sad, really. The living room is back here."

I didn't know what to say, so I kept my mouth shut and followed her into the hallway and through a narrow doorway at the

end of the hall. The living room was cozy, and furnished so taste-
fully that I had no doubt these were all Ivy's things. It was the first
softness and warmth I had seen in the entire place—even if everything was in shades of gray—and the windows were just plain
glass. Heavenly. I felt my tension loosen. Ivy snatched up a remote, and midnight jazz drifted into existence. Maybe this
wouldn't be so bad.

"You almost got tagged?" Ivy tossed the remote onto the coffee table and settled herself in one of the voluptuous gray suede
chairs beside the empty fireplace. "Are you all right?"

"Yeah," I admitted sourly, seeming to sink nearly to my ankles
in the expansive throw rug. "Is all this your stuff? A guy bumped
into me, slipped me a charm that wouldn't invoke until there were
no witnesses or causalities—other than me. I can't believe Denon
is serious about this. You were right." I worked hard to keep my
voice casual so Ivy wouldn't know how shaken I was. Hell, I
didn't want to know how shaken I was. I'd get the money to pay
off my contract somehow. "It was lucky as toast the old guy
across the street took it off me." I picked up a picture of Ivy and a
golden retriever. She was smiling to show her teeth; I stifled a
shiver.

"What old guy?" Ivy said quickly.

"Across the street. He's been watching you." I set the metal
frame down and adjusted the pillow in the chair opposite hers before I sat. Matching furniture; how nice. An old mantel clock
ticked, soft and soothing. There was a wide-screen TV with a
built-in CD player in one corner. The disc player under it had all
the right buttons. Ivy knew her electronics.

"I'll bring my things over once I get them dissolutioned," I
said, then winced, thinking how cheap my stuff would look next to
hers. "What will survive the dip," I added.

Survive the dip? I thought suddenly, closing my eyes and
scrubbing my forehead. "Oh no," I said softly. "I can't dissolution
my charms."

Ivy balanced her mug on a knee as she leafed through a magazine. "Hmm?"

"Charms," I half moaned. "The I.S. overlaid black spells on
my stash of charms. Dunking them in saltwater to break the spell
will ruin them. And I can't buy more." I grimaced at her blank
look. "If the I.S. got my apartment, I'm sure they've been to the
store, too. I should have brought a bunch yesterday before I quit,
but I didn't think they'd care if I left." I listlessly adjusted the

shade of the table lamp. They hadn't cared until Ivy had left with me. Depressed, I tossed my head back and looked at the ceiling.

"I thought you already knew how to make spells," Ivy said warily.

"I do, but it's a pain in the butt. And where am I going to get the raw materials?" I closed my eyes in misery. I was going to have to *make* all my charms.

There was a rustle of paper, and I lifted my head to see Ivy perusing her magazine. There was an apple and Snow White on the cover. Snow White's leather corset was cut to show her belly button. A drop of blood glittered like a jewel at the corner of her mouth. It put a whole new twist on the enchanted sleep thing. Mr. Disney would be appalled. Unless, of course, he had been an Inderlander. That would explain a lot.

"You can't just buy what you need?" Ivy asked.

I stiffened at the touch of sarcasm in her voice. "Yeah, but everything will have to be dunked in saltwater to make sure it hasn't been tampered with. It'll be nearly impossible to get rid of all the salt, and that will make the mix wrong."

Jenks buzzed out of the fireplace with a cloud of soot and an irritating whine. I wondered how long he had been listening in the flue. He landed on a box of tissue and cleaned a spot off his wing, looking like a cross between a dragonfly and a miniature cat. "My, aren't we obsessed," he said, answering my question as to whether he had been eavesdropping.

"You have the I.S. trying to nack you with black magic and see if you aren't a little paranoid." Anxious, I thwacked the box he was sitting on until he took to the air.

He hovered between me and Ivy. "Haven't seen the garden yet, have you, Sherlock?"

I threw the pillow at him, which he easily dodged. It knocked the lamp beside Ivy, and she casually reached out and caught it before it hit the floor. She never looked up from her magazine, never spilled a drop of her coffee perched on her knee. The hair on my neck prickled. "Don't call me that, either," I said to cover my unease. He looked positively smug as he hovered before me. "What?" I said snidely. "The garden has more than weeds and dead people?"

"Maybe."

"Really?" This would be the first good thing to happen to me today, and I got up to look out the back door. "Coming?" I asked Ivy as I reached for the handle.

Her head was bent over a page of leather curtains. "No," she said, clearly uninterested.

So it was Jenks who accompanied me out the back door and into the garden. The lowering sun was heady and strong, making the scents clear as it pulled moisture from the damp ground. There was a rowan somewhere. I sniffed deeply. And a birch and oak. What had to be Jenks's kids were darting noisily about, chasing a yellow butterfly over the rising mounds of vegetation. Banks of plants lined the walls of the church and surrounding stone fence. The man-high wall went completely around the property, to tactfully isolate the church from the neighbors.

Another wall low enough to step over separated the garden from the small graveyard. I squinted, seeing a few plants out among the tall grass and headstones, but only those that became more potent growing among the dead. The closer I looked, the more awestruck I became. The garden was complete. Even the rarities were there.

"It's perfect," I whispered, running my fingers through a patch of lemongrass. "Everything I could ever need. How did it all get here?"

Ivy's voice came from right behind me. "According to the old lady—"

"Ivy!" I said, spinning around to see her standing still and quiet on the path in a shaft of late amber sun. "Don't do that!" *Creepy vamp,* I thought. *I ought to put a bell on her.*

She squinted from under her hand, raised against the fading light. "She said their last minister was a witch. He put in the garden. I can get fifty taken off the rent if one of us keeps it up the way it is."

I looked over the treasure trove. "I'll do it."

Jenks flew up from a patch of violets. His purple trousers had pollen stains on them matching his yellow shirt. "Manual labor?" he questioned. "With those nails of yours?"

I glanced at the perfect red ovals my nails made. "This isn't work, this is—therapy."

"Whatever." His attention went to his kids, and he zoomed across the garden to rescue the butterfly they were fighting over.

"Do you think everything you need is here?" Ivy asked as she turned to go inside.

"Just about. You can't spell salt, so my stash is probably okay, but I'll need my good spell pot and all my books."

Ivy paused on the path. "I thought you had to know how to stir a brew by heart to get your witch license."

Now I was embarrassed, and I bent to tug a weed free from beside a rosemary plant. Nobody made their own charms if they could afford to buy them. "Yeah," I said as I dropped the weed, flicking the dirt from under my nails. "But I'm out of practice." I sighed. This was going to be harder than it looked.

Ivy shrugged. "Can you get them off the net? The recipes, I mean."

I looked askance at her. "Trust anything off the net? Oh, there's a good idea."

"There're some books in the attic."

"Sure," I said sarcastically. "One hundred spells for the beginner. Every church has a copy of that."

Ivy stiffened. "Don't get snotty," she said, the brown of her eyes disappearing behind her dilating pupils. "I just thought if one of the clergy was a witch, and the right plants were here, he might have left his books. The old lady said he ran off with one of the younger parishioners. That's probably his stuff in the attic in case he had the guts to come back."

The last thing I wanted was an angry vamp sleeping across the hall. "Sorry," I apologized. "I'll go look. And if I'm lucky, when I go out to the shed to find a saw to cut my amulets, there'll be a bag of salt for when the front steps get icy."

Ivy gave a little start, turning to look at the closet-sized shed. I passed her, pausing on the sill. "Coming?" I said, determined not to let her think popping in and out of vamp mode was shaking me. "Or will your owls leave me alone?"

"No, I mean yes." Ivy bit her lip. It was decidedly a human gesture, and my eyebrows rose. "They'll let you up there, just don't go making a lot of noise. I'll—I'll be right there."

"Whatever . . ." I muttered, turning to find my way up to the belfry.

As Ivy had promised, the owls left me alone. It turned out the attic had a copy of everything I had lost in my apartment, and then some. Several of the books were so old they were falling apart. The kitchen had a nest of copper pots, probably used, Ivy had claimed, for chili cook-offs. They were perfect for spell casting, since they hadn't been sealed to reduce tarnish. Finding everything I needed was eerie, so much so that when I went out to look for a saw in the shed, I was relieved to not find any salt. No, that was on the floor of the pantry.

Everything was going too well. Something had to be wrong.

Six

Ankles crossed, I sat atop Ivy's antique kitchen table and swung my feet in their fuzzy pink slippers. The sliced vegetables were cooked to perfection, still crisp and crunchy, and I pushed them around in the little white cardboard box with my chopsticks, looking for more chicken. "This is fantastic," I mumbled around my full mouth. Red tangy spice burned my tongue. My eyes watered. Grabbing the waiting glass of milk, I downed a third of it. "Hot," I said as Ivy glanced up from the box cradled in her long hands. "Cripes, it's really hot."

Ivy arched her thin black eyebrows. "Glad you approve." She was sitting at the table at the spot she had cleared before her computer. Looking into her own take-out box, her wave of black hair fell to make a curtain over her face. She tucked it behind an ear, and I watched the line of her jaw slowly move as she ate.

I had just enough experience with chopsticks to not look like an idiot, but Ivy moved the twin sticks with a slow precision, placing bits of food into her mouth with a rhythmic, somehow erotic, pace. I looked away, suddenly uncomfortable.

"What's it called?" I asked, digging into my paper box.

"Chicken in red curry."

"That's it?" I questioned, and she nodded. I made a small noise. I could remember that. I found another piece of meat. Curry exploded in my mouth, and I washed it down with a gulp of milk. "Where did you get it?"

"Piscary's."

My eyes widened. Piscary's was a combination pizza den and vamp hangout. Very good food in a rather unique atmosphere.

"This came from Piscary's?" I said as I crunched through a bamboo shoot. "I didn't know they delivered anything but pizza."

"They don't—generally."

The throaty pitch of her voice pulled my attention up, to find that she was absorbed in her food. She raised her head at my lack of movement and blinked her almond-shaped eyes at me. "My mother gave him the recipe," she said. "Piscary makes it special for me. It's no big deal."

She went back to eating. A feeling of unease drifted through me, and I listened to the crickets over the twin soft scraping of our sticks. Mr. Fish swam in his bowl on the windowsill. The soft, muted noise of the Hollows at night was almost unheard over the rhythmic thumps of my clothes in the dryer.

I couldn't bear the thought of wearing the same clothes again tomorrow, but Jenks told me it wouldn't be until Sunday that his friend could have my clothes despelled. The best I could do was wash what I had and hope I didn't run into anyone I knew. Right now I was in the nightgown and robe Ivy had lent me. They were black, obviously, but Ivy said the color suited me fine. The faint scent of wood ash on them wasn't unpleasant, but it seemed to cling to me.

My gaze went to the empty spot above the sink where a clock should be. "What time do you think it is?"

"A little after three," Ivy said, not glancing at her watch.

I dug around, sighing when I realized I had eaten all the pineapple. "I wish my clothes would get done. I am so tired."

Ivy crossed her legs and leaned over her dinner. "Go ahead. I'll get them out for you. I'll be up until five or so."

"No, I'll stay up." I yawned, covering my mouth with the back of my hand. "It isn't like I have to get up and go to work tomorrow," I finished sourly. A small noise of agreement came from Ivy, and my digging about in my dinner slowed. "Ivy, you can tell me to back off if it's none of my business, but why did you join the I.S. if you didn't want to work for them?"

She seemed surprised as she looked up. In a flat voice that spoke volumes, she said, "I did it to tick my mother off." A flicker of what looked like pain flashed over her, vanishing before I could be sure it existed. "My dad isn't pleased I quit," she added. "He told me I should have either stuck it out or killed Denon."

Dinner forgotten, I stared, not knowing if I was more surprised at learning her father was still alive or at his rather creative advice on how to get ahead at the office. "Uh, Jenks said you were the last living member of your house," I finally said.

Ivy's head moved in a slow, controlled nod. Brown eyes watching me, she moved her chopsticks between the box and her lips in a slow dance. The subtle display of sensuality took me aback, and I shifted uneasily on my perch on the table. She had never been this bad when we had worked together. Of course, we usually quit work before midnight.

"My dad married into the family," she said between dips into the box, and I wondered if she knew how provocative she looked. "I'm the last living blood member of my house. Because of the prenuptial, my mother's money is all mine, or it was. She is as mad as all hell I quit. She wants me to find a nice, living, high-blood vamp, settle down, and pop out as many kids as I can to be sure her living bloodline doesn't die out. She'll kill me if I croak before having a kid."

I nodded as if I understood, but I didn't. "I joined because of my dad," I admitted. Embarrassed, I put my attention into my dinner. "He worked for the I.S. in the arcane division. He'd come home every morning with these wild stories of people he had helped or tagged. He made it sound so exciting." I snickered. "He never mentioned the paperwork. When he died, I thought it would be a way to get close to him, sort of remember him by. Stupid, isn't it?"

"No."

I looked up, crunching through a carrot. "I had to do something. I spent a year watching my mother fall off her rocker. She isn't crazy, but it's like she doesn't want to believe he's gone. You can't talk to her without her saying something like, 'I made banana pudding today; it was your father's favorite.' She knows he's dead, but she can't let him go."

Ivy was staring out the black kitchen window and into a memory. "My dad's like that. He spends all his time keeping my mother going. I hate it."

My chewing slowed. Not many vamps could afford to remain alive after death. The elaborate sunlight precautions and liability insurance alone was enough to put most families on the street. Not to mention the continuous supply of fresh blood.

"I hardly ever see him," she added, her voice a whisper. "I don't understand it, Rachel. He has his entire life left, but he won't let her get the blood she needs from anyone else. If he's not with her, he's passed out on the floor from blood loss. Keeping her from dying completely is killing him. One person alone can't support a dead vampire. They both know that."

The conversation had taken an uncomfortable turn, but I couldn't just leave. "Maybe he's doing it because he loves her?" I offered slowly.

Ivy frowned. "What kind of love is that?" She stood, her long legs unfolding in a slow graceful movement. Cardboard box in hand, she vanished into the hall.

The sudden silence hammered on my ears. I stared at her empty chair in surprise. She walked out. How could she just walk out? We were talking. The conversation was too interesting to drop, so I slid from the table and followed her into the living room with my dinner.

She had collapsed into one of the gray suede chairs, sprawled out in a look of total unconcern, with her head on one of the thick arms and her feet dangling over the other. I hesitated in the doorway, taken aback at the picture she made. Like a lioness in her den, satiated from the kill. *Well,* I thought, *she is a vampire.* What did I expect her to look like?

Reminding myself that she wasn't a practicing vamp and that I had nothing to worry about, I cautiously settled in the chair across from her, the coffee table between us. Only one of the table lamps was on, and the edges of the room were indistinct and lost in shadow. The lights from her electronic equipment glowed. "So, joining the I.S. was your dad's idea?" I prompted.

Ivy had set her little white cardboard box atop her stomach. Not meeting my gaze, she lay on her back and indolently ate a bamboo shoot, looking at the ceiling as she chewed. "It was my mother's idea, originally. She wanted me to be in management." Ivy took another bite. "I was supposed to stay nice and safe. She thought it would be good for me to work on my people skills." She shrugged. "I wanted to be a runner."

I kicked off my slippers and tucked my feet under me. Curled up around my take-out box, I flicked a glance at Ivy as she slowly pulled her chopsticks out from between her lips. Most of the upper management in the I.S. were undead. I always thought it was because the job was easier if you didn't have a soul.

"It wasn't as if she could stop me," Ivy continued, talking to the ceiling. "So to punish me for doing what I wanted instead of what she wanted, she made sure Denon was my boss." A snicker escaped her. "She thought I'd get so ticked that I'd jump to a management position as soon as one opened up. She never considered I'd trade my inheritance to get out of my contract. I guess I showed her," she said sarcastically.

I shuffled past a tiny corncob to get to a chunk of tomato. "You threw away all your money because you didn't like your boss? I don't like him, either, but—"

Ivy stiffened. The force of her gaze struck me cold. My words froze in my throat at the hatred in her expression. "Denon is a ghoul," Ivy said, her words drawing the warmth from the room. "If I had to take his flack for one more day, I was going to rip his throat out."

I hesitated. "A ghoul?" I said, confused. "I thought he was a vamp."

"He is." When I said nothing, she swung herself upright to put her boots on the floor. "Look," she said, sounding bothered. "You must have noticed Denon doesn't look like a vamp. His teeth are human, right? He can't maintain an aura at noon? And he moves so loud you can hear him coming a mile away?"

"I'm not blind, Ivy."

She cradled her white paperboard box and stared at me. The night air coming in through the window was chilly for late spring, and I drew her robe tighter about my shoulders.

"Denon was bitten by an undead, so he has the vampire virus in him," Ivy continued. "That lets him do a few tricks and makes him real pretty, and I imagine he's as scary as all hell if you let him bully you, but he's someone's lackey, Rachel. He's a toy and always will be."

There was a small scrape as she put her white box on the coffee table between us and edged forward to the end of her chair so she could reach it. "Even if he dies and someone bothers to turn him into an undead, he'll be second-class," she said. "Look at his eyes next time you see him. He's afraid. Every time he lets a vamp feed on him, he has to trust that they'll bring him back as an undead if they lose control and accidentally kill him." She took a slow breath. "He should be afraid."

The red curry went tasteless. Heart pounding, I searched her gaze, praying it would just be Ivy staring back at me. Her eyes were still brown, but something was in them. Something old that I didn't understand. My stomach clenched, and I was suddenly unsure of myself. "Don't be afraid of ghouls like Denon," she whispered. I thought her words were meant to be soothing, but they tightened my skin until it tingled. "There are a lot more dangerous things to be afraid of."

Like you? I thought, but didn't say it. Her sudden air of repressed predator set off alarm bells in my head. I thought I should get up and leave. Get my scrawny witch butt back in the kitchen where it belonged. But she had eased herself back into her chair with her dinner, and I didn't want her to know she was scaring the crap out of me. It wasn't as if I hadn't seen Ivy go vampy before. Just not after midnight. In her living room. Alone.

"Things like your mother?" I said, hoping I hadn't gone too far.

"Things like my mother," she breathed. "That's why I'm living in a church."

My thoughts went to my tiny cross on my new bracelet with the rest of my charms. It never failed to impress me that something so small could stop so powerful a force. It wouldn't slow a living vamp down at all—only the undead—but I'd take whatever protection I could get.

Ivy put her boot heels on the edge of the coffee table. "My mother has been a true undead for the last ten years or so," she said, startling me from my dark thoughts. "I hate it."

Surprised, I couldn't help but ask, "Why?"

She pushed her dinner away in what was obviously a gesture of unease. There was a frightening emptiness in her face, and she wouldn't meet my gaze. "I was eighteen when my mother died," she whispered. Her voice was distant, as if she wasn't aware she was even talking.

"She lost something, Rachel. When you can't walk under the sun, you lose something so nebulous, you can't even say for sure what it is. But it's gone. It's as if she's stuck following a pattern of behavior but can't remember why. She still loves me, but she doesn't remember why she loves me. The only thing that brings any life to her is the taking of blood, and she's so damned savage about it. When she's sated, I can almost see my mother in what's left of her. But it doesn't last. It's never enough."

Ivy looked up from under her lowered brow. "You do have a crucifix, don't you?"

"Right here," I said with forced brightness. I wouldn't let her know she was putting me on edge; I wouldn't. Holding up my hand, I gave it a little shake so the robe's sleeve fell to my elbow to show my new charm bracelet.

Ivy put her boots on the floor. I relaxed at the less provocative position until she leaned halfway over the coffee table. Her hand went out with an unreal quickness, gripping my wrist before I knew she had moved. I froze, very aware of the warmth of her fingers. She studied the wood-inlaid metal charm intently as I fought the urge to pull away. "Is it blessed?" she asked.

Face cold, I nodded, and she released me, easing back with an eerie slowness. It seemed I could still feel her grip on me, an imprisoning firmness that wouldn't tighten unless I pulled away. "Mine, too," she said, drawing her cross out from behind her shirt.

Impressed anew with her crucifix, I set aside my dinner and scooted forward. I couldn't help but reach out for it. The tooled silver begged to be touched, and she leaned across the table so I could bring it closer. Ancient runes were etched into it, along with the more traditional blessings. It was beautiful, and I wondered how old it was.

Suddenly, I realized Ivy's warm breath was on my cheek.

I sat back, her cross still in my hand. Her eyes were dark and her face blank. There was nothing there. Frightened, I flicked my gaze from her to the cross. I couldn't just drop it. It would smack her right in the chest. But I couldn't set it gently down against her, either.

"Here," I said, terribly uncomfortable at her blank stare. "Take it."

Ivy reached out, her fingers grazing mine as she grasped the old metal. Swallowing hard, I scooted back into my chair and adjusted Ivy's robe to cover my legs.

Moving with a provocative slowness, Ivy took her cross off. The silver chain caught against the black sheen of her hair. She pulled her hair free, and it fell back in a cascading shimmer. She set the cross on the table between us. The click of the metal meeting the wood was loud. Eyes unblinking, she curled up in her chair opposite mine with her feet tucked under her and stared at me.

Holy crap, I thought in a sudden wash of understanding and panic. She was coming on to me. That's what was going on. How blind could I be?

My jaw clenched as my mind raced to find a way out of this. I was straight. Never a thought contrary to that. I liked my men taller than me and not so strong that I couldn't pin them to the floor in a surge of passion if I wanted. "Um, Ivy . . ." I started.

"I was born a vampire," Ivy stated softly.

Her gray voice ran down my spine, shutting off my throat. Breath held, I met the black of her eyes. I didn't say anything, afraid it might trigger her into movement, and I desperately didn't want her to move. Something had shifted, and I wasn't sure what was going on anymore.

"Both of my parents are vampires," she said, and though she didn't move, I felt the tension in the room swell until I couldn't hear the crickets. "I was conceived and born before my mother became a true undead. Do you know what that means—Rachel?" Her words were slow and precise, falling from her lips with the soft permanence of whispered psalms.

"No," I said, hardly breathing.

Ivy tilted her head so her hair made an obsidian wave that glistened in the low light. She watched me from around it. "The virus didn't have to wait until I was dead before shaping me," she said. "It molded me as I grew in my mother's womb, giving me a little of both worlds, the living and the dead."

Her lips parted, and I shuddered at the sight of her sharp teeth. I hadn't meant to. Sweat broke out on the small of my back, and as if in response, Ivy took a breath and held it. "It's easy for me to pull an aura," she said as she exhaled. "Actually, the trick is to keep it suppressed."

She uncurled from her chair, and my breath hissed in through my nose. Ivy jerked at the sound. Slow and methodical, she put her boots on the floor. "And although my reflexes and strength aren't as good as a true undead, they're better than yours," she said.

I knew all of this, and the question of why she was telling me increased my fear tenfold. Struggling not to show my alarm, I refused to shrink backward as she put her palms flat on the table to either side of her cross and leaned forward.

"What's more, I'm guaranteed to become an undead, even if I die alone in a field with every last drop of blood inside me. No worries, Rachel. I'm eternal already. Death will only make me stronger."

My heart pounded. I couldn't look away from her eyes. Damn. This was more than I wanted to know.

"And you know the best part?" she asked.

I shook my head, afraid my voice would crack. I was walking a knife edge, wanting to know what kind of a world she lived in but fighting to keep from entering it.

Her eyes grew fervent. Torso unmoving, she levered one of her knees up onto the coffee table, and then the other. God help me. She was coming at me.

"Living vamps can bespell people—if they want to be," she

whispered. The softness of her voice rubbed against my skin until it tingled. Double damn.

"What good is it if it only works on those who let you?" I asked, my voice harsh next to the liquid essence of hers.

Ivy's lips parted to show the tips of her teeth. I couldn't look away. "It makes for great sex—Rachel."

"Oh." The faint utterance was all I could manage. Her eyes were lost in lust.

"And I've got my mother's taste for blood," she said, kneeling on the table between us. "It's like some people's craving for sugar. It's not a good comparison but it's the best I can do unless you . . . try it."

Ivy exhaled, moving her entire body. Her breath sent a shock reverberating through me. My eyes went wide in surprise and bewilderment as I recognized it as desire. What the hell was going on? I was straight. Why did I suddenly want to know how soft her hair was?

All I'd have to do was reach out. She was inches from me. Poised. Waiting. In the silence, I could hear my heart pound. The sound of it echoed in my ears. I watched in horror as Ivy broke her gaze from mine, running it down my throat to where I knew my pulse throbbed.

"No!" I cried, panicking.

I kicked out, gasping in fear as I found her weight on me, pinning me to the chair.

"Ivy, no!" I shrieked. I had to get her off. I struggled to move. I took a lungful of air, hearing it explode from me in a cry of helplessness. How could I have been so stupid! She was a vampire!

"Rachel—stop."

Her voice was calm and smooth. Her one hand gripped my hair, pinning my head back to expose my neck. It hurt, and I heard myself whimper.

"You're making things worse," she said, and I wiggled, gasping as her grip on my wrist tightened until it hurt.

"Let me go. . . ." I panted, breathless, as if I had been running. "God, help me, Ivy. Let me go. Please. I don't want this." I was pleading. I couldn't help it. I was terrified. I'd seen the pictures. It hurt. God, it was going to hurt.

"Stop," she said again. Her voice was strained. "Rachel. I'm trying to let go of you, but you have to stop. You're making things worse. You have to believe me."

I took a gasping breath and held it. I flicked my gaze at what I could see of her. Her mouth was inches from my ear. Her eyes were black, the hunger in them a frightening contrast to the calm sound of her voice. Her gaze was fixed to my neck. A drop of saliva dropped warm onto my skin. "God, no," I whispered, shuddering.

Ivy quivered, her body trembling where it touched mine. "Rachel. Stop," she said again, and terror swept me at the new edge of panic in it. My breath came in a ragged pant. She really was trying to get off me. And by the sound of it, she was losing the battle.

"What do I do?" I whispered.

"Close your eyes," she said. "I need your help. I didn't know it was going to be this hard."

My mouth went dry at the little-lost-girl sound of her voice. It took all my will to close my eyes.

"Don't move."

Her voice was gray silk. Tension slammed through me. Nausea gripped my stomach. I could feel my pulse pushing against my skin. For what felt like a full minute I lay under her, all my instincts crying out to flee. The crickets chirped, and I felt tears slip from under my fluttering eyelids as her breath came and went on my exposed neck.

I cried out when her grip on my hair loosened. My breath came in a ragged gasp as her weight lifted from me. I couldn't smell her anymore. I froze, unmoving. "Can I open my eyes?" I whispered.

There was no answer.

I sat up to find myself alone. There was the faintest sound of the sanctuary door closing and the fast cadence of her boots on the sidewalk, then nothing. Numb and shaken, I reached up to first wipe my eyes and then my neck, smearing her saliva into a cold spot. My eyes rove over the room, finding no warmth in the soft gray. She was gone.

Drained, I stood up, not knowing what to do. I clutched my arms about myself so tight it hurt. My thoughts went back to the terror, and before that, the flash of desire that had washed through me, potent and heady. She had said she could only bespell the willing. Had she lied to me, or had I really wanted her to pin me to the chair and rip open my throat?

Seven

The sun was no longer slanting into the kitchen, but it was still warm. Not warm enough to reach the core of my soul, but nice. I was alive. I had all my body parts and fluids intact. It was a good afternoon.

I was sitting at the uncluttered end of Ivy's table, studying the most battered book I had found in the attic. It looked old enough to have been printed before the Civil War. Some of the spells I'd never heard of. It made for fascinating reading, and I would admit the chance to try one or two of them filled me with a dangerous titillation. None even hinted at the dark arts, which pleased me to no end. Harming someone with magic was foul and wrong. It went against everything I believed in—and it wasn't worth the risk.

All magic required a price paid by death in various shades of severity. I was strictly an earth witch. My source of power came gently from the earth through plants and was quickened by heat, wisdom, and witch blood. As I dealt only in white magic, the cost was paid by ending the life of plants. I could live with that. I wasn't going to delve into the morality of killing plants, otherwise I'd go insane every time I cut my mom's lawn. That wasn't to say that there weren't black earth witches—there were—but black earth magic had nasty ingredients like body parts and sacrifices. Just gathering the materials needed to stir a black spell was enough to keep most earth witches white.

Ley line witches, however, were another story. They drew their power right from the source, raw and unfiltered through living things. They, too, required death, but it was a subtler death—the slow death of the soul, and it wasn't necessarily theirs. The soul-death needed by white ley line witches wasn't as severe as that required by black witches, going back to the cutting the grass analogy vs. slaughtering goats in your basement. But creating a powerful spell designed to harm or kill left a definite wound on one's being.

Black ley line witches got around that by fostering that payment onto someone else, usually attaching it right on the charm to give the receiver a double whammy of bad luck. But if the person was insanely "pure of spirit" or more powerful, the cost, though not the charm, came right back to the maker. It was said that enough black on one's soul made it easy for a demon to pull you involuntarily into the ever-after.

Just as my dad had been, I thought as I rubbed my thumb against the page before me. I knew with all my being that he had been a white witch to the end. He would have had to be able to find his way back into reality, even though he didn't last to see the next sunrise.

A small sound jerked my attention up. I stiffened upon finding Ivy in a black silk robe, slumped against the doorframe. The memory of last night washed through me, knotting my stomach. I couldn't stop my hand from creeping up to my neck, and I changed the motion to adjusting my earring as I pretended to study the book before me. " 'Morning," I said cautiously.

"What time is it?" Ivy asked in a ragged whisper.

I flicked a glance at her. Her usually smooth hair was rumpled, waves from her pillow creasing it. Her eyes had dark circles under them, and her oval face was slack. Early afternoon lassitude had completely overwhelmed her air of stalking predator. She held a slim leather-bound book in her hand, and I wondered if her night had been as sleepless as mine.

"It's almost two," I said warily as I used a foot to push out a chair across the table from me so she wouldn't sit beside me. She seemed all right, but I didn't know how to treat her anymore. I was wearing my crucifix—not that it would stop her—and my silver ankle knife—which wasn't much better. A sleep amulet would drop her, but they were in my bag, sitting out of easy reach on a chair. It would take a good five seconds to invoke one. In all honesty, though, she didn't look like much of a threat right now.

"I made muffins," I said. "They were your groceries. I hope you don't mind."

"Uh," she said, shuffling across the shiny floor to the coffeepot in her black slippers. She poured herself a cup of lukewarm brew, leaning back against the counter to sip it. Her wish was gone from around her neck. I wondered what she had wished for. I wondered if it had anything to do with last night. "You're dressed," she whispered as she slumped into the chair I had kicked out for her in front of her computer. "How long have you been up?"

"Noon." *Liar*, I thought. I'd been up all night pretending to sleep on Ivy's couch. I decided to officially start my day when I put my clothes back on. Ignoring her, I turned a yellowing page. "Spent your wish, I see," I murmured cautiously. "What was it?"

"None of your business," she said, the warning obvious.

My breath left me in a slow exhalation, and I kept my eyes lowered. An uncomfortable silence descended and I let it grow, refusing to break it. I had almost left last night. But the certain death waiting for me outside Ivy's protection outweighed the possible death at Ivy's hands. Maybe. Maybe I wanted to know what it felt like for her teeth to sink into me.

This was *not* where I wanted my thoughts to go. Ivy had scared the crap out of me, but seeing her in the bright light of post noon, she looked human. Harmless. Dare I say, a grump?

"I have something I want you to read," she said, and I looked up as the thin book she had been holding hit the table between us. There was nothing written on the cover, the embossing almost completely worn away.

"What is it?" I said flatly, not reaching for it.

Eyes dropping, she licked her lips. "I'm sorry about last night," she said, and my gut tightened. "You probably won't believe me, but it scared me, too."

"Not as much as you scared me." Working with her for a year hadn't prepared me for last night. I'd only seen her professional side. I hadn't considered she was different away from the office. I flicked my eyes up at her and away. She looked entirely human. Neat trick, that.

"I haven't been a practicing vamp for three years," she said softly. "I wasn't prepared for . . . I didn't realize—" She looked up, her brown eyes pleading. "You have to believe me, Rachel. I didn't want that to happen. It's just that you were sending me all wrong signals. And then you got frightened, and then you panicked, and then it got worse."

"Worse?" I said, deciding anger was better than fear. "You nearly ripped out my throat!"

"I know," she implored. "I'm sorry. But I didn't."

I fought to keep from shuddering as I remembered the warmth of her saliva on my neck.

She nudged the book closer. "I know we can avoid a repeat of last night. I want this to work. There's no reason it can't. I owe you something for taking one of your wishes. If you leave, I can't protect you against the vamp assassins. You don't want to die at their hands."

My jaw clenched. No. I didn't want to die at the hands of a vampire. Especially one who would say she was sorry while killing me.

I met her gaze across the cluttered table. She sat in her black robe and kick-off slippers, looking as dangerous as a sponge. Her need for me to accept her apology was so raw and obvious, it was painful. I couldn't do it. Not yet. I reached a finger out to pull the book closer. "What is it?"

"A—uh—dating guide?" she said hesitantly.

I took a quick breath and drew my hand back as if stung. "Ivy. No."

"Wait," she said. "That's not what I mean. You're giving me mixed signals. My head knows you don't mean it, but my instincts . . ." Her brow furrowed. "It's embarrassing, but vampires, whether living or dead, are driven by instincts triggered mostly by . . . smell?" she finished apologetically. "Just read up on the turn-ons, okay? And don't do them."

I settled back into my chair. Slowly, I pulled the book closer, seeing how old it was by the binding. She had said instincts, but I thought hunger was more accurate. It was only the realization of how hard it had been for her to admit that she could be manipulated by something as stupid as smell that kept me from throwing the book back in her face. Ivy prided herself on her control, and to have confessed such a weakness to me told me more than a hundred apologies that she was really sorry. "All right," I said flatly, and she gave me a relieved, closed-lipped smile.

She took a muffin and pulled the evening edition of the *Cincinnati Enquirer* that I had found against the front door to her. The air was still tense, but it was a start. I didn't want to leave the security of the church, but Ivy's protection was a double-edged sword. She had bottled up her blood lust for three years. If she broke, I might be just as dead.

" 'Councilman Trenton Kalamack blames I.S. negligence in secretary's death,' " she read, clearly trying to change the subject.

"Yeah," I said cautiously. I put her book in the pile with my spell books to read later. My fingers felt dirty, and I wiped them on my jeans. "Ain't money grand? There's another story of him being cleared of all suspicion of dealing in Brimstone."

She said nothing, turning pages between bites of muffin until she found the article. "Listen to this," she said softly. "He says, 'I was shocked to learn of Mrs. Bates's second life. She seemed the model employee. I will, of course, pay for her surviving son's education.' " Ivy gave a short snort of mirthless laughter. "Typical." She turned to the comics. "So will you be spell crafting today?"

I shook my head. "I'm going to the records vault before they close for the weekend. This," I flicked a finger at the paper, "is useless. I want to see what really happened."

Ivy set down her muffin, thin eyebrows high in question.

"If I can prove Trent is dealing in Brimstone and give him to the I.S.," I said, "they'll forget about my contract. They have a standing warrant for him." *And then I can get the hell out of this church,* I added silently.

"Prove Trent runs Brimstone?" Ivy scoffed. "They can't even prove if he's human or Inderlander. His money makes him slipperier than frog spit in a rainstorm. Money can't buy innocence, but it can buy silence." She picked at her muffin. Dressed in her robe and with her sloppy hair, she could have been any of my sporadic roommates over the past years. It was unnerving. Everything changed when the sun was up.

"These are good," Ivy said as she held up a muffin. "Tell you what. I'll buy groceries if you make dinner. Breakfast and lunch I can get on my own, but I don't like cooking."

I made a face in understanding and agreement—I didn't appreciate the finer arts of culinary expertise, either—but then I thought about it. It would take up my time, but not having to go to the store sounded great. Even if Ivy only offered so I wouldn't have to put my life on the line for a can of beans, it sounded fair. I'd be cooking either way, and cooking for two was easier than cooking for one. "Sure," I said slowly. "We can try it for a while."

She made a soft noise. "It's a deal."

I glanced at my watch. It was one-forty. My chair squeaked across the linoleum as I stood up and grabbed a muffin. "Well, I'm out of here. I've got to get a car or something. This bus thing is awful."

Ivy laid out the comics atop the clutter surrounding her computer. "The I.S. isn't going to let you just walk in."

"They have to. Public record. And no one's going to tag me with a bunch of witnesses they will have to pay off. Cuts into their profits," I finished bitterly.

The arch to Ivy's eyebrows said more clearly than words she wasn't convinced.

"Look," I said as I pulled my bag from atop a chair and sorted through it. "I was going to use a disguise spell, all right? And I'll leave at the first sign of trouble."

The amulet I waved in the air seemed to satisfy her, but as she went back to her comics, she muttered, "Take Jenks with you?"

It really wasn't a question, and I grimaced. "Yeah. Sure." I knew he was a babysitter, but as I poked my head out the back door and yelled for him, I decided it would be nice having the company, even if it was a pixy.

Eight

I scrunched deeper into the corner of the bus seat, trying to make sure no one could look over my shoulder. The bus was crowded, and I didn't want anyone to know what I was reading.

"If your vampire lover is sated and won't be stirred," I read, "try wearing something of his or hers. It needn't be much, perhaps as little as a handkerchief or tie. The smell of your sweat mingling is something even the most restrained vampire can't resist."

Okay. Don't wear Ivy's robe or nightgown anymore.

"Often the mere washing of your clothes together leaves enough of a scent to let your lover know you care."

Fine. Separate loads.

"If your vampire lover moves to a more private location in the middle of a conversation, be assured that he or she isn't spurning you. It's an invitation. Go all out. Take some food or drink with you to get the jaws loosened up and the saliva moving. Don't be a flirt. Red wine is passé. Try an apple or something equally crunchy."

Damn.

"Not all vampires are alike. Find out if your lover likes pillow talk. Foreplay can take many forms. A conversation about past ties and bloodlines is sure to strike a chord and stir pride unless your lover is from a secondary house."

Double damn. I was a harlot. I was a freaking vampire hussy.

Eyes closed, I let my head fall against the back of the seat. A warm breath tickled my neck. I jerked upright, spinning. The heel of my hand was already in motion. It smacked into the palm of an attractive man. He laughed at the resounding pop, raising his hands in placation. But it was the soft, speculative amusement in his eyes that stopped me.

"Have you tried page forty-nine?" he asked, leaning forward to rest his crossed arms on the back of my seat.

I stared blankly at him, and his smile grew seductive. He was almost too pretty, his smooth features holding a childlike eagerness. His gaze slipped to the book in my hand. "Forty-nine," he repeated, his words dropping in pitch. "You'll never be the same."

On edge, I flipped to the right page. Oh—my—God. Ivy's book was illustrated. But then I hesitated, squinting as I became confused. Was there a third person in there? And what the hell was that bolted to the wall?

"This way," the man said, reaching over the seat and turning the book sideways in my grip. His cologne was woodsy and clean. It was as nice as his easy voice and soft hand intentionally brushing mine. He was the classic vampire flunky: nice build, dressed in black, and a frightening need to be liked. Not to mention his lack of understanding personal space.

I tore my gaze from his when he tapped the book. "Oh," I said, as it suddenly made sense. "Oh!" I exclaimed, warming as I slammed the book shut. There were two people. Three if you count the one with the . . . whatever it was.

My eyes rose to his. "You survived that?" I asked, not sure if I should be appalled, horrified, or impressed.

His gaze went almost reverent. "Yeah. I couldn't move my legs for two weeks, but it was worth it."

Heart pounding, I shoved the book into my bag. He rose with a charming smile and ambled forward to get off. I couldn't help but notice that he limped. I was surprised he could walk. He watched me as he descended the stairs, his deep eyes never leaving mine.

Swallowing hard, I forced myself to look away. Curiosity got the better of me, and even before the last of the people had gotten off the bus, I had pulled Ivy's book back out. My fingers were cold as I thumbed it open. I ignored the picture, reading the small print under the cheerful "How to" instructions. My face went cold and my stomach knotted.

It was a warning to not allow your vampire lover to coerce you into it until you had been bit at least three times. Otherwise, there might not be enough vamp saliva in your system to overwhelm the pain receptors, fooling your brain into thinking pain was pleasure. There were even instructions on how to keep from passing out if you indeed didn't have enough vamp saliva and you found yourself in agonizing pain. Apparently if the blood pressure dropped, so did the enjoyment of your vampire lover. Nothing on how to get him or her to stop, though.

Eyes closing, I let my head thump against the window. The chatter of the oncoming passengers pulled my eyes open, and I blinked as my gaze went to the sidewalk. The man was standing there, watching me. I clasped an arm about myself, chilled. He was smiling as if his groin hadn't been delicately incised and his blood pulled from him and consumed as if in communion. He had enjoyed it, or at least he thought he had.

He held up three fingers in the Boy Scout's salute, touched the tips of them to his lips, and blew me a kiss. The bus jerked into motion, and he walked away, the hem of his duster swinging.

Staring out the window, I felt nauseated. Had Ivy ever been a part of something like that? Maybe she had accidentally killed someone. Maybe that's why she wasn't practicing anymore. Maybe I should ask her. Maybe I should keep my mouth shut so I could sleep at night.

Closing the book, I pushed it to the bottom of my bag, starting as I found a slip of paper slid between the pages with a phone number on it. Crumpling it, I shoved it and the book in my bag. I looked up to see Jenks flitting back from where he had been talking with the driver.

He landed on the back of the seat in front of me. Apart from a gaudy red belt, he was wearing head-to-toe black: his work clothes. "No spells aimed at you on the new riders," he said cheerfully. "What did that guy want?"

"Nothing." I pushed the memory of that picture out of my mind. Where was Jenks last night when Ivy had pinned me? That's what I wanted to know. I would have asked him but was afraid he might tell me last night had been my fault.

"No, really," Jenks insisted. "What did he want?"

I stared at him. "No, really. Nothing. Now, drop it," I said, thankful I was already under my disguise spell. I did *not* want Mr. Page Forty-nine recognizing me on the street at some future date.

"All right, all right," he said, darting to land on my earring. He was humming "Strangers in the Night," and I sighed, knowing the song would be running in my head for the rest of the day. I pulled out my hand mirror and pretended to primp my hair, careful to whack the earring Jenks was sitting on at least twice.

I was a brunette now, with a big nose. A rubber band held my now brown hair back in a ponytail. It was still long and frizzy.

Some things are harder to spell than others. My jeans jacket was turned inside out to show a flowered paisley. I had a leather Harley-Davidson cap on. I'd be giving it back to Ivy with many apologies as soon as I saw her, and would never wear it again. With all the no-no's I'd pulled last night, it was no wonder Ivy had lost it.

The bus entered the shadow of tall buildings. My stop was next, and I gathered my things and stood. "I've got to get some transportation," I said to Jenks as my boots hit the sidewalk and I scanned the street. "Maybe a bike," I grumbled, timing it so I didn't have to touch the glass-paneled door to enter the lobby of the I.S. records building.

From my earring came a snort. "I wouldn't," he advised. "It's too easy to tamper with a motorbike. Stick with public transport."

"I could park it inside," I protested, nervously eyeing the few people in the small foyer.

"Then you couldn't ride it, Sherlock," he said sarcastically. "Your boot is untied."

I looked down. It wasn't. "Very funny, Jenks."

The pixy muttered something I couldn't hear. "No," he said impatiently. "I meant, pretend to tie your boot while I see if you're passably safe."

"Oh." I obediently went to a corner chair and retied my boot. I could hardly track Jenks as he hovered over the few runners that were about, sniffing for spells aimed at me. My timing had been precise. It was Saturday. The vault was open only as a courtesy, and only for a few hours. Still, a few people were about: dropping off information, updating files, copying stuff, trying to make a good impression by working on the weekend.

"Smells okay," Jinks said as he returned. "I don't think they expected you to come here."

"Good." Feeling more confident than I had any right to, I strode to the front desk. I was in luck. Megan was working. I gave her a smile and her eyes widened. She quickly reached to adjust her glasses. The wood-framed spectacles were spelled to see through almost everything. Standard issue for I.S. receptionists. There was a blur of motion before me, and I jerked to a halt.

"Heads up, woman!" Jenks shouted, but it was too late. Someone brushed against me. Instinct alone kept me standing as a foot slipped between my feet to trip me up. Panicked, I spun around into a crouch. My face went cold as I landed, ready for anything.

It was Francis. *What the Turn was he doing here?* I thought, rising to a stand as he held a hand to his stomach and laughed at me. I should have ditched my bag. But I hadn't expected to see anyone who knew me under my disguise charm.

"Nice hat, Rachel," Francis all but whined as he flicked the collar of his loud shirt back up. His tone was a disgusting mix of bravado and fading fright at me having nearly attacked him. "Hey, I bought six squares in the office pool yesterday. Is there any way you could die tomorrow between seven and midnight?"

"Why don't you tag me yourself?" I said with a sneer. Either the man had no pride or he didn't realize how ridiculous he looked, standing with one of his boat shoes untied and his stringy hair falling out of the spell-enhanced wave. And how could he have a stubble that thick this early in the day? He must have spray-painted it on.

"If I tagged you myself, I'd lose." Francis adopted his more usual air of superiority, a look entirely wasted on me. "I don't have time to talk with a dead witch," he said. "I have an appointment with Councilman Trenton Kalamack and need to do some research. You know, research? Ever done any of that?" He sniffed through his thin nose. "Not that I've heard."

"Go stuff a tomato, *Francis,*" I said softly.

He glanced down the hall that led to the vault. "Ooooh," he drawled. "I'm scared. You'd better leave now if you want any chance of getting back to your church alive. If Meg didn't trip the alarm that you're here, I will."

"Quit screaming into my jazz," I said. "You're really starting to tick me off."

"See you later, Rachel-me-gal. Like in the obituaries." His laugh was too high-pitched.

I gave him a withering look, and he signed the log-in book before Megan with a flourish. He turned and mouthed, "Run, witch. Run." Pulling out his cell phone, he punched a few buttons and strutted past the VIP's dark offices to the vault. Megan winced apologetically as she buzzed him through the gate.

My eyes closed in a long blink. When I opened them, I gave Megan a wave to say, "Just a minute," and sat in one of the lobby's chairs to dig in my bag as if looking for something. Jenks landed on my earring. "Let's go," he said, sounding worried. "We'll come back tonight."

"Yeah," I agreed. Denon spelling my apartment had been simple harassment. Sending an assassin team would be too expensive. I wasn't worth it. But why take chances?

"Jenks," I whispered. "Can you get in the vault without the cameras seeing you?"

"'Course I can, woman. Sneaking around is what pixies do best. 'Can I get past the cameras?' she asks. Who do you think does the maintenance on them? I'll tell you. Pixies. And do we ever get an ounce of credit? No-o-o-o-o. It's the lunker of a re-pairman who sits on his lard-butt at the bottom of the ladder, who drives the truck, who opens the toolbox, who scarfs down the doughnuts. But does he ever *do* anything? No-o-o-o-o—"

"That's great, Jenks. Shut up and listen." I glanced at Megan. "Go see what records Francis looks at. I'll wait for you as long as I can, but if there's any sign of a threat, I'm leaving. You can get home from here all right, can't you?"

Jenks's wings made a breeze, shifting a strand of hair to tickle my neck. "Yeah, I can do that. You want I should pix him for you while I'm in there?"

My eyebrows rose. "Pix him? You can do that? I thought it was a—uh—fairy tale."

He hovered before me, his small features smug. "I'll give him the itch. It's what pixies do second best." He hesitated, grinning roguishly. "No, make that third."

"Why not?" I said with a sigh, and he silently rose on his drag-onfly wings, studying the cameras. He hung for a moment to time their sweep. Shooting straight up to the ceiling, he arched down the long hallway, past the offices and to the vault's door. If I hadn't been watching, I'd never have seen him go.

I pulled a pen out of my bag, tugged the tie closed, and strode to Megan. The massive mahogany desk completely separated the lobby from the unseen grunt offices behind it. It was the final bastion between the public and the nitty-gritty workforce that kept the records straight. The sound of a female voice raised in laughter filtered out through the open archway behind Megan. No one did much work on Saturday. "Hi, Meg," I said as I drew closer.

"Good afternoon, Ms. Morgan," she said overly loudly as she adjusted her glasses.

Her attention was fixed over my shoulder, and I fought the urge to turn around. *Ms. Morgan?* I thought. *Since when was I Ms. Morgan?* "What gives, Meg?" I said, glancing behind me to the empty lobby.

She held herself stiffly. "Thank God you're still alive," she whispered from between her teeth, her lips still curled in a smile. "What are you doing here? You should be hiding in a basement." Before I could answer, she cocked her head like a spaniel, smiling like the blonde she wished she was. "What can I do for you to-day—Ms. Morgan?"

I made a quizzical face, and Megan sent her eyes meaning-fully over my shoulder. A strained look came over her. "The cam-era, idiot," she muttered. "The camera."

My breath slipped from me in understanding. I was more worried about Francis's phone call than the camera. No one looked at the tapes unless something happened. By then it would be too late.

"We're all pulling for you," Megan whispered. "The odds are running two hundred to one you make it through the week. Per-sonally, I give you a hundred to one."

I felt ill. Her gaze jumped behind me, and she stiffened. "Someone's behind me, aren't they?" I said, and she winced. I sighed, swinging my bag to rest against my back and out of the way before I turned on a slow heel.

He was in a tidy black suit, starched white shirt, and thin black tie. His arms were confidently laced behind his back. He didn't take his sunglasses off. I caught the faint scent of musk, and by the soft reddish beard, I guessed he was a werefox.

Another man joined him, standing between me and the front door. He didn't take his shades off, either. I eyed them, sizing them up. There would be a third somewhere, probably behind me. Assassins always worked in threes. *No more. No less. Always three*, I thought dryly, feeling my stomach tighten. Three against one wasn't fair. I looked down at the hall to the vault. "See you at home, Jenks," I whispered, knowing he couldn't hear me.

The two shades stood straighter. One unbuttoned his jacket coat to show a holster. My brow rose. They wouldn't gun me down in cold blood in front of a witness. Denon might be ticked, but he wasn't stupid. They were waiting for me to run.

I stood with my hands on my hips and my feet spread for bal-ance. Attitude is everything. "Don't suppose we could talk about this boys?" I said tartly, my heart hammering.

The one who had unbuttoned his coat grinned. His teeth were small and sharp. A mat of fine red hair covered the back of his hand. Yup. A werefox. Great. I had my knife, but the point was to stay far enough away that I wouldn't have to use it.

From behind me came Megan's irate shout, "Not in my lobby. Take it outside."

My pulse leapt. Meg would help? *Maybe,* I thought as I vaulted over her counter in a smooth move, *she just didn't want a stain on her carpet.*

"That way." Megan pointed behind her to the archway to the back offices.

There was no time for thanks. I darted through the doorway, finding myself in an open office area. Behind me were muffled thumps and shouted curses. The warehouse-sized room was divided with corporate's favorite four-foot walls, a maze of biblical proportions.

I smiled and waved at the startled faces of the few people working, my bag whacking into the partitions as I ran. I shoved the water cooler over in passing, shouting an insincere "Sorry" as it tipped. It didn't shatter but did come apart. The heavy glugging of water was soon overpowered by the cries of dismay and calls for a mop.

I glanced behind me. One of the shades was entangled with three office workers struggling to gain control of the heavy bottle. His weapon was hidden. So far, so good. The back door beckoned. I ran to the far wall, flinging open the fire door, relishing the colder air.

Someone was waiting. She was pointing a wide-mouth weapon at me.

"Crap!" I exclaimed, backpedaling to slam the door shut. Before it closed, a wet splat hit the partition behind me, leaving a gelatinous stain. The back of my neck burned. I reached up, crying out when I found a blister the size of a silver dollar. My fingers touching it burned.

"Swell," I whispered as I wiped the clear goo off on the hem of my jacket. "I don't have time for this." Kicking the emergency lock into place, I darted back into the maze. They weren't using delayed spells anymore. These were primed and loaded into splat balls. Just freaking great. My guess was it had been a spontaneous combustion spell. Had I gotten more than a back splash, I'd be dead. Nice little pile of ash on the Berber carpet. There was no way Jenks could have smelled this coming, even if he had been with me.

Personally, I'd rather be killed by a bullet. That, at least, was romantic. But it was harder to track down the maker of a lethal spell than it was to identify the manufacturer of a bullet or conventional gun. Not to mention that a good charm left no evidence. Or in the case of spontaneous combustion spells, not much of a body. No body. No crime. No need to do time.

"There!" someone shouted. I dove under a desk. Pain jolted my elbow as I landed on it. My neck felt like it was on fire. I had to get some salt on it, neutralize the spell before it spread.

My heart pounded as I shimmied out of my jacket. Splatters of goo decorated it. If I hadn't been wearing it, I'd probably be dead. I jammed it into someone's trashcan.

The calls for a mop were loud as I dug a vial of saltwater out of my bag. My fingers were burning and my neck was in agony. Hands shaking, I bit off the tube's plastic top. Breath held, I dumped the vial across my fingers and then my bowed neck. My breath hissed out at the sudden sting and whiff of sulfur as the black spell broke. Saltwater dripped from me to the floor. I spent one glorious moment relishing the cessation of pain.

Shaking, I dabbed at my neck with the hem of my sleeve. The blister under my careful fingers hurt, but the throb from the salt-water was soothing compared to the burn. I stayed where I was, feeling like an idiot as I tried to figure out how I was going to get out of there. I was a good witch. All my charms were defensive, not offensive. Slap 'em up and keep them off their feet until you subdue them was the name of the game. I'd always been the hunter, never the hunted. My brow furrowed as I realized I had nothing for this.

Megan's overloud fussing told me exactly where everyone was. I felt my blister again. It wasn't spreading. I was lucky. My breath caught at the soft pacing a few cubicles over. I wished I wasn't sweating so much. Weres have excellent noses, but one-track minds. It was probably only the lingering scent of sulfur that had kept him from finding me already. I couldn't stay here. A faint pounding on the back door told me it was time to go.

Tension throbbed in my head as I cautiously peeked over the walls to see shade number one padding through the cubicles to let shade number three in. Taking a soft breath, I moved the opposite way in a crouched run. I was betting my life that the assassins had kept one of their number at the front door and that I wouldn't bump into him halfway there.

Thanks to Megan's nonstop harangue about the water on the floor, I made it to the archway to the lobby with no one the wiser. Face cold, I looked around the doorframe to find the reception desk deserted. Papers littered the floor. Pens rolled under my feet.

Megan's keyboard hung from its cord, still swaying. Hardly breathing, I skulked my way to the opening in the counter where it flipped up. Still at ground level, I shot a quick glance past the front desk.

My heart gave a quick pound. There was a shade fidgeting by the door, looking surly at having been left behind. But getting past one was better odds than getting past two.

Francis's whiny voice came faint from the vault. "Here? Denon set them on her here? He must be pissed. Nah, I'll be right back. I gotta see this. It ought to be worth a laugh."

His voice was getting closer. *Maybe Francis would like to go for a stroll with me,* I thought, hope bringing my muscles tight. One thing you could count on with Francis was that he was curious *and* stupid, a dangerous combination in our profession. I waited, adrenaline singing through me, until he lifted the counter panel and came behind the desk.

"What a mess," he said, more interested in the clutter on the floor than me rising behind him. He never saw me coming, too busy scratching. Like clockwork, I slipped an arm about his neck, wrenching one of his arms back behind him, nearly lifting him off his feet.

"Ow! Damn it, Rachel!" he shouted, too cowed to know how easy it would be to elbow me in the gut and get away. "Lemme go! This isn't funny."

Swallowing, I sent my frightened eyes to the shade by the door, his weapon pulled and aimed. "No it isn't, cookie," I breathed in Francis's ear, painfully aware how close to death we were. Francis didn't have a clue, and the thought he might do something stupid scared me more than the gun. My heart pounded and I felt my knees go loose. "Hold still," I told him. "If he thinks he can get a shot off on me, he might take it."

"Why should I care?" he snarled back.

"You see anyone else out here but you, me, and the gun?" I said softly. "Wouldn't be hard to get rid of one witness, now would it?"

Francis stiffened. I heard a small gasp as Megan appeared in the doorway to the back offices. More people peered over and around her, whispering loudly. I sent my gaze darting over them, feeling the pinch of panic. There were too many people. Too many opportunities for something to go wrong.

I felt better when the shade eased from his crouch and tucked his pistol away. He put his arms to his side, palms out in an insincere gesture of acquiescence. Tagging me before so many witnesses would be too costly. Stalemate.

I kept Francis before me as an unwilling shield. There was a whisper of sound as the other two shades ghosted out of the office area. They held themselves against the back wall of Megan's office. One had a drawn weapon. He took in the situation and holstered it.

"Okay, Francis," I said. "It's time for your afternoon constitutional. Nice and slow."

"Shove it, Rachel," he said, his voice shaking and sweat beading his forehead.

We edged out from behind the desk, me struggling to keep Francis upright as he slipped on the rolling pens. The Were by the door obligingly stepped aside. His attitude was clear enough. They were in no hurry. They had time. Under their watchful eyes, Francis and I backed out the door and into the sun.

"Lemme go," Francis said, beginning to struggle. Pedestrians gave us a wide birth, and the passing cars slowed to watch. I hate rubberneckers, but maybe it would work for me. "Go on, run," Francis said. "That's what you do best, Rachel."

I tightened my grip until he grunted. "You got that right. I'm a better runner than you'll ever be." The surrounding people were starting to scatter, realizing this was more than a lover's quarrel. "You might want to start running, too," I said, hoping to add to the confusion.

"What the hell are you talking about?" His sweat stank over his cologne.

I dragged Francis across the street, weaving between the slowed cars. The three shades had come out to watch. They stood with taut alertness by the door in their dark glasses and black suits. "I imagine they think you're helping me. I mean really," I taunted, "a big, strong witch like you not able to get away from a frail wisp of a girl like me?" I heard his quick intake of breath in understanding. "Good boy," I said. "Now run."

With the traffic between me and the shades, I dropped Francis and ran, losing myself in the pedestrian traffic. Francis took off the other way. I knew if I got enough distance between us, they wouldn't follow me home. Weres were superstitious and wouldn't violate the sanctuary of holy ground. I'd be safe—until Denon sent something else after me.

Nine

"Something else," I mused as I turned a brittle yellow page that smelled of gardenias and ether. A spell of inconspicuousness would be great, but it called for fern seed. Not only didn't I have time to gather enough, but also it wasn't the right season. Findlay Market would have it, but I didn't have the time. "Get real, Rachel," I breathed, shutting the book and straightening my back painfully. "You can't stir anything that difficult."

Ivy was lounging across from me at the kitchen table, filling out the change of address forms she had picked up and crunching through the last of her celery and dip. It was all the supper I had time to make. She didn't seem to care. Maybe she was going out later and pick up a snack. Tomorrow, if I lived to see it, I'd make a real supper. Maybe pizza. The kitchen was not conducive to food preparation tonight.

I was spelling; I'd made a mess. Half-chopped plants, dirt, green-stained bowls with strained gratings left to cool, and dirty copper pots overflowed the sink. It looked like Yoda's kitchen meets the *Galloping Gourmet.* But I had my detection amulets, sleep inducers, even some new disguise charms to make me look old instead of younger. I couldn't help a wash of satisfaction for having made them myself. As soon as I found a strong enough spell to break into the I.S. records vault, Jenks and I were out of here.

Jenks had come in that afternoon with a slow, shaggy Were of a man trailing after him, his friend who had my stuff. I bought the musty-smelling cot he had with him, thanking him for bringing over the few articles of clothing that hadn't been spelled: my winter coat and a pair of pink sweats that were stuck in a box in the back of my closet. I had told the man not to bother with anything else right now but my clothes, music, and kitchen stuff, and he shuffled away with a hundred clutched in his grip, promising to at least have my clothes by tomorrow.

Sighing, I looked up from my book, past Mr. Fish on the windowsill and into the black garden. My hand cupped over the blister on my neck, and I pushed the book away to make room for the next. Denon must have been seriously ticked to set the Weres after me in broad daylight, when they were at a severe disadvantage. If it had been night, I'd probably be dead—new moon or not. That he was wasting money told me he must have been taken apart for letting Ivy go.

After eluding the Weres, I had splurged for a cab home. I justified it by saying it was to avoid the possible hit men on the bus, but the reality was, I didn't want anyone to see me with the shakes. They started three blocks after I got in the cab and didn't quit until I was in the shower long enough to have drained all the hot water from the water heater. I had never been on the hunted end of the game. I didn't like it. But what scared me almost as much was the thought that I might have to make and use a black spell to keep myself alive.

Much of my job had entailed bringing in "gray spell" crafters—witches who took a perfectly good spell like a love charm and turned it to a bad use. But the serious black magic users were out there, and I'd brought them in, too: the ones specializing in the darker forms of entrapment, the people who could make you go missing—and for a few dollars more, spell your relatives into not remembering you even existed—the handful of Inderlanders driving Cincinnati's underground power struggles. Sometimes the best I had been able to do was to cover up the ugly reality so that humanity never knew how difficult it was to rein in the Inderlanders who thought of humans as free-range cattle. But never had I had anyone come at me like that before. I wasn't sure how to keep myself safe and my karma clean at the same time.

The last of my daylight hours had been spent in the garden. Messing about in the dirt with pixy children getting in the way is a great way to ground oneself, and I found I owed Jenks a very large thank-you—in more ways than one. It wasn't until I went inside with my spell-crafting materials and a sunburnt nose that I found out what their cheerful shouts and calls had been about. They hadn't been playing hide and seek; they were intercepting splat balls.

The small pyramid of splat balls neatly stacked by the back

door had shocked the peas out of me. Each one held my death. I hadn't known. Not a freaking clue. Seeing them there ticked me off, making me angry instead of afraid. Next time the hunters found me, I vowed, I'd be ready.

After my whirlwind of spell crafting, my bag was full of my usual charms. The dowel of redwood from work had been a lifesaver. Any wood can store spells, but redwood lasts the longest. The amulets not in my bag hung from the cup hooks in the otherwise empty cupboard. They were all great spells, but I needed something stronger. Sighing, I opened the next book.

"Transmutation?" Ivy said, setting the forms aside and pulling her keyboard closer. "You're that good?"

I ran a thumbnail under a fingernail to get the dirt out from under it. "Necessity is the mother of courage," I mumbled. Not meeting her eyes, I scanned the index. I needed something small, preferably that could defend itself.

Ivy returned to her surfing with a loud crunch of celery. I had been watching her closely since sundown. She was the model roommate, clearly making an effort to keep her normal vampy reactions to a minimum. It probably helped that I had rewashed my clothes. The moment she started looking seductive, I was asking her to leave.

"Here's one," I said softly. "A cat. I need an ounce of rosemary, half a cup of mint, one teaspoon of milkweed extract gathered after the first frost . . . Well, that's out. I don't have any extract, and I'm not about to go to the store now."

Ivy seemed to swallow back a chuckle, and I flipped to the index. Not a bat; I didn't have an ash tree in the garden, and I'd probably need some of the inner bark. Besides, I wasn't going to spend the rest of the night learning to fly by echolocation. The same went for birds. Most of those listed didn't fly at night. A fish was just silly. But maybe . . .

"A mouse," I said, turning to the proper page and looking over the list of ingredients. Nothing was exotic. Almost everything I needed was already in the kitchen. There was a handwritten note at the bottom, and I squinted to read a faded, masculine-looking script: *Can be safely adapted for any rodent.* I glanced at the clock. This would do.

"A mouse?" Ivy said. "You're going to spell yourself into a mouse?"

I stood, went to the stainless steel island in the center of the kitchen, and propped the book up. "Sure. I've got everything but the mouse hair." My eyebrows rose. "Do you think I could have one of your owl's pellets? I need to strain the milk past some fur."

Ivy tossed her wave of black hair over her shoulder, her thin eyebrows high. "Sure. I'll get you one." Shaking her head, she closed the site she was looking at and rose with a stretch tall enough to show her bare midriff. I blinked at the red jewel piercing her belly button, then looked away. "I need to let them out anyway," she said as she collapsed in on herself.

"Thanks." I turned back to my recipe, going over exactly what I needed and gathering it on the kitchen island. By the time Ivy padded down from the belfry, everything was measured and waiting. All that was left was the stirring.

"It's all yours," she said, setting a pellet on the counter and going to wash her hands.

"Thank you," I whispered. I took a fork and teased the felt mass apart, pulling three hairs from among the tiny bones. I made a face, reminding myself that it hadn't gone all the way through the owl, just been regurgitated.

Grabbing a fistful of salt, I turned to her. "I'm going to make a salt circle. Don't try to cross it, okay?" She stared, and I added, "It's a potentially dangerous spell. I don't want anything to get into the pot by accident. You can stay in the kitchen, just don't cross the circle."

Looking unsure, she nodded. "Okay."

I kind of liked seeing her off balance, and I made the circle bigger than usual, enclosing the entirety of the center island with all my paraphernalia. Ivy levered herself up to sit on a corner of the counter. Her eyes were wide with curiosity. If I was going to do this a lot, I might want to blow off the security deposit and etch a groove in the linoleum. What good is a security deposit if you're dead from a misaligned spell?

My heart beat fast. It had been a while since I'd closed a circle, and Ivy watching made me nervous. "All right, then . . ." I murmured. I took a slow breath, willing my mind to empty and my eyes to close. Slowly, my second sight wavered into focus.

I didn't do this often, as it was confusing as all get-out. A wind that wasn't from this side of reality lifted the lighter strands of my hair. My nose wrinkled at the smell of burnt amber. Immediately I felt like I was outside as the surrounding walls vanished to silvery hints. Ivy, even more transitory than the church, was gone. Only the landscape and plants remained, their outlines quavering with the same reddish glow that thickened the air. It was as if I stood in the same spot before mankind found it. My skin crawled when I realized the gravestones existed in both worlds, as white and solid looking as the moon would be if it were up.

Eyes still closed, I reached out with my second sight, searching for the nearest ley line. "Holy crap," I murmured in surprise, finding a reddish smear of power running right through the graveyard. "Did you know there's a ley line running through the cemetery?"

"Yes," Ivy said softly, her voice coming from nowhere.

I stretched out my will and touched it. My nostrils flared as force surged into me, backwashing at my theoretical extremities until the power equalized. The university was built on a ley line so big that it could be drawn upon almost anywhere in Cincinnati. Most cities are built on at least one. Manhattan has three of considerable size. The largest ley line on the East Coast runs through a farm outside of Woodstock. Coincidence? I think not.

The ley line in my backyard was tiny, but it was so close and underused that it gave me more strength than the university's ever had. Though no real breeze touched me, my skin prickled from the wind blowing in the ever-after.

Tapping into a ley line was a rush, albeit a dangerous one. I didn't like it. Its power ran through me like water, seeming to leave an ever-growing residue. I couldn't keep my eyes closed any longer, and they flew open.

The surreal red vision of the ever-after was replaced by my humdrum kitchen. I stared at Ivy perched on the counter, seeing her with the earth's wisdom. Sometimes a person looks totally different. I was relieved to see Ivy looked the same. Her aura—her real aura, not her vamp aura—was streaked with sparkles. How very odd. She was looking for something.

"Why didn't you tell me there was a ley line so close?" I asked.

Ivy's eyes flicked over me. Shrugging, she crossed her legs and kicked off her shoes to land them under the table. "Would it have made any difference?"

No. It didn't make any difference. I shut my eyes to strengthen my fading second sight while I closed the circle. The heady flood of latent power made me uncomfortable. With my will, I moved the narrow band of salt from this dimension into the ever-after. It was replaced with an equal ring of ever-after reality.

The circle snapped shut with a skin-tingling jolt, and I jumped. "Cripes," I whispered. "Maybe I used too much salt." Most of the force I had pulled from the ever-after now flowed through my circle. What little remained eddying through me still made my skin crawl. The residue would continue to grow until I broke the circle and disconnected from the ley line.

I could feel the barrier of ever-after reality surrounding me as a faint pressure. Nothing could cross the quickly shifting bands of alternate realities. With my second sight, I could see the shimmering wave of smudged red rising up from the floor to arch to a close just over my head. The half sphere went the same distance beneath me. I would do a closer inspection later to be sure I wasn't bisecting any pipes or electrical lines, making the circle vulnerable to breakage should anything actively try to get through that way.

Ivy was watching me when I opened my eyes. I gave her a mirthless smile and turned away. Slowly my second sight diminished to nothing, overwhelmed by my usual vision. "Locked down tight," I said as her aura seemed to vanish. "Don't try to cross it. It'll hurt."

She nodded, her placid face solemn. "You're—witchier," she said slowly.

I smiled, pleased. Why not let the vamp see the witch had teeth, too? Taking the smallest copper mixing bowl, about the size of my cupped hands, I set it over the lit campfire-in-a-can that Ivy had bought for me earlier. I had used the stove for crafting my lesser spells, but again, a working gas line would have left an opening in the circle. "Water . . ." I murmured, filling my graduated cylinder with spring water and squinting to make sure I read it properly. The vat sizzled as I added it, and I raised the bowl up from the flame. "Mouse, mouse, mouse," I mused, trying not to show how nervous I was. This was the hardest spell I had tried outside of class.

Ivy slipped from the counter, and I stiffened. The hair on the back of my neck rose as she came to stand behind my shoulder but still out of the circle. I stopped what I was doing and gave her a look. Her smile went sheepish and she moved to the table.

"I didn't know you tapped into the ever-after," she said, settling before her monitor.

I looked up from the recipe. "As an earth witch, I don't very often. But this spell will physically change me, not just give the illusion I'm a mouse. If something gets in the pot by accident, I might not be able to break it, or end up only halfway changed . . . or something."

She made a noncommittal noise, and I set the mouse hair into a sieve to pour milk over. There is an entire branch of witchcraft that uses ley lines instead of potions, and I had spent two semesters cleaning up after one of my professor's labs so I wouldn't have to take more than the basic course. I had told everyone it was because I didn't have a familiar yet—which was a safety requirement—but the truth of it was, I simply didn't like them. I'd lost a good friend when he decided to major in ley lines and drifted into a bad crowd. Not to mention my dad's death had been linked to them. And it didn't help that the ley lines were gateways to the ever-after.

It's claimed the ever-after used to be a paradise where the elves had dwelt, popping into our reality long enough to steal human children. But when demons took over and trashed the place, the elves were forced to bide here for good. Of course, that was even before Grimm was writing his fairy tales. It's all there in the older, more savage stories/histories. Almost every one of them ends with, "And they lived happy in the ever-after." Well . . . that's the way it's supposed to go. Grimm lost the "in the" part somewhere. That some witches use ley lines probably accounted for the longstanding misinterpretation that witches aligned themselves with demons. I shudder to think how many lives that mistake had ended.

I was strictly an earth witch, dealing solely with amulets, potions, and charms. Gestures and incantations were in the realm of ley line magic. Witches specializing in this branch of craft tapped directly into ley lines for their strength. It was a harsher magic, and I thought less structured and beautiful, since it lacked much of the discipline earth enchantment had. The only benefit I could see in ley line magic was that it could be invoked instantly with the right word. The drawback was that one had to carry around a slice of ever-after in their chi. I didn't care that there were ways to isolate it from your chakras. I was convinced that the demonic taint from the ever-after left some sort of accumulated smut on your soul. I'd seen too many friends lose their ability to clearly see what side of the fence their magic was on.

Ley line magic was where the greatest potential for black magic lay. If a charm was hard to trace back to its maker, finding out who cursed your car with ley line magic was nigh impossible. That's not to say all ley line witches were bad—their skills were in high demand in the entertainment, weather control, and security industries—but with such a close association with the ever-after and the greater power at one's disposal, it was easy to lose one's morals.

My lack of advancement with the I.S. might be placed at the feet of my refusal to use ley line magic to apprehend the big bad uglies. But what was the difference if I tagged them with a charm instead of an incantation? I had gotten very good fighting ley line magic with earth, though one wouldn't be able to tell that looking at my tag/run ratio.

The memory of that pyramid of splat balls outside my back door twinged through me, and I poured the milk over the mouse hair and into the pot. The mixture was boiling, and I raised the bowl even higher on its tripod, stirring it with a wooden spoon. Using wood while spelling wasn't a good idea, but all my ceramic spoons were still cursed, and to use metal other than copper would be inviting disaster. Wood spoons tended to act like amulets, absorbing spell and leading to embarrassing mistakes, but if I soaked it in my vat of saltwater when done, I'd be fine.

Hands on my hips, I read over the spell again and set the timer. The simmering mix was starting to smell musky. I hoped that was all right.

"So," Ivy said as she clicked and clacked at her keyboard. "You're going to sneak into the records vault as a mouse. You won't be able to open the file cabinet."

"Jenks says he has a copy of everything already. We just have to go look at it."

Ivy's chair creaked as she leaned back and crossed her legs, her doubt that we two midgets would be able to handle a keyboard obvious in how she had her head cocked. "Why don't you just change back to a witch once you're there?"

I shook my head as I double-checked the recipe. "Transformations invoked by a potion last until you get a solid soaking in saltwater. If I wanted, I could transform using an amulet, break into the vault, take it off, find what I need as a human, and then put the amulet back on to get out. But I'm not going to."

"Why not?"

She was just full of questions, and I looked up from adding the fuzz of a pussytoes plant. "Haven't you ever used a transformation spell?" I questioned. "I thought vamps used them all the time to turn into bats and stuff."

Ivy dropped her eyes. "Some do," she said softly.

Obviously Ivy had never transformed. I wondered why. She certainly had the money for it. "It's not a good idea to use an amulet for transforming," I said. "I'd have to tie the amulet to me or wear it around my neck, and all my amulets are bigger than a mouse. Kind of awkward. And what if I was in a wall and dropped it? Witches have died from despelling back to normal and solidifying with extra parts—like a wall or cage." I shuddered, giving the brew a quick clockwise stir. "Besides," I added softly, "I won't have any clothes on when I turn back."

"Ha!" Ivy barked, and I jerked. "Now we hear the real reason. Rachel, you're shy!"

What could I say to that? Mildly embarrassed, I closed my spell book and shelved it under the island with the rest of my new library. The timer dinged, and I blew out the flame. There wasn't much liquid left. It wouldn't take long to reach room temperature.

Wiping my hands off on my jeans, I reached across the clutter for a finger stick. Many a witch before the Turn had feigned a mild case of diabetes in order to get these little gems for free. I hated them, but it was better than using a knife to open a vein, as they had in less enlightened times. Poised to jab myself, I suddenly hesitated. Ivy couldn't cross the circle, but last night was still very real in my thoughts. I'd sleep in a salt circle if I could, but the continuous connection to the ever-after would make me insane if I didn't have a familiar to absorb the mental toxins the lines put out. "I—uh—need three drops of my blood to quicken it," I said.

"Really?" Her look entirely lacked that intent expression that generally proceeded a vamp's hunting aura. Still, I didn't trust her.

I nodded. "Maybe you should leave."

Ivy laughed. "Three drops drawn from a finger stick isn't going to do anything."

Still I hesitated. My stomach clenched. How could I be sure she knew her limits? Her eyes narrowed and red spots appeared on her pale cheeks. If I insisted she leave, she would take offense, I could tell. And I wasn't about to show I was afraid of her. I was absolutely safe within my circle. It could stop a demon; stopping a vamp was nothing.

I took a breath and stuck my finger. There was a flicker of black in her eyes and a chill through me, then nothing. My shoulders eased. Emboldened, I massaged three drops into the brew. The brown, milky liquid looked the same, but my nose could tell the difference. I closed my eyes, bringing the smell of grass and grain deep into my lungs. I would need three more drops of my blood to prime each dose before use.

"It smells different."

"What?" I jumped, cursing my reaction. I had forgotten she was there.

"Your blood smells different," Ivy said. "It smells woody. Spicy. Like dirt, but dirt that's alive. Human blood doesn't smell like that, or vampire."

"Um," I muttered, quite sure I didn't like that she could smell three drops of my blood from halfway across the room through a barrier of ever-after. But it was reassuring to know she had never bled a witch.

"Would my blood work?" she asked intently.

I shook my head as I gave the brew a nervous stir. "No. It has to be from a witch or warlock. It's not the blood but the enzymes that are in it. They act as a catalyst."

She nodded, clicking her computer into sleep mode and sitting back to watch me.

I rubbed the tip of my finger to smear the slick of blood to nothing. Like most, this recipe made seven spells. The ones I didn't use tonight, I'd store as potions. If I cared to put them in amulets, they would last a year. But I wouldn't transform with an amulet for anything.

Ivy's eyes were heavy on me as I carefully divided the brew into the thumb-sized vials and capped them tightly. Done. All that was left was to break the circle and my connection to the ley line. The former was easy, the second was a tad more difficult.

Giving Ivy a quick smile, I reached out with my fuzzy pink slipper and pushed a gap into the salt. The background thrum of ever-after power swelled. My breath hissed in through my nose as all the strength that had been flowing through the circle now flowed through me.

"What's the matter?" Ivy asked from her chair, sounding alert and concerned.

I made a conscious effort to breathe, thinking I might hyperventilate. I felt like an overinflated balloon. Eyes on the floor, I waved her away. "Circle's broken. Stay back. Not done yet," I said, feeling both giddy and unreal.

Taking a breath, I started to divorce myself from the line. It was a battle between the baser desire for power and the knowledge that it would eventually drive me insane. I had to force it from me, pushing it out from my head to my toes until the power returned back to the earth.

My shoulders slumped as it left me, and I staggered, reaching out for the counter.

"Are you okay?" Ivy asked, close and intent.

Gasping, I looked up. She was holding my elbow to keep me

upright. I hadn't seen her move. My face went cold. Her fingers were warm through my shirt. "I used too much salt. The connection was too strong. I—I'm all right. Let go of me."

The concern in her face vanished. Clearly affronted, she let me go. The sound of the salt crunching under her feet was loud as she went back to her corner and sat in her chair, looking hurt. I wasn't going to appologize. I hadn't done anything wrong.

Heavy and uncomfortable, the silence weighed on me as I put all but one vial away in the cabinet with my extra amulets. As I gazed at them, I couldn't help but feel a twinge of pride. I had made them. And even if the insurance I'd need to sell them was more than I made in a year at the I.S., I could use them.

"Do you want some help tonight?" Ivy asked. "I don't mind covering your back."

"No," I blurted. It was a little too quick, and her features folded into a frown. I shook my head, smiling to soften my refusal, wishing I could bring myself to say, "Yes, please." But I still couldn't quite trust her. I didn't like putting myself in a situation where I had to trust anyone. My dad had died because he trusted someone to get his back. "Work alone, Rachel," he had told me as I sat beside his hospital bed and gripped his shaking hand as his blood lost its ability to carry oxygen. "Always work alone."

My throat tightened as I met Ivy's eyes. "If I can't lose a couple of shades, I deserve to be tagged," I said, avoiding the real issue. I put my collapsible bowl and a bottle of saltwater into my bag, adding one of my new disguise amulets that no one from the I.S. had seen.

"You aren't going to try one first?" Ivy asked when it became obvious I was leaving.

I nervously brushed a curling strand of hair back. "It's getting late. I'm sure it's fine."

Ivy didn't seem very happy. "If you aren't back by morning, I'm coming after you."

"Fair enough." If I wasn't back by morning, I'd be dead. I snagged my long winter coat from a chair and shrugged into it. I gave Ivy a quick, uneasy smile before I slipped out the back door. I'd go through the graveyard and pick up the bus on the next street over.

The spring night air was cold, and I shivered as I eased the screen door shut. The pile of splat balls at my feet was a reminder I didn't appreciate. Feeling vulnerable, I slipped into the shadow of the oak tree to wait for my eyes to adjust to a night with no moon. It was just past new and wouldn't be up until nearly dawn. *Thank you, God, for small favors.*

"Hey, Ms. Rachel!" came a tiny buzz, and I turned, thinking for an instant it was Jenks. But it was Jax, Jenks's oldest son. The preadolescent pixy had kept me company all afternoon, nearly getting snipped more times than I would care to recall as his curiosity and attention to "duty" brought him perilously close to my scissors while his father slept.

"Hi, Jax. Is your dad awake?" I asked, offering him a hand to alight upon.

"Ms. Rachel?" he said, his breath fast as he landed. "They're waiting for you."

My heart gave a thump. "How many? Where?"

"Three." He was glowing pale green in excitement. "Up front. Big guys. Your size. Stink like foxes. I saw them when old man Keasley chased them off his sidewalk. I would've told you sooner," he said urgently, "but they didn't cross the street, and we already stole the rest of their splat balls. Papa said not to bother you unless someone came over the wall."

"It's okay. You did good." Jax took flight as I eased into motion. "I was going to cut across the backyard and pick up the bus on the other side of the block anyway." I squinted in the faint light, giving Jenks's stump a soft tap. "Jenks," I said softly, grinning at the almost subliminal roar of irritation that flowed from the old ash stump. "Let's go to work."

Ten

The pretty woman sitting across from me on the bus stood to get off. She paused, standing too close to me for comfort, and I looked up from Ivy's book. "Table 6.1," she said as I met her gaze. "It's *all* you need to know." Her eyes closed, and she shuddered as if in pleasure.

Embarrassed, I thumbed to the back. "Jiminy Cricket," I whispered. It was a table of accessories and suggested uses. My face warmed. I wasn't a prude, but some of it . . . and with a vampire? Maybe with a witch. If he was drop-dead gorgeous. Without the blood. *Maybe.*

I jerked as she crouched in the aisle. Leaning far too close, she dropped a black business card into the open book. "In case you want a second," she whispered, smiling with a quick kinship I didn't understand. "Newbies shine like stars, bringing out the best in them. I don't mind playing second fiddle to your first night. And I could help you . . . afterward. Sometimes they forget." A flash of fear crossed her, quick but very real.

Jaw hanging, I could say nothing as she stood and walked away and down the stairs.

Jenks flitted close, and I snapped the book shut. "Rache," he said as he landed on my earring. "Whatcha reading? You've had your nose in it since we got on the bus."

"Nothing," I said, feeling my pulse hammer. "That woman. She was human, right?"

"The one talking to you? Yeah. By the smell of it, she's a vamp flunky. Why?"

"No reason," I said as I shoved the book to the bottom of my bag. I was never reading this thing in public again. Fortunately, my stop was next. Ignoring Jenks's nonstop inquisition, I strode into the mall's food court. My long coat flapped about my ankles as I immersed myself in the hustle of predawn Sunday shopping. I invoked my old lady disguise in the bathroom, hoping to throw off anyone who might have recognized me. Still, I thought it prudent to lose myself in a crowd before I headed to the I.S.: kill some time, gather my courage, pick up a hat to replace the one of Ivy's I'd lost today—buy some soap to cover any lingering smell of her on me.

I strode past an amulet outlet without my usual, wistful hesitation. I could make anything I wanted, and if someone was looking for me, that's where they would watch. *But no one would expect me to buy a pair of boots,* I thought, my steps slowing as I passed a window. The leather curtains and dim lights said more clearly than the name of the shop that it catered to vamps.

What the heck? I thought. *I live with a vamp.* The sales associate couldn't be any worse than Ivy. I was savvy enough to buy something without leaving any blood behind. So, ignoring Jenks's complaints, I went in. My thoughts flicked from Table 6.1 to the flirtatious, handsome clerk who had warned the other salesmen off after taking a peek at me through a pair of wood-rimmed glasses. His name tag said VALENTINE, and I ate up his attention with a spoon as he helped me choose a good pair of boots, ooohing over my silk stockings and caressing my feet with his strong, cool fingers. Jenks waited in the hall in a potted plant, sullen and bad-tempered.

God help me, but Valentine was pretty. It had to be in the vamp job description, like wearing black and knowing how to flirt without triggering any of my proximity alarms. It didn't hurt to look, right? I could look and still not join the club, yes?

But as I walked out in my new, too expensive boots, I wondered at my sudden curiosity. Ivy had as much as admitted to me that she was driven by smell. Perhaps they all put out pheromones to subliminally soothe and lure the unsuspecting. It would make it far easier to seduce their prey. I had thoroughly enjoyed myself with Valentine, as relaxed as if he had been an old friend, letting him take teasing liberties with his hands and words that I normally wouldn't. Shaking the uncomfortable thought away, I continued my shopping.

I had to stop at the Big Cherry for some pizza sauce. Humans would boycott any store that sold tomatoes—even though the T-4

Angel variety was long extinct—so the only place you could get them was a specialty shop where it wouldn't matter if half the world's population refused to cross your threshold.

It was nerves that made me stop at the sweet shop. Everyone knows chocolate soothes the jitters; I think they did a study on it. And for five glorious minutes, Jenks stopped talking while he ate the caramel I bought him.

Stopping at The Bath and Body was a must—I wouldn't use Ivy's shampoo and soap anymore. And that led me to a scent shop. With Jenks's grudging help, I picked out a new perfume that helped hide Ivy's lingering scent. Lavender was the only thing that came close. Jenks said I stank like an explosion in a flower factory. I didn't especially like it, either, but if it kept me from triggering Ivy's instincts, I'd drink it, much less simply bathe in it.

Two hours before sunup I was back on the street and headed for the records vault. My new boots were deliciously quiet, seeming to float me above the pavement. Valentine had been right. I turned onto the deserted street with no hesitation. My old lady spell was still working—which might account for the odd looks in the leather shop—but if no one saw me, all the better.

The I.S. chose their buildings carefully. Nearly all of the offices on this street kept to a human clock and had been closed since Friday night. Traffic hummed two streets away, but here it was quiet. I glanced behind me as I slipped into the alley between the records building and the adjacent insurance tower. My heart pounded as I passed the fire door where I had nearly been tagged. I wouldn't bother trying to get in that way. "See a drainpipe, Jenks?" I asked.

"I'll check around," he said, flitting ahead to do a little reconnaissance.

I followed at a slower pace, angling for the faint tapping of metal that I heard now. Thoroughly enjoying the rush of adrenaline, I slid between a truck-sized trashcan and a pallet of cardboard. A smile edged over me as I spotted Jenks sitting on the curve of a downspout, tapping it with his boot heels. "Thanks, Jenks," I said, taking off my bag and setting it on the dew-damp cement.

"No problem." He flitted up to sit on the edge of a Dumpster. "For the love of Tink," he moaned, holding his nose. "You know what's in here?" I flicked a glance at him. Encouraged, he said, "Three-day-old lasagna, five varieties of yogurt cups, burnt popcorn . . ." He hesitated, his eyes closing as he sniffed. ". . . south of the border style, a million candy wrappers, and someone has an almost unholy need for superchunk burritos."

"Jenks? Shut up." The soft hiss of wheels on pavement warned me into immobility, but even the best night vision would have a difficult time spotting me back there. The alley stunk so bad, I didn't have to worry about Weres. Even so, I waited until the street was quiet before I dug in my bag for a detection spell and finger stick. The sharp jab of it made me jump. I squeezed the required three drops onto the amulet. They soaked in immediately, and the wooden disk glowed a faint green. I let out a breath I hadn't known I had been holding. No sentient creature but Jenks was within a hundred feet of me—and I had my doubts about Jenks. It was safe enough to spell myself into a mouse.

"Here, watch this and tell me if it turns red," I told Jenks as I balanced the disk beside him on the rim of the Dumpster.

"Why?"

"Just do it!" I whispered. Sitting on a bundle of cardboard, I unlaced my new boots, took off my socks, and set a bare foot on the cement. It was cold and damp from last night's rain, and a small sound of disgust slipped from me. I shot a quick glance to the end of the alley, then arranged my boots out of sight behind a bin of shredded paper with my winter coat. Feeling like a Brimstone addict, I crouched in the gutter and pulled out my vial of brew. "Way to go, Rache," I whispered as I remembered I hadn't set up my dissolution bowl yet.

I was confident Ivy would know what to do if I showed up as a mouse, but she'd never let me live it down. The saltwater glugged nosily into the bowl, and I tucked the empty jug away. The screw top to the vial went plinking into the Dumpster, and I winced as I massaged another three drops of blood out of my throbbing finger. But my discomfort paled as my blood hit the liquid and the warm meadow fragrance arose.

My stomach clenched as I mixed the vial by hitting the side with a series of gentle thwacks. Nervous, I wiped a hand on my jeans and glanced at Jenks. Making a spell is easy. It's trusting you did it right that's hard. When it came down to it, courage was the only thing separating a witch from a warlock. *I am a witch,* I told myself, my feet going cold. *I did this right. I will be a mouse, and I will be able to turn back with a dip in saltwater.*

"Promise you won't tell Ivy if this doesn't work?" I asked Jenks, and he grinned, roguishly tugging his cap lower over his eyes.

"Whatcha going to give me?"

"I won't lace your stump with ant killer."

He sighed. "Just do it," he encouraged. "I'd like to get home before the sun goes nova. Pixies sleep at night, you know."

I licked my lips, too anxious to come up with a retort. I had never transformed before. I'd taken the classes, but tuition didn't cover the cost to buy a professional-grade transformation spell, and liability insurance hadn't allowed us students to sample our own brew. Liability insurance. You gotta love it.

My fingers tightened on the vial and my pulse hammered. This was going to really hurt.

In a sudden rush, I closed my eyes and downed it. It was bitter, and I swallowed it in one gulp, trying not to think of the three mouse hairs. Yuck.

My stomach cramped and I bent double. I gasped as I lost my balance. The cold cement rushed up, and I put a hand out to stop my fall. It was black and furry. *It's working!* I thought in both delight and fright. This wasn't so bad.

Then a sharp pain ripped through my spine. Like blue flame it ran from my skull to my backbone. I cried out, panicking as a guttural shriek tore my ears. Hot ice ran through my veins.

I convulsed, agony taking my breath from me. Terror struck me as my vision went black. Blind, I reached out, hearing a terrifying scrabbling. "No!" I shrieked. The pain swelled, driving everything from me, swallowing me up.

Eleven

"**R**ache? Rachel, wake up. Are you all right?"

A warm, low, unfamiliar voice was a black thread pulling me back to consciousness. I stretched, feeling different muscles work. My eyes flashed open to see shades of gray. Jenks stood in front of me with his hands on his hips and his feet spread wide. He looked six feet tall. "Crap!" I swore, hearing it come out as a harsh squeak. I was a mouse. I was a freaking mouse!

Panic raced through me as I remembered the pain of transforming. I was going to have to go through it all again to turn back. No wonder transforming was a dying art. It hurt like hell.

My fear slowed, and I wiggled out from under my clothes. My heart was pounding terribly fast. That awful lavender perfume was thick on my clothes, choking me. I wrinkled my nose and tried not to gag as I realized I could smell the alcohol used to carry the flowery scent. Under it was that incenselike ash smell I identified with Ivy, and I wondered if a vamp's nose was as sensitive as a mouse's.

Wobbling on four legs, I sank down to a crouch and looked at the world through my new eyes. The alley was the size of a warehouse, the black sky above threatening. Everything was shades of gray and white; I was color-blind. The sound of the distant traffic was loud, and the reek of the alley was an assault. Jenks was right. Someone really liked burritos.

Now that I was facedown in it, the night seemed colder. Turning to my pile of clothes, I tried to hide my jewelry. Next time I'd leave everything at home but my ankle knife.

I turned back to Jenks, jerking in surprise. *Whoa, baby!* Jenks was hell on wings. He had strong, clearly defined shoulders to support his ability to fly. He had a thin waist and a muscular physique. His shock of fair hair fell artfully over his brow to give him a devil-may-care attitude. A spiderweb of glitters laced his wings. Seeing him from his size-perspective, I could see why Jenks had more kids than three pairs of rabbits.

And his clothes . . . Even in black and white his clothes were stunning! The hem and collar of his shirt was embroidered with the likeness of foxgloves and ferns. His black bandanna, which had once looked red, was inlaid with tiny shimmers in an eye-riveting pattern.

"Hey, Hot Stuff," he said cheerfully, his voice surprisingly low and rich to my rodent ears. "It worked. Where did you find a spell for a mink?"

"Mink?" I questioned, hearing only a squeak. Tearing my gaze from him, I looked at my hands. My thumbs were small, but my fingers were so dexterous it didn't seem to matter. Tiny savage nails tipped them. I reached up to feel a short triangular muzzle, and I turned to see my long, luxurious, flowing tail. My entire body was one sleek line. I'd never been this skinny. I lifted a foot, to find that my feet were white with little white pads. It was hard to judge sizes, but I was a great deal bigger than a mouse, more like a large squirrel.

A mink? I thought, sitting up and running my front paws over my dark fur. How cool was that? I opened my mouth to feel my teeth. Nasty sharp teeth. I wouldn't have to worry about cats—I was almost as big as one. Ivy's owls were better hunters than I thought. My teeth clicked shut and I looked up at the open sky. Owls. I still had to worry about owls. And dogs. And anything else bigger than me. What had a mink been doing in the city?

"You look good, Rache," Jenks said.

My eyes jerked to him. *So do you, little man.* I idly wondered if there was a spell to turn people pixy size. If Jenks was any indication, it might be nice to take a vacation as a pixy and troll Cincinnati's better gardens. Color me Thumbelina and I'd be a happy girl.

"I'll see you up on the roof, okay?" he added, grinning as he noticed my ogling. Again I nodded, watching him flit upward. *Maybe I could find a spell to make pixies bigger?*

My wistful sigh came out as a rather odd squeak, and I scampered to the drainpipe. There was a puddle from last night's rain at the bottom, and my whiskers brushed the sides as I easily crawled up. My nails, I was pleased to note, were sharp and could find purchase in what seemed smooth metal. They were as good a potential weapon as my teeth.

I was panting by the time I reached the flat roof. I practically flowed out of the drainpipe, gracefully loping to the dark shadow of the building's air conditioner and Jenks's loud hail. My hearing was better, otherwise I would never have heard him.

"Over here, Rache," he called. "Someone's bent the intake screen."

My silky tail was twitching in excitement as I joined him at the air conditioner. One corner of the screen was missing a screw. Even more helpful, the screen was bent. It wasn't hard to squeeze in with Jenks levering it open for me. Once through, I crouched in the more certain dark and waited for my eyes to adapt as Jenks flitted about. Slowly another mesh screen came into focus. My rodent eyebrows rose as Jenks pulled aside a triangular cut in the wire. Clearly we had found the I.S. vault's unadvertised back door.

Full of a new confidence, Jenks and I explored our way into the building's air ducts. Jenks never shut up, his unending commentary about how easy it would be to become lost and die of starvation no help at all. It became clear that the maze of ductworks was used frequently. The drops and steeper inclines actually had quarter-inch rope tied to the top of them, and the old smell of other animals was strong. There was only one way to go—down—and after a few false turns, we found ourselves looking out into the familiar expanse of the record vault.

The vent we peered from was directly over the terminals. Nothing moved in the soft glow from the copiers. Sterile rectangular tables and plastic chairs were scattered across the ugly red carpet. Built into the walls were the files themselves. These were only the active records, a measly fraction of the dirt the I.S. had on the Inderland and human populations, both living and dead. Most were stored electronically, but if a file was pulled, a paper copy stayed in the cabinets for ten years, fifty for a vampire.

"Ready, Jenks?" I said, forgetting it would come out as a squeak. I could smell burnt coffee and sugar from the table by the door, and my stomach growled. Lying down, I stretched an arm through the vent's slats, scraping my elbow to awkwardly reach the opening lever. It gave way with an unexpected suddenness, swinging with a loud squeak to hang by its hinges. Crouched in the shadows, I waited until my pulse slowed before poking my nose out.

Jenks stopped me as I went to push a waiting coil of rope out of the duct. "Hold on," he whispered. "Let me trip the cameras." He hesitated, his wings going dark. "You, ah, won't tell anyone about this, right? It's kind of a—uh—pixy thing. It helps us get around unnoticed." He gave me a chagrined look, and I shook my head.

"Thanks," he said, and he dropped into space. I waited a breathless moment before he zipped back up and settled himself on the edge of the opening and dangled his feet. "All set," he said. "They will record a fifteen-minute loop. Come on down. I'll show you what Francis looked at."

I pushed the rope out of the ductwork and started to the floor. My nails made it easy.

"He made an extra copy of everything he wanted," Jenks was saying, waiting by the copier's recycle bin. He grinned as I tipped the can over and began rifling through the papers. "I kept tripping the copier from inside. He couldn't figure out why it was giving him two of everything. The intern thought he was an idiot."

I looked up, just about dying to say, "Francis is an idiot."

"I knew you would be all right," Jenks said as he began arranging the papers in a long line on the floor. "But it was really hard to sit here and do nothing when I heard you run. Don't ask me to do that again, all right?"

His jaw was clenched. I didn't know what to say, so I nodded. Jenks was more of a help than I had thought to give him credit for. Feeling bad for having discounted him, I tugged the scattered pages into order. There wasn't much, and the more I read, the more discouraged I became.

"According to this," Jenks said, standing on the first page with his hands on his hips, "Trent is the last of his family. His parents died under circumstances reeking of magic. Almost the entire house staff was under suspicion. It took three years before the FIB and the I.S. gave up and decided to officially look the other way."

I skimmed the statement of the I.S. investigator. My whiskers twitched when I recognized his name: Leon Bairn, the same who ended up as a thin smear on the sidewalk. Interesting.

"His parents refused to claim kinship to human or Inderland," Jenks said, "as does Trent. And there wasn't enough left of them to do an autopsy. Just like his parents, Trent employs Inderlanders as well as humans. Everyone but pixies and fairies."

It wasn't surprising. Why risk a discrimination lawsuit?

"I know what you're thinking," Jenks said. "But he doesn't seem to lean either way. His personal secretaries are always warlocks. His nanny was a human of some repute, and he roomed at Princeton with a pack of Weres." Jenks scratched his head in thought. "Didn't join the fraternity, though. You won't find it in the records, but the word is he's not a Were, or a vamp, or anything." Seeing my shrug, he continued. "Trent doesn't smell right. I've talked to a pixy who got a whiff of him while backing up a runner out at Trent's stables. She says it's not that Trent doesn't smell human, but that something subtle about him screams Inderlander."

I thought of the spell I had used to disguise my looks tonight. Opening my mouth to ask Jenks about that, I shut it with a snap. I couldn't do anything but squeak. Jenks grinned, and pulled a broken pencil lead from a pocket. "You're going to have to spell it," he said, writing down the alphabet on the bottom of one of the pages.

I bared all my teeth, which only made him laugh. But I had little choice. Skittering across the page like it was a Ouija board, I pointed out, "Charm?"

Jenks shrugged. "Maybe. But a pixy could smell through it, just as I can smell witch under the mink stink. But if it's a disguise, it would explain the warlock secretary. The more you use magic, the stronger you smell." I looked at him quizzically, and he added, "All witches smell alike, but those who work the most magic smell stronger, more unearthly. You, for example, reek from your recent spelling. You pulled on the ever-after tonight, didn't you?"

It wasn't a question, and I sat back on my haunches, surprised. He could tell from my smell?

"Trent might have another witch invoke his spells for him," Jenks said. "That way, he could be able to cover his smell with a charm. The same goes for a Were or vamp."

Struck by a sudden idea, I spelled out, "Ivy's smell?"

Jenks flitted uneasily into the air before I had even finished. "Uh, yeah," he stammered. "Ivy stinks. Either she's a dabbler that quit sipping blood last week or an intense practitioner that quit last year. I can't tell. She's probably somewhere in between—probably."

I frowned—as much as a mink can frown. She'd said it had been three years. She must have been very, very intense. Swell.

I glanced to the vault clock. We were running out of time. Impatient, I turned to Trent's skimpy record. According to the I.S., he lived and worked in a huge estate outside the city. He raised racehorses on the property, but most of his income came from farming: orange and pecan groves in the south, strawberries on the coast, wheat in the Midwest. He even had an island off the Eastern seaboard that grew tea. I already knew this. It was standard newspaper fodder.

Trent grew up as an only child, losing his mother when he was ten and his father when he was a freshman at college. His parents had two other children that didn't survive infancy. The doctor wouldn't give up the records without being subpoenaed, and shortly after the request, the office had burnt to the ground. Tragically, the doctor had been working late and hadn't made it out. *The Kalamacks,* I thought dryly, *played for keeps.*

I sat up from the records and snapped my teeth. There was nothing here I could use. I had a feeling the FIB records, if I could by some miracle see them, would be even less helpful. Someone had gone to a lot of trouble to ensure that very little was known about the Kalamacks.

"Sorry," Jenks said. "I know you were really counting on the records."

I shrugged, pushing and tugging the papers back into the bin. I wouldn't be able to put the basket upright, but at least it would look like it fell over and hadn't been rifled through.

"You want to go with Francis on his interview concerning his secretary's death?" Jenks asked. "It's this coming Monday at noon."

Noon, I thought. What a safe hour. It wasn't ridiculously early in the day for most Inderlanders, and a perfectly reasonable time for humans. Maybe I could tag along with Francis and help. I felt my rodent lips pull back across my teeth in a smile. Francis wouldn't mind. It might be my only chance to dig something up on Trent. Nailing him as a distributor of Brimstone would be enough to pay off my contract.

Jenks flew up to stand on the rim of the basket, his wings moving fitfully to keep his balance. "Mind if I come with you to get a good sniff of Trent? I bet I could tell what he is."

My whiskers brushed the air as I thought about it. It'd be nice having a second pair of eyes. I could hitch a ride with Francis. Not as a mink, though. He would probably scream like a sissy and throw things if he found me hiding in the backseat. "Talk later," I spelled out. "Home."

Jenks's smile grew sly. "Before we go, do you want to see your record?"

I shook my head. I had seen my record lots of times. "No," I wrote. "I want to shred it."

Twelve

"I've got to get a car," I whispered as I lurched off the bus steps. I snatched my coat out of the closing doors and held my breath as the diesel engine roared to life and the bus lumbered off. "Soon," I added, pulling my bag closer.

I hadn't slept well in days. Salt had dried all over me and I itched everywhere. It seemed I couldn't go five minutes without accidentally hitting the blister on my neck. Coming off the caramel-induced sugar high, Jenks was cranky. In short, we were very good company.

A false dawn had brightened the eastern sky, giving the thin blue a beautiful translucence. The birds were loud and the streets were hushed. The chill in the air made me glad for my coat. I would guess the sun was only an hour from rising. Four in the morning in June was a golden hour when all good vampires are tucked into bed and wise humans hadn't yet poked their noses out to find the early edition of the paper. "I am so ready for bed," I whispered.

"Evening, Ms. Morgan," came a gravely voice, and I spun, falling into a crouch.

Jenks made a snuff of sarcastic laughter from my earring. "It's the neighbor," he said dryly. "Jeez, Rache. Give me some credit."

Heart pounding, I slowly stood, feeling as old as I was supposed to be under my age spell. Why wasn't he in bed? "'Morning, rather," I said, stepping even with Keasley's gate. He was unmoving in his rocker, his face shadowed and unseen.

"Been shopping?" He wiggled his foot to tell me he noticed my boots were new.

Tired, I leaned on the top of the chain-link fence. "Would you like a chocolate?" I asked, and he motioned for me to enter.

Jenks hummed in worry. "A splat ball's range is longer than my sense of smell, Rache."

"He's a lonely old man," I whispered as I unlatched the gate. "He wants a chocolate. Besides, I look like an old hag. Anyone watching will think I'm his date." I eased the lock down quietly, and I thought I saw Keasley hide a smile behind a yawn.

A tiny, dramatic sigh slipped from Jenks. I settled my bag on the porch and sat down on the uppermost stair. Twisting, I pulled a paper sack from my coat pocket and extended it.

"Ah . . ." he said, his gaze on the horse-and-rider trademark. "Some things are worth risking your life for." As I expected, he chose a dark piece. A dog barked in the distance. Jaw moving, he looked past me into the silent street. "You've been to the mall."

I shrugged. "Among other places."

Jenks's wings fanned my neck. "Rachel . . ."

"Cool your jets, Jenks," I said, peeved.

Keasley got to his feet with a pained slowness. "No. He's right. It's late."

Between Keasley's obtuse comments and Jenks's instincts, I became decidedly wary. The dog barked again, and I lurched to my feet. My thoughts returned to that pile of splat balls outside my door. Maybe I should have hiked in through the graveyard, disguised or not.

Keasley moved with a pained slowness to his door. "Watch your step, Ms. Morgan. Once they know you can slip past them, they'll change tactics." He opened the door and went inside. The screen shut without a sound. "Thank you for the chocolate."

"You're welcome," I whispered as I turned away, knowing he could hear me.

"Creepy old man," Jenks said, making my earring swing as I crossed the street and headed for the motorbike parked in front of the church. The false dawn glinted on its chrome, and I wondered if Ivy had gotten her bike back from the shop.

"Maybe she'll let me use it," I mused aloud, eyeing it appreciatively in passing. It was all shiny and black, with its gold trim and silky leather; a Nightwing. Yummy. I ran an envious hand across the seat, leaving a smear where I wiped the dew away.

"Rache!" Jenks shrilled. "Drop!"

I dropped. Heart pounding, my palms hit the pavement. There was the hiss of something overhead where I had stood. Adrenaline surged, making my head hurt. I shoved myself into a roll, putting the bike between me and the opposite street.

I held my breath. Nothing moved among the shrubs and overgrown bushes. I pushed my bag in front of my face, my hands searching inside.

"Stay down," Jinks hissed. His voice was tight, and a purple glow laced his wings.

The prick of the finger stick jolted me to my toes. My sleep charm was invoked in 4.5 seconds; my best time yet. Not that it would do me much good if whoever it was stayed in the bushes. Maybe I could throw it at him. If the I.S. was going to make a habit of this, I might want to invest in a splat gun. I was more of a confront-them-directly-and-knock-them-unconscious kind of a gal. Hiding in the bushes like a sniper was cheesy, but when in Rome . . .

I gripped the charm by the cord so it wouldn't affect me and waited.

"Save it," Jenks said, relaxing as we were abruptly surrounded by a host of darting pixy children. They swirled over us, talking so fast and high I couldn't keep up. "They're gone," Jenks added. "Sorry about that. I knew they were there, but—"

"You knew they were there?" I exclaimed, my neck hurting as I peered up at him. A dog barked, and I lowered my voice. "What the hell were you doing?"

He grinned. "I had to flush them out."

Peeved, I got to my feet. "Great. Thanks. Let me know next time I'm bait." I shook out my long coat, grimacing as I realized I'd squished my chocolates.

"Now, Rache," he cajoled, hovering by my ear. "If I had told you, your reactions would have been off and the fairies would have just waited until I wasn't watching."

My face went slack. "Fairies?" I said, chilled. Denon must be off his rocker. They were expe-e-e-ensive. Perhaps they gave him a discount because of the frog incident.

"There're gone," Jenks said, "but I wouldn't stay out here for long. The word is the Weres want another crack at you." He took off his red bandanna and handed it to his son. "Jax, you and your sisters can have their catapult."

"Thanks, Papa!" The small pixy rose up two feet in excitement. Wrapping the red scarf around his waist, he and about six other pixies broke from the group and zipped across the street.

"Be careful!" Jenks shouted after them. "It might be booby-trapped!"

Fairies, I thought as I clutched my arms about me and looked over the quiet street. Crap.

The remainder of Jenks's kids was clustered around him, all talking at once as they tried to drag him around back. "Ivy's with someone," Jenks said as he started to drift upward, "but he checks out okay. You mind if I call it a night?"

"Go ahead," I said, glancing at the bike. It wasn't Ivy's after all. "And, uh, thanks."

They rose like a swarm of fireflies. Close behind them were Jax and his sisters, working together to carry a catapult as small as they were. With a dry clattering of wings and shouts, they flew up and beyond the church, leaving a hard silence in the morning street.

I turned my back and shuffled up the stone stairs. Glancing across the road, I saw a curtain fall against the single lit window. *Show's over. Go to sleep, Keasley,* I thought, tugging open the heavy door and slipping inside. Easing it shut, I slid the oiled dead bolt in place behind me, feeling better despite knowing most of the I.S.'s assassins wouldn't use a door. *Fairies? Denon must be royally ticked.*

Blowing wearily, I leaned back against the thick timbers, to shut out the coming morning. All I wanted was to take a shower and go to bed. As I slowly crossed the empty sanctuary, the sound of soft jazz and Ivy's voice raised in anger filtered out from the living room.

"Damn it, Kist," I heard as I entered the dark kitchen. "If you don't get your butt out of that chair right now, I'm going to sling you halfway to the sun."

"Aw, lighten up, Tamwood. I'm not gonna do anything," came a new voice. It was masculine, deep but with a hint of a whine, as if whomever it came from was indulged in almost everything. I paused to dump my used amulets into the pot of saltwater beside the refrigerator. They were still good, but I knew better than to leave active amulets lying around.

The music snapped off with a jarring suddenness. "Out," Ivy said softly. "Now."

"Ivy?" I called loudly, curiosity getting the better of me. Jenks said whoever it was had the all clear. Leaving my bag on the kitchen counter, I headed for the living room. My exhaustion spilled into a tinge of anger. We had never discussed it, but I assumed that until the price was off my head, we would try to keep a low profile.

"Ooooh," the unseen Kist mocked. "She's back."

"Behave yourself," Ivy threatened him as I entered the room. "Or I'll have your hide."

"Promise?"

I took three steps into the living room and jerked to a halt. My anger vanished, washed away in a surge of primal instinct. A leather-clad vamp sprawled in Ivy's chair, looking like he belonged. His immaculate boots were on the coffee table, and Ivy shoved them off in disgust. She moved quicker than I'd ever seen before. She took two steps from him and fumed, her hip cocked and her arms crossed aggressively. The mantel clock ticked loudly.

Kist couldn't be a dead vamp—he was on holy ground and it was almost sunup—but burn my britches if he didn't come close. His feet hit the floor with an exaggerated slowness. The indolent look he gave me went right to my core, settling over me like a wet blanket to tighten my gut. And yeah, he was pretty. Dangerously so. My thoughts jerked back to Table 6.1, and I swallowed.

His face was lightly stubbled, giving him a rugged appearance. Straightening, he tossed his blond hair out of his eyes in a movement of artful grace that must have taken him years to perfect. His leather jacket was open to show a black cotton shirt pulled tight over an attractively muscled chest. Twin stud earrings glittered from one ear. The other had a single earring and a long-healed tear. Otherwise, he hadn't a visible scar anywhere. I wondered if I would be able to feel them if I ran my finger down his neck.

My heart pounded, and I dropped my gaze, promising myself I wouldn't look again. Ivy didn't scare me as much as this one did. He moved on feral instinct, governed by whim.

"Aw," Kist said, scooting himself up in the chair. "She's cute. You should have told me she was such a dar-r-r-rling." I felt him take a deep breath, as if tasting the night. "She reeks of you, Ivy love." His voice dropped in pitch. "Isn't that the sweetest?"

Cold, I clutched the collar of my coat closed and backed up until I was in the threshold.

"Rachel," Ivy said dryly. "This is Kisten. He's leaving. Aren't you, Kist."

It wasn't a question, and my breath caught as he got to his feet with a fluid, animal grace. Kist stretched, his hands reaching for the ceiling. His lean body moved like a cord to show every gorgeous curve of muscle on him. I couldn't look away. His arms fell and our eyes met. They were brown. His lips parted in a soft smile as he knew I had been watching him. His teeth were sharp like Ivy's. He wasn't a ghoul. He was a living vamp. I looked away even though living vamps couldn't bespell the wary. "You have a taste for vamps, little witch?" he whispered.

His voice was like wind over water, and my knees went loose at the compulsion he put in it. "You can't touch me," I said, unable to resist looking at him as he tried to bespell me. My voice sounded like it was coming from inside my head. "I haven't signed any papers."

"No?" he whispered. His eyebrows were raised in sultry confidence. He eased close, his steps soundless. Heart pounding, I looked at the floor. I felt behind me to touch the doorframe. He was stronger than me, and faster. But a knee in the groin would drop him like any man.

"The courts won't care," he breathed as he drifted to a stop. "You're already dead."

My eyes widened as he reached for me. His scent washed over me, the musty scent of black earth. My pulse pounded, and I stepped forward. His hand cupped my chin, warm. A shock went through me, buckling my knees. He gripped my elbow, supporting me against his chest. Anticipation of an unknown promise made my blood race. I leaned into him, waiting. His lips parted. A whisper of words I couldn't understand came from him, beautiful and dark.

"Kist!" Ivy shouted, startling both of us. A flash of ire filmed his eyes, then vanished.

My will flowed back with a painful swiftness. I tried to jerk away, finding myself held. I could smell blood. "Let go," I said, almost panicking when he didn't. "Let go!"

His hand dropped. He turned to Ivy, completely dismissing me. I fell back to the archway, shaking, but unable to voluntarily leave until I knew he was gone.

Kist stood before Ivy calm and collected, a study in opposites to Ivy's agitation. "Ivy, love," he persuaded. "Why do you torment yourself? Your scent covers her, but her blood still smells pure. How can you resist? She's asking for it. She's screaming for it. She'll bitch and moan the first time, but she'll thank you for it in the end."

Expression going coy, he gently bit his lip. Crimson ran, wiped away with a slow, taunting, deliberate tongue. My breath sounded harsh even to me, and I held it.

Ivy went furious, her eyes going to black pits. The tension wouldn't let me breathe. The crickets outside chirped faster. With an exaggerated slowness, Kist cautiously leaned toward Ivy. "If you don't want to break her in," he said, his voice low with anticipation, "give her to me. I'll give her back to you." His lips parted to show his glistening canines. "Scout's honor."

Ivy's breath came in a quick pant. Her face was an unreal mix of lust and hatred. I could see her struggle to overcome her hunger, and I watched in a horrid fascination as it slowly vanished until only the hatred was left. "Get out," she said, her voice husky and wavering.

Kist took a slow breath. The tension flowed out of him as he exhaled. I found I could breathe again. I took quick, shallow breaths as my gaze darted between them. It was over. Ivy had won. I was—safe?

"It's stupid, Tamwood," Kist said as he adjusted his black leather jacket in a careful show of ease. "A waste of a good span of darkness for something that doesn't exist."

With swift, abrupt steps, Ivy went to the back door. Sweat trickled down the small of my back as the breeze from her passage touched me. Cold morning air spilled in, displacing the blackness that seemed to have filled the room. "She's mine," Ivy said as if I wasn't there. "She's under my protection. What I do or don't do with her is my business. You tell Piscary if I see one of his shadows at my church again, I'll assume he's making a bid of contention to what I hold. Ask him if he wants a war with me, Kist. You ask him that."

Kist passed between Ivy and me, hesitating on the sill. "You can't hide your hunger from her forever," Kist said, and Ivy's lips pressed together. "Once she sees, she'll run, and she'll be fair prey." In a clock-tick he slumped, a bad-boy look softening his features. "Come back," he cajoled with a sultry innocence. "I'm to tell you that you can have your old place again with only a minor concession. She's just a witch. You don't even know if she—"

"Out," Ivy said, pointing at the morning.

Kist stepped through the door. "An offer shunned makes dire enemies."

"An offer that really isn't one shames the one who makes it."

Shrugging, he pulled a leather cap from his back pocket and put it on. He glanced at me, his gaze going hungry. "Good-bye, love," he whispered, and I shuddered as if he had run a slow hand across my cheek. I couldn't tell if it was revulsion or desire. And he was gone.

Ivy slammed the door behind him. Moving with that same eerie grace, she crossed the living room and dropped into a chair. Her face was dark with anger, and I stared at her. *Holy crap. I was living with a vampire.* Nonpracticing or not, she was a vamp. What had Kist said? That Ivy was wasting her time? That I'd run when I saw her hunger? That I was hers? *Shit.*

Moving slowly, I edged backward out of the room. Ivy glanced up, and I froze. The anger drained from her face, replaced with what looked like alarm when she saw my fear.

Slowly, I blinked. My throat closed and I turned my back on her, going into the hallway.

"Rachel, wait," she called after me, her voice cajoling. "I'm sorry about Kist. I didn't invite him. He just showed up."

I strode into the hall, tensed to explode if she put a hand on me. Was this why Ivy had quit with me? She couldn't legally hunt me, but as Kist had said, the courts wouldn't care.

"Rachel . . ."

She was right behind me, and I spun. My stomach tightened. Ivy took three steps back. They were so quick it was hard to tell she had moved. Her hands were raised in placation. Her brow was pinched in worry. My pulse hammered, giving me a headache. "What do you want?" I asked, half hoping she would lie and tell me it was a mistake. From outside came the noise of Kist's bike. I stared at her as the sound of his departure faded.

"Nothing," she said, her brown eyes earnestly fixed to mine. "Don't listen to Kist. He's just jerking you around. He flirts with what he can't have."

"That's right!" I shouted so I wouldn't start shaking. "I'm yours. That's what you said, that I'm yours! I'm not anyone's, Ivy! Stay the hell away from me!"

Her lips parted in surprise. "You heard that?"

"Of course I heard that!" I yelled. Anger overpowered my fear, and I took a step forward. "Is that what you're really like?" I shouted, pointing to the unseen living room. "Like that—that animal? Is it? Are you hunting me, Ivy? Is this all about filling your gut with my blood? Does it taste better when you betray them? Does it?"

"No!" she exclaimed in distress. "Rachel, I—"

"You lied to me!" I shouted. "He bespelled me. You said a living vamp couldn't do that unless I wanted him to. And I sure as hell didn't!"

She said nothing, her tall shadow framed by the hallway. I could hear her breath and smell the sweet-sour tang of wet ash and redwood: our scents dangerously mingling. Her stance was tense, her very stillness sending a shock through me. Mouth dry, I backed up as I realized I was screaming at a vampire. The adrenaline spent itself. I felt nauseous and cold. "You lied to me," I whispered, retreating into the kitchen. She had lied to me. Dad was right. Don't trust anyone. I was getting my things and leaving.

Ivy's steps were overly loud behind me. It was obvious she was making an effort to hit the floor hard enough to make a sound. I was too angry to care.

"What are you doing?" she asked as I opened a cupboard and pulled a handful of charms off a hook, to put them in my bag.

"Leaving."

"You can't! You heard Kist. They're waiting for you!"

"Better to die knowing my enemies then to die sleeping innocently beside them," I retorted, thinking it was the stupidest thing I'd ever said. It didn't even make sense.

I jerked to a halt as she slipped in front of me and shut the cupboard. "Get out of my way," I threatened, my voice low so she wouldn't hear it shake.

Dismay pinched her eyes and furrowed her brow. She looked utterly human, and it scared the crap out of me. Just when I thought I understood her, she did something like this.

With my charms and finger sticks out of reach, I was helpless. She could throw me across the room and crack my head open on the oven. She could break my legs so I couldn't run. She could tie me to a chair and bleed me. But what she did was stand before me with a pained, frustrated look on her pale, perfect, oval face. "I can explain," she said, her voice low.

I fought off the shakes as I met her gaze. "What do you want with me?" I whispered.

"I didn't lie to you," she said, not answering my question. "Kist is Piscary's chosen scion. Most of the time Kist is just Kist, but Piscary can—" She hesitated. I stared at her, every muscle in my body screaming to run. But if I moved, she would move. "Piscary is older than dirt," she said flatly. "He's powerful enough to use Kist to go places he can't anymore."

"He's a servant," I spat. "He's a freaking lackey for a dead vamp. Does his daylight shopping for him, brings Papa Piscary humans to snack on."

Ivy winced. The tension was easing from her, and she took a more relaxed stance—still between me and my charms. "It's a great honor to be asked to be a scion for a vampire like Piscary. And it's not all one-sided. Because of it, Kist has more power than a living vamp should have. That's how he was able to bespell you. But Rachel," she rushed as I made a helpless noise, "I wouldn't have let him."

And I should be happy for that? That you don't want to share? My pulse had slowed, and I sank down into a chair. I didn't think my knees would support me anymore. I wondered how much of my weakness was from the spent adrenaline and how much was Ivy pumping the air full of soothing pheromones. *Damn, damn, damn!* I was in way over my head. Especially if Piscary was involved.

Piscary was said to be one of the oldest vampires in Cincinnati. He didn't cause trouble and kept his few people in line. He worked the system for all it was worth, doing all the paperwork and making sure every take his people made was legal. He was far more than the simple restaurant owner he pretended to be. The I.S. had a "Don't ask, don't tell" policy on the master vampire. He was one of the aforementioned people who moved in Cincinnati's unseen power struggles, but as long as he paid his taxes and kept his liquor license current, there was nothing anyone could—or wanted to—do. But if a vampire looked harmless, it only meant they were smarter than most.

My eyes flicked to Ivy, standing with her arms clasped about herself as if she were upset. *Oh, God. What was I doing here?*

"What's Piscary to you?" I asked, hearing my voice tremble.

"Nothing," she said, and I made a scoffing noise. "Really," she insisted. "He's a friend of the family."

"Uncle Piscary, huh?" I said bitterly.

"Actually," she said slowly, "that's more accurate than you might think. Piscary started my mother's living-vamp bloodline in the 1700s."

"And has been bleeding you slowly ever since," I said bitterly.

"It's not like that," she said, sounding hurt. "Piscary's never touched me. He's like a second father."

"Maybe he's letting the blood age in the bottle."

Ivy ran her hand over her hair in an unusual show of worry. "It's not like that. Really."

"Swell." I slumped to put my elbows on the table. Now I had to worry about chosen scions invading my church with the strength of a master? Why didn't she tell me this before? I didn't want to play the damn game if the rules kept changing.

"What do you want with me?" I asked again, afraid she might tell me and I'd have to leave.

"Nothing."

"Liar," I said, but when I looked up from the table, she was gone.

My breath came in a quick sound. Heart pounding, I stood, my arms clasped about myself as I stared at the empty counters and silent walls. I hated it when she did that. Mr. Fish on the windowsill wiggled and squirmed, not liking it, either.

Slow and reluctant, I put my charms away. My thoughts swirled back to the fairy attack on my front steps, the Were splat balls stacked on my back porch, and then to Kist's words that the vamps were just waiting for me to leave Ivy's protection. I was trapped, and Ivy knew it.

Thirteen

I tapped on the outside of the passenger window of Francis's car to get Jenks's attention. "What time is it?" I said softly, since even whispers echoed down in the parking deck. Cameras were recording me, but no one watched the films unless someone complained of a break-in.

Jenks dropped from the visor and wedged the button for the power window down. "Eleven-fifteen," he said as the glass lowered. "Do you think they rescheduled Kalamack's interview?"

I shook my head and glanced over the tops of the cars to the elevator doors. "No. But if he makes me late, I'm going to be ticked." I tugged at the hem of my skirt. Much to my relief, Jenks's friend had come through with my clothes and jewelry yesterday. All my clothes were hanging in neat rows or resting in tidy piles in my closet. It felt good seeing them there. The Were had done a nice job washing, drying, and folding everything, and I wondered how much he'd charge to do my laundry every week.

Finding something to wear that was both conservative and provocative had been harder than I thought. I had finally settled on a short red skirt, plain tights, and a white blouse whose buttons could be undone or fastened according to need. My hoop earrings were too small for Jenks to perch on, which the pixy had spent the first half hour complaining about. With my hair piled atop my head and a snappy pair of red heels, I looked like a perky coed. The disguise spell helped; I was a big-nosed brunette again, reeking of that lavender perfume. Francis would know who I was, but then, I wanted him to.

I nervously picked at the dirt under my nails, making a mental note to repolish them. The red enamel had vanished when I turned into a mink. "Do I look okay?" I asked Jenks as I fussed with my collar.

"Yeah, fine."

"You didn't even look," I complained as the elevator chimed. "That might be him," I said. "Are you set with that potion?"

"I only have to nudge the top and it will be all over him." Jenks rolled the window up and darted into hiding. I had a vial of "sleepy-time" potion balanced between the ceiling of the car and the visor. Francis, though, would be led to believe it was something more sinister. It was incentive for him to agree to let me take his place at the Kalamack interview. Hijacking a full-grown man, wuss or not, was tricky. It wasn't quite as if I could knock him out and lug him into the trunk. And leaving him unconscious where anyone could find him would get me caught.

Jenks and I had been in the parking deck for an hour now, making small but telling modifications to Francis's sports car. It had taken Jenks only a few moments to short out the alarm and rig the driver's door and window locks. And while I had to wait outside the car for Francis, my bag was already tucked under the passenger seat.

Francis had earned himself a real cherry of a car: a red convertible with leather seats. There were dual climate controls. The windows could go opaque—I knew, because I had tried them. There was even a built-in cell phone whose batteries were now in my bag. The vanity plate read, BUSTED. The hateful thing had so many gadgets, all it needed was clearance to take off. And it still smelled new. A bribe, I wondered with a stab of jealousy, or hush money?

The light over the elevators went out. I ducked behind the pylon, hoping it was Francis. The last thing I wanted was to be late. My pulse settled into a fast, familiar pace, and a smile eased over me as I recognized Francis's quick footsteps. He was alone. There was a jangle of keys and a surprised "Huh" when the car didn't make the expected welcoming chirp as he disengaged the alarm. My fingertips tingled in anticipation. This was going to be fun.

His car door squeaked open, and I sprang around the pylon. As one, Francis and I slid into either side of the vehicle, our doors slamming shut simultaneously.

"What the hell?" Francis exclaimed, only now realizing he had company. His narrow eyes squinted and he flicked his limp hair out of his eyes. "Rachel!" he said, nearly oozing misplaced confidence. "You are so dead."

He went for the door. I reached across him to grip his wrist, pointing up to Jenks. The pixy grinned. His wings were a blur of anticipation as he patted the vial of brew. Francis went white. "Tag," I whispered, letting go of him and locking the doors from my side. "You're it."

"Wh-What do you think you're doing?" Francis stuttered, pale under his nasty stubble.

I smiled. "I'm taking your run to interview Kalamack. You just volunteered to drive."

He stiffened, a hint of backbone showing. "You can just Turn yourself," he said, his eyes on Jenks and the potion. "Like you'd dip into black magic and make something fatal. I'm tagging you right now."

Jenks made a disgusted sound and tilted the vial. "Not yet, Jenks!" I shouted, lunging across the seat. Nearly in Francis's lap, I snaked my right arm around the scrawny man's windpipe, gripping the headrest to pin him to the seat in a headlock. His fingers clutched at my arm but he couldn't do anything in the close confines. His sudden sweat mixed with the scrape of his polyester jacket against my arm, and I thought it more vile than my perfume. "Idiot!" I hissed into Francis's ear, glancing up at Jenks. "Do you know what that is, dangling above your crotch? You want to chance that it might be irreversible?"

Red-faced, he shook his head, and I eased myself closer despite the gearshift jabbing my hip. "You wouldn't make anything fatal," he said, his voice higher than usual.

From the visor, Jenks complained, "Aw, Rache. Let me spell him. I can coach you on how to drive a stick."

The fingers digging into my arm jerked. I tensed, using the pain as impetus to pin him to the seat all the tighter. "Bug!" Francis exclaimed. "You're a—" His words choked off with a rasp as I jerked my arm.

"Bug?" Jenks shouted, incensed. "You sack of sweat stink. I've got farts that smell sweeter than you. Think you're better than me? Poop ice cream cones, do you? Call me a *bug*! Rachel, let me do him now!"

"No," I said softly, my dislike for Francis dipping into real aversion. "I'm sure Francis and I can come to an understanding. All I want is a ride out to Trent's estate and that interview. Francis won't get into trouble. He's a victim, right?" I smiled grimly at Jenks, wondering if I could keep him from dosing Francis after such an insult. "And you aren't going to nack him afterward. Hear me, Jenks? You don't kill the donkey after he plows the field. You might need him next spring." I leaned into Francis, breathing into his ear. "Right, cookie?"

He nodded as much as he could, and I slowly let him go. His eyes were on Jenks.

"You squish my associate," I said, "and that vial will spill on you. You drive too fast, the vial will spill. If you attract attention—"

"I'll dump it all over you," Jenks interrupted, the light playfulness in his voice replaced with a hot anger. "You tick me off again, I'll spell you good." He laughed, sounding like evil wind chimes. "Got it, *Francine*?"

Francis's eyes squinted. He resettled himself in his seat, touching the collar of his white shirt before he pushed the sleeves of his jacket to his elbows and took the wheel. I thanked God that Francis had left his Hawaiian shirts at home in deference to his interview with Trent Kalamack.

Face tight, he jammed the keys in the ignition and started the car. Music blared, and I jumped. The sullen way Francis cranked the wheel and threw the car into gear made it obvious he hadn't given up; he was playing along until he could find a way out. I didn't care. All I needed was to get him away from the city. Once clear, it would be nappies for Francis.

"You're not going to get away with this," he said, sounding like a bad movie. He waved his parking pass at the automated gate, and we eased into the bright light and late morning traffic with Don Henley's "Boys of Summer" blasting. If I hadn't been wound so tight, I might have enjoyed it.

"Think you could put more of that perfume on, Rachel?" Francis said, a sneer twisting his narrow face. "Or are you wearing it to cover your pet bug's stench?"

"Shut him up!" Jenks shouted. "Or I will."

My shoulder tensed. This was so stupid. "Pix him if you want, Jenks," I said as I turned down the music. "Just don't let any of that brew hit him."

Jenks grinned and flipped Francis off. Pixy dust fanned over him, unseen by Francis but clearly visible from my angle, since it reflected the sun. Francis reached up to scratch behind an ear.

"How long does it take?" I asked Jenks.

" 'Bout twenty minutes."

Jenks was right. By the time we had gotten out from under the shadow of buildings, through the burbs, and into the country, Francis put two and two together. He couldn't sit still. His comments got nastier and nastier, and his scratching more and more intense, until I pulled the duct tape out of my purse and threatened to tape his mouth shut. Red welts had appeared where his clothes met his skin. They oozed a clear liquid, looking like a bad case of poison ivy. When we hit deep country, he was scratching so much it seemed a struggle to keep the car on the road. I had been watching him intently. Driving a stick didn't look hard.

"You *bug*," he said with a snarl. "You did this to me Saturday, too, didn't you!"

"I'm gonna spell him!" Jenks said, the high pitch of his voice making my eyes ache.

Tired of it all, I turned to Francis. "All right, cookie. Pull it over."

Francis blinked. "What?"

Idiot, I thought. "How long do you think I can keep Jenks from tagging you if you keep insulting him? Pull over." Francis glanced nervously between the road and me. We hadn't seen a car in the last five miles. "I said, *pull over!*" I shouted, and he swerved to the dusty shoulder in a rattling of pebbles. I turned the car off and yanked the keys from the ignition. We lurched to a stop, my head smacking against the rearview mirror. "Out," I said, unlocking the doors.

"What? Here?" Francis was a city boy. He thought I was going to make him walk back. The idea was tempting, but I couldn't run the risk of him being picked up or finding his way to a phone. He got out with a surprising eagerness. I realized why when he started scratching.

I popped the trunk, and Francis's thin face went blank. "No way," he said, his skinny arms raised. "I'm not getting in there."

I felt the new bump on my forehead, waiting. "Get into the trunk or I'm going to teach you how I spell mink and make a pair of earmuffs out of you." I watched him think that over, wondering if he would make a run for it. I almost wished he would. It'd feel good to tackle him again. It had nearly been two whole days. I'd get him into the trunk somehow.

"Run," Jenks said, circling above his head with the vial. "Go on. Dare you, stink bag."

Francis seemed to deflate. "Oh, you'd like that, eh, bug?" he said with a sneer. But he wedged himself into the tiny space. He even gave me no trouble when I duct-taped his hands in front of him. We both knew he could get out of the wraps given enough time. But his superior look faltered as I held my hand up and Jenks landed on it with the vial.

"You said you wouldn't," he stammered. "You said it would turn me into a mink!"

"I lied. Both times."

The look Francis gave me was murderous. "I won't forget this," he said, his jaw clenching to make him look even more ridiculous than his boat shoes and wide-cuffed slacks. "I'm coming after you myself."

"I hope you do." I smiled, dumping the vial over his head. "Nighty night."

He opened his mouth to say more, but his expression slackened as soon as the fragrant liquid hit him. I watched, fascinated, as he fell asleep amid the scent of bay leaf and lilac. Satisfied, I slammed the trunk shut and called it good.

Settling uneasily behind the wheel, I adjusted the seat and mirrors. I hadn't ever driven a stick before, but if Francis could do it, I sure as heck could.

"Put it in first," Jenks said, sitting on the rearview mirror and mimicking what I should do. "Then give it more gas than you think you need while you let up on the clutch."

I gingerly pushed the stick back and started the car.

"Well?" Jenks said from the mirror. "We're waiting. . . ."

I pushed the gas pedal and let up on the clutch. The car lurched backward, slamming into a tree. Panicking, I pulled my feet from the pedals, and the car stalled. I stared wide-eyed at Jenks as he laughed. "It's in reverse, witch," he said, darting out the window.

Through the rearview mirror, I watched him zip to the back and assess the damage. "How bad is it?" I asked as he came back.

"It's okay," he said, and I felt a wash of relief. "Give it a few months, and you won't be able to see where it was hit," he added. "The car's busted, though. You broke a taillight."

"Oh," I said, realizing he'd been talking about the tree, not the car. My nerves were jittery as I jammed the stick forward, double-checked it, and started the car again. Another deep breath, and we lurched forward on our way.

Fourteen

Jenks turned out to be a passable instructor, enthusiastically shouting advice through the window as I practiced starting from a dead stop until I got the hang of it. My newfound confidence evaporated as I turned onto Kalamack's drive, slowing at the gatehouse. It was low and formidable looking, the size of a small jail. Tasteful plantings and low walls hid the security system that prevented anyone from driving around it.

"And how did you plan to get past that?" Jenks said as he flitted to hide atop the visor.

"No problem," I said, my mind whirling. Visions of Francis in the trunk assailed me, and smiling my prettiest at the guard, I brought the car to a halt before the white stick across the road. The amulet beside the guard's watch stayed a nice green. It was a spell checker, much cheaper than the wood-framed glasses that could see through charms. I had been very careful to keep the amount of magic used in my disguise spell below the level of most vanity charms. As long as his amulet stayed green, he would assume I was under a standard makeup spell, not a disguise.

"I'm Francine," I said on the spur of the moment. I pitched my voice high, smiling brainlessly, as if I had been planting Brimstone all night. "I have an appointment with Mr. Kalamack?" Trying to look like a nitwit, I twirled a stray strand of hair. I was a brunette today, but it probably still worked. "Am I late?" I asked, tugging my finger free of the knot I had accidentally put in my hair. "I didn't think it would take me this long. He lives a long way out!"

The gateman was unaffected. Maybe I was losing my touch.

Maybe I should have undone another button on my blouse. Maybe he liked men. He looked at his clipboard, then me.

"I'm from the I.S.," I said, putting my tone somewhere between petulance and spoiled annoyance. "Do you want to see my ID?" I rummaged in my bag for my nonexistent badge.

"Your name isn't on the list, ma'am," the stone-faced guard said.

I flopped back with a huff. "Did that guy in dispatch put me down as Francis again? Darn him!" I exclaimed, hitting the wheel with an ineffective fist. "He's always doing that, ever since I refused to go on a date with him. I mean, really. He didn't even have a car! He wanted to take me to the movies on a bus. Ple-e-e-ease," I moaned. "Can you see me on a *bus*?"

"Just a moment, ma'am." He picked up a phone and began speaking. I waited, trying to keep my ditzy smile in place, praying. The gateman's head bobbed in an unconscious expression of agreement. Still, his face was seriously empty when he turned back.

"Up the drive," he said, and I struggled to keep my breath even. "Third building on the right. You can park in the visitor lot directly off the front steps."

"Thank you," I sang merrily, sending the car lurching forward when the white bar rose. Through the rearview mirror I watched the guard go back inside. "Easy as pie," I muttered.

"Getting out might be harder," Jenks said dryly.

Up the drive was three miles through an eerie wood. My mood went subdued as the road wound between the close, silent sentinels. Despite the overpowering impression of age, I began to get the feeling that everything had been planned out, even to the surprises, like the waterfall I found around a bend in the road. Disappointed somehow, I continued on as the artificial woods thinned and turned into rolling pasture. A second road joined mine, well-traveled and busy. Apparently I had come in the back way. I followed the traffic, taking an offshoot labeled VISITORS PARKING. Rounding a turn in the road, I saw the Kalamack estate.

The huge fortress of a building was a curious mix of modern institution and traditional elegance, with glass doors and carved angels on the downspouts. Its gray rock was softened by old trees and bright flower beds. There were several low buildings attached to it, but the main one rose three stories up. I brought the car to a halt in one of the visitor parking spots. The sleek vehicle next to mine made Francis's car look like a toy from the bottom of a cereal box.

Dropping Francis's wad of keys into my bag, I eyed the gardener tending the bushes surrounding the lot. "Still want to split up?" I breathed as I primped in the rearview mirror, carefully picking out that knot I'd put in my hair. "I don't like what happened at the front gate."

Jenks flitted down onto the stick shift and stood with his hands on his hips in his Peter Pan pose. "Your interview runs the usual forty minutes?" he said. "I'll be done in twenty. If I'm not here when you're done, wait about a mile down from the gatehouse. I'll catch up."

"Sure," I said as I tightened the string on my bag. The gardener was wearing shoes, not boots, and they were clean. What gardener has clean shoes? "Just be careful," I said, nodding to the small man. "Something smells off."

Jenks snickered. "The day I can't elude a gardener is the day I become a baker."

"Well, wish me luck." I cracked the window for Jenks and got out. My heels clacked smartly as I went to take a peek at the back of Francis's car. As Jenks had said, one of the taillights was broken. There was a nasty dent, too. I turned away with a flash of guilt. Taking a steadying breath, I strode up the shallow steps to the twin, double doors.

A man stepped from a recessed nook as I approached, and I jerked to a halt, startled. He was tall enough to need two looks to see all of him. And thin. He reminded me of a starving post-Turn refugee from Europe: prim, proper, and stuck-up. The man even had a hawklike nose and permanent frown cemented to his lightly wrinkled face. Gray brushed his temples, marring his otherwise coal black hair. His inconspicuous gray slacks and white business shirt fitted him perfectly, and I tugged my collar straight. "Ms. Francine Percy?" he said, his smile empty and his voice slightly sarcastic.

"Yes, hello," I said, purposely giving the man a limp-wristed handshake. I could almost see him stiffen in aversion. "I have a noon meeting with Mr. Kalamack."

"I'm Mr. Kalamack's publicity adviser, Jonathan," the man said. Apart from taking great care in his pronunciation, he had no accent. "If you would accompany me? Mr. Kalamack will meet with you in his back office." He blinked, his eyes watering. I imagined it was from my perfume. Maybe I had overdone it, but I wasn't going to risk triggering Ivy's instincts.

Jonathan opened the door for me, motioning me to go before him. I stepped through, surprised to find the building brighter inside than out. I had expected a private residence, and this wasn't it. The entryway looked like the headquarters of any Fortune-twenty business, with the familiar glass and marble motif. White pillars held up the distant ceiling. An impressive mahogany desk stretched before the twin staircases that rose to the second and third floors. Light streamed in. Either it was piped in from the roof or Trent was spending a fortune on natural-light bulbs. A soft, mottled green carpet muffled any echo. There was a buzz of muted conversations and a steady but sedate flow of people going about their business.

"This way, Ms. Percy," my escort said softly.

I dragged my eyes from the man-sized pots of citrus trees and followed Jonathan's measured pace past the front desk and through a series of hallways. The farther we went, the lower the ceilings, the darker the lighting, and the more comforting the colors and textures became. Almost unnoticed, the soothing sound of running water drifted into existence. We hadn't met anyone since leaving the front entryway, and I felt a touch uneasy.

Clearly we had left the public face behind and entered the more private areas. What, I wondered, was going on? Adrenaline shook me as Jonathan paused and put a fingertip to his ear.

"Excuse me," he murmured, stepping a few feet away. His wrist, I noticed as he raised his hand to his ear, had a microphone on his watchband. Alarmed, I strained to catch his words as he had turned to prevent me from reading his lips.

"Yes, Sa'han," he whispered, his tone respectful.

I waited, holding my breath so I could hear.

"With me," he said. "I was informed you had an interest, so I have taken the liberty of escorting her to your back porch." Jonathan shifted uncomfortably. He gave me a long, sideways look of disbelief. "Her?"

I wasn't sure to take that as a compliment or insult, and I pretended to be busy rearranging the back of my stockings and pulling another strand of hair from my topknot to dangle beside my earring. I wondered if someone had investigated the trunk. My pulse quickened as I realized how quickly this could come tumbling down about me.

His eyes widened. "Sa'han," he said urgently, "accept my apologies. The gatehouse said—" His words cut off and I could see him stiffen under what must be a rebuke. "Yes, Sa'han," he said, tilting his head in an unconscious show of deference. "Your front office."

The tall man seemed to gather himself as he turned back to me. I shot him a dazzling smile. There was no expression in his blue eyes as he stared at me as if I was a puppy present on the new rug. "If you would return that way?" he said flatly, pointing.

Feeling more like a prisoner than a guest, I took Jonathan's subtle directions and retraced our path to the front. I led the way. He kept himself behind me. I didn't like this at all. It didn't help that I felt short next to him or that my footsteps were the only ones I could hear. Slowly, the soft colors and textures returned to corporate walls and bustling efficiency.

Keeping those same three steps behind me, Jonathan directed me down a small hallway just off the lobby. Frosted-glass doors were set on either side. Most were propped open and had people working inside, but Jonathan indicated the end office. Its door was wood, and he almost seemed to hesitate before he reached in front of me to open it. "If you would wait here," he said, a hint of a threat in his precise voice. "Mr. Kalamack will be with you shortly. I'll be at his secretary's desk if you need anything."

He pointed to a conspicuously empty desk tucked in a recessed nook. I thought of Ms. Yolin Bates, clay-cold dead in the I.S. lockup three days ago. My smile grew forced. "Thank you, Jon," I said brightly. "You've been a dear."

"It's Jonathan." He shut the door firmly behind me. There was no click of a lock.

I turned, glancing over Kalamack's front office. It looked normal enough—in a disgustingly wealthy executive sort of way. There was a bank of electronic equipment inlaid in the wall next to his desk that held so many buttons and switches it would put a recording studio to shame. The opposite wall had a huge window, the sun spilling in to set the soft carpet glowing. I knew I was too far into the building for the window and its accompanying sunbeam to be real, but it was good enough to warrant a severe going-over.

I set my bag beside the chair opposite the desk and went to the "window." Hands on my hips, I eyed the shot of yearlings arguing over fallen apples. My eyebrows rose. The engineers were off. It was noon, and the sun wasn't low enough to be casting beams that long.

Finding satisfaction in their error, I turned my attention to the freestanding fish tank against the back wall behind the desk. Starfish, blue damsels, yellow tangs, and even sea horses coexisted peacefully, seemingly unaware the ocean was five hundred miles east. My thoughts turned to my Mr. Fish, swimming contentedly in his little glass bowl. I frowned, not jealous, but annoyed at the fickleness of the luck of the world.

Trent's desk had the usual stuff on top, complete with a small fountain of black rock for the water to chatter over. His computer's screen saver was a scrolling line of three numbers: twenty, five, one. A rather enigmatic message. Stuck in the corner where the walls met the ceiling was a conspicuous camera, its red light winking at me. I was under surveillance.

My thoughts went back to Jonathan's conversation with his mysterious Sa'han. Clearly my story of Francine had been breached. But if they wanted me arrested, they would have done it by now. It seemed I had something Mr. Kalamack wanted. *My silence?* I ought to find out.

Grinning, I waved at the camera and settled myself behind Trent's desk. I imagined the stir I was causing as I began rummaging about. The datebook was first, laid invitingly open on the desktop. Francis's appointment had a line through his name and a question mark penciled beside it. Wincing, I leafed back to the day where Trent's secretary had been tagged with Brimstone. There was nothing out of the ordinary. The phrase "Huntingtons to Urlich" caught my eye. Was he smuggling people out of the country? Big whoop.

The top drawer held nothing unusual: pencils, pens, sticky notepads, and a gray touchstone. I wondered what Trent could possibly be concerned about to warrant that. The side drawers contained color-coded files concerning his off-estate interests. As I waited for someone to stop me, I browsed, learning his pecan groves had suffered from a late frost this year but that his strawberries on the coast made up the loss. I slammed the drawer shut, surprised no one had come in yet. Perhaps they were curious as to what I was looking for? I knew I was.

Trent had a thing for maple candy and pre-Turn whiskey, if the stash I found in a lower drawer meant anything. I was tempted to crack the near forty-year-old bottle and sample it but decided that would bring my watchers out faster than anything else would.

The next drawer was full of neatly arranged discs. *Bingo!* I thought, opening it farther.

"Alzheimer's," I whispered, running a finger across a hand-made label. "Cystic fibrosis, cancer, cancer . . ." In all, there were eight labeled cancer. Depression, diabetes . . . I continued until I found Huntington. My gaze went to the datebook and I shut the drawer. *Ahhhh . . .*

Settling back into Trent's plush chair, I pulled his appointment book onto my lap. I started at January, turning pages slowly. Every fifth day or so a shipment went out. My breath quickened as I noticed a pattern. Huntington went out the same day every month. I flipped back and forth. They all went out on the same day of the month, within a few days of each other. Taking a slow breath, I glanced at the drawer of discs. Sure I was on to something, I popped one into the computer and jiggled the mouse. Damn. Password protected.

There was a small click of a latch. Jumping to my feet, I jabbed the eject button.

"Good afternoon, Ms. Morgan."

It was Trent Kalamack, and I tried not to flush as I slipped the small disc into a pocket. "Beg pardon?" I said, turning the ditzy charm on full. They knew who I was. Big surprise.

Trent adjusted the lowest button on his gray linen jacket as he shut the door behind him. A disarming smile curved over his clean-shaven features, giving him the air of someone my age.

His hair had a transparent whiteness to it that some children have, and he was comfortably tan, looking as if it wouldn't take much to get him poolside. He looked far too pleasant to be as wealthy as he was rumored to be. It wasn't fair to have money and good looks both.

"You'd rather be Francine Percy?" Trent said, eyeing me over his wire-rimmed glasses.

I tucked an escaped curl behind an ear, striving for an air of nonchalance. "Actually—no," I admitted. I must still have a few cards to play or he wouldn't be bothering with me.

Trent moved to the back of his desk with a preoccupied poise, forcing me to retreat to the other side. He held his dark blue tie to himself as he sat. Glancing up, he looked charmingly surprised as he noticed I was still standing. "Please sit," he said, flashing me small, even teeth. He pointed a remote at the camera. The red light went out, and he tucked the remote away.

Still I stood. I didn't trust his casual acceptance. Warning bells were going off in my head, making my stomach clench. *Fortune* magazine had put him on its cover as last year's most eligible bachelor. It had been a head-to-knee shot, with him leaning casually against a door with his company name on it in gold letters. His smile had been a compelling mix of confidence and secrecy. Some women are drawn to a smile like that. Me, I get wary. He gave me the same smile now as he sat, his hand tucked under his chin as his elbow rested on the desktop.

I watched the short hair about his ears drift, and I thought his carefully styled hair had to be incredibly soft if just the draft from the vent could lift it like that.

Trent's lips tightened as he saw my attention on his hair, then returned to that smile. "Let me apologize for the mistake at the front gate, and then with Jon," he said. "I wasn't expecting you for at least another week."

I sat down as my knees went weak. *He was expecting me?* "I'm sure I don't understand," I said boldly, relieved my voice didn't crack.

The man reached for a pencil with a casual ease, but his eyes jerked to mine when I shifted my feet. If I'd known him better, I would have said he was wound tighter than I was. He meticulously erased the question mark by Francis's name and wrote mine in. Setting the pencil down, he ran a hand over his head to get his hair to lay flat.

"I'm a busy man, Ms. Morgan," he said, his voice rising and falling pleasantly. "I have found it more cost-effective to lure key employees from other companies rather than raise them up from scratch. And where I would be loath to suggest I was in competition with the I.S., I've found their training methods and the skill sets they foster are commensurate with my needs. In all honesty, I would have preferred to see if you had the ingenuity to survive an I.S. death threat before I brought you in. Perhaps nearly finding your way to my back porch is enough."

I crossed my legs and arched my eyebrows. "Are you offering me a job, Mr. Kalamack? You want me for your new secretary? Type your letters? Fetch your coffee?"

"Heavens, no," he said, ignoring my sarcasm. "You smell too strongly of magic for a secretarial position, despite trying to cover it with that—mmm—perfume?"

I flushed, determined not to drop from his questioning gaze.

"No," Trent continued matter-of-factly. "You're too interesting to be a secretary, even one of mine. Not only have you quit the I.S., but you're baiting them. You went shopping. You broke into their records vault to shred your file. Locking a runner unconscious in his own car?" he said with a carefully cultivated laugh.

"I like that. But even better is your quest to improve yourself. I applauded your drive to expand your horizons, learn new skills. The willingness to explore options most shun is a mind-set I strive to instill in my employees. Though reading that book on the bus shows a certain lack of . . . judgment." A sliver of dark humor showed behind his eyes. "Unless your interest in vampires has an earthier source, Ms. Morgan?"

My stomach tightened, and I wondered if I had enough charms to fight my way out of here. How had Trent found all that out when the I.S. couldn't even keep tabs on me? I forced myself to be calm as I realized how deep in the pixy dust I was. What had I been thinking, walking in here? The man's secretary was dead. He ran Brimstone, no matter how generous he was during charity fundraisers or that he golfed with the mayor's husband. He was too smart to be content running a good third of Cincinnati's manufacturing. His hidden interests webbed the underworld, and I was pretty sure he wanted to keep it that way.

Trent leaned forward with an intent expression, and I knew he was done with the idle chitchat. "My question, Ms. Morgan," he said softly, "is what do you want with me?"

I said nothing. My confidence trickled away.

He gestured to his desk. "What were you looking for?"

"Gum?" I said, and he sighed.

"For the sake of eliminating a great deal of wasted time and effort, I suggest we be honest with each other." He took off his glasses and set them aside. "Inasmuch as we need to. Tell me why you risked death to visit me. You have my word the record of your actions today will be—misplaced? I simply want to know where I stand. What have I done to warrant your attention?"

"I walk free?" I said, and he leaned back in his seat, nodding. His eyes were a shade of green I had never seen before. There was no blue in them. Not even a whisper.

"Everyone wants something, Ms. Morgan," he said, each word precise but flowing into the next like water. "What is it you want?"

My heart pounded at his promise of freedom. I followed his gaze to my hands and the dirt under my nails. "You," I said, curling my fingertips under my palms to hide them. "I want the evidence that you killed your secretary. That you're dealing in Brimstone."

"Oh . . ." he said with a poignant sigh. "You want your freedom. I should have guessed. You, Ms. Morgan, are more complex than I gave you credit for." He nodded, his silk-lined suit making a soft whisper as he moved. "Giving me to the I.S. would certainly buy your independence. But you can understand I won't allow it." He straightened, becoming all business again. "I'm in the position of offering you something just as good as freedom. Perhaps better. I can arrange for your I.S. contract to be paid off. A loan, if you will. You can work it off over the course of your career with me. I can set you up in a decent establishment, perhaps a small staff."

My face went cold, then hot. He wanted to buy me. Not noticing my slow anger, he opened a file from his in-box. Pulling a pair of wood-rimmed glasses from an inner pocket, he balanced them on his small nose. I grimaced as he looked me over, clearly seeing past my disguise. He made a small sound before he bent his fair head to read what it contained. "Do you like the beach?" he asked lightly, and I wondered why he was even pretending he needed the glasses to read. "I have a macadamia plantation I have been looking to expand. It's in the South Seas. You could even pick out the colors for the main house."

"You can go Turn yourself, Trent," I said, and he looked up over his glasses, seemingly surprised. It made him look charming, and I forced the thought from me. "If I wanted someone tugging on my leash, I would have stayed with the I.S. Brimstone is grown on those islands. And I might as well be human that close to the sea. I couldn't even bring up a love charm there."

"Sun," he said persuasively as he tucked his glasses away. "Warm sand. Setting your own hours." He closed the file and put a hand upon it. "You can bring your new friend. Ivy, is it? A Tamwood vampire. Quite a catch." A wry smile flickered over him.

My temper burned. He thought he could buy me off. The trouble was, I was tempted, and that made me angry with myself. I glared, my hands stiff in my lap.

"Be honest," Trent said, his long fingers twirling a pencil with a mesmerizing dexterity. "You're resourceful, perhaps even skilled, but no one eludes the I.S. permanently without help."

"I have a better way," I said as I struggled to remain seated. I had nowhere to go until he let me. "I'm going to tie you to a post in the center of the city. I'm going to prove you were involved with your secretary's death and you're dealing in Brimstone. I quit my job, Mr. Kalamack, not my morals."

Ire flickered behind his green eyes, but his face remained calm as he set his pencil back in the cup with a sharp tap. "You can trust me to keep my word. I always keep my word, promises or threats."

His voice seemed to pool on the floor, and I fought the idiotic urge to lift my feet from the carpet. "A businessman has to," he intoned, "or he won't be in business very long."

I swallowed, wondering what the hell he was. He had the grace, the voice, the quickness, and the confident power of a vampire. And as much as I disliked the man, the raw attraction was there, heightened by his personal strength rather than a teasing manner and sexual innuendos. But he wasn't a living vampire. Though warm and good-natured on the surface, he had a very large personal space that most vampires lacked. He kept people at arm's length, too far to seduce with a touch. No, he wasn't a vamp, but maybe . . . a human scion?

My eyebrows rose. Trent blinked, seeing the idea crossing me and not knowing what it was. "Yes, Ms. Morgan?" he murmured, seeming uncomfortable for the first time.

My heart pounded. "Your hair is floating again," I said, trying to jolt him. His lips parted, and he seemed at a loss for words.

I jumped as the door opened and Jonathan strode in. He was stiff and angry, with the attitude of a protector fettered by the very one he has been pledged to defend. In his hands was a head-sized glass ball. Jenks was inside it. Frightened, I stood, clutching my bag to myself.

"Jon," Trent said, smoothing his hair as he got to his feet. "Thank you. If you would please escort Ms. Morgan and her associate out?"

Jenks was so angry his wings were a black blur. I could see him mouthing something but couldn't hear him. His gestures, though, were unmistakable.

"My disc, Ms. Morgan?"

I spun, gasping as I realized Trent had come around his desk and was right behind me. I hadn't heard him move. "Your what?" I stammered.

His right hand was outstretched. It was smooth and unworked but carried a taut strength. He had a single gold band on his ring finger. I couldn't help but notice that he was only a few inches taller than me. "My disc?" he prompted, and I swallowed.

Tensed to react, I dug it from my pocket with two fingers and handed it to him. Something swept over him. It was as subtle as a shade of blue, as indistinguishable as a snowflake among thousands, but it was there. In that instant I knew it wasn't Brimstone that Trent was afraid of. It was something on that disc.

My thoughts shot to his neatly arranged discs, and it was with an incredible resolve that I kept my eyes on his instead of following my suspicions to his desk drawer. God, help me. The man ran biodrugs along with Brimstone. The man was a freaking biodrug lord. My heart hammered and my mouth went dry. You were jailed for running Brimstone. But you were staked, burned, and scattered for running biodrugs. And he wanted me to work for him.

"You've shown an unexpected capacity to plan, Ms. Morgan," Trent said, interrupting my racing thoughts. "Vampire assassins won't attack you while under a Tamwood's protection. And arranging a pixy clan to protect you against fairies as well as living in a church to keep the Weres at bay are beautiful in their simplicity. Let me know when you change your mind about working for me. You would find satisfaction here—and recognition. Something the I.S. has been most remiss with."

I steeled my face, concentrating on keeping my voice from shaking. I hadn't planned anything. Ivy had, and I wasn't sure what her motives were. "With all due respect, Mr. Kalamack, you can go Turn yourself."

Jonathan stiffened, but Trent simply nodded and went back behind his desk.

A heavy hand hit my shoulder. I instinctively grabbed it, crouching to fling whoever had touched me over my shoulder and to the floor. Jonathan hit with a surprised grunt. I was kneeling on his neck before I realized I had moved. Frightened for what I had done, I rose and backed away. Trent glanced up in unconcern from replacing the disc in the drawer.

Three other people had entered at Jonathan's heavy thump. Two centered about me, one stood before Trent.

"Let her go," Trent said. "It was Jon's error." He sighed with mild disappointment. "Jon," he added tiredly, "she isn't the fluff she pretends to be."

The tall man had risen smoothly to his feet. He tugged his shirt straight and ran his hand to smooth his hair. He eyed me with hatred. Not only had I bested him before his employer, but he had also been rebuked in front of me. The angry man scooped Jenks up with bad grace and motioned to the door.

I walked free, back out into the sun, more afraid of what I had turned down than of having left the I.S.

Fifteen

I yanked at the pizza dough, taking my frustrations concerning my fabulous afternoon out on the helpless yeast and flour. A crackle of stiff paper came from Ivy's wooden table. My attention jerked to her. Head bowed and brow furrowed, she kept her attention on her map. I'd be a fool not to recognize that her reactions had quickened with sunset. She moved with that unnerving grace again, but she looked irate, not amorous. Still, I was aware of her every move.

Ivy had a real run, I thought sourly as I stood at the center island and made pizza. Ivy had a life. Ivy wasn't trying to prove the city's most prominent, beloved citizen was a biodrug lord and play head cook at the same time.

Three days on her own, and Ivy had already got a run to find a missing human. I thought it odd a human would come to a vamp for help, but Ivy had her own charms, or scary competence, rather. Her nose had been buried in her map of the city all night, plotting the man's usual haunts with colored markers and drawing out the paths he would likely take while driving from home to work and such.

"I'm no expert," Ivy said to the table, "but is that how you're supposed to do that?"

"You want to make dinner?" I snapped, then looked at what I was doing. The circle was more of a lopsided oval, so thin in places it almost broke through. Embarrassed, I pushed the dough to fill in the thin spot and tugged it to fit the baking stone properly. As I fussed with the edges, I surreptitiously watched her. At her first sultry glance or overly quick move, I was going out the door to hide behind Jenks's stump. The jar of sauce opened with a loud pop. My eyes flicked to Ivy. Seeing no change, I dumped most of it onto the pizza and recapped the jar.

What else should go on it? I wondered. It would be a miracle if Ivy let me top it with everything I usually did. Deciding not to even attempt the cashews, I pulled out the mundane toppings. "Peppers," I muttered. "Mushrooms." I glanced at Ivy. She looked like a meat kind of a gal. "Bacon left from breakfast."

The marker squeaked as Ivy drew a purple line from the campus to the Hollow's more hazardous strip of nightclubs and bars by the riverfront. "So," she drawled. "Are you going to tell me what's bothering you, or am I going to have to order pizza in after you burn that one?"

I put the pepper in the sink and leaned against the counter. "Trent runs biodrugs," I said, hearing the ugliness anew as I said it. "If he knew I was going to try and tag him with that, he'd kill me quicker than the I.S."

"But he doesn't." Ivy drew another line. "All he knows is you think he runs Brimstone and had his secretary murdered. If he was worried, he wouldn't have offered you that job."

"Job?" I said, turning my back to her as I washed the pepper. "It's in the South Seas—running his Brimstone plantations, no doubt. He wants me out of the way, that's all."

"How about that," she said as she capped her pen by pounding it on the table. Startled, I spun, flinging drops of water everywhere. "He thinks you're a threat," she finished, making a show of brushing away the water I had accidentally hit her with.

I gave her a sheepish smile, hoping she couldn't tell she had me on edge. "I hadn't thought about it that way," I said.

Ivy went back to her map, frowning as she dabbed at the stains the water had made on her crisp lines. "Give me some time to check around," she said in a preoccupied voice. "If we can get ahold of his financial records and a few of his buyers, we can find a paper trail. But I still say it's just Brimstone."

I yanked open the fridge for the Parmesan and mozzarella. If Trent didn't run biodrugs, then I was a pixy princess. There was a clatter as Ivy tossed one of her markers into the cup beside her monitor. My back was to her, and the noise startled me.

"Just because he has a drawer full of discs labeled with diseases once helped by biodrugs doesn't mean he's a drug lord," Ivy said, throwing another. "Maybe they're client lists. The man is big into philanthropy. Keeps half a dozen country hospitals running alone with his donations."

"Maybe," I said, unconvinced. I knew about Trent's generous contributions. Last fall he had been auctioned off in Cincinnati's For the Children charity for more money than I used to make in a year. Personally, I thought his efforts were a publicity front. The man was dirt.

"Besides," Ivy said as she leaned back in her chair and tossed another one of her markers into the cup in an unreal show of hand-eye coordination. "Why would he be running biodrugs? The man is independently wealthy. He doesn't need any more money. People are motivated by three things, Rachel. Love . . ." A red marker clattered in with the rest. "Revenge . . ." A black one landed next to it. "And power," she finished, tossing in a green one. "Trent has enough money to buy all three."

"You forgot one," I said, wondering if I should just keep my mouth shut. "Family."

Ivy grabbed the pens out of the cup. Leaning back in her chair to balance on two legs, she started tossing them again. "Doesn't family come in with love?" she asked.

I watched her from the corner of my sight. *Not if they were dead,* I thought, my memories turning to my dad. *In that case, it might come under revenge.*

The kitchen went silent as I sprinkled a thin dusting of Parmesan on the sauce. Only the clacks of Ivy's pens broke the stillness. Every single one went in, the sporadic rattles getting on my nerves. The pens stopped, and I froze in alarm. Her face was shadowed. I couldn't see if her eyes were going black. My heartbeat quickened, and I didn't move, waiting.

"Why don't you just stake me, Rachel?" she said in exasperation as she flipped her hair aside to show me irate brown eyes. "I'm not going to jump you. I said Friday was an accident."

Shoulders easing, I rummaged loudly in the drawer for a can opener for the mushrooms. "A pretty freaking scary accident," I muttered under my breath as I drained them.

"I heard that." She hesitated. A pen landed in the cup with a rattle. "You, ah, did read the book, right?" she asked.

"Most of it," I admitted, then went alarmed. "Why, am I doing something wrong?"

"You're ticking me off, that's what you're doing wrong," she said, her voice raised. "Stop watching me. I'm not an animal. I may be a vampire, but I still have a soul."

I bit my tongue so I wouldn't even mouth an answer to that. There was a clatter as she dropped her remaining markers in the pencil cup. The silence grew heavy as she pulled her maps to her. I turned my back on her to prove I trusted her. I didn't, though. Putting the pepper on the cutting board, I yanked open a drawer and banged noisily about until I found a huge knife. It was too big to cut peppers, but I was feeling vulnerable and that was the knife I was going to use.

"Uh . . ." Ivy hesitated. "You're not putting peppers on that, are you?"

My breath slipped from me and I set the knife down. We probably wouldn't have anything on our pizza but cheese. Silently, I put the pepper back in the refrigerator. "What's a pizza without peppers?" I whispered under my breath.

"Edible," was her prompt response, and I grimaced. She wasn't supposed to hear that.

My eyes traveled over the counter and my assembled goodies. "Mushrooms okay?"

"Can't have pizza without them."

I layered slices of slimy brown atop the Parmesan. Ivy rattled her map, and I snuck an unhelped glance at her.

"You never did tell me what you did with Francis," she said.

"I left him in his open trunk. Someone will douse him in salt-water. I think I broke his car. It doesn't accelerate anymore, no matter what gear I put it in and how loud I race it."

Ivy laughed and my skin crawled. As if daring me to object, she rose, coming to lean against the counter. My tension flowed back. It doubled when she eased herself up with a controlled slowness to sit on the counter beside me. "So," she said, opening the bag of pepperoni and provocatively placing a slice in her mouth. "What do you think he is?"

She was eating. Great.

"Francis?" I asked, surprised she had to ask. "He's an idiot."

"No, Trent."

I held my hand out for the pepperoni and she set the bag on my palm. "I don't know, but he isn't a vamp. He thought my perfume was to cover up my witch smell, not—uh—yours." I felt awkward with her that close, and I dealt the pepperoni like cards onto the pizza. "And his teeth aren't sharp enough." Finished, I put the bag in the refrigerator, out of Ivy's reach.

"They could be capped." Ivy stared at the refrigerator and the unseen pepperoni. "It would be harder to be a practicing vamp, but it's been done."

My thoughts went back to Table 6.1, with its too helpful diagrams, and I shuddered, disguising it in my reach for the tomato. Ivy bobbed her head in agreement as my hand hovered over it in question. "No," I said confidently, "he doesn't have that lack of understanding of personal space every living vamp I've met besides you seems to have."

As soon as I said it, I wished I could take it back. Ivy stiffened, and I wondered if the unnatural distance she put between herself and everyone had everything to do with her being a nonpracticing vamp. It must be frustrating, second-guessing your every move, wondering if your head prompted it or your hunger. No wonder Ivy had a tendency to fly off the handle. She was fighting a thousand year instinct with no one to help her find her way. I hesitated, then asked, "Is there a way to tell if Trent is a human scion?"

"Human scion?" she said, sounding surprised. "There's a thought."

I sent the knife through the tomato to make little red squares. "It sort of fits. He has the inner strength, grace, and personal power of a vampire but without the touchy feely. And I'd stake my life that he's not a witch or warlock. It's more than him lacking even the barest hint of a redwood smell. It's the way he moves, the light in the back of his eyes. . . ." I went still as I recalled his unreadable green eyes.

Ivy slipped off the counter, pilfering a pepperoni off the pizza. I casually moved it to the other side of the sink and away from her. She followed, taking another. There was a soft buzz as Jenks flew in through the window. He had a mushroom in his arms almost as large as himself, bringing the smell of dirt into the kitchen. I glanced at Ivy, and she shrugged.

"Hey, Jenks," Ivy said as she moved back to her chair in the corner of the kitchen. Apparently we'd passed the "I can stand right next to you and not bite you" test. "What do you think? Is Trent a Were?"

Jenks dropped the mushroom, his tiny face shifting with anger. His wings blurred to nothing. "How should I know if Trent is a Were?" he snapped. "I didn't get close enough. I got caught. Okay? Jenks got caught. Happy now?" He flew to the window. Standing beside Mr. Fish with his hands on his hips, he stared into the dark.

Ivy shook her head with a look of disgust. "So you got caught. Big freaking deal. They knew who Rachel was, and you don't see her whining over it."

Actually, I had thrown my tantrum on the way home, which

might have accounted for the odd noise Francis's car was making when I left it in the mall parking lot in the shade of a tree.

Jenks darted to hover three inches before Ivy's nose. His wings were red in anger. "You have a *gardener* trap you in a glass ball and see if it doesn't give you a new outlook on life, Little Miss Merry Sunshine."

My bad mood slipped away as I watched a four-inch pixy confront a vamp. "Knock it off, Jenks," I said lightly. "I don't think he was a real gardener."

"Really?" he said sarcastically, flying to me. "You think?"

Behind him, Ivy pretended to squish Jenks between her finger and thumb. Rolling her eyes, she returned to her maps. A silence grew, not comfortable, but not awkward, either. Jenks flitted down to his mushroom and brought it to me, dirt and all. He was dressed in a loose, very casual outfit. The flowing silk was the color of wet moss, and the cut of it made him look like a desert sheik. His blond hair was slicked back and I thought I smelled soap. I'd never seen a pixy relaxing at home. It was kind of nice.

"Here," he said awkwardly, rolling the mushroom to a stop beside me. "I found it in the garden. I thought you might want it. For your pizza tonight."

"Thanks, Jenks," I said, brushing off the dirt.

"Look," he said as he backed away three steps. His wings were a confusing flash of motion and stillness. "I'm sorry, Rachel. I was supposed to back you up, not get caught."

How embarrassing, I thought. Having someone no bigger than a dragonfly apologizing for not protecting me. "Yeah, well, we both screwed up," I said sourly, wishing Ivy wasn't witnessing this. Ignoring her puff of noise, I rinsed off his mushroom and sliced it. Jenks seemed satisfied and went to make annoying circles around Ivy's head until she swatted at him.

Abandoning her, he came back to me. "I'm going to find out what Kalamack smells like if it kills me," Jenks said as I placed his contribution on the pizza. "It's personal now."

Well, I thought, *why not?* I took a deep breath. "I'm going back tomorrow night," I said, thinking about my death threat. Eventually I was going to make a mistake. And unlike Ivy, I couldn't come back from the dead. "Want to go with me, Jenks? Not as a backup, but as a partner."

Jenks rose up, his wings shifting to purple. "You can bet your mother's panties I will."

"Rachel!" Ivy exclaimed. "What do you think you're doing?"

I tore open the bag of mozzarella and dumped it over the pizza. "I'm making Jenks a full partner. Got a problem with that? He's been working too much overtime for anything less."

"No," she said, staring at me across the kitchen. "I mean going back to Kalamack's!"

Jenks hovered next to me to make a united front. "Shut your mouth, Tamwood. She needs a disc to prove Kalamack is a bio-drug runner."

"I don't have a choice," I said, pushing the cheese so hard it spilled over the edge.

Ivy leaned back in her chair with an exaggerated slowness. "I know you want him, but think it through, Rachel. Trent can accuse you of everything from trespassing to impersonating I.S. personnel to looking at his horses cross-eyed. If you get caught, you're toast."

"If I accuse Trent without solid proof, he will slide through the courts on a technicality." I couldn't look at her. "It has to be fast and idiot proof. Something the media can get their teeth into and run with." My motions were jerky as I picked up the cheese I had spilled and put it back on the pizza. "I have to get one of those discs, and tomorrow I will."

A small noise of disbelief came from Ivy. "I can't believe you're rushing back, no plans, no preparations. Nothing. You already tried the no-thinking approach and you got caught."

My face burned. "Just because I don't plan out my trips to the bathroom, it doesn't mean I'm not a good runner," I said tightly.

Her jaw clenched. "I never said you weren't a good runner. I only meant a little planning might save you some embarrassing mistakes, like what happened today."

"Mistakes!" I exclaimed. "Look here, Ivy. I'm a damn fine runner."

She arched her thin eyebrows. "You haven't had a clean tag in the last six months."

"That wasn't me, that was Denon! He admitted it. And if you are so unimpressed with my abilities, why did you beg that I let you come with me?"

"I didn't," Ivy said. Her eyes narrowed and spots of anger appeared on her cheeks.

Not wanting to argue with her, I turned to put the pizza in the oven. The dry whoosh of air made my cheeks tighten and sent wisps of my hair floating into my eyes. "Yes, you did," I muttered, knowing she could hear me, then said louder, "I know exactly what I'm going to do."

"Really?" she said from right behind me. I stifled a gasp and whipped around. Jenks was standing on the windowsill next to Mr. Fish, white-faced. "So tell me," she said, her voice dripping with sarcasm. "What's your *perfect plan?*"

Not wanting her to know she had scared me, I brushed past her, deliberately showing her my back as I scraped the flour off the counter with that big knife. The hair on the back of my neck rose, and I turned to find her just where I had left her, even if her arms were crossed and a dark shadow was flitting behind her eyes. My pulse quickened. I knew I shouldn't have been arguing with her.

Jenks darted between Ivy and me. "How are we going to get in, Rachel?" he asked, alighting beside me on the counter.

I felt safer with him watching her, and I purposely turned my back on Ivy. "I'm going in as a mink." Ivy made a noise of disbelief and I stiffened. Brushing the loosened flour into my hand, I dumped it into the trash. "Even if I'm spotted, they won't know it's me. It will be a simple snatch and dash." Trent's words about my activities flitted through me, and I wondered.

"Burglarizing the office of a councilman is not a simple snatch and dash," Ivy said, the tension seeming to ooze from her. "It's grand theft."

"With Jenks, I'll be in and out of his office in two minutes. Out of the building in ten."

"And buried in the basement of the I.S. tower in an hour," Ivy said. "You're nuts. Both of you are bloody nuts. It's a fortress in the middle of the freaking woods! And that's not a plan—it's an idea. Plans are on paper."

Her voice had become scornful, pulling my shoulders tight. "If I used plans, I'd be dead three times over," I said. "I don't need a plan. You learn all you can, then you just do it. Plans can't take into account surprises!"

"If you used a plan, you wouldn't have any surprises."

Ivy stared at me, and I swallowed. More than a hint of black swirled in her eyes, and my stomach clenched.

"I have a more enjoyable path if you're looking for suicide," she breathed.

Jenks landed on my earring, jolting my eyes from Ivy. "It's the first smart thing she's done all week," he said. "So back off, Tamwood."

Ivy's eyes narrowed, and I took a quick step back as she was distracted. "You're as bad as her, pixy," she said, showing her teeth. Vamp teeth were like guns. You didn't pull them unless you were going to use them.

"Let her do her job!" Jenks shouted back.

Ivy went wire tight. A cold draft hit my neck as Jenks shifted his wings as if to fly. "Enough!" I cried, before he could leave me. I wanted him right were he was. "Ivy. If you have a better idea, tell me. If not—shut up."

Together Jenks and I looked at Ivy, stupidly thinking we were stronger together than alone. Her eyes flashed to black. My mouth went dry. They were unblinking, alive with a promise as yet only hinted at. A tickle in my belly swirled up to close my throat. I couldn't tell if it was fear or anticipation. She fixed upon my eyes, not breathing. *Don't look at my neck,* I thought, panicking. *Oh. God. Don't look at my neck.* "Rot and hell," Jenks whispered.

But she shuddered, turning away to lean over the sink. I was shaking, and could swear I heard a sigh of relief from Jenks. This, I realized, could have been really, really bad.

Ivy's voice sounded dead when she next spoke. "Fine," she said to the sink. "Go get yourself killed. Both of you." She jerked herself into motion and I jumped. Hunched and pained-looking, she stalked out of the kitchen. Too soon to be believed came the sound of the church's front door slamming, then nothing.

Someone, I thought, *was going to get hurt tonight.*

Jenks left my earring, alighting on the windowsill. "What's with her?" he asked belligerently into the sudden quiet. "You would almost think she cared."

Sixteen

I woke from a sound sleep, jolted by the distant sound of glass breaking. I could smell wood incense. My eyes flashed open.

Ivy was bending over me, her face inches from mine.

"No!" I shouted, punching out in a blind panic. My fist caught her in the gut. Ivy clutched her middle and fell to the floor, struggling to breathe. I scrambled to crouch on my bed. My eyes darted from the gray window to the door. My heart pounded, and I went cold in a painful rush of adrenaline. She was between me and my only way out.

"Wait," she gasped, her robe sleeve falling to her elbow as she reached to catch me.

"You backstabbing, bloodsucking vamp," I hissed.

My breath caught in surprise as Jenks—no, it was Jax—flitted from the windowsill to hover before me. "Ms. Rachel," he said, distracted and tense. "We're under attack. Fairies." He nearly spat the last word.

Fairies, I thought in a wash of cold fear as I glanced at my bag. I couldn't fight fairies with my charms. They were too fast. The best I could do would be to try and squish one. Oh God. I'd never killed anyone in my entire life. Not even by accident. I was a runner, damn it. The idea was to bring them in alive, not dead. But fairies . . .

My gaze shot to Ivy, and I flushed as I realized what she was doing in my room. With as much grace as I could find, I got off my bed. "Sorry," I whispered, offering her a hand up.

Her head tilted so she could see me past the curtain of her hair. Pain barely hid her anger. A white hand darted out and yanked me down. I hit the floor with a yelp, panicking again as she covered my mouth with a firm hand. "Shut up," she wheezed, her breath on my cheek. "You want to get us killed? They're already inside."

Eyes wide, I whispered around her fingers, "They won't come inside. It's a church."

"Fairies don't recognize holy ground," she said. "They couldn't care less."

They were already inside. Seeing my alarm, Ivy took her hand from my mouth. My eyes went to the heating vent. Reaching out a slow hand, I closed it, wincing at the squeak.

Jax lit upon on my pajama-covered knee. "They invaded our garden," he said, the murderous cast on his childlike face looking terribly wrong. "They're going to pay. And here I am, stuck babysitting you two lunkers." He flitted to the window in disgust.

There was a bump from the kitchen, and Ivy yanked me down as I tried to rise. "Stay put," she said softly. "Jenks will take care of them."

"But—" I bit back my protest as Ivy turned to me, her eyes black in the dim light of the early morning. What could Jenks do against fairy assassins? He was trained in backup, not guerrilla warfare. "Look, I'm sorry," I whispered. "For hitting you, I mean."

Ivy didn't move. A seething mix of emotion had gathered behind her eyes, and I felt my breath catch. "If I wanted you, little witch," she said, "you couldn't stop me."

Chilled, I swallowed hard. It sounded like a promise.

"Something's changed," she said, her attention on my closed door. "I didn't expect this for another three days."

A sick feeling washed over me. The I.S. had changed its tactics. I had brought this on myself. "Francis," I said. "It's my fault. The I.S. knows I can slip past their watchers now." I pressed my fingertips into my temples. Keasley, the old man across the street, had warned me.

There was a third crash, louder this time. Ivy and I stared at the door. I could hear my heartbeat. I wondered if Ivy could, too. After a long moment, there was a tiny knock at the door. Tension slammed into me, and I heard Ivy take a slow breath, gathering herself.

"Papa?" Jax said softly. There was a whine of noise from the hall, and Jax darted to the door. "Papa!" he shouted.

I lurched to my feet, shoulders slumping. I flicked on the light, squinting in the sudden glare at the clock Ivy had lent me. Five-thirty. I'd only been asleep an hour.

Ivy rose with startling quickness, opening the door and stalking out with the hem of her robe furling. I winced as she left. I hadn't meant to hurt her. No, that wasn't true. I had. But I thought she was making me into an early morning snack.

Jenks careened in, nearly crashing into the window as he tried to land.

"Jenks?" I said, deciding my apology to Ivy could wait. "Are you all right?"

"We-e-e-e-ell," he drawled, sounding as if he were drunk. "We won't have to worry about fairies for a while." My eyes widened at the length of steel in his hand. It had a wooden handle and was the size of one of those sticks they put olives on. Staggering, he sat down hard, accidentally bending his lower set of wings under him.

Jax pulled his father to his feet. "Papa?" he said, worried. Jenks was a mess. One of his upper wings was in tatters. He was bleeding from several scratches, one right under his eye. The other was swollen shut. He leaned heavily on Jax, who was struggling to keep his father upright.

"Here," I said, tucking my hand under and behind Jenks, forcing him to sit on my palm. "Let's get you to the kitchen. The light's better in there. Maybe we can tape your wing."

"No light there," Jenks slurred. "Broke 'em." He blinked, struggling to focus. "Sorry."

Worried, I cupped my hand over him, ignoring his muffled protests. "Jax," I said, "get your mom." He grabbed his father's sword and darted out just below the ceiling. "Ivy?" I called as I edged my way through the dark hall. "What do you know about pixies?"

"Apparently not enough," she said from right behind me, and I jumped.

I elbowed the light switch as I entered the kitchen. Nothing. The lights were busted.

"Wait," Ivy said. "There's glass all over the floor."

"How can you tell?" I said in disbelief, but I hesitated, not willing to chance my bare feet in the dark. Ivy brushed past me in a whisper of black, and I shuddered as the breeze of her passage chilled me. She was going vampy. There was the crunch of glass, and the fluorescent bulb over the oven flickered into life, illuminating the kitchen in an uncomfortable glow.

Thin, fluorescent lightbulb glass littered the floor. There was a pungent haze in the air. My eyebrows rose as I realized it was a cloud of fairy dust. It caught in my throat, and I put Jenks on the counter before I sneezed and accidentally dropped him.

Breath held, I picked my way to the window to open it farther. Mr. Fish was lying helpless in the sink, his bowl shattered. I gingerly plucked him from between the thick shards, filling a plastic cup and plunking him in. Mr. Fish wiggled, shuddered, and sank to the bottom. Slowly his gills moved back and forth. He was okay.

"Jenks?" I said, turning to find him standing where I had left him. "What happened?"

"We got 'em," he said, barely audible, listing to the side.

Ivy took the broom from the pantry and began sweeping the glass into a pile.

"They thought I didn't know they were there," Jenks continued as I rummaged for some tape, starting as I found a severed fairy wing. It looked like a Luna moth's wing rather than a dragonfly's. The scales rubbed off on my fingers, staining them green and purple. I carefully set the wing aside. There were several very complicated spells that called for fairy dust.

Jeez, I thought, turning away. I was going to be sick. Someone had died, and I was considering using part of him to spell.

"Little Jacey spotted them first," Jenks said, his voice falling into an eerie cadence. "On the far side of the human graves. Pink wings in the lowering moon as the earth slipped 'round her silver light. They reached our wall. Our lines were strung. We held our land. What's said is done."

Bewildered, I looked at Ivy standing silent with her unmoving broom. Her eyes were wide. This was weird. Jenks wasn't swearing; he sounded poetic. And he wasn't done.

"The first went down beneath the oak, stung by the taste of steel in his blood. The second on holy ground did fall, stained with the cries of his folly. The third in the dust and salt did fail, sent back to his master, a silent warning given." Jenks looked up, clearly not seeing me. "This ground is ours. So it is said with broken wing, poisoned blood, and our unburied dead."

Ivy and I stared at each other through the ugly light. "What the hell?" Ivy whispered, and Jenks's eyes cleared. He turned to us, touched his head in salute, and slowly collapsed.

"Jenks!" Ivy and I cried, jolted into motion. Ivy got there first. She cupped Jenks into her hands and turned to me with a panicked look. "What do I do?" she cried.

"How should I know?" I shouted back. "Is he breathing?"

There was a sound of jangling wind chimes, and Jenks's wife darted into the room, trailing a wake of at least a dozen pixy children. "Your living room is clean," she said brusquely, her silk fog-colored cloak billowing to a stop around her. "No charms. Take him there. Jhem, go turn the light on ahead of Ms. Ivy, then help Jinni fetch my kit here. Jax, take the rest of this lot through the church. Start in the belfry. Don't miss a crack. The walls, the pipes, the cable and phone lines. Watch the owls, and mind you check that priest hole. You even think you smell a spell or one of those fairies, you sing out. Clear? Now go."

The pixy children scattered. Ivy, too, obediently followed the tiny woman's order and hotfooted it into the living room. I would have thought it amusing but for Jenks unmoving on her palm. Limping, I followed them.

"No, love," the tiny woman directed as Ivy went to set Jenks on a cushion. "The end table, please. I need a hard surface to cut against."

Cut against? I thought, moving Ivy's magazines off the table and onto the floor to make room. I sat down on the closest chair and tilted the lamp shade. My adrenaline was fading, leaving me light-headed and cold in my flannel pajamas. What if Jenks was really hurt? I was shocked he had actually killed two fairies. *He had killed them.* I had put people in the hospital before, sure, but kill someone? I thought back to my fear as I huddled in the dark next to a tense vampire and wondered if I could do the same.

Ivy set Jenks down as if he were made of tissue paper, then backed to the door. Her tall stance hunched, making her look nervous and out of place. "I'll check outside," she said.

Mrs. Jenks smiled, showing an ageless warmth in her smooth, youthful features. "No, love," she said. "It's safe now. We have at least a full day before the I.S. can find another fairy clan willing to breach our lines. And there's not enough money to get pixies to invade other pixies' gardens. It just proves fairies are uncouth barbarians. But you go search if you like. The youngest bairn could dance among the flowers this morning."

Ivy opened her mouth as if to protest, then realizing the pixy was entirely serious, she dropped her eyes and slipped out the back door.

"Did Jenks say anything before he passed out?" Mrs. Jenks asked as she arranged him so his wings were awkwardly splayed. He looked like a pinned bug on display, and I felt ill.

"No," I said, wondering at her calm attitude. I was nearly frantic. "He started in like he was reciting a sonnet or something." I pulled my pajama top tighter to my throat and hunched into myself. "Is he going to be all right?"

She sank to her knees beside him, her relief obvious as she ran a careful finger under her husband's swollen eye. "He's fine. If he was cursing or reciting poetry, he's fine. If you told me he was singing, I'd be worried." Her hands slowed their motion over him, and her eyes went distant. "The one time he came home singing, we nearly lost him." Her eyes cleared. Pressing her lips together in a mirthless smile, she opened the bag her children had brought.

I felt a flush of guilt. "I'm really sorry about this, Mrs. Jenks," I said. "If it hadn't been for me, this never would have happened. If Jenks wants to break his contract, I'll understand."

"Break his contract!" Mrs. Jenks fixed her eyes on me with a frightening intensity. "Heavens, child. Not over a little bit of a thing like this."

"But Jenks shouldn't have to fight them," I protested. "They could've killed him."

"There were only three," she said, spreading a white cloth next to Jenks like a surgical kit, laying bandages, salve, even what looked like artificial wing membrane on it. "And they knew better. They saw the warnings. Their deaths were legitimate." She smiled, and I could see why Jenks had used his wish to keep her. She looked like an angel, even with the knife she held.

"But they weren't after you," I insisted. "They were after me."

Her head shook to send the tips of her wispy hair waving. "Doesn't matter," she said in her lyrical voice. "They would have gotten the garden regardless. But I think they did it for the *money*." She nearly spat the word. "It took a lot of I.S. money to convince them to try my Jenks's strength." She sighed, cutting out portions of the thin membrane to match the holes in Jenks's wing with the coolness of someone mending a sock.

"Don't fret," she said. "They thought that because we had just taken possession, they could catch us off balance." She turned a smug eye to me. "They found out wrong, didn't they?"

I didn't know what to say. The pixy/fairy animosity went far deeper than I had imagined. Being of the mind-set that no one could own the earth, pixies and fairies shunned the idea of property titles, relying upon the simple adage might makes right. And because they weren't in competition with anyone but each other, the courts turned a blind eye to their affairs, allowing them to settle their own disagreements, up to and including killing each other, apparently. I wondered what had happened to whoever had the garden before Ivy rented the church.

"Jenks likes you," the small woman said, rolling up the wing membrane and packing it away. "Calls you his friend. I'll give you the same title out of respect for him."

"Thanks," I stammered.

"I don't trust you, though," she said, and I blinked. She was as direct as her husband, and just about as tactful. "Is it true you made him a partner? For real and not just a cruel prank?"

I nodded, more serious than I had been all week. "Yes, ma'am. He deserves it."

Mrs. Jenks took a pair of tiny scissors in hand. They looked more like an heirloom than a functional piece of equipment, their wooden handles carved into the shape of a bird. The beak was metal, and my eyes widened as she took the cold iron and knelt before Jenks. "Please stay asleep, love," I heard her whisper, and I watched in astonishment as she delicately trimmed the frayed edges of Jenks's wing. The smell of cauterized blood rose thick in the shut-up room.

Ivy appeared in the doorway as if having been summoned. "You're bleeding," she said.

I shook my head. "It's Jenks's wing."

"No. You're bleeding. Your foot."

I straightened, squashing a flash of angst. Breaking eye contact, I swung my foot up to look at its underside. A red smear covered my heel. I had been too busy to notice.

"I'll clean it up," Ivy said, and I dropped my foot, shrinking back. "The *floor*," Ivy said in disgust. "You left bloody footprints all over the *floor*." My gaze went to where she pointed to the hallway, my footprints obvious in the growing light of the new day. "I wasn't going to touch your foot," Ivy muttered as she stomped out.

I flushed. Well . . . I had woken up with her breathing on my neck.

There was a thumping of cupboard doors and a rush of water from the kitchen. She was mad at me. Maybe I ought to apologize. But for what? I already said I was sorry for hitting her.

"You sure Jenks is going to be okay?" I asked, avoiding the problem.

The pixy woman sighed. "If I can get the patches in place before he wakes up." She sat back on her heels, closed her eyes, and said a short prayer. Wiping her hands on her skirt, she took up a dull blade with a wooden handle. She set a patch in place and ran the flat of the blade along the edges, melting it to Jenks's wing. He shuddered, though didn't wake. Her hands were shaking when she finished, and pixy dust sifted from her to make her glow. An angel indeed.

"Children?" she called, and they appeared from everywhere. "Bring your father along. Josie, if you would go and make sure the door is open?"

I watched as the children descended upon him, lifting him up and carrying him out through the flue. Mrs. Jenks wearily got to her feet as her eldest daughter packed everything away in the bag. "My Jenks," she said, "sometimes reaches for more than a pixy ought to dream for. Don't get my husband killed in his folly, Ms. Morgan."

"I'll try," I whispered as she and her daughter vanished up the chimney. I felt guilty, as if I were intentionally manipulating Jenks to protect myself. There was a sliding clatter of glass into the trashcan, and I rose, glancing out the window. The sun was up, shining on the herbs in the garden. It was way past my bedtime, but I didn't think I could go back to sleep.

Feeling weary and out of control, I shuffled into the kitchen. Ivy was on her hands and knees in her black robe, swabbing up my footprints. "I'm sorry," I said, standing in the middle of the kitchen with my arms clasped around myself.

Ivy looked up with narrowed eyes, playing the part of the martyr well. "For what?" she said, clearly wanting to drag me through the entire apology process.

"For, er, hitting you. I wasn't awake yet," I lied. "I didn't know it was you."

"You already apologized for that," she said, going back to the floor.

"For you cleaning up my footprints?" I tried again.

"I offered to."

I bobbed my head. She had. I wasn't going to delve into the possible motives behind that, but just accept her offer as her being nice. But she was mad about something. I hadn't a clue what. "Um, help me out here, Ivy," I finally said.

She rose and went to the sink, methodically rinsing the rag out. The yellow cloth was carefully set over the faucet to dry. She turned, leaning back against the counter. "How about a little trust? I said I wasn't going to bite you, and I'm not."

My mouth dropped open. Trust? Ivy was upset about trust?

"You want trust?" I exclaimed, finding I needed to be angry to talk to Ivy about this. "Then how about more control from you. I can't even contradict you without you going vampy on me!"

"I do not," she said, her eyes widening.

"You do, too," I said, gesturing. "It's just like that first week we worked together and we would argue over the best way to bring in a shoplifter at the mall. Just because I don't agree with you doesn't mean I'm wrong. At least listen to me before you decide that I am."

She took a breath, then slowly let it out. "Yes. You're right."

I jerked back at her words. She thought I was right? "And another thing," I added, slightly mollified. "Stop with the running away during an argument. You stormed out of here tonight like you were going to rip someone's head off, then I wake up with you bending over me? I'm sorry for punching you, but you have to admit, you kind of deserved it."

A faint smile crossed her, then disappeared. "Yeah. I suppose." She rearranged the rag over the spigot. Turning, she clasped her arms around herself, gripping her elbows. "Okay, I won't leave in the middle of an argument, but you're going to have to not get so excited during them. You're jerking me around until I don't know which floor to stand on."

I blinked. Did she mean excited as in scared, angry, or both? "Beg pardon?"

"And maybe get a stronger perfume?" she added apologetically.

"I—I just bought some," I said in surprise. "Jenks said it covered everything."

A sudden distress pinched Ivy's face as she met my gaze. "Rachel . . . I can still smell me thick on you. You're like a big chocolate-chip cookie sitting all alone on an empty table. And when you get all agitated, it's as if you just came out of the oven, all warm and gooey. I haven't had a cookie in three years. Could you just calm down so you don't smell so damn good?"

"Oh." Suddenly cold, I sank down in my chair at the table. I didn't like being compared to food. And I'd never be able to eat another chocolate-chip cookie again. "I rewashed my clothes," I said in a small voice. "I'm not using your sheets or soap anymore."

Ivy's eyes were on the floor when I turned around. "I know," she said. "I appreciate it. It helps. This isn't your fault. A vampire's scent lingers on anyone they live with. It's a survival trait that tends to lengthen the life of a vampire's companion by telling other vamps to back off. I didn't think I would notice it, seeing as we were sharing floor space, not blood."

A shudder went through me as I recalled from my basic Latin class that the word companion stemmed from the word for food. "I don't belong to you," I said.

"I know." She took a careful breath, not looking at me. "The lavender is helping. Maybe if you hung satchels of it in your closet it would be enough. And tried not to get so emotional, especially when we're—discussing alternative actions?"

"Okay," I said softly, realizing how complex this arrangement was going to be.

"Are you still going out to Kalamack's tomorrow?" Ivy asked.

I nodded, relieved at the change of topics. "I don't want to go without Jenks, but I don't think I can wait for him to be flightworthy."

Ivy was silent for a long moment. "I'll drive you out. As close as you want to risk it."

My mouth dropped open for a second time. "Why? I mean, really?" I quickly amended, and she shrugged.

"You're right. If you don't get this done quickly, you won't last another week."

Seventeen

"You aren't going, *dear,*" Mrs. Jenks said tightly.

I dumped my last swallow of coffee down the sink, gazing uncomfortably into the garden, bright with the early afternoon sun. I would rather be anywhere else right now.

"The devil I'm not," Jenks muttered.

I turned around, too tired from a morning with not enough sleep to enjoy watching Jenks get henpecked. He was standing on the stainless steel island with his hands aggressively on his hips. Beyond him, Ivy was hunched at her wooden table as she planned three routes to the Kalamack estate. Mrs. Jenks was beside her. Her stiff stance said it all. She didn't want him to go. And looking the way she did, I wasn't about to contradict her.

"I say you aren't going," she said, a cord of iron laced through her voice.

"Mind your place, woman," he said. A hint of pleading ruined his tough-guy stance.

"I am." Her tone was severe. "You're still broken. What I say goes. That's our law."

Jenks gestured plaintively. "I'm fine. I can fly. I can fight. I'm going."

"You aren't. You can't. You're not. And until I say, you're a gardener, not a runner."

"I can fly!" he exclaimed, his wings blurring into motion. He lifted a mere fingerbreadth off the counter and back down. "You just don't want me to go."

She stiffened. "I'll not have it said you were killed because of my failings. Keeping you alive is my responsibility, and I say *you're broken*!"

I fed Mr. Fish a crushed flake. This was embarrassing. If it had been up to me, I'd let Jenks go, flightless or not. He was recovering faster than I would have believed possible. Still, it had been less than ten hours since he was spouting poetry. I looked at Mrs. Jenks with an inquiring arch to my eyebrows. The pretty pixy woman shook her head. That was it, then.

"Jenks," I said. "I'm sorry, but until you have the green, you're garden-bound."

He took three steps, stopping at the edge of the counter. His fists clenched.

Uncomfortable, I joined Ivy at the table. "So," I said awkwardly. "You said you have an idea of how I can get in?"

Ivy took the end of the pen out from between her teeth. "I did some research this morning on the net—"

"You mean after I went back to bed?" I interrupted.

She looked up at me with her unreadable brown eyes. "Yes." Turning away, she rifled through her maps, pulling out a colored brochure. "Here, I printed this out."

I sat down as I took it. She had not only printed it out, but had folded it into the usual brochure folds. The colorful pamphlet was an advertisement for guided tours of the Kalamack botanical gardens. " 'Come stroll among the spectacular private gardens of Councilman Trenton Kalamack,' " I read aloud. " 'Call ahead for ticket prices and availability. Closed on the full moon for maintenance.' " There was more, but I had my way in.

"I've got another one for the stables," Ivy said. "They run tours all year, except for spring, when the foals are born."

"How considerate." I ran a finger over the crayon-bright sketch of the grounds. I had no idea Trent was interested in gardening. Maybe he *was* a witch. There was a loud, very obvious whine as Jenks flew the short distance to the table. He could fly, but barely.

"This is fantastic," I said, ignoring the belligerent pixy as he walked over the paper and into my line of sight. "I was planning on you dropping me off somewhere in the woods so I could hike my way in, but this is great. Thanks."

Ivy gave me an honest, closed-lipped smile. "A little research can save a lot of time."

I stifled a sigh. If Ivy had her way, we would have a six-step plan posted over the john for what to do if it backed up. "I could fit in a big purse," I said, warming to the idea.

Jenks sniffed. "A really big-ass purse."

"I have someone who owes me a favor," Ivy said. "If she bought the ticket, my name wouldn't be on the roster. And I could wear a disguise." Ivy grinned to show a faint slip of teeth. I returned it weakly. She looked altogether human in the bright afternoon light.

"Hey," Jenks said, glancing at his wife. "I could fit in a purse, too."

Ivy tapped her pen on her teeth. "I'll take the tour, and misplace my purse somewhere."

Jenks stood on the brochure, his wings moving in abrupt fits of motion. "I'm going."

I jerked the pamphlet out from under him, and he stumbled back. "I'll meet you tomorrow past the front gate in the woods. You could pick me up just out of sight."

"I'm going," Jenks said louder, ignored.

Ivy leaned back in her chair with a satisfied air. "Now *that* sounds like a plan."

This was really odd. Last night Ivy had nearly bit my head off when I suggested nearly the same thing. All she needed was to have some input. Pleased for having figured this small bit of Ivy out, I rose and opened my charm cupboard. "Trent knows about you," I said as I looked my spells over. "Only heaven knows how. You definitely need a disguise. Let's see . . . I could make you look old."

"Is no one listening to me?" Jenks shouted, his wings an angry red. "I'm going. Rachel, tell my wife I'm fit enough to go."

"Uh, hold up," Ivy said. "I don't want to be spelled. I've got my own disguise."

I turned, surprised. "You don't want one of mine? It doesn't hurt. It's just an illusion. It's not anything like a transformation charm."

She wouldn't meet my gaze. "I have something in mind already."

"I said," Jenks shouted, "I'm going!"

Ivy scrubbed a hand over her eyes.

"Jenks—" I began.

"Tell her," he said, darting a glance at his wife. "If you say it's okay, she'll let me go. I'll be able to fly by the time I need to."

"Look," I said. "There will be other times—"

"To break into Kalamack's estate?" he cried. "Don't freaking think so. Either I go now, or never. This is my only shot at finding out what Kalamack smells like. No pixy or fairy has been able to tell what he is. And not you, or anyone else, is going to take that chance from me." A wisp of desperation had crept into his voice. "Neither of you are big enough."

I looked past him to Mrs. Jenks, my eyes pleading. He was right. There would be no other time. It would be too chancy to risk even my life if it hadn't already been in the blender and waiting for someone to push the button. The pretty pixy's eyes closed, and she clasped her arms about herself. Looking pained, she nodded. "All right," I said, my attention back on Jenks. "You can come."

"What?" Ivy yelped, and I shrugged helplessly.

"She says it's okay," I said, nodding to Mrs. Jenks. "But only if he promises to bug out the second I say. I'm not going to risk him any more than he can fly."

Jenks's wings blurred to an excited purple. "I'll leave when I decide."

"Absolutely not." I stretched my arms out along the table, putting my fists to either side of him and glaring. "We are going in under my discretion, and we will leave on the same terms. This is a witchocracy, not a democracy. Clear?"

Jenks tensed, his mouth open to protest, but then his eyes slid from mine to his wife's. Her tiny foot was tapping. "'Kay," he said meekly. "But only this time."

I nodded and pulled my arms back to myself. "Will that fit in with your *plan*, Ivy?"

"Whatever." Chair scraping, she got to her feet. "I'll call for the ticket. We have to leave in time to get to my friend's house and out to the main bus station by four. The tours run from there." Her pace was edging into vamp mode as she strode from the kitchen.

"Jenks, dear?" the small pixy woman said softly. "I'll be in the garden if you—" Her last words choked off, and she flew out through the window.

Jenks spun, a heartbeat too late. "Matalina, wait," he cried, his wings blurring to nothing. But he was nailed to the table, unable to keep up with her. "The Turn take it! It's my only chance," he shouted after her.

I heard Ivy's muffled voice in the living room as she argued with someone on the phone. "I don't care if it is two in the afternoon. You owe me." There was a short silence. "I could come down there and take it out of your hide, Carmen. I've nothing to do tonight." Jenks and I jumped at the thunk of something hitting the wall. I think it was the phone. It seemed everyone was having a fabulous afternoon.

"All set!" she shouted with what was obviously forced cheerfulness. "We can pick up the ticket in a half hour. That gives us just enough time to change."

"Great," I said with a sigh, rising to pluck a mink potion from the cupboard. I couldn't imagine mere clothes would make a good enough disguise for a vamp. "Hey, Jenks?" I said softly as I rummaged in the silverware drawer for a finger stick. "How does Ivy smell?"

"What?" he all but snarled, clearly still upset about his wife.

My eyes shot to the empty hall. "Ivy," I said, even more softly so she couldn't possibly hear. "Before the fairy attack, she stormed out of here like she was going to rip someone's heart out. I'm not going to put myself in her purse until I know if . . ." I hesitated, then whispered, "Has she started practicing again?"

Jenks turned serious. "No." He steeled himself and made the short flight to me. "I sent Jax to watch her. Just to make sure no one slipped her a charm aimed at you." Jenks puffed with parental pride. "He did well on his first run. No one saw him. Just like his old man."

I leaned closer. "So where did she go?"

"Some vamp bar on the river. She sat in the corner, snarling at anyone who got close, and drank orange juice all night." Jenks shook his head. "It's really weird, if you ask me."

There was a small sound in the doorway, and Jenks and I straightened with a guilty quickness. I looked up, blinking in surprise. "Ivy?" I stammered.

She smiled weakly, with a pleased embarrassment. "What do you think?"

"Uh, great!" I managed. "You look great. I never would have recognized you." And I might not have.

Ivy was wrapped in a skintight yellow sundress. The thin straps holding it up stood out sharp against her shockingly white skin. Her black hair was a wave of ebony. Bright red lipstick was the only color to her face, making her look more exotic than usual. She had sunglasses on, and a wide-brimmed yellow hat that matched her high heels. Over her shoulders was a purse big enough to carry a pony.

She spun in a slow circle, looking like a stoic model on the runway. Her heels made a sharp click-clack, and I couldn't help but watch. I made a mental note—no more chocolate for me. Coming to a stop, she took her sunglasses off. "Think this will do?"

I shook my head in disbelief. "Uh, yeah. You actually wear that?"

"I used to. And it won't set off any spell-check amulets, either."

Jenks made a face as he levered himself up on the sill. "Much as I enjoy this horrific outpouring of estrogen, I'm going to go say good-bye to my wife. Let me know when you're ready. I'll be in the garden—probably next to the stink weed." He wobbled into flight and out the window. I turned back to Ivy, still amazed.

"I'm surprised it still fits," Ivy said as she looked down at herself. "It used to be my mother's. I got it when she died." She eyed me with a severe frown. "And if she ever shows up on our doorstep, don't let on I have it."

"Sure," I offered weakly.

Ivy tossed her purse to the table and sat with her legs crossed at the knees. "She thinks my great aunt stole it. If she knew I had it, she'd make me give it back." Ivy harrumphed. "Like she could wear it anymore. A sundress after dark is so tacky."

She turned, a bright smile on her face. I stifled a shudder. She looked like a human. A wealthy, desirable human. This, I realized, was a hunting dress.

Ivy went still at my almost horrified look. Her eyes dilated, sending my pulse hammering. That awful black drifted over her as her instincts were jerked into play. The kitchen faded from my awareness. Though she was across the room, Ivy seemed right before me. I felt myself go hot, then cold. She was pulling an aura in the middle of the freaking afternoon.

"Rachel . . ." she breathed, her gray voice enticing a shudder from me. "Stop being afraid."

My breath came quick and shallow. Frightened, I forced myself to turn so my back was almost to her. *Damn, damn, damn!* This wasn't my fault. I hadn't done anything! She had been so normal . . . and then this? From the corner of my sight I watched Ivy hold herself still, scrambling for control. If she moved, I was going out the window.

But she didn't move. Slowly my breath came easier. My pulse slowed, and her tension decreased. I took a deep breath, and the black in her eyes diminished. I flipped my hair out of my face and pretended to wash my hands, and she slumped to her chair by the table. Fear was an aphrodisiac to her hunger, and I had been unwittingly feeding it to her.

"I shouldn't have put this on again," she said, her voice low and strained. "I'll wait in the garden while you invoke your spell." I nodded, and she drifted to the door, clearly making a conscious effort to move at a normal speed. I hadn't noticed her standing up, but there she was, moving into the hallway. "And Rachel," she said softly, standing in the threshold. "If I ever do start practicing again, you'll be the first to know."

Eighteen

"I don't think I'll ever get my nose clear of the stink in that sack." Jenks took a dramatic breath of the night air.

"Purse," I said, hearing the word come out as a bland squeak. It was all I could manage. I had recognized right off what Ivy's mother's purse smelled like, and the thought that I had spent a good portion of my day in it gave me the willies.

"You ever smell anything like that?" Jenks continued blithely.

"Jenks, shut up." Squeak, squeak, chirp. Guessing what a vamp carried when she went hunting wasn't high on my list. I tried really hard not to think about Table 6.1.

"No-o-o-o," he drawled. "It was more of a musky, metallic kind of—oh."

But the night air was pleasant enough. It was edging toward ten, and Trent's public garden had the lush smell of rising damp. The moon was a thin sliver lost behind the trees. Jenks and I were hidden in the shrubbery behind a stone bench. Ivy was long gone.

She had tucked her purse under the seat this afternoon, pretending to be faint. After blaming her weariness on low blood sugar, half the men on the tour had offered to run up to the pavilion to fetch her a cookie. I had nearly blown our cover laughing at Jenks's nonstop, overly dramatic parody of what was going on outside her purse. Ivy had left in a swirl of manly concern. I hadn't known whether to be worried or amused at how easily she had swayed them.

"This feels as wrong as Uncle Vamp at a sweet-sixteen party,"

Jenks said as he edged out of the shadows and onto the path. "I haven't heard a bird all afternoon. No fairies or pixies, either." He peered up at the black canopy from under his hat.

"Let's go," I squeaked as I looked down the abandoned path. Everything was in shades of gray. I still wasn't used to it.

"I don't think there *are* any fairies or pixies," Jenks continued. "A garden this size could support four clans, easy. Who takes care of the plants?"

"Maybe that way," I said, needing to talk even though he couldn't understand me.

"You've got that right," he said, continuing his one-sided conversation. "Lunkers. Thick-fingered clumsy oafs who rip out an ailing plant instead of giving it a dose of potash. Uh, present company excepted, of course," he added.

"Jenks," I chittered, "you're a real piece of work."

"You're welcome."

I didn't trust Jenks's belief that there might be no fairies or pixies, and I half expected them to descend upon us at any moment. Having seen the aftermath of a pixy/fairy skirmish, I wasn't in any hurry to experience it. Especially not when I was the size of a squirrel.

Jenks craned his neck and studied the upper branches as he adjusted his hat. He had told me earlier that it was a flaming red, and that the conspicuous color was a pixy's only defense when entering another clan's garden. It was a promise of good intent and quick departure. His constant fussing with it since leaving Ivy's purse had nearly driven me crazy. Being stuck behind a bench all afternoon had done nothing for my nerves, either. Jenks had spent most of the day sleeping, stirring back to wakefulness when the sun neared the unseen horizon.

A flash of excitement raced through me and was gone. Pushing the feeling away, I chittered for Jenks's attention and started toward the smell of carpet. The time spent in Ivy's purse, and then under the bench, had done Jenks a lot of good. Still, though, he was lagging behind. Worried the slight noise of his labored flight might alert someone, I came to a rolling halt, motioning Jenks to get on my back.

"Whatsa matter, Rache," he said, tugging his hat back down, "got an itch?"

I gritted my teeth. Crouched on my haunches, I pointed to him, then my shoulders.

"No freaking way." He glanced at the trees. "I won't be carted about like a baby."

I don't have time for this, I thought. I pointed again, this time straight up. It was our agreed sign that he was to go home. Jenks's eyes narrowed, and I bared my teeth. Surprised, he took a step back.

"Okay, okay," he grumbled. "But if you tell Ivy, I'm going to pix you every night for a week. Got it?" His light weight hit my shoulders, and he gripped my fur. It was an odd sensation, and I didn't like it. "Not too fast," he muttered, clearly uncomfortable as well.

Apart from his death grip on my fur, I hardly noticed him. I went as fast as I dared. I didn't like that there might be unfriendly eyes holding fairy steel watching us, and I immediately struck out off the path. The sooner we were inside, the better. My ears and nose worked nonstop. I could smell everything, and it wasn't as cool as one might think.

The leaves would shiver at every gust, making me freeze or dart deeper into the foliage. Jenks was singing a bothersome song under his breath. Something about blood and daisies.

I wove my hesitant way through a barrier of loose stone and brambles and slowed. Something was different. "The plants have changed," Jenks said, and I bobbed my head.

The trees I wove between as I moved downhill were markedly more mature. I could smell mistletoe. Old, well-conditioned earth held firmly established plants. Scent, not visual beauty, seemed more important. The narrow path I found was hard-packed dirt instead of brick. Ferns crowded the trail until only one person could pass. Somewhere, water ran. More wary, we continued until a familiar smell brought me to an alarmed standstill. Earl Grey tea.

From under the shadow of a wood lily, I stood motionless and searched for the smell of people. It was silent but for the night insects. "Over there," Jenks breathed. "A cup on the bench." He slipped from me to melt back into the shadows.

I eased forward, whiskers twitching and ears straining. The grove was empty. With a smooth motion, I flowed up onto the bench. There was a swallow of tea left in the cup, its rim decorated with dew. Its silent presence was as telling as the change in plant life. Somehow we had left the public gardens behind. We were in Trent's backyard.

Jenks perched himself upon the handle, his hands on his hips, scowling. "Nothing," he complained. "I can't smell squat off a teacup. I have to get inside."

I leapt from the bench to make an easy landing. The stink of habitation was stronger to the left, and we followed the dirt path through the ferns. Soon the scent of furniture, carpet, and electronics grew pungent, and it was with no surprise that I found the open-air deck. I looked up, making out the silhouette of a lattice-work cover. A night-blooming vine trailed over it, its fragrance fighting to be recognized over the stink of people.

"Rachel, wait!" Jenks exclaimed, yanking my ear as I stretched to step onto the moss-covered planks. Something brushed my whiskers, and I drew back, running my paws over them. It was sticky. It caught in my paws, and I accidentally glued my ears flat to my eyes. Panicking, I sat back on my haunches. I was stuck!

"Don't rub it, Rache," Jenks said urgently. "Hold still."

But I couldn't see. My pulse raced. I tried to shout, but my mouth was glued shut. The smell of ether caught at my throat. Frantic, I lashed out, hearing an irate buzz. I could barely breathe! What the devil was this stuff?

"Turn it all, Morgan," Jenks all but hissed. "Stop fighting me. I'll get it off you."

I yanked my instincts back and sank into a crouch, my breath fast and shallow. One of my paws was stuck to my whiskers and it hurt. It was all I could do not to go rolling in the dirt.

"Okay." There was a breeze from Jenks's wings. "I'm going to touch your eye."

My paws twitched as he pulled the stuff off an eyelid. His fingers were gentle and deft, but from the amount of pain, he was ripping half my eyelid off. Then it was gone and I could see. I squinted through one eye as Jenks rub his palms together, a small ball between them. Pixy dust sifted from him to make him glow. "Better?" he said, glancing at me.

"Heck yeah," I squeaked. It came out more mangled than usual, seeing as my mouth was still glued shut.

Jenks tossed the ball away. It was that sticky stuff, caked with dust. "Hold still, and I'll have the rest off you faster than Ivy can pull an aura." He yanked at my fur, turning the sticky stuff into little balls. "Sorry," he said as I yelped when he jerked my ear. "I did warn you."

"What?" I chirped, and for once he seemed to understand.

"About the sticky silk." Grimacing, he gave a hard yank, pulling a tuft of my hair out. "That's how I got caught yesterday," he said angrily. "Trent has sticky silk lacing his lobby ceiling just above human height. It's expensive stuff. I'm surprised he uses it anywhere else." Jenks flitted to my other side. "It's a pixy/fairy deterrent. You can get it off, but it takes time. I bet the entire canopy is netted. That's why there's nothing here that flies."

I twitched my tail to show I understood. I had heard of sticky silk, but the thought that I might run into it never crossed my mind. To anyone larger than a child, it felt like spiderweb.

Finally he was done, and I felt my nose, wondering if it was the same shape. Jenks took off his hat and shoved it under a rock. "Wish I had brought my sword," he said. Such was the territorial drive between pixies and fairies that if Jenks had trashed the conspicuous hat, I could stake my life that the garden was pixy and fairy free.

The slightly submissive air he had affected all afternoon vanished. From his point of view, the entire garden was probably now his, since there was no one to say different. He stood beside me with his hands on his hips, severely eyeing the deck.

"Watch this," Jenks said as he shook a cloud of pixy dust from him. His wings blurred to nothing, blowing the glowing dust toward the deck. The faint haze seemed to catch in the air. As if by magic, the pixy dust fixed itself to the silk, outlining a patch of net. Jenks gave me a sideways, satisfied smirk. "Good thing I brought Matalina's scissors," he said, pulling from his pocket the wooden-handled pair of sheers. He confidently strode up to the shimmering net and cut a mink-sized hole. "After you." He gestured grandly, and I flowed up onto the deck.

My heart gave a thump of excitement before settling down to a slow, deliberate pace. It was just another run, I told myself. Emotion was an expense I couldn't afford. Ignore that my life was involved. My nose twitched, searching for human or Inderlander. Nothing.

"I think it's a back office," Jenks said. "See, there's a desk."

Office? I thought, feeling my furry eyebrows rise. It was a deck. Or was it? Jenks lurched excitedly about, like a rabid bat. I followed at a more sedate pace. After about fifteen feet the mossy planking turned into a mottled carpet enclosed by three walls. Well-maintained potted plants were everywhere. The small desk against the far wall didn't look like much work was done there. There was a long couch and chairs arranged beside a wet bar, making the room a very comfortable place to relax or do a bit of light work. The room was a slice of outdoors, a feeling heightened by opening onto the shaded deck and in turn the garden.

"Hey!" Jenks said in excitement. "Look what I found."

I turned from the orchids I had been jealously eyeing to see Jenks hovering over a bank of electronic equipment. "It was hidden in the wall," Jenks explained. "Watch this." He flew feet first into a button set into the wall. The player and its accompanying discs slid back into hiding. Delighted, Jenks hit it again, and the equipment reappeared. "Wonder what that button does," he said, and distracted by the promise of new toys, he darted across the room.

Trent, I decided, had more music discs than a sorority house: pop, classical, jazz, new age, even some head-banger stuff. No disco, though, and my respect for him went up a notch.

I longingly ran a paw over a copy of *Takata's Sea*. The disc sank out of sight and into the player, and I jerked back. Alarmed, I jumped up to hit the button with a scrabbling of nails to send everything back into the wall.

"There's nothing here, Rache. Let's go." Jenks looked pointedly at the door and alighted on the handle. But it wasn't until I jumped up to add my weight that it clicked open. I fell to the floor in an awkward thump. Jenks and I listened at the crack for a breathless moment.

Pulse racing, I nosed the door open enough for Jenks to slip out. In a moment he buzzed back. "It's a hallway," he said. "Come on out. I've already fixed the cameras."

He disappeared around the door again, and I followed, needing all my weight to pull the door shut. The click of the lock was loud, and I cowered, praying it went unheard. I could hear running water and the rustling of night creatures being piped in from unseen speakers. Immediately I recognized the hallway as the one I had been in yesterday. The sounds had probably been there before, but so soft they were subliminal to anything but a rodent's hearing. My head bobbed in understanding. Jenks and I had found Trent's back office where he entertained his "special" guests.

"Which way?" Jenks whispered, hovering beside me. Either his wing was fully functional or he didn't want to risk being spotted riding a mink. I confidently started up the corridor. At every juncture I took the path less appealing and more sterile. Jenks played vanguard, setting every camera for a fifteen-minute loop so we were unseen. Fortunately, Trent went by a human clock—at least publicly—and the building was deserted. Or so I thought.

"Crap," Jenks whispered the same instant I froze. Voices were coming from up the hall. My pulse raced. "Go!" Jenks said urgently. "No! To the right. That chair and the potted plant."

I loped forward. The smell of citrus and terra-cotta blossomed, and I tucked behind the earthen pot as soft footsteps moved along the floor. Jenks flitted up to hide in the plant's branches.

"As much as that?" Trent's voice came sharp to my sensitive ears as he and another turned the corner. "Find out what Hodgkin is doing to get such an increase in productivity. If it's something you think can be applied to other sites, I want a report."

I held my breath as Trent and Jonathan walked past.

"Yes, Sa'han." Jonathan scribbled on an electronic notepad. "I've finished screening the potential applicants for your new secretary. It would be relativity simple to clear your calendar tomorrow morning. How many would you like to see?"

"Oh, limit it to the three you think are best suited and one you don't. Anyone I know?"

"No. I had to go out of state this time."

"Wasn't today your day off, Jon?"

There was a pause. "I opted to work, seeing as you lacked your usual secretary."

"Ah," Trent said with a comfortable laugh as they turned a corner. "So there's the reason for your zeal in finishing the interviews."

Jonathan's soft denial was the merest hint as they walked out of sight.

"Jenks," I squeaked. There was no response. "Jenks!" I squeaked again, wondering if he had gone and done something stupid like following them.

"I'm still here," he grumbled, and I felt a wash of relief. The tree shuddered as he shimmied down the trunk. He sat on the edge of the pot and dangled his feet. "I got a good sniff of him," he said, and I sank back on my haunches in expectation.

"I don't know what he is." Jenks's wings shifted to a dismal shade of blue as his circulation slowed and his mood dulled. "He smells meadowy, but not like a witch. There's no hint of iron, so he's not a vamp." Jenks's eyes crinkled in confusion. "I could smell his body rhythms slowing down, which means he sleeps at night. That rules out Weres or any other nocturnal Inderlander. Turn it all, Rache. He doesn't smell like anything I recognize. And you know what's more odd? That guy with him? He smells just like Trent. It's got to be a spell."

My whiskers twitched. Odd wasn't the word. "Squeak," I said, meaning, "I'm sorry."

"Yeah, you're right." He rose on slow dragonfly wings, slipping out to the middle of the hallway. "We should finish the run and get out of here."

A jolt shook me. *Out of here,* I thought as I left the security of the citrus tree. I was willing to bet we couldn't get out the way we came in. But I'd worry about that after I burgled Trent's office. We had already done the impossible. Getting out would be a snap.

"This way," I chittered, turning down a familiar hallway just before the lobby. I could smell the salt from the fish tank in Trent's office. The frosted glass doors we passed were black and empty. No one was working late. Trent's wooden door was predictably shut.

Swift and silent, Jenks went to work. The lock was electronic, and after a few moments of tinkering behind the panel bolted to the doorframe, the lock clicked and the door cracked open. "Standard stuff," Jenks said. "Jax could have done it."

The soft gurgling of the desk fountain drifted into the hall. Jenks pushed his way in first, taking care of the camera before I followed him in.

"No, wait," I squeaked as he angled feet first at the light switch. The room was bathed in a painful glare. "Hey!" I squeaked, hiding my face behind my paws.

"Sorry." The light went out.

"Turn on the light over the fish tank," I chittered, trying to see with my light-shocked eyes. "The fish tank," I repeated uselessly, sitting back on my haunches and pointing.

"Rache. Don't be stupid. You don't have time to eat." Then he hesitated, dropping an inch. "Oh! The light. Hee hee. Good idea."

The light flickered on, illuminating Trent's office in a soft green glow. I scrambled onto his swivel chair and then the desk, awkwardly flipping his datebook back a few months and tearing out a page. My pulse raced as I sent it to the floor, following it down.

Whiskers twitching, I pried open the desk drawer and found the discs. I wouldn't have put it past Trent to move everything. *Maybe,* I thought with a stab of pride, *he didn't think I was that much of a threat.* Taking the disc marked ALZHEIMERS, I eased back to the carpet and threw my weight against the drawer to shut it. His desk was made of a scrumptious cherry wood, and I dismally thought of the coming embarrassment of my pressboard furniture among Ivy's.

Sitting back on my haunches, I gestured to Jenks for the string. Jenks had already folded the paper into a wad he could manage, and as soon as I had the disc tied to me, we'd be gone.

"String, right?" Jenks dug in a pocket.

The overhead light exploded into existence, and I froze, cowering. Breath held tight, I crouched to look under the desk toward the door. There were two pairs of shoes—a soft slipper and an uncomfortable leather—framed in the light spilling into the hall.

"Trent," Jinks mouthed as he landed next to me with the folded paper.

Jonathan's voice was angry. "They're gone, Sa'han. I'll alert the grounds."

There was a tight sigh. "Go. I'll see what they took."

My pulse pounded, and I scrunched under the desk. The leather shoes turned and went into the hall. My adrenaline rushed as I considered darting out, but I couldn't run with the disc in my front paws. And I wasn't going to leave it behind.

The door to Trent's office closed, and I cursed my hesitation. I edged to the back panel of the desk. Jenks and I exchanged glances. I gave him the sign to go home, and he nodded emphatically. We scrunched down as Trent came around and stood before his fish tank.

"Hello, Sophocles," Trent breathed. "Who was it? If you could only tell me."

He had lost his business jacket, making him look vastly more informal. I wasn't surprised at the firm definition in his shoulders as they bunched under his lightweight shirt at his slightest movement. Sighing, he sat in his chair. His hand went to the drawer with the discs, and I felt myself go weak. I swallowed hard as I realized he was humming the first track to *Takata's Sea. Double damn. I had given myself away.*

" 'Is it no wonder the newborn cry?' " Trent said, whispering the lyrics. " 'The choice was real. The chance is a lie.' "

He went still, his fingers on the discs. Slowly he pushed the drawer shut with a foot. Its small click made me jump. He tucked closer under the desk, and I heard the sound of the datebook scraping across the desktop. He was so close, I could smell the outside on him. "Oh," he said with a soft surprise. "Imagine that.

"Quen!" he said loudly.

I stared at Jenks in confusion until a masculine voice came echoing into the room from a hidden speaker. "Sa'han?"

"Loose the hounds," Trent said. His voice reverberated with power, and I shivered.

"But it isn't the full of the—"

"Loose the hounds, Quen," Trent repeated, his voice no louder but carrying a deep anger. Under the desk, his foot began to shift rhythmically.

"Yes, Sa'han."

Trent's foot stilled. "Wait." I heard him take a deep breath, as if tasting the air.

"Sir?" came the hidden voice.

Trent sniffed again. He slowly rolled his chair away from the desk. My heart pounded, and I held my breath. Jenks flitted up to hide behind the back of a drawer. I froze as Trent stood, backed from his desk, and crouched down. I had nowhere to go. Trent's eyes met mine, and he smiled. Fear paralyzed me. "Belay that," he said softly.

"Yes, Sa'han." The speaker went dead with a soft pop.

I stared at Trent, feeling as if I was going to burst.

"Ms. Morgan?" Trent said, inclining his head cordially, and I shivered. "I wish I could say it was a pleasure." Still he smiled, inching forward. I bared my teeth and chittered. His hand drew back and he frowned. "Come out of there. You have something that belongs to me."

I felt the presence of the disc beside me. Being caught, I went from successful thief to village idiot in a heartbeat. How could I have thought I could get away with it? Ivy was right.

"Come along, Ms. Morgan," he said, reaching under the desk.

I sprang into the empty spaces behind the drawers, trying to escape. Trent reached up after me. I squeaked as a tight grip fastened on my tail. My nails grated as he pulled. Terrified, I twisted, sinking my teeth into the fatty part of his hand.

"You canicula!" he shouted, pulling me out in a helpless scrabbling. The world spun as he rose to his feet. Violently shaking his hand, he smacked me into the desk. Stars exploded into existence, seeming to go with the dusky cinnamon taste of his blood. The pain in my head loosened my jaws, and I spun from my tail as he held me.

"Let her go!" I heard Jenks cry.

The world gyrated in quick swings. "You brought your bug," Trent said calmly, slamming the flat of his hand against a panel on his desk. A faint smell of ether tickled my nose.

"Get out, Jenks!" I squeaked, recognizing the smell of sticky web.

Jonathan flung open the door. He stood in the threshold, his eyes wide. "Sa'han!"

"Shut the door!" Trent shouted.

I twisted frantically to escape. Jenks darted out just as my teeth closed upon Trent's thumb again. "Damn you, witch!" Trent shouted, swinging me into the wall. Stars exploded anew, dying to black embers. The embers grew, and I watched, numb, as they slowly overtook my sight until there was nothing else. I was warm, and I couldn't move.

I was dying.

I had to be.

Nineteen

"So, Ms. Sara Jane, the split schedule isn't an issue for you?"

"No sir. I don't mind working until seven if I have the afternoon for errands and such."

"I appreciate your flexibility. Afternoons are for contemplation. My best work is done in the morning and evening. I keep only a small staff after five, and I find the lack of distractions helps me concentrate."

The sound of Trent's smooth, public persona slipped into my awareness, jarring me awake. I opened my eyes, not understanding why everything was glaringly white and gray. Then I remembered. I was a mink. But I was alive. Barely.

The alternating high and low voices of Trent and Sara Jane's interview continued as I shakily got to my feet to find I was in a cage. My stomach tightened at a wave of nausea. I sank down, struggling not to vomit. "I am so wasted," I whispered as Trent flicked glances at me over his wire-rim glasses as he talked with a trim young woman in a pale interview suit.

My head hurt. If I didn't have a concussion, it was close. My right shoulder where I had hit his desk was sore, and it hurt to breathe. I tucked my front paw close and tried not to move. Staring at Trent, I tried to figure things out. Jenks was nowhere. *That's right,* I remembered in relief. He had made it out. He would have gone home to Ivy. Not that they could do anything for me.

My cage held a bottle of water, a bowl of pellets, a ferret hut large enough to curl up in, and an exercise wheel. *Like I would ever use it,* I thought bitterly.

I was sitting on a table at the back of Trent's office. According to the fake sunlight from the window, it was only a few hours after sunrise. Too early for me. And though it stuck in my craw, I was going to slink into that hut and go to sleep. I didn't care what Trent thought.

Taking a deep breath, I stood. "Ow! Ow!" I squeaked, wincing.

"Oh, you have a pet ferret," Sara Jane exclaimed softly.

I shut my eyes in misery. I wasn't a pet ferret; I was a pet mink. *Get it straight, lady.*

I heard Trent rise from behind his desk and felt, more than saw, both of them come close. Apparently the interview was over. Time to ogle the pet mink. The light was eclipsed, and I opened my eyes. They stood above me, staring.

Sara Jane looked professional in her classy interview dress, her long, fair hair falling midway to her elbows in a simple, sparse cut. The petite woman was cute as a button, and I imagined most people didn't take her seriously with her upturned nose, her high little-girl voice, and her short stature. But I could tell from the intelligent look in her wide-set eyes that she was used to working in a man's world and knew how to get things done. I imagined that if someone misjudged her, she wasn't opposed to using it to her advantage.

The woman's perfume was strong, and I sneezed, clenching in pain.

"This is—Angel," Trent said. "She's a mink." His sarcasm was subtle but loud in my ears. His left hand massaged his right. It was bandaged. *Three cheers for the mink,* I thought.

"She looks ill." Sara Jane's carefully polished fingernails were worn to almost the quick, and her hands looked unusually strong, almost like a laborer's.

"You don't mind rodents, Sara Jane?"

She straightened, and I shut my eyes as the light fell upon them. "I despise them, Mr. Kalamack. I hale from a farm. Vermin are killed on sight. But I'm not about to lose a potential position because of an animal." She took a slow breath. "I need this job. My entire family scrimped to put me through school, to get me out of the fields. I have to pay them back. I have a younger sister. She's too smart to spend her life digging sugar beets. She wants to be a witch, to get her degree. I can't help her unless I get a good job. I *need* this job. Please, Mr. Kalamack. I know I don't have the experience, but I'm smart and I know how to work hard."

I cracked an eyelid. Trent's face was serious in thought. His fair hair and complexion stood out sharply against his dark business suit, and he and Sara Jane made a handsome couple, though she was rather short beside him. "Nicely said, Sara Jane," he said, smiling warmly. "I appreciate honesty above all in my employees. When can you start?"

"Immediately," she said, her voice quavering. I felt ill. Poor woman.

"Wonderful." His gray voice sounded genuinely pleased. "Jon has a few papers for you to sign. He will walk you through your responsibilities, shadow you for your first week. Go to him with any questions. He's been with me for years and knows me better than I know myself."

"Thank you, Mr. Kalamack," she said, her narrow shoulders raised in excitement.

"My pleasure." Trent took her elbow and walked her to the door. *He touched her,* I thought. *Why hadn't he touched me?* Scared I might figure out what he was, maybe?

"Do you have a place to stay yet?" he was asking. "Be sure to ask Jon about the off-site housing we have available for employees."

"Thank you, Mr. Kalamack. No, I don't have an apartment yet."

"Fine. Take what time you need to get settled. If you like, we can arrange for a portion of your compensation to be put in a trust fund for your sister, pretax."

"Yes, please." The relief in Sara Jane's voice was obvious, even from the hall. She was caught. Trent was a god to her, a prince rescuing her and her family. He could do no wrong.

My stomach roiled. The room was empty, though, and I dragged myself into my hut. I circled once to get my tail in place, then collapsed with my nose poking out. The door to Trent's office clicked shut, and I jumped, all my hurts starting up again.

"Good morning, Ms. Morgan," Trent said as he breezed past my cage. He sat at his desk and began sorting through the strewn papers. "I was going to keep you here only until I got a second opinion on you. But I don't know. You are *such* the conversation starter."

"Go Turn yourself," I said, baring my teeth. Again, it was all chirps and chitters.

"Really." He sat back and twirled his pencil. "That couldn't have been complimentary."

A knock made me scrunch out of sight. It was Jonathan, and Trent became busy as he came in. "Yes, Jon?" he said, his attention firmly on his calendar.

"Sa'han." The unusually tall man stood at a respectful distance. "Ms. Sara Jane?"

"She has exactly the qualifications I need." Trent put down his pencil. Leaning back in his chair, he took off his glasses and chewed idly on the tip of the earpiece until he noticed Jonathan watching with a prim, unspoken disapproval. Trent tossed them to the desktop with a bothered look. "Sara Jane's younger sister wants off the farm to become a witch," he said. "We must help excellence along in any way we can."

"Ah." Jonathan's narrow shoulders relaxed. "I see."

"If you would, find the asking price on Sara Jane's home farm. I may like to dabble in the sugar industry. Get the taste of it, as it were? Keep the labor force. Move Hodgkin in as foreman for six months to train the present foreman in his methods. Instruct him to watch Sara Jane's sister. If she has a brain, have him move her to where she has some responsibilities."

I wedged my head out my door, worried. Jonathan looked down his narrow nose at me in disgust. "With us again, Morgan?" he mocked. "If it had been up to me, I would have stuffed you down the garbage disposal in the employees' break room and flicked the switch."

"Bastard," I chittered, then flipped him off to make sure he understood.

Jonathan's few wrinkles deepened as he frowned. Long arm swinging, he smacked my cage with the folder in his hand.

Ignoring my pain, I lunged at him, clinging to the bars with my teeth bared.

He fell back in obvious shock. Flushing, the gaunt man pulled his arm back again.

"Jon," Trent said softly. Though his voice was a whisper, Jonathan froze. I clung to the bars, heart pounding. "You forget your place. Leave Ms. Morgan alone. If you misjudge her and she fights back, it's not her fault but yours. You've made this mistake before. Repeatedly."

Seething, I dropped to the floor of the cage and growled. I hadn't known I could growl, but there it was. Slowly, Jonathan's clenched hand loosened. "It's my place to protect you."

Trent's eyebrows rose. "Ms. Morgan isn't in the position to harm anyone. Stop it."

Eyes going from one to the other, I watched the older man take Trent's rebuke with an acceptance I wouldn't have expected. The two had a very odd relationship. Trent was clearly in charge, but remembering the bother in Trent's face when Jonathan expressed his disapproval of Trent chewing his glasses, it seemed it hadn't always been so. I wondered if Jonathan had seen to Trent's upbringing, however briefly, when his mother, and then his father, had died.

"Accept my apologies, Sa'han," Jonathan said, actually inclining his head.

Trent said nothing, returning to his papers. Though clearly dismissed, Jonathan waited until Trent looked up. "Is there something else?" Trent asked.

"Your eight-thirty is early," he said. "Shall I accompany Mr. Percy back?"

"Percy!" I squeaked, and Trent glanced at me. *Not Francis Percy!*

"Yes," Trent said slowly. "Please do."

Swell, I thought as Jonathan ducked into the hallway and eased the door shut behind him. Francis's interrupted interview. I paced the perimeter of my cage, nervous. My muscles were loosening, and the movement felt painfully good. I stopped as I realized Trent hadn't taken his gaze off me. Under his questioning look, I slunk into my hut, ashamed somehow.

I found Trent was still watching me as I curled my tail about myself, draping it across my nose to keep it warm. "Don't be angry with Jon," he said softly. "He takes his station seriously—as he should. If you push him too far, he'll kill you. Let's hope you don't need to learn the same lesson he does."

I lifted my lip to show my teeth, not liking him giving me wise-old-man crap.

A whiny voice pulled both our attentions to the hallway. Francis. I had told him I could turn into a mink. If he made the right connection, I was as good as dead. Well, more dead than I was. I didn't want him to see me. Neither, apparently, did Trent.

"Mmmm, yes," he said, hastily getting up and shifting one of his floor plants to hide my cage. It was a peace lily, and I could see past its wide leaves and still stay hidden. There was a knock, and Trent called, "Come in."

"No, really," Francis was saying as Jonathan all but pushed him in.

From behind the plant, I watched Francis meet Trent's eyes and swallow hard. "Uh, hello, Mr. Kalamack," he stammered, coming to an awkward standstill. He looked more unkempt than usual, one of his laces peeping out from under his pants almost undone, and his stubble having grown from potentially attractive to ugly. His black hair lay flat, and his squinty eyes had faint, tired lines at the corners. It was likely Francis hadn't been to bed yet, coming out for his interview at Trent's convenience rather than the I.S.'s.

Trent said nothing. He went to sit, easing behind his desk with the relaxed tension of a predator settling in beside the water hole.

Francis glanced at Jonathan, his shoulders hunched. There was the sound of sliding polyester as he pushed up his jacket sleeves, then pulled them back down. Tossing his hair from his eyes, Francis edged to the chair and sat on the very end. Stress drew the features on his triangular face tight, especially when Jonathan closed the door and stood behind him with his arms crossed and his feet spread wide. My attention flicked between them. What was going on?

"Would you explain yesterday to me?" Trent said with a smooth casualness.

Confusion made me blink, then my mouth dropped open in understanding. Frances worked for Trent? It would explain his fast advancement, not to mention how a short-order cook such as himself made witch. A chill ran through me. This arrangement wasn't with the I.S.'s blessing. The I.S. had no idea. Francis was a mole. The cookie was a freaking mole!

I looked at Trent through the wide leaves. His shoulders shifted slightly, as if agreeing with my thoughts. My nausea came rolling back. Francis wasn't good enough for anything this slimy. He was going to get himself killed.

"Uh—I—" Frances stammered.

"My head of security found you spelled in your own trunk," Trent said calmly, the barest hint of a threat in his voice. "Ms. Morgan and I had an interesting conversation."

"She—She said she would turn me into an animal," Frances interrupted.

Trent took a deep breath. "Why," he said with a tired patience, "would she do that?"

"She doesn't like me."

Trent said nothing. Francis cringed as he probably realized how childish that sounded.

"Tell me about Rachel Morgan," Trent demanded.

"She's a pain in the—um—butt," he said, flicking a nervous look at Jonathan.

Trent took a pen in hand and twirled it. "I know that. Tell me something else."

"That you don't already know?" Francis blurted. His pinched eyes were riveted to the revolving pen. "You've probably had your finger on her longer than on me. Did you give her a loan for tuition?" he said, sounding almost jealous. "Whisper in her I.S. interviewer's ear?"

I stiffened. How dare he suggest it. I had *worked* for my schooling. I'd gotten my job on *my own*. I looked to Trent, hating them all. I didn't owe anyone anything.

"No. I didn't." Trent set his pen down. "Ms. Morgan was a surprise. But I did offer her a job," he said, and Francis seemed to sink in on himself. His mouth worked, but nothing came out. I could smell the fear on him, sour and sharp.

"Not your job," Trent said, his disgust obvious. "Tell me what she is afraid of. What makes her angry? What does she cherish most in the world?"

Francis's breath came in a relieved sound. He shifted, going to cross his legs but hesitating at the last, awkward moment. "I don't know. The mall? I try to stay away from her."

"Yes," Trent said in his liquid voice. "Let's talk about that for a moment. After reviewing your activities the past few days, one might question your loyalties—Mr. Percy."

Francis crossed his arms. His breathing increased and he began to fidget. Jonathan took a menacing step closer, and Francis tossed his hair from his eyes again.

Trent went frighteningly intense. "Do you know how much it cost me to quiet the rumors when you ran from the I.S. records vault?"

He licked his lips. "Rachel said they'd think I was helping her. That I should run."

"And so you ran."

"She said—"

"And yesterday?" Trent interrupted. "You drove her to me."

The tight anger in his voice pulled me out of my hut. Trent leaned forward, and I swear I heard Francis's blood freeze. The businessman aura fell from Trent. What was left was domination. Natural, unequivocal domination.

I stared at the change. Trent's mien was nothing like a vamp's aura of power. It was like unsweetened chocolate: strong and bitter and oily, leaving an uncomfortable aftertaste. Vamps used fear to command respect. Trent simply demanded it. And from what I could see, the thought never crossed his mind that it would be denied.

"She used you to get to me," he whispered, his eyes unblinking. "That is inexcusable."

Francis cowered in his chair, his thin face drawn and his eyes wide. "I—I'm sorry," he stammered. "It won't happen again."

Trent's breath slipped into him in a slow gathering of will, and I watched in horrified fascination. The yellow fish in the tank splashed at the surface. The hair on my back pricked. My pulse raced. Something rose, as nebulous as a whiff of ozone. Trent's face went empty and ageless. A haze seemed to edge him, and I wondered in a sudden shock if he were pulling on the ever-after. He'd have to be a witch or human to do that. And I would've sworn he was neither.

I tore my eyes from Trent. Jonathan's thin lips were parted. He stood behind Francis, watching Trent with a slack mix of surprise and worry. This raw show of anger wasn't expected, even by him. His hand rose in protest, hesitant and fearful.

As if in response, Trent's eye twitched and his breath eased out. The fish hid behind the coral. My skin eerily rippled, settling my fur flat. Jonathan's fingers trembled, and he made fists of them. Still not looking from Francis, Trent intoned, "I know it won't."

His voice was dust upon cold iron, the sounds sliding from one meaning to the next in a liquid grace that was mesmerizing. I felt out of breath. Shuddering, I crouched where I was. What the blazes had happened? Had almost happened?

"What do you plan on doing now?" Trent asked.

"Sir?" Francis said, his voice cracking as he blinked.

"That's what I thought." Trent's fingertips quivered with his repressed anger. "Nothing. The I.S. is watching you too closely. Your usefulness is beginning to fade."

Francis's mouth opened. "Mr. Kalamack! Wait! Like you said, the I.S. is watching me. I can draw their attention. Keep them from the customs docks. Another Brimstone take will put me in the clear and distract them at the same time." Francis shifted on the edge of his seat. "You can move your—things?" he finished weakly.

Things, I thought. Why didn't he just say biodrugs? My whiskers quivered. Francis distracted the I.S. with a token amount of

Brimstone while Trent moved the real moneymaker. How long? I wondered. How long had Francis worked for him? Years?

"Mr. Kalamack?" Francis whispered.

Trent placed his fingertips together as if in careful thought. Behind him, Jonathan furrowed his thin eyebrows, the worry that had filled him almost gone.

"Tell me when?" Francis begged, edging closer on his chair.

Trent pushed Francis to the back of his chair with a three-second glance. "I don't give chances, Percy. I take opportunities." He pulled his datebook closer, paging a few days ahead. "I would like to schedule a shipment on Friday. Southwest. Last flight before midnight to L.A. You can find your usual take at the main bus station in a locker. Keep it anonymous. My name has been in the papers too often lately."

Francis jumped to his feet in relief. He stepped forward as if to shake Trent's hand, then glanced at Jonathan and backed up. "Thank you, Mr. Kalamack," he gushed. "You won't be sorry."

"I can't imagine I would." Trent looked at Jonathan, then the door. "Enjoy your afternoon," he said in dismissal.

"Yes sir. You, too."

I felt as if I was going to be sick as Francis bounced out of the room. Jonathan hesitated in the threshold, watching Francis make obnoxious noises at the ladies he passed in the hall.

"Mr. Percy has made himself more of a liability than an asset," Trent breathed tiredly.

"Yes, Sa'han," Jonathan agreed. "I strongly urge you to remove him from the payroll."

My stomach clenched. Francis didn't deserve to die just because he was stupid.

Trent rubbed his fingertips into his forehead. "No," he finally said. "I'd rather keep him until I arrange for a replacement. And I may have other plans for Mr. Percy."

"As you like, Sa'han," Jonathan said, and softly closed the door.

Twenty

"Here, Angel," Sara Jane coaxed. A carrot wiggled through the bars of my cage. I stretched to take it before she could let it drop. Aspen chips didn't season them at all.

"Thanks," I chittered, knowing she couldn't understand me, but needing to say something regardless. The woman smiled and cautiously extended her fingers through the cage. I grazed my whiskers across them because I knew she would like it.

"Sara Jane?" Trent questioned from his desk, and the petite woman turned with a guilty swiftness. "I employ you to manage my office affairs, not be a zookeeper."

"Sorry sir. I was taking the opportunity to try and rid myself of my irrational fear of vermin." She brushed at her knee-length cotton skirt. It wasn't as crisp or professional as her interview suit, but still new. Just what I'd expect a farm girl would wear on her first day on the job.

I chewed ravenously on the carrot left over from Sara Jane's lunch. I was starving, since I refused to eat those stale pellets. *What's the matter, Trent?* I thought between chews. *Jealous?*

Trent adjusted his glasses and returned his attention to his papers. "When you're through ridding yourself of your irrational fears, I'd like you to go down to the library."

"Yes sir."

"The librarian has collated some information for me. But I want you to screen it for me. Bring up what you think is most pertinent."

"Sir?"

Trent set down his pen. "Information regarding the sugar beet industry." He smiled with a genuine warmth. I wondered if he had a patent on it. "I may be branching out in that direction, and need to learn enough to make an informed decision."

Sara Jane beamed, tucking her fair hair behind an ear in pleased embarrassment. Obviously she guessed Trent might be buying the farm her family was serfed upon. *You're a smart woman,* I thought darkly. *Follow it down. Trent will own your family. You'd be his, body and soul.*

She turned back to my cage and dropped a last celery stick. Her smile faded. Worry creased her brow. It would have looked endearing on her childlike face, except the woman's family was in real danger. She took a breath to say something, then closed her mouth. "Yes sir," she said, her eyes distant. "I'll bring the information up right away."

Sara Jane closed the door as she left, her footsteps sounding slow in the hallway.

Trent gave his door a suspicious glance as he reached for his cup of tea: Earl Grey, no sugar or milk. If he followed yesterday's pattern, it would be phone conversations and paperwork from three until seven, when the few people he kept late went home. I imagined it was easier to run illegal drugs from your office when no one was around to see you.

Trent had returned that afternoon from his three-hour lunch break with his wispy hair freshly combed and smelling of the outdoors. He had been decidedly refreshed. If I hadn't known better, I would have assumed he spent his midday break napping in his back office.

Why not? I thought as I stretched out on the hammock my cell had come with. He was wealthy enough to set his own hours.

I yawned, my eyes slipping shut. It was the second day of my captivity, and I was quite sure it wouldn't be my last. I had spent last night thoroughly investigating my cage, only to find that it was Rachel proof. It had been designed for ferrets, and the two-story wire cage was surprisingly secure. My hours spent prying at the seams left me bone tired. It was pleasant to do nothing. My hope that Jenks or Ivy might rescue me was thin. I was on my own. And it might be a while before I managed to convey to Sara Jane that I was a person and get out of there.

I cracked an eyelid as Trent rose from his desk and strode restlessly to his music discs arranged in a recessed shelf beside the player. He cut a nice figure as he stood before them, so intent on his choice that he didn't realize I was rating his backside: 9.5 out of 10. I took the .5 off for most of his physique being hidden behind a business suit that cost more than some cars.

I'd gotten another yummy look at him last night when he took off his jacket after everyone went home. The man had a very strong back. Why he kept it hidden behind that jacket was both a mystery and a crime. His tight stomach was even better. He had to work out, though I don't know where he found the time. I would have given anything to see him in a bathing suit—or less. His legs had to be just as muscular, being the expert rider he was reputed to be. And if it sounded like I was a sex-starved nympho . . . Well, I didn't have anything to do but watch him.

Trent had worked long after sunset yesterday, seemingly alone in the silent building. The only light had been from that fake window. It slowly paled as the sun went down, mirroring the natural light outside until he clicked on the desk lamp. I had caught myself drowsing several times, waking up when he turned a page or the printer hummed to life. He hadn't quit until Jonathan came by to remind him to eat. I guess he earned his money, same as I did. 'Course, he had two jobs, being a reputable businessman and drug lord both. Probably filled up one's day right nicely.

My hammock swayed as I watched Trent choose a disc. It spun up, and the soft cadence of drums drifted into existence. Eyeing me, Trent adjusted his gray linen suit and smoothed his wispy hair as if daring me to say anything. I gave him a sleepy thumbs-up, and his frown deepened. It wasn't the stuff I liked, but it was okay. This was older, carrying a forgotten sound of bound intensity, of lost sorrow chained to stir the soul. It wasn't half bad.

I could get used to this, I mused as I carefully stretched my healing body. I hadn't slept this well since I quit the I.S. It was ironic that here, in a cage in a drug lord's office, I was safe from my I.S. death threat.

Trent settled himself back at his work, his pen occasionally accompanying the drums as he paused in thought. Obviously this was one of his favorites. I slipped in and out of sleep as the afternoon wore on, soothed by the rumble of drums and whisper of music. The occasional phone call sent Trent's mellow voice to rise and fall in a soothing sound, and I found myself eagerly waiting for the next interruption just so I could hear it.

It was a commotion in the hall that jerked me from sleep. "I know where his office is," boomed an overly confident voice, reminding me of one of my more arrogant professors.

There was a half-heard scolding from Sara Jane, and Trent met my inquiring gaze.

"Turn it all to hell," he muttered, the corners of his expressive eyes crinkling. "I told him to send one of his assistants." He dug about in a drawer with unusual haste, the clatter bringing me fully awake. I blinked the sleep from me as he pointed a remote at the player. The pipes and drums ceased. He tossed the remote back into the drawer with a resigned air. If I didn't know better, I would have thought that Trent liked having someone to share his day with, someone he didn't have to pretend to be anything but what he was—*whatever* he was. His anger at Francis had set my creepy meter off the scale.

Sara Jane knocked and came in. "Mr. Faris is here to see you, Mr. Kalamack?"

Trent took a slow breath. He didn't look happy. "Send him in."

"Yes sir." She left the door open and her heels clicked away. They soon returned as she escorted in a heavyset man wearing a dark gray lab coat. The man looked huge standing beside the small woman. Sara Jane left, her eyes pinched in a lingering worry.

"Can't say I like your new secretary," Faris grumbled as the door closed. "Sara, is it?"

Trent rose to his feet and extended his hand, his distaste hidden behind his sincere-looking smile. "Faris. Thanks for coming on such short notice. It's only a small matter. One of your assistants would have been fine. I trust I haven't interrupted your research too badly?"

"Not at all. I'm always glad to get up into the sun," he puffed as if winded.

Faris squeezed the bites I had given Trent yesterday, and Trent's smile froze. The heavy man wedged himself into the chair across from Trent's desk as if he owned it. He propped an ankle up on one knee, sending his lab coat to fall open to show dress slacks and shiny shoes. A dark stain spotted his lapel, and the smell of disinfectant flowed from him, almost hiding the scent of redwood. Old pocketmarked scars were scattered across his cheeks and the skin visible on his beefy hands.

Trent returned to behind his desk and leaned back, hiding his bandaged hand under the other one. There was a moment of silence.

"So, what do you want?" Faris demanded, his voice rumbling.

I thought I saw a flash of annoyance cross Trent. "Direct as usual," he said. "Tell me what you can about this?"

He had pointed to me, and my breath caught. Disregarding my lingering stiffness, I lurched into my hut. Faris levered himself to his feet with a groan, and the sharp scent of redwood crashed over me as he came close. "Well well," he said. "Aren't you the stupid one."

Annoyed, I looked up at his dark eyes, almost lost among the folds of skin. Trent had come around to the front of his desk, sitting against it. "Recognize her?" he asked.

"Personally? No." He gave the bars of my cage a soft thunk with a thick finger.

"Hey!" I shouted from my hut. "I'm really getting tired of that."

"Shut up, you," he said disdainfully. "She's a witch," Faris continued, dismissing me as if I were nothing. "Just keep her out of your fish tank, and she won't be able to change back. It's a powerful spell. She must have the backing of a large organization, as only they could afford it. And she's stupid."

The last was directed at me, and I fought the urge to throw pellets at him.

"How so?" Trent went to rummage in his lower drawer, the chiming of lead crystal ringing out before he poured two shots of that forty-year-old whiskey.

"Transformation is a difficult art. You have to use potions rather than amulets, which means you stir an entire brew for only one occasion. The rest gets thrown away. Very expensive. You could pay your assistant librarian's salary for what this stirring cost, and staff a small office for the liability insurance to sell it."

"Difficult, you say?" Trent handed Faris a glass. "Could you make such a spell?"

"If I had the recipe," he said, puffing up his substantial chest, his pride clearly affronted. "It's old. Preindustry, perhaps? I don't recognize who stirred this spell." He leaned close, breathing deeply. "Lucky for him, or I might have to relieve the witch of his library."

This, I thought, *is becoming a very interesting conversation.*

"So you don't think she made it herself?" Trent asked. He was again sitting back against his desk, looking incredibly trim and fit next to Faris.

The heavyset man shook his head and sat back down. The shot glass was completely unseen, enfolded by his thick hands. "I'd stake my life on it. You can't be smart enough to competently stir a spell like that and be dumb enough to be caught. Doesn't make sense."

"Maybe she was impatient," Trent said, and Faris exploded into laughter. I jumped, covering my ears with my paws.

"Oh, yes," Faris said between guffaws. "Yes. She was impatient. I like that."

I thought Trent's usual polish was starting to look thin as he returned behind his desk and set his untasted drink aside.

"So who is she?" Faris asked, leaning forward like a mock conspirator. "An eager reporter trying for the story of her life?"

"Is there a spell that will allow me to understand her?" Trent asked, ignoring Faris's question. "All she does is squeak."

Faris grunted as he leaned to set his emptied glass on the desk in an unspoken request for more. "No. Rodents don't have vocal cords. You plan on keeping her for any length of time?"

Trent spun his glass in his fingers. He was alarmingly silent.

Faris smiled wickedly. "What's cooking in that nasty little head of yours, Trent?"

The creak of Trent's chair as he leaned forward seemed very loud. "Faris, if I didn't need your talents so badly, I would have you whipped in your own lab."

The large man grinned, sending the folds in his face to fall into each other. "I know."

Trent put the bottle away. "I may enter her in Friday's tournament."

Faris blinked. "The city's tournaments?" he said softly. "I've seen one of those. The bouts don't end until one is dead."

"So I've heard."

Fear pulled me to the wire mesh. "Whoa, wait a moment," I chittered. "What do you mean, dead? Hey! Someone talk to the mink!"

I threw a pellet at Trent. It went about two feet before arching down to the carpet. I tried again, this time kicking it rather than throwing it. It hit the back of his desk with a plink. "The Turn take you, Trent!" I shouted. "Talk to me."

Trent met my gaze, his eyebrows raised. "The rat fights, of course."

My heart gave a thump. Chilled, I sank back on my haunches. The rat fights. Illegal. Backroom. Rumors. To the death. I was going to be in the ring—fighting a rat to the death.

I stood in confusion, my long, white-furred feet planted on the wire mesh of my cage. I felt betrayed, of all things. Faris looked ill. "You're not serious," he whispered, his fat cheeks turning white. "You're really going to play her? You can't!"

"Why ever not?"

Faris's jowls dropped as he struggled for words. "She's a person!" he exclaimed. "She won't last three minutes. They'll rip her to shreds."

Trent shrugged with an indifference I knew wasn't faked. "Surviving is her problem, not mine." He put on his wire glasses and bent his head over his papers. "Good afternoon, Faris."

"Kalamack, this is too far. Even you aren't above the law."

As soon as he said it, both Faris and I knew it was a mistake. Trent pulled his gaze up. Silent, he eyed Faris from over his lenses. He leaned forward, an elbow on his accumulated work. I waited breathlessly, the tension making my fur rise. "How is your youngest daughter, Faris?" Trent asked, his beautiful voice unable to hide the ugliness of his question.

The large man went ashen. "She's fine," he whispered. His rough confidence had vanished, leaving only a frightened, fat man.

"What is she? Fifteen?" Trent eased back in his chair, set his glasses beside his in/out-box, and laced his long fingers over his middle. "Wonderful age. She wants to be an oceanographer, yes? Talk to the dolphins?"

"Yes." It was hardly audible.

"I can't tell you how pleased I am that the treatment for her bone cancer worked."

I looked at the back of Trent's drawer where the incriminating discs lay. My gaze lifted to Faris, taking in his lab coat with a new understanding. Cold struck through me, and I stared at Trent. He wasn't just running biodrugs, he was making them. I wasn't sure if it horrified me more that Trent was actively flirting with the same technology that wiped out half the world's population, or that he was blackmailing people with it, threatening their loved ones. He was so pleasant, so charming, so damned likable with his confident personality. How could something so foul lie next to something so attractive?

Trent smiled. "She's been in remission for five years now. Good physicians willing to explore illegal techniques are hard to find. And expensive."

Faris swallowed. "Yes—sir."

Trent eyed him with a questioning arch to his eyebrows. "Good afternoon—Faris."

"Slime," I hissed, ignored. "You are a slime, Trent! Scrapings from under my boot."

Faris moved shakily to the door. I tensed when I smelled a sudden defiance. Trent had backed him into a corner. The large man had nothing to lose.

Trent must have sensed it, too. "You're going to run now, aren't you," he said as Faris opened the door. The sound of office chatter filtered in. "You know I can't let you."

Faris turned with a hopeless look. Astonished, I watched Trent unscrew his pen and stick a small tuft in the empty barrel. With a short puff of air, he shot it at Faris.

The large man's eyes widened. He took a step toward Trent, then put his hand to his throat. A soft rasp came from him. His face began to swell. I watched, too shocked to be afraid, as Faris dropped to his knees. The heavy man grasped at a shirt pocket. His fingers fumbled, and a syringe fell to the floor. Faris reached for it, collapsing, stretching for the syringe.

Trent rose. His face blank, he nudged the syringe out of Faris's grasp with a foot.

"What did you do to him?" I squeaked, watching as Trent put his pen back together. Faris was turning purple. A ragged gasp came from him, then nothing.

Trent slipped his pen in a pocket and stepped over Faris to reach the open door. "Sara Jane!" he called out. "Call the paramedics. Something's wrong with Mr. Faris."

"He's dying!" I squeaked. "That's what's wrong with him! You freaking killed him!"

The sound of worried chatter rose as everyone came out of his or her office. I recognized Jonathan's fast footsteps. He lurched to a stop in the threshold, grimacing at Faris's bulk on the floor, then frowning at Trent in disapproval.

Trent was crouched beside Faris, feeling for a pulse. He shrugged at Jonathan and injected the syringe's contents into Faris's thigh through his slacks. I could tell it was too late. Faris wasn't making noises anymore. Faris was dead. Trent knew it.

"The paramedics are coming," Sara Jane said from the hall, her footsteps coming closer. "Can I get—" She stopped behind Jonathan and put a hand to her mouth, staring down at Faris.

Trent stood, the syringe slipping from him to fall dramatically to the floor. "Oh, Sara Jane," he said softly as he drew her back into the hallway. "I'm so sorry. Don't look. It's too late. I think it was a bee sting. Faris is allergic to bees. I tried to give him his antitoxin, but it didn't act soon enough. He must have brought a bee in with him unaware. He slapped his leg just before he collapsed."

"But he . . ." she stammered, glancing back once as Trent moved her away.

Jonathan crouched to pluck a tuft of fuzz from Faris's right leg. The fluff went into a pocket. The tall man met my eyes, a wry, sarcastic look on his face.

"I'm so sorry," Trent said from the hall. "Jon?" he called, and Jonathan rose. "Please see that everyone leaves early. Clear the building."

"Yes sir."

"This is terrible, just awful," Trent said, seeming to really mean it. "Go on home, Sara Jane. Try not to think about it."

I heard her choke back a sob as her hesitant footsteps retreated.

It had only been moments since Faris had been standing. Shocked, I watched Trent step over Faris's arm. Cool as broccoli, he went to his desk and pushed the intercom. "Quen? I'm sorry to disturb you, but will you please come up to my front office? There is a paramedic team on their way into the grounds, and after that, probably someone from the I.S."

There was a slight hesitation, and Quen's voice crackled from the speaker. "Mr. Kalamack? Yes. I'll be right there."

I stared at Faris, swollen and prostrate on the floor. "You killed him," I accused. "God help me. You killed him. Right in your office. In front of everyone!"

"Jon," Trent said softly, rummaging in apparent unconcern in a drawer. "See that his family gets the upgraded benefits package. I want his youngest daughter to be able to go to the school of her choice. Keep it anonymous. Make it a scholarship."

"Yes, Sa'han." His voice was casual, as if dead bodies were an everyday occurrence.

"That's real generous of you, Trent," I chittered. "She'd rather have her father, though."

Trent looked at me. There was a bead of sweat at his hairline. "I want to meet with Faris's assistant before the day is out," he said lightly. "What was his name . . . Darby?"

"Darby Donnelley, Sa'han."

Trent nodded, rubbing his forehead as if bothered. When his hand dropped, the sweat was gone. "Yes. That's it. Donnelley. I don't want this to put me behind schedule."

"What do you want me to tell him?"

"The truth. Faris is allergic to bee stings. His entire staff knows it."

Jonathan nudged Faris with a toe and left. His steps were loud now that there was no background noise. The floor had emptied shockingly fast. I wondered how often this happened.

"Like to reconsider my previous offer?" Trent said, addressing me. He had his untasted shot of whiskey in his fingers. I wasn't sure, but I thought they were trembling. He considered the drink for a moment, then tossed it back with a smooth motion. The glass was set gently down. "The island is out," he said. "Having you closer would be prudent. The way you infiltrated my compound was impressive. I think I could persuade Quen to take you on. He laughed himself breathless watching you duct-tape Mr. Percy in his trunk, then almost murdered you after I told him you had broken into my front office."

Shock blanked my mind. I couldn't say anything. Faris was *dead on the floor,* and Trent was asking me to work for him?

"But Faris was quite struck with your stirring," he continued. "Deciphering pre-Turn gene-splicing techniques can't be much harder than stirring a complex spell. If you don't want to explore your limits in the physical arena, you could go toward the mental. Such a mix of skills you have, Ms. Morgan. It makes you curiously valuable."

I sank back on my haunches, dumbfounded.

"You see, Ms. Morgan," he was saying. "I'm not a bad man. I offer all my employees a fair situation, a chance for advancement, the opportunity to reach their full potential."

"Opportunity? Chance for advancement?" I sputtered, not caring that he couldn't understand me. "Who do you think you are, Kalamack? God? You can go Turn yourself."

"I think I got the gist of that." He gave me a quick smile. "If nothing else, I've taught you to be honest." He shifted his chair closer to his desk. "I'm going to break you, Morgan, until you will do anything to get out of that cage. I do hope it takes a while. Jon took nearly fifteen years. Not as a rat, but a slave all the same. I imagine you will break a lot faster."

"Damn you, Trent," I said, seething.

"Don't be crass." Trent picked up his pen. "I'm sure your moral fiber is as strong as if not stronger than Jon's. But he didn't have rats trying to rip him apart. I had the luxury of time with Jon. I went slowly, and I wasn't as good then." Trent's eyes went distant in thought. "Even so, he never knew I was breaking him. Most don't. He still doesn't. And if you suggested it, he would kill you."

Trent's distant gaze cleared. "I quite like having all the cards faceup on the table. It adds to the satisfaction, don't you think? Not having to be delicate about it. Both of us knowing what's going on. And if you don't survive, it's no great loss. I haven't invested that much in you. A wire cage? Food chips? Wood shavings?"

The feeling of being in a cage crashed over me. Trapped. "Let me out!" I shouted, pulling at the mesh of my cell. "Let me out, Trent!"

There was a knock on the doorframe and I spun. Jonathan entered, sidestepping Faris. "The medical team is parking their van. They can get rid of Faris. The I.S. wants a statement, nothing more." His eyes flicked disparagingly at me. "What's wrong with your witch?"

"Let me out, Trent," I chittered, growing frantic. "Let me out!" I ran to the bottom of my cage. Heart pounding, I ran back up to the second floor. I threw myself against the bars, trying to knock the cage over. I had to get out!

Trent smiled, his expression calm and collected. "Ms. Morgan just realized how persuasive I can be. Hit her cage."

Jonathan hesitated in confusion. "I thought you didn't want me to torment her."

"Actually, I said not to react in anger when you misjudge how a person will respond. I'm not acting out of anger. I'm teaching Ms. Morgan her new place in life. She's in a cage; I can do anything I want to her." His cold eyes were fixed to mine. "Hit—her—cage."

Jonathan grinned. Taking the folder he had in his hand, he swung it against the wire mesh. I cowered at the loud smack even though I knew it was coming. The cage shook, and I gripped the mesh floor with all four of my paws.

"Shut up, witch," Jonathan added, a pleased gloating in his eye. I slunk to hide in my hut. Trent had just given him permission to torment me all he wanted. If the rats didn't kill me, Jonathan would.

Twenty-one

"**C**ome on, Morgan. Do something," Jonathan breathed. The stick poked me, almost shoving me over. I trembled as I tried not to react.

"I know you're mad," he said, shifting his crouch to jam the dowel into my flank.

The floor of my cage was littered with pencils—all chewed in half. Jonathan had been tormenting me on and off all morning. After several hours of hissing and lunging at him, I realized not only was my frenzy exhausting, but it also made the sadistic freak all the more enthusiastic. Ignoring him was nowhere near as satisfying as yanking pencils out of his grip and gnawing them in half, but I was hoping he would eventually tire and go away.

Trent had left for his lunch/nap about thirty minutes ago. The building was quiet, as everyone slacked off when Trent left the floor. Jonathan, though, showed no sign of leaving. He had been content to stay and harass me between forkfuls of pasta. Even moving to the center of my cage hadn't helped. He had simply gotten a longer stick. My hut was long gone.

"Damn witch. Do something." Jonathan shifted his stick to tap me on the head. It hit me once, twice, three times, right between my ears. My whiskers quivered. I could feel my pulse begin to pound and my head ache with the struggle to do nothing. On the fifth tap I broke, rearing back and snapping the stick in two with a frustrated bite.

"You're dead!" I squeaked, throwing myself at the wire mesh. "Hear me? When I get out of here, you're dead!"

He straightened, his fingers running through his hair. "I knew I could get you to move."

"Try that when I'm out of here," I whispered, quivering with rage.

The sound of high heels in the hallway grew loud, and I crouched in relief. I recognized the cadence. Apparently so did Jonathan, as he straightened and took a step back. Sara Jane strode into the office without her usual knock. "Oh!" she exclaimed softly, her hand going to the collar of the new business suit she had bought yesterday. Trent paid his employees in advance. "Jon. I'm sorry. I didn't think anyone would still be here." There was an awkward silence. "I was going to give Angel the leftovers from my lunch before I ran my errands."

Jonathan looked down his nose at her. "I'll do it for you."

Oh please, no, I thought. He'd probably dip them in ink first, if he did at all. The leftovers from Sara Jane's lunches were the only thing I'd eat, and I was half starved.

"Thank you, but no," she said, and I sank to a relieved crouch. "I'll lock up Mr. Kalamack's office if you want to go."

Yes, leave, I thought, my pulse racing. *Go so I can try to tell Sara Jane I'm a person.* I'd been trying all day, but the one time I attempted it when Trent had been watching, Jonathan "accidentally" knocked my cage so hard it fell over.

"I'm waiting for Mr. Kalamack," Jonathan said. "Are you sure you don't want me to give them to her?" A smug look crossed his usually stoic face as he moved behind Trent's desk and pretended to tidy it. My hope that he would leave vanished. He knew better.

Sara Jane crouched to bring her eyes level with mine. I thought they were blue, but I couldn't be sure. "No. It won't take long. Is Mr. Kalamack working through lunch?" she asked.

"No. He just asked me to wait."

I crept forward at the smell of carrots. "Here, Angel," the small woman said, her high voice soothing as she opened a fold of napkin. "It's just carrots today. They were out of celery."

I glanced at Jonathan suspiciously. He was checking the sharpness of the pencils in Trent's pencil cup, so I cautiously reached for the carrot. There was a sharp bang, and I jumped.

A smirk quirked the corners of Jonathan's thin lips. He had dropped a file on the desk. Sara Jane's look was wrathful enough to curdle milk. "Just stop it," she said indignantly. "You've been pestering her all day." Lips pursed, she pushed the carrots through the mesh. "Here you go, sweetie," she soothed. "Take your carrots. Don't you like your pellets?" She dropped the carrots and left her fingers poking through the mesh.

I sniffed them, allowing her cracked and work-worn nails to brush the top of my head. I trusted Sara Jane, and my trust didn't come easily. I think it was because we were both trapped, and we both realized it. That she knew about Trent's biodrug dealings seemed unlikely, but she was too smart to not be worried about how her predecessor died. Trent was going to use her as he had Yolin Bates, leaving her dead in an alley somewhere.

My chest tightened as if I was going to cry. A faint scent of redwood came from her, almost overwhelmed by her perfume. Miserable, I pulled the carrots farther in and downed them as fast as I could. They smelled sharply of vinegar, and I wondered at Sara Jane's choice of salad dressing. She had only given me three. I could've eaten twice that.

"I thought you farmers hated chicken killers," Jonathan said, pretending indifference as he watched me for any unminklike behavior.

Sara Jane's cheeks colored, and she rose quickly from her crouch. Before she could say anything, she reached out an unsteady hand and braced herself against my cage. "Oooh," she said, her eyes going distant. "I got up too fast."

"Are you all right?" he asked, his flat tone sounding as if he didn't care.

She put a hand to her eyes. "Yes. Yes, I'm fine."

I paused my chewing, hearing soft pacing in the hall, and Trent walked in. He had taken his coat off, and it was only his clothes that made him look like a Fortune-twenty executive rather than a head lifeguard. "Sara Jane, aren't you on lunch?" he asked amiably.

"Just leaving now, Mr. Kalamack," she said. She glanced worriedly between Jonathan and me before she left. Her heels thumped dimly in the hallway and vanished. I felt a wash of relief. If Trent was here, Jonathan would probably leave me alone and I could eat.

The haughty man folded himself carefully into one of the chairs opposite Trent's desk. "How long?" he said, putting an ankle on his knee and glancing at me.

"Depends." Trent fed his fish something from a freezer-dried pouch. The Yellow Tang bumped against the surface, making soft sounds.

"It must be strong," Jonathan said. "I didn't think it would affect her at all."

I paused in my chewing. *Her? Sara Jane?*

"I thought it might," Trent said. "She'll be fine." He turned, his face creased in thought. "In the future, I may have to be more direct in my dealings with her. All the information she brought up concerning the sugar beet industry was slanted toward a bad business venture."

Jonathan cleared his throat, making it sound patronizing. Trent closed the pouch and tucked it away in the cabinet under the tank. He went to stand behind his desk, his fair head bowed as he arranged his papers.

"Why not a spell, Sa'han?" Jonathan unfolded his long legs and stood, tugging out the creases in his dress pants. "I would imagine it would be more certain."

"It's against the rules to spell animals in competition." He scribbled a note in his planner.

A dry smile crossed Jonathan's face. "But drugs are all right? That makes perverted sense."

My chewing slowed. They were talking about me. The bitter taste of vinegar was stronger on this last carrot. And my tongue was tingling. Dropping the carrot, I touched my gums. They were numb. *Damn. It was Friday.*

"You bastard!" I shouted, throwing the carrot at Trent, only to have it bounce back against the mesh. "You drugged me. You drugged Sara Jane to get me!" Furious, I flung myself at the door, wedging my arm out, trying to reach the latch. Nausea and dizziness rose.

The two men came close, peering down at me, Trent's expression of domination sending a chill through me. Terrified, I raced up the ramp to the second level, then downstairs. The light hurt my eyes. My mouth was numb. I staggered, losing my balance. *He'd drugged me!*

A realization clawed through my panic. The door was going to open. This might be my only chance. I froze in the center of my cage, panting. Slowly, I tipped over. *Please,* I thought desperately. *Please open the door before I really do pass out.* My lungs heaved and my heart raced. Whether it was from my efforts or the drugs, I couldn't tell.

The two men were silent. Jonathan poked me with a pencil. I allowed my leg to quiver as if I was unable to move it. "I think she's down," he said. Excitement tinged his voice.

"Give it some time." The light hit my eyes as Trent moved away, and I slit them.

Jonathan, though, was blessedly impatient. "I'll get the carrying case."

The cage trembled as he unlatched the door. My pulse raced as Jonathan's long fingers closed about my body. I wiggled to life, my teeth bearing down on his finger.

"You little canicula!" Jonathan swore, yanking his hand out and pulling me with him. I loosened my hold, hitting the floor with a bone-shaking thump. Nothing hurt. Everything was numb. I leapt for the door, sprawling as my legs wouldn't work.

"Jon!" Trent exclaimed. "Get the door!"

The floor trembled, quickly followed by the slamming of the door. I hesitated, unable to think. I had to run. Where the hell was the door?

The shadow of Jonathan came close. I bared my teeth, and he hesitated, cowed by my tiny incisors. The sharp stink of fear was on him. He was afraid, the bully. Darting forward, he grasped the scruff of my neck. I twisted, sinking my teeth in the fatty part of his thumb.

He grunted in pain and let go. I hit the floor. "Damn witch!" he shouted. I staggered, unable to run. Jonathan's blood was thick on my tongue, tasting of cinnamon and wine.

"Touch me again," I panted, "and I'll take off your entire thumb."

Jonathan drew back, afraid. It was Trent who scooped me up. Deep under the drug, I could do nothing. His fingers were blessedly cold as he cradled me in his hands. He set me gently into the carrier and latched the door. It clicked shut, shaking the entire cage.

My mouth was fuzzy and my stomach was twisting. The carrier was lifted, swinging in a smooth arc until it landed on the desk. "We have a few minutes until we have to leave. Let's see if Sara Jane has any antibiotic cream in her desk for those bites of yours."

Trent's mellow voice grew as fuzzy as my thoughts. The darkness became overwhelming, and I lost my grip on consciousness, cursing myself for my stupidity.

Twenty-two

Someone was talking. I understood that. Actually, there were two voices, and now that I was regaining the ability to think, I realized they'd been alternating with each other for some time. One was Trent, and his wonderfully liquid voice lured me back to consciousness. Beyond him was the high-pitched squeaking of rats.

"Aw, hell," I whispered, having it come out as a thin moan of a squeak. My eyes were open, and I forced them closed. They felt as dry as sandpaper. A few more painful blinks and the tears started to flow again. Slowly the gray wall of my carrier swam into focus.

"Mr. Kalamack!" called a welcoming voice, and the world spun as the carrier turned. "The upstairs told me you were here. I'm so pleased." The voice got closer. "And with an entry! Wait and see, wait and see," the man nearly gushed as he pumped Trent's offered hand up and down. "Having an entry makes the games vastly more entertaining."

"Good evening, Jim," Trent said warmly. "Sorry for just dropping in on you."

The mellow cadence of Trent's voice was a balm, soothing my headache away. I both loved and hated it. How could something so beautiful belong to someone so foul?

"You're always welcome here, Mr. Kalamack." The man smelled like wood chips, and I scrunched back, bracing myself in the corner. "Have you checked in, then? Do you have your placing for the first round?"

"There will be more than one fight?" Jonathan interrupted.

"Indeed sir," Jim said brightly as he gently turned the grate of the carrier to face him. "You play your rat until it's dead or you pull it. Oh!" he said as he saw me. "A mink. How very—continental of you. This will change your odds, but no worry. We've fought badgers and snakes before. We thrive on individuality, and everyone loves it when an entrant is eaten."

My pulse quickened. I had to get out of there.

"Are you sure your animal will fight?" Jim asked. "The rats here have been bred for aggression, though we have a street rat making a surprising showing the last three months."

"I had to sedate her to get her in the carrier," Trent said, his voice tight.

"Oooh, a feisty one. Here," Jim offered solicitously as he snagged a notebook from a passing official. "Let me change your first round to one of the later matches so she has a chance to fully shake her sedation. No one wants those slots anyway. There's not much time for your animal to recover before the next bout."

I inched to the front of the carrier in helplessness. Jim was a nice-looking man with round cheeks and an ample belly. It would only take a small charm to make him into the mall Santa Claus. What was he doing in Cincinnati's underground?

The jovial man's gaze went over Trent's unseen shoulder and he gave someone a merry wave. "Please keep your animal with you at all times," he said, his eyes on the new arrival. "You have five minutes to place your entrant in the pit after you're called or you forfeit."

Pit, I thought. *Swell.*

"All I need to know now," Jim said, "is what you call your animal."

"Angel." Trent said it with a mocking sincerity, but Jim wrote it down without a moment of hesitation.

"Angel," he repeated. "Owned and trained by Trent Kalamack."

"You don't own me!" I squeaked, and Jonathan thunked my carrier.

"Back upstairs, Jon," Trent said as Jim shook his hand and left. "The noise of these rats is going right through my head."

I dropped to all fours to steady myself as the carrier swung. "I'm not going to fight, Trent," I squeaked loudly. "You can just forget it."

"Oh, do be still, Ms. Morgan," Trent said softly as we rose. "It's not as if you haven't been trained for this. Every runner knows how to kill. Working for me, working for them . . . There's no difference. It's only a rat."

"I've never killed anyone in my life!" I shouted, rattling the gate. "And I'm not going to start for you." But I didn't think I had a choice. I couldn't reason with a rat, tell it there'd been a big mistake and why couldn't we all just get along?

The noise of the rats dulled under loud conversations as we found the top of the stairs. Trent paused, taking it in. "Look there," he murmured. "There's Randolph."

"Randolph Mirick? Jonathan said. "Haven't you been trying to arrange a meeting with him about increasing your water rights?"

"Yes." Trent almost seemed to breathe the word. "For the last seven weeks. He's apparently a very busy man. And look there. That woman holding that vile little dog? She's the CEO of the glass factory we're contracted with. I'd very much like to speak with her about the possibility of getting a volume discount. I had no idea this would be an opportunity to network."

We drifted into motion, moving through the crowd. Trent kept his conversation light and friendly, showing me off as if I was a prize mule. I huddled in the back of my cage and tried to ignore the sounds the women made at me. My mouth felt like the inside of a hair dryer, and I could smell old blood and urine. And rats.

I could hear them, too, squeaking in voices higher than most people's hearing. The battles were beginning already, though anyone on two legs couldn't know it. Bars and plastic might separate the participants, but threats of violence were already being promised.

Trent found a seat next to the freaking mayor of the city, and after tucking me between his feet, he talked to the woman in a sideways fashion about the overall benefits of rezoning his property as industry rather than commercial, seeing as a good portion of his land was used for industrial gain in some way or other. She wasn't listening until Trent commented he might have to move his more sensitive industries to more friendly pastures.

It was a nightmarish hour. The ultrasonic squeaks and shrieks cut through the lower sounds, going unheard by the crowd. Jonathan kept up a colorful commentary for my benefit, embellishing the monstrosities taking place in the pit. None of the rounds took long—ten minutes at best. The sudden hush followed by the watchers' wild explosions was barbaric. Soon I could smell the blood Jonathan seemed to enjoy expounding upon, and I was jumping at every shift of Trent's feet.

The audience politely applauded the official results of the latest bout. It was an obvious win. Thanks to Jonathan, I knew the victorious rat had ripped open the belly of its opponent before the loser had given up and died, its teeth still clamped upon the winning rat's foot.

"Angel!" Jim called, his voice deeper, carrying more showmanship over the loudspeaker. "Owned and trained by Kalamack."

My legs trembled at the rush of adrenaline. *I can best a rat,* I thought as the crowd cheered my adversary, the Bloody Baron, to the floor. I would not be killed by a rat.

My gut tightened as Trent slipped onto the empty bench beside the pit. The smell was a hundred times worse here. I knew even Trent could smell it as his smooth face wrinkled in distaste. Jonathan shifted eagerly from foot to foot behind him. For a prim and proper snob who pressed his collars and starched his socks, the man had a taste for blood sports. The squeaks of the rats were almost nonexistent now that half were dead and half were licking their wounds.

There was a moment or two of pleasantries between the owners, followed by a dramatic buildup of excitement orchestrated by Jim. I wasn't listening to his ringmaster patter, more concerned with my first view of the pit.

The circle was about the size of a kiddie wading pool with three-foot walls. The floor was sawdust. Dark splotches decorated it, the scatter pattern telling me it was probably blood. The scent of urine and fear rose so strong, I was surprised I couldn't see it as a haze in the air. Someone's warped humor had put animal toys in the arena.

"Gentlemen?" Jim said dramatically, yanking my attention back. "Place your entrants."

Trent pulled the grate close to his face. "I've changed my mind, Morgan," he murmured. "I don't want you as a runner. You're more valuable to me killing rats than you could ever be killing my competition. The contacts I can make here are astounding."

"Go Turn yourself," I snarled.

At my harsh squeak, he unlatched the grate and dumped me out.

I hit the sawdust softly. A quick shadow of movement at the far side of the pit heralded the arrival of the Bloody Baron. The crowd oohed over me, and I made a liquid hop to hide behind a ball. I was a hindsight more attractive than a rat.

Face down in it, the arena was awful: blood, urine, death. All I wanted was out. My eyes fell upon Trent, and he smiled knowingly. He thought he could break me; I hated him.

The audience cheered, and I turned to see old Bloody himself galloping toward me. He wasn't as long as I was, but was stockier. I guessed we weighed about the same. Squeaks came from him nonstop as he ran. I froze, not knowing what to do. At the last moment I jumped out of the way, kicking him as he went by. It was an attack I had used as a runner hundreds of times. It was instinctive, though as a mink it lacked effectiveness and grace. I finished the spin kick in a crouch, watching the rat skid to a halt.

Baron hesitated, nuzzling his side where I struck him. He had gone silent.

Again he rushed me, the crowd urging him on. This time I aimed with more precision, scoring on his long face as I jumped aside. I landed in a crouch, my forepaws automatically moving into a block as if I was fighting a person. The rat slid to a faster halt, squeaking and weaving his head as if trying to focus. A rat's eyesight must be minimal. I could use that.

Chittering like a mad thing, Baron rushed me a third time. I tensed, planning to jump straight up, land on his back, and choke him into unconsciousness. I was nauseous and sick at heart. I wouldn't kill for Trent. Not even a rat. If I sacrificed one principle, one ethic, he would have me body and soul. If I gave in on rats, tomorrow it would be people.

The noise of the crowd swelled as Baron ran. I jumped. "Crap!" I squeaked as he slid to a stop under me, twisting onto his back. I was going to fall right on top of him!

I hit with a soft thunk, squealing as his teeth latched onto my nose. Panicking, I tried to pull away. But he held on, exerting just enough pressure that I couldn't break free. Twisting off him, I pawed at his grip, pummeling his belly with my feet. Squeaking in time with my strikes, he took the abuse, slowly loosening his hold. He finally let go enough that I could wiggle away.

I backed up, rubbing my nose and wondering why he hadn't taken it clean off.

Baron flipped to his feet. He touched his side where I had first stuck him, then his face, and then his middle where my feet had hit him, cataloging the list of hurts I'd given him. His paw reached up to rub his nose, and with a start I realized he was mimicking me. Baron was a person!

"Holy crap!" I squeaked, and Baron bobbed his head once. My breath came fast and my gaze darted to the surrounding walls and the people pressed against them. Together we might get out where alone we couldn't. Baron made soft noises at me, and the crowd went quiet.

There was no way I was going to lose this chance. He twitched his whiskers and I lunged. We rolled about the floor in a harmless tussle. All I had to do was figure out how to get out of there and communicate it to Baron without Trent realizing it.

We knocked into an exercise wheel and broke apart. I found my feet and turned, looking for him. Nothing. "Baron!" I shouted. But he was gone! I spun, wondering if a descending hand had plucked him out. A rhythmic scratching came from a nearby tower of blocks. I fought the urge to turn. Relief flooded me. He was still here. And now I had an idea.

The only time the hands came down was when the game was over. One of us was going to have to pretend to die.

"Hey!" I shouted as Baron crashed down on me. Sharp teeth latched onto my ear, tearing it. Blood coursed into my eyes, half blinding me. Furious, I flung him over my shoulder. "What the hell is wrong with you?" I cried as he tumbled to a halt. The crowd cheered wildly, clearly dismissing our previous unrodent-like behavior.

Baron started in with a long series of squeaks, no doubt trying to explain his thinking. I lunged, latching on to his windpipe and shutting him up. His hind feet pummeled me as I cut off his air supply. Twisting, he reached my nose, gouging it with his nails. I eased my grip under the needles of his claws, allowing air to him.

He went limp in understanding. "You're not supposed to be dead yet," I said, my squeaks mangled from his fur in my mouth. I clamped down until he squealed and began to inefficiently struggle. The crowd surged into noise, presumably thinking Angel was going to score her first win. I glanced at Trent. My heart gave a thump at his suspicious look. This wasn't going to work. Baron might escape, but not me. I was going to have to die, not Baron.

"Fight me," I squeaked, knowing he wouldn't understand. I loosened my hold until my jaws were slipping. Not understanding, Baron went limp. I jabbed a hind foot into his crotch.

He yelped in pain, yanking from my loose grip. I rolled away. "Fight me. Kill me," I chittered. Baron's head wove as he tried to focus. I gave my head a toss toward the crowd. He blinked, seeming to get it, and attacked. His jaws clamped about my windpipe, cutting off my air. I flailed about, sending us crashing into the walls. I heard the shouts of the people over the sound of the blood pulsing in my head.

His grip was tight, too tight to breathe. *Any time now,* I thought desperately. *You can let me breathe any time.* I sent us thumping into a ball, and still he wouldn't let up. Fear stirred. He was a person, wasn't he? I hadn't just let a rat get a death grip on me, had I?

I started to struggle in earnest. His grip tightened. My head felt as if it was going to explode. My blood pounded. I twisted and squirmed, clawing at an eye until the tears ran, but still he wouldn't let up. Flipping wildly, I sent us crashing into the walls. I found his neck and clamped down. Immediately he loosened his grip. I took a grateful gulp of air.

Furious, I bit hard, tasting his blood on my teeth. He bit me back, and I squeaked in pain. I eased my grip. He did the same. The noise of the crowd pressed down, almost as strong as the heat from the lights. We lay on the floor in the sawdust, struggling to slow our breathing so as to look as though we were suffocating each other. I finally understood. His owner knew he was a person as well. We both had to die.

The crowd was shouting, wanting to know who won or if we were both dead. I looked through cracked eyelids to find Trent. He didn't look happy, and I knew our ruse was halfway to being successful. Baron lay very still. A tiny squeak slipped from him, and I carefully answered. A pulse of excitement raced through me and was gone.

"Ladies! Gentlemen!" Jim's professional voice layered over the noise. "It seems we have a draw. Will the owners please retrieve their animals?" The crowd hushed. "We will have a short break to determine if either contestant is alive."

My heart raced as the shadows of hands came closer. Baron made three short squeaks and exploded into motion. I belatedly followed, grasping the first hand I found.

"Look out!" someone shouted. I was flung into the air as a hand jerked away. I arched through the air, tail whipping in frantic circles. I glimpsed a surprised face and landed on a man's chest. He screamed like a girl and brushed me off. I hit the floor hard, stunned. I took three quick breaths, then lurched under his chair.

The noise was astounding. One would think a lion was loose, not two rodents. People scattered. The rush of feet past the chair was unreal. Someone smelling of wood chips reached down. I bared my teeth and he drew back.

"I've got the mink," an official shouted over the noise. "Get me a net." He glanced away, and I ran. Pulse so fast it was almost a hum, I dodged feet and chairs, nearly slamming head first into the far wall. The blood from my ear was dripping into my eye, blurring my vision. How was I going to get out of there?

"Everyone remain calm!" came Jim's voice over the loud-speaker. "Please return to the lobby for refreshments while a search is made. We ask that you keep the outer doors closed until we have regained the contestants." There was a pause. "And some-body get that dog out of here," he finished loudly.

Doors? I thought as I peered into the madhouse. I didn't need a door. I needed Jenks.

"Rachel!" came a call from above me. I squeaked as Jenks landed on my shoulders with a light thump. "You look like crap," he shouted into my torn ear. "I thought that rat nacked you. When you jumped up and grabbed Jonathan's hand, I nearly pissed my pants!"

"Where's the door?" I tried to ask. How he found me would have to wait.

"Don't have a hissy," he said defensively. "I left like you said. I just came back. When Trent left with that cat box, I knew you were in it. I hitched a ride under the bumper. Betcha didn't know that's how pixies get around the city, did you? You'd better get your furry ass moving before someone sees you."

"Where!" I squeaked. "Where do I go!"

"There's a back way out. I did a survey during the first fight. Man, those rats are vicious. Did you see that one bite the other's foot right off? If you follow this wall for about twenty feet, then down three stairs, you'll come to a hallway."

I started moving. Jenks gripped my fur tighter.

"Ugh. Your ear is a mess," he said as I flowed down the three stairs. "Okay. Go down the hallway to the right. There's an open-ing—No! Don't take it," he shouted as I did just that. "It's the kitchen."

I turned, freezing at the sound of feet on the stairs. My pulse raced. I wouldn't be caught. I wouldn't.

"The sink," Jenks whispered. "The cupboard door isn't closed. Hurry!"

Spotting it, I scurried across the tile floor, my claws scraping softly. I wedged myself inside. Jenks flitted to peek around the door. Backing away to hide behind a bucket, I listened.

"They aren't in the kitchen," a voice shouted, sounding muf-fled. I felt a knot of worry loosen. He had said "they." Baron was still free.

Jenks turned, his wings an unseen blur as he stood in the cupboard. "Damn, it's good to see you. Ivy's done nothing but stare at a map of Trent's compound she dug up," he whispered. "All night muttering and scribbling on paper. Every sheet ends up crumpled in the corner. My kids are having a blast playing hide-and-seek in the pile she's made. I don't think she knows I'm gone. She just sits at that map of hers, drinking orange juice."

I smelled dirt. As Jenks babbled like a Brimstone addict needing his fix, I explored the smelly cupboard to find that the pipe from the sink went under the house through a wood floor. The crack between the iron and the floor was just wide enough for my shoulder. I started chewing.

"I said, get that dog out of here," a muffled voice shouted. "No. Wait. You have a lead for him? He can find them."

Jenks came close. "Hey, the floor. That's a good idea! Let me help." Jenks alighted next to me, getting in my way.

"Get Baron," I tried to squeak.

"I can so help." Jenks pried a toothpick-sized stick of wood from around the hole.

"The rat," I chittered. "He can't see." Frustrated, I knocked over a canister of sink cleaner. The powder spilled out, and the smell of pine became overwhelming. Snatching Jenks's toothpick, I wrote out, "Get rat."

Jenks took to the air, a hand over his nose. "Why?"

"Man," I scrawled. "Can't see."

Jenks grinned. "You found a friend! Wait till I tell Ivy."

I bared my teeth, pointing at the door with my stick. Still he hesitated. "You'll stay here? Keep making that hole bigger?"

Frustrated, I threw the stick at him. Jenks hovered backward. "All right, all right! Don't lose your panties. No, wait. You don't have any, do you?"

His laughter chimed out, sounding like freedom itself, as he slipped past the crack in door. I went back to chewing the floor. It tasted awful, a putrid mix of soap, grease, and mold. I just knew I was going to get sick. Tension strung through me. The sudden thumps and crashes from up front jerked me. I was waiting for the triumphant cry of capture. Fortunately it seemed the dog didn't know what was expected of it. It wanted to play, and tempers were getting short.

My jaws ached, and I stifled a cry of frustration. Soap had gotten into the cut on my ear, and it was a flaming misery. I tried to stick my head through the hole and into the crawl space. If my head could make it, my body probably could, too. But it wasn't big enough yet.

"Look!" someone shouted. "He's working now. He's got their scent."

Frantic, I yanked my head out of the hole. My ear scraped and started bleeding again. There was a sudden scratching in the hallway, and I redoubled my efforts. Jenks's voice came faintly over the sounds of my gnawing. "It's the kitchen. Rachel is under the sink. No. The next cupboard. Hurry! I think they saw you."

There was a sudden rush of light and air, and I sat up, spitting pulpy wood from me.

"Hi! We're back! I found your rat, Rache."

Baron glanced at me. His eyes were bright. Immediately he bounded over. His head dipped into the hold and he started gnawing. There wasn't enough room for his wider shoulders. I continued to widen the hole at the top. The yapping of the dog came from the hall. We froze for a heartbeat, then chewed. My stomach clenched.

"Is it big enough?" Jenks shouted. "Go! Hurry!"

Pushing my head into the hole next to Baron's, I gnawed furiously. There was a scratching at the cupboard door. Shafts of light flickered as the door bumped against the frame. "Here!" a loud voice shouted. "He's got one in here."

Hope dying, I pulled my head up. My jaws ached. The pine soap had matted my fur and was burning my eyes. I turned to face the scrabbling of paws. I didn't think the opening was big enough yet. A sharp squeak drew my attention. Baron was crouched beside it, pointing down.

"It's not big enough for you," I said.

Baron lunged at me, yanking me to the hole and stuffing me down. The sound of the dog grew suddenly louder, and I dropped into space.

Arm and legs outstretched, I tried to snag the pipe. A front paw reached a welded seam. I jerked to a stop. Above me the dog barked wildly. There was a scrabble of claws on the wood floor, then a yelp. I started losing my hold. I dropped to the dry earth. I lay there, listening for Baron's death scream.

I should have stayed, I thought desperately. *I never should have let him shove me down that hole.* I knew it hadn't been big enough for him.

There was a quick scratching and a thump in the dirt beside me.

"You made it!" I squeaked, seeing Baron sprawled in the dirt.

Jenks flitted down, glowing in the dim light. There was a dog whisker in his hand. "You should have seen him, Rache," he said excitedly. "He bit that dog right on the nose. He-yah! Pow! Slam-bam, thank you, ma'am!"

The pixy continued his circles around us, too hyper to sit still. Baron, however, seemed to have the shakes. Curled into a huddled ball of fur, he looked like he was going to be sick. I crept forward, wanting to say thanks. I touched him on his shoulder, and he jumped, staring at me with wide black eyes.

"Get that dog out of here!" came an angry voice through the floor, and we looked up at the faint spot of light. The yapping grew faint, and my pulse eased. "Yup," Jim said. "Those are fresh chewings. One got out this way."

"How do we get down there?" It was Trent, and I cowered, pressing myself into the dirt.

"There's a trapdoor in the hallway, but the crawl space is open to the street through any of the vents." Their voices grew distant as they moved away. "I'm sorry, Mr. Kalamack," Jim was saying. "We've never had an escapee before. I'll get someone to go down there right away."

"No. She's gone." His voice held a controlled, soft frustration, and I felt a stir of victory. Jonathan wasn't going to have a very pleasant drive back. I straightened from my crouch and heaved a sigh. My ear and eyes were burning. I wanted to go home.

Baron squeaked for my attention, pointing to the ground. I looked to find he had written in careful letters, "Thanks."

I couldn't help my smile. Crouched beside him, I wrote, "You're welcome." My letters looked sloppy next to his.

"You two are *so sweet,*" Jenks mocked. "Can we get out of here now?"

Baron leapt to the screen across the vent, latching on with all four feet. Choosing carefully, he began to pull at the seams with his teeth.

Twenty-three

My spoon scraped the bottom of the cottage cheese container. Hunching over it, I pushed what remained into a pile. My knee was cold, and I tugged my midnight-blue, terry-cloth robe back over it. I was stuffing my face while Baron changed back into a person and showered in the second bathroom Ivy and I had independently determined was mine. I could hardly wait to see what he really looked like. Ivy and I agreed that if he had survived the rat fights for who knew how long, he had to be a hunk. God knew he was brave, chivalrous, and not fazed by vampires—the last one being the most intriguing, seeing as Jenks had said he was human.

Jenks had called Ivy collect from the first phone we found. The sound of her motorcycle—just out of the shop from her having slid it under a truck last week—had been like a choir singing. I almost cried at her concern when she swung from the seat wearing head-to-toe biker leather. Someone cared if I lived or died. It didn't matter if it was a vampire whose motives I still didn't understand.

Neither Baron or I would get into the box she had brought, and after a five-minute discussion consisting of her protests and our squeaks, she finally threw the box into the back of the alley with a grunt of frustration and let us ride up front. She hadn't been in the best of moods when she tooled on out of the alley, a mink and a rat standing on her gas tank with our forepaws on the tiny dash. By the time we cleared the worst of Friday rush-hour traffic and were able to pick up speed, I knew why dogs hung their heads out the window.

Riding a bike was always a thrill, but as a rodent, it was a scent-ual rush. Eyes squinting and my whiskers bent back by the wind, I rode home in style. I didn't care that Ivy was getting odd looks and people kept blowing their horns at us. I was sure I was going to have a brain orgasm from the overload of input. I almost regretted it when Ivy had turned onto our street.

Now, with a finger, I pushed the last bit of cheese onto the spoon, ignoring Jenks's pig noises from the ladle hanging over the center island. I hadn't stopped eating since losing my fur, but as I'd had only carrots for the last three and a half days, I was entitled to a little binge.

Setting the empty container aside on the dirty plate before me, I wondered if it hurt more or less to transform if you were a human. From the muffled, masculine groan of pain that had emanated from the bathroom before the shower started, I'd say it hurt just about the same.

Though I had scrubbed myself twice, I thought I still smelled mink under my perfume. My torn ear throbbed, my neck had red-rimmed punctures where Baron had bitten me, and my left leg was bruised from falling into the exercise wheel. But it was good to be a person again. I glanced at Ivy doing the dishes, wondering if I should have taped up my ear.

I still hadn't brought Ivy and Jenks entirely up to speed on my last few days, telling them only about my captivity, not what I had learned during it. Ivy had said nothing, but I knew she was dying to tell me I had been an idiot for not having a backup plan for escape.

She reached for the tap, turning it off after she rinsed the last glass. Setting it to drain, she turned and dried her hands on the dish towel. Seeing a tall, thin, leather-clad vamp doing dishes was almost worth the price of admission to my crazy life. "Okay, let me get this straight," she said as she leaned against the counter. "Trent caught you red-handed, and instead of turning you in, he put you in the city's rat fights to try and break you so you'd agree to work for him?"

"Yup." I stretched to reach the bag of frosted cookies next to Ivy's computer.

"Figures." She pushed herself into motion to get my empty plate. Washing it, she set it next to the glasses to drip. Apart from my dishes, there had been no plates, silverware, or bowls. Just twenty or so glasses, all with a drop of orange juice in the bottom.

"Next time you go up against someone like Trent, can we at least have a plan for when you get caught?" she asked, her back to me and her shoulders tense.

Annoyance pulled my head up from my bag of cookies. I took a breath to tell her she could take her plans and use them for toilet paper, then hesitated. Her shoulders were as tight as her stance was rigid. I remembered how worried Jenks said she was, and what she had said about how me flying off the handle jerked her instincts into play. Slowly my breath slipped out. "Sure," I said hesitantly. "We can have a fail-safe plan for when I screw up, as long as we have one for you, too."

Jenks snickered and Ivy flicked a glance at him. "We don't need one for me," she said.

"Write it out and post it by the phone," I said casually. "I'll do the same." I was halfway kidding, but I wondered if in all her anal-retentive glory she just might do it.

Saying nothing, Ivy, not content to let the glasses and plates drain by themselves, began to dry them. I crunched my ginger-snaps, watching her shoulders ease and her motions lose their hair-trigger quickness. "You were right," I said, thinking I owed her at least that much. "I've never had anyone I could count on be-fore. . . ." I hesitated. "I'm not used to it."

Ivy turned, surprising me with the relief in her stance. "Hey, don't sweat it."

"Oh, save me," Jenks said from the utensils rack. "I think I'm going to puke."

Ivy snapped her towel at him, her lips quirked in a wry smile I watched her closely as she went back to drying. Keeping calm and compromising made all the difference. Now that I thought about it, compromising had been how we got through our year working together. It was harder, though, to keep my cool when I was sur-rounded by all her stuff and none of mine. I had felt vulnerable and on edge.

"You should have seen her, Rachel," Jenks said in a loud, con-spiratorial whisper. "Sitting day and night at her maps to find a way to get you free from Trent. I told her all we had to do was keep watch and help if we could."

"Shut up, Jenks." Ivy's voice was suddenly thick with warn-ing. I shoved the last cookie in my mouth and rose to throw the bag away.

"She had this grandiose plan," Jenks said. "She swept it up from the floor when you were showering. She was going to call in all her favors. She even talked to her mother."

"I'm going to get a cat," Ivy said tightly. "A big, black cat."

I pulled the bag of bread from the counter and dug the honey out from the back of the pantry, where I had hidden it from Jenks. Taking it all to the table, I sat and arranged everything.

"Good thing you escaped when you did," Jenks said, swinging the ladle to send gleams of light about the kitchen. "Ivy was about to throw what little she has left after you—again."

"I will call my cat Pixy Dust," Ivy said. "I will keep it in the garden and not feed it."

My gaze shifted from Jenks's suddenly closed mouth to Ivy. We had just had a warm and fuzzy discussion without getting bit, vampy, or scared. Why did Jenks have to ruin it? "Jenks," I said with a sigh. "Don't you have something to do?"

"No." He dropped down, extending a hand into the stream of honey I was drizzling on a piece of bread. He sank an inch from the weight, then rose. "So, you gonna keep him?"

I looked blankly at Jenks, and he laughed.

"Your new bo-o-o-oyfriend," he drawled.

My lips pursed at the amusement in Ivy's eyes. "He's not my boyfriend."

Jenks hovered over the open jar of honey, pulling glistening strands up and into his mouth. "I saw you with him on that bike," he said. "Um, this is good." He took another handful, his wings starting to hum audibly. "Your tails were touching," he mocked.

Annoyed, I flicked my hand at him. He darted out of reach, then back. "You should have seen them, Ivy. Rolling around on the floor, biting each other." He laughed, and it turned into a high-pitched giggle. I slowly tilted my head as he listed to the left. "It was love at first bite."

Ivy turned. "He bit you on the neck?" she said, deadpan serious but for her eyes. "Oh, then it's got to be love. She won't let *me* bite her neck."

What was this? Pick on Rachel night? Not entirely comfortable, I pulled another piece of bread out to finish my sandwich and waved Jenks off the honey. He bobbed and weaved erratically, struggling to maintain an even flight as the sugar rush made him drunk.

"Hey, Ivy," Jenks said as he drifted sideways and licked his fingers. "You know what they say about the size of a rat's tail, don't you? Da longer da tail, da longer his—"

"Shut up!" I cried. The shower went off, and my breath caught. A surge of anticipation brought me up straight in my chair.

I flicked a glance at Jenks, giggling-drunk on the honey. "Jenks," I said, not wanting to subject Baron to an intoxicated pixy. "Leave."

"Nuh-uh," he said, scooping up a handful. Peeved, I recapped the jar. Jenks made a small noise of distress, and I waved him up into the hanging utensils. With any luck, he would stay there until he threw off his drunk. That would be about four minutes, tops.

Ivy walked out, muttering about glasses in the living room. The collar of my robe was damp from my hair, and I tugged at it. I wiped the honey from my fingers, fidgeting in what felt like blind date jitters. This was stupid. I'd already met him. We had even had a rodent's version of a first date: a resounding stint at the gym, a brisk run from people and dogs, even a bike ride through the park. But what do you say to a guy you don't know who saved your life?

I heard the bathroom door creak open. Ivy jerked to a stop in the hall, her face blank as she stood with two mugs dangling from her fingers. I pulled my robe over my shins, wondering if I should stand up. Baron's voice eased past her and into the kitchen. "You're Ivy, right?"

"Um . . ." Ivy hesitated. "You're—uh—in my robe," she finished, and I winced. Great. He had her smell all over him. Nice start.

"Oh. Sorry." His voice was nice. Kind of resonate and rumbly. I could hardly wait to see him. Ivy seemed positively at a loss for words. Baron took a noisy breath. "I found it on the dryer. There wasn't anything else to wear. Maybe I should go put on a towel. . . ."

Ivy hesitated. "Um, no," she said, the unusual sound of amusement in her voice. "You're all right. You helped Rachel escape?"

"Yeah. Is she in the kitchen?" he questioned.

"Come on in." Her eyes were rolling as she preceded him into the room. "He's a geek," she mouthed, and my face froze. *A geek had saved my life?*

"Uh, hi," he said, standing awkwardly just inside the doorway.

"Hi," I said, too disconcerted to say more as I ran my gaze over him. Calling him a geek wasn't fair, but compared to what Ivy was used to dating, he might be.

Baron was as tall as Ivy, but his build was so sparse he seemed taller. The pale arms showing past Ivy's black robe had the occasional faint scar, presumably from prior rat fights. His cheeks were clean-shaven—I'd have to get a new razor; the one I'd borrowed from Ivy was probably ruined. The rims of his ears were notched. Two puncture marks on either side of his neck stood out red and sore looking. They matched mine, and I felt a flush of embarrassment.

Despite, or maybe because of, his narrow frame he looked nice, kind of bookish. His dark hair was long, and the way he kept brushing it from his eyes led me to think he usually kept it shorter. The robe made him look soft and comfortable, but the way the black silk stretched across his lean muscles kept my eyes roving. Ivy was being overly critical. He had too many muscles to be a geek.

"You have red hair," he said, shifting into motion. "I thought it would be brown."

"I thought you were—ah—shorter." I stood up as he approached, and after an awkward moment, he extended his hand across the corner of the table. Okay, so he wasn't Arnold Schwarzenegger. But he had saved my life. Maybe somewhere between a short, young Jeff Goldblum and untidy Buckaroo Banzai.

"My name is Nick," he said as he took my hand. "Well, it's Nicholas, actually. Thanks for he!ping me get out of that rat pit."

"I'm Rachel." He had a nice grip. Just the right amount of firmness without trying to prove how strong he was. I motioned to one of the kitchen chairs, and we both sat. "And don't mention it. We kind of helped each other out. You can tell me it's none of my business, but how on earth did you end up as a rat in the city fights?"

Nick rubbed a thin hand behind an ear and looked at the ceiling. "I—uh—was cataloging a vamp's private book collection. I found something interesting and made the mistake of taking it home." He met my eyes with a sheepish expression. "I wasn't going to keep it."

Ivy and I exchanged looks. *Just borrowing it. Ri-i-i-i-ight.* But if he had worked with vampires before, that might explain his ease around Ivy.

"He changed me into a rat when he found out," Nick continued, "then gave me to one of his business associates as a gift. He was the one who put me in the fights, knowing as a human, I'd have the smarts advantage. I made him a lot of money, if nothing else. How about you?" he asked. "How did you get there?

"Um," I stammered. "I made a spell to turn myself into a mink and got put in the fights by mistake." It wasn't really a lie. I hadn't planned it, so it was an accident. Really.

"You're a witch?" he said, a smile curving over his face. "Cool. I wasn't sure."

A smile crossed me. I'd run into a few humans like him who thought Inderlanders were merely the other side to the humanity coin. Every time it was a surprise and a delight.

"What are those fights?" Ivy asked. "Some sort of crime clearinghouse where you can get rid of people without getting blood on your hands?"

Nick shook his head. "I don't think so. Rachel was the first person I ran into. And I was there for three months."

"Three months," I said, appalled. "You were a rat for three months?"

He shifted in his chair and tightened the tie on his robe. "Yeah. I'm sure all my stuff has been sold to pay my back rent. But hey, I've got hands again." He held them up, and I noticed that though thin, they were heavily callused.

I winced in sympathy. In the Hollows it was standard practice to sell your renter's things if they disappeared. People went missing all too frequently. He didn't have a job anymore, either, seeing as he was "fired" from his last one.

"You really live in a church?" he asked.

My gaze followed his, roving over the clearly institutional kitchen. "Yeah. Ivy and I moved in a few days ago. Don't mind the bodies buried in the backyard."

He smiled a charming half smile. God save me, but it made him look like a little lost boy. Ivy, at the sink again, snickered under her breath.

"Honey," Jenks's tiny voice moaned from the ceiling, jerking my attention upward. He peered down from the ladle, his wings blurring to nothing when he noticed Nick. Flying unsteadily, he almost fell to the table. I cringed, but Nick smiled.

"Jenks, right?" Nick asked.

"Baron," Jenks said, stumbling as he tried to take his best Peter Pan pose. "Glad you can do something other than squeak. Gives me a headache. Squeak, squeak, squeak. That ultrasonic stuff goes right through my head."

"It's Nick. Nick Sparagmos."

"So, Nick," he said, "Rachel wants to know what it was like having balls as big as your head that drag on the floor."

"Jenks!" I shouted. *Oh, God help me.* Head shaking violently in denial, I looked at Nick, but he seemed to have taken it in stride, his eyes glinting as his long face grinned.

Jenks took a hasty breath, darting out of the way as I made a snatch for him. He was rapidly regaining his balance. "Hey, that's one bad-ass scar on your wrist," he said quickly. "My wife—she's a sweet girl—patches me up. She's a wonder with her stitching."

"Do you want something to put on your neck?" I asked, trying to change the subject.

"No. It's all right," Nick said. He stretched out slowly, as if he were stiff, abruptly straightening when there was a soft touch on my slippered foot. I tried not to be too obvious as I looked him over. Jenks was a lot more blunt.

"Nick," Jenks said, landing next to him on the table. "Have you ever seen a scar like this?" Jenks pushed his sleeve up to show a puckered zigzag from his wrist to his elbow. Jenks always wore a long-sleeved silk shirt and matching pants. I hadn't known he had scars.

Nick whistled appreciatively, and Jenks beamed. "I got that from a fairy," Jenks said. "He was shadowing the same take my runner was. A few seconds at the ceiling with the butterfly-winged pansy, and he took his runner somewhere else."

"No kidding." Nick seemed impressed as he leaned forward. He smelled good: manly without dipping into Were, and no hint of blood at all. His eyes were brown. Nice. I liked human eyes. You could look at them and never see anything but what you might expect.

"What about that one?" Nick pointed to a round scar on Jenks's collarbone.

"Bee sting," Jenks said. "Had me in bed for three days with the shivers and jerks, but we kept our claim on the southside flower boxes. How did you get that one?" he asked, taking to the air to point at the softly welted scar ringing Nick's wrist.

Nick glanced at me and away. "A big rat named Hugo."

"Looks like he nearly took your hand off."

"He tried."

"Lookie here." Jenks tugged at his boot, yanking it off along with a nearly transparent sock to show a misshapen foot. "A vamp pulped my foot when I didn't dodge fast enough."

Nick winced, and I felt ill. It must be hard to be four inches in a six-foot world. Parting the upper part of his robe, he showed his shoulder and a hint of a curve of muscle. I leaned forward to get a better look. The light crisscrossing of scars appeared to be nail gouges, and I tried to see how far down they might go. I decided

Ivy was wrong. He wasn't a geek. Geeks don't have washboard stomachs. "A rat named Pan Peril gave me these," Nick said.

"How about this?" Jenks let his shirt fall completely about his waist. I felt my amusement fade as Jenks's scarred and battered body came to light. "See here?" he said, pointing to a concave, round scar. "Look. It goes right through to the other side." He turned to show a smaller scar on his lower back. "Fairy sword. It probably would have killed me, but I had just married Matalina. She kept me alive until the toxins worked their way out."

Nick shook his head slowly. "You win," he said. "I can't beat that."

Jenks rose several inches in pride. I didn't know what to say. My stomach rumbled, and in the obvious silence afterward I murmured, "Nick, can I make you a sandwich or something?"

His brown eyes meeting mine were warm. "If it's not too much trouble."

I rose and shuffled in my pink fuzzy slippers to the fridge. "No trouble at all. I was going to make myself something to eat anyway."

Ivy finished putting the last of the glasses away and started cleaning the sink with scouring powder. I gave her a sour look. The sink didn't need cleaning. She was just being nosy. Upon opening the fridge, I silently assessed the take-out bags from four different restaurants. Apparently Ivy had been grocery shopping. Shuffling about, I found the bologna and a head of browning lettuce. My eyes went to the tomato on the windowsill and I bit my lower lip, hoping Nick hadn't seen it yet. I didn't want to offend him. Most humans wouldn't touch a tomato with a gloved hand. Shifting to block his view, I hid it behind the toaster.

"Still eating, are we?" Ivy murmured under her breath. "A moment on the lips . . ."

"I'm hungry," I muttered back. "And I'm going to need all my strength tonight." I stuck my head back in the fridge for the mayonnaise. "I could use your help if you have the time."

"Help with what?" Jenks asked. "Getting tucked into bed?"

I turned with my hands full of sandwich stuff and elbowed the fridge shut. "I need your help bringing in Trent. And we only have until midnight to do it."

Jenks's flight bobbled. "What?" he said flatly, every drop of humor gone.

I pulled my weary gaze up to Ivy. I knew she wasn't going to like this. If the truth be told, I'd been waiting until Nick was present, hoping that with a witness, she wouldn't make a scene.

"Tonight?" Ivy put the back of her wrist on her leather hip huggers and stared. "You want to make a run for him tonight?" Her eyes went to Nick and back to me. Tossing her rag into the sink, she dried her hands on a dish towel. "Rachel, can I talk to you in the hallway?"

My brow furrowed at her implied insult that Nick couldn't be trusted. But then heaving a sigh of exasperation, I dumped everything in my arms onto the counter. "Excuse me," I said, giving Nick an apologetic grimace.

Peeved, I followed her out. I abruptly slowed at the sight of her standing halfway down to our rooms, her waspish outline looking dangerous in the dark hallway. The overpowering smell of incense in the close confines pulled me wire-tight. "What?" I said shortly.

"Letting Nick know about your little problem isn't a good idea," she said.

"He has been a rat for three months," I said, backing up. "How on earth could he be an I.S. assassin? The poor man doesn't even have any clothes, and you're worried about him killing me?"

"No," she protested, moving closer until I found my back against the wall. "But the less he knows about you, the safer you *both* will be."

"Oh." My face went cold. She was too close. Having lost her sense of personal space was not a good sign.

"And what are you going to accuse Trent of?" she demanded. "Keeping you as a mink? Putting you in the city's fights? If you go whining to the I.S. for that, you're dead."

Her speech had slowed to a sultry drawl. I had to get out of this hallway. "After three days with him, I have more than that."

From the kitchen came Nick's voice. "The I.S.?" he said loudly. "Are they the ones that put you in the rat fights, Rachel? You aren't a black witch, are you?"

Ivy jerked. Her eyes flashed to brown. Looking disconcerted, she backed up. "Sorry," she said softly. Clearly not pleased, Ivy returned to the kitchen. Relieved, I followed, to find Jenks on Nick's shoulder. I wondered if Nick had acute hearing or if Jenks had relayed everything to him. I was betting on the latter. And Nick's question about black witchcraft had been disturbing in its casualness.

"Nah," Jenks said, sounding smug. "Rachel's witchcraft is whiter than her ass. She quit the I.S. and took Ivy with her. Ivy was their best. Denon, her boss, put a price on Rachel's head for spite."

"You *were* an I.S. runner," Nick said. "I get it. But how did you end up in the rat fights?"

Still on edge, I looked to Ivy, who was industriously scrubbing the sink again, and she shrugged. So much for keeping rat boy in the dark. Shuffling back to the counter, I pulled out six pieces of bread. "Mr. Kalamack caught me in his office looking for evidence of him moving biodrugs," I said. "He thought it would be more fun putting me in the rat fights than turning me in."

"Kalamack?" Nick asked, his large eyes going wider. "You're talking about Trent Kalamack? The councilman? He runs bio-drugs?" Nick's robe had parted about his knees, and I wished he'd turn ju-u-u-ust a little more.

Smug, I layered two slices of bologna each on three slices of bread. "Yup, but while I was trapped I found out Trent isn't simply running biodrugs." I hesitated dramatically. "He's *making* them, too," I finished.

Ivy turned. Rag hanging forgotten in her slack grip, she stared at me from across the kitchen. I could hear kids playing tag next door, it was so quiet. Enjoying her reaction, I picked at the lettuce until I got to the green parts.

Nick was ashen-faced. I didn't blame him. Humans were terrified of genetic manipulation, for obvious reasons. And having Trent Kalamack dabbling in it was very worrisome. Especially when it wasn't clear which side of the human/Inderlander fence he was on. "Not Mr. Kalamack," the distraught man said. "I voted for him. Both times. Are you sure?"

Ivy, too, looked worried. "He's a bioengineer?"

"Well, he funds them," I said. *And kills them, and leaves them to rot on his office floor.* "He's got a shipment going out on Southwest tonight. If we can intercept it and tie it to him, I can use it to pay off my contract. Jenks, you still have that page from his datebook?"

The pixy nodded. "It's hidden in my stump."

I opened my mouth to protest, then decided it wasn't a bad spot. The sound of the knife was loud as I slathered mayonnaise on the bread and finished the sandwiches.

Nick pulled his head up from his hands. His long face was drawn and he looked pale. "Genetic engineering? Trent Kalamack has a biolab? The councilman?"

"You're going to love this next part," I said. "Francis is the one working the I.S. angle."

Jenks yelped, zipping up to the ceiling and down again. "Francis? You sure you weren't knocked on the head, Rache?"

"He works for Trent as sure as I just spent the last four days eating carrots. I saw him. You know those Brimstone takes Francis has been running? The promotion? *That car?*" I didn't finish my thoughts, allowing Jenks and Ivy to figure it out.

"Son of a pup!" Jenks exclaimed. "The Brimstone runs are distractions!"

"Yup." I cut the sandwiches in half. Pleased with myself, I put one on a plate for me and two on a plate for Nick; he was thin. "Trent keeps the I.S. and the FIB busy with Brimstone while the real moneymaker goes out on the other side of the city."

Ivy's motions were slow in thought as she washed her hands free of the scouring powder once more. "Francis isn't that smart," she said as she dried her fingers and set the dish towel aside again.

I went still. "No, he isn't. He's going to get himself tagged and bagged."

Jenks landed beside me. "Denon's gonna piss his pants when he hears this," he said.

"Wait up." Ivy's attention sharpened. The ring of brown in her eyes was shrinking, but it was in excitement, not hunger. "Who's to say Denon isn't on Trent's payroll, too? You'll need proof before going to the I.S. They kill you before helping you tag him. And catching him is going to take more than us two and an afternoon of planning."

My brow pinched in worry. "This is my only shot, Ivy," I protested. "High risk or not."

"Um." Nick's hand was shaking as he reached for a sandwich. "Why don't you go to the FIB?"

Ivy and I turned in a poignant silence. Nick took a bite and swallowed. "The FIB would go into a Hollow slum at midnight on a tip concerning bioengineered drugs—especially if Mr. Kalamack was being implicated. If you have any proof at all, they'll take a look."

I turned to Ivy in disbelief. Her face looked as blank as mine felt. *The FIB?*

My brow smoothed and I felt a smile come over me. Nick was right. The rivalry alone between the FIB and the I.S. would be enough to get them interested. "Trent will fry, my contract will be paid off, and the I.S. will look like a fool. I like it." I took a bite of my sandwich, wiping the mayonnaise from the corner of my mouth as I met Nick's eyes.

"Rachel," Ivy said warily. "Can I talk to you for a moment?"

I glanced at Nick, feeling my ire rise again. What did she want now? But she had already walked out. "Excuse me," I said, lurching to my feet and nervously tightening the tie on my robe. "The princess of paranoia wants a word with me." Ivy looked okay. It should be all right.

Nick brushed a crumb from his front, unperturbed. "You mind if I make some coffee? I've been dying for a cup the last three months."

"Sure. Whatever," I said, glad he wasn't insulted by Ivy's mistrust. I was. Here he came up with a great plan, and Ivy didn't like it because she didn't think of it first. "The coffee is in the fridge," I added as I followed Ivy into the hallway.

"What is your problem?" I said even before I reached her. "He's just some guy with sticky fingers. And he's right. Convincing the FIB to go after Trent is a heck of a lot safer than trying to get the I.S. to help me."

I couldn't see the color of Ivy's eyes in the dim light. It was getting dark outside, and the hallway was an uncomfortable black with her in it. "Rachel, this isn't a raid on the local vamp hangout," she said. "It's an attempt to bring down one of the city's most powerful citizens. One wrong word out of Nick and you'll be dead."

My gut clenched at the reminder. I took a breath, then slowly let it out. "Keep talking."

"I know Nick wants to help," she said. "He wouldn't be human if he didn't want to repay you somehow for helping him escape. But he's going to get hurt."

I said nothing, knowing she was right. We were professionals and he wasn't. I'd have to get him out of the way somehow. "What do you suggest?" I asked, and her tension eased.

"Why don't you take him up and see if those clothes in the belfry fit him while I book a seat on that plane?" she asked. "What flight did you say it was?"

I tucked a stray curl behind my ear. "Why? All we need to know is when it leaves."

"We might need more time. It's going to be close as it is. Most airlines will hold a plane if you tell them you have daylight restrictions. They blame it on the weather or a small maintenance issue. They won't take off until the sun isn't shining at 38,000 feet."

Daylight restrictions? That explained a lot. "Last flight to L.A. before midnight," I said.

Ivy's face grew intent as she fell into what I remembered as her "planning mode." "Jenks and I will go to the FIB and explain everything," she said in a preoccupied voice. "You can meet us there for the actual take."

"Whoa, wait a minute. I'm going to the FIB. It's my run."

Her frown was obvious in the dark of the hallway, and I stepped back, uncomfortable. "It's still the FIB," she said dryly. "Safer, yes. But they might tag you for the prestige of nailing a runner the I.S. couldn't. Some of those guys would love to kill a witch, and you know it."

I felt ill. "Okay," I agreed slowly, my mouth starting to water at the sound of gurgling coffee. "You're right. I'll stay out of it until you've told the FIB what we're doing."

Ivy's determined look shifted to one of shock. "You think I'm right?"

The smell of coffee was pulling me into the kitchen. Ivy followed me in, her footsteps soundless. I clasped my arms around myself as I entered the brighter room. The memory of hiding in the dark from fairy assassins quashed any feeling of excitement that the prospect of tagging Trent had given me. I needed to make some more spells. Strong ones. Different ones. Really different ones. Maybe . . . maybe black. I felt sick.

Nick and Jenks had their heads together as Jenks tried to convince him to open the jar of honey. By Nick's grin and continuous soft refusals, I guessed he knew something about pixies as well as vamps. I went to stand by the coffeemaker, waiting for it to finish. Ivy opened the cupboard and handed me three mugs, the question in her eyes demanding an answer as to why I was suddenly on edge. She was a vamp; she read body language better than Dr. Ruth.

"The I.S. is still spelling for me," I said softly. "Whenever the FIB moves to make a major play, the I.S. always follows to get involved. If I'm going to make a public appearance, I need something to protect myself from them. Something strong. I can make it while you're at the FIB, then join you at the airport," I said slowly.

Ivy stood at the sink, her arms crossed suspiciously. "That sounds like a good idea," she prompted. "Some prep work. Fine."

Tension pulled me tight. Black earth magic always involved killing something before adding it to the mix. Especially the strong spells. Guess I was about to find out if I could do that.

Dropping my eyes, I arranged the mugs in a straight row. "Jenks?" I questioned. "What's the assassin lineup like outside?"

The wind from his wings shifted my hair as he landed by my hand. "Real light. It's been four days since you've been spotted. It's just the fairies now. Give my kids five minutes, and we'll distract them enough that you can slip out if you need to."

"Good. I'm going out to find some new spells as soon as I get dressed."

"What for?" Ivy asked, her tone going wary. "You have plenty of spell books."

I felt the dampness of sweat on my neck. I didn't like that Ivy knew it was there. "I need something stronger." I turned, finding Ivy's face curiously slack. Dread pulled my shoulders tight. I took a deep breath and dropped my eyes. "I want something I can use for an offensive," I said in a small voice. With one hand cupping an elbow, I put a hand over my collarbone.

"Whoa, Rache," Jenks said, his wings clattering as he forced himself into my line of sight. His tiny features were pinched in worry, doing nothing for my sense of well-being. "That's dipping kind of close to dark magic, isn't it?"

My heart was pounding, and I hadn't even done anything yet. "Dipping? Hell, it is," I said. I flicked a glance at Ivy. Her posture was carefully neutral. Nick, too, didn't seem upset as he rose, coming close at the promise of coffee. Again, the thought of him practicing black magic raced through me. Humans could tap into ley lines, though wizards and sorceresses were thought of as little more than a joke in most Inderland circles.

"The moon is waxing," I said, "so that will be on my side, and I wouldn't be making spells to hurt anyone in particular. . . ." My words trailed off. The silence was uncomfortable.

Ivy's relatively mild response was unnerving. "Are you sure, Rachel?" she asked, only the barest hint of warning in her voice.

"I'll be fine," I said as I looked away from her. "I'm not doing this out of malice but to save my life. There's a difference." *I hope. God save my soul if I'm wrong.*

Jenks's wings blurred in fitful spurts as he landed on the ladle. "It doesn't matter," he said, clearly agitated. "They burned all the black spell books."

Nick pulled the coffee carafe out from under the stream of coffee and slipped a mug in its place. "The university library has some," he said as the hot plate sizzled against what spilled in the bare second it took.

We all turned to Nick, and he shrugged. "They keep them in the ancient book locker."

A wisp of fear tugged at me. *I shouldn't be doing this*, I thought. "And you have a key, right?" I said sarcastically, taken aback when he nodded.

Ivy exhaled in a puff of disbelief. "You have a key," she scoffed. "You were a rat an hour ago, and you have a key to the university's library."

He suddenly looked far more dangerous as he casually stood in my kitchen with Ivy's black robe hanging loose on his tall, lean body. "I did my work-study there," he said.

"You went to the university?" I asked, pouring myself a cup after Nick.

He took a sip of coffee, his eyes closed in what looked like bliss. "Full scholarship," he said. "I majored in data acquisition, organization, and distribution."

"You're a librarian," I said in relief. That's how he knew about the black spell books.

"Used to be. I can get you in and out, no problem. The lady in charge of us work-study peons hid keys to locked rooms near the doors so we wouldn't keep bothering her." He took another sip, and his eyes glazed as the caffeine hit him.

Only now did Ivy look worried, her brown eyes pinched. "Rachel, can I talk to you?"

"No," I said softly. I didn't want to go into that hallway again. It was dark. I was on edge. That my heart was pounding because I was afraid of black magic and not her would mean nothing to her instincts. And going to the library with Nick was a sight less dangerous than making a black spell—for which she didn't seem to have any care. "What do you want?"

She eyed Nick, then me. "I was only going to suggest you take Nick up to the belfry. We've got some clothes up there that might fit him."

I pushed myself from the counter, my untasted coffee tight in my grip. *Liar*, I thought. "Give me a minute to get dressed, Nick, and I'll take you up. You don't mind wearing a minister's hand-me-downs, do you?"

Nick's look of startlement eased into question. "No. That would be great."

"Fine," I said, my head pounding. "After you're dressed, you and I will go out to the library and you can show me all their black magic books."

I glanced at Ivy and Jenks as I walked out. Jenks was very pale, clearly not liking what I was doing. Ivy looked concerned, but what worried me most was Nick's casual ease with everything Inderlander, and now black magic. He wasn't a practitioner, was he?

Twenty-four

I stood on the sidewalk waiting for Nick to get out of the cab, estimating what I had left in my wallet before putting it away. My last paycheck was dwindling. If I wasn't careful, I'd have to send Ivy to the bank for me. I was burning it faster than usual, and I couldn't understand why. All my expenses were less. *Must be the cabs,* I thought, vowing to use the bus more.

Nick had found a pair of work-faded jeans up in the belfry. They were baggy on him, held up with one of my more conservative belts; our long-departed minister had been a large man. The gray sweatshirt with the University of Cincinnati's logo was equally outsized, and the gardening boots had been hopelessly too big. But Nick had them on his feet, clomping about like a bad Frankenstein movie. Somehow, with his tall height and casual good looks, he made slovenly seem attractive. I always just looked like a slob.

The sun wasn't down yet, but the streetlights were on since it was cloudy. It had taken longer to get the minister's small wardrobe into the wash than it had to get here. I held the collar of my winter coat closed against the chill air and scanned the headlight-illuminated street as Nick said a few last words to the cabbie. Nights could be chill in late spring, but I would have worn the long coat anyway to cover up the brown gingham dress I had on. It was supposed to go along with my old lady disguise. I had only worn it once before, to a mother-daughter banquet I was somehow roped into.

Nick unfolded himself out of the cab. He slammed the door shut and smacked the top of the car. The driver gave him a casual hand toss and drove away. Cars flowed around us. The street was busy in the hours of twilight when both humanity and Inderlander were in force.

"Hey," Nick said, peering at me in the unsure light. "What happened to your freckles?"

"Uh . . ." I stammered, fingering my pinky ring. "I don't have any freckles."

Nick took a breath to say something, then hesitated. "Where's Jenks?" he finally asked.

Flustered, I pointed across the street to the library steps with my chin. "He went ahead to check things out." I eyed the few people filing in and out of the library. Studying on a Friday night. Some people have an insatiable desire to ruin the curve for the rest of us. Nick took my elbow, and I tugged away from him. "I can walk across the street by myself, thank you."

"You look like an old lady," he muttered. "Stop swinging your arms, and slow down."

I sighed, trying to move slowly as Nick crossed in the middle of the street. Horns blew, and Nick ignored them. We were in student territory. If we had crossed at the intersection, we would have attracted attention. Even so, I was tempted to give a few one-fingered waves, but decided it might blow the old lady image. Then again, maybe not.

"Are you sure no one will recognize you?" I asked as we moved up the marble stairs and to the glass doors. Cripes, no wonder old people died. It took them twice as long to do anything.

"Yup." He pulled the door open for me and I shuffled in. "I haven't worked here for five years, and the only people working on Friday are the freshmen. Now hunch your back and try not to attack anyone." I gave him a nasty smile, and he added a cheerful, "That's better."

Five years meant he wasn't much older than I was. It was about what I had guessed, though it was hard to tell under the rat-induced wear and tear.

I stood in the entryway to get my bearings. I like libraries. They smell good and are quiet. The fluorescent light in the entrance looked too dim. It was usually supplemented by the natural light coming in through the big windows running the entire two stories up. The gloom of sunset dampened everything.

My gaze jerked to a blur falling from the ceiling. It was headed right for me! Gasping, I ducked. Nick clutched my arm. Thrown off balance, my heels slipped on the marble floor. Crying out, I went down. Sprawled with my legs every which way, my face burned as Jenks hovered before me, laughing. "Damn it all to hell!" I shouted. "Watch what you're doing!"

There was a collective gasp, and everyone looked at me. Jenks hid himself in my hair, his merry laughter ticking me off. Nick bent and took my elbow. "Sorry, Grandmum," he said loudly. He gave everyone a sheepish look. "Grandmum can't hear very well," he said in a conspiratorial whisper, "the old bat." He turned to me, his face serious but his brown eyes glinting. "We're in the library now!" he shouted. "You have to be quiet!"

Face warm enough to make toast, I mumbled something and let him help me up. There was a nervous patter of amusement, and everyone returned to whatever they were doing.

An uptight, pimply-faced adolescent rushed up to us, worried about a lawsuit, no doubt. Amid more fuss than it warranted, he ushered us to the back offices, babbling about slippery floors, that they had just been waxed, and he would talk to the janitor immediately.

I hung on Nick's arm, moaning about my hip and playing the old lady to the hilt. The flustered kid buzzed us through a semisecure area. Red-faced, he fussed over me as he sat me down and propped my feet up on a swivel chair. The silver knife strapped to my ankle gave him a slight pause. I whispered faintly something about water, and he fled to find some. It took him three tries to get through the buzzed door. Silence descended as the door clicked shut behind him. Grinning, I met Nick's eyes. It wasn't exactly how we had planned it, but here we were.

Jenks came out from hiding. "Slicker than snot on a doorknob," he said, darting up to inspect the cameras. "Ha!" he exclaimed. "They're fake."

Nick took my hand and drew me to my feet. "I was going to take you down through the access in the employees' break room, but this will work." I looked blankly at him and he flicked his eyes to a gray fire door. "The basement is through there."

A smile curved over me as I saw the lock. "Jenks?"

"On it," he said, dropping down and starting to tinker. He had it sprung in three seconds flat. "Here goes . . ." Nick murmured as he turned the knob. The door opened to show a dark stairway. Nick flicked on the lights and listened. "No alarms," he said.

I pulled out a detection amulet and quickly invoked it. It stayed warm and green in my hand. "No silent alarms, either," I murmured, hanging it about my neck.

"Hey," Jenks complained. "This is first-year stuff."

We started down. The air was cold in the narrow stairwell, with none of the comforting smell of books. Every twenty feet a bare bulb burned, sending sickly yellow beams to show the dirt in the lee of the steps. A foot-wide band of grime made a stripe on the walls to either side of me at hand height, and my lip curled. There was a banister, but I wouldn't use it.

The way ended at an echoing dark hallway. Nick looked at me, and I glanced at my amulet. "We're clear," I whispered, and he flicked on the lights to illuminate a hallway with a low ceiling, the walls stark cinder block. Floor to ceiling wire gates ran down the length of the hall, doing nothing to hide the racks of books behind them.

Jenks buzzed confidently ahead of us. Heels clacking, I followed Nick to a locked wire door. The ancient-book section. While Jenks flitted in and out between the diamond-shaped holes, I laced my fingers through the mesh and stood on tiptoe, all senses soaking it in. A frown pinched my brow. It was my imagination, of course, but it seemed I could smell the magic flowing out from the racks of books, all but visible as it eddied about my ankles. The feeling of old power emanating from the locked room was as different from the smell upstairs as a chocolate kiss is to a premium Belgium sweet. Heady, rich, and oh-so-bad for you.

"So where's that key?" I asked, knowing Jenks wouldn't be able to shift the heavy tumblers of the older, mechanical lock. Sometimes it's the older safeguards that work best.

Nick ran his fingers under a nearby shelf, his eyes glinting in a past frustration as his hand stopped. "Not enough seniority to go into the book locker, eh?" he muttered under his breath as he pulled out a key with a bit of sticky tack on it. Eyes tight, he looked at the skeleton key laying heavy in his hand before opening the wire-meshed door.

My heart gave a pound and settled as the door squeaked. Nick put the key in his pocket with an abrupt, determined motion. "After you," he said as he turned on the fluorescent lights.

I hesitated. "Is there any other way out of here?" I asked, and when he shook his head, I turned to Jenks. "Stay here," I said. "Watch my—back. . . ." I bit my lip. "Will you watch my back, Jenks?" I said, my stomach clenching.

The pixy must have heard the hint of a quaver in my voice as he lost his excitement and landed on my proffered hand. At eye level, he nodded. The sparkles in his black silk shirt caught the light, adding to the glow his blurring wings put out. "Gotcha, Rache," he said solemnly. "Nothing is going to come through here unless you know about it. Promise."

I took a nervous breath. Nick's eyes were confused. Everyone in the I.S. knew how my dad had died. I appreciated Jenks not saying anything, just telling me that he would be there for me.

"Okay," I said as I took off my detecting amulet and hung it where Jenks could see it. I followed Nick in, ignoring the creepy sensation of my skin tingling. Whether they contained black arts or white, they were just books. The power came from using them.

The door squeaked shut, and Nick brushed past me, gesturing me to follow. I took off my disguise amulet and dropped it into my bag, then undid the bun my hair was in and shook it all out. Fluffing it, I felt half a century younger.

I glanced at the passing titles as I passed them, slowing as the aisle opened up to a good-sized room hidden from the hallway by racks of books. There was an institutional-looking table and three mismatched swivel chairs that weren't even good enough for an intern's desk.

Nick strode unhesitatingly to the glass-door cabinet across the room. "Here, Rachel," he said as he pulled it open. "See if what you want is here." He turned, brushing the shock of black hair from his eyes. I blinked at the intent, sly look shadowing his long face.

"Thanks. This is great. I really appreciate it," I said as I dropped my bag on the table and came to stand beside him. Worry pinched me, and I pushed it aside. If the spell was too disgusting, I just wouldn't do it.

Carefully, I worked the oldest-looking book out. The binding had been torn off the spine, and I had to use two hands to manage the unwieldy tome. I set it at the corner of the table and dragged a chair up to it. It was as cold as a cave down here, and I was glad for my coat. The dry air smelled faintly like potato chips. Squelching my nervousness, I opened the book. The title page had been ripped out, too. Using a spell from a book with no name was disturbing. The index was intact, though, and my eyebrows rose. *A spell to talk to ghosts? Cool . . .*

"You aren't like most humans I've spent any time with," I said as I scanned the index.

"My mom was a single parent," he said. "She couldn't afford anything uptown and so was more inclined to let me play with witches and vampires than the kids of heroin addicts. The Hollows was the lesser of two evils." Nick had his hands in his back pockets and was rocking heel to toe as he read the titles of a row of books. "I grew up there. Went to Emerson."

I glanced at him, intrigued. Growing up in the Hollows would explain why he knew so much about Inderlanders. To survive, you had to. "You went to Inderland Hollows's high school?" I asked.

He jiggled the locked door of a tall free-standing closet. The wood looked red in the glow from the fluorescent lights. I wondered what was so dangerous that it had to be locked inside a closet, inside a locked vault, behind a locked door, at the bottom of a government building.

Picking at the heat-warped lock, Nick shrugged. "It was all right. The principal bent the rules for me after I got a concussion. They let me carry a silver dagger to get the Weres to back off, and rinsing my hair in holy water kept the living vamps from being too obnoxious. It didn't stop them, but the bad case of B.O. it gave me worked almost as well."

"Holy water, huh?" I said, deciding I'd stick with my lilac perfume rather than have a body odor that only vamps could smell.

"It was only the warlocks and witches that gave me trouble," he added as he gave up on the lock and sat in one of the chairs, his long legs straight out before him. I gave him a sideways smirk. I could well imagine the witches gave him trouble. "But the practical jokes stopped after I befriended the biggest, meanest, ugliest warlock in school." A faint smile played about his eyes, and he looked tired. "Turk. I did his homework for four years. He should have graduated a long time ago, and the teachers were glad to look the other way to get him out of the system. Because I didn't go whining to the principal all the time like the handful of other humans enrolled there, I was cool enough to hang with the Inderlanders. My friends took care of me, and I learned a lot I might not have."

"Like that you don't have to be afraid of a vamp," I said, thinking it was odd a human would know more about vamps than I did.

"Not at noon, anyway. But I'll feel better once I take a shower and get Ivy's smell off me. I didn't know that was her robe, earlier." He clumped over. "What are you looking for?"

"Not sure," I said, nervous as he peered over my shoulder. There had to be something I could use that wouldn't send me too far down the wrong side of the "Force." A nervous amusement flashed through me. *You're not my father, Darth, and I'll never join you!*

Nick's eyes began to water at the strength of my perfume, and he backed off. We had driven over with the windows down. Now I knew why he hadn't said anything about it.

"You haven't lived with Ivy very long, have you?" he asked. I looked up from the index, surprised, and his long face went slack. "I, uh, sorta got the idea that you and she weren't . . ."

I flushed, dropping my eyes. "We aren't," I said. "Not if we can help it. We're just roommates. I'm on the right side of the hall, she's on the left."

He hesitated. "Do you mind if I make a suggestion, then?"

Mystified, I stared at him, and he went to sit on the corner of the table. "You might want to try a perfume with a citrus base instead of a flower."

My eyes widened. This was not what I had been expecting, and my hand crept up to cover my neck where I had dumped a splash of that awful perfume. "Jenks helped me pick it out," I said in explanation. "He said it covered Ivy's smell pretty good."

"I'm sure it does." Nick winced apologetically. "But it has to be strong to work. The ones based on citrus neutralize a vamp's odor, not just cover it up."

"Oh . . ." I breathed, recalling Ivy's fondness for orange juice.

"A pixy's nose is good, but a vamp's is specialized. Go shopping with Ivy next time. She'll help you pick out something that works."

"I'll do that," I said, thinking I could have avoided offending everyone if I had just asked for her help the first time. Feeling stupid, I closed the unnamed book and rose to get another.

I pulled the next book off the shelf, tensing when it was heavier than I thought it should be. It hit the table with a thump and Nick cringed. "Sorry," I said, pushing the cover straight to hide that I had torn the rotting binding. Sitting down, I opened the book.

My heart gave a thump and I froze, feeling the hair on my neck stand on end. It wasn't my imagination. Worried, I looked up to see if Nick had noticed it, too. He was staring over my shoulder at one of the aisles the book racks made. The eerie feeling wasn't coming from the book. It was coming from behind me. *Damn.*

"Rachel!" came a tiny call from the hall. "Your amulet went red, but no one's out here!"

I shut the book and stood. There was a flickering in the air. My heart pounded when half a dozen books in the aisle pushed themselves to the back of the shelves. "Uh, Nick?" I questioned. "Is there a history of ghosts in the library?"

"Not that I know of."

Double damn. I moved to stand beside him. "Then what the hell is that?"

He gave me a wary look. "I don't know."

Jenks flitted in. "There's nothing in the hallway, Rache. You sure that charm you gave me is working?" he asked, and I pointed at the disturbance in the aisle.

"Holy crap!" he exclaimed, hovering between Nick and me as the air started to take on a more solid form. As one, the books slid back to the front of the shelves. That was even creepier.

The mist turned yellow, then became firm. My breath hissed in through my teeth. It was a dog. That is, if dogs can be as big as ponies and have canines longer than my hand and tiny horns coming out of their heads, then it was a dog. I backed up a step with Nick, and it tracked us. "Tell me this is the library's security system," I whispered.

"I don't know what it is." Nick was ashen-faced, his slow confidence shattered. The dog was between us and the door. Saliva dripped from its jaw, and I swear it hissed when it hit the floor. Yellow smoke rose from the puddle. I could smell sulfur. What the devil was this thing?

"Do you have anything in your purse for this?" Nick whispered, stiffening as the dog's ears pricked.

"Anything to stop a yellow dog from hell?" I asked. "No."

"If we show no fear, maybe it won't attack."

The dog opened its jaws and said, "Which one of you is Rachel Mariana Morgan?"

Twenty-five

I gasped, my heart pounding.

The dog yawned with a little whine at the end. "Must be you," it said. Its skin rippled like amber fire, then it leapt at us.

"Look out!" Nick shouted, pushing me clear as the slavering dog landed on the table.

I hit the floor, rolling to a crouch. Nick cried out in pain. There was a crash as the table slid into the racks. It shifted back when the dog jumped off it. The heavy plastic shattered.

"Nick!" I cried, seeing him crumpled in a heap. The monster stood over him, nosing him. Blood stained the floor. "Get off him!" I shouted. Jenks was at the ceiling, powerless.

The dog turned to me. My breath caught. Its irises were red surrounded by a sickly orange color, and its pupils were slit sideways like a goat's. Never taking my eyes off it, I backed up. Fingers fumbling, I pulled my silver dagger from my ankle. I swear a doggy smile curved around its savage canines as I shrugged out of my coat and kicked off my old lady heels.

Nick groaned and moved. He was alive. A wash of relief swept me. Jenks was on his shoulder, yelling in his ear to get up.

"Rachel Mariana Morgan," the dog said, its voice black and honey sweet. I shivered in the basement's cold air, waiting. "One of you is afraid of dogs," it said, sounding amused. "I don't think it's you."

"Come find out," I said boldly. My heart was pounding, and I adjusted my grip on my dagger as I began to tremble. Dogs shouldn't talk. They shouldn't.

It took a step forward. I stared, mouth agape, as its front legs lengthened, pushing itself upward into a walking position. It thinned out, becoming manlike. Clothes appeared: artfully torn blue jeans, a black leather jacket, and a chain running from its belt loop to its wallet. It had spiked hair, colored red to match its ruddy complexion. Eyes were hidden behind black plastic sunglasses. I couldn't move from the shock of it as a bad-boy swagger came into its steps.

"I was sent to kill you," it said in a seedy London accent, still approaching as it finished turning into a cobbled-street gang member. "I was told to make sure you died afraid, sweet. Wasn't given much to go on. Might take a while."

I lurched back, only now realizing it was almost on me.

With motion almost too quick to be seen, its hand jerked forward like a piston. It hit me before I knew it had moved. My cheek exploded into a fiery agony, then went numb. A second blow to the shoulder lifted me. My stomach dropped, and I crashed backward into a book rack.

I struck the floor, books pummeling me as they fell. Shaking the stars from my vision, I rose. Nick had dragged himself between two racks of books. Blood ran from under his hair and down his neck. His face wore a look of awe and fear. He touched his head, looking at the blood as if it meant something. I met his eyes across the room. The thing was between us.

I gasped as it sprang, its hands grasping. I dropped to a knee. I swung my knife, lurching as it went right through it. Horrified, I scrambled out of its reach. It kept coming. Its entire face had gone misty, reforming as my knife passed through. *What the hell was it?*

"Rachel Mariana Morgan," it mocked. "I'm here for you."

It reached out and I turned to run. A heavy hand grabbed my shoulder. It whipped me back around. The thing held me, and I froze as its other red-skinned hand folded into a murderous-looking fist. Grinning to show startling white teeth, it pulled its arm back. It was going for my middle.

I barely got my arm down to block it. Its fist hit my arm. The sudden shock of pain took my breath away. I fell to my knees, a scream ripping from me as I clutched my arm. It followed me down. Arm held close, I rolled away.

It landed heavy and hot to crush me under it. Its breath was steam upon my face. Its long fingers gripped my shoulder until I cried out. Its free hand snaked its way under my dress and up my inner thigh, roughly searching. My eyes widened in astonishment. *What the hell?*

Its face was inches before mine. I could see my shock mirrored in its sunglasses. A tongue slipped past its teeth. Warm and disgusting, it ran its tongue from my chin to my ear. Nails dug at my underwear. It savagely pulled at them, making them cut into me.

Jolted into action, I knocked the sunglasses askew. My nails dug at its orange irises.

Its surprised cry bought me a quick breath. In the instant of confusion, I pushed it off me and rolled away. A heavy boot smelling of ash lashed out, striking my kidney. Gasping, I huddled in a fetal position curved around my knife. That time I had gotten it. It had been too distracted to turn misty. If it could feel pain, then it could die.

"Not afraid of rape, sweet?" it said, sounding pleased. "You're one tough little bitch."

It grasped my shoulder, and I fought back, helpless against the long red fingers that pulled me stumbling up. My eyes flicked to Nick and the sound of heavy blows. He was hammering at the locked wooden cabinet with a leg from the table. His blood was everywhere. Jenks was on his shoulder, his wings red in fear.

The air blurred before me, and I staggered as I realized the thing had changed again. The hand now gripping my shoulder was smoothed. Panting, I looked up to see it had become a tall, sophisticated young man dressed in a formal frock and coat. A pair of smoked glasses was perched on its narrow nose. I was sure I had hit it, but what I could see of its eyes looked undamaged. Was it a vamp? A really old vampire?

"Perhaps you're afraid of pain?" the vision of an elegant man said, its accent now proper enough for even Professor Henry Higgins.

I jerked away, stumbling into a book rack. Grinning, it reached after me. It picked me up and threw me across the room at Nick, who was still hammering at the cabinet.

My back hit it with enough force to knock the air from me. The clatter of my knife on the floor was loud as my fingers lost their grip. Struggling to breathe, I slid down the broken cabinet, ending up half sitting on the shelves behind the shattered doors. I was helpless as the thing lifted me by my dress front.

"What are you?" I rasped.

"Whatever scares you." It smiled to show flat teeth. "What scares you, Rachel Mariana Morgan?" it asked. "It isn't pain. It isn't rape. It doesn't seem to be monsters."

"Nothing," I panted, spitting at it.

My saliva sizzled as it hit its face. Reminded of Ivy's saliva on my neck, I shuddered.

Its eyes went wide in pleasure. "You're afraid of the soulless shadows," it whispered in delight. "You're afraid of dying in the loving embrace of a soulless shadow. Your death is going to be a pleasure for both of us, Rachel Mariana Morgan. Such a twisted way to die—in pleasure. It might have been better for your soul had you been afraid of dogs."

I lashed out, striking its face to leave four scratch marks. It didn't flinch. Blood oozed out, too thick and red. It twisted both my arms behind me, gripping my wrists with one hand. Nausea doubled me over as it pulled on my arm and shoulder. It pushed me up against the wall, crushing me. I got my good hand free and swung.

It caught my wrist before I could reach it. I met its gaze and felt my knees go weak. The gentleman's frock had shrunk to a leather jacket and black pants. Blond hair and a lightly stubbled face replaced its ruddy complexion. Twin earrings caught the light. Kisten smiled at me, a red tongue beckoning. "You have a taste for vamps, little witch?" it whispered.

I twisted, trying to get away. "Not quite right," it murmured, and I struggled as its features shifted yet again. It grew smaller, only a head taller than I. Its hair grew long and straight and black. The blond stubble vanished, and the complexion paled to a ghost. Kisten's square jaw smoothed out to an oval.

"Ivy," I whispered, going slack in terror.

"You give me a name," it said, its voice becoming slow and feminine. "You want this?"

I tried to swallow. I couldn't move. "You don't scare me," I whispered.

Its eyes flashed black. "Ivy does."

I stiffened, trying to jerk away as it brought my wrist closer. "No!" I screamed as it opened its mouth to show fangs. It bit deep, and I screamed. Fire raced up my arm and into my body. It chewed at my wrist like a dog as I writhed, trying to pull away.

I felt skin tear as I twisted. I brought my knee up and pushed it away. It let go. I fell back panting, transfixed. It was as if Ivy stood before me, my blood dripping from her smile. A hand rose to brush the hair from its eyes, leaving a red smear across its forehead.

I couldn't . . . I couldn't deal with this. Taking a gasping breath, I ran for the door.

The thing snaked an arm out with a vampire's quickness and

jerked me back. Pain flared as it slammed me against the cement wall. Ivy's pale hand pinned me. "Let me show you what vamps do behind locked doors, Rachel Mariana Morgan," it breathed.

I realized I was going to die in the basement of the university library.

The thing that was Ivy leaned close. I could feel my pulse pushing at my skin. My wrist tingled warmly. Ivy's face was inches from mine. It was getting better at pulling images out of my head. There was a crucifix around its neck, and I could smell orange juice. Its eyes were smoky with a remembered look of sultry hunger. "No," I whispered. "Please, no."

"I can have you anytime I want, little witch," it whispered, the gray silk of its voice twin to Ivy's.

I panicked, struggling helplessly. The thing that looked like Ivy grinned to show teeth. "You are so afraid," it whispered lovingly, tilting its head so its black hair brushed my shoulder. "Don't be so afraid. You'll like it. Didn't I say you would?"

I jerked as something touched my neck. A small sound escaped me as I realized it was a quick tongue. "You're going to love it," it said in Ivy's throaty whisper. "Scout's honor."

Images of being pinned to Ivy's chair flooded back. The thing holding me against the wall groaned in pleasure and nuzzled my head aside. Terrified, I screamed.

"Oh, please," the thing moaned as I felt the cool, icy sharpness of teeth graze my neck. "Oh, please. Now . . ."

"No!" I shrieked, and it drove its teeth into me. Three times it lunged with rapid, hungry motions. I buckled in its grip. Still fastened to me, we dropped to the floor. It crushed me under it against the cold cement. Fire burned at my neck. A twin sensation rose up my wrist, joining it in my head. Shudders racked me. I could hear it sucking at me, feel the rhythmic pulls as it tried to take more than my body could give.

I gasped as a tangy sensation broke over me. I stiffened, unable to separate pain from pleasure. It was . . . was . . .

"Get off her!" Nick shouted.

I heard a thump and felt a jarring. The thing pulled itself off me.

I couldn't move. I didn't want to. I lay sprawled on the floor, transfixed and numb under the vampire-induced stupor. Jenks hovered over me, the breeze on my neck from his wings sending tingling jolts through me.

Nick stood with blood dripping into his eyes. He had a book in his hands. It was so large, he was struggling with it. He was mumbling under his breath, looking pale and frightened. His eyes darted from the book to the thing beside me.

It melted back into a dog. Snarling, it leapt at Nick.

"Nick," I whispered as Jenks fanned pixy dust onto my neck. "Look out . . ."

"Laqueus!" Nick shouted, juggling the book against a raised knee as he flung out a hand.

The dog slammed into something and fell to the ground. I watched from the floor as it picked itself up and shook its head as if dazed. Snarling, it jumped at him again, falling back a second time. "You bound me!" it raged, melting from one form to another in a grotesque kaleidoscope of shapes. It looked to the floor and the circle Nick had made of his own blood. "You don't have the knowledge to call me from the ever-after!" it shouted.

Hunched over the book, Nick licked his lips. "No. But I can bind you in a circle once you're here." He sounded hesitant, as if he wasn't sure.

As Jenks stood on my outstretched palm and sifted pixy dust onto my ravaged wrist, the thing hammered against the unseen barrier. Smoke curled from the floor where its feet touched the cement. "Not again!" it raged. "Let me out!"

Nick swallowed hard and strode past the blood and fallen books to me. "My God, Rachel," he said as the book dropped to the floor with the sound of tearing pages. Jenks was dabbing at the blood on my face, singing a fast-paced lullaby about dew and moonbeams.

I looked from the broken book on the floor to Nick. "Nick?" I quavered, riveted to his silhouette against the ugly fluorescent lights. "I can't move." Panic washed through me. "I can't move, Nick! I think it paralyzed me!"

"No. No," he said, glancing at the dog. Settling himself behind me, he pulled me up to sit slumped against him. "It's the vampire saliva. It will wear off."

Cradled in his arms and half in his lap, I felt myself start to go cold. Numb, I gazed up at him. His brown eyes were pinched. His jaw was clenched in worry. The blood ran from his scalp, making a slow rivulet down his face to soak his shirt. His hands were red and sticky, but his arms around me were warm. I started to shiver.

"Nick?" I quavered. My attention followed his to the thing. It was a dog again. It stood there, staring at us. Saliva dripped from it. Its muscles quivered. "Is that a vampire?"

"No," he said tersely. "It's a demon, but if it's strong enough, it has the abilities of whatever form it assumes. You'll be able to move in a minute." His long face screwed up in distress as he looked at the blood splattered about the room. "You're going to be all right." Still keeping me in the cradle of his lap, he used my silver knife to rip the bottom of his shirt. "You're going to be all right," he whispered as he tied the rag around my wrist and set it gently in my lap. I moaned at the unexpected bliss that rose from my wrist at the rough movement.

"Nick?" There were black sparkles between me and the lights. It was fascinating. "There aren't any more demons. There hasn't been a demon attack since the Turn."

"I took three years of Demonology as a Second Language to help me with my Latin," he said, stretching to reach my bag as Jenks tugged it out from the wreck of the table. "That thing is a demon." Keeping my head in his lap, he clattered through my things. "Do you have anything for pain in here?"

"No," I said dreamily. "I like pain." Face going slack, Nick's gaze shot to mine and then to Jenks's. "No one takes demonology," I protested weakly, wanting to giggle. "It's, like, the most useless thing in the world." My gaze drifted to the cabinet. The doors were still shut, but the panels had been broken by Nick's hammering and me being thrown into it. Beyond the splintered wood was an empty spot the size of the book on the floor beside me. *So that's what they hide in a locked cabinet, in a locked room, behind a locked door, in the basement of a government building.* I squinted at Nick. "You know how to call demons?" I questioned. God help me, but I felt good. All light and airy. "You're a black practitioner. I arrest people like you," I said, trying to run a finger down his jawline.

"Not exactly." Nick took my hand and set it down. Shaking the cuff of his sweatshirt past his hand, he used it to brush the blood from my face. "Don't try to talk, Rachel. You lost a lot of blood." He turned to Jenks, his eyes frightened. "I can't take her on the bus like this!"

Jenks's face looked pained. "I'll get Ivy." He dropped to my shoulder and whispered, "Hold on, Rache. I'll be right back." He flitted to Nick, the breeze from his wings sending more waves of euphoria through me. I closed my eyes and rode it, hoping it would never end.

"If you let her die here, I'll kill you myself," Jenks threatened, and Nick nodded. Jenks left with the sound of a thousand bees. The sound echoed in my head even after he was gone.

"It can't get out?" I asked, opening my eyes as my emotions swung from one extreme to the other and tears welled.

Nick shoved the big book of demon spells in my bag. His bloody handprints were all over both of them. "No. And when the sun rises, poof, it's gone. You're safe. Hush." He tucked my knife in my bag and stretched for my coat.

"We're in a basement," I protested. "There's no sun down here."

Nick ripped the lining from my coat and pressed it against my neck. I cried out as a pulse of ecstasy shot through me from the lingering effects of the vampire saliva. The bleeding had slowed, and I wondered if it was from Jenks's pixy dust. Apparently it could do more than make people itch.

"It's not sunlight that pulls a demon back to the ever-after," Nick said, clearly thinking he had hurt me. "It's something about gamma rays or protons. . . . Damn it, Rachel. Stop asking me so many questions. It was taught as an aid to understand language development, not to learn how to control demons."

The demon was Ivy again, and I shuddered as it licked its red lips with a bloodstained tongue, taunting me. "What grade did you get, Nick?" I asked. "Please tell me it was an A."

"Uh . . ." he stammered as he covered me with my coat. Looking frantic, he gathered me up in his arms, almost rocking me. My breath hissed in as my wrist throbbed in time with the pulses from my neck. "Easy," he shushed. "You'll be all right."

"Are you sure?" came a cultured voice from the corner.

Nick's head came up. Cradled in Nick's arms, I stared at the demon. It was back to wearing a gentleman's frock. "Let me out. I can help you," the demon said, all congeniality.

Nick hesitated. "Nick?" I said, suddenly frightened. "Don't listen to it. Don't!"

The demon smiled over its smoked glasses, showing flat, even teeth. "Break the circle and I'll take you to her Ivy. Otherwise . . ." The demon's brow furrowed as if it was worried. "It almost looks as if there's more blood outside of her than in."

Nick's gaze darted over the blood splattered on the walls and books. His grip on me tightened. "You were trying to kill her," he said, his voice cracking.

It shrugged. "I was compelled to. By binding me in your circle, you rubbed out the one that was used to summon me. With it went any compulsion to do his bidding. I'm all yours, little wizard." It grinned, and my breath came in a quick, fear-laced pant.

"Nicky . . ." I whispered as my blood-loss induced stupor was stripped away. This was bad. I knew this was bad. The remembered terror as it savaged me rose high. My pulse faltered as my heart tried to beat faster.

"Can you get us back to her church?" Nick asked.

"The one by the small ley line?" The demon's outline wavered as its expression turned startled. "Someone closed a circle with it six nights ago. The ripple it sent through the ever-after shook the cups on my saucers, so to speak." It tilted its head in speculation. "That was you?"

"No," Nick said weakly.

I felt ill. I had used too much salt. God help me. I didn't know demons could sense it when I drew on a ley line. If I lived through this, I'd never use them again.

The demon gazed at me. "I can take you there," it said. "But in return I want no compulsion put on me to return to the ever-after."

Nick's grip tightened. "You want me to let you loose in Cincinnati for the entire night?"

A power-filled smile edged over the demon. It exhaled slowly, and I heard the joints in its shoulder crack. "I mean to kill the one who summoned me. Then I'll leave. It smells over here." It looked over its smoked glasses, shocking me with its alien eyes. "You won't ever call me—will you, little wizard? I could teach you so much that you want to know."

Fear fought with the pain in my shoulder as Nick hesitated before shaking his head.

"You won't hurt us," Nick said. "Mentally, physically, or emotionally. You will take the most direct path and do nothing to endanger us afterward."

"Nick Nicky," the demon pouted. "One might think you didn't trust me. I can even get you there before her Ivy leaves if I take you through a ley line. But you'd better hurry. Rachel Mariana Morgan seems to be failing fast."

Through the ever-after? I thought in panic. *No!* That's what had killed my dad.

Nick swallowed, his Adam's apple bobbing. "No!" I tried to shout, squirming to get out of his grip. The stupor from its saliva was almost gone, and with the return of movement came pain. I welcomed the hurt, knowing the pleasure had been a lie. Nick was white-faced as he tried to keep me unmoving and hold the lining of my coat against my neck.

"Rachel," he whispered. "You've lost so much blood. I don't know what to do!"

My throat was too parched to swallow. "Don't—Don't let it out," I insisted. "Please," I pleaded as I pushed his hands off of me. "I'm fine. The bleeding has stopped. I'll be all right. Leave me here. Go call Ivy. She'll pick us up. I don't want to go through the ever-after."

The demon's brow furrowed as if it was concerned. "Mmmm," he mused gently, touching the lace at his throat. "Sounds like she's going incoherent. Not good. Tick-tock, Nick Nicky. Better decide quick."

Nick's breath hissed in and he tensed. His gaze roved over the pool of blood on the floor and then me. "I've got to do something," he whispered. "You're so cold, Rachel."

"Nick, no!" I shouted as he set me on the floor and lurched into a stand. Reaching out with a foot, he smeared the line of blood.

I heard a frightened wail. I covered my mouth as I realized it was coming from me. Terror pulsed through me as the demon shuddered. It slowly stepped across the line. It ran a hand across the bloodstained wall and licked its finger, never taking its eyes off of me.

"Don't let it touch me!" My voice was high-pitched. I could hear the hysteria in it.

"Rachel," Nick soothed as he knelt beside me. "It said it won't hurt you. Demons don't lie. It was in every text I copied."

"They don't tell the truth, either!" I exclaimed.

Ire flickered behind the demon's eyes, smothered in a wave of false concern for me before Nick could see. It came forward, and I struggled to push myself back. "Don't let it touch me!" I cried. "Don't make me do this!"

The fear in Nick's eyes was for how I was acting, not from the demon. He didn't understand. He thought he knew what he was doing. He thought his books had all the answers. He didn't know what he was doing. I did.

Nick gripped my shoulder and turned to the demon. "Can you help her?" he asked it. "She's going to kill herself."

"Nick, no!" I shrieked as the demon knelt to put its grinning face next to mine.

"Sleep, Rachel Mariana Morgan," it breathed, and I remembered no more.

Twenty-six

"What happened? Where is Jenks?" Ivy's voice penetrated my daze, close and worried. I could feel myself moving forward in a rocking motion. I had been warm, and now I was cold again. The smell of blood was thick. The memory of something more foul lingered in me: carrion, salt, and burnt amber. I couldn't open my eyes.

"She was attacked by a demon." It was terse and soft. Nick.

That's right, I thought, starting to piece everything together. I was in his arms. That's what that one good smell was, all masculine and sweaty. And that was his bloody sweatshirt pushing against my swollen eye, rubbing it even more sore. I started to shiver. Why was I cold?

"Can we get off the street?" Nick asked. "She's lost a lot of blood."

There was a warm touch on my forehead. "A demon did this?" Ivy said. "There hasn't been a demon attack since the Turn. Damn it, I knew I shouldn't have let her off the grounds."

The arms about me tensed. My weight shifted forward and back as he stopped. "Rachel knows what she's doing," Nick said tightly. "She isn't your child—in any sense of the word."

"No?" Ivy said. "She acts like one. How could you let her get mauled like this?"

"Me? You cold-blooded vamp!" Nick shouted. "You think I let this happen?"

My stomach clenched in a wave of nausea, and I tried to pull my coat over me with my good hand. I cracked my eyes, squinting in the glow of the streetlight. Couldn't they finish their argument after they put me to bed?

"Ivy," Nick said slowly. "I'm not afraid of you, so save the aura crap and back off. I know what you're up to, and I won't let you do it."

"What are you talking about?" Ivy stammered.

Nick leaned toward her, and I slumped unmoving between them. "Rachel seems to think you moved in the same day she did," he said. "She might be interested to know all your magazines are addressed to you at the church." I heard Ivy's quick intake of breath, and he added in an intent voice, "How long have you been living here waiting for Rachel to quit? A month? A year? Are you hunting her slow, Tamwood? Hoping to making her your scion when you die? Doing a little long-term planning, are we? Is that it?"

I struggled to turn my head from Nick's chest so I could hear better. I tried to think, but I was so confused. Ivy had moved in the same day I did, hadn't she? Her computer hadn't been hooked up to the net yet, and she had all those boxes in her room. How come her magazines had the church's address on them? My thoughts went to the perfect witch-garden out back and the spell books in the attic complete with alibi. God save me, I was a fool.

"No," Ivy said softly. "This isn't what it looks like. Please don't tell her. I can explain."

Nick lurched into motion, jostling me as he went up the stone stairs. My memory was returning. Nick had made a deal with the demon. Nick had let it out. It had made me go to sleep. It had made me go through the ley lines. Damn. The slam of the sanctuary door jolted me, and I moaned at the pulse of pain.

"She's coming around," Ivy said tersely, her voice echoing. "Put her in the living room."

Not the couch, I thought as the peaceful feeling of the sanctuary infused me. I didn't want to get my blood all over Ivy's couch, but then I decided it had probably seen blood before.

My stomach dropped as Nick crouched. I felt the gentle give of the cushions beneath my head. My breath hissed as Nick pulled his arms out from under me. There was the click of the table lamp, and I puckered my face at the sudden warmth and glare through my closed eyelids.

"Rachel?"

It was close, and someone gently touched my face.

"Rachel." The room got quiet. It was the hush that really woke me up. I opened my eyes, squinting to see Nick kneeling beside me. Blood still seeped from under his hairline, and a dried rivulet of it flaked from his jawline and neck. His hair was mussed and disheveled, and his brown eyes were pinched. He was a mess. Ivy was behind him, close in worry.

"It's you," I whispered, feeling light-headed and unreal. Nick leaned back with a relieved puff. "Can I have some water?" I rasped. "I don't feel so good."

Ivy leaned forward to eclipse the light. Her eyes roved over me with a professional detachment that cracked when she lifted the edge of Nick's makeshift bandage on my neck. Her eyes went puzzled. "It's almost stopped bleeding."

"Love, trust, and pixy dust," I slurred, and Ivy nodded.

Nick got to his feet. "I'll call an ambulance."

"No!" I exclaimed. I tried to sit up, forced back by fatigue and Nick's hands. "I'll get tagged there. The I.S. knows I'm alive." I fell back panting. The bruise on my face where the demon hit me pulsed in time with my heart. A twin throb came from my arm. I was dizzy. My shoulder hurt when I inhaled, and the room darkened when I exhaled.

"Jenks dusted her," Ivy said, as if that explained everything. "As long as she doesn't start bleeding again, she probably won't get any worse. I'll get a blanket." She rose with that eerie, fast grace of hers. She was going vampy, and I was in no condition to do anything about it.

I looked at Nick as she left. He seemed ill. The demon had tricked him. We had gotten home as promised, but now a demon was loose in Cincinnati when all Nick had needed to do was wait for Jenks and Ivy.

"Nick?" I breathed.

"What? What can I do?" His voice was worried and soft, tinged with guilt.

"You're an ass. Help me sit up."

He winced. With hands hesitant and cautious, he helped me inch my way up until my back was against the arm of the couch. I sat and stared at the ceiling while the black spots danced and quivered until they went away. Taking a slow breath, I looked at myself.

Blood splattered my dress where it showed past my coat draped over me like a blanket. Maybe now I could throw it away. A brown film of blood had stuck my nylons to my feet. My arm with the bite looked gray where it wasn't streaked with sticky blood. The hem of Nick's shirt was still tied around my wrist, and blood dripped wetly from it with the speed of a dripping faucet: plink, plink, plink. Maybe Jenks had run out of dust before he got to it. My other arm was swollen, and my shoulder felt like it was broken. The room got too cold, then hot. I stared at Nick, feeling myself go distant and unreal.

"Oh, shit," he muttered, glancing at the hallway. "You're going to pass out again." He grasped my ankles and slowly pulled me down until my head was supported by the arm of the couch. "Ivy!" he shouted. "Where's that blanket?"

I stared at the ceiling until it stopped spinning. Nick stood hunched in a corner with his back to me, one hand clenched about his middle, the other holding his head. "Thanks," I whispered, and he turned.

"What for?" His voice was bitter, and he looked ragged with dried blood on his face. His hands were black with it, the lines on his palms showing a stark white.

"For doing what you thought was best." I shivered under my coat.

He smiled sickly, his pale face going longer. "There was so much blood. I guess I panicked. Sorry." His gaze went to the hallway, and I wasn't surprised when Ivy strode in with a blanket over one arm, a stack of pink towels under the other, and a pan of water in her hands.

Unease overwhelmed my pain. I was still bleeding. "Ivy?" I quavered.

"What?" she snapped as she set the towels and water on the coffee table and tucked the blanket around me as if I was a child.

I swallowed hard, trying to get a good look at her eyes. "Nothing," I said meekly as she straightened and backed away. Apart from being paler than usual, she looked okay. I didn't think I could handle it if she vamped out on me. I was helpless.

The blanket was warm about my chin, and the light from the lamp piercing. I shivered as she sat on the coffee table and pulled the water closer. I wondered at the color of the towels until I realized pink didn't show old bloodstains.

"Ivy?" My voice edged into panic as she reached for the cloth pressed against my neck.

Her hand dropped, her perfect face going angry and insulted. "Don't be stupid, Rachel. Let me look at your neck."

She reached out again, and I shirked back. "No!" I cried as I jerked away. The demon's face flashed before me, mirroring hers. I hadn't been able to fight it. It almost killed me. Remembered terror soared high, and I found the strength to sit up. The pain in my neck seemed to cry out for release, for a return to that exquisite mix of pain and craving the vamp saliva had offered. It shocked and frightened me. Ivy's pupils swelled until her eyes went black.

Nick stepped between us, covered in drying blood and smelling of spent fear. "Back off, Tamwood," he threatened. "You're not touching her if you're pulling an aura."

"Relax, rat boy," Ivy exclaimed. "I'm not pulling an aura, I'm as mad as all hell. And I wouldn't bite Rachel right now even if she begged me. She stinks of infection."

That was more than I wanted to know. But her eyes were back to her normal brown as she wavered between anger and the need to be understood. I felt a flush of guilt. Ivy hadn't pinned me to the wall and bit me. Ivy hadn't taunted me, driving her teeth into me. Ivy hadn't sucked at my neck, moaning in pleasure as she held me down while I struggled. Damn it. It. Hadn't. Been. Her.

Still, Nick stood between us. "It's all right, Nick," I said, my voice trembling. He knew why I was afraid. "It's all right." I looked past him to Ivy. "I'm sorry. Please—look at it?"

Immediately Ivy seemed to lose her tension. She scooted closer with a quick, vindicated motion as Nick stepped out of the way. I let out my held breath as she gently worked at the soggy fabric. "Okay," Ivy warned. "This may tug a little."

"Ouch!" I cried as it pulled when she lifted, then I bit my lip to keep from doing it again. Ivy set the ugly wad on the table beside her. My stomach twisted. It was black with moist blood, and I swear there were bits of flesh sticking to the inside of it. I shivered at the cold feel of air on my neck. There was the shivery sensation of a slow flow of blood.

Ivy saw my face. "Get that out of here, will you?" she murmured, and Nick left with the soggy wad.

Face blank, Ivy put a hand towel across my shoulder to catch the renewed oozing. I stared at the black TV as she soaked a washcloth and rung it out over the pan of water. Her touch was gentle as she began to dab at the outskirts of the damage and worked her way in. Still, I couldn't help my occasional jerk. The threatened rim of black around my vision began to grow.

"Rachel?" Her voice was soft, and my attention darted to her, worried at what I would find. But her face was carefully neutral as her eyes and fingers probed the bite marks on my neck. "What happened?" she asked. "Nick said something about a demon, but this looks like—"

"It looks like a vampire bite," I finished blandly. "It made itself look like a vampire and did that to me." I took a shaky breath. "It made itself look like you, Ivy. I'm sorry if I'm a little flaky for a while. I know it wasn't you. Just give me some slack until I can convince my unconscious you didn't try to kill me, okay?"

I met her eyes, feeling a pulse of shared fear as understanding flashed over her. For all accounts, I had been ravaged by a vampire. I had been initiated into a club that Ivy was trying to stay out of. Now we both were. I thought about what Nick had said concerning her wanting to make me her scion. I didn't know what to believe.

"Rachel, I—"

"Later," I said as Nick came back in. I felt ill, and the room was starting to go gray again. Matalina was with him along with two of her children lugging a pixy-sized bag. Nick knelt at my head. Hovering in the center of the room, Matalina silently took in the situation, then took the bag from her children and bundled them to the window. "Hush, hush," I heard her whisper. "Go home. I know what I said, but I changed my mind." Their protests carried a horrified fascination, and I wondered how bad I looked.

"Rachel?" Matalina hovered right in front of me, moving back and forth until she found where my eyes were focusing. The room had gone alarmingly quiet, and I shivered. Matalina was such a pretty little thing. No wonder Jenks would do anything for her. "Try not to move, dear," she said.

A soft whir from the window pulled her up out of my sight. "Jenks," the small pixy woman said in relief. "Where have you been?"

"Me?" He dropped into my line of sight. "How did you get here before me?"

"We took a direct bus," Nick said sarcastically.

Jenks's face was weary and his shoulders were slumped. I felt a smile curve over me. "Is pretty pixy man too pooped to party?" I breathed, and he came so close I had to squint.

"Ivy, you gotta do something," he said, his eyes wide and worried. "I dusted her bites to slow the bleeding, but I've never seen anyone that was this white before and still alive."

"I am doing something," she growled. "Get out of my way."

I felt the air shift as Matalina and Ivy bent close over me. I found the idea of a pixy and a vamp inspecting the bloody mess of my neck reassuring. Since infection was a turnoff, I ought to be safe. Ivy would know if it was life-threatening or not. *And Nick,* I thought, feeling a faint need to giggle. *Nick would rescue me if Ivy lost control.*

Ivy's fingers touched my neck and I yelped. She jerked back, and Matalina took to the air. "Rachel," Ivy said worriedly. "I can't fix this. Pixy dust will hold you together for only so long. You need to be stitched. We have to get you to Emergency."

"No hospital," I said with a sigh. I had stopped shivering, and my stomach felt all funny. "Runners go in, but they don't come out." I gave in to my desire to giggle.

"You would rather die on my couch?" Ivy said, and Nick began to pace behind her.

"What is wrong with her?" Jenks whispered loudly.

Ivy stood up and crossed her arms to look severe and pissy. A pissy vampire. Yeah, that was funny enough to laugh at, and I giggled again.

"It's the blood loss," Ivy said impatiently. "She's going to yo-yo between lucidity and irrationality until she stabilizes or passes out. I hate this part."

My good hand crept up to my neck, and Nick forced it back under the blanket.

"I can't fix this, Rachel!" Ivy exclaimed in frustration. "There's too much damage."

"I'll make something," I said firmly. "I'm a witch." I leaned to roll off the couch and get to my feet. I had to go to the kitchen. I had to cook dinner. I had to cook dinner for Ivy.

"Rachel!" Nick shouted, trying to catch me. Ivy leapt forward, easing me into the cushions. I felt myself go white. The room spun. Wide-eyed, I stared at the ceiling, willing myself not to pass out. If I did, Ivy would take me to Emergency.

Matalina drifted within my sight. "Angel," I whispered. "Beautiful angel."

"Ivy!" Jenks shouted, fear in his voice. "She's getting delusional."

The pixy angel smiled a blessing on me. "Someone should go get Keasley," she said.

"The old lunker—uh—witch across the street?" Jenks said.

Matalina nodded. "Tell him Rachel needs medical help."

Ivy, too, seemed bewildered. "You think he can do something?" she asked, the edge of fear in her voice. Ivy was afraid for me. Maybe I should have been afraid for me, too.

Matalina flushed. "He asked—the other day—if he might have a few cuttings from the garden. There's no harm in that." The pretty pixy fussed with her dress, her eyes downcast. "They were all plants with strong properties. Yarrow, vervain, that sort. I thought perhaps if he wanted them, he might know what to do with them."

"Woman . . ." Jenks said warningly.

"I stayed with him the entire time," she said, her eyes defiant. "He didn't touch but what I said he could. He was very proper. Asked after everyone's health."

"Matalina, it's not our garden," Jenks said, and the angel grew angry.

"If you won't get him, I will," she said sharply, and she darted out the window. I blinked, staring at the spot where she had been.

"Matalina!" Jenks shouted. "Don't you fly from me. That's not our garden. You can't treat it as if it was." He dropped into my line of sight. "I'm sorry," he said, clearly embarrassed and angry. "She won't do it again." His face hardened, and he darted out after her. "Matalina!"

" 'S okay," I whispered, though neither of them were there anymore. "I say it's okay. The angel can ask anyone she wants into the garden." I closed my eyes. Nick put a hand on my head, and I smiled. "Hi, Nick," I said softly, opening my eyes. "Are you still here?"

"Yes, I'm still here."

"Good," I said. " 'Cause when I can stand up, I'm going to give you a bi-i-i-g kiss."

Nick's hand fell from me and he took a step back.

Ivy grimaced. "I hate this part," she muttered. "I hate it. I hate it."

My hand crept up to my neck, and Nick forced it back down. I could hear the faucet dripping again on the carpet: plink, plink, plink. The room began to revolve majestically, and I watched it spin, fascinated. It was funny, and I tried to laugh.

Ivy made a frustrated sound. "If she's giggling, she's going to be all right," she said. "Why don't you take a shower?"

"I'm okay," he said. "I'll wait until I know for sure."

Ivy was silent for three heartbeats. "Nick," she said, her voice thick with warning. "Rachel stinks of infection. You stink of blood and fear. Go take a shower."

"Oh." There was a long hesitation. "Sorry."

I smiled up at Nick as he edged to the door. "Go wash, Nick

Nicky," I said. "Don't make Ivy go all black and scary. Take as long as you want. There's soap in the dish, and . . ." I hesitated, trying to remember what I was saying. ". . . and towels on the dryer," I finished, proud of myself.

He touched my shoulder, his eyes flicking from me to Ivy. "You should be all right."

Ivy crossed her arms before her, impatiently waiting for him to leave. I heard the shower go on. It made me a hundred times more thirsty. Somewhere, I could feel my arm pounding and my ribs throbbing. My neck and shoulder were one solid ache. I turned to watch the curtain move in the breeze, fascinated.

A loud boom from the front of the church pulled my attention to the black hallway. "Hello?" came Keasley's distant voice. "Ms. Morgan? Matalina said I could walk in."

Ivy's lips pursed. "Stay here," she said, bending over me until I had no choice but to look at her. "Don't get up until I get back, okay? Rachel? Do you hear me? *Don't get up.*"

"Sure." My gaze drifted past her to the curtain. If I squinted ju-u-u-u-ust right, the gray shifted to black. "Stay here."

Giving me a last look, she gathered up all her magazines and left. The sound of the shower drew me. I licked my lips. I wondered, if I tried really hard, could I reach the sink in the kitchen?

Twenty-seven

There was the rattle of a paper bag in the hallway, and I tilted my head up from the arm of the couch. The room held steady this time, and a fog seemed to lift from me. Keasley's hunched figure came in, Ivy close behind. "Oh, good," I whispered breathlessly. "Company."

Ivy pushed past Keasley and sat on the end of the chair nearest me. "You look better," she said. "Are you back yet or still in la-la land?"

"What?"

She shook her head, and I gave Keasley a wan smile. "Sorry I can't offer you a chocolate."

"Ms. Morgan." His gaze lingered on my exposed neck. "Have an argument with your roommate?" he said dryly as he ran a hand over his tightly curled black hair.

"No," I said hurriedly as Ivy stiffened.

He arched his eyebrows in disbelief and set his paper bag on the coffee table. "Matalina didn't say what I needed, so I brought a little of everything." He squinted at the table lamp. "Do you have anything brighter than that?"

"I've got a clip-on fluorescent." Ivy slipped to the hall and hesitated. "Don't let her move or she'll go incoherent again."

I opened my mouth to say something, but she vanished, to be replaced by Matalina and Jenks. Jenks looked positively incensed, but Matalina was unrepentant. They hovered in the corner, their conversation so fast and high-pitched I couldn't follow it. Finally Jenks left, looking like he was going to murder a pea pod.

Matalina adjusted her flowing white dress and flitted to the arm of the couch beside my head.

Keasley sat down on the coffee table with a weary sigh. His three-day-old beard was going white. It made him look like a vagrant. The knees of his overalls were stained with wet earth, and I could smell the outside on him. His dark-skinned hands, though, were raw from an obvious scrubbing. He pulled a newspaper out from his bag and spread it open like a tablecloth. "So who's that in the shower? Your mother?"

I snorted, feeling the tightness of my swollen eye. "His name is Nick," I said as Ivy appeared. "He's a friend."

Ivy made a rude sound as she attached a small light to the shade of the table lamp and plugged it in. I winced, squinting as heat and light poured out.

"Nick, eh?" Keasley said as he dug in his bag, laying amulets, foil-wrapped packages, and bottles onto the newsprint. "A vamp, is he?"

"No, he's a human," I said, and Keasley peered mistrustingly at Ivy.

Not seeing his look, Ivy crowded close. "Her neck is the worst. She's lost a dangerous amount of blood—"

"I can tell." The old man stared belligerently at Ivy until she backed up. "I need more towels, and why don't you get Rachel something to drink? She needs to replace her fluids."

"I know that," Ivy said, taking a faltering step backward before turning to go into the kitchen. There was the clatter of a glass and the welcoming sound of liquid. Matalina opened her repair kit and silently compared her needles to Keasley's.

"Something warm?" Keasley reiterated loudly, and Ivy slammed the freezer door shut. "Let's take a look," he said as he aimed the light at me. He and Matalina were silent for a long time. Easing back, Keasley let his breath slip from him. "Perhaps something to dull that pain, first," he said softly, reaching for an amulet.

Ivy appeared in the archway. "Where did you get those spells?" she said suspiciously.

"Relax," he said with a distant voice as he inspected each disk carefully. "I bought these months ago. Make yourself useful and boil up a pan of water."

She snuffed and spun about, storming back into the kitchen. I heard a series of clicks followed by the whoosh of the gas igniting. The taps ran full force as she filled a pan, and a faint yelp of surprise came from my bathroom.

Keasley had bloodied his finger and invoked the spell before I realized it. The amulet settled around my neck, and after looking me square in the eye to gauge its effectiveness, he turned his attention to my neck. "I really appreciate this," I said as the first fingers of relief eased into my body and my shoulders drooped. Salvation.

"I'd hold off on the thanks till you get my bill," Keasley murmured. I frowned at the old joke, and he smiled, crinkling the folds around his eyes. Resettling himself, he prodded my skin. The pain broke through the spell, and I took a sharp breath. "Still hurt?" he asked needlessly.

"Why don't you just put her out?" Ivy asked.

I started. Damn it, I hadn't even heard her come in. "No," I said sharply. I didn't want Ivy convincing him to take me to Emergency.

"It wouldn't hurt, then," Ivy said, standing belligerently in her leather and silk. "Why do you have to do things the hard way?"

"I'm not doing things the hard way, I just don't want to be put out," I argued. My vision darkened, and I concentrated on breathing before I put myself out.

"Ladies," Keasley murmured into the tension. "I agree sedating Rachel would be easier, especially on her, but I'm not going to force it."

"Thanks," I said listlessly.

"A few more pans of water, perhaps, Ivy?" Keasley asked. "And those towels?"

The microwave dinged, and Ivy spun away. What bee had stung her bonnet? I wondered.

Keasley invoked a second amulet and settled it next to the first. It was another pain charm, and I slumped into the double relief and closed my eyes. They flashed open as Ivy set a mug of hot chocolate on the coffee table, closely followed by a stack of more pink towels. With a misplaced frustration, she returned to the kitchen to slam about under the counter.

From under the blanket, I slowly pulled out the arm the demon had struck. The swelling had gone down, and a small knot of worry loosened. It wasn't broken. I wiggled my fingers, and Keasley put the hot chocolate into my grip. The mug was comfortingly warm, and the hot chocolate slid down my throat with a protective feeling.

While I sipped my drink, Keasley packed the towels around my right shoulder. Taking a squeeze bottle from his bag, he washed the last of the blood from my neck, soaking the towels. His brown eyes intent, he began to probe the tissue. "Ow!" I yelped, nearly spilling my hot chocolate as I jerked away. "Do you really need to do that?"

Keasley grunted and put a third amulet around my neck. "Better?" he asked. My sight had blurred at the strength of the spell. I wondered where he got such a strong charm, then remembered he had arthritis. It took one heck of a strong spell to touch pain like that, and I felt guilty that he was using his medicinal charm on me. This time I only felt a dull pressure as he poked and prodded, and I nodded. "How long since you were bit?" he asked.

"Um," I murmured, fighting off the drowsy state the amulet was instilling. "Sunset?"

"It's what, just after nine now?" he said, glancing at the clock on the disc player. "Good. We can stitch you all the way up." Settling himself, he took on the air of an instructor, beckoning Matalina close. "Look here," he said to the pixy woman. "See how the tissue has been sliced rather than torn? I'd rather stitch up a vamp bite than a Were bite any day. Not only is it cleaner, but you don't have to de-enzyme it."

Matalina drifted closer. "Thorn spears leave cuts like this, but I've never been able to find anything to hold the muscle in place while the ends reattach."

Blanching, I gulped my hot chocolate, wishing they would stop talking as if I was a science experiment or slab of meat for the grill.

"I use vet-grade dissolvable sutures, myself," Keasley said.

"Vet-grade?" I said, startled.

"No one keeps track of animal clinics," he said absently. "But I've heard the vein that runs the stem of a bay leaf is strong enough for fairies and pixies. I wouldn't use anything but catgut for the wing muscles, though. Want some?" He dug in his bag and put several small paper envelopes on the table. "Consider it payment for those slips of plants."

Matalina's wings colored a delicate rose. "Those weren't my plants to give."

"Yes, they were," I interrupted. "I'm getting fifty taken off my rent for keeping up the garden. I guess that makes it mine. But you're the ones tending it. I say that makes it yours."

Keasley looked up from my neck. A shocked stare came over Matalina.

"Consider it Jenks's income," I added. "That is, if you think he might want to sublet the garden as his pay."

For a moment there was silence. "I think he might like that," Matalina whispered. She shifted the small envelopes to her bag. Leaving them, she darted to the window and back again, clearly torn. Her fluster at my offer was obvious. Wondering if I had done something wrong, I looked over Keasley's paraphernalia laid out on the newspaper.

"Are you a doctor?" I asked, setting my empty mug down with a thump. I had to remember to get the recipe for this spell. I couldn't feel a thing—anywhere.

"No." He wadded up the water and blood-soaked towels, throwing them to the floor.

"Then where did you get all this stuff?" I prodded.

"I don't like hospitals," he said shortly. "Matalina? Why don't I do the interior stitching and you close the skin? I'm sure your work is more even than mine." He smiled ruefully. "I'd wager Rachel would appreciate the smaller scar."

"It helps to be an inch from the wound," Matalina said, clearly pleased to have been asked.

Keasley swabbed my neck with a cold gel. I studied the ceiling as he took a pair of scissors and trimmed what I assumed were ragged edges. Making a satisfied noise, he chose a needle and thread. There was a pressure on my neck followed by a tug, and I took a deep breath. My eyes flicked to Ivy as she came in and bent close over me, almost blocking Keasley's light.

"What about that one?" she said, pointing. "Shouldn't you stitch that first?" she said. "It's bleeding the most."

"No," he said, making another stitch. "Get another pot of water boiling, will you?"

"Four pots of water?" she questioned.

"If you would," he drawled. Keasley continued stitching, and I counted the tugs, my gaze on the clock. The chocolate wasn't sitting as well as I would have liked. I hadn't been stitched since my ex–best friend had hidden in my school locker pretending to be a werefox. The day had ended with us both being expelled.

Ivy hesitated, then scooped up the wet towels and took them into the kitchen. The water ran, and another cry followed by a muffled thump came from my shower. "Will you stop doing that!" came an annoyed shout, and I couldn't help my smirk. All too soon Ivy was back peering over Keasley's shoulder.

"That stitch doesn't look tight," she said.

I shifted uncomfortably as Keasley's wrinkled brow furrowed. I liked him, and Ivy was being a bloody nuisance. "Ivy," he murmured, "why don't you do a perimeter check?"

"Jenks is outside. We're fine."

Keasley's jaw clenched, the folds of skin on his jaw bunching. He slowly pulled the green thread tight, his eyes on his work. "He might need help," he said.

Ivy straightened with her arms crossed and black hazing her eyes. "I doubt that."

Matalina's wings blurred to nothing as Ivy bent close, blocking Keasley's light.

"Go away," Keasley said softly, not moving. "You're hovering."

Ivy pulled back, her mouth opening in what looked like shock. Her wide eyes went to mine, and I smiled in an apologetic agreement. Stiffening, she spun round. Her boots clacked on the wood floor in the hallway and into the sanctuary. I winced as the loud boom of the front door reverberated through the church.

"Sorry," I said, feeling someone ought to apologize.

Keasley stretched his back painfully. "She's worried about you and doesn't know how to show it without biting you. Either that or she doesn't like being out of control."

"She's not the only one," I said. "I'm starting to feel like a failure."

"Failure?" he breathed. "How do you stir that?"

"Look at me," I said sharply. "I'm a wreck. I've lost so much blood I can't stand up. I haven't done anything by myself since I left the I.S. except get caught by Trent and made into rat chow." I didn't feel much like a runner anymore. *Dad would be disappointed*, I thought. I should have stayed where I was, safe, secure, and bored out of my mind.

"You're alive," Keasley said. "That's no easy trick while under an I.S. death threat." He adjusted the lamp until it shone right in my face. I closed my eyes, starting as he dabbed a cold pad at my swollen eyelid. Matalina took over stitching my neck, her tiny tugs almost unnoticed. She ignored us with the practiced restraint of a professional mother.

"I'd be dead twice over if it wasn't for Nick," I said, looking toward the unseen shower.

Keasley aimed the lamp at my ear. I jerked as he dabbed at it with a soft square of damp cotton. It came away black with old blood. "You would have escaped Kalamack eventually," he said.

"Instead, you took a chance and got Nick out as well. I don't see the failure in that."

I squinted at him with my unswollen eye. "How do you know about the rat fight?"

"Jenks told me on the way over."

Satisfied, I winced as Keasley dabbed a foul-smelling liquid on my torn ear. It throbbed dully under the three pain amulets. "I can't do anything more about this," he said. "Sorry."

I had all but forgotten about my ear. Matalina flitted up to eye level, her gaze shifting from Keasley to me. "All done," she said in her china-doll voice. "If you can finish up all right, I would like to, um . . ." Her eyes were charmingly eager. An angel with glad tidings. "I want to tell Jenks about your offer to sublet the garden."

Keasley nodded. "You go right ahead," he said. "There's not much left but her wrist."

"Thanks, Matalina," I offered. "I didn't feel a thing."

"You're welcome." The tiny pixy woman darted to the window, then returned. "Thank you," she whispered before vanishing through the window and into the dark garden.

The living room was empty but for Keasley and me. It was so quiet, I could hear the lids popping on the pots of water in the kitchen. Keasley took the scissors and cut the soaked cotton off my wrist. It fell away, and my stomach roiled. My wrist was still there, but nothing was in the right place. No wonder Jenks's pixy dust couldn't stop it from bleeding. Chunks of white flesh were lumped into mounds, and little craters were filled with blood. If my wrist looked like that, what had my neck looked like? Closing my eyes, I concentrated on breathing. I was going to pass out. I knew it.

"You've made a strong ally there," he said softly.

"Matalina?" I held my breath, trying not to hyperventilate. "I can't imagine why," I said as I exhaled. "I've continually put her husband and family at risk."

"Mmmm." He put Ivy's pan of water on his knees and gently lowered my wrist into it. I hissed at the bite of the water, then relaxed as the pain amulets dulled it. He prodded my wrist and I yelped, trying to jerk away. "You want some advice?" he asked.

"No."

"Good. Listen anyway. Looks to me like you've become the leader here. Accept it. Know it comes with a price. People will be doing things for you. Don't be selfish. Let them."

"I owe Nick and Jenks my life," I said, hating it. "What's so great about that?"

"No, you don't. Because of you, Nick no longer has to kill rats to stay alive, and Jenks's life expectancy has nearly doubled."

I pulled away, and this time he let me go. "How do you figure that?" I said suspiciously.

The resonate *tang* of the pan hitting the coffee table was sharp as Keasley set it aside. He tucked a pink towel under my wrist, and I forced myself to look at it. The tissue looked more normal. A slow welling of blood rose to hide the damage, spilling over my wet skin to flow messily onto the towel.

"You made Jenks a partner," he said as he ripped open a gauze pad and dabbed at me. "He has more at risk than a job, he has a garden. Tonight you made it his for as long as he wants. I've never heard of leasing property to a pixy, but I would wager it will hold up in a human or Inderland court if another clan challenged it. You guaranteed that *all* his children have a place to survive until adulthood, not just the few firstborn. I think that's worth an afternoon of hide-and-seek in a room full of lunkers to him."

I watched him thread a needle and forced my eyes to the ceiling. The tugs and pinches started up with a slow rhythm. Everyone knew pixies and fairies vied with each other for a good bit of earth, but I had no idea the reasons went so deep. I thought about what Jenks had said about risking death by a bee sting for a pair of measly flower boxes. Now he had a garden. No wonder Matalina had been so matter-of-fact about the fairy attack.

Keasley fell into a pattern of two stitches, one dab. The thing wouldn't stop bleeding. I refused to watch, my eyes roving over the gray living room until they fell upon the empty end table where Ivy's magazines had once sat. I swallowed hard, feeling nauseous. "Keasley, you've lived here awhile, right?" I questioned. "When did Ivy move in?"

He looked up from his stitching, his dark, wrinkled face blank. "The same day you did. You quit the same day, didn't you?"

I caught myself before I could nod my agreement. "I can see why Jenks is risking his life to help me, but . . ." I looked at the hallway. "What is Ivy getting out of this?" I whispered.

Keasley looked at my neck in disgust. "Isn't it obvious? You let her feed off you, and she won't let the I.S. kill you."

My mouth opened in outrage. "I already told you Ivy didn't do this!" I exclaimed, my heart pounding in the effort to raise my voice. "It was a demon!"

He didn't look as surprised as I would have expected. He stared at me, waiting for more. "I left the church to get a recipe for a spell," I said softly. "The I.S. sent a demon after me. It made itself into a vampire to kill me. Nick bound it in a circle or it would have." I slumped, exhausted. My pulse hammered. I was too weak to even be angry.

"The I.S.?" Keasley cut his needle free and glanced at me from under his lowered brow. "Are you sure it was a demon? The I.S. doesn't use demons."

"They do now," I said sourly. I looked at my wrist, then quickly away. It was still bleeding, the blood oozing from between the green stitches. I reached up to find my neck at least had stopped. "It knew all three of my names, Keasley. My middle name isn't even on my birth certificate. How did the I.S. find out what it was?"

Keasley's eyes were worried as he blotted at my wrist. "Well, if it was a demon, you won't have to worry about any residual vamp ties from your bites—I'd imagine."

"Small favors," I said bitterly.

He took my wrist again, pulling the lamp closer. He cupped a towel under it to catch the still-dripping blood. "Rachel?" he murmured.

Alarm bells rang in the back of my mind. I'd always been Ms. Morgan to him. "What?"

"About the demon. Did you make a deal with it?"

I followed his gaze to my wrist and went frightened. "Nick did," I said quickly. "He agreed to let it out of the circle if it got me back here alive. It took us through the ley lines."

"Oh," he said, and I felt myself go cold at his flat tone. He knew something I didn't.

"Oh, what?" I demanded. "What's the matter?"

He took a slow breath. "This isn't going to heal on its own," he said softly, setting my wrist on my lap.

"What?" I exclaimed, holding my wrist as my stomach churned and the chocolate threatened to come back up. The shower went off, and I felt a flash of panic. What had Nick done to me?

Keasley opened a medicated adhesive bandage and applied it over my eye. "Demons don't do anything for free," he said. "You owe it a favor."

"I didn't agree to anything!" I said. "It was Nick! I told Nick not to let it out!"

"It's not anything Nick did," Keasley said as he took my bruised arm and gently prodded it until my breath hissed in. "The demon wants additional payment for taking you through the ley lines. You have a choice, though. You can pay for your passage by having your wrist drip blood the rest of your life, or you can agree to owe the demon a favor and it will heal. I'd suggest the former."

I collapsed into the cushions. "Swell." Just freaking great. I'd told Nick it was a bad idea.

Keasley pulled my wrist to him and started winding a roll of gauze bandage around it. Blood soaked it almost as quickly as it went about my wrist. "Don't let it tell you that you don't have a say in the matter," he said as he used the entire roll, fastening the end with a bit of white medical tape. "You can dicker about how to pay for your passage until you both agree on something. Years, even. Demons always give you choices. And they're patient."

"Some choice!" I barked. "Agree to owe him a favor or walk around like I've got stigmata the rest of my life?"

He shrugged as he gathered his needles, thread, and scissors on his newspaper and folded it up. "I think you did pretty well for your first run-in with a demon."

"First run-in!" I exclaimed, then lay back panting. *First? Like there was ever going to be a second.* "How do you know all this?" I whispered.

He stuffed the newspaper in the bag and rolled the top down. "You live long enough, you hear things."

"Great." I looked up as Keasley pulled the heavy-duty pain amulet from around my neck. "Hey," I objected as all my pains started back in with a dull throbbing. "I need that."

"You'll do fine with just two." He stood up and dropped my salvation into a pocket. "That way, you won't hurt yourself by trying to do anything. Leave those stitches in for about a week. Matalina can tell you when to take them out. No shape shifting, meantime." He pulled out a sling and set it on the coffee table. "Wear it," he said simply. "Your arm is bruised, not broken." He arched his white eyebrows. "Lucky you."

"Keasley, wait." I took a quick breath, trying to gather my thoughts. "What can I do for you? An hour ago I thought I was dying."

"An hour ago, you were dying." He chuckled, then shifted from foot to foot. "It's important you don't owe anyone anything, isn't it?" He hesitated. "I envy you for your friends. I'm old enough not to be afraid to say that. Friends are a luxury I haven't indulged in for a long time. If you let me trust you, consider us even."

"But that's nothing," I protested. "Do you want more plants from the garden? Or a mink potion? They're good for a few days more, and I won't be using them again."

"I wouldn't count on that," he said, glancing into the hall at the sound of my bathroom door creaking open. "And being someone I trust might be expensive. I might call in my marker someday. Are you willing to risk it?"

"Of course," I said, wondering what an old man like Keasley could be running from. It couldn't be worse than what I was facing. The door to the sanctuary boomed shut, and I straightened. Ivy was done sulking and Nick was out of the shower. They were going to be at each other again in a moment, and I was too tired to play referee. Jenks buzzed in through the window, and I closed my eyes to gather my strength. All three of them at once might kill me.

Bag in hand, Keasley shifted as if to go. "Please, don't leave yet," I pleaded. "Nick might need something. He has a nasty cut on his head."

"Rache," Jenks said as he flew circles around Keasley in greeting. "What the devil did you say to Matalina? She's flitting over the garden as if she's on Brimstone, laughing and crying all at the same time. Can't get a straight word out of the woman." He jerked to a stop, hovering in midair, listening.

"Oh, great," he muttered. "They're at it again already."

I exchanged a weary look with Keasley as the muttered conversation in the hall came to an intent but quiet finish. Ivy walked in with a satisfied look. Nick was quick behind her. His scowl melted into a smile when he saw me upright and clearly feeling better. He had changed into an oversized white cotton T-shirt and a clean pair of baggy jeans fresh from the dryer. His charming half smile didn't work on me. The thought of why my wrist was bleeding was too real.

"You must be Keasley?" Nick asked, holding out his hand over the table as if nothing was wrong. "I'm Nick."

Keasley cleared his throat and took his hand. "Nice to meet you," he said, his words at odds with the disapproving look on his old face. "Rachel wants me to look at your forehead."

"I'm fine. It quit bleeding in the shower."

"Really." The old man's eyes narrowed. "Rachel's wrist won't quit."

Nick's face went slack. His gaze darted to me. His mouth opened, then shut. I glared at him. Damn it all to hell. He knew exactly what that meant. "It—um . . ." he whispered.

"What?" Ivy prompted. Jenks landed on her shoulder, and she brushed him off.

Nick ran a hand over his chin and said nothing. Nick and I were going to talk. . . . We were going to talk real soon. Keasley aggressively shoved his paper bag into Nick's chest. "Hold this while I get Rachel's bath started. I want to make sure her core temp is where it should be."

Nick meekly backed up. Ivy looked suspiciously between the three of us. "A bath," I said brightly, not wanting her to know anything was wrong. She'd probably kill Nick if she knew what had happened. "That sounds great." I pushed my blanket and coat off of me and swung my feet to the floor. The room darkened and I felt my face go cold.

"Slow up," Keasley said as he put a dark hand on my shoulder. "Wait until it's ready."

I took a deep breath, refusing to put my head between my knees. It was so undignified.

Nick looked sick as he stood in the corner. "Uh," he stammered. "You might have to wait for that bath. I think I used all the hot water."

"Good," I breathed, "that's what I told you to do." But inside I was withering.

Keasley harrumphed. "That's what the pans of water are for."

Ivy scowled. "Why didn't you say so," she grumbled as she walked out. "I'll do it."

"Mind that her bath isn't too hot," Keasley called after her.

"I know how to treat severe blood loss," she yelled belligerently.

"That you probably do, missy." Straightening, he backed a startled Nick into the wall. "You tell Ms. Morgan what she can expect concerning her wrist," he said, taking his bag back.

Nick nodded once, looking surprised by the short, innocuous-seeming witch.

"Rache," Jenks said, buzzing close. "What's going on with your wrist?"

"Nothing."

"What's going on with your wrist, Hot Stuff?"

"Nothing!" I waved him away, almost panting from the effort.

"Jenks?" Ivy called loudly over the distant sound of water flowing. "Get me that black bag on my dresser, will you? I want to put it in Rachel's bath."

"The one that stinks like vervain?" he called, rising up to hover before me.

"You've been in my stuff!" she accused, and Jenks grinned sheepishly. "And hurry up about it," she added. "The sooner Rachel is in the tub, the sooner we can get out of here. As long as she's all right, we need to see about finishing her run."

The recollection of Trent's shipment came flooding back. I looked at the clock and sighed. There was still time to get to the FIB and nail him. But I was not going to be taking part in it in any way, shape, or form.

Swell.

Twenty-eight

Bubbles, I thought, *ought to be marketed as a medicinal inducement for well-being.* I sighed, scooting myself up before my neck could slip under the water. Dulled by amulets and warm water, my bruises had retreated to a background throb. Even my wrist, propped high and dry on the side of the tub, felt reasonable. Faintly through the walls, I could hear Nick talking to his mother on the phone, telling her that work had gotten really hectic the last three months and that he was sorry he hadn't called. Otherwise, the church was quiet. Jenks and Ivy were gone. "Out doing my job," I whispered, my complacent mood going sour.

"What's that, Ms. Rachel?" Matalina piped up. The small pixy woman was perched on a towel rack, looking like an angel in her flowing white silk dress as she embroidered dogwood blossoms on an exquisite shawl for her eldest daughter. She had been with me since I got in the tub, making sure I didn't pass out and drown.

"Nothing." I laboriously lifted my bruised arm and drew a mound of bubbles closer. The water was going cold and my stomach was rumbling. Ivy's bathroom looked eerily like my mother's, with tiny soaps in the shape of shells, and lacy curtains over the stained-glass window. A vase of violets rested on the back of the commode, and I was surprised a vamp cared about such things. The tub was black, contrasting nicely with the pastel walls and rosebud wallpaper.

Matalina set her stitching aside and flitted down to hover over black porcelain. "Should your amulets get wet like that?"

I glanced at the pain charms draped around my neck, thinking

I looked like a drunken prostitute at Mardi Gras. "It's okay," I breathed. "Soapy water won't dissolution them like saltwater does."

"Ms. Tamwood wouldn't tell me what she put in your bath," Matalina said primly. "There might be salt in it."

Ivy hadn't told me, either, and to tell the truth, I didn't want to know. "No salt. I asked."

With a small harrumph, Matalina landed on my big toe, poking above the water. Her wings blurred to nothing, and a clear spot formed as the bubbles melted. Gathering her skirts, she cautiously bent to dip a hand, to bring a drop up to her nose. Tiny ripples spread out from her touch on the water.

"Vervain," she said in her high voice. "My Jenks was right, there. Bloodroot. Goldenseal." Her eyes met mine. "That's used to cover up something potent. What is she trying to hide?"

I looked at the ceiling. If it took away the pain, I really didn't care.

There was a creak of floorboards in the hall, and I froze. "Nick?" I called, looking at my towel just out of reach. "I'm still in the tub. Don't come in!"

He scuffed to a halt, the thin veneered wood between us. "Uh, hi, Rachel. I was just, uh, checking on you." There was a hesitation. "I—um—need to talk to you."

My stomach clenched, and my attention fell upon my wrist. It was still bleeding through a wad of gauze an inch thick. The rivulet of blood on the black porcelain looked like a welt. Maybe that's why Ivy had a black tub. Blood didn't show up as well on black as it did on white.

"Rachel?" he called into the quiet.

"I'm okay," I said loudly, my voice echoing off the pink walls. "Give me a minute to get out of the tub, all right? I want to talk to you, too—little wizard."

I said the last snidely, and I heard his feet shift. "I'm not a wizard," he said faintly. He hesitated. "Are you hungry? Can I make you something to eat?" He sounded guilty.

"Yeah. Thanks," I replied, wishing he would get away from the door. I was ravenous. My appetite probably had everything to do with that cakelike cookie Ivy made me eat before she left. It was as appetizing as a rice pancake, and only after I had choked it down did Ivy bother to tell me it would increase my metabolism, especially my blood production. I could still taste it on the back of my throat. Sort of a mix between almonds, bananas, and shoe leather.

Nick scuffed away, and I stretched with my foot for the tap to warm the water. The water heater was probably hot by now.

"Don't warm it, dear," Matalina warned. "Ivy said to get out once it went cold."

A wave of irritation swept me. I knew what Ivy had said. But I refrained from comment.

I slowly sat up and moved to sit on the edge of the tub. The room seemed to darken around the edges, and I abruptly wrapped a fluffy pink towel around myself in case I passed out. When the room stopped going gray, I pulled the plug on the tub and carefully stood. It drained noisily, and I wiped the mist from the mirror, leaning against the sink to look at myself.

A sigh shifted my shoulders. Matalina came to rest on my shoulder, watching me with sad eyes. I looked as if I'd fallen out of the back of a truck. One side of my face was welted with a purple bruise that spread up into my eye. Keasley's bandage had fallen off, showing a red gash following the arc of my eyebrow, to make me look lopsided. I didn't even remember getting cut. I leaned closer, and the victim in the mirror mimicked me. Gathering my resolve, I pulled my damp, stringy hair away from my neck.

A sound of resignation slipped from me. The demon hadn't made clean punctures, but rather, three sets of tears that melted into each other like rivers and tributaries. Matalina's tiny stitches looked like a little railroad trellis running down to my collarbone.

The remembrance of the demon pulled a shudder from me; I had nearly died under it. Just that thought was enough to scare the hell out of me, but what was going to keep me awake at night was the niggling awareness that for all the terror and pain, the vampire saliva it had pumped into me had felt good. Lie or not, it had felt . . . staggeringly wonderful.

I gripped the towel closer around me and turned away. "Thank you, Matalina," I whispered. "I don't think the scars will be that noticeable."

"You're welcome, dear. It was the least I could do. Would you like me to stay and make sure you get dressed all right?"

"No." The sound of a mixer came from the kitchen. I opened the door and peeked into the hall. The smell of eggs was thick in the air. "I think I can manage, thanks."

The small pixy nodded and flitted out with her needlework, her wings making a soft hum. I listened for a long moment, and deciding Nick was safely occupied, I hobbled to my room, breathing a sigh of relief upon reaching it undetected.

My hair dripped as I sat on the edge of my cot to catch my breath. The thought of putting on pants made me cringe. But I wasn't going to wear a skirt and nylons, either. I finally settled on my "fat jeans" and a blue button-up plaid shirt that was easy enough to get into without bringing on too much pain from my shoulder and arm. I wouldn't be caught dead in such an outfit on the street, but it wasn't as if I was trying to impress Nick.

The floor kept shifting under my feet as I dressed, and the walls tilted if I moved fast, but eventually I emerged with my damp amulets clanking about my neck. I scuffed down the hallway in my slippers, wondering if I ought to try to cover my bruise with a complexion spell. Standard makeup wasn't going to cut it.

Nick blundered out of the kitchen, almost running me down. He had a sandwich in his hand. "There you are," he said, his eyes wide as he ran his gaze down to my pink slippers and back up again. "Do you want an egg sandwich?"

"No, thanks," I said, my stomach rumbling again. "Too much sulfur." The thought flashed through me how he had looked, that black book in his grip as he flung out his hand and stopped that demon dead in its tracks: frightened, scared . . . and powerful. I'd never seen a human look powerful. It had been surprising. "I could use some help changing my wrist bandage, though," I finished bitingly.

He cringed, thoroughly destroying the picture in my head. "Rachel, I'm sorry—"

I pushed past him and went into the kitchen. His steps were light behind me, and I leaned against the sink as I fed Mr. Fish. It was fully dark outside, and I could see tiny flashes of light as Jenks's family patrolled the garden. I froze as I saw that the tomato was back on the windowsill. A wash of worry hit me as I mentally cursed Ivy—then my brow furrowed. Why did I care what Nick thought? It was my house. I was an Inderlander. If he didn't like it, tuff toads.

I could feel Nick behind me at the table. "Rachel, I'm really sorry," he said, and I turned, bracing myself. My outrage would lose all its effect if I passed out. "I didn't know it would demand payment from you. Honest."

Angry, I brushed the damp hair from my eyes and stood with my arms crossed. "It's a demon mark, Nick. A freaking demon mark."

Nick folded his lanky body into one of the hard-back chairs. Elbows on the table, he dropped his head into the cup his hands made. Looking at the table, he said flatly, "Demonology is a dead art. I didn't expect to be putting the knowledge to practical use. It was only supposed to be a painless way to fulfill one of my ancient language requirements."

He looked up, meeting my eyes. His worry, the need for me to listen and understand, halted my next caustic outburst. "I'm really, really sorry," he said. "If I could move your demon mark to me, I would. But I thought you were dying. I couldn't just let you bleed to death in the back of some cab."

My anger trickled away. He had been willing to take a demon mark to save me. No one made him do it. I was an ass.

Nick lifted the hair from over his left temple. "Look. See?" he said hopefully. "It stops."

I peered at his scalp. Right where the demon had hit him was a newly closed wound, red-rimmed and sore looking. The half circle had a line through it. My stomach clenched. A demon mark. Damn it all to hell, I was going to have to wear a demon mark. Black ley line witches had demon marks, not white earth witches. Not me.

Nick let his shock of dark hair fall. "It will vanish after I pay back my favor. It's not forever."

"A favor?" I asked.

His brown eyes were pinched, pleading for understanding. "It will probably be information or something. At least, that's what the texts say."

One hand clasped about my middle, I pushed my fingertips into my forehead. I really didn't have a choice. It wasn't as if Kotex made a pad for this kind of a thing. "So how do I let this demon know I agree to owe it a favor?"

"Do you?"

"Yes."

"You just did, then."

I felt ill, not liking that a demon had such a tie to me that it would know the moment I agreed to its terms. "No paperwork?" I said. "No contracts? I don't like verbal agreements."

"You want it to come here and fill out paperwork?" he asked. "Think about it hard enough and it will."

"No." My gaze dropped to my wrist. There was a small tickle. My face went slack as it grew to an itch and then a slight burning. "Where are the scissors?" I said tightly. He looked around blankly, and my wrist started to flame. "It's burning!" I shouted. The pain in my wrist continued to grow, and I pushed at the gauze, frantically trying to get it off.

"Get it off! Get it off!" I shouted. Spinning, I flipped the tap on full and shoved my wrist under the water. The cold water soaked through, quenching the burning sensation. I leaned over the sink, my pulse pounding as the water flowed, pulling away the pain.

The damp night air breezed in past the curtains, and I stared past the dark garden and into the graveyard, waiting for the black spots to go away. My knees were weak, and it was only the rush of adrenaline that kept me upright. There was a soft scraping sound as Nick slid a pair of scissors to me across the counter.

I turned off the tap. "Thanks for the warning," I said bitterly.

"Mine didn't hurt," he said. He looked worried and confused, and oh so bewildered. Grabbing a dish towel and the scissors, I went to my spot at the table. Wedging the blade through the gauze, I sawed at the soggy wrap. I flicked a glance up at him. Tall and awkward, he stood by the sink, guilt seeming to pour from his hunched posture. I slumped.

"I'm sorry for being such a crab, Nick," I said as I gave up on cutting it off and started to unwind it instead. "I would have died if it hadn't been for you. I was lucky you were there to stop it. I owe you my life, and I'm really thankful for what you did." I hesitated. "That thing scared the hell out of me. All I wanted was to forget about it, and now I can't. I don't know how to react, and yelling at you is very convenient."

A smile quirked the corner of his mouth, and he turned a chair so he could sit before me. "Let me get that for you," he said, reaching for my hand.

I hesitated, then let him pull my wrist onto his lap. He bowed his head over my wrist, and his knees almost touched mine. I really owed him more than a simple thanks. "Nick? I mean it. Thank you. That's twice you saved my life. This demon thing will be all right. I'm sorry you got a demon mark helping me."

Nick looked up, his brown eyes searching mine. I was suddenly very conscious of how close he was. My memory went back to feeling his arms around me, carrying me into the church. I wondered if he had held me all the way through the ever-after.

"I'm glad I was there to help," he said softly. "It was kind of my fault."

"No, it would have found me no matter where I was," I said. Finally the last wrap was gone. Swallowing hard, I stared at my wrist. My stomach twisted. It was entirely healed. Even the green stitches were gone. The raised white scar looked old. Mine was in the shape of a full circle with that same line running through it.

"Oh," Nick murmured, leaning back. "The demon must like you. It didn't heal me, just stopped the bleeding."

"Swell." I rubbed the mark on my wrist. It was better than a bandage—I guess. It wasn't as if anyone would know what the scar was from; no one had been dealing with demons since the Turn. "So now I just wait until it wants something?"

"Yeah." Nick's chair scraped as he stood up and went to the stove.

I propped my elbows up on the table and felt the air slip in and out of my lungs. Nick stood at the stove with his back to me and stirred a stewpot. An uncomfortable silence grew.

"Do you like student food?" Nick said suddenly.

I straightened. "Beg pardon?"

"Student food." His eyes went to the tomato on the sill. "Whatever's in the refrigerator over pasta."

Understandably concerned, I pushed myself upright and tottered over to see what was on the stove. Macaroni spun and rolled in the pot. A wooden spoon sat next to it, and my eyebrows rose. "Have you been using that spoon?"

Nick nodded. "Yeah. Why?"

I reached for the salt and dumped the entire canister into it.

"Whoa!" Nick cried. "I already salted the water. You don't need that much."

Ignoring him, I tossed the wooden spoon into my dissolution vat and pulled out a metal one. "Until I get my ceramic spoons back, it's metal for cooking and wooden for spells. Rinse the macaroni well. It ought to be okay."

Nick's eyebrows rose. "I would think you would use metal spoons for spells and wooden for cooking since spells don't stick to metal."

I made my slow way to the fridge, feeling my heart pound from even this little exertion. "And why do you suppose spells don't stick to metal? Unless it's copper, metal screws everything up. I'll do the spell crafting if you don't mind; you do dinner."

Much to my surprise, Nick didn't get all huffy and testosterone laden but only gave me that lopsided smile of his.

A jolt of pain broke through the amulets as I tugged the fridge open. "I can't believe how hungry I am," I said as I looked for something that wasn't wrapped in paper or plastic foam. "I think Ivy may have slipped me something."

There was a whoosh of water as Nick dumped the macaroni to drain. "Little cake thing?"

I pulled my head out and blinked at him. Had Ivy given him one, too? "Yes."

"I saw it." His eyes were fixed on the tomato, steam billowing around him as he rinsed the macaroni. "When I was doing my master's thesis, I had access to the rare-book vault." His brow pinched. "It's right next to the ancient-book locker. Anyway, the architectural designs of preindustrial cathedrals are boring, and one night I found a diary of a seventeenth-century British priest. He had been tried and convicted of murdering three of his prettiest parishioners."

Nick dumped the pasta back in the bowl and opened a jar of alfredo. "He made reference to such a thing. Said it made the vampire's orgies of blood and lust possible on a nightly basis. From a scientific point of view, you should consider yourself lucky. I imagine it's only rarely offered to someone not under their sway and compelled to keep their mouth shut about it."

I frowned in unease. What the devil had Ivy given me?

His eyes still on the tomato, Nick dumped the sauce over the pasta. A rich smell filled the kitchen, and my stomach growled. He stirred it in, and I watched Nick watch the tomato. He was starting to look rather sick. Exasperated with humanity's groundless revulsion of tomatoes, I closed the fridge and hobbled to the window. "How did this get in here?" I muttered, pushing it through the pixy hole and into the night. It hit with a soft thud.

"Thanks," he said, taking a relieved breath.

I returned to my chair with a heavy sigh. One would think Ivy and I had a decaying sheep's head on our counter. But it was nice to know he had at least one human hang-up.

Nick puttered about, adding mushrooms, Worcestershire sauce, and pepperoni to the concoction. I smiled as I realized it was the last of my pizza fixings. It smelled wonderful, and as he plucked the ladle from the island rack, I asked, "Enough for two?"

"It's enough for a dorm room." Nick slid a bowl before me and sat down, curling his arm protectively about his bowl. "Student food," he said around a full mouth. "Try it."

I glanced at the clock above the sink as I dipped my spoon. Ivy and Jenks were probably at the FIB right now, trying to convince

282 • This Witch for Hire

the front guy they weren't loons, and here I was, eating macaroni alfredo with a human. It didn't look right. The food, I mean. It would have been better in a tomato sauce. Dubious, I took a taste. "Hey," I said, pleased. "This is good."

"Told you."

For a few moments there was only the scraping of spoons and the sound of the crickets in the garden. Nick's pace slowed, and he glanced at the clock over the sink. "Hey, uh, I've got a big favor to ask," he said hesitantly.

I swallowed as I looked up, knowing what was coming. "You can crash here for the night if you want," I said. "Though there are no guarantees you'll wake up with all your fluids intact or even at all. The I.S. is still spelling for me. Right now it's just those tenacious fairies, but as soon as the word gets out that I'm still alive, we might be up to our armpits in assassins. You'd be safer on a park bench," I finished wryly.

His smile was relieved. "Thanks, but I'll risk it. I'll get out of your hair tomorrow. See if my landlord has anything left that's mine. Go visit my mom." His long face puckered, looking as worried as when he thought I was bleeding to death. "I'll tell her I lost everything in a fire. This is going to be a rough one."

I felt a stab of sympathy. I knew what it was like to find yourself on the street with only a box left of your life. "Sure you don't want to stay with her tonight?" I asked. "It'd be safer."

He went back to eating. "I can take care of myself."

I bet you can, I thought, my mind going back to that demon book he took from the library. It wasn't in my bag anymore, a tiny smear of blood the only thing to say it had ever been there. I wanted to come right out and ask if he worked black magic. But he might say yes, and then I'd have to decide what I was going to do about it. I didn't want to do that right yet. I liked Nick's easy confidence, and the novelty of seeing that in a human was decidedly . . . intriguing.

A part of me knew and despised that the attraction probably stemmed from my "hero rescuing the damsel in distress syndrome," but I needed something safe and secure in my life right now, and a magic-working human who could keep demons from tearing my throat out fit the bill nicely. Especially when he looked as harmless as he did.

"Besides," Nick said, ruining it, "Jenks will pix me if I leave before he gets back."

My breath slipped from me in bother. He was a babysitter. How nice.

The sound of the phone ringing echoed through the walls. I looked up at Nick and didn't move. I was sore, darn it.

He gave me that half smile of his and stood. "I'll get it." I took another bite as I watched his vanishing backside, thinking I might offer to go shopping with him when he bought himself some new clothes. Those jeans he had on were way too loose.

"Hello," Nick said, his voice dropping and taking on a surprisingly professional tone. "You've reached Morgan, Tamwood, and Jenks. Vampiric Charms Runner Service."

Vampiric Charms Runner Service? I thought. A little of Ivy, a little of me. It was as good as anything else, I suppose. I blew on a spoonful, thinking his cooking wasn't bad, either.

"Jenks?" Nick said, and I hesitated, looking up as Nick appeared in the hallway with the phone. "She's eating. You're at the airport already?"

There was a long pause, and I sighed. The FIB was more open-minded and eager for Trent than I had anticipated.

"The FIB?" Nick's tone had shifted to concern, and I stiffened as he added, "She did what? Is anyone dead?"

My eyes closed in a long blink and I set my spoon aside. Nick's concoction went sour in my stomach, and I swallowed hard.

"Um, sure," Nick said, the skin around his expressive eyes crinkling as he met my gaze. "Give us a half hour." The beep of the phone as he turned it off was loud. He turned to me and blew out his breath. "We have a problem."

Twenty-nine

I fell against the side of the cab as it made a tight turn. Pain broke past my amulets, and I clutched one-handed at my bag in misery. The driver was human, and he had made it painfully clear he didn't like driving out to the Hollows after dark. His constant muttering hadn't abated until he crossed the Ohio River and was back where "decent people kept themselves." In his eyes, my and Nick's only saving grace was that he had picked us up at a church and that we were going to the FIB, "A fine and decent establishment upholding the right side of the law."

"Okay," I said as Nick helped ease me upright. "So those fine and decent people at the FIB were harassing Ivy, playing good-cop/bad-cop. Someone touched her and—"

"She exploded," Nick finished. "It took eight officers to bring her down. Jenks says three are in the hospital for observation. Four more were treated and released."

"Idiots," I muttered. "What about Jenks?"

Nick put an arm out, bracing himself as we lurched to a stop before a tall stone and glass building. "They'll release him to a responsible person." His grin looked a tad nervous. "And in the absence of one, they said you would do."

"Ha ha," I said dryly. Peering up through the dirty glass of the cab, I read FEDERAL INDERLANDER BUREAU engraved deeply over the two sets of doors. Nick sidled out to the sidewalk first and extended a hand to help me. I slowly worked my way out and tried to find my bearings as he paid the cabbie with the money I slipped him. It was bright under the streetlights, and the streets themselves had remarkably light traffic for that hour. Clearly we were deep into the human district of Cincinnati. Looking up to find the top of the imposing building, I felt very much the minority and on edge.

I scanned the black windows around me for any sign of attack. Jax had said the fairy assassins left right after my phone call. *To get reinforcements, or to set up an ambush here?* I didn't like the idea that fairy catapults might be winching back as I waited. Even a fairy wouldn't be so bold as to tag me inside the FIB building, but on the sidewalk I was fair game.

Then again, they could have been taken off the run, seeing as the I.S. was sending demons now. I felt a flash of satisfaction, knowing the demon had ripped apart its summoner. They wouldn't send another any time soon. Black magic always swings back to get you. Always.

"You really ought to take better care of your sister," the driver said as he took the money, and Nick and I looked blankly at each other. "But I guess you Inderlanders don't care about each other as much as us decent folks. I'd pulp anyone who dared touch my sister with the back of his hand," he added before driving off.

I stared at his taillights in confusion until Nick said, "He thinks someone beat you and I'm bringing you in to file a complaint."

I was too nervous to laugh—besides, it would have made me pass out—but I managed a choking snicker, taking his arm before I fell over. Brow pinched, Nick gallantly pulled the glass door open and held it for me. A flash of angst went through me as I stepped over the threshold. I had put myself in the questionable position of having to trust a human-run establishment. It was shaky ground. I didn't like it.

But the sound of loud conversations and the smell of burnt coffee were familiar and soothing. Institution was written everywhere, from the gray tiled floor, to the chatter of loud conversation, to the orange chairs the anxious parents and unrepentant thugs sat in. It felt like coming home, and my shoulders eased.

"Um, over there," Nick said, pointing to the front counter. My arm was throbbing in its sling and my shoulder hurt. Either my sweat was diluting my amulets or my exertions were starting to cancel them out. Nick walked almost behind me, and it was bothersome.

The desk clerk looked up as we approached, her eyes widening. "Oh, sweetheart!" she exclaimed softly. "What happened to you?"

"I, uh . . ." I winced as I put my elbows on the counter to steady myself. My complexion charm wasn't enough to blur my black eye or stitches. Just what was I supposed to tell her? That demons were loose in Cincinnati again? I glanced behind me, but Nick was no help, turned away to the doors. "Um," I stammered. "I'm here to pick someone up."

She reached to scratch her neck. "Not the one who did that to you."

I couldn't help my smile at her concern. I was a sucker for pity. "No."

The woman tucked a strand of graying hair behind her ear. "I hate to tell you this, but you need to go to the Hillman Street office. And you'll have to wait until tomorrow. They won't release anyone after normal business hours."

I sighed. I hated the maze of bureaucracy with a passion, but I've found the best way to deal with it is to smile and act stupid. That way, no one gets confused. "But I talked to someone less than twenty minutes ago," I objected. "I was told to come here."

Her mouth made a round O of understanding. A wary expression settled around her eyes. "Ah," she said, looking at me sideways. "You're here for the—" She hesitated. "—pixy." She rubbed the beginnings of a small blister behind her neck. She'd been pixed.

Nick cleared his throat. "His name is Jenks," he said tightly, his head lowered. Clearly he had heard the hesitation, thinking she had almost said "bug."

"Yes," she said slowly, leaning to scratch her ankle. "Mr. Jenks. If you would take a seat over there," she pointed, "someone will be with you as soon as Captain Edden is available."

"Captain Edden." I took Nick's arm. "Thank you." Feeling old and creaky, I angled to the orange monstrosities lined up against the lobby's walls. The woman's attitude shift wasn't unexpected. In a breath I had gone from honey to whore.

Though having lived openly with humans for forty years, tensions ran high at times. They were afraid, and probably for good reason. It's not easy waking up to find your neighbors are vampires and your fourth-grade teacher really was a witch.

Nick's eyes roved over the lobby as he helped me sit. The chairs were as unpleasant as I had expected: hard and uncomfortable. Nick sat beside me, perched on the edge with his long legs bent at the knees. "How are you doing?" he asked as I groaned while trying to find a halfway comfortable position.

"Fine," I said shortly. "Just dandy." I winced, tracking two uniformed men passing through the lobby. One was on crutches.

The other's black eye was just starting to purple up, and he was scratching vigorously at his shoulders. *Thanks a heap, Jenks and Ivy.* My unease filtered back. How was I supposed to convince the captain of the FIB to help me now?

"You want something to eat?" Nick said, yanking my attention back. "I, uh, could go across the street for some Graeter's. You like butter-pecan ice cream?"

"No." It came out more brusque than I had intended, and I smiled to soften my words. "No, thank you," I amended, my worry settling in my belly to stay.

"How about something from the candy machine, then? Salt and carbohydrates?" he prompted hopefully. "The food of champions."

I shook my head and set my bag between my feet. Trying to keep my breathing shallow, I stared at the scuffed tile floor. If I ate one more thing, I thought I was gonna ralph. I had eaten another bowl of Nick's macaroni before the cab picked us up, but that wasn't the problem.

"Amulets wearing off?" Nick guessed, and I nodded.

A pair of scuffed brown shoes came to a slow halt within my range. Nick slid to the back of his chair with his arms crossed, and I slowly pulled my head up.

It was a stocky man in a white dress shirt and khakis, trim and carrying the polish of an ex-marine gone civilian. He wore plastic-framed glasses, the lenses looking too small against his round face. There was the smell of soap about him, and his close-cropped hair was damp and stuck up like a baby orangutan's. My guess was he had been pixed and knew enough to wash before the blisters could start. His bandaged right wrist was in a sling identical to mine. Short black hair, short gray mustache. I hoped he had a long temper. "Ms. Morgan?" he said, and I straightened with a sigh. "I'm Captain Edden."

Great, I thought, struggling to stand up. Nick helped. I found I could look Edden right in the eye, making him rather short for all his official presence. I would almost say he had some troll blood in him if such a thing were biologically possible. My eyes lingered on the weapon holstered on his hip, and I spared a wish for my I.S.-issue cuffs. Eyes scrunched from my too strong perfume, he stuck out his left hand instead of the usual right, seeing as we were both unable to use them.

My pulse quickened as we shook left hands; it felt wrong, and I would rather use my bruised right arm than do it again. "Good evening, Captain," I said, trying to hide my nervousness. "This is Nick Sparagmos. He's helping keep me upright today."

Edden gave Nick a short nod, then hesitated. "Mr. Sparagmos? Have we met before?"

"No. I don't think so."

Nick's words were a shade too fast, and I ran my gaze down his carefully casual stance. Nick had been here before, and I didn't think it had been to pick up his tickets to the FIB's yearly fund-raising dinner.

"You sure?" the man questioned, running a quick hand over his bristly hair.

"Yeah."

The older man eyed him. "Yes," he said abruptly. "I'm thinking of someone else."

Nick's posture eased almost imperceptibly, piquing my interest further.

Captain Edden's gaze turned to my neck, and I wondered if I ought to try and cover my stitches with a scarf or something. "If you would come back with me?" the stocky man said. "I'd like to speak with you before I release the pixy to your custody."

Nick stiffened. "His name is Jenks," he muttered, just audible over the lobby noise.

"Yes. Mr. Jenks." Edden paused. "If you would come back to my office?"

"What about Ivy?" I asked, reluctant to leave the public lobby behind. My pulse was racing with just the effort to stand here. If I had to move quickly, I'd pass out.

"Ms. Tamwood will remain where she is. She's to be turned over to the I.S. for prosecution in the morning."

Anger overpowered my caution. "You knew better than to touch an angry vamp," I said. Nick's grip tightened on my arm, and it was all I could do to not try to jerk away from him.

A hint of a smile drifted over Edden. "It still remains that she assaulted FIB personnel," he said. "My hands are tied concerning Tamwood. We aren't equipped to deal with Inderlanders." He hesitated. "Would you come with me to my office? We can discuss your options."

My worry deepened; Denon would love to get Ivy incarcerated dead to rights. Nick handed me my bag, and I nodded. This was not good. It almost seemed as if Edden had goaded Ivy into losing her temper to get me to come down here with my hat in my hand. But I followed Edden to a glass-walled corner office off the lobby. At first it looked tucked out of the way, but with the blinds up, he would have a view of everything. Right now, they were closed to make his corner less of a fishbowl than it was. He left the door open, and the noise filtered in.

"Have a seat," he said, gesturing to the two green upholstered chairs opposite his desk. I gratefully sat, finding the flat padding marginally more comfortable than the plastic chairs in the lobby. As Nick stiffly lowered himself, I ran my eyes over Edden's office, noting the dust-covered bowling trophies and stacks of folders. File cabinets lined one wall, photo albums stacked on top of them to nearly the ceiling. A clock hung behind Edden's desk, ticking loudly. There was a picture of him and my old boss, Denon, shaking hands outside City Hall. Edden looked short and common next to Denon's vampire grace. They were both smiling.

I brought my attention back to Edden. He was slouched in his chair, clearly waiting for me to finish my evaluation of his office. If he cared to ask, I would have told him he was a slob. But his office had a cluttered efficiency about it that said real work was done here. It was as far from Denon's gadget-strewn, sterile office as my old desk was from a churchyard. I liked it. If I had to trust someone, I'd rather it be someone as unorganized as me.

Edden pulled himself straight. "I'll admit my conversation with Tamwood was intriguing, Ms. Morgan," he said. "As a former I.S. operative, I'm sure you know what bringing Trent Kalamack in under the suspicion of anything—much less manufacturing and distributing illegal bioproducts—could do for the FIB's image."

Right to the point. Snap my fingers if I wasn't starting to like this guy. Still I said nothing as my stomach knotted. He wasn't done.

Edden put an arm on his desk, hiding his sling in his lap. "But you understand I can't ask my people to arrest Councilman Kalamack under the advice of a former I.S. runner. You're under a death threat, illegal or not."

My breathing quickened to match my whirling thoughts. I had been right. He had thrown Ivy into custody to get me down here. For one panicked instant I wondered if he was stalling me. If he had the I.S. on their way to tag me. The thought vanished in a painful rush of adrenaline. The FIB and the I.S. were in a bitter rivalry. If Edden was going to claim the bounty on my head, he'd do it himself, not invite the I.S. into his building. Edden had brought me down here to evaluate me. For what? I wondered, my worry tightening.

Deciding to take control of the conversation, I smiled, wincing as the swelling on my eye pulled. Giving up on my dazzle-them-to-distraction approach, I faced him squarely, pushing the tension from my shoulders down to my stomach, where he couldn't see it. "I'd like to apologize for my associate's behavior, Captain Edden." I looked at his bandaged wrist. "Did she break it?"

The barest wisp of surprise crossed him. "Worse. It's fractured in four places. They'll tell me tomorrow if I have to get a cast or simply wait for it to heal. Damn infirmary won't let me take anything stronger than an aspirin. It's a full moon next week, Ms. Morgan. Do you realize how far behind I will be if I have to take even one day off?"

This chitchat was going nowhere. My pain was starting to flow back, and I had to find out what Edden wanted before it was too late to move on Kalamack. It had to be more than Trent; he could have dealt with Ivy alone if that was all he wanted.

Steadying myself, I took off one of my amulets and pushed it across the desk. My bag was full of spells, but not one of them was for pain. "I understand, Captain Edden. I'm sure we can come to an agreement that would be mutually beneficial." My fingers left the small disk, and I struggled to keep my eyes from widening at the rush of pain. Nausea twisted my stomach, and I felt three times as weak. I hoped I hadn't made a mistake offering it to him. As witnessed by the desk clerk, few humans approved of Inderlanders, much less their magic. I thought it worth the risk. Edden seemed unusually open-minded. It remained to be seen how far.

His eyes showed only curiosity as he reached for the charm. "You know I can't accept this," he said. "As an FIB officer, it would be considered . . ." His face went slack as his fingers closed upon the amulet and the pain in his wrist was deadened. ". . . a bribe," he finished softly.

His dark eyes met mine, and I smiled despite my pain. "A trade." I arched my eyebrows, ignoring the pull of tape. "An aspirin for an aspirin?" If he was smart, he'd understand I was testing the waters. If he was stupid, it didn't matter, and I'd be dead by the end of the week. But if there was no way to convince him to act on my "tip," I wouldn't be sitting in his office.

For a moment Edden sat as if afraid to move and break the spell. Finally an honest smile came over him. He leaned to his open door and bellowed out into the hall, "Rose! Get me a couple of aspirin. I'm dying in here." He leaned back, grinning as he hung the amulet about his neck and hid it behind his shirt. His relief was obvious. It was a start.

My worry grew as a harried-looking woman walked in, her heels clicking on the gray tile. She visibly jerked at finding us in Edden's office. Pulling her eyes from me, she held out two paper cups, and he pointed to the desk. The woman's brow furrowed, and she set them next to his hand and silently left. Edden reached a foot out after her and kicked the door shut. He waited, shifting his glasses higher up his nose before crossing his good arm over his bad.

I swallowed hard as I reached for the two cups. Now it was my turn for trust. There might be anything in those tiny white pills, but finding relief from my pain was beyond expectation. The pills rattled as I brought the cup close and peered down at them.

I'd heard about pills. I'd had a roommate who swore by them, keeping a bottle of white tablets next to her toothbrush. She said they worked better than amulets, and you didn't have to stick your finger. I had watched her take one once. You were supposed to swallow them whole.

Nick leaned close. "You can palm it if you want," he whispered, and I shook my head. I quickly upended the cup with the aspirin, tasting the bitter bite of willow bark as I took a swallow of tepid water. I struggled not to cough as I felt the pills go down, clenching at the pain the sudden movement brought on. This was supposed to make me feel better?

Nick patted me hesitantly on the back. Through my watering eyes I could see Edden all but laughing at my ineptness. I waved Nick off and forced myself to sit up straight. A moment passed, then another. Still the aspirin didn't take effect. I sighed. Nothing. No wonder humans were so suspicious. Their medicines didn't work.

"I can give you Kalamack, Captain Edden." I glanced at the clock behind him. Ten forty-five. "I can prove he's dealing in illegal drugs. Both manufacturing and distribution."

Edden's eyes went alight. "Give me the proof, and we will go to the airport."

I felt my expression freeze. Ivy had told him nearly everything, and he still wanted to talk to me? Why hadn't he taken the information and brought some glory for himself? God knew it would be cheaper. What was he up to? "I don't have all of it," I admitted. "But I heard him discussing the arrangements. If we find the drugs, that's proof enough."

Edden pressed his lips together to make his mustache move. "I won't go out on circumstantial evidence. I've been a fool for the I.S. before."

I glanced at the clock again. Ten forty-six. His eyes met mine as I looked away, and I bit back a flash of annoyance. Now he knew I was in a hurry. "Captain," I said, trying to keep the imploring from my voice. "I broke into Trent Kalamack's office to get the proof but got caught. I spent the last three days as an unwilling guest. I overheard several meetings that substantiated my beliefs. He's a manufacturer and distributor of illegal biodrugs."

Calm and collected, Edden leaned back and swiveled his chair. "You spent three days with Kalamack and expect me to believe he was speaking the truth in front of you?"

"I was a mink," I said dryly. "I was supposed to die in the city's rat fights. I wasn't supposed to escape."

Nick shifted uneasily beside me, but Edden nodded as if I had confirmed his suspicions.

"Trent is running a rainbow of biodrugs out nearly every week," I said, forcing my hand down from playing with my hair. "Blackmailing anyone who can afford it and who is in the unfortunate situation of needing them. You could chart his hidden profits by plotting the I.S. Brimstone takes. He's using them as a—"

"Distraction," Edden finished for me. He hit the nearby file cabinet, leaving a small dent. Both Nick and I jumped. "Damn! No wonder we never catch a break."

I nodded. It was now or never. Whether I trusted him or not was irrelevant. If he didn't help me, I was dead. "It gets better," I said, praying I was doing the right thing. "Trent has an I.S. runner on his payroll who has been heading most of the I.S. Brimstone takes."

Edden's round face went hard behind his glasses. "Fred Perry."

"Francis Percy," I corrected him, a sudden flash of anger warming me.

Eyes narrowed, Edden shifted in his chair. Clearly he didn't like a bad cop any more than I did. I took a shaky breath. "A shipment of biodrugs is going out tonight. With me, you can nail them both. The FIB gets the credit for the tag, the I.S. looks like a fool, and your department quietly pays off my contract." My head hurt, and I prayed I hadn't just flushed my only chance down the toilet. "You could make it a consultant fee. An aspirin for an aspirin."

Lips pressed tight, Edden looked at the acoustic-tiled ceiling.

Slowly his face calmed, and I waited, stilling myself as I realized I was clicking my nails together in time with the ticking of the clock.

"I'm tempted to bend the rules for you, Ms. Morgan," he said, and my heart gave a thump. "But I need more. Something the higher-ups can chart on their profit and loss statements that will show value for more than a quarter."

"More!" Nick exclaimed, sounding angry.

My head throbbed. *He wanted more?* "I don't have anything more, Captain," I said forcefully, frustration riding high in me.

He smiled wickedly. "But you do."

My eyebrows tried to go up, halted by the tape.

Edden glanced at his closed door. "If this works out—catching Kalamack, I mean . . ." A thick hand reached to rub his forehead. When his fingers dropped, the easy, self-assured confidence of an FIB captain was gone, replaced with an eager, intelligent gleam that set me back a pace. "I've been working for the FIB since I left the service," he said softly. "I worked my way up by seeing what was missing, and finding it."

"I'm not a commodity, Captain," I said hotly.

"Everyone is a commodity," he said. "My departments at the FIB are at a great disadvantage, Ms. Morgan. Inderlanders have evolved knowing human weaknesses. Hell, you're probably responsible for half our mental hang-ups. The frustrating truth is, we can't compete."

He wanted me to rat on my fellow Inderlanders. He should have known better. "I don't know anything you can't find in a library," I said, gripping my bag tightly. I wanted to get up and storm out, but he had me right where he wanted me, and I could do nothing but watch him smile. His flat teeth were startlingly human compared to the predatory gleam in his eye.

"I'm sure that's not entirely true," he said. "But I'm asking for advice, not a betrayal." Edden leaned back in his chair, seeming to collect his thoughts. "Occasionally," he said, "tonight with Ms. Tamwood, for example, an Inderlander comes to us seeking help or with information they don't feel—prudent—taking to the I.S. To be honest, we don't know how to deal with them. My people are so suspicious that they can't gain any useful information. On the rare occasion when we do understand, we don't know how to capitalize on it. The only reason we were able to contain Ms. Tamwood is because she agreed to be incarcerated once it was explained we would be more willing to listen to you if she did. Up until today we have reluctantly turned situations like this over to the I.S." His eyes met mine. "They make us look like fools, Ms. Morgan."

He was offering me a job, but my tension swelled instead of easing. "If I wanted a boss, I would have stayed with the I.S., Captain."

"No," he protested quickly, his chair creaking as he sat upright. "Having you here would be a mistake. Not only would my officers want my head on a pole, but it's against the I.S./FIB convention to have you on the payroll." His smile grew wicked, and I waited for it. "I want you as a consultant—occasionally—as the need demands."

I let my held breath out slowly, seeing for the first time what he was after.

"What did you say your firm was called?" Edden asked.

"Vampiric Charms," Nick said.

Edden chuckled. "Sounds like a dating service."

I winced, but it was too late to change it now. "And I get paid for these *occasional* services?" I asked, chewing on my lower lip. *This might work.*

"Of course."

Now it was my turn to stare at the ceiling, my pulse racing at the chance that I'd found a way out of this. "I'm part of a team, Captain Edden," I said, wondering if Ivy was having second thoughts about our partnership. "I can't speak for them."

"Ms. Tamwood has already agreed. I believe she said, 'If the little witch says yes, I'll go along with it.' Mr. Jenks expressed a similar feeling, but his exact words were substantially more—colorful."

I glanced at Nick and he shrugged uneasily. There was no guarantee, when all was said and done, that Edden wouldn't conveniently forget to pay off my contract. But something in his dry humor and honest reactions had convinced me he wouldn't. Besides, I had already made a pact with a demon tonight. This couldn't be any worse.

"Captain Edden, we have a deal," I said suddenly. "It's Southwest's 11:45 flight to L.A."

"Great!" His good hand hit the table with a thump, and I jumped again. "I knew you would. Rose!" he shouted to the closed door. Grinning, he leaned to open it. "Rose! Get a Brimstone dog team out to . . ." He looked at me. "Where's the Brimstone take?" he asked.

"Ivy didn't tell you?" I said in surprise.

"She may have. I want to know if she was lying."

"Main bus depot," I said, my heart hammering all the harder. *We were going to do this. I was going to tag Trent and get my death threat paid off.*

"Rose!" he shouted again. "The old bus depot. Who's pushing paper tonight who didn't go to the hospital?"

A feminine but robust voice cut over the accumulated clatter. "Kaman is here, but he's in the shower getting that bug dust off. Dillon, Ray—"

"Stop," Edden said. He stood, and, gesturing for Nick and me to join him, darted out of his office. I took a deep breath and lurched to my feet. Much to my surprise, my aches had retreated to dull throbs. We followed Edden down the hall, excitement making my pace quick. "I think the aspirin is finally working," I whispered to Nick as we caught up to Edden. He was hunched over a spotless desk, talking to the same woman who had brought me the pills.

"Call Ruben and Simon in," he said. "I need someone with a cooler head. Send them to the airport. Tell them to wait for me."

"You, sir?" Rose glanced over her glasses at Nick and me. Her frown said it all. She wasn't happy having two Inderlanders in the building, much less standing behind her boss.

"Yes, me. Get the unmarked van around front. I'm going out tonight." He hoisted his belt up over his hips. "No mistakes. This one has to be done right."

Thirty

The floor of the FIB van was surprisingly clean. There was a faint odor of pipe smoke, reminding me of my dad. Captain Edden and the driver, introduced as Clayton, were up front. Nick, Jenks, and I were on the middle bench. The windows were cracked to dilute my perfume. If I'd known they weren't going to release Ivy until after the deal was done, I wouldn't have put it on. As it was, I reeked.

Jenks was on a rampage, his tiny voice scraping along the inside of my skull as he ranted, winding my anticipation to new heights. "Put a sock in it, Jenks," I whispered as I ran the tip of my finger around the bottom of my tiny cellophane bag of nuts for the last of the salt. When the aspirin had dulled my pain, my hunger kicked in. I'd almost rather have done without the aspirin if it meant not being famished.

"Go Turn yourself," Jenks snarled from the cup holder where I had put him. "They stuffed me into a water cooler. Like I was a freak on display! They broke my fringing wing. Look at it! Snapped the main vein. I've got mineral spots on my shirt. It's ruined! And did you see my boots? I'll never get the coffee off them."

"They apologized," I said, but I knew it was a lost cause. He was on a roll.

"It's going to take me a week to grow my damn wing back. Matalina is gonna kill me. Everyone hides from me when I can't fly. Did you know that? Even my kids."

I tuned him out. The tirade had started the moment they released him and hadn't quit yet. Though Jenks hadn't been charged with a crime—seeing as he'd been at the ceiling cheering Ivy on while she pummeled the FIB officers—he had insisted on poking about where he shouldn't until they put him in an emptied water jug.

I was beginning to see what Edden had been talking about. He and his officers hadn't a clue as to how to handle Inderlanders. They could have trapped him in a cupboard or drawer as he nosed about. His wings never would have gotten wet and become as fragile as tissue paper. The ten-minute chase with a net wouldn't have happened. And half the officers on the floor wouldn't have been pixed. Ivy and Jenks had come to the FIB willingly, and they still ended up leaving a trail of chaos. What a violent, uncoopera-tive Inderlander might do was frightening.

"It doesn't make sense," Nick said loud enough for Edden in the front to hear. "Why is Mr. Kalamack padding his pocket with illegal gains? He's already independently wealthy."

Edden turned halfway around in his seat, his khaki nylon jacket sliding. He had a yellow FIB hat on, the only sign of his au-thority. "He must be funding a project he doesn't want to be found. Money is hard to trace when it's gotten from illegal means and spent on the same."

I wondered what it was. Something more going on in Faris's lab, perhaps?

The FIB captain brought his thick hand to his chin, his round face lit by the cars behind us. "Mr. Sparagmos," he questioned, "have you ever taken the ferry tour of the waterfront?"

Nick's face went still. "Sir?"

Edden shook his head. "It's the damnedest thing. I'm sure I've seen you before."

"No," Nick said, easing back into the corner of the seat. "I don't like boats."

Making a small sound, Edden turned back around in his seat. I exchanged a knowing look with Jenks. The small pixy made a sly face, catching on faster than I had. My empty bag of peanuts crumpled noisily, and I tucked it in my bag, not about to throw it onto the clean floor. Nick was shadowed and closed, the dim light from oncoming motorists blurring his sharp nose and thin face. Leaning close, I whispered, "What did you do?"

His eyes remained fixed out the window, his chest rising and falling in a smooth breath. "Nothing."

I glanced at the back of Edden's head. *Yeah, right. And I'm the I.S. poster girl.* "Look. I'm sorry I got you into this. If you want to just walk away when we get to the airport, I'll understand." On second thought, I didn't want to know what he had done.

He shook his head, giving me a quick flash of a smile. "It's all right," he said. "I'll see you through tonight. I owe you that for getting me out of that rat pit. One more week, and I was going to go insane."

Just imagining it gave me a chill. There were worse fates than being on an I.S. death list. I touched his shoulder briefly and eased back into my seat, surreptitiously watching him as he lost his hidden tension and his breath came easier. The more I knew about him, the larger his contrasts with most of humanity became. But instead of worrying me, it made me feel more secure. Back to my hero/damsel in distress syndrome. I'd read too many fairy tales as a child, and I was too much a realist not to enjoy being rescued once in a while.

An uncomfortable silence settled in, and my anxiety swelled. What if we were too late? What if Trent changed the flight? What if it had all been an elaborate setup? *God help me,* I thought. I had gambled everything on the next few hours. If this didn't happen, I had nothing.

"Witch!" Jenks shouted, jerking my attention to him. I realized he had been trying to get my attention for the last few moments. "Pick me up," he demanded. "I can't see jack from here."

I offered him a hand and he clambered up. "I can't imagine why everyone avoids you when you can't fly," I said dryly.

"This never would have *happened*," Jenks said loudly, "if *someone* hadn't torn my freaking *wing* off."

I set him on my shoulder, where we could both watch the outgoing traffic as we headed into the Cincinnati–Northern Kentucky International Airport. Most people just called it the Hollows International, or even more simply, the "Big H.I." The passing cars were briefly lit by the scattered streetlights. The lights became more numerous the closer we came to the terminals. A flash of excitement went through me, and I straightened in my seat. Nothing was going to go wrong. I was going to nail him. Whatever Trent was, I was going to get him. "What time is it?" I asked.

"Eleven-fifteen," Jenks muttered.

"Eleven-twenty," Edden corrected, pointing to the van's clock.

"Eleven-fifteen," the pixy snarled back. "I know where the sun is better than you know what hole to pee out of."

"Jenks!" I said, aghast. Nick uncrossed his arms, a wisp of his confidence returning.

Edden raised a restraining hand. "It's all right, Ms. Morgan."

Clayton, an uptight cop who didn't seem to trust me, met my eyes in the rearview mirror. "Actually, sir," he said reluctantly, "that clock is five minutes fast."

"See?" Jenks exclaimed.

Edden reached for the car phone and snapped on the speaker so we all could hear. "Let's make sure that plane is grounded and everyone is in place," he said.

Anxious, I adjusted my arm sling as Edden punched three numbers into the phone. "Ruben," he barked into it, holding it like it was a mike. "Talk to me."

There was a brief hesitation, then a masculine voice crackled through the speakers. "Captain. We're waiting at the gate, but the plane isn't here."

"Not there!" I shouted, wincing as I yanked myself to the edge of the seat. "They should be boarding by now."

"It never came to the tunnel, sir," Ruben continued. "Everyone is waiting at the terminal. They say it's a minor repair and should only take an hour. This isn't your doing?"

I glanced from the speaker to Edden. I could almost see the ideas circulating behind his speculating expression. "No," he finally said. "Stay put." He broke the connection and the faint hiss disappeared.

"What is going on?" I shouted into his ear, and he gave me a black look.

"Get your butt back in your seat, Morgan," he said. "It's probably your friend's daylight restrictions. The airline won't make everyone wait on the tarmac when the terminal is empty."

I glanced at Nick, whose fingers were nervously tapping out the rhythm of an unheard beat. Still uneasy, I settled back. The landing beacon from the airport ran an arc across the underside of the clouds. We were nearly there.

Edden punched in a number from memory, a smile easing over his face as he took the phone off the speaker. "Hello, Chris?" he said, as I faintly heard a woman's voice answer. "Got a question for ya. Seems there's a Southwest flight stuck on the tarmac. Eleven forty-five to L.A.? What's up with it?" He hesitated, listening, and I found myself chewing on a hangnail. "Thanks, Chris." He chuckled. "How about the thickest steak in the city?" Again he chuckled, and I swear, his ears reddened.

Jenks snickered at something I couldn't hear. I glanced at Nick, but he was ignoring me.

"Chrissy," Edden drawled. "My wife might have a problem with that." Jenks laughed with Edden, and I tugged a curl, nervous. "Talk to you later," he said, and clicked the phone off.

"Well?" I asked from the edge of my seat.

The remnants of Edden's smile refused to leave him. "The plane is grounded. Seems the I.S. had a tip there's a bag of Brimstone on it."

"Turn it all," I swore. The bus was the decoy, not the airport. What was Trent doing?

Edden's eyes glinted. "The I.S. is fifteen minutes away. We could pull it right out from under them."

On my shoulder, Jenks started to swear.

"We aren't here for Brimstone," I protested, as everything started falling apart. "We're here for biodrugs!" Fuming, I went silent as a loud car approached us, heading back into the city.

"That one's above city code," Edden said. "Clayton, see if you can get a number off it."

Mind whirling, I waited for it to pass before I tried to speak again. The engine was racing as if the driver was doing thirty over the speed limit, but the car was hardly moving. The gears whined as it tried to shift in an all-too-familiar sound. *Francis*, I thought, my breath catching.

"That's Francis!" both Jenks and I shouted as I spun to see his broken taillight. My vision swam from the pain the quick movement started, but I half crawled to the far backseat, Jenks still on my shoulder. "That's Francis," I cried, my heart pounding. "Turn around. Stop! That's Francis."

Edden hit his fist into the dash. "Damn," he swore. "We're too late."

"No!" I shouted. "Don't you see? Trent is switching them. The biodrugs and Brimstone. The I.S. isn't there yet. Francis is switching them!"

Edden stared at me, his face alternating in the shadow and light as we continued up the long drive to the airport.

"Francis has the drugs! Turn around!" I shouted.

The van stopped at a traffic light. "Captain?" the driver prompted.

"Morgan," Edden said, "you're crazy if you think I'm going to pass up the chance to slip a Brimstone take right out from under the I.S. You don't even know if that was him or not."

Jenks laughed. "That was Francis. Rachel burned out his clutch right proper."

I grimaced. "Francis has the drugs. They're going out by bus. I'd bet my life on it."

Edden's eyes narrowed and his jaw clenched. "You have," he said shortly. "Clayton, turn around."

I slumped, letting out a breath I hadn't known I'd been holding. "Captain?"

"You heard me!" he said, clearly not happy. "Turn around. Do what the witch says." He turned to me, his face tight. "You'd better be right, Morgan," he nearly growled.

"I am." Stomach churning, I settled back, bracing myself at the sharp U-turn. *I had better be right,* I thought, glancing at Nick.

An I.S. truck passed us on its way to the airport, silent with its lights flashing. Edden hit the dash so hard it was a wonder the air bag didn't come out. He snatched up the radio. "Rose!" he bellowed. "Did the dog team find anything at the bus depot?"

"No, Captain. They're on their way in now."

"Get them back out there," he said. "Who do we have in the Hollows in plainclothes?"

"Sir?" She sounded confused.

"Who's in the Hollows that I didn't move to the airport?" he shouted.

"Briston is at the Newport mall in plainclothes," she said. The faint ringing of a phone intruded, and she shouted, "Someone get that!" There was hesitation. "Gerry is backing her up, but he's in uniform."

"Gerry," Edden muttered, clearly not pleased. "Move them to the bus depot."

"Briston and Gerry to bus depot," she repeated slowly.

"Tell them to use their ACGs," Edden added, shooting a glance at me.

"ACGs?" Nick asked.

"Anticharm gear," I said, and he nodded.

"We're looking for a white male, early thirties. Witch. Name is Francis Percy. I.S. runner."

"He's no better than a warlock," I interjected, bracing myself as we came to an abrupt halt at a red light.

"The suspect is probably carrying spells," Edden continued.

"He's harmless," I muttered.

"Do not approach unless he tries to leave," Edden said tightly.

"Yeah." I snorted as we lurched into motion again. "He might bore you to death."

Edden turned to me. "Will you shut your mouth?"

I shrugged, then wished I hadn't as my shoulder started to throb.

"Did you get that, Rose?" he said into the phone.

"Armed, dangerous, don't approach unless he tries to leave. Gotcha."

Edden grunted. "Thanks, Rose." He flicked the radio off with a thick finger.

Jenks yanked on my ear, and I let out a yelp.

"There he is!" the pixy shrilled. "Look. Right ahead of us."

Nick and I leaned forward to see. The broken taillight was like a beacon. We watched as Francis signaled, squealing his tires as he lurched into the bus depot. A horn blew, and I smirked. Francis had nearly been hit by a bus.

"Okay," Edden said softly as we circled to park on the far side of the lot. "We have five minutes until the dog team gets here, fifteen for Briston and Gerry. He will have to register the packages with the front desk. It will be a nice proof of ownership." Edden undid his seat belt and spun his bucket chair as the van halted. He looked as eager as a vamp with that toothy grin of his. "No one even look at him until everyone gets here. Got it?"

"Yeah, I got it," I said, jittery. I didn't like being under someone else's direction, but what he said made sense. Nervous, I slid across the seat to press my face to Nick's window and watch Francis struggle with three flat boxes.

"That him?" Edden said, his voice cold.

I nodded. Jenks walked down my arm and stood on the sill of the window. His wings were a blur as he used them for balance. "Yeah," the pixy snarled. "That's the pancake."

Glancing up, I realized I was almost in Nick's lap. Embarrassed, I put myself where I belonged. The aspirin was starting to wear off, and though my remaining amulet would be good for days, the pain was starting to break through with an unsettling frequency. But it was the fatigue I was really worried about. My heart was hammering as if I had just finished a race. I didn't think it was just from the excitement.

Francis kicked his car door shut and tottered into motion. He was the picture of self-importance as he strutted into the depot in his loud shirt with the turned-up collar. I smirked as he smiled at a woman coming out and got a quick brush-off. But on remembering his fear while sitting in Trent's office, my contempt took on a shade of pity for the insecure man.

"Okay, boys and girls," Edden said, pulling my attention back.

"Clayton, stay here. Send Briston in when she arrives. I don't want anyone out of plainclothes in sight of the windows." He watched Francis go through the double doors. "Have Rose move everyone in from the airport. Looks like the witch, er, Ms. Morgan was right."

"Yes sir." Clayton reluctantly reached for the car phone.

Doors started to open. It was obvious we weren't your typical group of bus patrons, but Francis was probably too stupid to notice. Edden stuffed his yellow FIB hat into a back pocket. Nick was a thin nobody; he looked like he belonged. But my bruises and sling drew more attention than if I had a bell and a card that said, "Will work for spells."

"Captain Edden?" I said as he slipped out and stood waiting. "Give me a minute."

Edden and Nick looked wonderingly back at me as I rummaged in my bag. "Rachel," Jenks said from Nick's shoulder. "You've got to be kidding. Ten makeup charms couldn't make you look better right now."

"Go Turn yourself," I muttered. "Francis will recognize me. I need an amulet."

Edden watched with interest. Feeling the press of adrenaline, I awkwardly rummaged with my good hand in my bag for an aging spell. Finally I dumped the bag onto the seat, grabbed the right charm and invoked it. As I set it around my neck, Edden made a sound of disbelief and admiration. His acceptance—no, approval—was gratifying. That he had taken my pain amulet earlier had a lot to do with me agreeing to owing him a favor or two. Whenever a human showed any appreciation for my skills, I got all warm and fuzzy. *Sucker.*

Jamming everything away in my bag, I creakily eased myself out of the van.

"Ready?" Jenks said sarcastically. "Sure you don't want to brush your hair?"

"Shove it, Jenks," I said as Nick offered me a hand. "I can get down by myself," I added.

Jenks made the jump from Nick to me, settling on my shoulder. "You look like an old woman," the pixy said. "Act like it."

"She is." Edden grabbed my shoulder to keep me from falling as my vamp boots hit the pavement. "She reminds me of my mother." His eyes scrunched as he made a face and waved his hand before his nose. "She even smells like her."

"Shut up, all of you," I said, hesitating as my deep breath

made me light-headed. The jarring pain from my landing had gone straight up my spine and into my skull, settling itself for a long stay. Refusing to let my fatigue get a foothold, I jerked away from Edden and hobbled to the doors. The two men followed, three paces behind. I felt like a slob in my fat jeans and that awful plaid shirt. Carrying the illusion of being old didn't help, either. I tugged at the door, unable to open it. "Someone open this door for me!" I exclaimed, and Jenks laughed.

Nick took my arm as Edden opened the door and a gust of overheated air billowed into us. "Here," Nick said. "Lean on me. You look more like an old lady that way."

The pain I could deal with. It was the fatigue that overwhelmed my pride and forced me to accept Nick's offered arm. It was either that or crawl into the bus station.

I shuffled in, a stir of excitement quickening my pulse as I scanned the long front counter for Francis. "There he is," I whispered.

Almost hidden behind a fake tree, Francis was talking to a young woman in a city uniform. The Percy charm was having its usual effect, and she looked annoyed. Three boxes were on the counter beside him. My continued existence was in those boxes.

Nick pulled gently on my good elbow. "Let's sit you down over here, Mother," he said.

"Call me that again and I'll take care of your family planning for you," I threatened.

"Mother," Jenks said, his wings fanning my neck in fitful spurts.

"Enough," Edden said softly, a new hardness in his voice. His eyes never left Francis. "All three of you are going to sit over there and wait. No one moves unless Percy tries to leave. I'm going to make sure those boxes don't get on a bus." His gaze still on Francis, he touched the weapon hidden behind his jacket and casually made his way to the counter. Edden beamed at a second clerk before he even got close.

Sit and wait? Yeah, I could do that.

I gave in to Nick's gentle pull and moved toward the bank of chairs. They were orange, same as at the FIB, and looked equally comfortable. Nick helped me ease down into one, taking the chair next to mine. He stretched out and pretended to nap, his eyes cracked to watch Francis. I sat stiffly with my bag on my lap, clutching it as I had seen old ladies do. Now I knew why. I hurt all over, and I felt like I would fall apart if I relaxed.

A kid shrieked, and I took a quick breath. My eyes drifted from Francis, busy making an ass of himself, to the other patrons. There was a tired mom with three kids—one still in diapers—arguing with a clerk over the interpretation of a coupon. A handful of businessmen absorbed in their business, striding importantly, as if this was only a bad dream and not the reality of their existence. Young lovers pressed dangerously close, probably fleeing parents. Vagrants. A tattered old man caught my eye and winked.

I started. This wasn't safe. The I.S. could be anywhere, ready to tag me.

"Relax, Rache," Jenks whispered as if reading my mind. "The I.S. isn't going to nack you with the captain of the FIB in the same room."

"How can you be so sure?" I said.

I felt the wind on my neck as he fanned his useless wings. "I'm not."

Nick opened his eyes and sat up. "How are you doing?" he asked quietly.

"I'm fine," Jenks said. "Thanks for asking. Did you know some lunker at the FIB snapped my freaking wing off? My wife is gonna kill me."

I managed a smile. "Hungry," I answered Nick. "Exhausted."

Nick glanced at me before returning his gaze to Francis. "You want something to eat?" He jingled the coins in his pocket, left over from the cab fare to the FIB. "You have enough for something out of the machine there."

I let a faint smile come over me. It was nice to have someone worried about me. "Sure. Thanks. Something with chocolate?"

"Chocolate," Nick affirmed, standing up. He glanced from the vending machines across the room to Francis. The snot was leaning halfway across the counter, probably trying to get her phone number. I watched Nick walk away. For someone so thin, he certainly moved with grace. I wondered what he had done to have gotten hauled into the FIB.

"Something with chocolate," Jenks drawled in a high falsetto. "Ohhhh, Nick. You're my hero!"

"Get stuffed," I said, more out of habit than anything else.

"Ya know something, Rache," Jenks said as he settled himself further on my shoulder. "You're going to make one really weird grandma."

I was too tired to come back with anything. I took a deep breath, making it slow so nothing would hurt. My eyes flicked from Francis and back to Nick, anticipation making my stomach feel tight. "Jenks," I said, watching Nick's tall shape as he stood before the candy machine, his head bowed over the change in his hand. "What do you think about Nick?"

The pixy snorted, then seeing I was serious, settled down. "He's okay," he said. "Won't do anything to hurt you. He's got this hero complex thing going, and you seem to need rescuing. You should have seen his face when you were flat out on Ivy's couch. I thought he was going to turn up his toes to the daisies. Just don't expect him to have your ideas of right or wrong."

My eyebrows pinched, hurting my face. "Black magic?" I whispered. "Oh God, Jenks. Don't tell me he's a practitioner?"

Jenks laughed, sounding like wind chimes. "No. I meant he doesn't have a problem stealing library books."

"Oh." I thought back to his unease in the FIB office and then in the van. Was that all it was? Somehow, I didn't think so. But pixies were known for their judge of character, no matter how flighty, flaky, or mouthy they were. I wondered if Jenks's opinion would change if he knew about my demon mark. I was afraid to ask. Hell, I was too afraid to show it to him.

I looked up as Francis laughed, writing something down on a paper and pushing it toward the ticket lady. He wiped a hand under his narrow nose and gave her a ratty grin. "Good girl," I whispered when she crumpled it up and tossed it over her shoulder as Francis headed for the door.

My heart seemed to catch. He was headed for the door! *Damn.*

I glanced up for help. Nick was struggling with the machine, his back to me. Edden was deep in conversation with an official-looking man in a bus uniform. The captain's face was red, and his eyes were fixed to the boxes behind the counter. "Jenks," I said tersely. "Get Edden."

"What? You want me to crawl over there, maybe?"

Francis was halfway to the door. I didn't trust Clayton outside to be able to stop a dog from taking a leak. I stood, praying that Edden would turn around. He didn't. "Get him," I muttered, ignoring Jenks's outrage as I plucked him from my shoulder and set him on the floor.

"Rachel!" Jenks shouted as I hobbled as fast as I could, trying to get between Francis and the door. I was too slow, and Francis cut ahead of me.

"Excuse me, young man?" I warbled, my pulse racing as I

reached out for him. "Would you tell me where the baggage area is?"

Francis spun on a quick heel. I struggled not to show my alarm that he might recognize me and my hatred for what he had done. "This is the bus depot, lady," he said, his thin lips twisted in annoyance. "There is no baggage area. Your stuff is on the curb outside."

"What's that?" I said loudly, mentally cursing Edden. *Where the hell was he?* I grabbed Francis arm in a tight grip, and he looked down at my spell-wrinkled hand.

"It's outside!" he shouted, trying to tug away, reeling as my perfume hit him.

But I wouldn't let go. From the corner of my sight I saw Nick beside the candy machine, staring blankly at my empty seat. His gaze rove over the people, finally catching mine. His eyes widened. He darted to Edden.

Francis had tucked his papers under his arm and was using his other hand to try and pry my fingers from him. "Lemme go, lady," he said. "There's no baggage claim."

My fingers cramped, and he jerked away. Panicking, I watched him tug his shirt straight. "Freaky old bat," he said with a huff. "What do you old hags do, swim in your perfume?" Then his mouth dropped open. "Morgan," he hissed, recognizing me. "He told me you were dead."

"I am," I said, my knees threatening to buckle. I was up on adrenaline alone.

His stupid grin told me he had no idea what was going on. "You're coming with me. Denon will give me a promotion when he sees you."

I shook my head. I had to do this by the book or Edden would be ticked. "Francis Percy, under the authority of the FIB, I am charging you with conspiring to willfully run biodrugs."

His grin vanished as his face went white under his ugly stubble. His gaze darted over my shoulder to the counter. "Shit," he swore, turning to run.

"Stop!" Edden cried out, too far back to be any good.

I lunged at Francis, grabbing the back of his knees. We went down in a painful thump. Francis squirmed, kicking me in the chest as he tried to get away. I gasped, hurting.

A whoosh of air streaked over us where my head had been. I jerked my attention up. Stars crossed my vision as Francis struggled to escape.

No, I thought as a blue ball of flame smashed into the far wall and exploded. *Those stars were real.*

The ground shook at the force of the blast. Women and children screamed, falling back to press against the walls. "What was that?" Francis stammered. He twisted under me, and for a heartbeat we watched, mesmerized, as the flickering blue flame plastered itself in a sunburst across the ugly yellow wall until it folded back in on itself and vanished with a pop.

Frightened for the first time, I turned to look behind me. Standing confidently by the hallway to the back offices was a short tidy man dressed in black, a red ball of ever-after in his hand. A wisp of a woman dressed the same blocked the main doors, her hand on her hip and her white teeth grinning. The third was a muscular man the size of a VW bug by the ticket counter.

It looked like the witch conference at the coast was over.

Swell.

Thirty-one

Francis's breath came in a gulp of understanding. "Let me go!" he shrieked, fear making his voice high and ugly. "Rachel, let me go! They're going to kill you!"

I dug my fingers into him as he struggled. Jaw gritted, I grunted in pain as his effort to flee pulled my stitches out. Blood flowed, and I fumbled in my bag for an amulet, watching from the corner of my sight as the short man's lips moved and the ball in his hand turned from ever-after red to blue. *Damn.* He was invoking his charm.

"I don't have time for this!" I muttered, angry as I lay half atop Francis, trying to tag him.

People were running now. They scattered into hallways and unhindered past the woman and into the parking lot. When witches dueled, only the quick survived. My breath hissed in through my nose as the man's lips stopped moving. Pulling his arm back, he threw the spell.

Gasping, I yanked Francis up and before me.

"No!" he shrieked, his mouth and eyes ugly in fear at the incoming charm.

The force of it slid us across the floor and to the chairs. His elbow jammed into my bruised arm and I grunted in pain. Francis's scream cut off in a frightening gurgle.

My shoulder turned to agony as I frantically pushed him off me. He sagged to the floor, senseless. Scooting backward, I stared. A pulsing blue sheet filmed him. A thin smear of it was on my sleeve. My skin crawled as the haze of blue ever-after reality slid from my sleeve to join that coating Francis. He was convulsing, covered in it. Then he went still.

Breath fast, I looked up. All three assassins were speaking Latin in tandem, their hands making unseen figures in the air. Their motions were graceful and deliberate, looking obscene.

"Rache!" Jenks shrilled from three chairs away. "They're making a net. Get out! You gotta get out!"

Get out? I thought, looking at Francis. The blue had vanished, leaving his arms and legs sprawled in unnatural angles on the floor. Horror flashed through me. I had made Francis take my hit. It had been an accident. I hadn't meant to kill him.

My stomach clenched, and I thought I might vomit. I pushed my fear aside, using my anger to get to my knees. I grasped for an orange chair, pulling on it to lever myself upright. They had made me make Francis take my hit. *Oh God. He was dead because of me.*

"Why did you make me do that?" I said softly, turning to the short man. I took a step forward as the air started to tingle. I couldn't say that what I'd done was wrong—I was alive—but I hadn't wanted to do that. "Why did you make me do that?" I said louder, anger swelling as the sensation of pinpricks broke over me like a wave. It was the beginnings of the net. I didn't care. I scooped up my bag as I passed it, kicking my uninvoked amulet out of the way.

The ley line witch's eyes grew wide in surprise as I came at him. Face going determined, he started chanting louder. I could hear the other two whispering like an ash-laden wind. It was easy to move in the center of the net, but the closer I got to the edge, the harder it became. We stood in a blue-tinted bowl of air. Past it, Edden and Nick struggled, trying to push their way in.

"You made me do that!" I shouted.

My hair lifted and fell in a breath of ever-after as their net went solid. Jaw clenched, I spared a glance beyond the haze of blue, seeing the muscle-bound mountain of a man outside it, keeping it in place even as he threw ley line spells at the hopelessly outclassed FIB officers who had swarmed in. I didn't care. Two of them in here with me. They weren't going anywhere.

I was angry and frustrated. I was tired of hiding in a church, tired of ducking splat balls, tired of dunking my mail in saltwater, and tired of being scared. And because of me, Francis was lying on the dirty cold floor of a cruddy bus depot. Worm that he was, he hadn't deserved that.

I swung my bag forward as I limped toward the short man. I

reached unseeing, feeling the notches of the amulets for a sleep charm. Mad as hell, I wiped it across my neck, letting it go to dangle from the cord. His lips started moving, and those long hands of his began sketching patterns. If it was a nasty spell, I had four seconds. Five, if it was strong enough to kill me.

"Nobody!" I exclaimed, staggering forward by will alone. His eyes widened as he saw my demon scar as I made a fist. "Nobody makes me kill anyone!" I shouted, swinging.

We both staggered as I connected with his jaw. Shaking my hand from the pain, I hunched into myself. The man stumbled back, catching himself. The gathering of power abruptly lessened. Furious, I gritted my teeth and swung again. He hadn't expected a physical attack—not many ley line witches did—and he raised his arm to block me. Grabbing his fingers, I gave them a backward twist, breaking at least three.

His scream of pain was echoed by the woman's cry of dismay from across the lobby. She started forward at a run. Still gripping his hand, I swung my foot up, yanking him forward to smack into it. His eyes bulged. Clutching his stomach, he fell back. His watering gaze tracked someone behind me. Still not breathing, he dropped and rolled to the right.

Gasping, I hit the ground and rolled to the left. There was a boom, and my hair blew back. I pulled my head up from the floor as the ball of green ever-after spread itself on the wall and down the hallway. I turned. The wisp of a woman was still coming, her face tight and her mouth going nonstop. A red ball of ever-after in her hand swelled, streaked with her own green aura as she tried to bend it to her will.

"You want a piece of me?" I shouted from the floor. "Do ya?" Staggering, I rose to put a hand to the wall to stay upright.

The man behind me said a word. I couldn't hear it. It was too alien for my mind to understand. It rolled into my head, and I struggled to make sense of it. Then my eyes opened wide and my mouth dropped in a silent scream as it exploded inside me.

Clutching my head, I fell to my knees, screaming. "No!" I shrieked, clawing at my scalp. "No! Get out!" Black-crusted red slashes. Squirming maggots. The sour taste of decayed flesh.

The memory of it burnt itself out from my subconscious. I looked up, panting. I was spent. There was nothing left. My heart pounded against my lungs. Black spots danced at the edges of my sight. My skin felt tingly, as if it wasn't mine. *What the hell had that been?*

The man and the woman stood together, her hand under his elbow as she supported him hunched over his broken hand. Their faces were angry, confident—and satisfied. He couldn't use his hand, but clearly he didn't need it to kill me. All he had to do was say that word again.

I was dead. The more-than-usual kind of dead. But I would take one of them with me.

"Now!" I heard Edden shout faintly as if through a fog.

All three of us started as the net went down. The shadow of blue hazing in the air fell into itself and vanished. That big witch outside the net was on the floor with his hands laced behind his head. Six FIB officers ringed him. Hope twanged through me, almost painful.

A darting shape drew my eye. Nick. "Here!" I shouted, grasping the cord of the invoked sleep charm from the floor where I had dropped it and winging it to him.

The assassin turned, but it was too late. White-faced, Nick dropped the loop over the head of the woman and backpedaled. She crumpled. The man fumbled for her, easing her to the floor. Mouth agape in surprise, he darted his glance over the room.

"This is the FIB!" Edden shouted, looking awkward in his sling and with his weapon held in his left hand. "Put your hands behind your head and stop moving your mouth or I'll blow it the hell off!"

The man blinked, shocked. He glanced at the woman at his feet. Taking a breath, he ran.

"No!" I cried. Still on the floor, I dumped my bag. I grabbed an amulet, smacked it against my bleeding neck, and threw it at his feet. Half the charms in my bag were tangled in it. Like a bola, it flew through the air at knee height. It hit him, wrapping around his leg like he was a cow. Tripping, he went down.

FIB personnel swarmed over him. Breath held, I watched, waiting. He stayed down. My charm had dropped him into a sweet, helpless sleep.

The noise of the FIB personnel beat at me. With a single-minded purpose, I crawled to Francis lying alone by the chairs. Fearing the worst, I rolled him over. His sightless eyes stared up at the ceiling. My face went slack. *God, no.*

But then his chest moved, and a stupid-ass smile quirked his thin lips as they shifted in whatever dream he was in. He was alive and breathing, deep under a ley line spell. Relief poured through me. I hadn't killed him.

"Tag!" I screamed into his unconscious, narrow, ratty face. "Do you hear me you sodden sack of camel dung? Tag! You're it!" *I hadn't killed him.*

Edden's scuffed brown shoes scraped to a halt beside me. My face went tight, and I wiped a blood-smeared hand under my eye. *I hadn't killed Francis.* Squinting, I ran my gaze up Edden's creased khakis and his blue arm sling. His hat was on, and I couldn't seem to take my eyes off the blue letters spelling out FIB glowing against the yellow background. A satisfied harrumph came out of him, and his wide grin made him look even more like a troll. Numb, I blinked as my lungs pressed against each other. It seemed to take an awful amount of effort to fill them.

"Morgan," the man said happily, extending a thick hand to help me up. "You okay?"

"No," I croaked. I reached for him, but the floor tilted. As Nick gasped a warning, I passed out.

Thirty-two

"Listen!" Francis shouted, spittle flying from him in his fervor. "I'll tell you everything. I want a deal. I want protection. I was only supposed to do Brimstone takes. That's all. But someone got spooked and Mr. Kalamack wanted the drops switched. He told me to switch the drops. That's all! I'm not a biodrug runner. Please. You gotta believe me!"

Edden said nothing, playing the silent bad cop as he sat across from me. The shipping papers Francis had signed were under his thick hand as an unspoken accusation. Francis cowered in a chair at the end of the table, two chairs down from us. His eyes were wide and frightened. He looked pathetic in his bright shirt and polyester jacket with the sleeves rolled up, trying to live the dream he wanted his life to be.

I carefully stretched my sore body, my gaze falling on the three cardboard boxes stacked ominously at one end of the table. A smile curved over me. Hidden under the table and in my lap was an amulet I'd taken from the head assassin. It glowed an ugly red, but if it was what I thought it was, it would go black when I was dead or in the event the contract on my life had been paid off. I was going home to sleep for a week as soon as the little sucker went out.

Edden had moved Francis and me into the employees' break room to stave off a repeat of the witch attack. Thanks to the local news van, everyone in the city knew where I was—and I was just waiting for fairies to crawl out of the ductwork. I had more faith in the ACG blanket draped over me than the two FIB officers standing around to make the long room seem cramped.

I tugged the blanket closer around my neck, appreciating its minor protection as much as its warmth. Spiderweb-thin strands of titanium were woven into it, guaranteed to dilute strong spells and break mild ones. Several of the FIB officers had yellow coveralls made out of a similar fabric, and I was hoping Edden would forget to ask for it back.

As Francis babbled, my eyes ran over the grimy walls decorated with sappy sentiments about happy workplaces and how to sue your employer. A microwave and a battered fridge took up one wall, a coffee-stained counter took up another. I eyed the decrepit candy machine, hungry again. Nick and Jenks were in the corner, both trying to stay out of the way.

The heavy door to the break room opened, and I turned as an FIB officer and a young woman in a provocative red dress slipped in. An FIB badge hung around her neck, and the yellow FIB hat perched on her overstyled hair looked like a cheap prop. I guessed they were Gerry and Briston from the mall. The woman's face scrunched up and she whispered a derisive, "Perfume." My breath puffed out. I'd love to explain, but it would probably do more harm than good.

The whispers of the FIB officers had lessoned dramatically after I'd ditched the old lady disguise and turned into a battered twenty-something with frizzy red hair and curves where they ought to be. I felt like a bean in a ma-raca, and with my sling, my black eye, and the blanket draped around me, I probably looked like a disaster refugee.

"Rachel!" Francis cried urgently, drawing my attention back to him. His triangular face was pale, and his dark hair had gone stringy. "I need protection. I'm not like you. Kalamack is going to kill me. I'll do anything! You want Kalamack; I want protection. I was only supposed to do Brimstone. It's not my fault. Rachel, you've got to believe me."

"Yeah." Tired beyond belief, I took a deep breath and looked at the clock. It was just after midnight, but it felt like nearly sunrise.

Edden smiled. His chair scraped as he got to his feet. "Let's open 'em up, people."

Two FIB officers eagerly stepped forward. I clutched the amulet in my lap and anxiously leaned to see. My continued existence was in those boxes. The sound of ripping tape was loud. Francis wiped his mouth, watching in what looked like a morbid fascination and fear.

"Sweet mother of God," one of the officers swore, backing away from the table as the box opened. "They're tomatoes."

Tomatoes? I lurched to my feet, grunting in pain. Edden was a breath ahead of me.

"It's inside them!" Francis babbled. "The drugs are inside. He hides the drugs in tomatoes so the custom dogs can't smell them." White-faced behind his stubble, he pushed his sleeves up again. "They're in there. Look!"

"Tomatoes?" Edden said, disgust crossing him. "He ships them out in tomatoes?"

Perfect red tomatoes with green stems stared back at me from their cardboard packing tray. Impressed, my lips parted. Trent must have wedged the vials into the developing fruit, and by the time it was ripe, the drug was safely hidden inside a faultless fruit no human would touch.

"Get over there, Nick," Jenks demanded, but Nick didn't move, his long face ashen. At the sink, two officers who had opened the boxes were violently scrubbing their hands.

Looking like he was going to be sick, Edden stretched to pick a tomato up, examining the red fruit. There was not a blemish or cut on the perfect skin. "I suppose we probably ought to open one up," he said reluctantly, setting it on the table and wiping his hand on his pants.

"I'll do it," I volunteered when no one spoke up, and someone slid a tarnished table knife across the table at me. I picked it up with my left hand, then remembering my other hand was in a sling, I looked for some help. Not one FIB officer would meet my gaze. Not one was willing to touch the fruit. Frowning, I set the knife aside. "Oh well," I breathed, raising my hand and bringing it down on top of the fruit.

It hit with a sodden splat. Red goo splattered over Edden's white shirt. His face went as gray as his mustache. There was a cry of disgust from the watching FIB officers. Someone gagged. Heart pounding, I took the tomato in one hand and squeezed. Pulp and seeds squirted from between my fingers. My breath caught as a cylinder the size of my pinky pressed against my palm. I dropped the mass of pulp and shook my hand. Shouts of dismay rose as the red flesh splattered against the table. It was only a tomato, but one would think I was pulping a decaying heart by the noise the big, strong FIB officers were making.

"Here it is!" I said triumphantly, picking out an institutional-looking vial gooped in tomato slime and holding it aloft. I'd never seen biodrugs before. I had thought there'd be more.

"Well, I'll be," Edden said softly, taking the ampule in a napkin. The satisfaction of discovery had overwhelmed his abhorrence.

A wisp of fear tightened Francis's eyes as his gaze darted from me to the boxes. "Rachel?" he whimpered. "You'll get me protection from Mr. Kalamack, right?"

Anger stiffened my back. He had betrayed me and everything I believed in—for money. I turned to him, the gray edging my sight as leaned over the table and I put myself in his face. "I saw you at Kalamack's," I said, and his lips went bloodless. Grabbing the front of his shirt, I left a red smear across the colorful fabric. "You're a black runner, and you're gonna burn." I pushed him back into his chair and sat down, my heart pounding from the effort—satisfied.

"Whoa!" Edden said softly. "Someone arrest him and read him his rights."

Francis's mouth opened and closed in alarm as Briston pulled her cuffs from her hip and snapped them around his wrists. I reached into my sling and awkwardly unhooked my charm bracelet. I tossed it to land next to her—just in case Francis had something nasty in his rolled-up sleeves—and at Edden's nod, she laced it on Francis's wrist as well.

The soft and certain pattern of the Miranda flowed out in a reassuring cadence. Francis's eyes were wide and fixed to the vial. I don't think he even heard the man at his elbow.

"Rachel!" he cried as he found his voice. "Don't let him kill me. He's going to kill me. I gave you Kalamack. I want a deal. I want protection! That's the way it works, right?"

My eyes met Edden's and I wiped my hand free of the last of the tomato on a scratchy napkin. "Do we have to listen to this right now?"

A wicked, not so nice smile came over Edden. "Briston, get this bucket of crap into the van. Put his confession on tape and paper. And read him his rights again. No mistakes."

Francis stood, his chair scraping the dirty tile. His narrow face was drawn and his hair had fallen into his eyes. "Rachel, tell them Kalamack is going to kill me!"

I looked at Edden, my lips pressed tight. "He's right."

At my words, Francis whimpered. His dark eyes looked haunted, as if unsure whether he should be happy or upset that someone was taking his worries seriously.

"Get him an ACG blanket," Edden said in a bothered tone. "Keep him secure."

My shoulders eased. If they got Francis tucked out of sight quick enough, he'd be safe.

Briston's gaze flicked to the boxes. "And the—uh—tomatoes, Captain?"

His grin widened as he leaned over the table, careful to keep his arms out of the splattered mess. "Let's leave that for the evidence crew."

Clearly relieved, Briston gestured for Clayton. "Rachel!" Francis babbled as they pulled him to the door. "You're going to help me, right? I'll tell them everything!"

All four of the FIB officers roughly escorted him out, Briston's heels clicking smartly. The door snicked shut, and I closed my eyes at the blessed silence. "What a night," I whispered.

Edden's chuckle pulled my eyes open. "I owe you, Morgan," he said, three paper napkins between his fingers and the tomato-slimed white vial. "After seeing you with those two witches, I don't know why Denon was so set on bringing you down. You're a hell of a runner."

"Thanks," I whispered around a long sigh, stifling a shudder as my thoughts returned to trying to fight two ley line witches at once. It had been close. If Edden hadn't jarred the concentration of that third witch to break the net, I would have been dead. "Thanks for getting my back, I mean," I said softly.

The absence of the FIB officers had pulled Nick from the corner, and he handed me a foam cup of something that might have once been coffee. He carefully lowered himself into the chair beside me, his gaze flicking between the three boxes and the tomato-smeared table. It seemed seeing Edden touch one had given him a measure of courage. I flashed him a tired smile and cupped my good hand about the coffee, taking advantage of its warmth.

"I'd appreciate it if you would inform the I.S. you're paying off my contract," I said. "Before I set foot out of this room," I added, tugging the ACG blanket closer.

Edden set the vial down with a reverent slowness. "With Percy's confession, Kalamack can't buy his way out of this." A smile played about his square face. "Clayton tells me we got the Brimstone at the airport, too. I ought to get out from behind my desk more often."

I sipped my coffee. The bitter swill filled my mouth, and I reluctantly swallowed. "How about that call?" I said as I set the cup down and looked at the red amulet glowing in my lap.

Edden sat up with a grunt and took out a slim cell phone. Cradling it in his left hand, he hit a single digit with his thumb. I looked at Jenks to see if he noticed. The pixy's wings blurred, and with an impatient look, he slid from Nick and walked stiffly down the table to me. I raised him up to my shoulder before he could ask. Levering himself close to my ear, Jenks whispered, "He's got the I.S. on speed dial."

"How about that," I said, the tape pulling on my eyebrow as I tried to raise it.

"I'm going to wring every drop of gloat out of this one," Edden said, slouching back in his chair as the phone rang. The white vial stood out before him like a tiny trophy. "Denon!" he shouted. "Full moon next week. How you doing?"

My jaw dropped. It wasn't the I.S. Edden had on speed dial. It was my old boss. And he was alive? The demon hadn't killed him? He must have had someone else do his dirty work.

Edden harrumphed, clearly misunderstanding my surprise, before turning his attention back to the phone. "That's great," he said, interrupting Denon. "Listen. I want you to call off the run you have on a Ms. Rachel Morgan. Maybe you know her? She used to work for you." There was a slight pause, and I almost caught what Denon said, it was so loud. On my shoulder, Jenks fanned his wings in agitation. A sly smile came over Edden.

"You *do* remember her?" Edden said. "Great. Call your people off. We're paying for it." Again a hesitation, and his smile grew. "Denon, I'm offended. She can't work for the FIB. I'll move the funds when the accounts open in the morning. Oh, and could you send one of your trolleys out to the main bus depot? I've three witches needing extradition to Inderlander custody. They were making a ruckus, and since we were in the neighborhood, we downed them for you."

There was a spate of angry conversation from the other end, and Jenks gasped. "Ooooh, Rachel," he stammered. "He's ticked."

"No," Edden said firmly, sitting straighter. He was clearly enjoying this. "No," he said again, grinning. "You should have thought about that before you set them on her."

The butterflies in my stomach wanted out. "Tell him to dissolution the master amulet keyed to me," I said, setting the amulet to clatter onto the table like a guilty secret.

Edden put a hand over the phone, drowning out Denon's irate voice. "A what?"

My eyes were fixed on the amulet. It was still glowing. "Tell him," I said, taking a slow breath, "I want the master amulet keyed to me dissolutioned. Every assassin team spelling for me has an amulet just like this one." I touched it with a finger, wondering if the tingle I felt was imagined or real. "As long as it's glowing, they won't stop."

His eyebrows arched. "A life-sign monitoring amulet?" he said, and I nodded, giving him a sour smile. It was a courtesy from one assassin trio to the next so no one would waste time plotting to murder someone already dead.

"Huh," Edden said, putting the phone to his ear. "Denon," he said cheerfully. "Be a good boy and dunk the charm monitoring Morgan's life signs so she can go home to bed."

Denon's angry voice was loud through the small speaker. I jerked when Jenks laughed, vaulting himself up to sit in the swing of my earring. Licking my lips, I stared at the amulet, willing it to go out. Nick's hand touched my shoulder, and I jumped. My eyes fixed back onto the amulet with a hungry intensity.

"There!" I exclaimed as the disk flickered and went out. "Look! It's gone!" Pulse hammering, my eyes closed in a long blink as I imagined them going out all over the city. Denon must have had the master amulet with him, wanting to know the exact moment the assassins were successful. He was one sick puppy.

Fingers shaking, I picked it up. The disk felt heavy in my hand. My gaze met Nick's. He seemed as relieved as I was, the smile on his face reaching his eyes. Exhaling, I fell back against the chair and slipped the disk into my bag. My death threat was gone.

Denon's angry questions echoed through the phone. Edden grinned all the wider. "Turn on your TV, Denon, my friend," he said, holding the speaker away from his ear for a moment. Drawing it close, he shouted, "Turn on your TV. I said, turn on your TV!" Edden's eyes flicked to mine. "Bye-bye, Denon," he said in a mocking falsetto. "See you at church."

The beep as the circuit broke was loud. Edden leaned back in his chair and crossed his good arm over the one in the sling. His smile was one of satisfaction. "You're a free witch, Ms. Morgan. How's it feel to come back from the dead?"

My hair swung forward as I looked down at myself, every scratch and bruise complaining for attention. My arm throbbed in its sling, and my face was one solid ache. "Great," I said, managing a smile. "It feels just great." It was over. I could go home and hide under my covers.

Nick stood and put a hand on my shoulder. "Come on, Rachel," he said softly. "Let's get you home." His dark eyes rose to Edden's briefly. "She can do the paperwork tomorrow?"

"Sure." Edden rose, taking the vial cautiously between two fingers and dropping it into a shirt pocket. "I'd like you to be at Mr. Percy's interrogation, if you could manage it. You have a lie-detecting amulet, don't you? I'm curious to see how they compare to our electronic devices."

My head bobbed, and I tried to find the strength to rise. I didn't want to tell Edden how much trouble it was to make those things, but I wasn't going to go spell shopping for at least a month, to give the charms aimed at me a chance to filter out of the marketplace. Maybe two months. I looked at the black amulet on the table and stifled a shudder. *Maybe never.*

A soft boom of sound shifted the air and the floor trembled. There was a heartbeat of absolute silence, then the faint noise of people shouting filtered through the thick walls. I looked at Edden. "That was an explosion," he breathed, a hundred thoughts racing behind his eyes. But only one struck me. *Trent.*

The door to the break room flung open, smashing into the wall. Briston fell into the room, catching herself at the chair Francis had recently occupied. "Captain Edden," she gasped. "Clayton! My God, Clayton!"

"Stay with the evidence," he said, then darted out the door almost as fast as a vamp. The sound of people shouting drifted in before the door majestically closed. Briston stood in her red dress, her knuckles white as she clenched the back of the chair. Her head was bowed, but I could see her eyes welling up in what looked like grief and frustration.

"Rachel." Jenks prodded at my ear. "Get up. I want to see what happened."

"Trent happened," I whispered, my gut clenching. *Francis.*

"Get up!" Jenks shouted, tugging as if he could yank me up by my ear. "Rachel, get up!"

Feeling like a mule at the plow, I rose. My stomach lurched, and with Nick's help, I hobbled out into the noise and confusion. I hunched under my blanket and held my injured arm tight to me. I knew what I'd find. I'd seen Trent kill a man for less. Expecting him to sit idle as a legal noose slipped around his neck was ludicrous. But how had he moved so quickly?

The lobby was a confusing mess of broken glass and milling people. Cool night air came in through the gaping hole in the wall where glass once hung. Blue and yellow FIB uniforms were everywhere, not that they were helping matters. The stench of burning plastic caught at my throat, and the flickering black and orange of a fire beckoned from the parking lot where the FIB van burned. Red and blue lights flashed against the walls.

"Jenks," I breathed as he tugged on my ear to urge me on. "You keep doing that and I'll squish you myself."

"Then get your sorry little white witch behind out there!" he exclaimed in frustration. "I can't see squat from here."

Nick fended off the well-meaning efforts of good Samaritans who thought I'd been hurt in the explosion, but it wasn't until he scooped up an abandoned FIB hat and set it on my head that everyone left us alone. His arm curved around my waist, supporting me, we haltingly crunched over the broken glass, stepping from the yellow lights of the bus station into the harsher, uncertain come-and-go lights of the FIB's vehicles.

Outside, the local news was having a field day, sequestered in their little corner with bright lights and excited gestures. My stomach twisted as I realized that their presence had likely been responsible for Francis's death.

Squinting at the heat coming from the fire, I made my slow way to where Captain Edden stood quietly watching, thirty feet back from the flaming van. Saying nothing, I came to a standstill beside him. He didn't look at me. The wind gusted, and I coughed at the black taste of burnt rubber. There was nothing to say. Francis had been in there. Francis was dead.

"Clayton had a thirteen-year-old," Edden said, his eyes on the billowing smoke.

I felt as if I had been punched in the gut, and I willed myself to remain upright. Thirteen was not a good age to lose your father. I knew.

Edden took a deep breath and turned to me. The dead expression on his face chilled me. Flickering shadows from the fire pulled the few lines in his face into sharp relief. "Don't worry, Morgan," he said. "The deal was you give me Kalamack, the FIB pays off your contract." Emotion crossed his face, but I couldn't tell if it was rage or pain. "You gave him to me. I lost him. Without Percy's confession, all we have is a dead witch's word over his. And by the time I get a warrant, Kalamack's tomato fields will be plowed under. I'm sorry. He's going to walk. This . . ." He gestured to the fire. "This wasn't your fault."

"Edden—" I started, but he held up his hand.

Pulling away from me, he walked away. "No mistakes," he said to himself, looking more beaten than I felt. An FIB officer in a yellow ACG coverall rushed up to him, hesitating when Edden didn't acknowledge him. The crowd swallowed them up.

I turned back to the sudden bursts of gold and black, feeling ill. Francis was in there. Along with my charms. Guess they weren't so lucky after all.

"This wasn't your fault," Nick said, putting his arm around me again as my knees threatened to buckle. "You warned them. You did everything you could."

I leaned into his support before I fell over. "I know," I said flatly, believing it.

A fire engine wound between the parked cars, clearing the street and drawing an even larger crowd with its sporadic whoops of siren. "Rachel." Jenks tugged on my ear again.

"Jenks," I said in a bitter frustration. "Leave me alone."

"Blow it off your broomstick," the pixy snarled. "Jonathan is across the street."

"Jonathan!" Adrenaline rushed painfully through me, and I pulled from Nick. "Where?"

"Don't look!" Nick and Jenks said simultaneously. Nick put his arm back around me and started to turn me away.

"Stop!" I shouted, ignoring the pain as I tried to see behind me. "Where is he?"

"Keep walking, Rachel," Nick said tightly. "Kalamack might want you dead, too."

"Damn you all back to the Turn!" I shouted. "I want to see!" I went limp in an effort to make Nick stop. It sort of worked as I slipped from him and hit the pavement in an untidy pile.

Twisting, I scanned the opposite street. A familiar, hurried gait drew my attention. Darting between emergency personnel and rubberneckers was Jonathan. The tall, refined man was easy to spot, standing head and shoulders above most of the crowd. He was in a heap of hurry, headed for a car parked before the fire engine. Stomach clenching in worry, I stared at the long black car, knowing who was inside.

I swatted Nick out of the way as he tried to get me upright, cursing the cars and people who kept getting in my line of sight.

The back window rolled down. Trent met my eyes and my breath caught. By the light of the emergency vehicles, I could see his face was a mass of bruises and his head was bandaged. The anger in his eyes clenched my heart. "Trent," I hissed as Nick crouched to grip me under my arms and help me up.

Nick froze, and we both watched from the ground as Jonathan came to a halt beside the window. He bent to listen to Trent. My pulse raced as the tall man abruptly straightened, following Trent's gaze across the street to mine. I shivered at the hatred pouring from Jonathan.

Trent's lips moved, and Jonathan jumped. Giving me a final glare, Jonathan walked stiffly to the driver's door. I heard the door slam over the surrounding noise.

I couldn't take my eyes from Trent. His expression remained angry, but he smiled, and my worry tightened at the promise in it. The window went up and the car slowly drove away.

For a moment I could do nothing. The pavement was warm, and if I got up, I would only have to move. Denon hadn't sent the demon after me. Trent had.

Thirty-three

I bent to get the paper from the top step of the church's stoop. The smell of cut grass and damp pavement was almost a balm, filling my senses. There was a sudden rush on the sidewalk. Pulse pounding, I fell to a defensive crouch. The small-girl giggle following the pink bike and tinkly bell down the sidewalk was embarrassing. Her heels flashed as she peddled like the devil was after her. Grimacing, I slapped the paper against the palm of my hand as she disappeared around the corner. I swore, she waited for me every afternoon.

It had been a week since my I.S. death threat was officially nulled, and I was still seeing assassins. But then, more than the I.S. might want me dead.

Exhaling loudly, I willed the adrenaline from me as I yanked the door to the church closed behind me. The comforting crackle of newsprint echoed off the thick support beams and stark walls of the sanctuary as I found the classifieds. I tucked the rest of the paper under an arm and made my way to the kitchen, scanning the personals as I went.

"'Bout time you got up, Rache," Jenks said, his wings clattering as he flew annoying circles around me in the tight confines of the hall. I could smell the garden on him. He was dressed in his "dirt clothes," looking like a miniature Peter Pan with wings. "Are we going to go get that disc or what?"

"Hi, Jenks," I said, a stab of anxiety and anticipation running through me. "Yeah. They called for an exterminator yesterday." I laid the newsprint out on the kitchen table, pushing Ivy's colored pens and maps away to make room. "Look," I said, pointing. "I've got another one."

"Lemme see," the pixy demanded. He landed squarely on the paper, his hands on his hips.

Running my finger across the print, I read aloud, " 'TK seeking to reopen communication with RM concerning possible business venture.' " There was no phone number, but it was obvious who had written it. Trent Kalamack.

A weary unease pulled me to sit at the table, my gaze going past Mr. Fish in his new brandy snifter and out into the garden. Though I had paid off my contract and was reasonably safe from the I.S., I still had to contend with Trent. I knew he was manufacturing biodrugs; I was a threat. Right now he was being patient, but if I didn't agree to be on his payroll, he was going to put me in the ground.

At this point I didn't want Trent's head; I wanted him to leave me alone. Blackmail was entirely acceptable, and undoubtedly safer than trying to get rid of Trent through the courts. He was a businessman, if nothing else, and the hassle of disentangling himself from a trial was probably greater than his desire to have me work for him or see me safely dead. But I needed more than a page out of his daily planner. Today I would get it.

"Nice tights, Jenks," came Ivy's weak croak from the hall.

Startled, I jumped, then changed my motion to adjusting a curl of hair. Ivy was slumped against the doorframe, looking like an apathetic grim reaper in her black robe. Shuffling to the window, she shut the curtains and slumped against the counter in the new dimness.

My chair creaked as I leaned back in it. "You're up early."

Ivy poured a cold cup of coffee from yesterday, sinking down into a chair across from me. Her eyes were red-rimmed and her robe was tied sloppily about her waist. She listlessly fingered the paper where Jenks had left dirty footprints. "Full moon tonight. We doing it?"

I took a quick breath, my heart thumping. Rising, I went to dump out the coffee and make more before Ivy could drink the rest. Even I had higher standards than that. "Yes," I said, feeling my skin tighten.

"Are you sure you feel up to it?" she asked as her eyes settled on my neck.

It was my imagination, but I thought I felt a twinge from where her gaze rested. "I'm fine," I said, making an effort to keep my hand from rising to cover the scar. "Better than good. I'm great." Ivy's tasteless little cakes had made me alternatingly hungry and nauseous, but my stamina returned in an alarming three days rather than three months. Matalina had already removed the stitches from my neck to leave hardly a mark. Having healed that fast was worrisome. I wondered if I was going to pay for it later. And how.

"Ivy?" I asked as I got the grounds out of the fridge. "What was in those little cakes?"

"Brimstone."

I spun, shocked. "What?" I exclaimed.

Jenks snickered, and Ivy didn't drop my gaze as she got to her feet. "I'm kidding," she said flatly. Still I stared at her, my face cold. "Can't you take a joke?" she added, shuffling to the hall. "Give me an hour. I'll call Carmen and get her moving."

Jenks vaulted into the air. "Great," he said, his wings humming. "I'm going to go say good-bye to Matalina." He seemed to glow as a shaft of light pierced the kitchen as he slipped past the curtains.

"Jenks!" I called after him. "We aren't leaving for at least an hour!" It didn't take that long to say good-bye.

"Yeah?" came his faint voice. "You think my kids just popped out of the ground?"

Face warming, I flicked the switch and started the coffee brewing. My motions were quick with anticipation, and a glow settled in to burn in my middle. I had spent the last week planning Jenks's and my excursion out to Trent's in painful detail. I had a plan. I had a backup plan. I had so many plans I was amazed they didn't explode out my ears when I blew my nose.

Between my anxiety and Ivy's anal-retentive adherence to schedules, it was exactly an hour later that we found ourselves at the curb. Both Ivy and I were dressed in biker leather, giving us eleven feet, eight inches of bad-ass attitude between us—Ivy most of it. A version of those assassin life-monitoring amulets hung around our necks, tucked out of sight. It was my fail-safe plan. If I got in trouble, I'd break the charm and Ivy's amulet would turn red. She had insisted on them—along with a lot of other things I thought were unnecessary.

I swung up behind Ivy on her bike, with nothing but that fail-safe amulet, a vial of saltwater to break it, a mink potion, and Jenks. Nick had the rest. With my hair tucked under the helmet and the smoked faceplate down, we rode through the Hollows, over the bridge, and into Cincinnati. The afternoon sun was warm on my shoulders, and I wished we really were just two biker chicks headed into town for a Friday afternoon of shopping.

In reality, we were headed for a parking garage to meet Nick and Ivy's friend, Carmen. She would take my place for the day, pretending to be me while they drove around the countryside. I thought it overkill, but if it pacified Ivy, I'd do it.

From the garage, I would sneak into Trent's garden with the help of Nick playing lawn-service guy, spraying the bugs Jenks had seeded Trent's prize rosebushes with last Saturday. Once past Trent's walls, it would be easy. At least, that's what I kept telling myself.

I had left the church calm and collected, but every block deeper into the city wound me tighter. My mind kept going over my plan, finding the holes in it and the "what ifs." Everything we had come up with seemed foolproof from the safety of our kitchen table, but I was relying heavily upon Nick and Ivy. I trusted them, but it still made me uneasy.

"Relax," Ivy said loudly as we turned off the busy street and into the parking garage by the fountain square. "This is going to work. One step at a time. You're a good runner, Rachel."

My heart thumped, and I nodded. She hadn't been able to hide the worry in her voice.

The garage was cool, and she wove around the gate, avoiding the ticket. She was going to drive right on through as if using the garage as a side street. I took my helmet off upon catching sight of the white van plastered with green grass and puppies. I hadn't asked Ivy where she had gotten a lawn-care truck. I wasn't going to, either.

The back door opened as Ivy's bike lub-lub-lubbed closer, and a skinny vamp dressed like me jumped out, her hand grasping for the helmet. I handed it to her, sliding off as her leg took my place. Ivy never slowed the bike's pace. Stumbling, I watched Carmen stuff her blond hair under the helmet and grab Ivy's waist. I wondered if I really looked like that. Nah. I wasn't that skinny. "See you tonight, okay?" Ivy said over her shoulder as she drove away.

"Get in," Nick said softly, his voice muffled from inside the van. Giving Ivy and Carmen a last look, I jumped into the back, easing the door shut as Jenks flitted inside.

"Holy crap!" Jenks exclaimed, darting to the front. "What happened to you?"

Nick turned in the driver's seat, his teeth showing strong

against his makeup-darkened skin. "Shellfish," he said, patting his swollen cheeks. He had gone further in his charmless disguise, dying his hair a metallic black. With his dark complexion and his swollen face, he looked nothing like himself. It was a great disguise, which wouldn't set off a spell checker.

"Hi, Ray-ray," he said, his eyes bright. "How you doing?"

"Great," I lied, jittery. I shouldn't have involved him, but Trent's people knew Ivy, and he had insisted. "Sure you want to do this?"

He put the van into reverse. "I've an airtight alibi. My time card says I'm at work."

I looked askance at him as I pulled off my boots. "You're doing this on company time?"

"It's not as if anyone checks up on me. As long as the work gets done, they don't care."

My face went wry. Sitting on a canister of bug killer, I shoved my boots out of sight. Nick had found a job cleaning artifacts at the museum in Eden Park. His adaptability was a continual surprise. In one week he had gotten an apartment, furnished it, bought a ratty truck, got a job, and took me out on a date—a surprisingly nice date including an unexpected, ten-minute helicopter tour over the city. He said his preexisting bank account had a lot to do with how fast he had found his feet. They must pay librarians more than I thought.

"Better get changed," he said, his lips hardly moving as he paid the automated gate and we lumbered out into the sun. "We'll be there in less than an hour."

Anticipation pulled me tight, and I reached for the white duffel bag with the lawn care service logo on it. In it went my pair of lightweight shoes, my fail-safe amulet in a zippy bag, and my new silk/nylon bodysuit tightly packaged into a palm-sized bundle. I arranged everything to make room for one mink and an annoying pixy, tucking Nick's protective, disposable paper overalls on top. I was going in as a mink, but I would be damned if I was going to stay that way.

Conspicuous in their absence were my usual charms. I felt naked without them, but if caught, the most the I.S. could charge me with was breaking and entering. If I had even one charm that could act on a person—even as little as a bad-breath charm—it would bump me up to intent to do bodily harm. That was a felony. I was a runner; I knew the law.

While Nick kept Jenks occupied up front, I quickly stripped

down to nothing and jammed every last bit of evidence that I had been in the van into a canister labeled TOXIC CHEMICALS. I downed my mink potion with an embarrassed haste, gritting my teeth against the pain of transformation. Jenks gave Nick hell when he realized I'd been naked in the back of his van. I wasn't looking forward to changing back, suffering Jenks's barbs and jokes until I managed to get in my bodysuit.

And from there it went like clockwork.

Nick gained the grounds with little trouble, since he was expected—the real lawn service had gotten a cancellation call from me that morning. The gardens were empty because it was the full moon and they were closed for heavy maintenance. As a mink, I scampered into the thick rosebushes Nick was supposed to be spraying with a toxic insect killer but in actuality was saltwater to turn me back into a person. The thumps from Nick tossing my shoes, amulet, and clothes into the shrubs were unbelievably welcome. Especially with Jenks's lurid running commentary about acres of big, pale, naked women as he sat on a rose cane and rocked back and forth in delight. I was sure the saltwater was going to kill the roses rather than the aggressive insects Jenks had infected them with, but that, too, was in the plan. If by chance I was caught, Ivy would come in the same way with the new shipment of plants.

Jenks and I spent the better part of the afternoon squashing bugs, doing more than the saltwater to rid Trent's roses of pests. The gardens remained quiet, and the other maintenance crews stayed clear of Nick's caution flags stuck around the rose bed. By the time the moon rose, I was wound tighter than a virgin troll on his wedding night. It didn't help that it was so cold.

"Now?" Jenks asked sarcastically, his wings invisible but for a silver shimmer in the dark as he hovered before me.

"Now," I said, teeth chattering as I picked my careful way through the thorns.

With Jenks flying vanguard, we skulked from pruned bush to stately tree, finding our way in through a back door at the commissary. From there it was a quick dash to the front lobby, Jenks putting every camera on a fifteen-minute loop.

Trent's new lock on his office gave us trouble. Pulse pounding, I fidgeted by the door as Jenks spent an entire, unreal five minutes jigging it. Cursing like a furnace repairman, he finally asked for my help in holding an unbent paper clip against a switch. He didn't bother to tell me I was closing a circuit until after a jolt of electricity knocked me on my can.

"You ass!" I hissed from the floor, wringing my hand instead of wringing his neck like I wanted. "What the hell do you think you're doing?"

"You wouldn't have done it if I had told you," he said from the safety of the ceiling.

Eyes narrowed, I ignored his snarky, half-heard justifications and pushed open the door. I half expected to find Trent waiting for me, and I breathed easier upon finding the room empty, lit dimly from the fish tank behind the desk. Hunched with anticipation, I went right for the bottom drawer, waiting until Jenks nodded to tell me it hadn't been tampered with. Breath tight, I pulled it open to find—nothing.

Not surprised, I looked up at Jenks and shrugged. "Plan B," we said simultaneously as I pulled a wipe from a pocket and swabbed everything down. "To his back office."

Jenks flitted out the door and back. "Five minutes left on the loop. We gotta hurry."

I bobbed my head, taking a last look at Trent's office before I followed Jenks out. He buzzed ahead of me down the hallway at chest height. Heart pounding, I followed at a discreet distance, my shoes silent on the carpet as I jogged through the empty building. The fail-safe amulet about my neck glowed a nice, steady green.

My pulse increased and a smile curved over me as I found Jenks at the door to Trent's secondary office. This was what I had missed, why I had left the I.S. The excitement, the thrill of beating the odds. Proving I was smarter than the bad guy. This time, I'd get what I came for. "What's our clock?" I whispered as I came to a halt, pulling a strand of hair out of my mouth.

"Three minutes." He flitted up and then down. "No cameras in his private office. He's not there. I already checked."

Pleased, I slipped past the door, easing it closed as Jenks flew in behind me.

The smell of the garden was a balm. Moonlight spilled in, bright as early morning. I crept to the desk, my smile turning wry, since it now had the cluttered look of one that was being used. It took only a moment to find the briefcase beside the desk. Jenks jimmied the lock, and I opened it up, sighing at the sight of the discs in neat, tidy rows. "Are you sure they're the right ones?" Jenks muttered from my shoulder as I chose one and slipped it into a pocket.

I knew they were, but as I opened my mouth to answer, a twig snapped in the garden.

Pulse hammering, I jerked my thumb in the "Hide" gesture to Jenks. Wings silent, he flitted up to the row of light fixtures. Not breathing, I eased down to crouch beside the desk.

My hope that it might be a night animal died. Soft, almost inaudible footfalls on the path grew louder. A tall shadow moved with a confident quickness from the path to the porch. It took the three steps in one bound, moving with a content, happy motion. My knees went weak as I recognized Trent's voice. He was humming a song I didn't recognize, his feet moving to a spine-tingling beat. *Crap,* I thought, trying to shrink farther behind the desk.

Trent turned his back to me and rummaged in a closet. An uncomfortable silence replaced his humming as he sat on the edge of a chair between me and the porch, changing into what looked like tall riding boots. The moonlight made his white shirt seem to glow past his close-cut jacket. It was hard to tell in the dim light, but it looked as if his English riding outfit was green, not red. *Trent bred horses,* I thought, *and rode them at night?*

The twin thumps of his heels into his boots were loud. My breath coming faster, I watched him stand, seeming far taller than the extra inch the boots gave him. The light dimmed as a cloud passed before the moon. I almost missed it when he reached under the chair he had been sitting on.

In a smooth, graceful motion, he pulled a gun and trained it on me. My throat closed.

"I hear you," he said evenly, his voice rising and falling like water. "Come out. Now."

Chills raced down my arms and legs, setting my fingertips to tingle. I crouched beside the desk, not believing he had sensed me. But he was facing me squarely, his feet spread wide and his shadow looking formidable. "Put your gun down first," I whispered.

"Ms. Morgan?" The shadow straightened. He was actually surprised. I wondered who he had expected. "Why should I?" he asked, his mellow voice soothing despite the threat in it.

"My partner has a spell right over your head," I bluffed.

The shadow that was Trent shifted as he glanced up. "Lights, forty-eight percent," he said, his voice harsh. The room brightened, but not enough to ruin my night vision. Knees turning to water, I rose from my crouch, trying to look as if I had planned this as I leaned against his desk in my silk and spandex bodysuit and crossed my ankles.

Gun tight in his grip, Trent ran his gaze over me, looking disgustingly refined and smart in his green riding outfit. I forced myself to not look at the weapon pointing at me as my gut tightened. "Your gun?" I questioned, sending my gaze to the ceiling where Jenks waited.

"Drop it, Kalamack!" Jenks shrilled from the light fixture, his wings clattering in an aggressive noise.

Trent's stance eased to match my own tension-laced, casual poise. Motions sharp and abrupt, he took the bullets from the gun and tossed the heavy metal to my feet. I didn't touch it, feeling my breath come easier. The bullets clattered dully into a pocket of his riding jacket. In the stronger light, I could see evidence of his healing demon attack. A yellowing bruise decorated his cheekbone. The end of a blue cast poked beyond the cuff of his jacket. A healing scrape showed on his chin. I found myself thinking that despite it all, he looked good. It wasn't right that he should look so confident when he thought he had a lethal spell hanging over him.

"I only need to say one word, and Quen will be here in three minutes," he said lightly.

"How long do you take to die?" I bluffed.

His jaw clenched in anger, making him seem younger. "Is that what you are here for?"

"If it was, you'd already be dead."

He nodded, accepting that as truth. Standing wire-tight across the room, his gaze flicked to his open briefcase. "Which disc do you have?"

Feigning confidence, I brushed a strand of hair out of my eyes. "Huntington. If anything happens to me, it will go to six papers and three news studios along with the missing page of your planner." I pushed myself off from his desk. "Leave me alone," I threatened flatly.

His arms hung unmoving at his sides, his broken one at an angle. My skin pricked, though he made no move, and my veneer of confidence slipped. "Black magic?" he mocked. "Demons killed your father. Shame to see the daughter go the same way."

My breath hissed in. "What do you know of my dad?" I said, shocked.

His eyes slid to my wrist—the one with the demon scar—and my face went cold. My stomach knotted as I remembered the demon killing me slowly. "I hope it hurt you," I said, not caring that my voice quavered. Maybe he'd think it was in anger. "I don't know how you survived it. I almost didn't."

Trent's face went red and he pointed a finger at me. It was nice to see him act like a real person. "Sending a demon to attack me was a mistake," he said, his words sharp. "I don't deal in black magic, nor do I allow my employees to do so."

"You big fat liar!" I exclaimed, not caring if it sounded childish. "You got what you deserved. I didn't start this, but I'll be damned if I don't finish it!"

"I'm not the one with the demon mark, Ms. Morgan," he said icily. "A liar as well? How disappointing. I'm seriously considering withdrawing my offer of employment. Pray I don't, or I won't have any reason to tolerate your actions any longer."

Angry, I took a breath to tell him he was an idiot. But my mouth stopped. Trent thought I had summoned the demon that had attacked him. My eyes went wide as I figured it out. Someone had called two demons—one for me, one for him—and it hadn't been anyone at the I.S. I'd stake my life on it. Heart pounding, I reached out to explain, then shut my mouth.

Trent went wary. "Ms. Morgan?" he questioned softly. "What thought just percolated through that head of yours?"

I shook my head, licking my lips as I took a step back. If he thought I dealt in black magic, he'd leave me alone. And as long as I had proof of his guilt, he wouldn't risk killing me. "Don't back me into a corner," I threatened, "and I won't bother you again."

Trent's questioning expression hardened. "Get out," he said, moving from the porch in a graceful movement. Shifting as one, we exchanged places. "I'll give you a generous head start," he said as he reached his desk, snapping his briefcase shut. His voice was dusky, as rich and abiding as the scent of decaying maple leaves. "It may take ten minutes to reach my horse."

"Excuse me?" I asked, confused.

"I haven't run down two-footed prey since my father died." Trent adjusted his hunter-green coat with an aggressive motion. "It's the full moon, Ms. Morgan," he said, his voice thick with promise. "The hounds are loosed. You're a thief. Tradition says you should run—fast."

My heart pounded and my face went cold. I had what I came for, but it would do me no good if I couldn't escape with it. There was thirty miles of woods between me and the nearest source of help. How fast did a horse run? How long could I go before I dropped? Maybe I should have told him I hadn't sent the demon.

The distant sound of a horn lifted through the black. A baying hound answered it. Fear struck through me, as painful as a knife. It was an old, ancient fear, one so primal it couldn't be soothed with self-induced delusions. I didn't even know where it came from. "Jenks," I whispered. "Let's go."

"Right behind you, Rache," he said from the ceiling.

I took three running steps and dove off Trent's porch. I landed in a rolling crouch in the ferns. There was an explosion of a gun. The foliage beside my hand shattered. Lunging into the greenery, I bolted into a sprint.

Bastard! I thought, my knees almost giving way. What happened to my ten minutes?

Running, I fumbled for my vial of saltwater. I bit through the top and soaked my amulet. It flickered and went out. Ivy's would turn and stay red. The road was less than a mile. The gatehouse was three. The city was thirty. How long would it take Ivy to get here?

"How fast can you fly, Jenks?" I panted between foot strikes.

"Pretty damn fast, Rache."

I stuck to the paths until I reached the garden wall. A dog bayed as I climbed over it. Another answered. *Shit.*

Breathing in time with my strides, I ran over the manicured lawn and into that eerie wood. The sound of the dogs fell behind me. The wall was giving them trouble. They'd have to go around. Maybe I could do this. "Jenks," I panted as my legs began to protest. "How long have I been running?"

"Five minutes."

God, help me, I silently pleaded, feeling my legs begin to ache. It felt like twice that.

Jenks flew ahead, pixy dust sifting from him to show me the way. The silent pillars of dark trees loomed and vanished. My feet thumped rhythmically. My lungs ached and my side hurt. If I lived through this, I promised myself I was going to run five miles a day.

The calling of the dogs shifted. Though faint, their voices sang sweeter, truer, promising they'd soon be with me. It struck like a goad. I dug deeper, finding the will to keep to my pace.

I ran, pushing my heavy legs up and down. My hair stuck to my face. Thorns and brambles ripped my clothes and hands. The horns and dogs grew closer. I fixed my gaze on Jenks as he flew before me. A fire started in my lungs, growing to consume my chest. To stop would mean my death.

The stream was an unexpected oasis. I fell into the water and came up gasping. Lungs heaving, I pushed the water from my face so I could breathe. The pounding of my heart tried to outdo the hoarse sound of my breathing. The trees held a frightened hush. I was prey, and everything in the forest was silently watching, glad it wasn't them.

My breath rasped at the sound of the dogs. They were closer. A horn blew, pulling fear through me. I didn't know which sound was worse.

"Get up, Rachel!" Jenks urged, glowing like a will-o'-the-wisp. "Go down the stream."

I scrambled up, lurching into a slogging run in the shallows. The water would slow me down, but it would slow the dogs down, too. It would only be a matter of time before Trent would split the pack to search both sides of the stream. I wasn't going to get out of this one.

The pitch of the dogs singing faltered. I surged out onto the bank in a panic. They had lost the scent. They were right behind me. Visions of being torn apart by dogs spurred me on though my legs could hardly move. Trent would paint his forehead with my blood. Jonathan would save a lock of my hair in his top dresser drawer. I should have told Trent I hadn't sent that demon. Would he have believed me? He wouldn't now.

The burble of a motorbike brought a cry from me. "Ivy," I croaked, reaching out to support myself against a tree. The road was just ahead. She must have already been on her way. "Jenks, don't let her go past me," I said between gasps for air. "I'll be right behind you."

"Gotcha!"

He was gone. I stumbled into motion. The dogs were baying, soft and questing. I could hear the sound of voices and instructions. It pushed me into a run. A dog sang clear and pure. Another answered it. Adrenaline scoured through me.

Branches whipped my face and I fell into the road. My skinned palms stung. Too breathless to cry out, I forced myself up from my knees. Staggering, I looked down the road. A white light bathed me. The roar of a motorbike was an angel's blessing. Ivy. It had to be. She must have been on her way before I broke the amulet.

I got to my feet, listing as my lungs heaved. The dogs were coming. I could hear the thump of horses' hooves. I started a jolting, weaving jog toward the approaching light. It rushed upon me in a sudden surge of noise, sliding to a halt beside me.

"Get on!" Ivy shouted.

I could hardly lift my leg. She pulled me up behind her. The engine thrummed under me. I gripped her waist and struggled not to fall into the dry heaves. Jenks buried himself in my hair, his tight grip almost unnoticed. The bike lurched, spun, and leapt forward.

Ivy's hair flew back, stinging as it hit me. "Did you get it?" she shouted over the wind.

I couldn't answer. My body was trembling from the abuse. The adrenaline had spent itself out, and I was going to pay for it in spades. The road hummed under me. The wind pulled my heat away, turning my sweat cold. Fighting back the nausea, I reached with numb fingers to feel the reassuring bump of a disc in a front pocket. I patted her shoulder, unable to use my breath for anything other than breathing.

"Good!" she shouted over the wind.

Exhausted, I let my head rest against Ivy's back. Tomorrow I'd stay in bed and shake until the evening paper came. Tomorrow I'd be sore and unable to move. Tomorrow I'd put bandages on the welts from the branches and thorns. Tonight . . . I'd just not think about tonight.

I shivered. Feeling it, Ivy turned her head. "Are you all right?" she shouted.

"Yeah," I said into her ear so she could hear me. "Yeah, I am. Thanks for coming to get me." I pulled her hair out of my mouth and looked behind me.

I stared, riveted. Three horsemen stood on the ribbon of moonlit road. The hounds were milling about the horses' feet as they pranced with nervous, arched necks. I had just made it. Chilled to the core of my soul, I watched the middle rider touch his brow in a casual salute.

An unexpected pull went through me. I had bested him. He knew and accepted it, and had the nobility to acknowledge it. How could you not be impressed by someone that sure of himself. "What the hell is he?" I whispered.

"I don't know," Jenks said from my shoulder. "I just don't know."

Thirty-four

*M*idnight jazz goes very well with crickets, I thought as I sprinkled the chopped tomato on the tossed salad. Hesitating, I stared at the red globs among the leafy green. Glancing out the window at Nick standing before the grill, I picked them all out and tossed the lettuce again to hide what I had missed. Nick would never know. It wasn't as if it would kill him.

The sound and smell of cooking meat pulled at me, and I leaned past Mr. Fish on the sill to get a better look. Nick was wearing an apron that said "Don't stake the cook, cook the steak." Ivy's, obviously. He looked relaxed and comfortable as he stood at the fire in the moonlight. Jenks was on his shoulder, darting upward like fall leaves in the wind when the fire spurted.

Ivy was at the table, looking dark and tragic as she read the late edition of the *Cincinnati Enquirer* in the light of a candle. Pixy children were everywhere, their transparent wings making shimmering flashes when they reflected the moon, three days past full. Their shouts as they tormented the early fireflies broke into the muted roar of Hollows' traffic, making a comfortable mix. It was the sound of security, reminding me of my own family's cookouts. A vamp, a human, and a posse of pixies were an odd sort of family, but it was good to be alive in the night with my friends.

Content, I juggled the salad, a bottle of dressing, and the steak sauce and backed out the screen door. It slammed behind me, and Jenks's kids shrieked, scattering into the graveyard. Ivy looked up from the newsprint as I set the salad and bottles beside her. "Hey,

Rachel," she said. "You never did tell me how you got that van. Did you have any trouble taking it back?"

My eyebrows rose. "I didn't get the van. I thought you did."

As one, we turned to Nick, standing at the grill with his back to us. "Nick?" I questioned, and he stiffened almost imperceptibly. Full of a questioning speculation, I grabbed the steak sauce and eased up behind him. Waving Jenks away, I slipped an arm around Nick's waist and leaned close, delighted when his breath caught and he gave me a look of surprised speculation. *What the heck. He was a nice guy for a human.* "You stole that truck for me?" I asked.

"Borrowed," he said, blinking as he remained carefully unmoving.

"Thank you," I said, smiling as I handed the bottle of steak sauce to him.

"Oh, Nick," Jenks mocked in a high falsetto. "You're my hero!"

My breath slipped from me in bother. Sighing, I let my hand drop from around Nick's waist and stepped back. From behind us came Ivy's snort of amusement. Jenks made kissing noises as he circled Nick and me, and fed up, I darted my hand out.

Jenks jerked back, hovering in surprise as I almost got him. "Nice," he said, darting off to bother Ivy. "And how's your new job going?" he drawled as he landed before her.

"Shut up, Jenks," she warned.

"Job? You have another run?" I asked as she shook open the newsprint and hid behind it.

"Didn't you know?" Jenks said merrily. "Edden arranged it with the judge to give Ivy three hundred hours of community service for taking out half his department. She's been working at the hospital all this week."

Eyes wide, I went to the picnic table. The corner of the paper was trembling. "Why didn't you tell me?" I asked as I angled my legs past the bench and sat across from her.

"Maybe because they made her a candy striper," Jenks said, and Nick and I exchanged dubious looks. "I saw her on her way to work yesterday and followed her. She has to wear a short pink and white striped skirt and a frilly blouse." Jenks laughed, catching himself as he fell off my shoulder. "And white tights to cover her perky little ass. Looks real good on her bike."

A vampire candy striper? I thought, trying to picture it.

A chortle slipped from Nick, quickly turned into a cough. Ivy's knuckles as she gripped the paper turned white. Between the later hour and the relaxed atmosphere, I knew it was hard for her to keep from pulling an aura. This wasn't helping.

"She's at the Children's Medical Center, singing and having tea parties," Jenks gasped.

"Jenks," Ivy whispered. The paper slowly dropped, and I forced my face into a careful impassivity at the black hazing her.

Wings a blur, Jenks grinned and opened his mouth. Ivy rolled the paper. Quicker than sound, she slammed it at him. The pixy darted up into the oak, laughing.

We all turned at the creak of the wooden gate by the front walk. "Hello-o-o-o. Am I late?" came Keasley's voice.

"We're back here!" I shouted as I spotted Keasley's slow moving shadow making its way across the dew-wet grass past the silent trees and bushes.

"I brought the wine," he said as soon as he was closer. "Red goes with meat, right?"

"Thanks, Keasley," I said, taking the bottle from him. "You didn't have to do that."

He smiled, extending the padded envelope tucked under his arm. "This is yours, too," he said. "The delivery man didn't want to leave it on the steps this afternoon, so I signed for it."

"No!" Ivy shouted, reaching across the table to intercept it. Jenks, too, dropped from the oak, his wings making a harsh clattering. Looking annoyed, Ivy snatched it out of his grip.

Keasley gave her a dark look, then went to see how Nick was doing with the steaks.

"It's been over a week," I said, peeved as I wiped my hand free of the condensation from Keasley's wine. "When are you going to let me open my own mail?"

Ivy said nothing, pulling the citronella candle closer to read the return address. "As soon as Trent stops sending you mail," she said softly.

"Trent!" I exclaimed. Worried, I tucked a strand of hair behind my ear, thinking about the folder I'd given Edden two days ago. Nick turned from the steaks, his long face showing concern. "What does he want?" I muttered, hoping they couldn't tell how agitated I was.

Ivy glanced up at Jenks, and the pixy shrugged. "It's clean," he said. "Open it up."

"Of course it's clean," Keasley grumbled. "You think I'd give her a spelled letter?"

The envelope felt light in my grip as I took it from Ivy. Nervous, I slid a freshly painted nail under the flap, tearing it. There was a bump inside, and I shook the envelope over my hand.

My pinky ring slid out and fell into my grip. My face went slack in shock. "It's my ring!" I said. Heart pounding, I looked at my other hand, frightened to not see it there. Eyes rising, I took in Nick's surprise and Ivy's worry. "How . . ." I stammered, not remembering even having missed it. "When did he—Jenks, I didn't lose it in his office, did I?"

My voice was high, and my stomach tightened when he shook his head, his wings going dark. "You didn't have any jewelry that night," he said. "He must have taken it afterwards."

"Is there anything else?" Ivy asked, her tone carefully neutral.

"Yeah." I swallowed, and slipped my ring on. It felt odd for a moment, then comfortable. Fingers cold, I pulled out the thick slip of linen paper smelling of pine and apples.

" 'Ms. Morgan,' " I read softly in unease. " 'Congratulations on your newfound independence. When you see it for the illusion it is, I'll show you true freedom.' "

I let the paper fall to the table. My thick feeling of disquiet that he had seen me sleeping broke apart in the knowledge that that was all he did. My blackmail was tight. It had worked.

Slumping, I put my elbows on the table and dropped my forehead into my hands in relief. Trent had taken the ring from my sleeping finger for one reason only. To prove he could. I had infiltrated into his "house" three times, each one more intimate and unguarded than the last. That I could do it again whenever I wanted was probably intolerable to Trent. He had felt the need to retaliate, to show that he could do the same. I had gotten to him, and that went a long way toward ridding myself of my angry, vulnerable feeling.

Jenks darted down to hover over the note. "The sack of slug salt," he said, and angry pixy dust sifted from him. "He got past me. He got past me! How the hell did he do that?"

Steeling my face, I picked up the envelope, noticing the postmark was the day after I had escaped him and his dogs. The man worked fast. I'd give him that. I wondered if it had been him or Quen who did the actual pilfering. I was betting it was Trent.

"Rache?" Jenks landed on my shoulder, probably concerned at my silence. "You okay?"

I glanced at Ivy's worried expression across from me, thinking I ought to be able to get a laugh out of this situation. "I'm gonna get him," I bluffed.

Jenks flitted up and away, his wings clattering in alarm. Nick turned from the grill, and Ivy stiffened. "Whoa, wait a moment," she said, flicking Jenks a look.

"No one does that to me!" I added, clenching my jaw so I wouldn't smile and ruin it.

Keasley's brow furrowed. Eyes pinched, he sat back.

Ivy went paler than usual in the candlelight. "Slow down, Rachel," she warned. "He didn't do anything. He just wanted to get the last word. Let it go."

"I'm going back!" I shouted, standing to put some distance between us in case I was yanking her chain too hard and she came after me. "I'll show him," I said, waving an arm. "I'll sneak in. I'll steal his freaking glasses and mail them back to him in a freaking birthday card!"

Ivy stood, her eyes going black. "You do that, and he'll kill you!"

She actually thinks I'd go back? Was she nuts? My chin trembled as I tried not to laugh. Keasley saw it, and he chuckled, reaching for his unopened wine.

Ivy spun with a vamp quickness. "What are you laughing about, witch?" she said, leaning forward. "She's going to kill herself. Jenks, tell her she's going to kill herself. I'm not going to let you do this, Rachel. I swear, I'll tie you to Jenks's stump before I let you go back!"

Her teeth were a gleam in the moonlight and she was wound tight enough to pop. One more word, and she might make good her threat. "Okay," I said lightly. "You're right. I'll leave him alone."

Ivy froze. A heavy sigh slipped from Nick at the grill. Keasley's gnarly fingers were slow as they pulled the foil from the top of his bottle. "Oooh doggies, she got you, Tamwood," he said, laughing low and rich. "She got you good."

Ivy stared, her pale, perfect face marred with shock and the sudden realization that she'd been had. A stunned bewilderment, quickly followed by relief and then bother, crossed her. She took a breath. Holding it, her face went sullen. Eyes tight and angry, she dropped back down to the picnic table's bench and shook out the paper.

Jenks was laughing, making circles of pixy dust to sift down like sunbeams to glitter on her shoulders. Grinning, I rose and went to the grill. That had felt good. Almost as good as stealing the disc. "Hey, Nick," I said, slipping up behind him. Those steaks done yet?"

He gave me a sideways smile. "Coming right up, Rachel."

Good. I'd figure everything else out later.

THE GOOD, THE BAD, AND THE UNDEAD

*To the man who knows caffeine comes first,
chocolate comes second, romance comes third—
and when they ought to be reversed.*

Acknowledgments

I'd like to thank Will for his help and inspiration with the jewelry of the Hollows, and Dr. Carolinne White for her invaluable assistance with much of the Latin. But I'd especially like to thank my editor, Diana Gill, for giving me the freedom to push my writing into areas I'd never thought to go, and my agent, Richard Curtis.

One

I hitched the canvas strap holding the watering canister higher up on my shoulder and stretched to get the nozzle into the hanging plant. Sunlight streamed in, warm through my blue institutional jumpsuit. Past the narrow plate-glass windows was a small courtyard surrounded by VIP offices. Squinting from the sun, I squeezed the handle of the watering hose, and the barest hint of water hissed through.

There was a burst of clattering computer keys, and I moved to the next plant down. Phone conversation filtered in from the office past the reception desk, accompanied by a belly laugh that sounded like the bark of a dog. Weres. The higher up in the pack they were, the more human looking they managed, but you could always tell when they laughed.

I glanced down the row of hanging plants before the windows to the freestanding fish tank behind the receptionist's desk. Yup. Cream-colored fins. Black spot on right side. This was the one. Mr. Ray raised koi, showing them in Cincinnati's annual fish show. Last year's winner was always displayed in his outer office, but now there were two fish, and the Howlers' mascot was missing. Mr. Ray was a Den boy, a rival of Cincinnati's all Inderland baseball team. It didn't take much to put two and two together and get stolen fish.

"So," the cheerful woman behind the desk said as she stood to drop a ream of paper into the printer's hopper. "Mark is on vacation? He didn't tell me."

I nodded, not looking at the secretary dressed in her snappy cream-colored business suit as I dragged my watering equipment down another three feet. Mark was taking a short vacation in the stairwell of the building he had been servicing before this one. Knocked out with a short-term sleepy-time potion. "Yes, ma'am," I added, raising my voice and adding a slight lisp. "He told me what plants to water, though." I curled my red manicured nails under my palms before she spotted them. They didn't go with the working plant-girl image. I should have thought of that earlier. "All the ones on this floor, and then the arboretum on the roof."

The woman smiled to show me her slightly larger teeth. She was a Were, and fairly high up in the office pack by her amount of polish. And Mr. Ray wouldn't have a dog for a secretary when he could pay a high enough salary for a bitch. A faint scent of musk came from her, not unpleasant. "Did Mark tell you about the service elevator at the back of the building?" she said helpfully. "It's easier than lugging that cart up all those stairs."

"No, ma'am," I said, pulling the ugly cap with the plant-man logo on it tighter to my head. "I think he's making everything just hard enough that I don't try to take his territory." Pulse quickening, I pushed Mark's cart with its pruning shears, fertilizer pellets, and watering system farther down the line. I had known of the elevator, along with the placement of the six emergency exits, the pulls for the fire alarm, and where they kept the doughnuts.

"Men," she said, rolling her eyes as she sat before her screen again. "Don't they realize that if we wanted to rule the world, we could?"

I gave her a noncommittal nod and squirted a tiny amount of water into the next plant. I kinda thought we already did.

A tight hum rose over the whirl of the printer and the faint office chatter. It was Jenks, my partner, and he was clearly in a bad mood as he flew out of the boss's back office and to me. His dragonfly wings were bright red in agitation, and pixy dust sifted from him to make temporary sunbeams. "I'm done with the plants in there," he said loudly as he landed on the rim of the hanging pot in front of me. He put his hands on his hips to look like a middle-aged Peter Pan grown up to be a trashman in his little blue jumpsuit. His wife had even sewn him a matching cap. "All they need is water. Can I help you out here with anything, or can I go back and sleep in the truck?" he added acerbically.

I took the watering canister off me, setting it down to unscrew the top. "I could use a fertilizer pellet," I prompted, wondering what his problem was.

Grumbling, he flew to the cart and started rummaging. Green twist ties, stakes, and used pH test strips flew everywhere. "Got one," he said, coming up with a white pellet as large as his head. He dropped it in the canister and it fizzed. It wasn't a fertilizer pellet but an oxygenator and slime-coat promoter. What's the point of stealing a fish if it dies in transport?

"Oh my God, Rachel," Jenks whispered as he landed on my shoulder "It's polyester. I'm wearing polyester!"

My tension eased as I realized where his bad mood came from. "It'll be okay."

"I'm breaking out!" he said, scratching vigorously under his collar. "I can't wear polyester. Pixies are allergic to polyester. Look. See?" He tilted his head so his blond hair shifted from his neck, but he was too close to focus on. "Welts. And it stinks. I can smell the oil. I'm wearing dead dinosaur. I can't wear a dead animal. It's barbaric, Rache," he pleaded.

"Jenks?" I screwed the cap lightly back onto the canister and hung it over my shoulder, pushing Jenks from me in the process. "I'm wearing the same thing. Suck it up."

"But it stinks!"

I eyed him hovering before me. "Prune something," I said through gritted teeth.

He flipped me off with both hands, hovering backward as he went. Whatever. Patting my back pocket of the vile blue jumpsuit, I found my snippers. While Miss Office Professional typed a letter, I snapped open a step stool and began to clip leaves off the hanging plant beside her desk. Jenks started to help, and after a few moments I breathed, "Are we set in there?"

He nodded, his eyes on the open door to Mr. Ray's office. "The next time he checks his mail, the entire Internet security system is gonna trip. It will take five minutes to fix if she knows what she's doing, four hours if she doesn't."

"I only need five minutes," I said, starting to sweat in the sun coming in the window. It smelled like a garden in there, a garden with a wet dog panting on the cool tile.

My pulse increased, and I moved down another plant. I was behind the desk, and the woman stiffened. I had invaded her territory, but she had to put up with it. I was the water girl. Hoping she attributed my rising tension to being so close to her, I kept working. My one hand rested on the lid of the watering canister. One twist and it would be off.

"Vanessa!" came an irate shout from the back office.

"Here we go," Jenks said, flying up to the ceiling and the security cameras.

I turned to see an irate man, clearly a Were by his slight size and build, hanging halfway out of the back office. "It did it again," he said, his face red and his thick hands gripping the archway. "I hate these things. What was wrong with paper? I like paper."

A professional smile wreathed the secretary's face. "Mr. Ray, you yelled at it again, didn't you? I told you, computers are like women. If you shout at them or ask them to do too many things at once, they shut down and you won't even get a sniff."

He growled an answer and disappeared into his office, unaware or ignoring that she had just threatened him. My pulse leapt, and I moved the stool right beside the tank.

Vanessa sighed. "God save him," she muttered as she got up. "That man could break his balls with his tongue." Giving me an exasperated look, she went into the back office, her heels thumping. "Don't touch anything," she said loudly. "I'm coming."

I took a quick breath. "Cameras?" I breathed.

Jenks dropped down to me. "Ten minute loop. You're clear."

He flew to the main door, perching himself on the molding above the lintel, to hang over and watch the exterior hallway. His wings blurred to nothing and he gave me a tiny thumbs-up.

My skin tightened in anticipation. I took off the fish tank lid, then pulled the green fishnet from an inner pocket of the jumpsuit. Standing atop the step stool, I pushed my sleeve to my elbow and plunged the net into the water. Immediately both fish darted to the back.

"Rachel!" Jenks hissed, suddenly at my ear. "She's good. She's halfway there."

"Just watch the door, Jenks," I said, lip between my teeth. *How long could it take to catch a fish?* I pushed a rock over to get to the fish hiding behind it. They darted to the front.

The phone started ringing, a soft hum. "Jenks, will you get that?" I said calmly as I angled the net, trapping them in the corner. "Got you now . . ."

Jenks zipped back from the door, landing feet first on the glowing button. "Mr. Ray's office. Hold please," he said in a high falsetto.

"Crap," I swore as the fish wiggled, slipping past the green net. "Come on, I'm just trying to get you home, you slimy finned

thing," I coaxed through gritted teeth. "Almost . . . almost . . ." It
was between the net and the glass. If it would just hold still . . .

"Hey!" a heavy voice said from the hall.

Adrenaline jerked my head up. A small man with a trim beard
and a folder of papers was standing in the hallway leading to the
other offices. "What are you doing?" he asked belligerently.

I glanced at the tank with my arm in it. My net was empty. The
fish had slipped past it. "Um, I dropped my scissors?" I said.

From Mr. Ray's office on my other side came a thump of heels
and Vanessa's gasp. "Mr. Ray!"

Damn. So much for the easy way. "Plan B, Jenks," I said,
grunting as I grabbed the top of the tank and pulled.

In the other room, Vanessa screamed as the tank tipped and
twenty-five gallons of icky fish water cascaded over her desk. Mr.
Ray appeared beside her. I lurched off the stool, soaked from the
waist down. No one moved, shocked, and I scanned the floor.
"Gotcha!" I cried, scrabbling for the right fish.

"She's after the fish!" the small man shouted as more people
came in from the hallway. "Get her!"

"Go!" Jenks shrilled. "I'll keep them off you."

Panting, I followed the fish in a hunched, scrabbling walk, trying to grab it without hurting it. It wiggled and squirmed, and my
breath exploded from me as I finally got my fingers around it. I
looked up as I dropped it into the canister and screwed the lid on
tight.

Jenks was a firefly from hell as he darted from Were to Were,
brandishing pencils and throwing them at sensitive parts. A four-
inch pixy was holding three Weres at bay. I wasn't surprised. Mr.
Ray was content to watch until he realized I had one of his fish.
"What the hell are you doing with my fish?" he demanded, his
face red with anger.

"Leaving," I said. He came at me, his thick hands reaching. I
obligingly took one of them, jerking him forward and into my
foot. He staggered back, clutching his stomach.

"Quit playing with those dogs!" I cried at Jenks, looking for a
way out. "We have to go."

Picking up Vanessa's monitor, I threw it at the plate-glass window. I'd wanted to do that with Ivy's for a long time. It shattered in
a satisfying crash, the screen looking odd on the grass. Weres
poured into the room, angry and giving off musk. Snatching the
canister, I dove through the window. "After her!" someone shouted.

My shoulders hit manicured grass and I rolled to my feet.

"Up!" Jenks said by my ear. "Over there."

He darted across the small enclosed courtyard. I followed, looping the heavy canister to hang across my back. Hands free, I climbed the trellis. Thorns pierced my skin, ignored.

My breath came in a quick pant as I reached the top. The snapping of branches said they were following. Hauling myself over the lip of the flat-topped, tar-and-pebble roof, I took off running. The wind was hot up here, and the skyline of Cincinnati spread out before me.

"Jump!" Jenks shouted as I reached the edge.

I trusted Jenks. Arms flailing and feet still going, I ran right off the roof.

Adrenaline surged as my stomach dropped. It was a parking lot! He sent me off the roof to land in a parking lot!

"I don't have wings, Jenks!" I screamed. Teeth gritted, I flexed my knees.

Pain exploded as I hit the pavement. I fell forward, scraping my palms. The canister of fish clanged and fell off as the strap broke. I rolled to absorb the impact.

The metal canister spun away, and still gasping from the hurt, I staggered after it, fingers brushing it as it rolled under a car. Swearing, I dropped flat on the pavement, stretching for it.

"There she is!" came a shout.

There was a ping from the car above me, then another. The pavement beside my arm suddenly had a hole in it, and sharp tingles of shrapnel peppered me. They were shooting at me?

Grunting, I wiggled under the car and pulled the canister out. Hunched over the fish, I backed up. "Hey!" I shouted, tossing the hair from my eyes. "What the hell are you doing? It's just a fish! And it isn't even yours!"

The trio of Weres on the roof stared at me. One hefted a weapon to his eye.

I turned and started running. This was not worth five hundred dollars anymore. Five thousand, maybe. *Next time,* I vowed as I pounded after Jenks, *I'd find out the particulars before I charge my standard fee.*

"This way!" Jenks shrilled. Bits of pavement were ricocheting up to hit me, echoing the pings. The lot wasn't gated, and as my muscles trembled from adrenaline, I ran across the street and into the pedestrian traffic. Heart pounding, I slowed to look behind me to see them silhouetted against the skyline. They hadn't jumped.

They didn't need to. I had left blood all over that trellis. Still, I didn't think they would track me. It wasn't their fish; it was the Howlers'. And Cincinnati's all Inderland baseball team was going to pay my rent.

My lungs heaved as I tried to match the pace of the people around me. The sun was hot, and I was sweating inside my polyester sack. Jenks was probably checking my back, so I dropped into an alley to change. Setting the fish down, I let my head thump back into the cool wall of the building. I'd done it. Rent was made for yet another month.

Reaching up, I yanked the disguise amulet from around my neck. Immediately I felt better, as the illusion of a dark-complected, brown-haired, big-nosed woman vanished, revealing my frizzy, shoulder-length red hair and pale skin. I glanced at my scraped palms, rubbing them together gingerly. I could have brought a pain amulet, but I had wanted as few charms as possible on me in case I was caught and my "intent to steal" turned into "intent to steal and do bodily harm." One I could dodge, the other I'd have to answer to. I was a runner; I knew the law.

While people passed at the head of the alley, I stripped off the damp coveralls and stuffed it into the Dumpster. It was a vast improvement, and I bent to unroll the hem of my leather pants down over my black boots. Straightening, I eyed the new scrape mark in my pants, twisting to see all the damage. Ivy's leather conditioner would help, but pavement and leather didn't mesh well. Better the pants scraped than me, though, which was why I wore them.

The September air felt good in the shade as I tucked in my black halter top and picked up the canister. Feeling more myself, I stepped into the sun, dropping my cap on a passing kid's head. He looked at it, then smiled, giving me a shy wave as his mother bent to ask him where he had gotten it. At peace with the world, I walked down the sidewalk, boot heels clunking as I fluffed my hair and headed for Fountain Square and my ride. I had left my shades there this morning, and if I was lucky, they'd still be there. God help me, but I liked being independent.

It had been nearly three months since I had snapped under the crap assignments my old boss at Inderland Security had been giving me. Feeling used and grossly unappreciated, I had broken the unwritten rule and quit the I.S. to start my own agency. It had seemed like a good idea at the time, and surviving the subsequent death threat when I couldn't pay the bribe to break my contract had been an eye opener. I wouldn't have made it if not for Ivy and Jenks.

Oddly enough, now that I was finally starting to make a name for myself, it was getting harder, not easier. True, I was putting my degree to work, stirring spells I used to buy and some I had never been able to afford. But money was a real problem. It wasn't that I couldn't get the jobs; it was that the money didn't seem to stay in the cookie jar atop the fridge very long.

What I made from proving a Werefox had been slipped some bane by a rival den had gone to renewing my witch license; the I.S. used to pay for that. I recovered a stolen familiar for a warlock and spent it on the monthly rider on my health insurance. I hadn't known that runners were all but uninsurable; the I.S. had given me a card, and I'd used it. Then I had to pay some guy to take the lethal spells off my stuff still in storage, buy Ivy a silk robe to replace the one I ruined, and pick up a few outfits for myself since I now had a reputation to uphold.

But the steady drain on my finances had to be from the cab fares. Most of Cincinnati's bus drivers knew me by sight and wouldn't pick me up, which was why Ivy had to come cart me home. It just wasn't fair. It had been almost a year since I accidentally removed the hair from an entire busload of people while trying to tag a Were.

I was tired of being almost broke, but the money for recovering the Howlers' mascot would put me in the clear for another month. And the Weres wouldn't follow me. It wasn't their fish. If they filed a complaint at the I.S., they'd have to explain where they had gotten it.

"Hey, Rache," Jenks said, dropping down from who knew where. "Your back is clear. And what is Plan B?"

My eyebrows rose and I looked askance at him as he flew alongside, matching my pace exactly. "Grab the fish and run like hell."

Jenks laughed and landed on my shoulder. He had ditched his tiny uniform, and he looked like his usual self in a long-sleeve hunter-green silk shirt and pants. A red bandana was about his forehead to tell any pixy or fairies whose territory we might walk through that he wasn't poaching. Sparkles glittered in his wings where the last of the pixy dust stirred up by the excitement remained.

My pace slowed as we reached Fountain Square. I scanned for Ivy, not seeing her. Not worried, I went to sit on the dry side of the fountain, running my fingers under the rim of the retaining wall for my shades. She'd be here. The woman lived and died by schedules.

While Jenks flew through the spray to get rid of the last of the "dead dinosaur stink," I snapped open my shades and put them on. My brow eased as the glare of the September afternoon was muted. Stretching my long legs out, I casually took off the scent amulet that was around my neck and dropped it into the fountain. Weres tracked by smell, and if they did follow me, the trail would end here as soon as I got in Ivy's car and drove away.

Hoping no one had noticed, I glanced over the surrounding people: a nervous, anemic-looking vampire lackey out doing his lover's daytime work; two whispering humans, giggling as they eyed his badly scarred neck; a tired witch—no, warlock, I decided, by the lack of a strong redwood smell—sitting at a nearby bench eating a muffin; and me. I took a slow breath as I settled in. Having to wait for a ride was kind of an anticlimax.

"I wish I had a car," I said to Jenks as I edged the canister of fish to sit between my feet. Thirty feet away traffic was stop-and-go. It had picked up, and I guessed it was probably after two o'clock, just beginning the span of time when humans and Inderlanders started their daily struggle to coexist in the same limited space. Things got a hell of a lot easier when the sun went down and most humans retired to their homes.

"What do you want with a car?" Jenks asked as he perched himself on my knee and started to clean his dragonfly-like wings with long serious strokes. "I don't have a car. I've never had a car. I get around okay. Cars are trouble," he said, but I wasn't listening anymore. "You have to put gas in them, and keep them in repair, and spend time cleaning them, and you have to have a place to put them, and then there's the money you lavish on them. It's worse than a girlfriend."

"Still," I said, jiggling my foot to irritate him. "I wish I had a car." I glanced at the people around me. "James Bond never had to wait for a bus. I've seen every one of his movies, and he never waited for a bus." I squinted at Jenks. "It kinda loses its pizzazz."

"Um, yeah," he said, his attention behind me. "I can see where it might be safer, too. Eleven o'clock. Weres."

My breath came fast as I looked, and my tension slammed back into me. "Crap," I whispered, picking up the canister. It was the same three. I could tell by their hunched stature and the way they were breathing deeply. Jaw clenched, I stood up and put the fountain between us. *Where was Ivy?*

"Rache?" Jenks questioned. "Why are they following you?"

"I don't know." My thoughts went to the blood I had left on the roses. If I couldn't break the scent trail, they could follow me all the way home. But why? Mouth dry, I sat with my back to them, knowing Jenks was watching. "Have they winded me?" I asked.

He left in a clatter of wings. "No," he said when he returned a bare second later. "You've got about half a block between you, but you gotta get moving."

Jiggling, I weighed the risk of staying still and waiting for Ivy with moving and being spotted. "Damn it, I wish I had a car," I muttered. I leaned to look into the street, searching for the tall blue top of a bus, a cab, anything. *Where the hell was Ivy?*

Heart pounding, I stood. Clutching the fish to me, I headed for the street, wanting to get into the adjacent office building and the maze I could lose myself in while waiting for Ivy. But a big black Crown Victoria slowed to a stop, getting in my way.

I glared at the driver, my tight face going slack when the window whined down and he leaned over the front seat. "Ms. Morgan?" the dark man said, his deep voice belligerent.

I glanced at the Weres behind me, then at the car, then him. A black Crown Victoria driven by a man in a black suit could only mean one thing. He was from the Federal Inderland Bureau, the human-run equivalent of the I.S. *What did the FIB want?* "Yeah. Who are you?"

Bother crossed him. "I talked to Ms. Tamwood earlier. She said I could find you here."

Ivy. I put a hand on the open window. "Is she all right?"

He pressed his lips together. Traffic was backing up behind him. "She was when I talked with her on the phone."

Jenks hovered before me, his tiny face frightened. "They winded you, Rache."

My breath hissed in through my nose. I glanced behind me. My gaze fell on one of the Weres. Seeing me watching him, he barked out a hail. The other two started to converge, loping forward with an unhurried grace. I swallowed hard. I was dog chow. That's it. Dog chow. Game over. Hit the reset button.

Spinning, I grabbed the door handle and jerked it up. I dove in, slamming the door behind me. "Drive!" I shouted, turning to look out the back window.

The man's long face took on a tinge of disgust as he glanced behind him in his rearview mirror. "Are they with you?"

"No! Does this thing move, or do you just sit in it and play with yourself?"

Making a low noise of irritation, he accelerated smoothly. I spun in my seat, watching the Weres come to a halt in the middle of the street. Horns blew from the cars forced to stop for them. Turning back around, I clutched my fish canister and closed my eyes in relief. I was going to get Ivy for this. I swear, I was going to use her precious maps as weed block in the garden. She was supposed to pick me up, not send some FIB flunky.

Pulse slowing, I turned to look at him. He was a good head taller than me, which was saying something—with nice shoulders, curly black hair cut close to his skull, square jaw, and a stiff attitude just begging for me to smack him. Comfortably muscled without going overboard, there wasn't even the hint of a gut on him. In his perfectly fitting black suit, white shirt, and black tie, he could be the FIB poster boy. His mustache and beard were cut in the latest style—so minimal that they almost weren't there—and I thought he might do better to lighten up on his aftershave. I eyed the handcuff pouch on his belt, wishing I still had mine. They had belonged to the I.S., and I missed them dearly.

Jenks settled himself at his usual spot on the rearview mirror where the wind wouldn't tear his wings, and the stiff-necked man watched him with an intentness that told me he had little contact with pixies. Lucky him.

A call came over the radio about a shoplifter at the mall, and he snapped it off. "Thanks for the ride," I said. "Ivy sent you?"

He tore his eyes from Jenks. "No. She said you'd be here. Captain Edden wants to talk you. Something concerning Councilman Trent Kalamack," the FIB officer added indifferently.

"Kalamack!" I yelped, then cursed myself for having said anything. The wealthy bastard wanted me to work for him or see me dead. It depended on his mood and how well his stock portfolio was doing. "Kalamack, huh?" I amended, shifting uneasily in the leather seat. "Why is Edden sending you to fetch me? You on his hit list this week?"

He said nothing, his blocky hands gripping the wheel so tight that his fingernails went white. The silence grew. We went through a yellow light shifting to red. "Ah, who are you?" I finally asked.

He made a scoffing noise deep in his throat. I was used to wary distrust from most humans. This guy wasn't afraid, and it was ticking me off. "Detective Glenn, ma'am," he said.

"Ma'am," Jenks said, laughing. "He called you ma'am."

I scowled at Jenks. He looked young to have made detective. The FIB must have been getting desperate. "Well, thank you, Detective Glade," I said, mangling his name. "You can drop me off anywhere. I can take the bus from here. I'll come out to see Captain Edden tomorrow. I'm working an important case right now."

Jenks snickered, and the man flushed, the red almost hidden behind his dark skin. "It's Glenn, *ma'am*. And I saw your important case. Want me to take you back to the fountain?"

"No," I said, slumping in my seat, thoughts of angry young Weres going through my head. "I appreciate the lift to my office, though. It's in the Hollows, take the next left."

"I'm not your driver," he said grimly, clearly unhappy. "I'm your delivery boy."

I shifted my arm inside as he rolled the window up from his control panel. Immediately it grew stuffy. Jenks flitted to the ceiling, trapped. "What the hell are you doing?" he shrilled.

"Yeah!" I exclaimed, more irate than worried. "What's up?"

"Captain Edden wants to see you now, Ms. Morgan, not tomorrow." His gaze darted from the street to me. His jaw was tight, and I didn't like his nasty smile. "And if you so much as reach for a spell, I'll yank your witch butt out of my car, cuff you, and throw you in the trunk. Captain Edden sent me to get you, but he didn't say what kind of shape you had to be in."

Jenks alighted on my earring, swearing up a blue streak. I repeatedly flicked the switch for the window, but Glenn had locked it. I settled back with a huff. I could jam my finger in Glenn's eye and force us off the road, but why? I knew where I was going. And Edden would see that I had a ride home. It ticked me off, though, running into a human who had more gall than I did. What was the city coming to?

A sullen silence descended. I took my sunglasses off and leaned over, noticing the man was going fifteen over the posted limit. Figures.

"Watch this," Jenks whispered. My eyebrows rose as the pixy flitted from my earring. The autumn sun coming in was suddenly full of sparkles as he surreptitiously sifted a glowing dust over the detective. I'd bet my best pair of lace panties it wasn't the usual pixy dust. Glenn had been pixed.

I hid a smile. In about twenty minutes Glenn would be itching so bad he wouldn't be able to sit still. "So, how come you aren't scared of me?" I asked brazenly, feeling vastly better.

"A witch family lived next door when I was a kid," he said warily. "They had a girl my age. She hit me with just about everything a witch can do to a person." A faint smile crossed his square face to make him look very un-FIBlike. "The saddest day of my life was when she moved away."

I made a pouty face. "Poor baby," I said, and his scowl returned. I wasn't pleased, though. Edden sent him to pick me up because he had known I couldn't bully him.

I hated Mondays.

Two

The gray stone of the FIB tower caught the late afternoon sun as we parked in one of the reserved slots right in front of the building. The street was busy, and Glenn stiffly escorted me and my fish in through the front door. Tiny blisters between his neck and collar were already starting to show a sore-looking pink against his dark skin.

Jenks noticed my eyes on them and snorted. "Looks like Mr. FIB Detective is sensitive to pixy dust," he whispered. "It's going to run through his lymphatic system. He's going to be itching in places he didn't know he had."

"Really?" I asked, appalled. Usually you only itched where the dust hit. Glenn was in for twenty-four hours of pure torture.

"Yeah, he won't be trapping a pixy in a car again."

But I thought I heard a tinge of guilt in his voice, and he wasn't humming his victory song about daisies and steel glinting red in the moonlight, either. My steps faltered before crossing the FIB emblem inlaid in the lobby floor. I wasn't superstitious—apart from when it might save my life—but I was entering what was generally humans-only territory. I didn't like being a minority.

The sporadic conversation and clatter of keyboards remind me of my old job with the I.S., and my shoulders eased. Justice's wheels were greased with paper and fueled by quick feet on the streets. Whether the feet were human or Inderlander was irrelevant. At least to me.

The FIB had been created to take the place of both local and federal authorities after the Turn. On paper, the FIB had been enacted to help protect the remaining humans from the—ah—more aggressive Inderlanders, generally the vamps and Weres. The reality was, dissolving the old law structure had been a paranoiac attempt to keep us Inderlanders out of law enforcement.

Yeah. Right. The out-of-the-closet, out-of-work Inderland police and Federal agents had simply started their own bureau, the I.S. After forty years the FIB was hopelessly outclassed, taking steady abuse from the I.S. as they both tried to keep tabs on Cincinnati's varied citizens, the I.S. taking the supernatural stuff the FIB couldn't.

As I followed Glenn to the back, I shifted the canister to hide my left wrist. Not many people would recognize the small circular scar on the underside of my wrist as a demon mark, but I preferred to err on the side of caution. Neither the FIB nor the I.S. knew I had been involved in the demon-induced incident that trashed the university's ancient-book locker last spring, and I'd just as soon keep it that way. It had been sent to kill me, but it ultimately saved my life. I'd wear the mark until I found a way to pay the demon back.

Glenn wove between the desks past the lobby, and my eyebrows rose in that not a single officer made one ribald comment about a redhead in leather. But next to the screaming prostitute with purple hair and a glow-in-the-dark chain running from her nose to somewhere under her shirt, we were probably invisible.

I glanced at the shuttered windows of Edden's office as we passed, waving at Rose, his assistant. Her face flashed red as she pretended to ignore me, and I sniffed. I was used to such slights, but it was still irritating. The rivalry between the FIB and the I.S. was long-standing. That I didn't work for the I.S. anymore didn't seem to matter. Then again, it could be she simply didn't like witches.

I breathed easier when we left the front behind and entered a sterile fluorescent-lit hallway. Glenn, too, relaxed into a slower pace. I could feel the office politics flowing behind us like unseen currents but was too dispirited to care. We passed an empty meeting room, my eyes going to the huge dry-marker board where the week's most pressing crimes were plastered. Pushing out the usual human-stalked-by-vamp crimes was a list of names. I felt ill as my eyes dropped. We were walking too fast to read them, but I knew what they had to be. I'd been following the papers just like everyone else.

"Morgan!" shouted a familiar voice, and I spun, my boots squeaking on the gray tile.

It was Edden, his squat silhouette hastening down the hallway toward us, arms swinging. Immediately I felt better.

"Slugs take it," Jenks muttered. "Rache, I'm outta here. I'll see you at home."

"Stay put," I said, amused at the pixy's grudge. "And if you say one foul word to Edden, I'll Amdro your stump."

Glenn snickered, and it was probably just as well I couldn't hear what Jenks muttered.

Edden was an ex–Navy SEAL and looked it, keeping his hair regulation short, his khaki pants creased, and his body under his starched white shirt honed. Though his thick shock of straight hair was black, his mustache was entirely gray. A welcoming smile covered his round face as he strode forward, tucking a pair of plastic-rimmed reading glasses into his shirt pocket. The captain of Cincinnati's FIB division came to an abrupt halt, wafting the smell of coffee over me. He was my height almost exactly— making him somewhat short for a man—but he made up for it in presence.

Edden arched his eyebrows at my leather pants and less-than-professional halter top. "It's good to see you, Morgan," he said. "I hope I didn't catch you at a bad time."

I shifted my canister and extended my hand. His stubby thick fingers engulfed mine, familiar and welcoming. "No, not at all," I said dryly, and Edden put a heavy hand on my shoulder, directing me down a short hallway.

Normally I would have reacted to such a show of familiarity with a delicate elbow in a gut. Edden, though, was a kindred spirit, hating injustice as much as I did. Though he looked nothing like him, he reminded me of my dad, having gained my respect by accepting me as a witch and treating me with equality instead of mistrust. I was a sucker for flattery.

We headed down the hallway shoulder-to-shoulder, Glenn lagging behind. "Good to see you flying again, Mr. Jenks," Edden said, giving the pixy a nod.

Jenks left my earring, his wings clattering harshly. Edden had once snapped Jenks's wing off while stuffing him into a water cooler, and pixy grudges went deep. "It's Jenks," he said coldly. "Just Jenks."

"Jenks, then. Can we get you anything? Sugar water, peanut butter . . ." He turned, smiling from behind his mustache. "Coffee, Ms. Morgan?" he drawled. "You look tired."

His grin banished the last of my bad mood. "That'd be great,"

I said, and Edden gave Glenn a directive look. The detective's jaw was clenched, and several new welts ran down his jawline. Edden grasped his forearm as the frustrated man turned away. Pulling Glenn down, Edden whispered, "It's too late to wash the pixy dust off. Try cortisone."

Glenn gave me a closed stare as he straightened and walked back the way we had come.

"I appreciate you dropping in," Edden continued. "I got a break this morning, and you're the only one I could call to capitalize on it."

Jenks made a scoffing laugh. "Whatsa matter, got a Were with a thorn in his paw?"

"Shut up, Jenks," I said, more from habit than anything else. Glenn had mentioned Trent Kalamack, and that had me itchy. The captain of the FIB drew to a stop before a plain door. Another equally plain door was a foot away. Interrogation rooms. He opened his mouth to explain, then shrugged and pushed the door open to show a bare room at half-light. He ushered me in, waiting until the door shut before turning to the two-way mirror and silently shifting the blinds.

I stared into the other room. "Sara Jane!" I whispered, my face going slack.

"You know her?" Edden crossed his short, thick arms on his chest. "That's lucky."

"There's no such thing as luck," Jenks snapped, the breeze from his wings brushing my cheek as he hovered at eye level. His hands were on his hips and his wings had gone from their usual translucence to a faint pink. "It's a setup."

I drew closer to the glass. "She's Trent Kalamack's secretary. What is she doing here?"

Edden stood beside me, his feet spread wide. "Looking for her boyfriend."

I turned, surprised at the tight expression on his round face. "Warlock named Dan Smather," Edden said. "Went missing Sunday. The I.S. won't act until he's gone for thirty days. She's convinced his disappearance is tied to the witch hunter murders. I think she's right."

My stomach tightened. Cincinnati was not known for its serial killers, but we had endured more unexplained murders in the last six weeks than the last three years combined. The recent violence had everyone upset, Inderlander and human alike. The one-way glass fogged under my breath and I backed up. "Does he fit the profile?" I asked, already knowing the I.S. wouldn't have brushed her off if he had.

"If he were dead he would. So far he's only missing."

The dry rasp of Jenks's wings broke the silence. "So why bring Rache into it?"

"Two reasons. The first being Ms. Gradenko is a witch." He nodded to the pretty woman past the glass, frustration thick in his voice. "My officers can't question her properly."

I watched Sara Jane look at the clock and wipe her eye. "She doesn't know how to stir a spell," I said softly. "She can only invoke them. Technically, she's a warlock. I wish you people would get it straight that it's your level of skill, not your sex, that makes you a witch or warlock."

"Either way, my officers don't know how to interpret her answers."

A flicker of anger stirred. I turned to him, my lips pressed. "You can't tell if she's lying."

The captain shrugged, his thick shoulders bunching. "If you like."

Jenks hovered between us, his hands on his hips in his best Peter Pan pose. "Okay, so you want Rache to question her. What's the second reason?"

Edden leaned a shoulder against the wall. "I need someone to go back to school, and as I don't have a witch on my payroll, that's you, Rachel."

For a moment I could only stare. "Beg pardon?"

The man's smile made him look even more like a conniving troll. "You've been following the papers?" he needlessly asked, and I nodded.

"The victims were all witches," I said. "All single except for the first two, and all experienced in ley line magic." I stifled a grimace. I didn't like ley lines, and I avoided using them whenever I could. They were gateways to the ever-after and demons. One of the more popular theories was that the victims had been dabbling in the black arts and simply lost control. I didn't buy that. No one was stupid enough to bind a demon—except Nick, my boyfriend. And that had been only to save my life.

Edden nodded, showing me the top of his head of thick black hair. "What has been kept quiet is that all of them, at one point or another, have been taught by a Dr. Anders."

I rubbed my scraped palms. "Anders," I murmured, searching my memory and coming up with a thin-faced, sour-looking woman with her hair too short and her voice too shrill. "I had a class with her." I glanced at Edden and turned to the one-way glass, embarrassed. "She was a visiting professor from the university while one of our instructors was on sabbatical. Taught Ley Lines for the Earth Witch. She's a condescending toad. Flunked me out on the third class because I wouldn't get a familiar."

He grunted. "Try to get a B this time so I can get reimbursed for tuition."

"Whoa!" Jenks shouted, his tiny voice pitched high. "Edden, you can just plant your sunflower seeds in someone else's garden. Rachel isn't going anywhere near Sara Jane. This is Kalamack trying to get his manicured fingers on her."

Edden pushed himself away from the wall, frowning. "Mr. Kalamack is not implicated in this whatsoever. And if you take this run gunning for him, Rachel, I'll sling your lily-white witch butt back across the river and into the Hollows. Dr. Anders is our suspect. If you want the run, you leave Mr. Kalamack out of this."

Jenks's wings buzzed an angry whine. "Did you all slip antifreeze in your coffee this morning?" he shrilled. "It's a setup! This has nothing to do with the witch hunter murders. Rachel, tell him this has nothing to do with the murders."

"This has nothing to do with the murders," I said blandly. "I'll take the run."

"Rachel!" Jenks protested.

I took a slow breath, knowing I would never be able to explain. Sara Jane was more honest than half the I.S. agents I had once worked with: a farm girl struggling to find her way in the city and help her indentured-servant family. Though she wouldn't know me from Jack, I owed her. She was the sole person who had shown me any kindness during my three days of purgatory trapped as a mink in Trent Kalamack's office last spring.

Physically, we were as unalike as two people could possibly be. Where Sara Jane sat stiffly upright at the table in her crisp business dress with every blond hair in place and makeup applied so well it was almost invisible, I stood in scraped-up leather pants with my frizzy red hair wild and untamed. Where she was petite, having a china-doll look with her clear skin and delicate features, I was tall with an athletic build that had saved my life more times than I have freckles on my nose. Where she was amply curved and padded in all the right places, I stopped at the curves, my chest not much more than a suggestion. But I felt a kinship with her. We were both trapped by Trent Kalamack. And by now she probably knew it.

Jenks hovered beside me. "No," he said. "Trent is using her to reach you."

Irritated, I waved him away. "Trent can't touch me. Edden, do you still have that pink folder I gave you last spring?"

"The one with the disc and datebook containing evidence that Trent Kalamack is a manufacturer and distributor of illegal genetic products?" The squat man grinned. "Yeah. I keep it by my bed for when I can't sleep at night."

My jaw dropped. "You weren't supposed to open it unless I went missing!"

"I peek at my Christmas presents, too," he said. "Relax. I won't do anything unless Kalamack kills you. I still say blackmailing Kalamack is risky—"

"It's the only thing keeping me alive!" I said hotly, then winced as I wondered if Sara Jane might have heard me through the glass.

"—but probably safer than trying to bring him to justice—at the present time. This, though?" He gestured to Sara Jane. "He's too smart for this."

If it had been anyone but Trent, I'd have to agree. Trent Kalamack was pristine on paper, as charming and attractive in public as he was ruthless and cold behind closed doors. I had watched him kill a man in his office, making it look like an accident with a swiftly implemented set of preparations. But as long as Edden didn't act on my blackmail, the untouchable man would leave me alone.

Jenks darted between me and the mirror. He came to a hovering standstill, worry creasing his tiny features. "This stinks worse than that fish. Walk away. You gotta walk away."

My gaze focused past Jenks, upon Sara Jane. She had been crying. "I owe her, Jenks," I whispered. "Whether she knows it or not."

Edden shifted to stand beside me, and together we watched Sara Jane. "Morgan?"

Jenks was right. There was no such thing as luck—unless you bought it—and nothing happened around Trent without reason. My eyes were fixed upon Sara Jane. "Yeah. Yeah, I'll do it."

Three

My gaze was drawn to Sara Jane's nails as she fidgeted across from me. Last time I had seen her, they were clean but worn down to the quick. Now they were long and shapely, polished a tasteful shade of red. "So," I said, looking from the fitfully flashing enamel to her eyes. They were blue. I hadn't known for sure. "You last heard from Dan on Saturday?"

From across the table, Sara Jane nodded. There hadn't been a flicker of recognition when Edden introduced us. Part of me was relieved, part disappointed. Her lilac scent pulled the unwelcome memory of helplessness I had felt while a mink caged in Trent's office.

The tissue in Sara Jane's hand was about the size of a walnut, clenched into a ball with her trembling fingers. "Dan called me as he was coming off of work," she said, the tremor reflected in her voice. She glanced at Edden, standing beside the closed door with his arms crossed and his white sleeves rolled up to his elbows. "Well, he left a message on my machine—it was four in the morning. He said he wanted to have dinner together, that he wanted to talk to me. He never showed up. That's why I know something's wrong, Officer Morgan." Her eyes went wide and her jaw clenched as she struggled not to cry.

"It's Ms. Morgan," I said uncomfortably. "I don't work for the FIB on a regular basis."

Jenks's wings shifted into motion as he remained perched on my foam cup. "She doesn't really work regularly at all," he said snidely.

"Ms. Morgan is our Inderland consultant," Edden said, frowning at Jenks.

Sara Jane dabbed at her eyes. The tissue still in her grip, she nudged her hair back. She had cut it, and it made her look even more professional as it bumped about her shoulders in a straight yellow sheet. "I brought a picture of him," she said, digging in her purse to pull out a snapshot and push it at me. I looked down to see her and a young man on the deck of one of the steamers that take tourists out on the Ohio River. They were both smiling. His arm was around her, and she was leaning into him. She looked happy and relaxed in blue jeans and a blouse.

I took a moment to study Dan's picture. He was clean-cut, sturdy looking, and wearing a plaid shirt. Just the kind of man one would expect a farm girl to bring home to Mom and Dad.

"Can I keep this?" I asked, and she nodded. "Thanks." I tucked it in my bag, not comfortable with how her eyes were fixed upon the picture as if she could bring him back by her will alone. "Do you know how we can get in touch with his relatives? He may have had a family emergency and needed to leave without notice."

"Dan is an only child," she said, dabbing at her nose with the crumpled tissue. "Both his parents are gone. They were serfed on a farm up north. Life expectancy isn't high for a farmer."

"Oh." I didn't know what else to say. "Technically, we can't enter his apartment until he's declared missing. You don't happen to have a key, do you?"

"Yes. I—" She blushed through her makeup. "I let his cat in when he works late."

I glanced down at the lie-detecting amulet in my lap as it briefly shifted from green to red. She was lying, but I didn't need an amulet to figure that out. I said nothing, not wanting to embarrass her further by making her admit she had the key for other, more romantic reasons.

"I was there today about seven," she said, eyes downcast. "Everything looked fine."

"Seven in the morning?" Edden uncrossed his arms and levered himself upright. "Isn't that when you—you witches, I mean—are tucked in bed?"

She gazed up at him and nodded. "I'm Mr. Kalamack's personal secretary. He works in the mornings and evenings, so my schedule is split. Eight to noon in the morning and four to eight in the afternoon. It took a while to become accustomed to it, but with four hours for myself in the afternoon, I was able to spend more time with . . . Dan," she finished.

"Please," the young woman pleaded suddenly, her gaze shifting between Edden and me. "I know something's wrong. Why won't anyone help me?"

I shifted uncomfortably as she struggled for control. She felt helpless. I understood her better than she knew. Sara Jane was the latest in Trent's long string of secretaries. As a mink I had listened in on her interview, unable to warn her as she was lured into believing Trent's half-truths. For all her intelligence, she hadn't a chance to escape his charm and extravagant offers. With his offer of employment, Trent had given her family a golden ticket out of their indentured servitude.

And Trent Kalamack was truly a benevolent employer, offering high wages and outstanding benefits. He gave people what they desperately wanted, asking in return nothing but their loyalty. By the time they realized how deep he demanded that loyalty go, they knew too much to extricate themselves.

Sara Jane had escaped the farm, but Trent had then bought it, probably to ensure that she would keep her mouth shut when she found out about his dealings in the illegal drug Brimstone, as well as the desperately sought-after genetic medicines outlawed during the Turn. I'd almost tagged him with the truth, but the sole other witness had died in a car explosion.

Publicly, Trent served on the city's council, untouchable because of his vast wealth and generous donations to charities and underprivileged children. Privately, no one even knew if he was a human or Inderlander. Even Jenks couldn't tell, which was unusual for a pixy. Trent quietly ran a good slice of Cincinnati's underworld, and both the FIB and the I.S. would sell their bosses to have a court date with him. And now Sara Jane's boyfriend was missing.

I cleared my throat, recalling the temptation of Trent's offer myself. Seeing Sara Jane under control again, I asked, "You said he works at Pizza Piscary's?"

She nodded. "He's a driver. That's how we met." She bit her lip and dropped her eyes.

The lie-detecting amulet was a steady green. Piscary's was an Inderland eatery serving everything from tomato soup to gourmet cheesecake. Piscary himself was said to be one of Cincinnati's master vampires. Nice enough, from what I'd heard: not greedy with his vamp takes, even-tempered, on record as being dead for the last three hundred years. 'Course, he was probably older than that, and the nicer and more civilized an undead vampire seemed, the more depraved he or she generally was. My roommate thought of him as sort of a friendly uncle, which made me feel oh-so-warm and fuzzy inside.

I handed Sara Jane another tissue, and she smiled weakly. "I can go out to his apartment today," I said. "Do you think you could meet me there with the key? Sometimes a professional can spot things others miss." Jenks snorted, and I shifted my legs, bumping the underside of the table to make him dart into the air.

Sara Jane showed relief. "Oh, thank you, Ms. Morgan," she gushed. "I can go right now. I just have to call my employer and let him know I'll be a little late." She gripped her purse, looking like she was ready to fly out of the room. "Mr. Kalamack told me to take all the time I need this afternoon."

I glanced at Jenks's attention-getting buzz. He had a worried I-told-you-so look. How nice of Trent to let his secretary take all the time she needs to find her boyfriend when he's probably stuffed in a closet so she'll keep her mouth shut. "Ah, let's make it tonight," I said, thinking of my fish. "I need to look up a few things." *And whip up a few antigoon spells, check my splat gun, and collect my fee . . .*

"Of course," she said, settling back as her expression clouded.

"And if nothing turns up there, we'll go on to the next step." I tried to make my smile reassuring. "I'll meet you at Dan's apartment a little after eight?"

Hearing the dismissal in my voice, she nodded and stood. Jenks flitted into the air, and I rose as well. "All right," she said. "It's out at Redwood—"

Edden shuffled his feet. "I'll tell Ms. Morgan where it is, Ms. Gradenko."

"Yes. Thank you." Her smile was starting to look stilted. "I'm just so worried. . . ."

I disguised putting my lie-detecting amulet away by digging through my bag and pulling out one of my cards. "Please let me or the FIB know if you hear from him in the meantime," I said as I handed it to her. Ivy had the cards professionally printed, and they looked slick.

"Yes. I will," she murmured, her lips moving as she read VAMPIRIC CHARMS, the name Nick had given my and Ivy's agency. She met my eyes as she tucked the card in her purse. I shook her hand, deciding her grip was firmer this time. Her fingers, though, were still cold.

"I'll show you out, Ms. Gradenko," Edden said as he opened the door. At his subtle gesture, I sank back into my chair to wait.

Jenks buzzed his wings for my attention. "I don't like it," he said as our eyes met.

A flash of ire took me. "She wasn't lying," I said defensively. He put his hands on his hips, and I waved him off my cup to take a sip of my lukewarm coffee. "You don't know her, Jenks. She hates vermin, but she tried to keep Jonathan from tormenting me though it might have meant her job."

"She felt sorry for you," Jenks said. "Pitiful little mink with a concussion."

"She gave me part of her lunch when I wouldn't eat those disgusting pellets."

"The carrots were drugged, Rache."

"She didn't know that. Sara Jane suffered as much as I did."

The pixy hovered six inches before me, demanding I look at him. "That's what I'm saying. Trent could be using her to get to you again, and she wouldn't even know it."

My sigh pushed him back. "She's trapped. I have to help her if I can." I looked up as Edden opened the door and poked his head in. He had an FIB hat on, and it looked odd with his white shirt and khakis as he gestured for me.

Jenks flitted to my shoulder. "You and your 'rescue impulses' are going to get you killed," he whispered as I found the hallway.

"Thanks, Morgan," Edden said as he grabbed my canister of fish and led me up front.

"No problem," I said as we entered the FIB's back offices. The hustle of people enfolded me, and my tension eased in the blessed autonomy it offered. "She wasn't lying about anything other than having a key to let his cat out. But I could have told you that without the spell. I'll let you know what I find out at Dan's apartment. How late can I call you?"

"Oh," Edden said loudly as we slipped past the front desk and headed for the sunlit sidewalk. "No need, Ms. Morgan. Thank you for your help. We'll be in touch."

I stopped short in surprise. A curl of escaped hair brushed my shoulder as Jenks's wings clattered against themselves in a harsh noise. "What the hell?" he muttered.

My face warmed as I realized he was brushing me off. "I did not come down here just to invoke a lousy lie-detecting amulet," I said as I jerked into motion. "I told you I'd leave Kalamack alone. Get out of my way and let me do what I'm good at."

Behind me, conversations were going quiet. Edden never hesitated in his slow stride to the door. "It's an FIB matter, Ms. Morgan. Let me help you out."

I followed, tight to his heels, not caring about the dark looks I was getting. "This run is mine, Edden," I almost yelled. "Your people will mess it up. These are Inderlanders, not humans. You can have the glory. All I want is to be paid." *And see Trent in jail,* I added silently.

He pushed open one of the glass double doors. The sun-warmed concrete threw up a wave of heat as I stomped out after him, almost pinning the short man against the building as he gestured for a cab. "You gave me this run and I'm taking it," I exclaimed, yanking a curl out of my mouth as the wind blew it up into my face. "Not some stuck-up, arrogant cookie in an FIB hat who thinks he's the greatest thing since the Turn!"

"Good," he said lightly, shocking me into taking a step back. Putting my canister on the sidewalk, he stuffed his FIB hat into his back pocket. "But from here on out, you are *officially* off the run."

My mouth opened in understanding. I was *officially* not here. Taking a breath, I willed the adrenaline out of my system. Edden nodded as he saw my anger fizzle out. "I'd appreciate your discretion on this," he said. "Sending Glenn out to Pizza Piscary's alone isn't prudent."

"Glenn!" Jenks shrilled, his voice scraping the inside of my skull, making my eyes water.

"No," I said. "I already have my team. We don't need Detective Glenn."

Jenks left me. "Yeah," he said as he flew between the FIB captain and me. His wings were red. "We don't play well with others."

Edden frowned. "This is an FIB matter. You will have an FIB presence with you when at all possible, and Glenn is the only one qualified."

"Qualified?" Jenks scoffed. "Why not admit he's the only one of your officers who can talk to a witch without pissing his pants?"

"No," I said firmly. "We work alone."

Edden stood beside my canister, his arms crossed to make his squat form look as immovable as a stone wall. "He's our new Inderland specialist. I know he's inexperienced—"

"He's an ass!" Jenks snapped.

A grin flashed over Edden. "I prefer rough around the edges, myself."

My lips pursed. "Glenn is a cocky, self-assured . . ." I fumbled, looking for something suitably derogatory. ". . . FIB flunky who is going to get himself killed the first time he runs into an Inderlander who isn't as nice as I am."

Jenks bobbed his head. "He needs to be taught a lesson."

Edden smiled. "He's my son, and I couldn't agree more," he said.

"He's what?" I exclaimed as an unmarked FIB car pulled up to the curb beside us. Edden reached for the handle of the back door and opened it. Edden was clearly from European decent, and Glenn . . . Glenn wasn't. My mouth worked as I tried to find something that couldn't be remotely construed as being racist. As a witch, I was sensitive to that kind of thing. "How come he doesn't have your last name?" I managed.

"He's used his mother's maiden name since joining the FIB," Edden said softly. "He's not supposed to be under my direction, but no one else would take the job."

My brow furrowed. Now I understood the cold reception in the FIB. It hadn't been all me. Glenn was new, taking a position everyone but his dad thought was a waste of time. "I'm not doing this," I said. "Find someone else to baby-sit your kid."

Edden put my canister into the back. "Break him in gently."

"You aren't listening," I said loudly, frustrated. "You gave me this run. My associates and I appreciate your offer to help, but you asked me here. Back off and let us work."

"Great," Edden said as he slammed the car's back door shut. "Thanks for taking Detective Glenn with you out to Piscary's."

A cry of disgust slipped from me. "Edden!" I exclaimed, earning looks from the passing people. "I said no. There is one sound coming past my lips. One sound. Two letters. One meaning. No!"

Edden opened the front passenger door and gestured for me to get in. "Thanks bunches, Morgan." He glanced into the backseat. "Why were you running from those Weres, anyway?"

My breath came in a slow, controlled sound. *Damn.*

Edden chuckled, and I put myself in the car and slammed the door, trying to get his stubby fingers in it. Scowling, I looked at the driver. It was Glenn. He looked as happy as I felt. I had to say something. "You don't look anything like your dad," I said snidely.

His gaze was fixed with a ramrod stiffness out the front window. "He adopted me when he married my mother," he said through clenched teeth.

Jenks zipped in trailing a sunbeam of pixy dust. "You're Edden's son?"

"You got a problem with that?" he said belligerently.

The pixy landed on the dash with his hands on his hips. "Nah. All you humans look alike to me."

Edden bent to put his beaming round face in the window. "Here's your class schedule," he said, handing me a yellow half page of paper with printer holes along the sides. "Monday, Wednesday, Friday. Glenn will buy any books you need."

"Hold it!" I exclaimed, alarm washing through me as the yellow paper crackled in my fingers. "I thought I was just going to poke around the university. I don't want to take a class!"

"It's the one Mr. Smather was taking. Be there, or you won't get paid."

He was smiling, enjoying this. "Edden!" I shouted as he backed up onto the sidewalk.

"Glenn, take Ms. Morgan and Jenks to their office. Let me know what you find at Dan Smather's apartment."

"Yes *sir!*" he barked. His knuckles gripping the wheel showed a fierce pressure. Pink patches of Ivy-Aid decorated his wrists and neck. I didn't that care that he had heard most of the conversation. He wasn't welcome, and the sooner he understood that, the better.

Four

"**R**ight at the next corner," I said, resting my arm on the open window of the unmarked FIB car. Glenn ran his fingertips through his close-cropped hair as he scratched his scalp. He hadn't said a word the entire way, his jaw slowly unclenching as he realized I wasn't going to make him talk to me. There was no one behind us, but he signaled before turning onto my street.

He had sunglasses on, taking in the residential neighborhood with its shady sidewalks and patchy lawns. We were well within the Hollows, the unofficial haven for most of Cincinnati's resident Inderlanders since the Turn, when every surviving human fled into the city and its false sense of security. There has always been some mingling, but for the most part humans work and live in Cincinnati since the Turn, and Inderlanders work and—uh—play in the Hollows.

I think Glenn was surprised the suburb looked like everywhere else—until you noticed the runes scratched in the hopscotch grid, and that the basketball hoop was a third again taller than NBA regulation. It was quiet, too. Peaceful. Some of that could be attributed to Inderland's schools not letting out until almost midnight, but most was self-preservation.

Every Inderlander over the age of forty had spent their earliest years trying to hide that they weren't human, a tradition that is unraveling with the cautious fear of the hunted, vampires included. So the grass is mown by sullen teenagers on Friday, the cars are dutifully washed on Saturday, and the trash makes tidy piles at the curb on Wednesday. But the streetlights are shot out by gun or charm as soon as the city replaces them, and no one calls the Humane Society at the sight of a loose dog, as it might be the neighbor's kid skipping school.

The dangerous reality of the Hollows remains carefully hidden. We know if we color too far out of humanity's self-imposed lines, old fears will resurface and they will strike out at us. They would lose—badly—and as a whole, Inderlanders like things balanced just as they are. Fewer humans would mean that witches and Weres would start taking the brunt of vampires' needs. And while the occasional witch "enjoyed" a vampiric lifestyle at his or her own discretion, we'd bind together to take them out if they tried to turn us into fodder. The older vampires know it, and so they make sure everyone plays by humanity's rules.

Fortunately, the more savage side of Inderlanders naturally gravitates to the outskirts of the Hollows and away from our homes. The strip of nightclubs along both sides of the river is especially hazardous since swarming, high-spirited humans draw the more predatorial of us like fires on a cold night, promising warmth and reassurance of survival. Our homes are kept as human looking as possible. Those who strayed too far from the Mr. and Mrs. Cleaver veneer were encouraged in a rather unique neighborhood intervention party to blend in a little more . . . or move out to the country where they couldn't do as much damage. My gaze drifted over the tongue-in-cheek sign peeping out from a bed of foxgloves. DAY SLEEPER. SOLICITORS WILL BE EATEN. *For the most part, anyway.*

"You can park up there on the right," I said, pointing.

Glenn's brow furrowed. "I thought we were going to your office."

Jenks flitted from my earring to the rearview mirror. "We are," he said snidely.

Glenn scratched his jawline, his short beard making a rasping sound under his nail. "You run your agency out of a house?"

I sighed at his patronizing lilt. "Sort of. Anywhere here is fine."

He pulled to the curb at Keasley's house, the neighborhood's "wise old man" who had both the medical equipment and know-how of a small emergency room for those who could keep their mouths shut about it. Across the street was a small stone church, its steeple rising high above two gigantic oaks. It sat on an unreal four city lots and had come with its own graveyard.

Renting out a defunct church hadn't been my idea but Ivy's. Seeing tombstones out the small stained-glass window of my bedroom had taken a while to get used to, but the kitchen it came with made up for having dead humans buried in the backyard.

Glenn cut the engine, and the new silence soaked in. I scanned the surrounding yards before I got out, a habit begun during my not-so-distant death threats, which I thought prudent to continue. Old man Keasley was on his porch as usual, rocking and keeping a sharp eye on the street. I gave him a wave and got a raised hand in answer. Satisfied he would have warned me if I had needed it, I got out and opened the back door for my canister of fish.

"I'll get it, ma'am," Glenn said as his door thumped shut.

I gave him a tired look over the car's roof. "Drop the ma'am, will you? I'm Rachel."

His attention went over my shoulder and he visibly stiffened. I whipped around expecting the worst, relaxing as a cloud of pixy children descended in a high-pitched chorus of conversation too fast for me to follow. Papa Jenks had been missed—as usual. My sour mood evaporated as the darting swooping figures in pale green and gold swirled about their dad in a Disney nightmare. Glenn took his sunglasses off, his brown eyes wide and his lips parted.

Jenks made a piercing whistle with his wings, and the horde broke enough for him to hover before me. "Hey, Rache," he said. "I'll be out back if you want me."

"Sure." I glanced at Glenn and muttered, "Is Ivy here?"

The pixy followed my gaze to the human and grinned, undoubtedly imagining what Ivy would do when meeting Captain Edden's son. Jax, Jenks's eldest child, joined his father. "No, Ms. Morgan," he said, pitching his preadolescent voice deeper than it normally fell. "She's doing errands. The grocery store, the post office, the bank. She said she'd be back before five."

The bank, I thought, wincing. She was supposed to wait until I had the rest of my rent. Jax flew three circles about my head, making me dizzy. "'Bye, Ms. Morgan," he called out, zipping off to join his siblings, who were escorting their dad to the back of the church and the oak stump Jenks had moved his very large family into.

My breath puffed out as Glenn came around the back of the car, offering to carry my canister. I shook my head and hefted it; it wasn't that heavy. I was starting to feel guilty for having let Jenks pix him. But then I hadn't known I was going to have to baby-sit him at the time. "Come on in," I said as I started across the street to the wide stone steps.

The sound of his hard-soled shoes on the street faltered. "You live in a church?"

My eyes narrowed. "Yeah. But I don't sleep with voodoo dolls."

"Huh?"

"Never mind."

Glenn muttered something, and my guilt deepened. "Thanks for driving me home," I said as I climbed the stone steps and pulled open the right side of the twin wooden doors for him. He said nothing, and I added, "Really. Thanks."

Hesitating on the stoop, he stared at me. I couldn't tell what he was thinking. "You're welcome," he finally said, his voice giving me no clue, either.

I led the way through the empty foyer into the even more empty sanctuary. Before we rented out the church, it had been used as a daycare. The pews and altar had been removed to make a large play area. Now all that remained were the stained-glass windows and a slightly raised stage. The shadow of a huge, long-gone cross spread across the wall in a poignant reminder. I glanced at the tall ceiling, seeing the familiar room in a new way as Glenn looked it over. It was quiet. I'd forgotten how peaceful it was.

Ivy had spread tumbling mats over half of it, leaving a narrow walkway running from the foyer to the back rooms. At least once a week we'd spar to keep fresh, now that we were both independents and not on the streets every night. It invariably ended with me a sweating mass of bruises and her not even breathing hard. Ivy was a living vamp—as alive as I was and in possession of a soul, infected by the vamp virus by way of her, at the time, still-living mother.

Not having to wait until she was dead before the virus began molding her, Ivy had been born possessing a little of both worlds, the living and dead, caught in the middle ground until she died and became a true undead. From the living she retained a soul, allowing her to walk under the sun, worship without pain, and live on holy ground if she wanted, which she did to tick her mother off. From the dead came her small but sharp canines, her ability to pull an aura and scare the crap out of me, and her power to hold spellbound those who allowed it. Her unearthly strength and speed were decidedly less than a true undead, but still far beyond mine. And though she didn't need blood to remain sane, as undead vampires did, she had an unsettling hunger for it, which she was continually fighting to suppress, since she was one of the few living vamps who had sworn off blood. I imagine Ivy must have had an interesting childhood, but I was afraid to ask.

"Come on in to the kitchen," I said as I went through the archway at the back of the sanctuary. I took off my shades as I passed my bathroom. It had once been the men's bathroom, the traditional fixtures replaced with a washer and dryer, a small sink, and a shower. This one was mine. The women's bathroom across the hall had been converted into a more conventional bathroom with a tub. That one was Ivy's. Separate bathrooms made things a heck of a lot easier.

Not liking the way Glenn was making silent judgments, I closed the doors to both Ivy's and my bedrooms as I passed them. They had once been clergy offices. He shuffled into the kitchen behind me, spending a moment or two taking it all in. Most people did.

The kitchen was huge, and part of the reason I had agreed to live in a church with a vampire. It had two stoves, an institutional-size fridge, and a large center island overhung with a rack of gleaming utensils and pots. The stainless steel shone, and the counter space was expansive. With the exception of my Beta in the brandy snifter on the windowsill, and the massive antique wooden table Ivy used for a computer desk, it looked like the set of a cooking show. It was the last thing one would expect attached to the back of church—and I loved it.

I set the canister of fish on the table. "Why don't you sit down," I said, wanting to call the Howlers. "I'll be right back." I hesitated as my manners clawed their way up to the forefront of my mind. "Do you want a drink . . . or something?" I asked.

Glenn's brown eyes were unreadable. "No, ma'am." His voice was stiff, with more than a hint of sarcasm, making me want to smack him a good one and tell him to lighten up. I'd deal with his attitude later. Right now I had to call the Howlers.

"Have a seat, then," I said, letting some of my own bother show. "I'll be right back."

The living room was just off the kitchen on the other side of the hallway. As I searched for the coach's number in my bag, I hit the message button on the answering machine.

"Hey, Ray-ray. It's me," came Nick's voice, sounding tinny through the recording. Shooting a glance at the hallway, I turned it down so Glenn couldn't hear. "I've got 'em. Third row back on the far right. Now you'll have to make good on your claim and get us backstage passes." There was a pause, then, "I still don't believe you've met him. Talk to you later."

My breath came in anticipation as it clicked off. I had met Takata four years ago when he spotted me in the balcony at a solstice concert. I had thought I was going to be kicked out when a thick Were in a staff shirt escorted me backstage while the warm-up band played.

Turned out Takata had seen my frizzy hair and wanted to know if it was spelled or natural, and if natural, did I have a charm to get something that wild to lie flat? Starstuck and repeatedly embarrassing myself, I admitted it was natural, though I had encouraged it that night, then gave him one of the charms my mother and I spent my entire high school career perfecting to tame it. He laughed then, unwinding one of his blond dreadlocks to show me his hair was worse than mine, static making it float and stick to everything. I hadn't straightened my hair since.

My friends and I had watched the show from backstage, and afterward, Takata and I led his bodyguards on a merry chase through Cincinnati the whole night. I was sure he would remember me, but I hadn't a clue as to how to get in touch with him. It wasn't as if I could call him up and say, "Remember me? We had coffee on the solstice four years ago and discussed how to straighten curls."

A smile twitched the corner of my mouth as I fingered the answering machine. He was all right for an old guy. 'Course, anyone over the age of thirty had seemed old to me at the time.

Nick's was the only message, and I found myself pacing as I picked up the phone and punched in the Howlers' number. I plucked at my shirt as the number rang. After running from those Weres, I had to take a shower.

There was a click, and a low voice nearly growled, "'Ello. Ya got the Howlers."

"Coach!" I exclaimed, recognizing the Were's voice. "Good news."

There was a slight pause. "Who is this?" he asked. "How did you get this number?"

I started. "This is Rachel Morgan," I said slowly. "Of Vampiric Charms?"

There was a half-heard shout directed off the phone, "Which one of you dogs called the escort service? You're athletes, for God's sake. Can't you pin your own bitches without having to buy them?"

"Wait!" I said before he could hang up. "You hired me to find your mascot."

"Oh!" There was a pause, and I heard several war whoops in the background. "Right."

I briefly weighed the trouble of changing our name against the fuss Ivy would raise: a thousand glossy black business cards, the page ad in the phone book, the matched oversized mugs she had imprinted our name on in gold foil. It wasn't going to happen.

"I recovered your fish," I said, bringing myself back. "When can someone pick it up?"

"Uh," the coach muttered. "Didn't anyone call you?"

My face went slack. "No."

"One of the guys moved her while they cleaned her tank and didn't tell anyone," he said. "She was never gone."

Her? I thought. *The fish was a her? How could they tell?* Then I got angry. I had broken into a Were's office for nothing? "No," I said coldly. "No one called me."

"Mmmm. Sorry about that. Thanks for your help, though."

"Whoa! Wait a moment," I cried, hearing the brush-off in his voice. "I spent three days planning this. I risked my life!"

"And we appreciate that—" the coach started.

I spun in an angry circle and stared out at the garden through the shoulder-high windows. The sun glinted on the tombstones beyond. "I don't think you do, *Coach.* We're talking bullets!"

"But she was never lost," the coach insisted. "You don't have our fish. I'm sorry."

"Sorry won't keep those Weres off my tail." Furious, I paced around the coffee table.

"Look," he said. "I'll send you some tickets to the exhibition game coming up."

"Tickets!" I exclaimed, astounded. "For breaking into Mr. Ray's office?"

"Simon Ray?" the coach said. "You broke into Simon's office? Damn, that's rough. 'Bye now."

"No, wait!" I shouted, but the phone clicked off. I stared at the humming receiver. Didn't they know who I was? Didn't they know I could curse their bats to crack and their pop flies to land foul? Did they think I would sit back and do nothing when they owed me my rent!

I flopped into Ivy's gray suede chair with a feeling of helplessness. "Yeah, right," I said softly. A noncontact spell required a wand. Tuition at the community college hadn't covered wand making, just potions and amulets. I didn't have the expertise, much less the recipe, for anything that complicated. I guess they knew who I was right enough.

The sound of a foot scraping linoleum came from the kitchen, and I glanced at the hall. Swell. Glenn had heard the entire thing. Embarrassed, I pulled myself up from the chair. I'd get the money from somewhere. I had almost a week.

Glenn turned as I entered the kitchen. He was standing next to that canister of useless fish. Maybe I could sell it. I put the phone beside Ivy's computer and went to the sink. "You can sit down, Detective Edden. We're going to be here a while."

"It's Glenn," he said stiffly. "It's against FIB policy to report to a member of your family, so keep it to yourself. And we're going to Mr. Smather's apartment now."

I made a scoffing bark of laughter. "Your dad just loves to bend the rules, doesn't he?"

He frowned. "Yes ma'am."

"We aren't going to Dan's apartment until Sara Jane gets off work." Then I slumped. Glenn wasn't the one I was angry with. "Look," I said, not wanting Ivy to find him while I was in the shower. "Why don't you go home and meet me back here about seven-thirty?"

"I'd prefer to stay." He scratched at the welt showing a light pink under his watchband.

"Sure," I said sourly. "Whatever. I gotta shower, though." Clearly he was concerned I'd go without him. The worry was well-founded. Leaning to the window over the sink, I shouted out into the lavish, pixy-tended garden, "Jenks!"

The pixy buzzed in through the hole in the screen so fast, I was willing to bet he'd been eavesdropping. "You bellowed, princess of stink?" he said, landing beside Mr. Fish on the sill.

I gave him a weary look. "Would you show Glenn the garden while I shower?"

Jenks's wings blurred into motion. "Yeah," he said, going to make wide wary circles around Glenn's head. "I'll baby-sit. Come on, cookie. You're going to get the five-dollar tour. Let's start in the graveyard."

"Jenks," I warned, and he gave me a grin, tossing his blond hair artfully over his eyes.

"This way, Glenn," he said, darting out into the hall. Glenn followed, clearly not happy.

I heard the back door shut, and I leaned to the window. "Jenks?"

"What!" The pixy darted back in the window, his face creased with irritation.

I crossed my arms in thought. "Would you bring in some mullein leaves and jewelweed flowers when you get the chance? And do we have any dandelions that haven't gone to seed?"

"Dandelions?" He dropped an inch in surprise, his wings clattering. "You going soft on me? You're going to make him an anti-itch spell, aren't you?"

I leaned to see Glenn standing stiffly under the oak tree, scratching his neck. He looked pitiful, and as Jenks kept telling me, I was a sucker for the underdog. "Just get them, all right?"

"Sure," he said. "He's not much good like that, is he?"

I choked back a laugh, and Jenks flew out the window to join Glenn. The pixy landed on his shoulder, and Glenn jumped in surprise. "Hey, Glenn," Jenks said loudly. "Head off toward those yellow flowers over there behind that stone angel. I want to show you to the rest of my kids. They've never met an FIB officer before."

A faint smile crossed me. Glenn would be safe with Jenks if Ivy came home early. She jealously guarded her privacy and hated surprises, especially ones in FIB uniforms. That Glenn was Edden's son wouldn't help. She was willing to let sleeping grudges lie, but if she felt her territory was being threatened, she wouldn't hesitate to act, her odd, political status of dead-vamp-in-waiting letting her get away with things that would put me in the I.S. lockup.

Turning, my eyes fell upon the fish. "What am I going to do with you—Bob?" I said around a sigh. I wasn't going to take him back to Mr. Ray's office, but I couldn't keep him in the canister. I cracked the top, finding that his gills were pumping and he was laying almost on his side. I thought perhaps I ought to put him in the tub.

Canister in hand, I went into Ivy's bathroom. "Welcome home, Bob," I murmured, dumping the canister into Ivy's black garden tub. The fish flopped in the inch of water, and I hurriedly ran the taps, jiggling the flow to try to keep it room temp. Soon Bob the fish was swimming in graceful sedate circles. I turned off the water and waited until it finished tinkling in and the surface grew smooth. He really was a pretty fish, striking against the black porcelain: all silver, with long, cream fins and that black circle decorating one side to look like a reverse full moon. I dabbled my fingertips in the water, and he darted to the other end of the tub.

Leaving him, I crossed the hall to my bathroom, got a change of clothes out of the dryer, and started the shower. As I picked the snarls out of my hair while waiting for the water to warm, my eyes fell upon the three tomatoes ripening upon the sill. I winced, glad they hadn't been anywhere for Glenn to see. A pixy had given them to me as payment for smuggling her across the city as she fled an unwanted marriage. And while tomatoes weren't illegal anymore, it was in bad taste to have them on display when one had a human guest.

It had been just over forty years since a quarter of the world's human population had been killed by a military-generated virus that had escaped and spontaneously fastened to a weak spot in a biogenetically engineered tomato. It was shipped out before anyone knew—the virus crossing oceans with the ease of an international traveler—and the Turn began.

The engineered virus had a varied effect upon the hidden Inderlanders. Witches, undead vampires, and the smaller species such as pixies and fairies, weren't affected at all. Weres, living vamps, leprechauns, and the like got the flu. Humans died by the droves, taking the elves with them as their practice of bolstering their numbers by hybridizing with humanity backfired.

The U.S. would have followed the Third World countries into chaos if the hidden Inderlanders hadn't stepped in to halt the spread of the virus, burn the dead, and keep civilization running until what was left of humanity finished mourning. Our secret was on the verge of coming out by way of the what-makes-these-people-immune question when a charismatic living vamp named Rynn Cormel pointed out that our combined numbers equaled humanity's. The decision to make our presence known, to live openly among the humans we had been mimicking to keep ourselves safe, was almost unanimous.

The Turn, as it came to be called, ushered in a nightmarish three years. Humanity took their fear of us out on the world's surviving bioengineers, murdering them in trials designed to legalize murder. Then they went further, to outlaw all genetically engineered products, along with the science that created them. A second, slower wave of death followed the first once old diseases found new life when the medicines humanity had created to battle everything from Alzheimer's to cancer no longer existed. Tomatoes are still treated like poison by humans, even though the virus is long gone. If you don't grow them yourself, you have to go to a specialty store to find them.

A frown pinched my forehead as I looked at the red fruit beading up with shower fog. If I was smart, I'd put it in the kitchen to see how Glenn would react at Piscary's. Bringing a human into an Inderland eatery wasn't a crackerjack idea. If he made a scene, we might not only get no information, we might get banned, or worse.

Judging that the water was hot enough, I eased into it with little "ow, ow, ows." Twenty minutes later I was wrapped in a big pink towel, standing before my ugly pressboard dresser with its dozen or so bottles of perfume carefully arranged on top. The blurry picture of the Howlers' fish was tucked between the glass and the frame. Sure looked like the same fish to me.

The delighted shrieks of pixy children filtered in through my open window to soften my mood. Very few pixies could manage to raise a family in the city. Jenks was stronger in spirit than most would ever know. He had killed before to keep his garden so his children wouldn't starve. It was good to hear their voices raised in delight: the sound of family and security.

"Which scent was it, now?" I murmured, fingers hovering over my perfumes as I tried to remember which one Ivy and I were currently experimenting with. Every so often a new bottle would show up without comment as she found something new for me to try.

I reached for one, dropping it when Jenks said from right beside my ear, "Not that one."

"Jenks!" I clutched my towel closer and spun. "Get the hell out of my room!"

He darted backward as I made a grab for him. His grin widened as he looked down at the leg I accidentally showed. Laughing, he swooped past me and landed on a bottle. "This one works good," he said. "And you're going to need all the help you can get when you tell Ivy you're going to make a run for Trent again."

Scowling, I reached for the bottle. Wings clattering, he rose, pixy dust making temporary sunbeams shimmer through the glittering bottles. "Thanks," I said sullenly, knowing his nose was better than mine. "Now get out. No, wait." He hesitated by my small stained-glass window, and I vowed to sew up the pixy hole in the screen. "Who's watching Glenn?"

Jenks literally glowed with parental pride. "Jax. They're in the garden. Glenn is shooting wild cherry pits straight up with a rubber band for my kids to catch before they hit the ground."

I was so surprised, I almost could ignore that my hair was dripping wet and I was wearing nothing but a towel. "He's playing with your kids?"

"Yeah. He's not so bad—once you get to know him." Jenks

vaulted through the pixy hole. "I'll send him inside in about five minutes, okay?" he said through the screen.

"Make it ten," I said softly, but he was gone. Frowning, I shut the window, locked it, and checked twice that the curtains hung right. Taking the bottle Jenks had suggested, I gave myself a splash. Cinnamon blossomed. Ivy and I had been working for the last three months to find a perfume that covered her natural scent mixing with mine. This was one of the nicer ones.

Whether undead or alive, vampires moved by instinct triggered by pheromones and scent, more at the mercy of their hormones than an adolescent. They gave off a largely undetectable smell that lingered where they did, an odoriferous signpost telling other vamps that this was taken territory and to back off. A far cry better than the way dogs did it, but living together the way we were, Ivy's smell lingered on me. She had once told me it was a survival trait that helped increase a shadow's life expectancy by preventing poaching. I wasn't her shadow, but there it was anyway. What it boiled down to was, the smell of our natural scents mingling tended to act like a blood aphrodisiac, making it harder for Ivy to best her instincts, nonpracticing or not.

One of Nick's and my few arguments had been over why I put up with her and the constant threat she posed to my free will if she forgot her vow of abstinence one night and I couldn't fend her off. The truth was, she considered herself my friend, but even more telling was that she had loosened the death grip she kept on her emotions and let me be her friend as well. The honor of that was heady. She was the best runner I'd ever seen, and I was continually flattered that she left a brilliant career at the I.S. to work with me/save my ass.

Ivy was possessive, domineering, and unpredictable. She also had the strongest will of anyone I had met, fighting a battle in herself that if she won would rob her of her life after death. And she was willing to kill to protect me because I called her my friend. God, how could you walk away from something like that?

Apart from when we were alone and she felt safe from recrimination, she either held herself with a cool stiffness or fell into a classic vampire mode of sexy domination that I had discovered was her way of divorcing herself from her feelings, afraid that if she showed a softening she would lose control. I think she had pinned her sanity on living vicariously through me as I stumbled through life, enjoying the enthusiasm with which I embraced everything, from finding a pair of red heels on sale to learning a spell to laying a big-bad-ugly out flat. And as my fingers drifted over the perfumes she had bought for me, I wondered again if perhaps Nick was right and our odd relationship might be slipping into an area I didn't want it to go.

Dressing quickly, I made my way back to the empty kitchen. The clock above the sink said it was edging toward four. I had loads of time to make a spell for Glenn before we left.

Pulling out one of my spelling books from the shelf under the center island counter, I sat at my usual spot at Ivy's antique wooden table. Contentment filled me as I opened the yellowed tome. The breeze coming in the window had a chill that promised a cold night. I loved it here, working in my beautiful kitchen surrounded by holy ground, safe from everything nasty.

The anti-itch spell was easy to find, dog-eared and spotted with old splatters. Leaving the book open, I rose to pull out my smallest copper vat and ceramic spoons. It was rare that a human would accept an amulet, but perhaps if he saw me making it, Glenn might. His dad had taken a pain amulet from me once.

I was measuring the springwater with my graduated cylinder when there was a scuffing on the back steps. "Hello? Ms. Morgan?" Glenn called as he knocked and opened the door. "Jenks said I could come right in."

I didn't look up from my careful measuring. "In the kitchen," I said loudly.

Glenn edged into the room. He took in my new clothes, running his eyes from my fuzzy pink slippers, up my black nylons to my matching short skirt, past my red blouse, to the black bow holding my damp hair back. If I was going to see Sara Jane again, I wanted to look nice.

In Glenn's hands was a wad of mullein leaves, dandelion blossoms, and jewelweed flowers. He looked stiffly embarrassed. "Jenks—the pixy—said you wanted these, ma'am."

I nodded to the island counter. "You can put them over there. Thanks. Have a seat."

With a stilted haste, he crossed the room and set the cuttings down. Hesitating briefly, he pulled out what was traditionally Ivy's chair and eased into it. His jacket was gone, and his shoulder holster with his weapon looked obvious and aggressive. In contrast, his tie was loose and the top button of his starched shirt was unfastened to show a wisp of dark chest hair.

"Where's your jacket?" I asked lightly, trying to figure out his mood.

"The kids . . ." He hesitated. "The pixy children are using it as a fort."

"Oh." Hiding my smile, I rummaged in my spice rack to find my vial of celandine syrup. Jenks's capacity to be a pain in the butt was inversely proportional to his size. His ability to be a stanch friend was the same. Apparently Glenn had won Jenks's confidence. How about that?

Satisfied the show of his gun wasn't intended to cow me, I added a dollop of celandine, swishing the ceramic measuring spoon to get the last of the sticky stuff off. An uncomfortable silence grew, accented by the whoosh of igniting gas. I could feel his gaze heavy upon my charm bracelet as the tiny wooden amulets gently clattered. The crucifix was self-explanatory, but he'd have to ask if he wanted to know what the rest were for. I had only a paltry three—my old ones were burnt to uselessness when Trent killed the witness wearing them in a car explosion.

The mix on the stove started to steam, and Glenn still hadn't said a word. "So-o-o-o," I drawled. "Have you been in the FIB long?"

"Yes ma'am." It was short, both aloof and patronizing.

"Can you stop with the ma'am? Just call me Rachel."

"Yes ma'am."

Ooooh, I thought, *it was going to be a fun evening.* Peeved, I snatched up the mullein leaves. Tossing them into my green-stained mortar, I ground them using more force then necessary. I set the mush to soak in the cream for a moment. *Why was I bothering to make him an amulet? He wasn't going to use it.*

The brew was at a full boil, and I turned the flame down, setting the timer for three minutes. It was in the shape of a cow, and I loved it. Glenn was silent, watching me with a wary distrust as I leaned my back against the edge of the counter. "I'm making you something to stop the itching," I said. "God help me, but I feel sorry for you."

His face hardened. "Captain Edden is making me take you. I don't need your help."

Angry, I took a breath to tell him he could take a flying leap off a broomstick, but then shut my mouth. "I don't need your help" had once been my mantra. But friends made things a lot easier. My brow furrowed in thought. What was it that Jenks did to persuade me? Oh, yeah. Swear and tell me I was being stupid.

"You can go Turn yourself for all I care," I said pleasantly. "But Jenks pixed you, and he says you're sensitive to pixy dust.

It's spreading through your lymph system. You want to itch for a week just because you're too stiff-necked to use a paltry itch spell? This is kindergarten stuff." I flicked the copper vat with a fingernail and it rang. "An aspirin. A dime a dozen." It wasn't, but Glenn probably wouldn't accept it if he knew how much one of these cost at a charm shop. It was a class-two medicinal spell. I probably should have put myself inside a circle to make it, but I'd have to tap into the ever-after to close one. And seeing me under the influence of a ley line would probably freak Glenn out.

The detective wouldn't meet my eyes. His foot twitched as if he was struggling to not scratch his leg through his pants. The timer dinged—or mooed, rather—and leaving him to make up his mind, I added the blossoms of jewelweed and dandelion, crushing them against the side of the pot with a clockwise—never wither-shins—motion. I was a white witch, after all.

Glenn gave up all pretense at trying not to scratch and slowly rubbed his arm through his shirtsleeve. "No one will know I've been spelled?"

"Not unless they did a spell check on you." I was mildly disappointed. He was afraid to openly show he was using magic. The prejudice wasn't unusual. But then, after having taken an aspirin once, I'd rather be in pain than swallow another. I guess I wasn't one to talk.

"All right." It was a very reluctant admission.

"Okey-dokey." I added the grated goldenseal root and turned it to a high boil. When the froth took on a yellow tint that smelled like camphor, I turned off the heat. Nearly done.

This spell made the usual seven portions, and I wondered if he'd demand I waste one on myself before trusting I wasn't going to turn him into a toad. That was an idea. I could put him in the garden to police the slugs from the hostas. Edden wouldn't miss him for at least a week.

Glenn's eyes were on me as I pulled out seven clean redwood disks about the size of a wooden nickle and arranged them on the counter where he could see. "Just about done," I said with a forced cheerfulness.

"That's it?" he questioned, his brown eyes wide.

"That's it."

"No lighting candles, or making circles, or saying magic words?"

I shook my head. "You're thinking of ley line magic. And it's Latin, not magic words. Ley line witches draw their power right from the line and need the trappings of ceremony to control it. I'm an earth witch." *Thank God.* "My magic is from ley lines, too, but it's naturally filtered through plants. If I was a black witch, much of it would come through animals."

Feeling as if I was back doing my graduate lab-work exam, I dug in the silverware drawer for a finger stick. The sharp prick of the blade on my fingertip was hardly noticeable, and I massaged the required three drops into the potion. The scent of redwood rose thick and musty, overpowering the camphor smell. I had done it right. I had known I had.

"You put blood in it!" he said, and my head came up at his disgusted tone.

"Well, duh. How else was I supposed to quicken it? Put it in the oven and bake it?" My brow furrowed, and I tucked a strand of my hair that had escaped my bow back behind my ear. "All magic requires a price paid by death, Detective. White earth magic pays for it by my blood and killing plants. If I wanted to make a black charm to knock you out, or turn your blood to tar, or even give you the hiccups, I'd have to use some nasty ingredients involving animal parts. The really black magic requires not just my blood but animal sacrifice." *Or human or Inderlander.*

My voice was harsher than I had intended, and I kept my eyes down as I measured out the doses and let them soak into the redwood disks. Much of my stunted career at the I.S. involved bringing in gray spell crafters—witches that took a white charm such as a sleep spell and turned it to a bad use—but I'd brought in black charm makers as well. Most had been ley line witches, since just the ingredients needed to stir a black charm were enough to keep most earth witches white. Eye of newt and toe of frog? Hardly. Try blood drawn from the spleen of a still-living animal and its tongue removed as it screamed its last breath into the ether. Nasty.

"I won't make a black charm," I said when Glenn remained silent. "Not only is it demented and gross, but black magic always comes back to get you." *And when I had my way, it involved my foot in his gut or my cuffs on his wrists.*

Choosing an amulet, I massaged three more drops of my blood onto it to invoke the spell. It soaked in quickly, as if the spell pulled the blood from my finger. I extended the charm to him, thinking of the time I had been tempted to stir a black spell. I survived, but came away with my demon mark. And all I'd done was look at the book. Black magic always swings back. Always.

"It's got your blood in it," he said in revulsion. "Make another, and I'll put mine in it."

"Yours? Yours won't do squat. It has to be witch blood. Yours doesn't have the right enzymes to quicken a spell." I held it out again, and he shook his head. Frustrated, I gritted my teeth. "Your dad used one, you whiny little human. Take it so we can all move on with our lives!" I thrust the amulet belligerently at him, and he gingerly took it.

"Better?" I said as his fingers encircled the wooden disk.

"Um, yeah," he said, his square-jawed face suddenly slack. "It is."

"Of course it is," I muttered. Slightly mollified, I hung the rest of my amulets in my charm cupboard. Glenn silently took in my stash, each hook carefully labeled thanks to Ivy's anal-retentive need to organize. Whatever. It made her happy and was no skin off my nose. I closed the door with a loud thump and turned.

"Thank you, Ms. Morgan," he said, surprising me.

"You're welcome," I said, glad he had finally dropped the ma'am. "Don't get any salt on it, and it should last for a year. You can take it off and store it if you want when the blisters go away. It works on poison ivy, too." I started to clean up my mess. "I'm sorry for letting Jenks pix you like that," I said slowly. "He wouldn't have if he had known you were sensitive to pixy dust. Usually the blisters don't spread."

"Don't worry about it." He stretched for one of Ivy's catalogs at the end of the table, pulling his hand back at the picture of the curved stainless-steel knives on special.

I slid my spelling book away under the center island counter, glad he was loosening up. "When it comes to Inderlanders, sometimes the smallest things can pack the hardest punch."

There was a loud boom of the front door closing. Stiffening, I crossed my arms before me, only now recognizing that it had been Ivy's motorcycle tooling up the road a moment before. Glenn met my eyes, sitting straighter as he recognized my alarm. Ivy was home.

"But not always," I finished.

Five

Eyes on the empty hallway, I motioned for Glenn to stay seated. I didn't have time to explain. I wondered how much Edden had told him, or if this was going to be one of his nasty but effective ways to smooth Glenn's edges.

"Rachel?" came Ivy's melodious voice, and Glenn stood, checking the creases in his gray slacks. *Yeah, that would help.* "Did you know there's an FIB car parked in front of Keasley's?"

"Sit down, Glenn," I warned, and when he didn't, I moved to stand between him and the open archway to the hall.

"Yuck!" Ivy exclaimed, her voice muffled. "There's a fish in my bathtub. Is it the Howlers'? When are they coming to get it?" There was a hesitation, and I managed a sick smile at Glenn. "Rachel?" she called out, closer. "Are you in here? Hey, we should go out to the mall tonight. Bath and Bodyworks is re-releasing an old scent with a citrus base. We need to hit the sample bottles. See how it works. You know, celebrate you making rent. What is that you have on now? The cinnamon? That's a nice one, but it only lasts three hours."

Would have been nice to have known that earlier. "I'm in the kitchen," I said loudly.

Ivy's tall, black-clad form strode past the opening. A canvas sack of groceries hung from her shoulder. Her black silk duster fluttered after her boot heels, and I could hear her looking for something in the living room. "I didn't think you would be able to pull the fish thing off," she said. There was a hesitation, then, "Where in hell is the phone?"

"In here," I said, crossing my arms uneasily.

Ivy pulled up short in the archway as she saw Glenn. Her somewhat Oriental features went blank in surprise. I could almost see the wall come down as she realized we weren't alone. The skin around her eyes tightened. Her small nose flared, taking in his scent, cataloging his fear and my concern in an instant. Lips tight, she put her canvas bag of groceries on the counter and brushed her hair out of her eyes. It fell to her mid-back in a smooth black wave, and I knew it was bother, not nerves, that had prompted her to tuck it behind an ear.

Ivy had once had money, and still dressed like it, but her entire early inheritance had gone to the I.S. to pay off her contract when she quit with me. Put simply, she looked like a scary model: lithe and pale, but incredibly strong. Unlike me, she wore no nail polish, no jewelry apart from her crucifix, twin black chain anklets about one foot, and very little makeup; she didn't need it. But like me, she was basically broke, at least until her mother finished dying and the rest of the Tamwood estate came to her. I was guessing that wouldn't be for about two hundred years—bare minimum.

Ivy's thin eyebrows rose as she looked Glenn over. "Bringing your work home again, Rachel?"

I took a breath. "Hi, Ivy. This is Detective Glenn. You talked to him this afternoon? Sent him to *pick me up?*" My look went pointed. We were going to talk about that later.

Ivy turned her back on him to unpack the groceries. "Nice to meet you," she said, her tone flat. Then to me, she muttered, "Sorry. Something came up."

Glenn swallowed hard. He looked shaky but was holding up. I guess Edden hadn't told him about Ivy. I really liked Edden. "You're a vampire," he said.

"Ooooh," Ivy said. "We've got a bright one here."

Fingers fumbling around the string of his new amulet, he pulled a cross from behind his shirt. "But the sun is up," he said, sounding as if he had been betrayed.

"My my my," Ivy said. "And a weatherman, too?" She turned with a snide look. "I'm not dead yet, Detective Glenn. Only the true undead have light restrictions. Come back in sixty years and I might be worried about a sunburn." Seeing his cross, she smiled patronizingly and pulled out from behind her black spandex shirt her own, extravagant crucifix. "That only works on undead vamps," she said as she turned back to the counter. "Where did you get your schooling? B-movies?"

Glenn backed up a step. "Captain Edden never said you worked with a vampire," the FIB officer stammered.

At Edden's name, Ivy spun. It was a blindingly fast motion, and I started. This wasn't going well. She was starting to pull an aura. *Damn.* I glanced out the window. The sun would be down soon. *Double damn.*

"I heard about you," the officer said, and I cringed at the arrogance in his voice, which he was using to cover his fear. Even Glenn couldn't be stupid enough to antagonize a vamp in her own house. That gun at his side wasn't going to do him any good. Sure, he could shoot her, and kill her, but then she'd be dead and she'd rip his freaking head off. And no jury in the world would convict her of murder, seeing as he killed her first.

"You're Tamwood," Glenn said, his bravado clearly scraped from a misplaced feeling of security. "Captain Edden gave you three hundred hours of community service for taking out everyone on his floor, didn't he? What was it he made you do? A candy striper, right?"

Ivy stiffened, and my mouth dropped open. He was that stupid.

"It was worth it," Ivy said softly. Her fingers were shaking as she set the bag of marshmallows gently on the counter.

My breath caught. *Shit.* Ivy's brown eyes had gone black as her pupils dilated. I stood, shocked at how quickly it had happened. It had been weeks since she vamped out on me, and never without warning. The angry shock of finding someone in an FIB uniform in her kitchen might have accounted for some of it, but in hindsight I had a sick feeling that letting her walk in on Glenn hadn't been the best thing. His fear had hit her hard and fast, giving her no time to prepare herself against temptation.

His sudden fright had filled the air with pheromones. They acted as a potent aphrodisiac only she could taste, jerking into play thousand-year-old instincts fixed deep in her virus-changed DNA. In a breath, they had turned her from my slightly disturbing roommate to a predator that could kill both of us in three seconds flat if the desire to sate her long-suppressed hunger outweighed the consequences of draining an FIB detective. It was that balance that frightened me. I knew where I was on her personal scale of hunger and reason. Where Glenn stood, I hadn't a clue.

Like flowing dust, her posture melted and she leaned back against the counter on one bent elbow, hip cocked. Deathly still, she ran her gaze up Glenn until it locked upon his eyes. Her head tilted with a sultry slowness until she was eyeing him from under her straight bangs. Only now did she take a slow, deliberate breath. Her long pale fingers flicked about the deep V-neck of her spandex shirt tucked into her leather pants.

"You're tall," she said, her gray voice pulling remembered fear from me. "I like that." It wasn't sex she was after, it was dominance. She would have bespelled him if she could have, but she'd have to wait until she was dead before she had power over the unwilling.

Swell, I thought as she pushed herself from the counter and headed for him. She'd lost it. It was worse than the time she found Nick and me snuggled up together on her couch not watching pro wrestling. I still didn't know what had set her off then—she and I had a concrete understanding that I wasn't her girlfriend, plaything, lover, shadow, or whatever the newest term for vampire flunky was these days.

My thoughts scrambled for a way to bring her back without making things worse. Ivy drifted to a stop before Glenn, the hem of her duster seeming to move in slow motion as it edged forward to touch his shoes. Her tongue slipped across her very white teeth, hiding them even as they flashed. With a recognizable restrained power, she put a hand to either side of him at head height, pinning him to the wall. "Mmmm," she said, breathing in through parted lips. "Very tall. Lots of leg. Beautiful, beautiful dark skin. Did Rachel bring you home for me?"

She leaned into him, almost touching. He was only a few inches taller than she was. She tilted her head as if to give him a kiss. A drop of sweat slid down his face and neck. He didn't move, tension pulling every muscle tight.

"You work for Edden," she whispered, her eyes fixed on the line of moisture as it pooled at his collarbone. "He'd probably be upset if you died." Her eyes darted to his at the sound of his quick breath.

Don't move, I thought, knowing if he did, instincts would take over. He was in trouble with his back to the wall like that. "Ivy?" I said, trying to distract her and avoid having to tell Edden why his son was in intensive care. "Edden gave me a run. Glenn is along for the ride."

I willed myself not to shudder as she turned the black pits her eyes had become to me. They tracked me as I put the island counter between us. She stood unmoving but for a hand tracing Glenn's shoulder and neck, her finger running a perfect half inch above him. "Uh, Ivy?" I said hesitantly. "Glenn might want to leave now. Let him go."

My request seemed to break through, and she took a quick, clean breath. Bending her elbow, she pushed herself away from the wall.

Glenn darted out from under her. Weapon drawn, he stood in the archway to the hall, his feet spread and his gun trained upon Ivy. The safety clicked off, and his eyes were wide.

Ivy turned her back on him and went to the bag of forgotten groceries. It might look as if she was ignoring him, but I knew she was aware of everything down to the wasp bumping about at the ceiling. Back hunched, she set a bag of shredded cheese on the counter. "Tell that bloodsack of a captain I said hi the next time you see him," she said, her soft voice carrying a shocking amount of anger. But the hunger—the need to dominate—was gone.

Knees weak, I let my breath out in a long puff of air. "Glenn?" I suggested. "Put the gun away before she takes it from you. And the next time you insult my roommate, I'm going to let her tear your throat out. Understand?"

His eyes flicked to Ivy before he holstered the weapon. He stayed in the archway, breathing hard.

Thinking the worst had to be over, I opened the fridge. "Hey, Ivy," I said lightly, to try and get everyone back to normal, "toss me the pepperoni?"

Ivy met my gaze from across the kitchen and blinked the last of her runaway instincts from her. "Pepperoni," she said, her voice huskier than usual. "Yeah." She felt a cheek with the back of her hand. Frowning at herself, she crossed the kitchen with what I recognized as a deliberately slow pace. "Thanks for bringing me down," she said softly as she handed me the pouch of cut meat.

"I should have warned you. I'm sorry." I put the pepperoni away and straightened, giving Glenn a black look. His face was grayed and drawn as he wiped the perspiration away. I think he just figured out we were in the same room with a predator held back by pride and courtesy. Maybe he learned something today. Edden would be pleased.

I shuffled through the groceries and pulled out the perishables. Ivy leaned close as she put a can of peaches away. "What's he doing here?" she asked, loud enough for Glenn to hear.

"I'm baby-sitting."

She nodded, clearly waiting for more. When it wasn't forthcoming, she added, "It's a paying job, right?"

I glanced at Glenn. "Uh, yeah. A missing person." I snuck a glance at her, relieved to see her pupils were almost back to normal.

"Can I help?" she asked.

Ivy had done almost nothing but run for missing persons since she quit the I.S., but I knew she would side with Jenks that it was a ploy of Trent Kalamack's once she learned it was Sara Jane's boyfriend. Putting off telling her would only make it worse, though. And I wanted her to come out to Piscary's with me. I'd get more information that way.

Glenn stood with an affected casualness as Ivy and I put the groceries away, not seeming to care that we were ignoring him. "Oh, come on, Rachel," the vamp cajoled. "Who is it? I'll put my feelers out." She looked as far from a predator now as a duck. I was used to the shifts in temperament, but Glenn looked bewildered.

"Uh, a witch named Dan." I tuned away, hiding my head in the fridge as I put the cottage cheese away. "He's Sara Jane's boyfriend, and before you get all huffy, Glenn is coming with me to look at his apartment. I figure we can wait until tomorrow to check out Piscary's; he works there as a driver. But no way is Glenn coming with me to the university." There was a heartbeat of silence, and I cringed, waiting for her shout of protest. It never came.

I looked past the door of the fridge, going slack in surprise. Ivy had put herself at the sink and was hunched over it, a hand to either side. It was her "count to ten" spot. It had never failed her yet. She pulled her eyes up and put them on me. My mouth went dry. It had failed.

"You are not taking this run," she said, the smooth monotone of her voice pulling the chill of black ice through me.

Panic flashed before settling into a churning burn in the pit of my stomach. All that existed was her pupil-black eyes. She inhaled, taking my warmth. Her presence seemed to swirl behind me until I fought to keep from turning around. My shoulders tensed and my breath came fast. She had pulled a full-blown, soul-stealing aura. Something was different, though. This wasn't anger or hunger I was seeing. This was fear. *Ivy was afraid?*

"I'm taking the run," I said, hearing a thin thread of fear in my voice. "Trent can't touch me, and I already told Edden I would."

"No you aren't."

Silk duster furling, she jerked into motion. I started, finding her right before me almost as soon as I noticed she had moved. Face whiter than usual, she pushed the fridge door shut. I jumped to get out of the way. I met her eyes, knowing if I showed the fright that was making my stomach knot, she would feed on it, making her fervor stronger. I'd learned a lot in the last three months, some of it the hard way, some of it I wished I hadn't needed to know.

"The last time you took on Trent, you almost died," she said, sweat trickling down her neck to disappear behind the deep V of her shirt. *She was sweating?*

"The key word there is 'almost,' " I said boldly.

"No. The key word is 'died.' "

I could feel the heat coming from her and stepped back. Glenn was in the archway, watching me with wide eyes as I argued with a vamp. There was a knack to it. "Ivy," I said calmly, though I was shaking inside. "I'm taking this run. If you want to come with Glenn and me when we talk to Piscary—"

My breath cut off. Ivy's fingers were around my throat. Gasping, my air exploded from me as she slammed me up against the kitchen wall. "Ivy!" I managed before she picked me up with one hand and pinned me there.

Air coming in short, insufficient pants, I hung off the floor.

Ivy put her face next to mine. Her eyes were black, but they were wide with fear. "You aren't going to talk to Piscary," she said, panic a silver ribbon through the gray silk of her voice. "You aren't taking this run."

I braced my feet against the wall and pushed. A breath of air made it past her fingers, and my back smacked back into the wall. I kicked out at her, and she shifted to the side. Her hold on me never altered. "What the hell are you doing?" I rasped. "Let me go!"

"Ms. Tamwood!" Glenn shouted. "Drop the woman and step to the center of the room!"

Digging my fingers into her one-handed grip, I looked past Ivy. Glenn was behind her, his feet braced, ready to shoot. "No!" my voice grated. "Get out. Get out of here!"

Ivy wouldn't listen to me if he was here. She was afraid. What the hell was she afraid of? Trent couldn't touch me.

There was a sharp whistle of surprise as Jenks darted in. "Howdy, campers," he said sarcastically. "I see Rachel told you about her run, huh, Ivy?"

"Get out!" I demanded, my head pounding as Ivy's grip tightened.

"Holy crap!" the pixy exclaimed from the ceiling, his wings flashing into a frightened red. "She's not kidding."

"I know . . ." Lungs hurting, I pried at the fingers around my neck, managing a ragged breath. Ivy's pale face was drawn. The

black of her eyes was total and absolute. And laced with fear. Seeing the emotion on her was terrifying.

"Ivy, let her go!" Jenks demanded as he hovered at eye level.
"It's not that bad, really. We'll just go with her."

"Get out!" I said, taking a clean breath as Ivy's eyes went confused and her grip faltered. Panic took me as her fingers shook.
Sweat trickled down her forehead, pinched in confusion. The
whites of her eyes showed strong against the black.

Jenks darted to Glenn. "You heard her," the pixy said. "Get
out."

My heart raced as Glenn hissed, "Are you crazy? We leave,
and that bitch will kill her!"

Ivy's breath came in a whimper. It was as soft as the first
snowflake, but I heard it. The smell of cinnamon filled my senses.

"We gotta get out of here," Jenks said. "Either Rachel will get
Ivy to let go, or Ivy will kill her. You might be able to separate
them by shooting Ivy, but Ivy will track her down and kill her the
first chance she gets if she overthrows Rachel's dominance."

"Rachel is dominant?"

I could hear the disbelief in Glenn's voice, and I frantically
prayed they'd get out before Ivy finished throttling me.

The buzz of Jenks's wings was as loud as my blood humming
in my ears. "How else do you think Rachel got Ivy to back off of
you? You think a witch could do that if she wasn't in charge? Get
out like she said."

I didn't know if dominant was the right word. But if they
didn't leave, the point would be moot. The honest to God's truth
was, in some twisted fashion Ivy needed me more than I needed
her. But the "dating guide" Ivy had given me last spring so I would
stop pressing her vamp-instinct buttons hadn't had a chapter on
"What to Do If You Find Yourself the Dominant." I was in un-
charted territory.

"Get—out," I choked as the edges of my sight shifted to black.

I heard the safety click back on. Glenn reluctantly holstered
his weapon. As Jenks flitted from him to the rear door and back
again, the FIB officer retreated, looking angry and frustrated. I
stared at the ceiling and watched the stars edging my sight as the
screen door squeaked shut.

"Ivy," I rasped, meeting her eyes. I stiffened at their black terror. I could see myself in their depths, my hair wild and my face
swollen. My neck suddenly throbbed under her fingers where they

pressed against my old demon bite. God help me, but it was starting to feel good, the remembrance of the euphoria that had surged through me last spring as the demon sent to kill me had ripped my neck open and filled it with vamp saliva.

"Ivy, open your fingers a little so I can breathe," I managed, spittle dripping down my chin. The heat from her hand made the smell of cinnamon stronger.

"You told me to let him go," she snarled, baring her teeth as her grip tightened until my eyes bulged. "I wanted him, and you made me let him go!"

My lungs tried to work, moving in short splurges as I struggled for air. Her hold slackened. I took a grateful gulp of air. Then another. Her face was grim, waiting. Dying with a vampire was easy. Living with one took more finesse.

My jaw ached where it rested upon her fingers. "If you want him," I whispered, "go get him. But don't break your fast in anger." I took another breath, praying it wouldn't be my last. "Unless it's for passion, it won't be worth it, Ivy."

She gasped as if I had hit her. Face thunderstruck, her grip loosened without warning. I fell into a heap against the wall.

Hunching into myself, I gagged on the air. I felt my throat, my stomach knotting as the demon bite on my neck continued to tingle in bliss. My legs were askew, and I slowly straightened them. Sitting with my knees to my chest, I shook my charm bracelet back to my wrist, wiped the spit from me, and looked up.

I was surprised to find Ivy still there. Usually when she broke down like this, she went running to Piscary. But then, she had never broken down quite like this before. She had been afraid. She had pinned me to the wall because she had been afraid. Afraid of what? Of me telling her she couldn't tear out Glenn's throat? Friend or not, I'd leave if I saw her take someone in my kitchen. The blood would give me nightmares forever.

"Are you okay?" I rasped, hunching into myself when it triggered a spate of coughing.

She didn't move, sitting at the table with her back to me. She had her head in her hands.

I had figured out shortly after we had moved in together that Ivy didn't like who she was. Hated the violence even as she instigated it. Struggled to abstain from blood even as she craved it. But she was a vampire. She didn't have a choice. The virus had fixed itself deep into her DNA and was there to stay. You are what you are. That she had lost control and let her instincts have sway meant failure to her.

"Ivy?" I got to my feet, listing slightly as I stumbled to her. I could still feel the impressions of her fingers around my neck. It had been bad, but nothing like the time she had pinned me to a chair in a cloud of lust and hunger. I pushed my black bow back where it belonged. "You all right?" I reached out, then drew back before touching her.

"No," she said as my hand dropped. Her voice was muffled. "Rachel, I'm sorry. I—I can't . . ." She hesitated, taking a ragged breath. "Don't take this run. If it's the money—"

"It's not the money," I said before she could finish. She turned to me, and my anger that she might try to buy me off died. A shiny ribbon of moisture showed where she had tried to wipe it away. I'd never seen her cry before, and I eased myself down in the chair beside her. "I have to help Sara Jane."

She looked away. "Then I'm going out to Piscary's with you," she said, her voice holding a thin memory of its usual strength.

I clutched my arms about myself, one hand rubbing the faint scar on my neck until I realized I was unconsciously doing it to feel it tingle. "I was hoping you would," I said as I forced my hand down.

She gave me a frightened, worried smile and turned away.

Six

Pixy children swarmed around Glenn as he sat at the kitchen table as far from Ivy as he could without looking obvious about it. Jenks's kids seemed to have taken an unusual liking to the FIB detective, and Ivy, sitting before her computer, was trying to ignore the noise and darting shapes. She gave me the impression of a cat sleeping before a bird feeder, seemingly ignoring everything but very aware if a bird should make a mistake and get too close. Everyone was overlooking that we had nearly had an incident, and my feelings for being saddled with Glenn had waned from dislike to a mild annoyance at his new, and unexpected, tact.

Using a diabetic syringe, I injected a sleepy-time potion into the last of the thin-walled, blue paint balls. It was after seven. I didn't like leaving the kitchen a mess, but I had to make these little gems up special, and there was no way I would go out to meet Sara Jane at a strange apartment unarmed. *No need to make it that easy for Trent,* I thought as I took off my protective gloves and tossed them aside.

From the nested bowls under the counter I pulled out my gun. I had originally kept it in a vat hanging over the island counter, until Ivy pointed out I'd have to put myself in plain sight to reach it. Keeping it at crawling height was better. Glenn perked up at the sound of iron hitting the counter, waving the chattering, green-clad adolescent pixy girls off his hand.

"You shouldn't keep a weapon out like that," he said scornfully. "Do you have any idea how many children are killed a year because of stupid stunts like that?"

"Relax, Mr. FIB Officer," I said as I wiped the reservoir out. "No one has died from a paint ball yet."

"Paint ball?" he questioned. Then he turned condescending. "Playing dress-up, are we?"

My brow furrowed. I liked my mini splat gun. It felt nice in my hand, heavy and reassuring despite its palm size. Even with its cherry red color, people generally didn't recognize it for what it was and assumed I was packing. Best of all, I didn't need a license for it.

Peeved, I shook a pinky-nail-sized red ball out from the box resting on the shelf above my charms. I dropped it in the chamber. "Ivy," I said, and she looked up from her monitor, no expression on her perfect, oval face. "Tag."

She went back to her screen, her head shifting slightly. The pixy children squealed and scattered, flowing out of the window and into the dark garden to leave shimmering trails of pixy dust and the memory of their voices. Slowly the sound of crickets came in to replace them.

Ivy wasn't the type of roommate who liked to play Parcheesi, and the one time I sat with her on the couch and watched *Rush Hour*, I had unwittingly triggered her vamp instincts and nearly got bitten during the last fight scene as my body temp rose and the smell of our scents mingling hit her hard. So now, with the exception of our carefully orchestrated sparing sessions, we generally did things with lots of space between us. Her dodging my splat balls gave her a good workout and improved my aim.

It was even better at midnight in the graveyard.

Glenn ran a hand over his close-cut beard, waiting. It was clear something was going to happen, he just didn't know what. Ignoring him, I set the splat gun on the counter and started to clean up the mess I'd made in the sink. My pulse increased and tension made my fingers ache. Ivy continued to shop on the net, the clicks of her mouse sounding loud. She reached for a pencil as something got her attention.

Snatching the gun, I spun and pulled the trigger. The puff of sound sent a thrill through me. Ivy leaned to the right. Her free hand came up to intercept the ball of water. It hit her hand with a sharp splat, breaking to soak her palm. She never looked up from her monitor as she shook the water from her hand and read the caption under the casket pillows. Christmas was three months away, and I knew she was stumped as to what to get her mother.

Glenn had stood at the sound of the gun, his hand atop his hol-

ster. His face slack, he alternated his gaze between Ivy and me. I
tossed him the splat gun, and he caught it. Anything to get his
hand away from his pistol. "If that had been a sleepy-time potion,"
I said smugly, "she'd be out cold."

I handed Ivy the roll of paper towels we kept on the island
counter for just this reason, and she nonchalantly wiped her hand
off and continued to shop.

Head bowed, Glenn eyed the paint-ball gun. I knew he was
feeling the weight of it, realizing it wasn't a toy. He walked to me
and handed it back. "They ought to make you license these
things," he said as it filled my grip.

"Yeah," I agreed lightly. "They should."

I felt him watching as I loaded it with my seven potions. Not
many witches used potions, not because they were outrageously
expensive and lasted only about a week uninvoked, but because
you needed to get a good soaking in saltwater to break them. It
was messy and took a heck of a lot of salt. Satisfied that I'd made
my point, I tucked the loaded splat gun into the small of my back
and put on my leather jacket to cover it. I kicked off my pink slippers and padded into the living room for my vamp-made boots by
the back door. "Ready to go?" I asked as I leaned against the wall
in the hallway and put them on. "You're driving."

Glenn's tall shape appeared in the archway, dark fingers ex-
pertly tying his tie. "You're going like that?"

Brow furrowing, I looked down at my red blouse, black skirt,
nylons, and ankle-high boots. "Something wrong with what I've
got on?"

Ivy made a rude snort from her computer. Glenn glanced at
her, then me. "Never mind," he said flatly. He snuggled his tie
tight to make him look polished and professional. "Let's go."

"No," I said, getting in his face. "I want to know what you
think I should put on. One of those polyester sacks you make your
female FIB officers wear? There's a reason Rose is so uptight, and
it has nothing to do with her having no walls or her chair having a
broken caster!"

Face hard, Glenn sidestepped me and headed up the hallway.
Grabbing my bag, I acknowledged Ivy's preoccupied wave good-
bye and strode after him. He took up almost the entire width of the
hall as he walked and put his arms into his suit's jacket at the same
time. The sound of the lining rubbing against his shirt was a soft
hush over the noise of his hard-soled shoes on the floorboards.

I kept to my cold silence as Glenn drove us out of the Hollows and back across the bridge. It would have been nice had Jenks come with us, but Sara Jane said something about a cat, and he prudently decided to stay home.

The sun was long down and traffic had thickened. The lights from Cincinnati looked nice from the bridge, and I felt a flash of amusement as I realized Glenn was driving at the head of a pack of cars too wary to pass him. Even the FIB's unmarked vehicles were obvious. Slowly my mood eased. I cracked the window to dilute the smell of cinnamon, and Glenn flipped the heater on. The perfume didn't smell as nice anymore, now that it had failed me.

Dan's apartment was a town house: tidy, clean, and gated. Not too far from the university. Good access to the freeway. It looked expensive, but if he was taking classes at the university, he could probably swing it just fine. Glenn pulled into the reserved spot with Dan's house number on it and cut the engine. The porch light was off and the drapes were pulled. A cat was sitting on the second-story balcony railing, its eyes glowing as it watched us.

Saying nothing, Glenn reached under the seat and moved it back. Closing his eyes, he settled in as if to nap. The silence grew, and I listened to the car's engine tick as it cooled off in the dark. I reached for the radio knob, and Glenn muttered, "Don't touch that."

Peeved, I sank back. "Don't you want to question some of his neighbors?" I asked.

"I'll do it tomorrow when the sun is up and you're at class."

My eyebrows rose. According to the receipt Edden had given me, class ran from four to six. It was an excellent time to be knocking on doors, when humans would be coming home, diurnal Inderlanders well up, and nightwalkers stirring. And the area felt like a mixed neighborhood.

A couple came out of a nearby apartment, arguing as they got into a shiny car and drove away. She was late for work. It was his fault, if I was following the conversation properly.

Bored, and a little nervous, I dug in my bag until I found a finger stick and one of my detection amulets. I loved these things—the detection amulet, not the finger stick—and after pricking my finger for three drops of blood to invoke it, I found that there was no one but Glenn and me within a thirty-foot radius. I draped it about my neck like my old I.S. badge as a little red car pulled into the lot. The cat on the railing stretched before dropping out of sight onto the balcony.

It was Sara Jane, and she whipped her car into the spot directly behind us. Glenn took notice, saying nothing as we got out and angled our paths to meet her.

"Hi," she said, her heart-shaped face showing her worry in the light from the street lamp. "I hope you weren't waiting long," she added, her voice carrying the professional air of the office.

"Not at all, ma'am," Glenn said.

I tugged my leather coat closer against the cold as she jingled her keys, fumbling for one that still carried a shiny, new-cut veneer and opened the door. My pulse increased, and I glanced at my amulet with thoughts of Trent going through me. I had my splat gun, but I wasn't a brave person. I ran away from big-bad-uglies. It increased my life span dramatically.

Glenn followed Sara Jane in as she flipped on the lights, illuminating the porch and apartment both. Nervous, I crossed the threshold, wavering between closing the door to keep anyone from following me in and leaving it open to keep my escape route available. I opted to leave it cracked.

"You got a problem?" Glenn whispered as Sara Jane made her confident way to the kitchen, and I shook my head. The town house had an open floor plan with almost the entire downstairs visible from the doorway. Stairs ran a straight, unimaginative pathway to the second floor. Knowing my amulet would warn me if anyone new showed up, I relaxed. There was no one here but us three and the cat yowling on the second-floor balcony.

"I'll go up and let Sarcophagus in," Sara Jane said as she headed for the stairs.

My eyebrows rose. "That's the cat, right?"

"I'll come with you, ma'am," Glenn offered, and he thumped upstairs after her.

I did a quick reconnaissance of the downstairs while they were gone, knowing we'd find nothing. Trent was too good to leave anything behind; I just wanted to see what kind of a guy Sara Jane liked. The kitchen sink was dry, the garbage can was stinky, the computer monitor was dusty, and the cat box was full. Clearly Dan hadn't been home in a while.

The floorboards above me creaked as Glenn walked through the upstairs. Perched on the TV was the same picture of Dan and Sara Jane aboard the steamer. I picked it up and studied their faces, setting the framed photo back on the TV as Glenn clumped downstairs. The man's shoulders took up almost the entirety of the narrow stairway. Sara Jane was silent behind him, looking small and walking sideways in her heels.

"Upstairs looks fine," Glenn said as he rifled through the stack of mail on the kitchen counter. Sara Jane opened the pantry. Like everything else, it was well-organized. After a moment of hesitation, she pulled out a pouch of moist cat food.

"Mind if I check his e-mails?" I asked, and Sara Jane nodded, her eyes sad. I jiggled the mouse to find that Dan had a dedicated, always-on line just like Ivy. Strictly speaking, I shouldn't have been doing this, but as long as no one said anything . . . From the corner of my eye I watched Glenn run his eyes over Sara Jane's smartly cut business dress as she tore the bag of cat food open, and then down my outfit as I bent over the keyboard. I could tell by his look that he thought my clothes were unprofessional, and I fought back a grimace.

Dan had a slew of unopened messages, two from Sara Jane and one with a university address. The rest were from a hard-rock chat room of some sort. Even I knew better than to open any of them, tampering with evidence should he turn up dead.

Glenn ran a hand across his short hair, seemingly disappointed that he had found nothing unusual. I was guessing it wasn't because Dan was missing but that he was a witch, and as such should have dead monkey heads hanging from the ceiling. Dan appeared to be an average, on his own young man. He was perhaps tidier than most, but Sara Jane wouldn't date a slob.

Sara Jane set a bowl of food on the placement next to a water bowl. A black cat slunk downstairs at the clink of porcelain. It hissed at Sara Jane, not coming to eat until she left the kitchen. "Sarcophagus doesn't like me," she said needlessly. "He's a one-person familiar."

A good familiar was like that. The best chose their owners, not the other way around. The cat finished the food in a surprisingly short amount of time, then jumped onto the back of the couch. I scratched the upholstery and he came close to investigate. He stretched out his neck and touched my finger with his nose. It was how cats greeted each other, and I smiled. I'd love to have a cat, but Jenks would pix me every night for a year if I brought one home.

Remembering my stint as a mink, I shuffled through my purse. Trying to be discreet, I invoked an amulet to do a spell check on the cat. Nothing. Not satisfied, I dug deeper for a pair of wire-rimmed glasses. Ignoring Glenn's questioning look, I popped open the hard case and carefully put the so-ugly-they-could-work-as-birth-control glasses on. I had bought them last month, spending three times my rent with the excuse that they were tax deductible. The ones that didn't make me look like a nerd reject would've cost me twice that.

Ley line magic could be bound in silver just as earth magic could be kept in wood, and the wire frames were spelled to let me see through disguises invoked by ley line magic. I felt kind of cheesy using them, thinking that it dumped me back into the realm of warlocks in that I was using a charm that I couldn't make. But as I scratched Sarcophagus's chin, sure now by the lack of any change that he wasn't Dan trapped in a cat's form, I decided I didn't care.

Glenn turned to the phone. "Would you mind if I listened to his messages?" he asked.

Sara Jane's laugh was bitter. "Go ahead. They're from me."

The snap of the hard case was loud as I put my glasses away. Glenn punched the button, and I winced as Sara Jane's recorded voice came into the silent apartment. "Hey, Dan. I waited an hour. It was Carew Tower, right?" There was a hesitation, then a distant, "Well, give me a call. And you'd better get some chocolate." Her voice turned playful. "You've got some serious groveling to do, farm boy."

The second was even more uncomfortable. "Hi, Dan. If you're there, pick up." Again a pause. "Um, I was just kidding about the chocolate. I'll see you tomorrow. Love you. 'Bye."

Sara Jane stood in the living room, her face frozen. "He wasn't here when I came over, and I haven't seen him since," she said softly.

"Well," Glenn said as the machine clicked off, "we haven't found his car yet, and his toothbrush and razor are still here. Wherever he is, he hadn't planned on staying. It looks like something has happened."

She bit her lip and turned away. Amazed at his lack of tact, I gave Glenn a murderous look. "You have the sensitivity of a dog in heat, you know that?" I whispered.

Glenn glanced at Sara Jane's hunched shoulders. "Sorry, ma'am."

She turned, a miserable smile on her. "Maybe I should take Sarcophagus home. . . ."

"No," I quickly assured her. "Not yet." I touched her shoulder in sympathy, and the smell of her lilac perfume pulled from me the chalky taste-memory of drugged carrots. I glanced at Glenn, knowing he wouldn't leave so I could talk to her alone. "Sara Jane," I asked hesitantly. "I have to ask you this, and I apologize. Do you know if anyone has threatened Dan?"

"No," she said, her hand rising to her collar and her face going still. "No one."

"How about you?" I asked. "Have you been threatened any way? Any way at all?"

"No. No of course not," she said quickly, her eyes dropping and her pale features going even whiter. I didn't need an amulet to know she was lying, and the silence grew uncomfortable as I gave her a moment to change her mind and tell me. But she didn't.

"A-Are we done?" she stammered, and nodding, I adjusted my bag on my shoulder. Sara Jane headed to the door, her steps quick and stilted. Glenn and I followed her out onto the cement landing. It was too cold for bugs, but a broken spiderweb stretched by the porch light.

"Thank you for letting us look at his apartment," I said as she checked the door with trembling fingers. "I'll be talking with his classmates tomorrow. Perhaps one of them will know something. Whatever it is, I can help," I said, trying to put more meaning into my voice.

"Yes. Thank you." Her eyes went everywhere but to mine, and she had fallen into her professional office tone again. "I appreciate you coming over. I wish I could be more help."

"Ma'am," Glenn said in parting. Sara Jane's heels clicked smartly on the pavement as she walked away. I followed Glenn to his car, glancing back to see Sarcophagus sitting in an upstairs window watching us.

Sara Jane's car gave a happy chirp before she set her purse inside, got in, and drove away. I stood in the dark beside my open door and watched her taillights vanish around a corner. Glenn was facing me, standing at the driver side with his arms resting on the roof of the car. His brown eyes were featureless in the buzz of the street lamp.

"Kalamack must pay his secretaries very well for the car she has," he said softly.

I stiffened. "I know for a fact he does," I said hotly, not liking what he was implying. "She's very good at her job. And she still has enough money to send home for her family to live like veritable kings compared to the rest of the farm's employees."

He grunted and opened his door. I got in, sighing as I fastened my belt and settled into the leather seats. I stared out the window at the dark lot, growing more depressed. Sara Jane didn't trust me. But from her point of view, why should she?

"Taking this kind of personal, aren't you?" Glenn asked as he started the car.

"You think because she's a warlock she doesn't deserve help?" I said sharply.

"Slow down. That's not what I meant." Glenn shot me a quick look as he backed the car into motion. He flipped the heater on full before he shifted into drive, and a strand of hair tickled my face. "I'm just saying you're acting like you have a stake in the outcome."

I ran a hand over my eyes. "Sorry."

"It's okay," he said, sounding as if he understood. "So . . ." He hesitated. "What gives?"

He pulled into traffic, and in the light of a street lamp I glanced at him, wondering if I wanted to be that open with him. "I know Sara Jane," I said slowly.

"You mean you know her type," Glenn said.

"No. I know her."

The FIB detective frowned. "She doesn't know you."

"Yeah." I rolled the window all the way down to get rid of the smell of my perfume. I couldn't stand it anymore. My thoughts kept returning to Ivy's eyes, black and frightened. "That's what makes it hard."

The brakes made a slow squeak as we stopped at a light. Glenn's brow was furrowed, and his beard and mustache made deep shadows on him. "Would you talk human, please?"

I gave him a quick mirthless smile. "Did your dad tell you about how we nearly brought Trent Kalamack in as a dealer and manufacturer of genetic drugs?"

"Yeah. That was before I transferred to his department. He said the only witness was an I.S. runner who died in a car bombing." The light changed, and we moved forward.

I nodded. Edden had told him the basics. "Let me tell you about Trent Kalamack," I said as the wind pushed against my hand. "When he caught me rifling through his office looking for a way to bring him into the courts, he didn't turn me in to the I.S., he offered me a job. Anything I wanted." Cold, I angled the vent toward me. "He'd pay off my I.S. death threat, set me up as an independent runner, give me a small staff, everything—if I worked for him. He wanted me to run the same system I had spent my entire professional life fighting. He offered me what looked like freedom. I wanted it so badly, I might have said yes."

Glenn was silent, wisely not saying anything. There wasn't a cop alive who hadn't been tempted, and I was proud that I had passed that test. "When I turned him down, his offer became a threat. I was spelled into a mink at the time, and he was going to torture me mentally and physically until I would do anything to get it to stop. If he couldn't have me willingly, he'd be satisfied with a warped shadow eager to please him. I was helpless. Just like Sara Jane is."

I hesitated to gather my resolve. I had never admitted that aloud before—that I had been helpless. "She thought I was a mink, but she gave me more dignity as an animal than Trent gave me as a person. I have to get her away from him. Before it's too late. Unless we can find Dan and get him safe, she doesn't have a chance."

"Mr. Kalamack is just a man," Glenn said.

"Really!" I said with a bark of sarcastic laughter. "Tell me, Mr. FIB Detective, is he human or Inderlander? His family has been quietly running a good slice of Cincinnati for two generations, and no one knows what he is. Jenks can't tell what he smells like, and neither can the fairies. He destroys people by giving them exactly what they want—and he enjoys it." I watched the passing buildings without seeing them.

Glenn's continued silence pulled my eyes up. "You really think Dan's disappearance has nothing to do with the witch hunter murders?" he asked.

"Yeah." I resettled myself, not comfortable with having told him so much. "I only took this run to help Sara Jane and pull Trent down. You going to run tattling to your dad now?"

The lights from oncoming traffic illuminated him. He took a breath and let it out. "You do anything in your little vendetta to jeopardize me proving Dr. Anders is the murderer, and I'll tie you to a bonfire in Fountain Square," he said softly in threat. "You will go to the university tomorrow, and you will tell me everything you learn." His shoulders eased. "Just be careful."

I eyed him, the passing lights illuminating him in flashes that seemed to mirror my uncertainty. It sounded as if he understood. Imagine that. "Fair enough," I said, settling back. My head turned as we turned left instead of right. I glanced at him with a feeling of déjà vu. "Where are we going? My office is the other way."

"Pizza Piscary's," he said. "There's no reason to wait until tomorrow."

I eyed him, not wanting to admit I'd promised Ivy I wouldn't go out there without her. "Piscary's doesn't open until midnight," I lied. "They cater to Inderlanders. I mean, how often does a human order a pizza?" Glenn's face went still in understanding, and I picked at my nail polish. "It will be at least two before they slow down enough to be able to talk to us."

"That's two in the morning, right?" he asked.

Well, duh, I thought. That was when most Inderlanders were hitting their stride, especially the dead ones. "Why don't you go home, sleep in, and we'll all go out tomorrow?"

He shook his head. "You'll go tonight without me."

A puff of affront escaped me. "I don't work like that, Glenn. Besides, if I do, you'll go out there alone, and I promised your dad I'd try to keep you alive. I'll wait. Witches' honor."

Lie, yes. Betray the trust of a partner—even unwelcome ones—no.

He gave me a quick, suspicious glance. "All right. Witches' honor."

Seven

"**R**ache," Jenks said from my earring. "Take a squint at that guy. Is he trolling or what?"

I tugged my bag up higher onto my shoulder and peered through the unseasonably warm September afternoon at the kid in question as I walked through the informal lounge. Music tickled my subconscious, the volume of his radio set too low to hear well. My first thought was that he must be hot. His hair was black, his clothes were black, his sunglasses were black, and his black duster was made of leather. He was leaning against a vending machine trying to look suave as he talked to a woman in a gothic black lace dress. But he was blowing it. No one looks sophisticated with a foam cup in his hand, no matter how sexy his two-day stubble is. And no one wore goth but out-of-control teen living vamps and pathetically sad vamp wannabes.

I snickered, feeling vastly better. The big campus and the conglomeration of youth had me on edge. I had gone to school at a small community college, taking the standard two-year program followed by a four-year internship with the I.S. My mother would have never been able to afford tuition at the University of Cincinnati on my dad's pension, extra death benefit aside.

I glanced at the faded yellow receipt Edden had given me. It had the time and days my class met, and right down at the lower right-hand corner was the cost of it all—tax, lab fees, and tuition all totaled up into one appalling sum. Just this one class was nearly as much as a semester at my alma mater. Nervous, I shoved the paper in my bag as I noticed a Were in the corner watching me. I looked out of place enough without wandering around with a class schedule in my grip. I might as well have hung a card around my neck saying, "Continuing Adult Education Student." God help me, but I felt old. They weren't much younger than I was, but their every move screamed innocence.

"This is stupid," I muttered to Jenks as I left the informal commissary. I didn't even know why the pixy was with me. Must be Edden had sicced him on me to make sure I went to class. My vamp-made boots clicked smartly as I strode through the windowed, elevated walkway connecting the Business Arts building with Kantack Hall. A jolt went through me as I realized my feet were hitting the rhythm of Takata's "Shattered Sight," and though I still couldn't really hear the music, the lyrics settled themselves deep into my head to drive me nuts. *Sift the clues from the dust, from my lives, of my will./ I loved you then. I love you still.*

"I should be with Glenn, interviewing Dan's neighbors," I complained. "I don't need to take the freaking class, just talk to Dan's classmates."

My earring swung like a tire swing, and Jenks's wings tickled my neck. "Edden doesn't want to give Dr. Anders any warning that she's a suspect. I think it's a good idea."

I frowned, my steps growing muffled as I found the carpeted hallway and began watching the numbers on the doors count up. "You think it's a good idea, do you?"

"Yeah. But there's one thing he forgot." He snickered. "Or maybe he didn't."

I slowed as I saw a group standing outside a door. It was probably mine. "What's that?"

"Well," he drawled, "now that you're taking the class, you fit the profile."

Adrenaline zinged through me and vanished. "How about that?" I murmured. *Damn Edden anyway.*

Jenks's laughter was like wind chimes. I shifted my heavy book to my other hip, scanning the small gathering for the person most likely to spill the best gossip. A young woman looked up at me, or Jenks rather, smiling briefly before turning away. She was dressed in jeans like me, with an expensive-looking suede coat over her T-shirt. Casual yet sophisticated. Nice combination. Dropping my bag to the carpet tile, I leaned back against the wall like everyone else, a noncommittal four feet away.

I surreptitiously looked at the book by the woman's feet. *Noncontact Extensions Using Ley Lines.* A tiny wash of relief went through me. I had the right book, at least. Maybe this wouldn't be so bad. I glanced at the frosted glass of the closed door, hearing a muted conversation from inside. Must be the previous class hadn't let out yet.

Jenks rocked my earring, pulling on it. I could ignore that, but when he started singing about inchworms and marigolds, I batted him off.

The woman beside me cleared her throat. "Just transfer in?" she asked.

"Beg pardon?" I asked as Jenks flitted back.

She popped her gum, her heavily made-up eyes going from me to the pixy. "There aren't many of us ley line students. I don't remember seeing you. Do you usually take night classes?"

"Oh." I pushed myself away from the wall and faced her. "No. I'm taking a class to, ah, move ahead at work."

She laughed as she tucked her long hair back. "Hey, I'm right there with you. But by the time I get out of here, there's probably not going to be any jobs left for a film production manager with ley line experience. Everyone seems to be minoring in art these days."

"I'm Rachel." I extended my hand. "And this is Jenks."

"Nice to meet you," she said, taking it for an instant. "Janine."

Jenks buzzed to her, alighting on her hastily raised hand. "Pleasure is all mine, Janine," he said, actually making a bow.

She beamed, utterly delighted. Obviously she hadn't had much contact with pixies. Most stayed outside the city unless employed in the few areas pixies and fairies excelled in: camera maintenance, security, or good old-fashioned sneaking around. Even so, fairies were far more commonly employed, since they ate insects instead of nectar and their food supply was more readily available.

"Uh, does Dr. Anders actually teach the class, or does she have an aide do it?" I asked.

Janine chuckled, and Jenks flitted back to my earring. "You've heard about her?" she asked. "Yes, she teaches, seeing as there's not that many of us." Janine's eyes pinched. "Especially now. We started with more than a dozen, but we lost four when Dr. Anders told us the murderer was taking only ley line witches and to be careful. And then Dan went and quit." She slumped back against the wall, sighing.

"The witch hunter?" I asked, stifling my smile. I had chosen the right person to stand beside. I made my eyes wide. "You're kidding. . . ."

Her face went worried. "I think that's some of the reason why Dan left. And it was a shame, too. The man was so hot, he could make a sprinkler spark in a rainstorm. He had a big interview. Wouldn't tell me anything. I think he was afraid I'd apply for it, too. Looks like he got the job."

My head bobbed as I wondered if this was the news he was going to tell Sara Jane on Saturday. But then a slow burn started in me that perhaps supper at Carew Tower had been a dump dinner, and he chickened out and left without telling her anything.

"Are you sure he quit?" I asked. "Maybe the witch hunter . . ." I left my sentence open, and Janine smiled reassuringly.

"Yes, he quit. He asked if I wanted to buy his magnetic chalk if he got the job. The bookstore won't take them back once you break the seal."

My face went slack in sudden, real alarm. "I didn't know I needed chalk."

"Oh, I've got one you can borrow," she said as she rummaged in her purse. "Dr. Anders usually has us sketching something or other: pentagrams, north/south apogees . . . you name it, we've traced it. She lumps the lab in with the lecture. That's why we meet here instead of a lecture hall."

"Thanks," I said as I accepted the metallic stick and gripped it along with my book. *Pentagrams?* I hated pentagrams. My lines were always crooked. I'd have to ask Edden if he would pay for a second trip to the bookstore. But then remembering the cost of the class he would probably never be reimbursed for, I decided to go pick up my old school supplies from my mom. Swell. Better give her a call.

Janine saw my sick look, and misunderstanding it, she rushed to say, "Oh, don't worry, Rachel. The murderer isn't after us. Really. Dr. Anders said to be careful, but he's only going for experienced witches."

"Yeah," I said, wondering if I would be considered experienced or not. "I guess."

The conversations around us ceased as Dr. Anders's voice shrilled from behind the door, "I don't know who's killing my students. I've been to too many funerals this month to listen to your foul accusations. And I'll sue you from here back to the Turn if you slander my name!"

Janine looked alarmed as she picked up her book and held it to her chest. The students in the hallway shifted from foot to foot and exchanged uneasy looks. From my earring Jenks whispered, "So much for keeping Dr. Anders in the dark about her possible suspect status." I nodded, wondering if Edden would let me drop the class now. "It's Denon in there with her," Jenks added, and I took a quick breath.

"What?"

"I can smell Denon," he reiterated. "He's in there with Dr. Anders."

Denon? I thought, wondering what my old boss was doing out from behind his desk.

There was a soft murmur, followed by a loud pop. Everyone in the hall but Jenks and me jumped. Janine reached up and touched her ear as if she had just been knocked a good one. "Didn't you feel that?" she asked me, and I shook my head. "She just set a circle without drawing a real one first."

I eyed the door along with everyone else. I didn't know you could set a circle without drawing it. I also didn't like that everybody but Jenks and I had been able to tell she had done it. Feeling as if I was in over my head, I picked my bag up.

The low rumble of my old boss's voice pulled a chill from me. Denon was a living vamp, like Ivy. But he was low-blood, rather than high, having been born a human and infected with the vamp virus later by one of the true undead. And where Ivy had political power because she'd been born a vamp and thus was guaranteed to join the undead even if she should die alone with every drop of blood in her, Denon would always be second-class, having to trust that someone would bother to finish turning him after he died.

"Get out of my room," Dr. Anders demanded. "Before I file harassment charges."

The students all shifted nervously. I wasn't surprised when the frosted glass darkened with a shape behind it. I stiffened with the rest when the door opened and Denon walked out. The man almost had to turn sideways to clear the door frame.

I still maintained my belief that Denon had been a boulder in a previous life—a smooth, river-worn boulder massing about a ton maybe? Being low-blood and having only human strength, he had to work hard to keep up with his dead brethren. The results were a trim waist and oodles of bunching muscles. They pulled at his white dress shirt as he sauntered into the hallway. The stark cotton stood in sharp contrast with his complexion, drawing my eye and holding it—just as he wanted.

The class fell back as he eased past. A cold presence seemed to flow out of the room and pool about him, the remnants of the aura he had probably pulled on Dr. Anders. A confident, dominating smile curved over him as his eyes fastened on me.

"Uh, Rachel?" Jenks muttered as he flitted to Janine. "I'll see you inside, okay?"

I said nothing, suddenly feeling too thin and vulnerable.

"I'll save you a seat," Janine said, but I didn't look from my old boss. There was a soft rustle as the hallway emptied.

I had been scared of the man, and I was ready and willing to be scared of him now, but something had changed. Though still moving with the grace of a predator, the ageless look he once carried was gone. The hungry cast in his eye, which he didn't bother to hide, told me he was still a practicing vamp, but I was guessing he had lost favor and was no longer tasting the undead, though they were probably still feeding upon him.

"Morgan," he said, his words seeming to backwash against the brick wall behind me and give me a shove forward. His voice was just like him, practiced, powerful, and full of a heavy promise. "I heard you were whoring for the FIB. Or are we just bettering ourselves?"

"Hello, Mr. Denon," I said, not dropping his pupil-black eyes. "You get bumped down to runner?" The hungry lust in his eyes faltered into anger, and I added, "Looks like you're doing the runs you gave me. Rescuing familiars out of trees? Checking for valid licenses? How are those homeless bridge trolls doing, anyway?"

Denon shifted forward, his eyes intent and his muscles tense. My face went cold, and I found my back against the wall. The sun streaming in from the distant walkway seemed to dim. Like a kaleidoscope, it swirled to look twice as far away as it was. My heart leapt, then settled back into its usual pace. He was trying to pull an aura, but I knew he couldn't do it without me giving him the fear to feed it. I wouldn't be afraid.

"Cut the crap, Denon," I said boldly, my stomach knotting. "I live with a vamp who could eat you for breakfast. Save the aura for someone who cares."

Still, he pressed close until he was the only thing I could see. I had to look up, and it ticked me off. His breath was warm, and I could smell the tang of blood on it. My pulse pounded, and I hated that he knew I was afraid of him still.

"Anyone here but you and me?" he said, his voice as smooth as chocolate milk.

Hand moving in a slow, controlled motion, I reached for the grip of my splat gun. The brick scraped my knuckles, but as my fingers touched the handle, my confidence raced back. "Just you, me, and my splat gun. Touch me, and I'll drop you." I smiled right back at him. "What do you suppose I put in my splat balls? Might be kind of hard to explain why someone from the I.S. had to come out here and hose you off with saltwater, huh? I'd say that would be good for a laugh for at least a year." I watched his eyes shift to hate.

"Back up," I said clearly. "If I pull it, I use it."

He backed up. "Walk away from this, Morgan," he threatened. "This is my run."

"That explains why the I.S. is spinning its wheels. Maybe you should go back to ticketing parked cars and let a professional take care of it."

His breath hissed out, and I found strength in his anger. Ivy was right. There was fear in the back of his soul. Fear that some-day the undead vampires that fed on him would lose control and kill him. Fear that they wouldn't bring him back as one of their brothers.

He should be afraid.

"This is an I.S. matter," he said. "Interfere, and I'll have you down in lockup." He smiled, flashing me his human teeth. "If you thought being in Kalamack's cage was bad, wait until you see mine."

My confidence cracked. The I.S. knew about that? "Don't get your falsies in a twist," I said snidely. "I'm here on a missing per-son, not your murders."

"Missing person," he mocked. "That's a good story. I'd stick with it. Try to keep your tag alive this time." He gave me a final glance before he started down the hallway to the sun and the dis-tant sound of the commissary. "You won't be Tamwood's pet for-ever," he said, not turning around. "Then, I'm coming for you."

"Yeah, whatever," I said even as a sliver of my old fear tried to surface. I quashed it as I pulled my hand away from the small of my back. I wasn't Ivy's pet, though living with her gave me a heap of protection from Cincinnati's vamp population. She wasn't in a position of power, but as the last living member of the Tamwood family, she had a leader-in-waiting status honored by wise vamps both living and dead.

I took a deep breath to try to dispel the weakness in my knees. Great. Now I had to go into class after they had probably started.

Thinking my day couldn't possibly get any worse, I gathered myself and walked into the room lit brightly from the bank of windows overlooking the campus. As Janine had said, it was set up like a lab, with two people sitting on stools at each of the high slate tables. Janine was by herself talking to Jenks, clearly having saved me the spot next to her.

Ozone from Dr. Anders's hastily constructed circle caught at me. The circle was gone, but my sinuses tingled at the remnants of power. I glanced at its source at the front of the room.

Dr. Anders sat at an ugly metal desk before a traditional black-board. She had her elbows on the table, her head in her hands. I could see her thin fingers trembling, and I wondered if it was from Denon's accusations or that she had pulled upon the ever-after strong enough to make a circle without the aid of a physical man-ifestation. The class seemed unusually quiet.

Her hair was back in a severe bun, gray streaks making unflat-tering lines through the black. She looked older than my mother, dressed in a conservative pair of tan slacks and a tasteful blouse. Trying not to draw attention to myself, I slipped past the first two rows of tables and sat beside Janine. "Thanks," I whispered.

Her eyes were wide as I tucked my bag under the table. "You work for the I.S.?"

I glanced at Dr. Anders. "I used to. I quit last spring."

"I didn't think you could quit the I.S.," she said, her face going even more full of wonder.

Shrugging, I pushed my hair out of the way so Jenks could land on his usual spot. "It wasn't easy." I followed her attention to the front of the room as Dr. Anders stood.

The tall woman was as scary as I remembered, with a long thin face, and a nose that wouldn't be out of place on a pre-Turn depiction of a witch. No wart, though, and her complexion wasn't green. She reeked of tenure, gathering the class's attention by simply standing. The tremor was gone from her hands as she took up a sheaf of papers.

Dropping a pair of wire-rimmed glasses down to perch on her nose, she made a show of studying her notes. I'd have been will-ing to bet they had a spell on them to see through ley line charms as well as correct her sight, and I wished I had the gall to put my own glasses on and see if she used ley line magic to make her look that unattractive or if it was all her. A sigh shifted her narrow shoulders as she looked up, her gaze going right to mine through her spelled glasses. "I see," she said, her voice making my spine crawl, "that we have a new face today."

I gave her a false smile. It was obvious she recognized me; her face had scrunched up like a prune.

"Rachel Morgan," she said.

"Here," I said, my voice flat.

A wisp of annoyance flashed over her. "I know who you are." Low heels clicking, she came to stand before me. Leaning forward, she peered at Jenks. "Who might you be, pixy sir?"

"Uh, Jenks, ma'am," he stammered, his wings moving fitfully to tangle in my hair.

"Jenks," she said, her tone bordering on the respectful. "I'm glad to make your acquaintance. You're not on my class list. Please leave."

"Yes ma'am," he said, and much to my surprise, the usually arrogant pixy swung himself off my earring. "Sorry, Rache," he said, hovering before me. "I'll be in the faculty lounge or the library. Nick might still be working."

"Sure. I'll find you later."

He gave Dr. Anders a head bob and zipped out the still open door.

"I'm sorry," Dr. Anders said. "Is my class interfering with your social life?"

"No, Dr. Anders. It's a pleasure seeing you again."

She pulled back at the faint sarcasm. "Is it?"

From the corner of my sight I saw Janine's mouth hanging open. What I could see of the rest of the class looked about the same. My face burned. I don't know why the woman had it in for me, but she did. She was as nice as a hungry crow to everyone else, but I got the ravenous badger.

Dr. Anders let her papers fall to my table with a slap. My name was circled in a thick red marker. Her thin lips tightened almost imperceptibly. "Why are you here?" she asked. "We are two classes into the semester."

"It's still add/drop week," I countered, feeling my pulse increase. Unlike Jenks, I had no problem fighting authority. But as the song went, authority always won.

"I don't even know how you managed to get the approval for taking this class," she said caustically. "You have none of the prerequisites."

"All my credits transferred in. And I got a year for life-experiences." True enough, but Edden was the real reason I had been able to skip right to a five-hundred-level class.

"You are wasting my time, Ms. Morgan," she said. "You are an earth witch. I thought I had made that very clear to you. You don't possess the control to work ley lines beyond what you need to close a modest circle." She leaned over me, and I felt my blood pressure rise. "I'm going to flunk you out of my class faster than before."

I took a steadying breath, glancing at the shocked faces. Clearly they had never seen this side of their beloved instructor. "I need this class, Dr. Anders," I said, not knowing why I was trying to appeal to her stunted compassion. Except that if I got kicked out, Edden might make me pay the tuition. "I'm here to learn."

At that, the prickly woman picked up her papers and retreated to the empty table behind her. Her gaze roved over the class before settling on me. "Having trouble with your demon?"

Several in the class gasped. Janine actually shrank away from me. *Damn that woman,* I thought, my hand going to cover my wrist. *Not even here for five minutes, and she alienates me from the entire class.* I should have worn a bracelet. My jaw clenched and my breathing increased as I fought to not respond.

Dr. Anders seemed satisfied. "You can't reliably hide a demon mark with earth magic," she said, her voice raised in the sound of instruction. "You need ley line magic for that. Is that why you're here, Ms. Morgan?" she mocked.

Shaking, I refused to drop her eyes. I hadn't known that. No wonder my charms to disguise it never worked past sundown.

Her wrinkles went deeper as she frowned. "Professor Peltzer's Demonology for Modern Practitioners is in the next building over. Perhaps you should excuse yourself and see if it's not too late to change classes. We do not deal in the black arts here."

"I am not a black witch," I said softly, afraid if I raised my voice, I would start shouting. I pushed up my sleeve to show my demon mark, refusing to be ashamed of it. "I did not call the demon who gave me this. I fought it off."

I took a slow breath, unable to look at anyone, most of all Janine, who had pushed as far from me as she could get. "I'm here to learn how to keep it off of me, Dr. Anders. I will not take any demonology classes. I'm afraid of them."

The last was a whisper, but I knew everyone heard. Dr. Anders seemed taken aback. I was embarrassed, but if it kept her off my case, then it was embarrassment well spent.

The woman's footsteps were loud as she clacked to the front of the room. "Go home, Ms. Morgan," she said to the blackboard.

"I know why you're here. I did not kill my past students, and I take offense in your unsaid accusation."

And with that pleasant thought, she turned, flashing the class a tight-lipped smile. "If the rest of you will please retain your copies of eighteenth century pentagrams? We will be having a quiz on them Friday. For next week, I want you to go over chapters six, seven, and eight in your texts and to do the even practices at the end of each. Janine?"

At the sound of her name, the woman jumped. She had been trying to get a good look at my wrist. I was still shaking, my fingers trembling as I wrote down the assignment.

"Janine, you would do well to do the odds on chapter six, as well. Your control in releasing stored ley line energy leaves something to be desired."

"Yes, Dr. Anders," she said, white-faced.

"And go sit by Brian," she added. "You can learn more from him than Ms. Morgan."

Janine didn't hesitate. Before Dr. Anders had even finished, Janine picked up her purse and book, moving to the next table. I was left alone, feeling sick. Janine's borrowed chalk sat next to my book like a stolen cookie.

"I would also like to evaluate your linkages with your familiars on Friday, as we will be starting a section on long-term protection over the next few weeks," Dr. Anders was saying. "So please bring them in. It will take some time to get through all of you. Those at the end of the alphabet can expect to be held beyond the usual class time."

There was a weary groan from some of the students, but it lacked a certain joviality that I sensed was usually there. My stomach dropped. I didn't have a familiar. If I didn't get one by Friday, she'd flunk me. Same as last time.

Dr. Anders smiled at me with the warmth of a doll. "Is that a problem, Ms. Morgan?"

"No," I said flatly, starting to want to pin the murders on her whether she had committed them or not. "No problem at all."

Eight

Thankfully, there was no line when we pulled up to Pizza Piscary's in Glenn's unmarked FIB car. Ivy and I slid out almost as soon as the car stopped. It hadn't been a very comfortable ride for either of us, the memory of her pinning me to the kitchen wall still new-penny bright. Her manner had been odd this evening, subdued but excited. I felt like I was going to meet her parents. In a way, I suppose I was. Piscary was the way-back originator of her living-vamp family line.

Glenn yawned as he slowly got out and put his jacket on, but he woke up enough to wave off Jenks, flitting around his head. He didn't seem at all uneasy about going into what was strictly an Inderland eatery. I could almost see the chip on his shoulder. Maybe he was a slow learner.

The FIB detective had agreed to exchange his stiff FIB suit for the jeans and faded flannel shirt Ivy had tucked in the back of her closet in a box labeled LEFTOVERS in a faded black marker. They fit Glenn exactly, and I didn't want to know where she had gotten them or why they had several neatly mended tears in some rather unusual places. A nylon jacket hid the weapon he refused to leave behind, but I had left my splat gun at home. It would be useless against a room full of vamps.

A van eased into the lot to take an empty space at the far end. My attention drifted from it to the brightly lit delivery/takeout window. As I watched, another pizza went out, the car lurching into the street and speeding away with the quickness that told of a large engine. Pizza drivers have made good money since they successfully lobbied for hazard pay.

Past the parking lot was the soft lapping of water on wood. Long strips of light glinted on the Ohio River, and the taller buildings of Cincinnati reflected in wide streaks on the flat water. Piscary's was waterfront property, situated in the middle of the more affluent strip of clubs, restaurants, and nightspots. It even had a landing where yacht-traveling patrons could tie up to—but getting a table overlooking the dock would be impossible this late.

"Ready?" Ivy said brightly as she finished adjusting her jacket. She was dressed in her usual black leather pants and silk shirt, looking lanky and predatory. The only color to her face was her bright red lipstick. A chain of black gold hung about her neck in place of her usual crucifix—which was now tucked in her jewelry box at home. It matched her ankle bracelets perfectly. She had gone further to paint her nails with a clear coat, giving them a subtle shine.

The jewelry and nail polish were unusual for her, and after seeing it, I had opted to wear a wide silver band instead of my usual charm bracelet to cover my demon mark. It felt nice to get dressed up, and I'd even tried to do something with my hair. The red frizz I ended up with almost looked intentional.

I kept a step behind Glenn as we moved to the front door. Inderlanders mixed freely, but our group was more odd than usual, and I was hoping to get in and out quickly with the information we came for before we attracted attention. The van that pulled in after us was a pack of Weres, and they were noisy as they closed the gap between us.

"Glenn," Ivy said as we reached the door. "Keep your mouth shut."

"Whatever," the officer said antagonistically.

My eyebrows rose and I took a wary step back. Jenks landed upon my big hoop earrings. "This ought to be good," he snickered.

Ivy grabbed Glenn's collar, picking him up and slamming him against the wooden pillar supporting the canopy. The startled man froze for an instant, then kicked out, aiming for Ivy's gut. Ivy dropped him to evade the strike. With a vamp quickness, she picked him back up and slammed him into the post again. Glenn grunted in pain, struggling to catch his breath.

"Ooooh," Jenks cheered. "That's going to ache in the morning."

I jiggled my foot and glanced at the pack of Weres. "Couldn't you have taken care of this before we left?" I complained.

"Look, you little snack," Ivy said calmly, putting herself in Glenn's face. "You will keep your mouth shut. You do not exist unless I ask you a question."

"Go to hell," Glenn managed, his face reddening under his dark skin.

Ivy shifted him a smidgen higher, and he grunted. "You stink like a human," she continued, her eyes shifting toward black. "Piscary's is all Inderlanders or bound humans. The only way you're going to get out of here with all your parts intact and unpunctured is if everyone thinks you're my shadow."

Shadow, I thought. It was a derogatory term. Thrall was another. Toy would be more accurate. It referred to a human recently bit, now little more than a walking source of sex and food, and mentally bound to a vamp. They were kept submissive as long as possible. Decades sometimes. My old boss, Denon, had been counted among them until he curried the favor of the one who had granted him a more free existence.

Face ugly, Glenn broke her hold and fell to the ground. "Go Turn yourself, Tamwood," he rasped, rubbing his neck. "I can take care of myself. This won't be any worse than walking into a good-old-boy's bar in deep Georgia."

"Yeah?" she questioned, pale hand on her cocked hip. "Anyone there want to eat you?"

The Were pack flowed past us and inside. One jerked, doing a double take as he saw me, and I wondered if my stealing that fish was going to be a problem. Music and chatter drifted out, cutting off as the thick door shut. I sighed. It sounded busy. Now we'd probably have to wait for a table.

I offered Glenn a hand up as Ivy opened the door. Glenn refused my help, tucking his anti-itch spell back behind his shirt as he struggled to find his pride, squished under Ivy's boots somewhere. Jenks flitted from me to his shoulder, and Glenn started. "Go sit somewhere else, pixy," he said around a cough.

"Oh, no," Jenks said merrily. "Don't you know a vamp won't touch you if there's a pixy on your shoulder? It's a well-known fact."

Glenn hesitated, and my eyes rolled. *What a crock.*

We filed in behind Ivy as the Were pack was being led to their table. The place was crowded, not unusual for a workday. Piscary's had the best pizza in Cincinnati, and they didn't take reservations. The warmth and noise relaxed me, and I took off my coat. The rough-cut, thick support beams seemed to prop up the low ceiling, and a rhythmic stomping to the beat of Sting's "Rehumanize Yourself" filtered down the wide stairs. Past them were wide windows looking out over the black river and the city beyond. A three-story, obscenely expensive motorboat was tied up, the docking lights shining on the name across the bow, SOLAR. Pretty college-age kids moved efficiently about in their skimpy uniforms, some more suggestive than others. Most were bound humans, since the vamp staff traditionally took the less supervised upstairs.

The host's eyebrows rose as he took Glenn in. I could tell he was the host because his shirt was only half undone and his name tag said so. "Table for three? Lighted or non?"

"Lighted," I interjected before Ivy could say different. I didn't want to be upstairs. It sounded rowdy.

"It will be about fifteen minutes, then. You can wait at the bar if you like."

I sighed. Fifteen minutes. It was always fifteen minutes. Fifteen little minutes that dragged to thirty, then forty, and then you were willing to wait ten more so you didn't have to go to the next restaurant and start all over again.

Ivy smiled to show her teeth. Her canines were no bigger than mine were, but sharp like a cat's. "We'll wait here, thanks."

Looking almost enraptured by her smile, the host nodded. His chest, showing beneath his open shirt, was scattered with pale scars. It wasn't what the hosts were wearing at Denny's, but who was I to complain? There was a soft look about him that I didn't like in my men but some women did. "It won't be long," he said, his eyes fixing to mine as he noticed my attention on him. His lips parted suggestively. "Do you want to order now?"

A pizza went by on a tray, and as I jerked my gaze from him, I glanced at Ivy and shrugged. We weren't there for dinner, but why not? It smelled great.

"Yeah," Ivy said. "An extra large. Everything but peppers and onions."

Glenn jerked his attention from what looked like a coven of witches applauding the arrival of their dinner. Eating at Piscary's was an event. "You said we weren't going to stay."

Ivy turned, black swelling within her eyes. "I'm hungry. Is that okay with you?"

"Sure," he muttered.

Immediately Ivy regained her composure. I knew she wouldn't vamp out here. It might start a cascading reaction from the surrounding vampires, and Piscary would lose his A rating on his MPL. "Maybe we can share a table with someone. I'm starved," she said, jiggling her foot.

MPL was short for Mixed Public License. What it meant was a strict enforcement of no blood drawn on the premises. Standard stuff for most places serving alcohol since the Turn. It created a safe zone that we frail "dead means dead" folk needed. If you had too many vamps together and one drew blood, the rest had a tendency to lose control. No problem if everyone's a vampire, but people didn't like it when their loved one's night on the town turned into an eternity in the graveyard. Or worse.

The clubs and nightspots without a MPL existed, but they weren't as popular and didn't make as much money. Humans liked MPL places, since they could safely flirt without someone else's bad decision turning their date into an out of control, bloodthirsty fiend. At least until the privacy of their own bedroom, where they might survive it. And vamps liked it too—it was easier to break the ice when your date wasn't uptight about you breaking his or her skin.

I looked around the semiopen room, seeing only Inderlanders among the patrons. MPL or not, it was obvious Glenn was attracting attention. The music had died, and no one had put in another quarter. Apart from the witches in the corner and the pack of Weres in the back, the downstairs was full of vamps in various levels of sensuality ranging from casual to satin and lace. A good part of the floor was taken up in what looked like a death-day party.

The sudden warm breath on my neck jerked me straight, and it was only Ivy's bothered look that kept me from smacking whoever it was. Spinning, my tart retort died. *Swell. Kisten.*

The living vamp was Ivy's friend, and I didn't like him. Some of that was because Kist was Piscary's scion, a loose extension of the master vampire who did his daylight work for him. It didn't help that Piscary had once bespelled me against my will through Kist, something I hadn't known was possible at the time. It also didn't help that he was very, very pretty, making him very, very dangerous by my reckoning.

If Ivy was a diva of the dark, then Kist was her consort, and God help me, he looked the part. Short blond hair, blue eyes, and chin holding enough stubble to give his delicate features a more rugged cast made him a sexy bundle of promised fun. He was dressed more conservatively than usual, his biker leather and chains replaced with a tasteful shirt and slacks. His I-should-care-what-you-think-because? attitude remained, though. The lack of biker boots put him a shade taller than me with the heels I had on, and the ageless look of an undead vampire shimmered in him like a promise to be fulfilled. He moved with a catlike confidence, having enough muscle to enjoy running your fingertips over but not so much that it got in the way.

Ivy and he had a past I didn't want to know about, since she had been a very practicing vamp at the time. I was always struck with the impression that if he couldn't have her, he'd be happy with her roommate. Or the girl next door. Or the woman he met on the bus this morning . . .

"Evening, love," he breathed in a fake English accent, his eyes amused because he had surprised me.

I pushed him back with a finger. "Your accent stinks. Go away until you get it right." But my pulse had increased, and a faint, pleasant tickle from the scar on my neck brought all my proximity alarms into play. *Damn it. I'd forgotten about that.*

He glanced at Ivy as if for permission, then playfully licked his lips as she frowned her answer. I scowled, thinking I didn't need her help fending him off. Seeing it, she made a puff of exasperated air and pulled Glenn to the bar, enticing Jenks to join them with the promise of a honeyed toddy. The FIB detective glanced at me over his shoulder as he went, knowing something had passed between the three of us but not what.

"Alone at last." Kist shifted to stand shoulder-to-shoulder with me and look across the open floor. I could smell leather, though he wasn't wearing any. That I could see, at least.

"Can't you find a better opening line than that?" I said, wishing I hadn't driven Ivy away.

"It wasn't a line."

His shoulder was too close to mine, but I wouldn't shift away and let him know it bothered me. I snuck a glance at him as he breathed with a heavy slowness, his eyes scanning the patrons even as he took in my scent to gauge my state of unease. Twin diamond earrings glittered from one ear, and I remembered the other had only one stud and a healed tear. A chain made out of the same stuff as Ivy's was the only hint of his usual bad-boy attire. I wondered what he was doing here. There were better places for a living vamp to pick up a date/snack.

His fingers moved with a restless motion, always pulling my eyes back to him. I knew he was throwing off vamp pheromones to soothe and relax me—all the better to eat you with, my dear—

but the prettier they are, the more defensive I get. My face went slack as I realized I had matched my breathing to his.

Subtle bespelling at its finest, I thought, purposely holding my breath to get us out of sync, and I saw him smile as he ducked his head and ran a hand over his chin. Normally only an undead vampire could bespell the unwilling, but being Piscary's scion gave Kist a portion of his master's abilities. He wouldn't dare try it here, though. Not with Ivy watching from the bar around her bottled water.

I suddenly realized he was rocking, moving his hips with a steady, suggestive motion. "Stop it," I said as I turned to face him, disgusted. "There's an entire string of women watching you at the bar. Go bother them."

"It's much more fun to bother you." Taking my scent deep into him, he leaned close. "You still smell like Ivy, but she hasn't bitten you. My God, you are a tease."

"We're friends," I said, affronted. "She's not hunting me."

"Then she won't mind if I do."

Annoyed, I pulled away. He followed me until my back found a support post. "Stop moving," he said as he put his hand against the thick post beside my head, pinning me though air still showed between us. "I want to tell you something, and I don't want anyone else to hear it."

"Like anyone could hear you over the noise," I scoffed, the fingers behind my back bending into a fist that wouldn't make my nails cut my palm if I had to slug him.

"You might be surprised," he murmured, his eyes intent. I fixed on them, looking for and recognizing the barest hint of swelling black, even as his nearness sent a promise of heat from my scar. I'd lived long enough with Ivy to know what a vamp looked like when they were close to losing it. He was fine, his instincts curbed and his hunger sated.

I was reasonably safe, so I relaxed, easing my shoulders down. His lust-reddened lips parted in surprise at my acceptance at how close he was. Eyes bright, he breathed languorously slow, tilting his head and leaning in so his lips brushed the curve of my ear. The light shimmered on the black chain around his neck, drawing my hand up. It was warm, and that surprise kept my fingers playing with it when I should have stopped.

The clatter of dishes and conversation retreated as I exhaled into his soft, unrecognizable whisper. A delicious feeling ran through me, sending the sensation of molten metal through my veins. I didn't care that it was from him triggering my scar into play; it felt so good. And he hadn't even said a word I recognized yet.

"Sir?" came a hesitant voice from behind him.

Kist's breath caught. For three heartbeats he held himself still, unmoving as his shoulders tensed in annoyance. My hand dropped from his neck.

"Someone wants you," I said, looking beyond him to the host, shifting nervously. A smile edged over me. Kist was tempting a break in the MPL, and someone had been sent to rein him in. Laws were good things. They kept me alive when I did something stupid.

"What," Kist said flatly. I'd never heard his voice carry anything but sultry petulance before, and the power in it sent a jolt through me, its unexpectedness making it all the more demanding.

"Sir, the party of Weres upstairs? They're starting to pack."

Oh? I thought. That was not what I had expected.

Kist straightened his elbow and pushed away from the post, irritation flickering across him. I took a clean breath, my unhealthy disappointment mixing with a distressingly small waft of self-preserving relief.

"I told you to tell them we were out of bane," Kist said. "They came in reeking of it."

"We did, sir," the waiter protested, taking a step back as Kist pulled entirely away from me. "But they coerced Tarra into admitting there was some in the back, and she gave it to them."

Kist's annoyance turned into anger. "Who gave Tarra the upstairs? I told her to work the lower floor until that Were bite healed over."

Kist worked at Piscary's? Surprise, surprise. I hadn't thought the vamp had the presence of mind to do anything useful.

"She convinced Samuel to let her up there, saying she'd get better tips," the waiter said.

"Sam . . ." Kist said from between closed teeth. Emotion crossed him, the first hints of coherent thoughts that didn't revolve around sex and blood surprising me. Full lips pressed together, he scanned the floor. "All right. Pull everyone as if for a birthday and get her out of there before she sets them off. Cut off the bane. Complimentary desert for any who want it."

Blond stubble catching the light, he glanced up as if able to see through the ceiling to the noise upstairs. The music was high again, and Jeff Beck filtered down. "Loser." Somehow, it seemed to fit as they all slurred the lyrics together. The wealthier patrons in the lower floor didn't seem to mind.

"Piscary will have my hide if we lose our A rating over a Were bite," Kist said. "And as exciting as that might be, I want to be able to walk tomorrow."

Kist's easy admission of his relationship with Piscary took me aback, but it shouldn't have. Though I always equated the giving and taking of blood with sex, it wasn't, especially if the exchange was between a living and an undead vampire. The two held vastly different views, probably because one had a soul and the other didn't.

The "bottle the blood came in" mattered to most living vamps. They picked their partners with care, usually—but not always—following their sexual gender preferences on the happy chance that sex might be included in the mix. Even when driven by hunger, the giving and taking of blood often fulfilled an emotional need, a physical affirmation of an emotional bond in much the same way that sex could—but didn't always have to.

Undead vampires were even more meticulous, choosing their companions with the care of a serial killer. Seeking domination and emotional manipulation rather than commitment, gender didn't enter into the equation—though the undead wouldn't turn down the addition of sex, since it imparted an even more intense feeling of domination, akin to rape even with a willing partner. Any relationship that grew from such an arrangement was utterly one-sided, though the bitee usually didn't accept it, thinking their master was the exception to the rule. It gave me pause that Kist seemed eager for another encounter with Piscary, and I wondered, as I glanced at the young vampire beside me, if it was because Kist received a large measure of strength and status by being his scion.

Unaware of my thoughts, Kist furrowed his brow in anger. "Where's Sam?" he asked.

"The kitchen, sir."

His eye twitched. Kist looked at the waiter as if to say, "What are you waiting for?" and the man hurried away.

Bottled water in hand, Ivy snuck up behind Kist, pulling him farther from me. "And you thought I was stupid for majoring in security instead of business management?" she said. "You sound almost responsible, Kisten. Be careful, or you'll ruin your reputation."

Kist smiled to show his sharp canines, the air of harried

restaurant manager falling from him. "The perks are great, Ivy, love," he said, curving a hand around her backside with a familiarity she tolerated for an instant before hitting him. "You ever need a job, come see me."

"Shove it up your ass, Kist."

He laughed, dropping his head for an instant before bringing his sly gaze back to mine. A group of waiters and waitresses were headed up the wide stairway, clapping in time and singing some asinine song. It looked annoying and innocuous, nothing like the rescue mission it really was. My eyebrows rose. Kist was good at this.

Almost as if reading my mind, he leaned close. "I'm even better in bed, love," he whispered, his breath sending a delicious dart of sensation down to the pit of my being.

He shifted out of my reach before I could push him away, and still smiling, walked off. Halfway to the kitchen he turned to see if I was watching. Which I was. Hell, everything female in the place—alive, dead, or in between—was watching.

I pulled my attention from him to find a curiously closed look on Ivy. "You aren't afraid of him anymore," she said flatly.

"No," I said, surprised to find I wasn't. "I think it's because he can do something other than flirt."

She looked away. "Kist can do a lot of things. He gets off on being dominated, but when it comes to business, he'll slam you to the ground soon as look at you. Piscary wouldn't have a fool for a scion, no matter how good he is to bleed." Her lips pressed together until they went white. "Table's ready."

I followed her gaze to the single empty table against the far wall away from the windows. Glenn and Jenks had joined us when Kist left, and as a group we wove through the tables, settling on the half-circle bench with all our backs to the wall—Inderlander, human, Inderlander—and waited for the waiter to find us.

Jenks had perched himself on the low chandelier, and the light coming through his wings made green and gold spots on the table. Glenn silently took everything in, clearly trying not to look nonplussed at the sight of the scarred, well-put-together waiters and waitresses. Whether male or female, they were all young with smiling, eager faces that had me on edge.

Ivy didn't say anything more about Kist, for which I was grateful. It was embarrassing how quickly vamp pheromones acted on me, turning "get lost" to "get over here." Thanks to the excessive amount of vamp saliva the demon pumped into me while trying to kill me, my resistance to vamp pheromones was almost nil.

Glenn carefully put his elbows on the table. "You haven't told me how class went."

Jenks laughed. "It was hell on earth. Two hours of nonstop nitpicking and putdowns."

My mouth dropped open. "How do you know that?"

"I snuck back in. What did you do to that woman, Rachel? Kill her cat?"

My face burned. Knowing Jenks had witnessed it made it worse. "The woman is a hag," I said. "Glenn, if you want to string her up for killing those people, you go right ahead. She already knows she's a suspect. The I.S. was there stirring her into a tizzy. I didn't find anything that remotely resembled possible motive or guilt."

Glenn pulled his arms from the table and sat back. "Nothing?"

I shook my head. "Just that Dan had an interview after Friday's class. I'm thinking that was the big news he was going to spring on Sara Jane."

"He dropped all his classes Friday night," Jenks said. "Just made the add/drop with a full refund. Must have done it by e-mail."

I squinted up at the pixy sitting by the lightbulbs to stay warm. "How do you know?"

His wings blurred to nothing and he grinned. "I checked out the registrar's office during class break. You think the only reason I went was to look pretty on your shoulder?"

Ivy drummed her fingernails. "You three aren't going to talk shop all night, are you?"

"Ivy girl!" came a strong voice, and we all looked up. A short, spare man in a cook's apron was making a beeline for us from across the restaurant, weaving gracefully through the tables. "My Ivy girl!" he called over the noise. "Back already. And with friends!"

I glanced at Ivy, surprised to see a faint blush coloring her pale cheeks. *Ivy girl?*

"Ivy girl?" Jenks said from on high. "What the hell is that?"

Ivy rose to give him an embarrassed-looking hug as he halted before us, making an odd picture since he was nearly six inches smaller than she was. He returned it with a fatherly pat on the back. My eyebrows rose. She *hugged* him?

The cook's black eyes glittered in what looked like pleasure.

The scent of tomato paste and blood drifted to me. He was clearly a practicing vamp. I couldn't tell yet if he was dead.

"Hi, Piscary," Ivy said as she sat, and Jenks and I exchanged looks. This was Piscary? One of Cincinnati's most powerful vamps? I'd never seen such an innocuous looking vampire.

Piscary was actually an inch or two shorter than I was, and he carried his slight, well-proportioned build with a comfortable ease. His nose was narrow, and his wide-spaced, almond-shaped eyes and thin lips added to his exotic appearance. His eyes were very dark, and they shone as he took his chef's hat off and tucked it behind his apron ties. He kept his skull clean-shaven, and his honey-amber skin glinted in the light from over our table. The lightweight, pale shirt and pants he wore might have been off-the-rack, but I doubted it. They gave him the air of comfortable middle class, his eager smile enforcing the picture in my mind. Piscary ran much of the darker side of Cincinnati, but looking at him, I wondered how.

My usual healthy distrust of undead vamps sank to a wary caution. "Piscary?" I asked. "As in Pizza Piscary's?"

The vampire smiled, showing his teeth. They were longer than Ivy's—he was a true undead—and looked very white next to his dusky completion. "Yes, Pizza Piscary's is mine." His voice was deep for such a small frame, and it seemed to carry the strength of sand and wind. The faint remnants of an accent made me wonder how long he had been speaking English.

Ivy cleared her throat, jerking my attention away from his quick, dark eyes. Somehow the sight of his teeth hadn't instilled my usual knee-jerk alarm. "Piscary," Ivy said, "this is Rachel Morgan and Jenks, my business associates."

Jenks had flitted down to the hot-pepper shakers, and Piscary gave him a nod before turning to me. "Rachel Morgan," he said slowly and with care. "I've been waiting for my Ivy girl to bring you to see me. I think she's afraid I'll tell her she can't play with you anymore." His lips curved into a smile. "I'm charmed."

I held my breath as he took my hand with a high gentility that stood in sharp contrast to his looks. He lifted my fingers, bringing them close to his lips. His dark eyes were fixed on mine. My pulse quickened, but I felt as if my heart were somewhere else. He inhaled over my hand, as if scenting the blood humming within them. I stifled a shiver by clenching my jaw.

Piscary's eyes were the color of black ice. I boldly returned his gaze, intrigued at the hints beyond their depths. It was Piscary who looked away first, and I quickly pulled my hand from him. He was good. Really good. He had used his aura to charm rather than frighten. Only the old ones could do that. And there hadn't been even a twinge from my demon scar. I didn't know whether to take that as a good sign or bad.

Laughing good-naturedly at my sudden, obvious suspicion, Piscary sat down on the bench beside Ivy as three waiters struggled to get by with round platters. Glenn didn't seem at all upset Ivy hadn't introduced him, and Jenks kept his mouth shut. My shoulder pressed into Glenn as he shoved me down until I was nearly hanging off the edge to make room for Piscary.

"You should have told me you were coming," Piscary said. "I'd have saved you a table."

Ivy shrugged. "We got one okay."

Half turning, Piscary looked to the bar and shouted, "Bring up a bottle of red from the Tamwood cellar!" A sly grin came over him. "Your mother won't miss one."

Glenn and I exchanged a worried look. *A bottle of red?* "Uh, Ivy?" I questioned.

"Oh, good God," she said. "It's wine. Relax."

Relax, I thought. Easier said than done with my rear hanging half off the seat and surrounded by vampires.

"Have you ordered?" Piscary asked Ivy, but his gaze was on me, suffocating. "I have a new cheese that uses a just-discovered species of mold to age. All the way from the Alps."

"Yes," Ivy said. "An extra large—"

"With everything but onions and peppers," he finished, showing his teeth in a wide smile as he turned from me to her.

My shoulders slumped as his gaze left me. He looked like nothing more than a friendly pizza chef, and it was setting off more alarm bells than if he had been tall, thin, and slunk about seductively in lace and silk.

"Ha!" he barked, and I stifled my jump. "I'm going to make you dinner, Ivy girl."

Ivy smiled to look like a ten-year-old. "Thank you, Piscary. I'd like that."

"'Course you would. Something special. Something new. On the house. It will be my finest creation!" he said boldly. "I will name it after you and your shadow."

"I'm not her shadow," Glenn said tightly, shoulders hunched and his eyes on the table.

"I wasn't talking about you," Piscary said, and my eyes widened.

Ivy stirred uneasily. "Rachel . . . isn't my shadow . . . either."

She sounded guilty, and an instant of confusion crossed the old vamp's face. "Really?" he said, and Ivy visibly tensed. "Then what are you doing with her, Ivy girl?"

She wouldn't look up from the table. Piscary caught my eye again. My heart pounded as a faint tingle rippled across my neck at my demon bite. Suddenly the table was too crowded. I felt pressed upon at all sides, and the claustrophobic feeling beat at me. Shocked at the change, my breath left me and I held the next one. *Damn.*

"That's an interesting scar on your neck," Piscary said, his voice seeming to scour my soul. It hurt and felt good all at the same time. "Is it vamp?"

My hand rose unbidden to hide it. Jenks's wife had sewn me up, and the tiny stitches were almost invisible. I didn't like that he had noticed them. "It's demon," I said, not caring if Glenn told his dad. I didn't want Piscary thinking I'd been bitten by a vamp, Ivy or otherwise.

Piscary arched his eyebrows in a mild surprise. "It looks vampiric."

"So did the demon at the time," I said, my stomach tightening in the memory.

The old vamp nodded. "Ah, that would explain it." He smiled, chilling me. "A ravaged virgin whose blood has been left unclaimed. What a delectable combination you are, Ms. Morgan. No wonder my Ivy girl has been hiding you from me."

My mouth opened, but I could think of nothing to say.

He stood with no warning. "I'll have your dinner out in a moment." Leaning to Ivy, he murmured, "Talk to your mother. She misses you."

Ivy dropped her eyes. With a casual grace, Piscary snagged a stack of plates and breadsticks from a passing tray. "Enjoy your evening," he said as he set them on our table. He made his way back to the kitchen, stopping several times to greet the more well-dressed patrons.

I stared at Ivy, waiting for an explanation. "Well?" I said bitingly. "You want to explain why Piscary thinks I'm your shadow?"

Jenks snickered, taking his hands-on-hips Peter Pan pose atop the pepper shaker. Ivy shrugged in obvious guilt. "He knows we live under the same roof. He just assumed—"

"Yeah, I got it." Annoyed, I chose a breadstick and slumped against the wall. Ivy's and my arrangement was odd no matter what angle you looked at it. She was trying to abstain from blood, the lure to break her fast almost irresistible. As a witch, I could fend her off with my magic when her instincts got the better of her. I had dropped her once with a charm, and it was that memory that helped her master her cravings and keep her on her side of the hallway.

But what bothered me was that it was shame that made her let Piscary believe what he wanted—shame for turning her back on her heritage. She didn't want it. With a roommate, she could lie to the world, pretending she had a normal vamp life with a live-in source of blood yet remain true to her guilty secret. I told myself I didn't care, that it protected me against other vamps. But some-times . . . Sometimes it rankled me that everyone assumed I was Ivy's toy.

My sulk was interrupted by the arrival of the wine, slightly warm, as most vamps liked it. It had been opened already, and Ivy took control of the bottle, avoiding my look as she poured three glasses. Jenks made do with the drop on the mouth of the bottle. Still peeved, I settled back with my glass and watched the other guests. I wouldn't drink it because the sulfur it broke down into tended to wreak havoc with me. I'd have told Ivy, but it was none of her business. It wasn't a witch thing, just my own personal quirk that gave me headaches and made me so light sensitive that I had to hide in my room with a washcloth over my eyes. It was an oddly related lingering remnant of a childhood affliction that had me in and out of the hospital until puberty kicked in. I'd take the developed sulfur sensitivity any day in exchange for my misery as a child, weak and sickly as my body tried to kill itself.

The music had started again, and my unease at Piscary slowly filtered away, driven out by the music and background conversa-tions. Everyone could ignore Glenn now that Piscary had talked to us. The rattled human downed his wine as if it were water. Ivy and I exchanged glances as he refilled his glass with shaking hands. I wondered if he was going to drink until he passed out or try to tough it out sober. He took a sip of his next glass, and I smiled. He was going to split the difference.

Glenn gave Ivy a wary glance and leaned close to me. "How

could you meet his eyes?" he whispered, hard to hear above the surrounding noise. "Weren't you afraid he'd bespell you?"

"The man is over three hundred years old," I said, realizing Piscary's accent was Old English. "If he wanted to bespell me, he wouldn't have to look into my eyes."

Face going sallow behind his short beard, Glenn pulled away. Leaving him to mull that around for a bit, I jerked my head to get Jenks's attention. "Jenks," I said softly. "Why don't you take a quick peek in back? Check out the employees' break room? See what's up?"

Ivy topped her glass off. "Piscary knows we're here for a reason," she said. "He'll tell us what we want to know. Jenks will only get himself caught."

The small pixy bristled. "Get Turned, Tamwood," he snarled. "Why am I here if not to sneak around? The day I can't evade a baker is the day I—" He cut his thought short. "Uh," he reiterated, "yeah. I'll be right back." Pulling a red bandanna from a back pocket, he put it around his waist like a belt. It was a pixy's version of a white flag of truce, a declaration to other pixies and fairies that he wasn't poaching should he stumble into anyone's jealously guarded territory. He buzzed off just below the ceiling, headed for the kitchen.

Ivy shook her head. "He's going to get caught."

I shrugged and edged the breadsticks closer. "They won't hurt him." Settling back, I watched the contented people enjoy themselves, thinking of Nick and how long it had been since we'd been out. I'd started on my second breadstick when a waiter appeared. Already silent, the table went expectant as he cleared away the crumbs and used plates. The man's neck from behind the blue satin shirt was a mass of scars, the newest still red-rimmed and sore looking. His smile at Ivy was a little too eager, a little too much like a puppy. I hated it, wondering what his dreams had been before he became someone's plaything.

My demon bite tingled, and my gaze roved across the crowded room to find Piscary himself bringing our food. Heads turned as he passed, drawn by the fabulous smell that had to be emanating from the elevated platter. The level of conversation notably dropped. Piscary settled the platter before us, an eager smile hovering about him, his need for his cooking skills to be recognized looking odd on someone with so much hidden power. "I call it Temere's need," he said.

"Oh my God!" Glenn said in disgust, clear over the hush. "It's got tomatoes on it!"

Ivy elbowed him in the gut hard enough to knock the wind out of him. The room went silent except for the noise filtering down from upstairs, and I stared at Glenn. "Uh, how wonderful," he wheezed.

Sparing Glenn a glance, Piscary cut it into wedges with a professional flourish. My mouth watered at the smell of melted cheese and sauce. "That smells great," I said admiringly, my earlier distrust lulled by the prospect of food. "My pizzas never come out like this."

The short man raised his thin, almost nonexistent eyebrows. "You use sauce from a jar."

I nodded, then wondered how he knew.

Ivy looked to the kitchen. "Where is Jenks? He should be here for this."

"My staff is playing with him," Piscary said lightly. "I imagine he'll be out soon." The undead vamp slid the first piece onto Ivy's plate, then mine, then Glenn's. The FIB detective pushed his plate away with one finger in disgust. The other patrons whispered, waiting to see our reaction to Piscary's latest creation.

Ivy and I immediately picked our slices up. The smell of cheese was strong, but not enough to hide the odor of spice and tomatoes. I took a bite. My eyes closed in bliss. There was just enough tomato sauce to carry the cheese. Just enough cheese to carry the toppings. I didn't care if it had Brimstone on it, it was so good. "Oh, burn me at the stake now," I moaned, chewing. "This is absolutely wonderful."

Piscary nodded, the light shining on his shaven head. "And you, Ivy girl?"

Ivy wiped her chin free of sauce. "It's enough to come back from the dead for."

The man sighed. "I'll rest easy this sunrise."

I slowed my chewing, turning with everyone else to Glenn. He was sitting frozen between Ivy and me, his jaw clenched with a mix of determination and nausea. "Uh," he said, glancing down at the pizza. He swallowed, looking as if the nausea was winning out.

Piscary's smile vanished, and Ivy glared at him. "Eat it," she said loud enough for the entire restaurant to hear.

"And start at the point, not the crust," I warned him.

Glenn licked his lips. "It has tomatoes on it," he said, and my lips pursed. This was exactly what I had been hoping to avoid. One would think we had asked him to eat live grubs.

"Don't be an ass," Ivy said caustically. "If you really think the T4 Angel virus skipped forty tomato generations and appeared in an entirely new species for your benefit, I'll ask Piscary to bite you before we leave. That way you won't die but just turn vamp."

Glenn scanned the waiting faces, realizing he was going to have to eat some pizza if he wanted to walk out under his own power. Visibly swallowing, he awkwardly picked the slice up. His eyes screwed up and he opened his mouth. The noise from upstairs seemed loud as everyone downstairs watched, their breath held.

He took a bite, his face distorting wildly. The cheese made twin bridges from him to the pizza. He chewed twice before his eyes cracked open. His jaw slowed. He was tasting it now. His eye caught mine, and I nodded. Slowly he pulled the pizza away until the cheese separated.

"Yes?" Piscary leaned to put his expressive hands atop the table, genuinely interested in what a human thought of his cooking. Glenn was probably the first in four decades to sample it.

The man's face was slack. He swallowed. "Uh," he grunted from around a partially full mouth. "It's uh . . . good." He looked shocked. "It's really good."

The restaurant seemed to heave a sigh. Piscary straightened to all of his short height, clearly delighted as the conversations started up with a new, excited edge to them. "You're welcome here anytime, FIB officer," he said, and Glenn froze, clearly worried that he had been made.

Piscary grabbed a chair behind him and swung it around. Hunched over the table across from us, he watched us eat. "Now," he said as Glenn lifted the cheese to look at the tomato sauce under it. "You didn't come here for dinner. What can I do for you?"

Ivy set her pizza down and reached for her wine. "I'm helping Rachel find a missing person," she said, flicking her long hair needlessly back. "One of your employees."

"Trouble, Ivy girl?" Piscary asked, his resonate voice surprisingly gentle with regret.

I took a sip of wine. "That's what we want to find out, Mr. Piscary. It's Dan Smather."

Piscary's few wrinkles folded into a soft frown as he gazed at Ivy. With telltale motions so slight they were almost undetectable, she fidgeted, her eyes both worried and defiant.

My attention jerked to Glenn. He was pulling the cheese off his pizza. Appalled, I watched him gingerly pile it into a mound. "Can you tell us the last time you saw him, Mr. Piscary?" the man asked, clearly more interested in denuding his pizza than our questioning.

"Certainly." Piscary eyed Glenn, his brow furrowed as if not sure whether to be insulted or pleased as the man ate the pizza, now nothing more than bread and tomato sauce. "It was early Saturday morning after work. But Dan isn't missing. He quit."

My face went slack in surprise. It lasted for three heartbeats, then my eyes narrowed in anger. It was starting to fall together, and the puzzle was a lot smaller than I had thought. A big interview, dropping his classes, quitting his job, standing his girlfriend up at a "we have to talk" dinner. My eyes flicked to Glenn, and he gave me a brief, disgusted look as he came to the same conclusion. Dan hadn't disappeared; he had gotten a good job and ditched his small-town girlfriend.

Pushing my glass away, I fought off a feeling of depression. "He quit?" I said.

The innocuous-looking vamp looked over his shoulder to the front door as a rowdy group of young vamps swirled in and what looked like the entire wait staff flocked to them with loud calls and hugs. "Dan was one of my best drivers," he said. "I'm going to miss him. But I wish him luck. He said it was what he was going to school for." The slight man brushed the flour from the front of his apron. "Security maintenance, I think he said."

I exchanged weary looks with Glenn. Ivy straightened on the bench, her usual aloof mien looking strained. A sick feeling went through me. I didn't want to be the one to tell Sara Jane she had been dumped. Dan had gotten a career job and cut all his old ties, the cowardly sack of crap. I would have bet he had a second girlfriend on the side. He was probably hiding out at her place, letting Sara Jane think he was dead in an alley and laughing as she fed his cat.

Piscary shrugged, his entire body moving with the slight motion. "If I had known he was good at security, I might have made him a better offer, though it would be hard to give more than Mr. Kalamack. I'm just a simple restaurant owner."

At Trent's name, I started. "Kalamack?" I said. "He got a job with Trent Kalamack?"

Piscary nodded as Ivy sat stiffly on the bench, her pizza sitting untouched but for the first bite. "Yes," he said. "Apparently his girlfriend works for Mr. Kalamack, too. I believe her name is Sara? You might want to check with her if you are looking for him." His long-toothed smile went devious. "She's probably the one that got him the job, if you know what I mean."

I knew what he meant, but from the sound of it, Sara Jane hadn't. My heart pounded and I started to sweat. I knew it. Trent was the witch hunter. He lured Dan with a promise of employment and probably nacked him when Dan tried to back out, realizing what side of the law Trent worked. It was him. Damn him back to the Turn, I had known it!

"Thanks, Mr. Piscary," I said, wanting to leave so I could start cooking up some spells that night. My stomach tightened, the pleasant slurry of pizza and my gulp of wine going sour in my excitement. *Trent Kalamack*, I thought bitterly, *you are mine.*

Ivy set her empty wineglass onto the table. I met her eyes triumphantly, my pleased emotion faltering as she watched herself refill it. She never, *ever,* drank more than one glass, rightly concerned about lowered inhibitions. My thoughts went back to how she had flaked out in the kitchen after I told her I was going after Trent again.

"Rachel," Ivy said, her gaze fixed on the wine. "I know what you're thinking. Let the FIB handle it. Or give it to the I.S."

Glenn stiffened but remained silent. The memory of her fingers around my neck made it easy for me to find a flat tone. "I'll be fine," I said.

Piscary rose, his bare head coming below the hanging light. "Come see me tomorrow, Ivy girl. We need to talk."

That same wash of fear that I saw in her yesterday swept her. Something was going on that I wasn't aware of, and it wasn't something good. Ivy and I were going to have to have a talk, too.

Piscary's shadow fell over me, and I looked up. My expression froze. He was too close, and the smell of blood overwhelmed the sharp tang of tomato sauce. His black eyes fixed to mine, something shifted, as sudden and unexpected as ice cracking.

The old vamp never touched me, but a delicious tingle raced through me as he exhaled. My eyes widened in surprise. His whisper of breath followed his thoughts through my being, backwashing into a warm wave that soaked into me like water through sand. His thoughts touched the pit of my soul and rebounded as he whispered something unheard.

My breath caught as the scar on my neck suddenly throbbed in time with my pulse. Shocked, I sat unmoving as trails of promised ecstasy raced from it. A sudden need pulled my eyes wide, and my breath came fast.

Piscary's intent gaze was knowing as I took another breath, holding it against the hunger swelling in me. I didn't want blood. I wanted him. I wanted him to pull upon my neck, to savagely pin me to the wall, to force my head back and draw the blood from me, to leave behind a swelling sensation of ecstasy that was better than sex. It beat upon my resolve, demanding I respond. I sat stiffly, unable to move, my pulse pounding.

His potent gaze flowed down my neck. I shuddered at the sensation as my stance shifted, inviting him. The pull grew worse, tantalizingly insistant. His eyes caressed my demon bite. My eyes slipped shut at the tendrils of aching promise. If he would just touch me . . . I ached for even that. My hand crept unbidden to my neck. Abhorrence and blissful intoxication warred within me, drowned out by a hurting need.

Show me, Rachel, I felt his voice chime through me. Wrapped in the thought was compulsion. Beautiful, beautiful thoughtless compulsion. My need shifted to anticipation. I would have it all and more . . . soon. Warm and content, I traced a fingernail from my ear to my collarbone, poised on the brink of a shudder as my fingernail bumped over each and every scar. The hum of conversation was gone. We were alone, wrapped in a muzzy swirl of expectation. He had bespelled me. I didn't care. God help me; it felt so good.

"Rachel?" Ivy whispered, and I blinked.

My hand was resting against my neck. I could feel my pulse lifting rhythmically against it. The room and the loud noise snapped back into existence with a painful rush of adrenaline. Piscary was kneeling before me, one hand upon mine as he looked up. His pupil-black gaze was sharp and clear as he inhaled, tasting my breath as it flowed back through him.

"Yes," he said as I pulled my hand from his, my stomach in knots. "My Ivy girl has been most careless."

Almost panting, I stared at my knees, pushing my sudden fear down to mix with my fading craving for his touch. The demon scar on my neck gave a final pulse and faded. My held breath escaped me in soft sound. It carried a hint of longing, and I hated myself for it.

In a motion of smooth grace, he stood. I stared at him, seeing and loathing his understanding of what he had done to me. Piscary's power was so intimate and certain that the thought I could stand against it rightly never occurred to him. Beside him, Kist looked like a child, even when borrowing his master's abilities. *How could I ever be afraid of Kisten again?*

Glenn's eyes were wide and uncertain. I wondered if everyone knew what had happened.

Ivy's fingers gripped the stem of her empty wineglass, her knuckles white with pressure. The old vamp leaned close to her. "This isn't working, Ivy girl. You either get control of your pet or I will."

Ivy didn't answer, sitting with that same frightened, desperate expression.

Still shaking, I was in no position to remind them that I wasn't a possession.

Piscary sighed, looking like a tired father.

Jenks flitted erratically to our table with a faint whine. "What the hell am I here for?" he snarled as he landed on the salt shaker and started brushing himself off. What smelled like cheese dust sifted down to the table, and there was sauce on his wings. "I could be home in bed. Pixies sleep at night, you know. But no-o-o-o," he drawled. "I had to volunteer for baby-sitting. Rachel, give me some of your wine. Do you know how hard it is to get tomato sauce out of silk? My wife is gonna kill me."

He stopped his harangue, realizing no one was listening. He took in Ivy's distressed expression and my frightened eyes. "What the Turn is going on?" he said belligerently, and Piscary drew back from the table.

"Tomorrow," the old vamp said to Ivy. He turned to me and nodded his good-bye.

Jenks looked from me to Ivy and back again. "Did I miss something?"

Nine

"**W**here's my money, Bob?" I whispered as I dropped the stinky pellets into Ivy's bathtub. Jenks had sent his brood out to the nearest park yesterday to bring back a handful of fish food for me. The pretty fish gulped at the surface, and I washed the smell of fish oil off my hands. Fingers dripping, I looked at Ivy's perfectly arranged pink towels. After a moment of hesitation, I dried my hands, then smoothed them out so she couldn't tell I'd used one.

I spent a moment trying to arrange my hair under my leather cap, then strode out into the kitchen, boots thumping. My eyes went to the clock above the sink. Fidgeting, I went to the fridge, opening it to stare at nothing. Where the devil was Glenn?

"Rachel," Ivy muttered from her computer. "Stop. You're giving me a headache."

I shut the fridge and leaned against the counter. "He said he'd be here at one o'clock."

"So he's late," she said, one finger on the computer screen as she jotted down an address.

"An hour?" I exclaimed. "Cripes. I could have been out to the FIB and back by now."

Ivy clicked to a new page. "If he doesn't show, I'll loan you bus fare."

I turned back to the window and the garden. "That's not why I'm waiting for him," I said, even though it was.

"Yeah. Right." She clicked her pen open and shut so fast it almost hummed. "Why don't you make us some breakfast while you wait? I bought toaster waffles."

"Sure," I said, feeling a tug of guilt. I wasn't in charge of breakfast—just dinner—but seeing as we ate out last night, I felt I owed her something. The deal was, Ivy did the grocery shopping if I made supper. Originally the arrangement had been to keep me from running into assassins at the store and creating a new meaning to the phrase "cleanup in aisle three." But now, Ivy didn't want to cook and refused to renegotiate. Just as well. The way things were going, I wouldn't have enough for a can of Spam by week's end. And rent was due Sunday.

I opened the door to the freezer and pushed aside the half-empty cartons of ice cream to find the frozen waffles. The box hit the counter with a hard clunk. Yum, yum. Ivy gave me a raised eyebrow look when I struggled to open the damp cardboard. "So-o-o-o," she drawled as I dug my red nails into the top and tore it completely off when the handy-dandy pull-tab broke. "When are they coming to get the fish?"

My eyes darted to Mr. Fish swimming in his brandy snifter on the kitchen windowsill.

"The one in my bathtub?" she added.

"Oh!" I exclaimed, flushing. "Well . . ."

Her chair creaked as she leaned back. "Rachel, Rachel, Rachel," she lectured. "I've told you before. You have to get the money up front. *Before* the run."

Angry that she was right, I jammed two waffles into the toaster and shoved them down. They popped back up, and I smacked them down again. "It wasn't my fault," I said. "The stupid fish was never missing and no one bothered to tell me. But I'll have the rent by Monday. Promise."

"It's due Sunday."

There was a distant pounding at the front door. "There's Glenn," I said, striding out of the kitchen before she could say anything more. Boots clattering, I went down the hall and into the empty sanctuary. "Come on in, Glenn!" I shouted, voice echoing against the distant ceiling. The door remained shut, so I pushed it open, stopping short in surprise. "Nick!"

"Hey. Hi," he said, his lanky height looking awkward on the wide stoop. His long face was slack in question, and his thin eyebrows were high. Tossing his black, enviably straight bangs from his eyes, he asked, "Who's Glenn?"

A smile quirked the corners of my mouth at his hint of jealousy. "Edden's son."

Nick's face went empty, and I grinned, grabbing his arm and

pulling him inside. "He's an FIB detective. We're working together."

"Oh."

The volume of emotion behind that one word was better than a year's worth of dates. Nick edged past me, his sneakers hushed on the wooden floor. His blue plaid shirt was tucked into his jeans, and I caught him before he made it to the sanctuary, pulling him back into the dark foyer. The skin about his neck almost seemed to glow in the dusk, nicely tanned and so smooth it begged for my fingers to trace the outline of his shoulders. "Where's my kiss?" I complained.

The worried look pinching his eyes vanished. Giving me a lopsided smile, he put his long hands about my waist. "Sorry," he said. "You kind of threw me there."

"Aw," I gently kidded him. "What're you worried about?"

"Mmmm." He ran his gaze down me and back up. "Plenty." Eyes almost black in the dim light, he pulled me closer, sending the smell of musty books and new electronics to fill my senses. I tilted my head up to find his lips, a warm feeling starting in my middle. *Oh yeah. This was how I liked to start my day.*

Being narrow of shoulders and somewhat spare, Nick didn't exactly fit the white-knight-on-a-horse mold. But he had saved my life by binding an attacking demon, leading me to think a brainy man could be as sexy as a muscular one. It was a thought that solidified to fact the first time Nick had gallantly asked if he could kiss me, then left me breathless and pleasantly shocked after I'd said yes.

But by saying he wasn't muscle-bound, I didn't mean Nick was a weakling. His lanky build was surprisingly strong, as I learned the time we wrestled over the last spoon of Chunky Monkey and broke Ivy's lamp. And he was athletic in a lean sort of way, his long legs able to keep up with me whenever I coerced him into driving me out to the zoo for their early open hours for runners only; those hills were killers on the calves.

Nick's strongest appeal, though, was that his relaxed, flow-with-the-punches exterior hid a wickedly quick, almost frightening mind. His thoughts jumped faster than mine, taking them places I'd never think to go. Threat brought quick, decisive action with little regard to future consequences. And he wasn't afraid of anything. It was the last that I both admired and worried about. He was a magic-using human. He should be afraid. Of a lot. And he wasn't.

But best of all, I thought as I eased myself against him, *he didn't care one whit that I wasn't human.*

His lips were soft against mine, with a comfortable familiarity. Not a hint of a beard ruined our kiss. My hands linked behind his waist and I tugged him suggestively into me. Off balance, we shifted until my back hit the wall. Our kiss broke as I felt his lips curl against mine in a smile at my forwardness.

"You are a wicked, wicked witch," he whispered. "You know that, don't you? I came over here to give you the tickets, and here you are, getting me all bothered."

His bangs were a soft whisper against my fingertips. "Yeah? You probably ought to do something about that."

"I will." His grip on me loosened. "But you're just going to have to wait." His hand ran a deliciously light path across my backside as he stepped away. "Is that a new perfume?"

Playful mood faltering, I turned away. "Yes." I had thrown my cinnamon scent out that morning. Ivy hadn't said a word upon finding the thirty-dollar-an-ounce bottle making our trash smell like Christmas. It had failed me; I hadn't the stomach to wear it again.

"Rachel . . ."

It was the beginning of a familiar argument, and I stiffened. Being in the unusual circumstances of having been raised in the Hollows, Nick knew more about vamps and their scent-triggered hungers than I did. "I'm not moving out," I said flatly.

"Could you just . . ." He hesitated, his long pianist hands moving in short, jerky motions to show his frustration as he saw my jaw clench.

"We're doing okay. I'm very careful." Guilt for having not told him she had pinned me against the kitchen wall pulled my eyes down.

He sighed, his narrow body shifting. "Here." He twisted to reach into his back pocket. "You hold the tickets. I lose everything that lays around longer than a week."

"Remind me to keep moving, then," I quipped to lighten the mood as I took them. I glanced down at the seat numbers. "Third row. Fantastic! I don't know how you do it, Nick."

He flashed his teeth in a pleased smile, the hint of cunning swelling in his eyes. He'd never tell me where he'd gotten them. Nick could find anything, and if he couldn't, he knew someone who could. I had a feeling the guarded wariness he showed to authority stemmed from here. In spite of myself, I found this as yet unexplored part of Nick deliciously daring. And as long as I didn't know for sure . . .

"Do you want some coffee?" I asked, shoving the tickets into my pocket.

Nick glanced past me into the empty sanctuary. "Ivy still here?"

I said nothing, and he read my answer in the silence. "She really does like you," I lied.

"No thanks." He shifted to the door. Ivy and Nick didn't get along. I hadn't a clue why. "I've got to get back to work. I'm on lunch break."

Disappointment slumped my shoulders. "Okay." Nick worked full-time at the museum at Eden Park, cleaning artifacts when he wasn't moonlighting at the university library, helping them catalog and move their more sensitive volumes to a more secure location. I thought it amusing that our break-in to the university's ancient-book locker was probably what prompted the move. I was sure Nick had taken the job so he could "borrow" the very tomes they were trying to safeguard. He was working both jobs until the end of the month, and I knew it left him tired.

He turned to leave, and I reached after him with a sudden thought. "Hey, you still have my largest spell pot, don't you?" We'd used it for making chili three weeks ago for a Dirty Harry marathon at his place, and I'd never brought it back.

He hesitated, his hand on the door latch. "You need it?"

"Edden is making me take a ley line class," I said, not wanting to tell him that I was working on the witch hunter murders. Not yet. I wasn't going to ruin that kiss with an argument. "I need a familiar or the witch will flunk me. That means the big spell pot."

"Oh." He was silent, and I wondered if he was going to figure it out anyway. "Sure," he said slowly. "Tonight soon enough?" When I nodded, he added, "Okay. See you then."

"Thanks, Nick. 'Bye." Pleased I had wrangled a promise to see him tonight, I pushed the door open, stopping halfway when a masculine voice called out in protest. I looked to find Glenn on the stoop, juggling three sacks of fast food and a tray of drinks.

"Glenn!" I exclaimed, reaching for the drinks. "There you are. Come on in. This is Nick, my boyfriend. Nick, this is Detective Glenn." *Nick my boyfriend. Yeah, I liked that.*

Shifting the sacks to one hand, Glenn extended his hand. "How do you do," he said formally, still outside. He was dressed in a sharp-looking gray suit, making Nick's casual clothes seem untidy. My eyebrows rose at Nick's hesitation before shaking

Glenn's hand. I was positive it was because of Glenn's FIB badge. *Don't want to know. Don't want to know.*

"Nice to meet you," Nick said, then turned to me. "I'll, uh, see you tonight, Rachel."

"'Kay. 'Bye." It sounded a bit forlorn even to me, and Nick shifted from foot to foot before leaning forward to give me a kiss on the corner of my mouth. I thought it was more to prove his boyfriend status than any attempt to show affection. Whatever.

Sneakers silent, Nick hastened down the steps to his salt-rusted blue pickup at the curb. I felt a wash of worry at his hunched shoulders and stilted pace. Glenn, too, was watching, but his expression was more curious than anything else.

"Come on in," I repeated as I eyed the sacks of food and shifted the door wider.

Glenn took his sunglasses off, one hand tucking them into the inner breast pocket of his suit. With his athletic build and tidy beard, he looked like a pre-Turn Secret Service guy. "That's Nick Sparagmos?" he asked as Nick drove away. "The one who was a rat?"

My hackles rose at how he had said it, as if turning into a rat or mink was morally wrong. I put a hand on my hip, the tray of drinks tilting dangerously close to spilling ice and soda pop. Obviously his dad had told him more of the story than Glenn had let on. "You're late."

"I stopped to get us all lunch," he said stiffly. "Mind if I come in?"

I fell back, and he crossed the threshold. He hooked the door with his foot, closing it with a tug behind him. The smell of fries became overpowering in the sudden dusk in the foyer. "That's a nice little outfit," he said. "How long did it take you to paint it on?"

Affronted, I looked down at my leather pants and the red silk blouse tucked into them. Wearing leather before sunset had worried me until Ivy convinced me that the high quality of the leather I bought elevated the look from "white witch trash" to "wealthy witch class." She ought to know, but I was still sensitive to it. "This is what I wear to work," I snapped. "It saves on skin grafts if I have to run and end up sliding on pavement. Got a problem with it?"

Keeping his comments to a noncommittal grunt, he followed me to the kitchen. Ivy looked up from her map, silently taking in the burger bags and drinks. "Well," she drawled. "I see you survived the pizza. I could still have Piscary bite you if you want."

My mood lifted at Glenn's suddenly closed expression. He made an ugly noise deep in his throat, and I went to put the frozen waffles away, seeing that the toaster hadn't been plugged in. "You scarfed down that pizza fast enough last night," I said. "Admit it. You li-i-i-i-iked it."

"I ate it to stay alive." Motions sharp, he stood at the table and pulled the bags to him. Seeing a tall black man in an expensive suit and shoulder holster unpacking paper-wrapped food made an odd picture. "I went home and prayed to the porcelain god for two hours straight," he added, and Ivy and I exchanged amused looks.

Pushing her work aside, Ivy took the burger that was the most unsquished and the fullest envelope of fries. I slouched into a chair beside Glenn. He moved to the end of the table, not even trying to make it look casual. "Thanks for breakfast," I said, eating a fry before unwrapping my burger with a rustle of paper.

He hesitated, his death grip on his FIB officer persona loosening as he undid the lowest button to his jacket and sat. "The FIB is paying for it. Actually, this is my breakfast, too. I didn't get home until the sun was almost up. You put in a long day."

His faint tone of acceptance eased my shoulders another notch. "Not really. It just starts about six hours later than yours."

Wanting ketchup for my fries, I levered myself up and went to the fridge. I hesitated in my reach for the red bottle. Ivy caught my eye, shrugging after I pointed to it. *Yeah,* I thought. He was invading our lives. He ate the pizza last night. Why should Ivy and I suffer because of him? That decided, I pulled it out and set the bottle on the table with a bold thump. Much to my disappointment, Glenn didn't notice.

"So," Ivy said, reaching across the table and taking the ketchup. "You're going to baby-sit Rachel today? Don't take her on the bus. They won't stop for her."

He glanced up, starting as Ivy laced her burger with the red sauce. "Uh." He blinked, clearly having lost his thought. His eyes were fixed upon the ketchup. "Yes. I'm going to show her what we have so far on the murders."

A smile quirked the corner of my mouth at a sudden thought. "Hey, Ivy," I said lightly. "Pass me the clotted blood."

Not missing a beat, she pushed the bottle across the table. Glenn froze. "Oh my God!" he whispered harshly, his face going sallow.

Ivy snickered, and I laughed. "Relax, Glenn," I said as I

squirted ketchup over my fries. I lounged in my chair, giving him a sly look as I ate one. "It's ketchup."

"Ketchup!" He pulled his paper place mat with his food closer. "Are you insane?"

"Nearly the same stuff you were slurping last night," Ivy said.

I pushed the bottle toward him. "It won't kill you. Try some."

His eyes riveted to the red plastic, Glenn shook his head. His neck was stiff, and he pulled his food closer. "No."

"Aw, come on, Glenn," I coaxed. "Don't be a squish. I was kidding about the blood." *What's the point of having a human over if you can't jerk him around a little?*

He stayed sullen, eating his burger as if it were a chore, not an enjoyable experience. But without ketchup, it might be a job. "Look," I said persuasively as I edged closer and turned the bottle around. "Here's what's in it. Tomatoes, corn syrup, vinegar, salt . . ." I hesitated, frowning. "Hey, Ivy. Did you know they put onion and garlic powder in ketchup?"

She nodded, wiping a stray bit of ketchup off the corner of her mouth. Glenn looked interested, leaning closer to read the fine print above my freshly painted nail. "Why?" he asked. "What's wrong with onions and garlic?" He got a knowing look in his brown eyes and settled back. "Ah," he said wisely. "Garlic."

"Don't be stupid." I set the bottle down. "Garlic and onions have a lot of sulfur. So do eggs. They give me migraines."

"Mmmm," Glenn said smugly as he picked the ketchup bottle up between two fingers to read the label for himself. "What's natural flavors?"

"You don't want to know," Ivy said, her voice pitched dramatically.

Glenn set the bottle down. I couldn't help my snort of amusement.

The sound of an approaching motorcycle pulled Ivy to her feet. "That's my ride," she said, crumpling her wrapper and pushing her half-eaten carton of fries to the middle of the table. She stretched, her lanky body reaching for the ceiling. Glenn ran his attention over her, then looked away.

My gaze met Ivy's. It sounded like Kist's cycle. I wondered if this had anything to do with last night. Seeing my apprehension, Ivy grabbed her purse. "Thanks for breakfast, Glenn." She turned to me. "See you later, Rachel," she added as she breezed out.

Shoulders easing, Glenn looked at the clock above the sink,

then went back to eating. I was scraping the last of the ketchup up with a fry as Ivy's demand filtered in from the street, "Go Turn yourself, Kist. I'm driving." I smiled as the bike accelerated and the street grew quiet.

Finished, I crumpled my paper into a ball and stood. Glenn wasn't done, and as I cleared the table, I left the ketchup. From the corner of my sight, I watched him eye it. "It's good on burgers, too," I said, dropping to crouch beside the island counter and pick out a spell book. There was the sound of sliding plastic. Book in hand, I turned to find he had pushed the bottle away. He wouldn't meet my eyes as I sat down at the table. "Mind if I check on something before we leave?" I asked, opening to the index.

"Go ahead."

His voice had turned cold again, and deciding it was the spell book, I sighed and leaned over the faded print. "I want to stir a spell for the Howlers to change their mind about not paying me," I said, hoping he would relax if he knew what I was doing. "I thought I might pick up what I don't have in the garden while I'm out. You don't mind an extra stop, do you?"

"No." It was marginally less cold, and I took that as a good sign. He was noisily stirring the ice with his straw, and I purposely edged closer so he could see.

"Look," I said, pointing at the blurring print. "I was right. If I want to send their pop flies foul, I need a noncontact spell." For an earth witch such as myself, noncontact meant wands. I'd never made one before, but my eyebrows rose at the ingredients. I had everything but the fern seed and the wand. *How much could a dowel of redwood cost?*

"Why do you do it?"

His voice had a touch of belligerence, and blinking, I closed the book. Disappointed, I went to put it away, turning to face him with my back against the island counter. "Make spells? It's what I do. I'm not going to hurt anyone. Not with a spell, anyway."

Glenn set his super-sized cup down. His dark fingers loosened their grip and slid away. Leaning back in his chair, he hesitated. "No," he said. "How can you live with someone like that? Ready to explode with no warning?"

"Oh." I reached for my drink. "You just caught her on a bad day. She doesn't like your dad, and she took it out on you." *And you did ask for it, dickhead.* I slurped the last of my drink and threw the cup away. "Ready?" I said as I got my bag and coat from a chair.

Glenn stood and adjusted his suit coat before crossing in front of me to throw his stuff away under the sink. "She wants something," he said. "And every time she looks at you, I see guilt. Whether she means to or not, she's going to hurt you, and she knows it."

Affronted, I gave him an up-and-down look. "She's not hunting me." Trying to keep a lid on my anger, I headed down the hallway at a fast pace.

Glenn was close his hard-soled shoes a heartbeat behind mine. "Are you telling me yesterday was the first time she attacked you?"

My lips pursed, and the thumps of my boots went all the way up my spine. There had been lots of almosts before I figured out what pushed her buttons and quit doing it.

Glenn said nothing, clearly hearing the answer in my silence. "Listen," he said as we emerged into the sanctuary, "I may have looked like the dumb human last night, but I was watching. Piscary bespelled you easier than blowing out a candle. She pulled you from him by simply saying your name. That can't be normal. And he called you her pet. Is that what you are? It sure looks like it to me."

"I'm not her pet," I said. "She knows it. I know it. Piscary can think what he wants." Shoving my arms into my coat, I pushed my way out of the church and stormed down the steps. His car was locked, and I yanked at the handle. Angry, I waited for him to unlock it. "And it's none of your business," I added.

The FIB detective was silent as he opened his door, then paused to look at me over the roof of the car. He put on his shades, hiding his eyes. "You're right. It's not my business."

The door unlocked, and I got in, slamming it to make the car shake. Glenn slid softly in behind the wheel and shut his door.

"Damn right it isn't your business," I muttered in the closeness of his car. "You heard her last night. I'm not her shadow. She wasn't lying when she said that."

"I also heard Piscary say if she didn't get control of you, he would."

A flash of real fear tightened me, unwanted and unsettling. "I'm her friend," I asserted. "All she wants is a friend that isn't after her blood. Ever think of that?"

"A pet, Rachel?" he said softly as he started the car.

I said nothing, tapping my fingers on the armrest. I wasn't Ivy's pet. And not even Piscary could make her turn me into one.

Ten

The late September afternoon sun was warm through my leather jacket as I rested my arm on the car's window. The tiny vial of salt on my charm bracelet shifted in the wind to clink against my wooden cross, and reaching out, I adjusted the side mirror to watch the traffic hanging a car length behind. It was nice to have a vehicle at my beck and call. We'd be at the FIB in fifteen minutes, not the forty it would take by bus, afternoon traffic and all. "Take a right at the next light," I said, pointing.

I watched in disbelief as Glenn drove straight through the intersection. "What the Turn is wrong with you!" I exclaimed. "I have yet to get in this car and you go where I want you to."

Glenn's expression was smug behind his sunglasses. "Shortcut." He grinned, his teeth startlingly white. It was the first real smile I had seen on him, and it took me aback.

"Sure," I said, waving a hand in the air. "Show me your shortcut." I doubted it would be faster, but I wasn't going to say anything. Not after that smile.

My head turned to follow a familiar sign on one of the passing buildings. "Hey! Stop!" I shouted, spinning halfway around in my seat. "It's a charm shop."

Glenn checked behind him and made an illegal U-turn. I gripped the top of the window as he made another, pulling up right before the shop and parking at the curb. I opened the door and grabbed my bag. "I'll just be a minute," I said, and he nodded, moving his seat backward and leaning his head against the headrest.

Leaving him to nap, I strode into the shop. The bells above the door jingled, and I took a slow breath, feeling myself relax. I liked charm shops. This one smelled like lavender, dandelion, and the bite of chlorophyll. Bypassing the ready-made spells, I went straight to the back where the raw materials were.

"May I help you?"

I looked up from a posy of bloodroot to find a tidy, eager salesman leaning over the counter. He was a witch by the smell of him—though it was hard to tell with all the scents in there. "Yes," I said. "I'm looking for fern seed and a dowel of redwood suitable for a wand."

"Ah!" he said triumphantly. "We keep our seeds right over here."

I paralleled his path from my side of the counter to a display of amber bottles. He ran his fingers over them, bringing down one the size of my pinky and extending it. I wouldn't take it, indicating he should put it on the counter. He looked affronted as I dug about in my bag, then held an amulet over the bottle. "I assure you, ma'am," he said stiffly, "it's the highest quality."

I gave him a weak smile as the amulet glowed a faint green. "I was under a death threat this spring," I explained. "You can't blame me for being cautious."

The doorbells jingled, and I glanced back to see Glenn come in.

The salesman brightened, snapping his fingers and taking a step back. "You're Rachel. Rachel Morgan, right? I know you!" He pressed the bottle into my hands. "On the house. So glad to see you survived. What were the odds on you? Three hundred to one?"

"It was two hundred," I said, slightly offended. I watched his gaze dart over my shoulder to Glenn, his smile freezing as he realized he was human. "He's with me," I said, and the man gasped, trying to disguise it with a cough. His eyes lingered on Glenn's half-hidden weapon. *The Turn take it, I missed my cuffs.*

"The wands are over here," he said, his tone giving me clear indication he didn't approve of my choice of companions. "We store them in a desiccation box to keep them fresh."

Glenn and I followed him to a clear spot beside the cash register. The man pulled a wooden box the size of a violin case out, opened it, and turned it with a flourish so I could see.

I sighed as the sent of redwood came rolling out. My hand rose to touch them, dropping as the salesman cleared his throat. "What spell are you stirring, Ms. Morgan?" he asked, his tone going professional as he eyed me over his glasses. The rims were wood, and I'd bet my panties they were spelled to see through earth magic disguise charms.

"I want to try a noncontact spell. For . . . oh . . . breaking wood already under stress?" I said, stifling a tinge of embarrassment.

"Any of the smaller ones will do," he said, his gaze shifting between Glenn and me.

I nodded, my eyes fixed upon the pencil-size wands. "How much?"

"Nine hundred seventy-five," he said. "But to you, I'd sell it for nine."

Dollars? "You know," I said slowly, "I should make sure I have everything before I actually get the wand. No sense having it lay around and pick up moisture before I need it."

The salesman's smile turned stiff. "Of course." In one smooth motion he snapped the case closed and tucked it away.

I winced, withering inside. "How much for the fern seed?" I asked, knowing his earlier offer had been made only because I was buying a wand.

"Five-fifty."

I had that—I thought. Head bowed, I dug about in my bag. I had known wands were expensive, but not that expensive. Money in hand, I glanced up to find Glenn eyeing a rack of stuffed rats. As the salesman rang up my purchase, Glenn leaned close and, still staring at the rats, whispered, "What are those used for?"

"I have no idea." I got my receipt and jammed everything in my bag. Trying to find a shred of dignity, I headed for the door, Glenn trailing behind. The bells jingled as we reached the pavement. Again in the sun, I took a cleansing breath. I wasn't going to spend nine hundred bucks to possibly get my five-hundred-dollar fee.

Glenn surprised me by opening the car door for me, and as I settled in the seat, he leaned against the frame of the open window. "I'll be right back," he said, and strode inside. He was out in a moment with a small white bag. I watched him cross in front of the car—wondering. Timing himself between the traffic, he opened the door and slid in behind the wheel.

"Well?" I asked as he set the package between us. "What did you get?"

Glenn started the car and pulled out into traffic. "A stuffed rat."

"Oh," I said, surprised. What the devil was he going to do with it? Even I didn't know what it was for. I was dying to ask all the way to the FIB building but managed to keep my mouth shut even as we slipped into the cold shade of their underground parking.

Glenn had a reserved spot, and my heels echoed as I found the pavement. With the pained slowness I remembered from my dad, Glenn slowly unkinked himself as he got out and tugged the sleeves of his jacket down. He reached back in for his rat and gestured to the stairs.

Still silent, I followed him into the concrete stairway. We only had to go up one flight, and he held the door for me as we went in the back door. He took his shades off as we entered, and I pushed my hair out of my eyes and under my cap. The air conditioner was on, and I looked over the small entryway thinking it was worlds away from the busy front lobby.

Glenn plucked a visitor pass from behind a cluttered desk, signing me in and giving the man on the phone a nod. I clipped it on my lapel as I followed him to the open-aired offices.

"Hi, Rose," Glenn said as he came to Edden's secretary. "Is Captain Edden available?"

Ignoring me, the older woman put a finger on the paper she was typing from and nodded. "He's in a meeting. Want me to tell him you're here?"

Glenn took my elbow and started hustling me past her. "When he gets out. No rush. Ms. Morgan and I will be here for the next few hours."

"Yes sir," she said, going back to her typing.

Hours? I thought, not liking the way he hadn't let me talk to Rose; I wanted to find out what their dress code was. The FIB couldn't have that much information. The I.S. had primary jurisdiction of the crimes.

"My office is over there," Glenn said, pointing to the bank of offices with walls and a door that lined the cubicle-divided space. The few officers at their desks looked up from their paperwork as Glenn almost pushed me forward. I was getting the distinct impression that he didn't want anyone to know I was there.

"Nice," I said sarcastically as he ushered me into his office. The off-white room was almost barren, the dirt obvious in the corners. A new computer screen sat on a nearly empty desk. It had old speakers. A nasty chair sat behind it, and I wondered if there was a decent chair in the entire building. The desk was laminated white, but the grime embedded into it from past use made it almost gray. There was nothing in the wire trash can beside it.

"Watch the phone lines," Glenn said as he swept past me and

dropped his bag-o-rat on the file cabinet. His jacket came off and he meticulously hung it on a wooden hanger which then went on a hat tree. Looking over the ugly room, I wondered what his apartment was like.

The twin phone lines from the jack behind the long table ran across the open floor to his desk. It had to be an OSHA violation having them strung like that, but if he didn't care if someone pulled his phone off the desk by tripping on it, then why should I?

"Why don't you put your desk over there?" I asked, looking at the paper-cluttered table in the logical spot for a desk.

Standing hunched over his keyboard, he looked up. "My back would be to the door, and I wouldn't be able to see the main floor."

"Oh."

There were no knickknacks of any kind—nothing of a personal nature at all—the single shelf holding only folders leaking papers. It didn't look as if he had been here long. Light rectangular shadows showed where pictures had once hung. The only thing on the walls besides his detective certificate was a dusty bulletin board with hundreds of sticky notes thumbtacked to it, hanging right over that long table. They were faded and curling, with cryptic messages only Glenn could probably decipher.

"What are these?" I asked as he checked to see that the blinds on his window overlooking the open floor were closed.

"Notes from an old case I'm working on." He had a preoccupied tone in his voice as he edged back to his keyboard and typed in a string of letters. "Why don't you sit down?"

I stood in the middle of his office, staring at him. "Where?" I finally asked.

He looked up, reddening as he realized he was standing over the only chair. "I'll be right back." He moved around his desk, coming to an awkward halt before me until I got out of his way. His gait was stilted as he edged past me and strode out.

Thinking his office was the most inhospitable slice of FIB bureaucracy I had seen yet, I took off my hat and coat, hanging them on the nail sticking out from the back of his door. Bored, I wandered to his desk. A welcome screen with a blinking prompt waited.

A rattle preceded Glenn as he pushed a rolling swivel chair into his office. Giving me an apologetic look, he set it next to his. I dropped my bag on his barren desk and sat beside him, leaning forward to see. I watched him type in three passwords: dolphin, tulip, and Monica. Old girlfriend? I wondered. They showed up on the screen as asterisks, but he was a two-fingered typist and it wasn't hard to follow.

"Okay," he said, pulling to him a notepad with a list of names and ID numbers. I glanced at the first and looked back at the screen. With a painful slowness, he furrowed his brow and started to type them in. Tap. Pause. Tap, tap.

"Oh, just give me that," I said, pulling the keyboard close. Keys chattering happily, I typed in the first, then grabbed the mouse and clicked the All button, making the only limit to the retrieval being those entries made in the last twelve months.

A query came on the screen, and I hesitated. "Which printer?" I asked.

Glenn said nothing, and I turned to see him leaning back in his chair with his arms crossed before him. "I bet you take the remote away from your boyfriend, too," he said, pulling the keyboard back in front of him and reclaiming the mouse.

"Well it's my TV," I said hotly, then added, "Sorry." Actually, it was Ivy's. Mine was lost in the big salt dip. Which was just as well since it would have looked like a toy next to Ivy's.

Glenn made a small noise at the back of his throat. He slowly typed the next name in, checking it against the list before moving to the next. I impatiently waited. My eyes went to the crumpled bag on the file cabinet. An inane desire to take the rat out filled me. This must be why he had said we'd be here for hours. It'd be faster to cut the letters out and paste them in a note.

"That's not the same printer," I said, seeing he had switched them.

"I didn't know you wanted to look at everything," he said, his voice preoccupied as he picked letters off the keyboard. "I'm sending the rest to the basement's printer." Slowly he typed in the last string of numbers and hit Enter. "I don't want to hear about tying this floor's printer up," he added.

I fought to hide a smirk. *Didn't want to hear about it? How much could there be?*

Glenn stood, and I stared up at him. "I'll get them. Stay put till I get back."

I nodded as he left. Swiveling my chair from side to side, I waited, listening to the background chatter coming in. A smile eased over me. I hadn't realized how much I missed the camaraderie of my fellow I.S. runners. I knew if I went out of Glenn's office, the conversations would stop and the looks would go cold, but if I stayed here and listened, I could pretend someone might stop by to say hi, or ask my opinion on a tough case, or tell me a dirty joke to see me laugh.

Sighing, I rose to take Glenn's rat out of the bag. I set the ugly, beady-eyed thing on the cabinet where it could watch him. A scuffing at the door pulled me around. "Oh. Hi," I said, seeing that it wasn't Glenn.

"Ma'am." The heavy FIB officer eyed first my leather pants, then my visitor's badge. I shifted so he could see better. The badge, not my pants.

"I'm Rachel," I said. "I'm helping Detective Glenn. He's getting some printouts."

"Rachel Morgan?" he said. "I thought you were an old hag."

My mouth opened in anger, then shut in understanding. The last time he saw me, I probably did look like an old hag. "That was a disguise," I said as I crumpled the bag and threw it away. "This is the real me."

He ran his eyes over my outfit again. "Okay." He turned to leave, and I breathed easier.

He was gone when Glenn strode in, a decidedly preoccupied air about him. There was a nice-size packet of paper in his grip, and I thought the FIB's information gathering must be on par with the I.S. after all. He stood for a moment in the center of his office, then pushed the papers on his long table against the wall to one end. "Here's the first one," he said, dropping the reports on the cleared spot. "I'll be right back with the ones from the basement."

I froze in my reach for them. *The first one?* I had thought that was all of them. I took a breath to ask him, but he was gone. The thickness of the report was impressive. I wheeled my chair to the table and positioned it sideways so I wouldn't have my back to the door. Sitting, I crossed my legs and pulled the wad of pages into my lap.

I recognized the front picture of the first victim because the I.S. had released it to the papers. She had been a nice-looking older woman with a motherly smile. By the makeup and jewelry, it looked like they lifted her photo from a professional picture, like those poses you get for anniversaries and such. She had been three months from retiring from a security firm that designed magic-resistant safes. Died from "complications from rape." This was all old news. I shuffled to the coroner's report, my gaze dropping to the picture.

My gut clenched, and I flipped the report closed. Suddenly cold, I stared out of Glenn's door to the open offices. A phone rang, and someone picked it up. I took another breath, and held it. I forced myself to breathe, holding it again so I wouldn't hyperventilate.

I suppose, in a loose fashion, it could be considered rape. The woman's insides had been pulled out from between her legs and were dangling to her knees. I wondered how long she had stayed alive through the ordeal, then wished I hadn't. Stomach turning, I vowed to not look at any more pictures.

Fingers shaking, I tried to concentrate on the report. The FIB had been surprisingly through, leaving me with only one question. Stretching, I snagged the cordless phone from the desk. My jaw hurt from having clenched it too long as I dialed the number listed for next of kin.

An older man answered. "No," I assured him when he tried to hang up on me. "I'm not a dating service. Vampiric Charms is an independent runner firm. I'm currently working with the FIB to identify the person who attacked your wife."

The picture of her lying twisted and broken on the gurney flashed before me. I shoved it down to where it would probably stay until I tried to sleep. I hoped he hadn't seen the picture. I prayed he hadn't found her body.

"I apologize for calling, Mr. Graylin," I said in my best professional voice. "I have only one question. Did your wife happen to talk to a Mr. Trent Kalamack anytime before her death?"

"The councilman?" he said, his voice thick with astonishment. "Is he a suspect?"

"Perish the thought," I lied. "I'm following up one of the faint leads that we have concerning a stalker working his way up to him."

"Oh." There was a moment of silence, then, "Yes. As a matter of fact, we did."

The zing of adrenaline pulled me upright.

"We met him at a play this spring," the man was saying. "I remember because it was the *Pirates of Penzance*, and I thought the lead pirate looked like Mr. Kalamack. We had dinner afterwards at Carew Tower and laughed about it. He's not in any danger, is he?"

"No," I said, my heart pounding. "I'd ask you to keep our line of investigation quiet until we've proven it false. I'm very sorry about your wife, Mr. Graylin. She was a lovely woman."

"Thank you. I miss her." He hung up the phone in the uncomfortable silence.

I set the phone down, waiting three heartbeats before whispering an exuberant, "Yes!" Spinning my swivel chair around, I found Glenn standing in the doorway.

"What are you doing?" he asked, dropping another stack of papers before me.

I grinned, continuing to shift back and forth in my chair. "Nothing."

He went to his desk and punched a button on the phone's cradle, frowning as the last number called appeared on the tiny screen. "I never said you could call these people." His face went angry and his posture became stiff. "That man is trying to put this behind him. He doesn't need you dredging it up for him again."

"I only asked one question." Legs crossed, I swiveled, smiling.

Glenn glanced behind him into the open offices. "You are a guest here," he said roughly. "If you can't play by my rules—" He stopped. "Why are you still smiling?"

"Mr. and Mrs. Graylin had dinner with Trent a month before she was attacked."

The man straightened to his full height and drew back a step. His eyes narrowed.

"Mind if I call the next?" I asked.

He looked at the phone beside my hand, then back to the open floor. With a forced casualness, he shut his door halfway. "Keep it down."

Pleased with myself, I pulled the stack of papers closer. Glenn went back behind his computer, typing with an annoying slowness.

My mood quickly sobered as I scanned the coroner's report, skipping the picture portion this time. Apparently the man had been eaten alive from the extremities inward. They knew he had been alive at the time by the tearing pattern of the wounds. And they were fairly confident he had been eaten by the lack of body parts.

Trying to ignore the mental picture my imagination provided, I called the contact number. There was no answer, not even a machine. I called his former place of work next, my intuition settling into a nice groove at the name of the place: Seary Security.

The woman there was very nice, but she didn't know anything, telling me that Mr. Seary's wife was away at a "health resort" trying to relearn how to sleep. She did look in her files, though, telling me that they had been contracted to install a safe on the Kalamack estate.

"Security . . ." I murmured, pinning Mr. Seary's packet to the bulletin board atop Glenn's sticky notes to get it out of my way. "Hey, Glenn. You have any more of those sticky notes?"

He rummaged in his desk drawer, tossing me a pack, shortly followed by a pen. I scrawled the name of Mr. Seary's workplace and stuck it to his report. After a moment's thought, I did the same to the woman's, writing "safe designer" on it. I added a second sticky note with "Talked to T" circled in black ink.

A scuffing in the hallway brought my eyes up from the third report. I made a noncommittal smile recognizing the overweight cop, minibag of chips in hand. He acknowledged me and Glenn's nod, coming to a rest in the doorway. "Glenn's got you doing his secretary work?" he asked, his good-old-boy tone almost thick enough to cut.

"No," I said, smiling sweetly. "Trent Kalamack is the witch hunter, and I'm just taking a moment to tie the links together."

He grunted, eyeing Glenn. Glenn wearily returned his look, adding a shrug. "Rachel," he said, "this is Officer Dunlop. Dunlop, this is Ms. Morgan."

"Charmed," I said, not offering my hand lest I get it back covered in potato-chip grease.

Not getting the hint, the man walked in, crumbs falling to the tile floor. "Whatcha got?" he said, coming to peer at my thick reports stuck to the board atop Glenn's faded sticky notes.

"Too soon to say." I pushed him out of my space with a finger in his gut. "Excuse me."

He backed up but didn't leave, going instead to see what Glenn was doing. Heaven save me from cops on break. The two talked over Glenn's suspicions concerning Dr. Anders, their rising and falling voices soothing.

I blew chip crumbs off my papers, my pulse quickening as I saw that the third victim had worked at the city racetrack in weather control. It was a very difficult field of work, heavy in ley line magic. The man had been pressed to death while working late, stirring up a fall shower to dampen down the track for the next day's race. The actual implement of death was unknown. There had been nothing in the stables heavy enough. I didn't look at that picture, either.

It had been at this point that the media realized the three deaths were connected despite the varying methods of death and named the sadistic freak the "witch hunter."

A quick phone call got me his sister, who said of course he

knew Trent Kalamack. That the councilman often called her brother to ask about the state of the track, but that she hadn't heard if he had talked to Mr. Kalamack before his death or not, and that she was just sick about her brother's death, and did I know how long it took for insurance checks to come in?

I finally got my condolences wedged in between her chattering and hung up on her. Everyone handled death differently, but that was offensive.

"Did he know Mr. Kalamack?" Glenn asked.

"Yup." I pinned the packet to the board and stuck a note to it with the words "weather maintenance" on it.

"And his job is important because . . ."

"It takes a heckuva lot of ley line skill to manipulate the weather. Trent raises racehorses. He could have easily been out there and talked to him and no one would have given it a second thought." I added another note with "Knew T" on it.

Old Dunlop-the-cop made an interested noise and ambled over. He hung a respectful three feet behind me this time. "Done with this one?" he asked, fingering the first.

"For now," I said, and he pulled it from the board. Some of Glenn's notes fluttered down to fall behind the table. Glenn's jaw tightened.

Feeling like someone was starting to take me seriously, I sat straighter. The overweight man ambled back to Glenn, making noises as he found the pictures. He dropped the report onto Glenn's desk, and I heard the patter of chip crumbs. Another officer came in, and an impromptu meeting seemed to be taking shape as they clustered around Glenn's computer screen. I turned my back on them and looked at the next report.

The fourth victim had been found in early August. The papers had said the cause of death was severe blood loss. What they hadn't said was that the man had been disemboweled, torn apart as if ravaged by animals. His boss had found him in the basement of his workplace, still alive and trying to push his insides back into him where they belonged. It was more difficult than usual since he only had one arm, the other hanging by his underarm skin.

"Here you go, ma'am," a voice said at my elbow, and I jerked. Heart pounding, I stared at a young FIB officer. "Sorry," he said as he extended a sheaf of papers. "Detective Glenn asked me to bring these up when they finished. Didn't mean to startle you." His eyes dropped to the report in my hand. "Nasty, isn't it?"

"Thank you," I said, accepting the reports. My fingers were

trembling as I dialed the number for the victim's boss when there was no next of kin.

"Jim's," a tired voice said after the third ring.

My greeting froze in my throat. I recognized his voice. It was the announcer at Cincinnati's illegal rat fights. Heart pounding, I hung up, missing the button the first time. I stared at the wall. The room had gone silent.

"Glenn?" I said, my throat tight. I turned to see him surrounded by three officers, all looking at me.

"Yeah?"

My hands shook as I extended the report across the small space. "Will you look at the crime scene photos for me?"

His face blank, he took it. I turned to his wall of sticky notes, listening to the pages turn. Feet shuffled. "What am I looking for?" he asked.

I swallowed hard. "Rat cages?" I asked.

"Oh my God," someone whispered. "How did she know?"

I swallowed again. I couldn't seem to stop. "Thanks."

With motions slow and deliberate, I took the report and stuck it to the bulletin board. My handwriting was shaky as I wrote "T availability" and stuck it on the pages. The report said he had been a bouncer at a dance club, but if he was one of Dr. Anders's students, he had been skilled with ley lines and was more likely the head of security at Jim's rat fights.

I reached for the fifth packet with a grim feeling. It was Trent—I knew it was Trent—but the horror of what he had done was killing any joy I might find in it.

I felt the men behind me watching as I leafed through the report, recalling that the fifth victim, found three weeks ago, had died the same way as the first. A call to her tearful mother told me she had met Trent in a specialty bookstore last month. She remembered because her daughter had been surprised that such a young, important man was interested in collectable, pre-Turn fairy-tale anthologies. After confirming that her daughter had been employed in a security subscription firm, I gave her my condolences and hung up.

The background murmurs of the excited men added to my numb state. I carefully wrote my big T, making sure the lines were clear and straight. I stuck it beside the copy of the woman's work ID picture. She had been young, with straight blond hair to her shoulders and a pretty, oval face. Just out of college. The memory of the picture I had seen of the first woman on the gurney flashed into my mind. I felt the blood drain from me. Cold and light-headed, I stood.

The men's conversations stopped as if I had rung a bell. "Where's the ladies' room?" I whispered, my mouth dry.

"Turn left. Go to the back of the room."

I didn't have time to say thanks. Low heels clacking, I strode out of the room. I looked neither left nor right, moving faster as I saw the door at the end of the room. I hit the door at a run, reaching the toilet just in time.

Retching violently, I lost my breakfast. Tears streamed down my face, the salt mixing with the bitter taste of vomit. How could anyone do that to another person? I wasn't prepared for this. I was a witch, damn it. Not a coroner. The I.S. didn't teach its runners how to deal with this. Runners were runners, not murder investigators. They brought their tags in alive, even the dead ones.

My stomach was empty, and when the dry heaves finally stopped, I stayed where I was, sitting on the floor of the FIB bathroom with my forehead against the cold porcelain, trying not to cry. I suddenly realized someone was holding my hair out of the way, and had been for a while.

"It will go away," Rose whispered, almost to herself. "Promise. Tomorrow or the next day, you'll close your eyes and it will be gone."

I looked up. Rose dropped her hand and took a step back. Beyond the propped-open door was the row of sinks and mirrors. "Really?" I said miserably.

She smiled weakly. "That's what they say. I'm still waiting. I think they all are."

Feeling foolish, I awkwardly got to my feet and flushed the toilet. I brushed myself off, glad the FIB kept their bathroom cleaner than I kept mine. Rose had gone to a sink, giving me a moment to gather myself. I left the stall feeling embarrassed and stupid. Glenn would never let me live this down.

"Better?" Rose asked as she dried her hands, and I gave her a loose-necked nod, ready to burst into tears again because she wasn't calling me a newbie or making me feel inadequate or that I wasn't strong. "Here," she said, taking my purse from a sink and handing it to me. "I thought you might want your makeup."

I nodded again. "Thanks, Rose."

She smiled, the age lines in her face making her look even more comforting. "Don't worry about it. This is a bad one."

She turned to go, and I blurted, "How do you deal with it?

How do you keep from falling apart? That— What happened to them is horrible. How can a person do that to another?"

Rose took a slow breath. "You cry, you get angry, then you do something about it."

I watched her leave, the clack of her quick heels sounding sharp before the door closed.

Yeah. I can do that.

Eleven

It took more courage than I wanted to admit to walk out of the ladies' bathroom. I wondered if everybody knew I had lost it. Rose had been unexpectedly kind and understanding, but I was sure the FIB officers would use it against me. *Pretty little witch too soft to play with the big boys?* Glenn would never look past it.

I darted a nervous glance over the open-air offices, my steps faltering as I didn't find mocking, knowing faces but empty desks. No, everyone was standing outside of Glenn's office, peering in. Loud voices were coming from inside.

"Excuse me," I murmured, holding my bag close to myself as I pushed past the uniformed FIB officers. I halted just over the threshold, finding the room full of arguing people with weapons and handcuffs.

"Morgan." The cop who had been eating chips grabbed my arm and pulled me farther in. "You all right now?"

I caught myself, stumbling at my abrupt entrance. "Yes," I said hesitantly.

"Good. I called the last one for you." Dunlop met my eyes. They were brown—and it seemed I could see right to his soul, they were so frank. "Hope you don't mind. I was dying of curiosity." He ran a hand across his mustache, wiping the grease from it as his gaze went to the six reports tacked over Glenn's notes.

My gaze swept the room. Every man and woman glanced at me as the weight of my eyes fell on them, recognizing me before going back to his or her conversation. They all knew I had spewed my guts, but by their lack of comment, it seemed I had broken the ice in some twisted fashion. Perhaps falling apart proved to them that I was just as human as they were—sort of.

Glenn was sitting at his desk with his arms crossed, saying nothing as he watched the separate arguments. He gave me a wry, eyebrow-raised look. By the sound of it, most of the room wanted to arrest Trent, but a few were too cowed by his political muscle and wanted more. There was less tension in the room than I would have expected, seeing as they were all shouting at each other. Humans appeared to enjoy doing things by loud committee.

I put my purse on the floor beside the table and sat down to look at the last report. The paper had said the latest victim had been a former Olympic swimmer. He'd died in his bathtub. Drowning. He worked for a local TV station as the celebrity weatherman but had gone to school for ley line manipulation. The note stuck to it said in a stilted print that his brother didn't know if he talked to Trent or not. I pulled the report from the board and made myself look it over, paying more attention to the conversations around me than the print.

"He's laughing at us," a street-hardened, swarthy woman said as she argued with a thin, nervous-looking officer. Everyone but Glenn and I were standing, and I felt like I was at the bottom of a well.

"Mr. Kalamack isn't the witch hunter," the man protested in a nasally voice. "He gives more to Cincinnati than Santa Claus."

"That fits the profile," Dunlop butted in. "You've seen the reports. Whoever is doing this is certifiable. Twin lives, probably a schizophrenic."

There was a soft murmur from the surrounding officers as the arguments swirled down to just this one. For what it was worth, I agreed with Dunlop. Whoever was doing this was an itsy-bitsy-skitzy. Trent filled that description nicely.

The nervous man straightened, gaze darting about the room for support. "Okay, the murderer is mental, yes," he admitted in an irritating whine. "But I've met Mr. Kalamack. The man is no more a murderer than my mother is."

I flipped to the coroner's report, learning that our Olympic swimmer had indeed died in his bathtub, but that it had been full of witch blood. A bad feeling started to push out the horror. It takes a lot of blood to fill a bathtub. A lot more than one person has; more like two dozen. Where had it all come from? A vampire wouldn't have wasted it like that.

The discussion concerning the thin cop's mother became loud, and I wondered if I should tell them about benevolent Mr. Kalamack killing his lead geneticist and blaming it on a bee sting. Nice, neat, and tidy. Murder without hardly lifting a hand. Trent had given the widowed wife and orphaned fifteen-year-old-girl the upgraded benefits package and an anonymous, full university scholarship.

"Stop thinking with your wallet, Lewis," Dunlop said, swinging his ample middle around aggressively. "Just because the man gives to the FIB charity auction, that doesn't make him a saint. I say that makes him more suspicious. We don't even know if he's human."

Glenn flicked a glance at me. "What does that have to do with anything?"

Dunlop started, clearly remembering I was here. "Absolutely nothing!" he said loudly, as if the volume of his voice could erase the hidden, underlying racial slur. "But the man has something to hide."

I silently agreed, starting to like the overweight cop despite his lack of tact.

The officers clustered at the door looked over their shoulders into the open offices. They exchanged looks and backed up. One of them said, "Afternoon, Captain," as he ducked out of the way, and I wasn't surprised when Edden's squat bulk replaced theirs in the doorframe.

"What is going on?" he said, pushing his round-framed glasses back up his nose.

Another FIB officer made a silent farewell to me and slipped out.

"Hi, Edden," I said, not getting up from my swivel chair.

"Ms. Morgan," the short man said, a hint of anger on him as he shook my offered hand and raised his eyebrows at my leather pants. "Rose said you were here. I'm not surprised to find you in the middle of an argument." He looked at Glenn, and the tall FIB officer shrugged, not a bit apologetic as he got to his feet.

"Captain," Glenn said, taking a deep breath. "We were conducting a free-flow exercise concerning the possible alternate suspects for the witch hunter murders."

"No you weren't," Edden said, and my eyes went to his at the anger in his voice. "You were gossiping about Councilman Kalamack. He's not a suspect."

"Yes sir," Glenn agreed as Dunlop gave me an unreadable look and edged quietly out of the room, surprisingly agile for his size. "But I believe Ms. Morgan is entertaining a valid thought path."

Surprised at the support, I blinked at Glenn.

Edden didn't even look at me. "Stop the college psycho-babble, Glenn. Dr. Anders is our prime suspect. You'd better have a good reason for pulling your energies from there."

"Yes sir," Glenn said, not at all upset. "Ms. Morgan has found a direct link from four of the six victims to Mr. Kalamack, and a probable window of opportunity for contact with Mr. Kalamack in the other two."

Instead of being excited as I would have expected, Edden slumped. I stood up as he came close to look at the records tacked to the wall. His tired eyes went from one to the next. The last of the FIB officers left, and I went to stand beside Glenn. With a united front, maybe he might stop wasting our time and let us go after Trent.

Feet spread wide, Edden put his hands on his hips and stared at the sticky notes tacked to the reports. I found I was holding my breath, and let it out. Unable to resist, I said, "All but the last victim used ley lines heavily in their daily work. And there's a slow progression from those highly skilled down to those just out of school and not yet using their degrees."

"I know." Edden's voice was flat. "Which is why Dr. Anders is a suspect. She is the last ley line witch of any repute left in Cincinnati actively practicing. I think she's getting rid of the competition. Especially as most of the victims were working in security related fields."

"Or Trent just hasn't gotten to her yet," I said softly. "The woman is a cactus."

Edden turned, putting his back to the reports. "Morgan, why would Trent Kalamack be killing ley line witches? He has no motive."

"He has the same motive you've given Dr. Anders," I said. "Getting rid of the competition. Maybe he offered them a job, and when they refused, he killed them? It would fit in with Sara Jane's missing boyfriend." *Not to mention what he did to me.*

Creases appeared in Edden's forehead. "Which brings up the question as to why he would let his secretary come to the FIB."

"I don't know," I said, my voice rising as I became frustrated. "Maybe the two are unrelated. Maybe she lied about him knowing she came to us. Maybe the man is crazy and wants to get caught. Maybe he's so sure we can't find our asses in the dark that he's thumbing his nose at us. He had them killed, Edden. I know it. He talked to them before they died. What more do you need!"

I was almost shouting. I knew it wouldn't get me anywhere with Edden, but this bureaucracy was part of the reason I had quit the I.S. And it rankled to find myself trying to "convince the boss" again. Head bowed and hand on his chin, Glenn took a step back, leaving me alone. I didn't care.

"It's not against the law to talk to Trent Kalamack," Edden said, his eyes level with mine. "Half the city knows him."

"You're going to ignore that he talked to every one of these people?" I protested.

His face went red behind his eyeglasses. They looked too small for his round face. "I can't accuse a councilman of phone calls and casual conversations," he said. "That's his job."

My pulse quickened. "Trent killed those people," I said softly. "And you know it."

"What you know isn't worth goose shit, Rachel. It's what I can prove. And I can't prove anything with this." He flicked a hand at the nearest report, making it flutter.

"Then search his compound," I demanded.

"Morgan!" Edden shouted, shocking me. "I won't authorize a search on the evidence that he talked to the victims. I need more."

"Then let me talk to him. I'll get it."

"God bless it!" he swore. "You want me fired, Rachel? Is that it? Do you know what will happen if I let you go through his compound and find nothing?"

"Nothing," I said.

"Wrong! I will have accused a well-respected man of murder. He is a councilman. A benefactor of most of the charities and hospitals on both sides of the state line. The FIB will become a foul word in human and Inderland households alike. My reputation will be shot!"

Frustrated, I stood toe-to-toe with him, able to look the man right in the eye. "I didn't know you became an FIB officer to better your reputation."

Glenn shifted, making a soft sound of warning. Edden stiffened, his jaw clenching until white spots appeared on his forehead. "Rachel," he said with a soft threat, "this is an official FIB investigation, and we are going to do it *my* way. You've allowed yourself to become emotionally involved, and your judgment is compromised."

"My judgment?" I shouted. "He stuck me in a freaking cage and put me in the rat fights!"

Edden took a step closer. "I'm not," he said, pointing at me, "going to let you waltz into his office and telegraph your vendetta-based suspicions while we're gathering evidence. Even if we do question him, you will—not—be—there!"

"Edden!" I protested.

"No!" he barked, rocking me back a step. "This conversation is over."

I took a breath to tell him it wasn't over until I said so, but he had walked out. Angry, I struck out after him. "Edden," I called after his swiftly vanishing shadow. For a squat man, he moved fast. A door slammed. "Edden!"

Ignoring the watching FIB officers, I stormed through the open offices, past Rose, and to his closed door. I reached for the handle, then hesitated. It was his office; angry or not, I couldn't barge in. Frustrated, I stood outside his door and shouted, "Edden!" I tucked a strand of hair behind my ear. "You and I both know Trent Kalamack is able and willing to commit murder. If you won't let me talk to him through the FIB, then I quit!"

I took off my visitor's badge as if it meant something and threw it on Rose's desk. "You hear me? I'll go talk to him by myself."

Edden's door jerked open, and I took a step back. He stood before me, his khaki slacks creased and his plaid shirt starting to come untucked. He loomed out into the hallway, pushing me almost into Rose's desk with a stubby finger. "I told you if you came into this gunning for Mr. Kalamack, I'd sling your witch ass back across the river and into the Hollows. You made a commitment to work with Detective Glenn on this, and I'm holding you to it. But if you talk to Mr. Kalamack, I'll toss you in my own lockup for harassment."

I took a breath to protest, but my resolve faltered.

"Now get out of here," Edden almost growled. "You have a class tomorrow, and I'll deduct the tuition from your compensation if you don't go."

Thoughts of rent money intruded. Despising that money, not what was right, would be what stopped me. I glared at him. "You know he killed those people," I said tightly.

Shaking in unspent adrenaline, I walked away. I passed through the silent FIB officers at their desks on my way to the front. I'd take the bus home.

Twelve

I fell hard as Ivy cut my legs from under me. I rolled away, already aching where my hip had hit the floor. My heart pounded in time with the twin pains on the back of my calves. I tossed a strand of hair that had escaped my exercise band from my eyes. Putting a hand against the wall of the sanctuary, I used it for balance as I got to my feet. Lungs heaving, I ran the back of my hand across my forehead to wipe the sweat from me.

"Rachel," Ivy said from eight feet away. "Pay attention. I almost hurt you that time."

Almost? I shook my head to clear my vision. I had never seen her move away, she was so quick. Of course, I might not have seen her move since I was falling on my can at the time.

Ivy took three loping steps toward me. Eyes wide, I twisted my body in a tight circle to the left, sending my right foot into her midsection.

Grunting, she clutched her stomach and stumbled backward. "Ow," she complained, retreating. I hunched over, putting my hands on my knees to signal I wanted a breather. Ivy obediently moved farther away and waited, trying not to show that I had hurt her.

From my position, I glanced at her standing in a band of green and gold afternoon sun streaming in through the sanctuary's windows. The black body stocking and soft slippers she wore when we sparred with each other made her look more predatory than usual. Her straight black hair was tied back, accentuating her tall, lean appearance. Face blank and pale, she waited for me to catch my breath so we could continue.

The practice was more for me than her. She insisted it would extend my life expectancy should I run up against a big-bad-ugly without my spells or a direction to run. I always came away from of our sparring bruised and headed for my charm cupboard. How that extended my life was beyond me. More practice making pain amulets, maybe?

Ivy had arrived home early from her afternoon with Kist, surprising me with the offer to work out. I was still seething over Edden's refusal to let me question Trent and needed to burn off some anger and so said yes. As usual, within fifteen minutes I was hurting and breathing hard while she had yet to break a sweat.

Ivy danced impatiently from foot to foot. Her eyes were a nice steady brown. I kept a close watch on her when we worked out together, not wanting to push her too close to her limits. She was fine. "What's up?" she asked as I straightened. "You're more aggressive than usual."

I bent my leg back to stretch my leg muscle and pull the cuff of my sweatpants back down about my ankle. "Every one of the victims talked to Trent before they died," I said, stretching the truth. "Edden won't let me question him." I pulled the other leg, then nodded.

Ivy's breath quickened. I dropped to a crouch as she darted forward. Too quick for thought, I ducked her blow, sweeping my leg at her feet. Calling out, she flung herself in a backflip to avoid it, landing on her hands and then feet. I jerked back to keep her foot from hitting my jaw on the way by.

"So?" Ivy questioned softly, waiting as I stood up.

"So Trent is the murderer."

"Can you prove it?"

"Not yet." I lunged for her. She danced out of the way, jumping onto the thin windowsill. As soon as her feet landed, she pushed off, somersaulting right over me. I spun to keep her in view. Red spots of exertion were starting to show on her. She was dipping into her vamp repertoire to evade me. Encouraged, I followed up, striking with my fists and elbows.

"So quit and finish the run yourself," Ivy said between blocks and counterstrikes.

My wrists smacking into her blocks hurt, but I kept at it. "I told him . . . that's what I was going to do . . ." Strike, block, block, strike. ". . . and he threatened to lock me up for harassment. Told me I should concentrate on Dr. Anders." Pull six feet back. Pant. Sweat. *Why was I doing this again?*

A smile, real and unusual flashed across her face and was gone. "Sneaky bastard," she said. "I knew God had put him on earth to be more than a happy meal."

"Edden?" I wiped at the sweat dripping from my nose. "He's more of a big kid's meal, isn't he?" I gestured for her to come get me. Eyes glinting in amusement, she obliged, attacking with a barrage of blows ending with a strike to my solar plexus that sent me reeling.

"Your concentration is slipping," she said, breathing hard as she watched me kneel, gasping, on the floor. "You should have seen that coming."

I had, but my arm was going numb and slow from having been hit too many times. "I'm all right," I wheezed. This was the first time I'd seen her break a sweat, and I wasn't going to stop now. I shakily got to my feet and held up two fingers, then one. My hand went down, and she lunged with a supernatural quickness.

Alarmed, I blocked her vamp-quick blows, retreating off the mats and almost into the foyer. She grabbed my arm as I reached the threshold, flinging me over her and back onto the mats. My back hit with a thump, knocking the wind from me. I felt her feet padding after me. Adrenaline surged. Still not breathing, I rolled until I hit the wall. She was hot after me, landing to pin me there.

Eyes alight, she leaned over me. "Edden is a wise man," she said between breaths, a strand of hair that had escaped her tie tickling my face. Sweat dampened her brow. "You should listen to him and leave Trent alone."

"Et tu, brute?" I wheezed. Grunting, I jerked my knee up to her groin.

She sensed it coming and fell back. I had known she was too fast to let it land, but it got her off me—which was what I'd wanted.

Ivy stood her usual eight feet back and waited for me to rise. It was slower this time. I rubbed my shoulder as I took her in, avoiding eye contact to let her know I wasn't ready.

"Not bad," she admitted. "But you didn't follow it up. Mr. Big Bad Ugly isn't going to stand aside and wait for you to regain your balance, and neither should you."

I gave her a weary look from around my red frizz of hair. Trying to keep up with her, much less best her, was hard. I'd never had to think about overcoming a vampire before since the I.S. didn't send witches to tag them. And whatever else, the I.S. took care of its own, on or off the job. Unless they wanted you dead.

"What are you going to do?" she asked as I felt my ribs through my sweatshirt.

"About Trent?" I said, breathless. "Talk to him without Edden or Glenn knowing."

Ivy's rocking motion faltered. With a warning shout, she leapt forward.

Instinct and practice saved me as I ducked. She spun in a tight circle, and I jerked out of the way. Ivy followed with a series of blows that backed me to the wall. Her voice echoed against the empty walls of the sanctuary, filling it with sound.

Shocked at her sudden ferocity, I pushed myself from the wall and fought back using every trick that she had taught me. I became angry that she wasn't even trying. With her vamp speed and strength, I was a moving target dummy.

My eyes widened as Ivy's face went savage. She was going to show me something new. Swell.

She shouted and spun. I foolishly did nothing as her foot slammed into my chest, sending me into the wall of the church.

My breath whooshed out and pain crushed my lungs. She darted away, leaving me to hang gasping. Staring at the floor, I saw the green and gold sunbeams shake as the stained-glass windows to either side of me shivered. Still not breathing, I looked up to see Ivy sauntering away. Her slow, mocking pace ticked me off.

Anger burned, giving me strength. Still having not caught my breath, I jumped her.

Ivy cried out in surprise as I landed on her back. Grinning savagely, my legs went around her waist. I grabbed a fistful of her hair and jerked her head back, sliding an arm around her throat to choke her.

Gasping, she backpedaled. I let go, knowing she was going to slam me against the wall again. I dropped to the floor, and she tripped over me. She went down. I grappled for her, catching her around the neck again. She bucked against the floor, twisting her body at an impossible angle, breaking my hold.

Heart pounding, I flipped myself to my feet, finding Ivy standing eight feet away—waiting. My exhilaration at having surprised her vanished as I realized something had shifted. She was moving from foot to foot with an unnerving, fluid grace, the first sign of her vamp background getting the better of her.

Immediately I straightened and waved my arms in surrender. "That's it," I panted. "I have to get cleaned up. I'm done. I've got to do my homework."

But instead of backing off as she always did, she started to circle. Her movements were languorously slow and her eyes were fixed to mine. My heart pounded and I spun to keep her in view. Tension laced through me, tightening my muscles one by one. She came to a halt in a sunbeam, the light glinting on her black body stocking like it was oil. Her hair was free, the black band lying between us where I had accidentally ripped it off her.

"That's the trouble with you, Rachel," she said, her soft voice echoing. "You always quit when it starts to get good. You're a tease. Nothing but a goddamned tease."

"Excuse me?" I asked, the pit of my stomach clenching. I knew exactly what she meant, and it scared the crap out of me.

Her face tightened. Forewarned, I braced myself as she lunged. I blocked her fists, driving her away with a foot aimed at her knees. "Knock it off, Ivy!" I shouted as she jerked out of my reach. "I said I'm done!"

"No you aren't." Her gray voice settled over me like silk. "I'm trying to save your life, little witch. A big bad vamp isn't going to stop because you tell him to. He's going to keep coming until he gets what he wants or you drive him away. I'm going to save your life—one way or another. You'll thank me when it's over."

She darted forward. Catching my arm, she twisted it, trying to force me to the floor. I gasped and kicked her legs from under her. We went down, my breath exploding out of me. Panicking, I pushed away and rolled to my feet.

I found her waiting her usual eight feet back—circling. A subtle heat had soaked into her movements. Her head was lowered and she was eyeing me from around her hair. Her lips were parted, and I could almost see her breath passing through them.

I backed away. Fear grew as the ring of brown around her pupils flashed to black. *Damn.*

Swallowing, I ran a hand over myself, foolishly trying to wipe her sweat off. I had known better than to jump her. I had to get her smell off me, and now. My fingers touched the demon scar on my neck, and my breath caught. It was tingling from the pheromones she was pumping into the air. *Double damn.*

"Stop, Ivy," I said, cursing the quaver that had crept into my voice. "We're done." Knowing my life hung on what happened in the next few seconds, I turned my back on her in a false show of confidence. Either I would make it to my room and its two locks or I wouldn't.

The hair on the back of my neck prickled as I paced past her.

My heart pounded, and I held my breath. She did nothing as I neared the hallway, and my breath slipped out.

"No, we aren't," she whispered.

The sound of moving air pulled me around.

She attacked silently, her eyes lost in black. I fended off her blows by instinct. She wasn't even trying. Ivy caught my arm, and I cried out in pain as she spun me around, crushing my back against her. I leaned forward as if trying to break her grip. As her arms tightened and her body leaned to find our balance, I slammed my head backward into her chin.

Grunting, she dropped her grip and stumbled back. Adrenaline sang through me. She was between me and my spells. If I went for the front door, I'd never make it. This was my fault. Damn it back to the Turn, I shouldn't have jumped her. I shouldn't have become aggressive. She was driven by instinct, and I had pushed her too far.

I stood, watching her come to a swaying halt in a sunbeam. Standing sideways, she tilted her head and touched the corner of her mouth.

My stomach clenched as her fingertip came away colored in blood. Her eyes met mine as she rubbed the blood between her fingers and smiled. I shuddered at the sight of her sharp canines. "First blood, Rachel?"

"Ivy, no!" I shouted as she lunged.

She caught me before I had moved a step. Gripping my shoulder, she flung me to the front of the church. I hit the wall where the altar had once stood, slipping down to the floor. I struggled for air as she paced to me. Everything hurt. Her eyes were black pits. Her movements were smooth with power. I tried to roll away. She caught me, yanking me up.

"Come on, witch," Ivy said gently, her black, owl-feather voice in stark contrast to her painful grip on my shoulder. "I taught you better. You're not even trying."

"I don't want to hurt you," I panted, one arm clutched around my middle.

She held me to the wall under the shadow of a long gone cross. The blood from her lip made a red jewel caught at the corner of her mouth. "You can't," she whispered.

Heart pounding, I jerked to get away, failing. "Let me go, Ivy," I panted. "You don't want to do this." A cloying scent of incense pulled the memory of her pinning me to her chair last spring. "If you do this," I said frantically, "I'll leave. You'll be alone."

She leaned close, putting the flat of her free forearm against the wall by my head. "If I do this, you won't leave." A heated smile curved over her—showing a hint of teeth—and she pressed closer. "But you could get away if you really wanted to. What do you think I've been teaching you the last three months? Do you want to get away—Rachel?"

Panic lanced deep into me. My heart beat wildly, and Ivy sucked her breath in as if I had slapped her. Fear was an aphrodisiac, and I'd just given her a jolt. Lost in the blackness of instinct and need, her muscles went tension-wire tight. "Do you want to get away, little witch?" she murmured, her breath against my demon scar sending a surge of tingling through me.

My intake of breath went to my core, seeming to turn my blood to liquid metal as it conducted a pulse through me. "Get off," I panted, the delicious feeling coursing from my neck to fill me. It was my scar. She was playing on my demon scar as Piscary had done.

She licked her lips. "Make me." She hesitated, the hard hunger shifting to something more playful and insidious. "Tell me it doesn't feel good when I do this." Breath easing from her in a sigh, she watched my eyes as her finger ran a trail from my ear, across my neck, and down my collarbone.

I almost buckled at the sensation of her nail finding the faint bumps of scar tissue, stimulating the scar back into full play. My eyes closed as I remembered that the demon had taken Ivy's face when it ripped out my throat, filling the wound with a dangerous cocktail of neurotransmitters to make pain into pleasure. "Yes," I breathed, almost moaning. "God help me. It does. Please . . . stop."

Her body shifted against mine. "I know how it feels," she said. "The hunger racing from it to fill your body, the need it stirs, until the only thought burning in you is to touch the craving to fulfill it."

"Ivy?" I whimpered. "Stop. I can't. I don't want to."

My eyes flashed open at her silence. The drop of blood at the corner of her mouth was gone. I could feel the blood pounding through me. I knew my reactions were tied to the demon scar, that she was sending out pheromones to restimulate the pseudovamp saliva that remained in me to make pain into pleasure. I knew it was one of the survival adaptations vamps relied upon to bind people to them, ensuring that they had a willing supply of blood. I knew all of this, but it was getting harder to remember. Harder to care. It wasn't sexual. It was need. Hunger. Heat.

Ivy put her forehead against the wall beside mine as if to gather her resolve. Her hair made a silk curtain between us. I felt the warmth from her through her body stocking. I couldn't move, wire-tight with fear and want, wondering if she would sate it or if I would be strong enough of will to push her away.

"You don't know what it's been like living beside you, Rachel," she said, her whisper coming from behind her hair as if from a confessional grate. "I knew you'd be frightened if you knew how vulnerable your scar makes you. You've been marked for pleasure, and unless you have a vampire to claim and protect you, they all will take advantage of it, taking what they want and passing you to the next until you're nothing but a puppet begging to be bled. I was hoping you might be able to say no. That if I taught you enough, you would be able to drive a hungry vampire away. But you can't, dear heart. The neurotoxins have soaked in too far. It's not your fault. I'm sorry. . . ."

My breath came in small pants, each one sending the promise of coming pleasure through me, flowing back to renew that which ebbed, building on those that came before. I held my breath, trying to find the will to tell her to get off me. *Oh God, I was failing.*

Ivy's voice went soft, persuasive. "Piscary said this is the only way to keep you. To keep you alive. I would be kind, Rachel. I wouldn't ask anything you didn't want to give. You wouldn't be like those pathetic shadows at Piscary's, but strong, an equal. He showed me when he bespelled you that it wouldn't hurt." Her voice went little girl soft. "The demon already broke you. The pain is over. It will never hurt again. He said you would respond, and my God, Rachel, you did. It's as if a master broke you. And you're mine."

Fear flashed through me at her hard, possessive tone. She turned her head, her hair falling back to show her face. Her black eyes were an ancient hunger, faultless in their innocence. "I saw what happened under Piscary, what you felt with no more than a finger touching your skin."

I was too frightened and enraptured by the waves of feeling coming off my neck in time with my pulse to move. "Imagine," she whispered, "what it's like when it's not your finger but my teeth—slicing clean and pure through you."

The thought sent a pulse of heat through me. I went slack in her grip, my body rebelling against my railing thoughts. Tears slipped down my face, warm on my cheeks to fall on my collarbone. I couldn't tell if they were tears of fear or need.

"Don't cry, Rachel," she said, tilting her head to brush her lips upon my neck in time with her words. I almost passed out from the ache of desire. "I didn't want it to be like this, either. But for you," she whispered, "I'd break my fast."

Her teeth grazed my neck, taunting. I heard a soft moan, shocked to realize it came from me. My body cried out for it, but my soul screamed no. The eager, pliant faces at Piscary's intruded. Lost dreams. Wasted lives. Existence turned to serve someone else's need. I tried to push her away, but failed. My will was a ribbon of cotton, falling apart with the slightest tug. "Ivy," I protested, hearing my whisper. "Wait." *I couldn't say no. But I could say wait.*

She heard, pulling away to look at me. She was lost in a haze of anticipation and rapture. Numb terror struck through me. "No," I said, panting as I fought the pheromone-induced high. *I had said it. Somehow I had said it.*

Wonder and hurt crossed her face, a breath of awareness returning to her black eyes. "No?" She sounded like a hurt child.

My eyes closed in the ripples of ecstasy that flowed from my neck as her fingernails continued to trace the scars where her lips had let off. "No . . ." I managed, feeling unreal and disconnected as I weakly tried to push her away. "No."

My eyes flashed open as her grip on my shoulder tightened. "I don't think you mean that," she snarled.

"Ivy!" I shrieked as she pulled me against her. Adrenaline scoured my veins. Pain followed it, punishing me for my defiance. Terrified, I found the strength to keep her from my neck. She pulled me with an increasing power. Her lips drew back from her teeth. My muscles began to shake. Slowly she pulled me closer. Her soul was lost from her eyes. Her hunger shone like a god. My arms trembled, ready to give out.

God save me, I thought desperately, my eyes finding the cross incorporated into the ceiling.

Ivy jerked as a metallic *bong* reverberated through the air.

She stiffened. The need in her flickered. Her eyebrows rose in bewilderment and her focus wavered. Breath held, I felt her grip slacken. Fingers slipping from me, she collapsed at my feet with a sigh.

Behind her stood Nick with my largest copper spell pot.

"Nick," I whispered, tears blurring my vision. I took a breath and reached out for him, passing out as he touched my hand.

Thirteen

It was warm and stuffy. I could smell cold coffee. Starbucks: two sugars, no cream. I opened my eyes to find a red stringy mass of my hair blocking my sight. My arm aching, I pushed it out of the way. It was quiet, with only the hushed sound of traffic and the familiar hum of Nick's alarm clock to break the stillness. I wasn't surprised to find I was in his bedroom, safe on my occasional side of the bed, facing both the window and the door. Nick's dilapidated dresser with the missing knob never looked so good.

The light slanting in past the drawn curtains was faint. I was guessing it was getting close to sunset. A glance at his clock showed 5:35. I knew it was accurate. Nick was a gadget guy, and the clock received a signal from Colorado every midnight to reset it from the atomic clock there. His watch was the same way. Why someone had to be that accurate was beyond me. I didn't even wear my wristwatch.

The gold and blue afghan Nick's mother had crocheted him was snuggled under my chin, smelling faintly of ivory soap. What I recognized as a pain amulet lay on the nightstand—right beside the finger stick. Nick thought of everything. If he could have invoked it, he would have.

I sat up looking for him, knowing by the scent of coffee that he was probably nearby. The afghan pooled about me as I swung my feet to the floor, Muscles protesting, I reached for the amulet. My ribs hurt and my back was sore. Head bowed, I pricked my finger for the three drops of blood to invoke the charm. Even before I slipped the cord over my head, I felt myself relax in immediate relief. It was all muscle aches and bruises, nothing that wouldn't heal.

I squinted in the artificial dusk. An abandoned coffee cup pulled my eyes to a slump of clothes on the chair. It moved in a gentle rhythm, becoming Nick asleep with his long legs sprawled out before him. He was sock-footed, since he wouldn't let shoes on his carpet, and his big feet pulled a smile from me.

I sat, content to do nothing for the moment. Nick's day started six hours earlier than mine, and a faint stubble made early shadows on his long face slack in slumber. His chin rested on his chest, his short black hair falling to hide his eyes. They opened as a primitive part of him felt my gaze on him. My smile grew as he stretched in the chair, a sigh slipping from him.

"Hi, Ray-ray," he said, his voice pooling like brown puddle-warm water about my ankles. "How are you doing?"

"I'm okay." I was embarrassed that he had witnessed what happened, embarrassed he'd saved me, and heartily glad he had been there to do both.

He came to sit beside me, his weight making me slide into him. My breath made a relieved, contented sound as I fell against him. He put his arm around me and gave me a sideways squeeze. I rested my head against his shoulder, taking the scent of old books and sulfur deep into me. Slowly my heartbeat became obvious as I sat and did nothing, taking strength simply from his presence.

"Are you sure you're all right?" he asked, his hand buried deep in my hair as he held me.

I pulled away to look at him. "Yes. Thanks. Where's Ivy?" He didn't say anything, and my face went slack in alarm. "She didn't hurt you, did she?"

His hand dropped from my hair. "She's on the floor where I left her."

"Nick!" I protested, pushing myself away from him so I could sit straight. "How could you just leave her there?" I stood, looking for my bag and realizing he hadn't brought it. I was still barefoot, too. "Take me home," I said, knowing the bus wouldn't pick me up.

Nick had risen when I did. His face flashed into alarm and his eyes dropped. "Shit," he said under his breath. "I'm sorry. I thought you said no to her." His gaze flicked to mine and away, his long face looking pained, disappointed, and red with embarrassment. "Aw, shit, shit, shit," he muttered. "I'm really sorry. Yeah. Yeah, come on. I'll get you home. Maybe she hasn't woken up yet. I'm really, really sorry. I thought you said no. Oh God. I shouldn't have interfered. I thought you said no!"

He was hunched with discomfort, and bewildered, I reached

out and pulled him back before he could walk out the bedroom door. "Nick?" I said as he jerked to a halt. "I did say no."

Nick's eyes widened even farther. His lips parted and he stood there, seeming unable to even blink. "But . . . you want to go back?"

I sat on the bed and looked up at him. "Well, yeah. She's my friend." I gestured in disbelief. "I can't believe you just left her lying there!"

Nick hesitated, confusion thick in his pinched eyes. "But I saw what she tried to do," he said. "She almost bit you, and you want to go back?"

My shoulders slumped and I dropped my gaze to the stain-spotted, ugly yellow carpet. "It was my fault," I said softly. "We were sparring and I was angry." I glanced up. "Not with her. With Edden. Then she got cocky, and it ticked me off, so I jumped her, catching her off guard . . . landed on her back, pulled her head back by her hair and breathed on her neck."

His lips pressed together, Nick lowered himself to sit on the edge of the chair and put his elbows on his knees. "Let me get this straight. You decided to spar with her while you were angry. You waited until you were both emotionally charged, and then you jumped her?" He exhaled loudly through his nose. "Are you sure you didn't *want* her to bite you?"

I made a sour face at him. "I did say it wasn't her fault." Not wanting to argue with him, I got up and moved his arms to make a spot for me in his lap. He made a surprised grunt, then curved his arms about me as I sat down. I tucked my head against his cheek and shoulder, breathing in his masculine scent. The memory of the vamp-saliva-induced euphoria flickered through me and was gone. I hadn't wanted her to bite me—I hadn't—but a niggling thought wouldn't go away that the baser, pleasure-driven side of me might have. I had known better. It hadn't been her fault. And as soon as I could convince myself of that and get out of Nick's lap, I was going to call and tell her so.

I snuggled and listened to the traffic as Nick ran a hand over my head. He seemed inordinately relieved. "Nick?" I questioned. "What would you have done if I hadn't said no?"

He took a slow breath. "Put your spell pot just inside the door and left," he said, his voice rumbling up through me.

I straightened, and he winced as my body weight shifted against him. "You would have let her tear out my throat?"

He wouldn't meet my eyes. "Ivy wouldn't have drained you

and left you for dead," he said reluctantly. "Even in the frenzy you had her whipped up to. I heard what she offered you. That was no one night stand. It was a life commitment."

My demon scar tingled at his words, and frightened, I pushed the feeling away. "Just how long were you standing there?" I asked, going cold with the thought that the nightmare might have been far more than Ivy simply losing control.

His grip around me tightened as his eyes failed to reach mine. "Long enough to hear her ask to make you her scion. I wasn't going to stand in your way if it was something you wanted."

My mouth dropped open and I pulled my arm from around behind him. "You would have walked away and let her make me into a plaything?"

A flash of anger flickered in his brown eyes. "A scion, Rachel. Not a shadow or plaything, or even a thrall. There's a world of difference."

"You would have walked away?" I exclaimed, not willing to get out of his lap for fear pride might make me leave his apartment. "You would have done nothing?"

His jaw clenched but he made no move to dump me onto the floor. "I am not the one living in a church with a vamp!" he said. "I don't know what you want. I can only go on what you tell me and what I see. You live with her. You date me. What am I supposed to think?"

I said nothing, and he added in a softer voice, "What Ivy wants is not wrong or unusual, it's a cold, scary fact. She's going to need a trustworthy scion in about forty years or so, and she likes you. To tell you the truth, it's a damn fine offer. But you had better make up your mind as to what you want before time and vamp pheromones make it for you." His voice grew halting, reluctant. "You wouldn't be a plaything. Not with Ivy. And you would be safe with her, untouchable by just about every nasty thing Cincinnati has."

Gaze distant, my thoughts lit on small, seemingly unrelated instances of friction between Ivy and Nick, seeing them in a new light. "She's been hunting me all this time," I whispered, feeling the first hints of real fear.

The wrinkles around Nick's eyes creased. "No. It's not just blood she's after, though an exchange is involved. But I have to be honest. You complement each other like no vamp and scion pair I've seen." A flicker of unknown emotion swelled and died within his eyes. "It's a chance at greatness—if you're willing to give up your dreams and bind yourself to hers. You would always be second. But you would be second to a vamp slated to rule Cincinnati."

Nick's hand ceased its motion over my hair. "If I made a mistake," he said carefully, not looking at me, "and you want to be her scion, then fine. I'll drive you and your toothbrush home and walk away, letting you two finish what I interrupted." His hand began moving again. "My only regret will be that I wasn't enough to lure you away from her."

My eyes drifted across Nick's hodgepodge of furniture, hearing the busy traffic outside his apartment. It was so unlike Ivy's church with its wide open spaces and breathing room. All I had wanted was to be her friend. She desperately needed one, unhappy with herself and wanting to be something more, something clean and pure, something untouched and unsullied. She was trying so hard to escape her vampiric existence, and I knew she harbored a belief that someday I might find a spell to help her. I couldn't leave and destroy the one thing that kept her going. God save me if I was a fool, but I admired her indomitable will and belief that someday she'd find what she sought.

Despite the potential threat she posed, her asinine demands for organization, and her strict adherence to structure, she was the first person I'd roomed with who said nothing about my mindslips, like draining the water heater or neglecting to turn off the heat before opening the windows. I'd lost too many friends over such petty arguments. I didn't want to be alone anymore. The scary thing was that Nick was right. We did do well together.

And now I had a new fear. I hadn't realized the threat of my vamp scar until she told me. Marked for pleasure and unclaimed. Passed from vampire to vampire until I begged to be bled. Remembering the waves of euphoria and how hard it had been to say no, I saw how easy Ivy's prediction could turn real. Though she hadn't bitten me, I was sure the word on the streets was that I was taken goods and to back off. *Damn. How did I get to this place?*

"Do you want me to take you back?" Nick whispered, pulling me close.

I shifted my shoulder to mold myself into him. If I was smart, I'd ask his help in moving my stuff out of the church tonight, but what came out of my mouth was a small, "Not yet. I'll call to make sure she's all right, though. I'm not going to be her scion, but I can't leave her to be alone. I said no, and I think she'll respect that."

"What if she doesn't?"

I tucked in closer. "I don't know. . . . Maybe I'll put a bell on her."

He chuckled, but I thought I heard a trace of pain in it. I felt his amusement fade. His chest shifted my head as he breathed. What happened had scared me more than I wanted to admit. "You aren't under a death threat anymore," he whispered. "Why don't you leave?"

I didn't move, hearing his heartbeat. "I don't have the money," I protested softly. We'd been over this before.

"I told you that you can move in with me."

I smiled, though he couldn't see it, my cheek scraping against his cotton shirt. His apartment was small, but that wasn't why I had always kept our sleepovers to the weekends. He had his own life, and I would get in his way if he had to take me in more than small doses. "It would last for a week, and then we would hate each other," I said, knowing from experience it was true. "And I'm the only thing keeping her from falling back into being a practicing vamp."

"So let her fall. She's a vampire."

I sighed, not finding the strength to get angry. "She doesn't want to be. I'll be more careful. It'll be all right." I put a confident, persuasive tone in my voice, but was left wondering if I was trying to convince him or me.

"Rachel . . ." Nick breathed, his breath shifting the hair atop my head. I waited, almost able to hear him trying to decide whether he should say anything more. "The longer you stay," he said reluctantly, "the harder it's going to be to resist the vamp-induced euphoria. That demon that attacked you last spring pumped more vamp saliva into you than a master vampire. If witches could be turned, you'd be one by now. As it is, I think Ivy could bespell you simply by saying your name. And she's not even dead yet. You're making unsafe rationalizations for staying in an unsafe situation. If you think you will ever want to leave, you should go now. Believe me, I know how good a vampire scar feels when a vamp's need kicks in. I know how deep the lie goes, and how strong the lure."

I sat up, my hand going to cover my neck. "You know?"

His eyes went sheepish. "I went to high school in the Hollows. You don't think I got through that without being bitten at least once?"

My brow rose at his almost guilty look. "You have a vamp bite? Where?"

He wouldn't meet my eyes. "It was a summer fling. And she wasn't dead so I didn't contract the vamp virus. There wasn't much saliva in it to begin with, so it stays pretty quiet unless I get in a situation where there are a lot of vampire pheromones. It's a trap. You know that, don't you?"

I slumped back into him, nodding. Nick was safe. His scar was old and made by a living vampire barely out of adolescence. Mine was new and laced with so much neurotoxin that Piscary could set it into play with just the weight of his eyes. Nick went still, and I wondered if his scar had flamed to life when he'd walked into the church. It might explain why he had said nothing and simply watched. How good had his scar felt? I wondered, unable to blame him.

"Where is it?" I asked slowly. "Your vamp scar?"

Nick jiggled me farther up onto his lap. "Never mind that—witch," he said playfully.

I suddenly became very aware of him pressing up against me, his arms draped around me to keep me from falling off. I glanced at the clock. I had to go to my mom's and get my old ley line stuff before I could do my homework. If I didn't do it tonight, it wouldn't get done. My gaze tilted to Nick's, and he smiled. He knew why I was looking at the clock.

"Is this it?" I asked. Shifting on his lap, I pulled the collar of his shirt aside to show a faint white scar on his upper shoulder from a deep scratch.

He grinned. "I don't know."

"Mmmm," I said. "Bet I could tell." As he laced his hands to cradle me about the hips, I undid the top button of his shirt. The angle was awkward, and I shifted to straddle his lap, my knees to either side of him. His hands moved to hold me a trifle lower, and arching my eyebrows at our new position, I leaned closer. My fingers went behind his neck and I nuzzled aside his collar to set my lips against the scar, leaving it with an audible pop.

Nick took a noisy breath, shifting under me into more of a slouch so he wouldn't have to hold me from falling. "That's not it," he said. His hand went to my back, tracing a trail down my spine, bumping as he found the waistband of my sweats.

"Okay," I murmured as his fingers tugged the hem of my sweatshirt. He reached up under it, his fingertips making a long tingle across my skin. "I know it isn't this one." Bending over him, I let my hair fall about his chest as I flicked my tongue against first one then the second puncture mark I had given him when I'd been a mink and thought he was a rat trying to kill me. He said nothing, and I carefully worried the three-month-old scar with gentle teeth.

"No," he said, his voice suddenly strained. "You gave me those."

"That's right," I breathed, my lips grazing his neck as I steadily worked my way to his ear with little hop-kisses. "Hmmm . . ." I breathed. "I guess I'll have to do some investigating. You are aware, Mr. Sparagmos, that I am professionally trained in the field of investigation?"

He said nothing, his free hand making a delicious sensation as he traced a path along the small of my back, testing.

I pulled back, and his hands followed the curves of my waist under my sweatshirt with an increasing pressure. I was glad it was near dark. So still and warm. An eager anticipation was in his gaze, and leaning forward to brush the tips of my hair over his face, I whispered, "Close your eyes."

His entire body shifted as he sighed, doing as I asked.

Nick's touch became more insistent, and I settled my forehead into the crook between his neck and shoulder. Eyes closed, I felt for the buttons on his shirt, enjoying the rising feeling of expectation as each one gave way. I struggled with the last, tugging his shirt out from his jeans.

His hands fell from me and he twisted to pull his shirt free. I tilted my head and gently bit his earlobe. "Don't you dare help," I whispered, his lobe still between my teeth. I shivered as he resumed his touch, his hands warm against my back. All the buttons were undone, and I ran my lips across the faint notches rimming his ear.

With a quick motion he reached up, pulling my face to his. His lips were demanding. A soft sound urged me to respond. *Had it been him or me? Don't know. Don't care.* One hand was buried deep in my hair, holding me to him as his lips and tongue explored. His motions grew aggressive, and I pushed him back into the chair, liking his rough touch. He hit the slats with a thump, pulling me down with him.

His stubble was prickly, and lips still on mine, he reached around, pulling me close. With a grunt of effort, he lurched to his feet, carrying me. My legs wrapped around him as he moved us to the bed. My lips felt cold as he pulled away, setting me down gently. His arms slipped from me as he knelt over me.

I looked up at him, his shirt still on, but open to show lean muscles running down to disappear beneath his waistband. I had tossed one of my arms artfully over my head, and I reached up with the other to draw a line from his chest downward, tugging at his jeans.

Button fly, I thought in a wash of impatience. God help me. I hated button fly. His dusky smile faltered and he almost shuddered as I gave up for a moment and reached behind him, tracing the curve of his back, following it as far as I could reach. It wasn't nearly far enough, and I pulled him down toward me. Slumping forward, Nick supported himself on the flat of a forearm. A sigh escaped me as I got my hands to where I wanted them to be.

Warm, and with the delightful mix of gentle pressure and rough skin, Nick sent his hand searching under my shirt. I ran my hand over his shoulders, feeling his muscles bunch and ease. He scooted lower, and I gasped in surprised as he nuzzled my midriff, his teeth searching for the hem of my sweatshirt.

My breath came faster, and a whispered pant of anticipation slipped from me as he tugged my shirt upward, his hands pushing against my waist. Hasty with a sudden need, I dropped my hands from fumbling at his button fly to help him get my shirt off. It scraped my nose in passing, taking my amulet with it. My held breath slipped out in a sound of relief. Nick's teeth were a teasing hint as he tugged at my tight-fitting exercise bra. I shuddered, arching my upper back in encouragement.

He buried his face at the base of my neck. My demon scar, running from my collarbone to my ear, gave a knife-edged pulse of feeling, and I froze into a frightened wariness. It had never done that before when I'd been with Nick. I didn't know whether to enjoy it or lump the feeling in with the terror of the scar's origin.

Sensing my sudden fear, Nick slowed, his body nudging mine once, twice, then halting. In a slow stillness, he brushed my scar with his lips. I couldn't move as waves of promise raced through me, settling low and insistent in my body. My heart pounded as I compared it to Ivy's vamp-pheromone induced ecstasy and found it identical. It felt too good to dismiss out of hand.

Nick hesitated, his breath harsh in my ear. Slowly the feeling ebbed. "Should I stop?" he whispered, his voice husky with need.

I closed my eyes, reaching downward to work almost frantically at his button fly. "No," I moaned. "It almost hurts. Be—careful."

His breath came in a quick sound, matching mine. More insistent, he ran a hand under my bra and made soft kisses against my scarred neck. An unhelped sound escaped me as I got the last of his buttons undone.

Nick's lips ghosted up the underside of my chin and found my mouth. His touch was gentle, and I lunged my tongue deep into him. He pushed back, his stubble harsh. Our breath came in tandem. His continuing gentle fingers on my neck sent a sudden spasm through me.

I traced my hands down his open shirt to find his jeans. Breath fast, I pushed his clothes down to where I could hook my foot into them and push them all the way off. Hungry for him, I sent my hands searching, stretching to find what I wanted.

Nick's breath caught as I grasped him, feeling the tight, smooth skin between my fingers and thumb. His head dropped from mine, burying it between my breasts, nuzzling, as my bra had somehow disappeared.

He pushed his hips against me, hinting, and I pushed pack. My heart pounded. Strong and insistent, my scar sent waves through me, though Nick's searching lips were nowhere near it.

I abandoned myself to the demon scar, letting the feeling flow through me. I'd figure out later if it was wrong or not. My hands quickened their motion against him, feeling the difference between him and a male witch, finding it roused me further. Leaving one hand to caress him, I grasped the hand not supporting his weight over me and led him to the drawstring on my sweats.

He snatched my wrist, pinning it up over my head on the pillow, refusing to accept my help. A jolt struck through me. He nipped at my neck and darted away, the barest hint of teeth bringing a gasp from me. Nick's hands tugged at my waistband, pulling my sweats and underwear off in a fierce need. I arched my back to help free them from my hips, and a heavy hand pinned my shoulder to the bed.

I opened my eyes, and Nick leaned over me and breathed, "My job, witch." But my sweats were gone.

I reached downward for him, and he shifted his weight, nudging his knee against the inside of my thigh. Again I arched my lower back, reaching, straining to find him. He fell to cover me. His lips on mine, we begin to move against each other.

Slowly, almost tauntingly, he moved inside of me. I clutched at his shoulders, racked with tingling jolts as his lips found my neck.

"My wrist," he panted in my ear. "Oh God, Rachel. She bit my wrist."

The surges of feeling came in time with our bodies' rhythm as I hungrily found his wrist. He moaned as I fastened on it. I grazed my teeth across it, sucking hungrily as he did the same on my neck. The ache rose in me, and out of my mind in need, I bit Nick's old scar, making it mine, trying to take it away from the one who first marked him.

Pain shot through my neck, and I cried out. Nick hesitated, then again pinched a fold of scarred skin between his teeth. I did the same with his wrist to tell him it was all right. Silent with a desperate need, his mouth lunged hungrily into me. Want crept up from within. I felt it swell. I seduced it closer, willing it to happen. *Now,* I thought, almost crying. *Oh God. Make it now.*

Together Nick and I shuddered, our bodies responding as one as a wave of euphoria washed from me into him. It rebounded, striking me with twofold strength. I gasped, clutching at him. He groaned as if in pain. Again the wave took us, pulling us back. Poised, we hung at the point of climax, trying to hold it forever.

Slowly it ebbed, jolts of dying pleasure sending tremors through us both as the tension eased from us in stages. Nick's weight gradually pressed down atop me. His breath was rough in my ear. Exhausted, I made a conscious effort to unkink my hands from his shoulder. The imprints of my fingers made red lines on his skin.

I lay for a moment, feeling a dying tingle from my neck. Then it was gone. I ran my tongue along the inside of my teeth. No blood. I hadn't broken his skin. *Thank God.*

Still atop me, Nick shifted his weight so I could breathe easier. "Rachel?" he whispered. "I think you almost killed me."

Breath slowing, I said nothing, thinking I could forego my three-mile run today. My heartbeat eased, filling me with a relaxed lassitude. I pulled his wrist close, eyeing the old scar showing a stark white against the red, roughened skin. I felt a twinge of embarrassment to see I had given him a hickey. No guilt, though, for having marked him. He'd probably known what would happen better than I had, and my neck was undoubtedly in a similar state.

Did I care? Not right now. Maybe later when my mom spotted it.

I gave his tender skin a kiss and set his arm down. "Why did it feel like one of us was a vampire?" I asked. "My demon scar was never that sensitive before. And you?" I left my sentence unfinished. I had nibbled a good share of his body over the last two months and never provoked such a response in him. Not that I was complaining.

Looking exhausted, he eased himself off me and fell groaning on the bed. "Must have been from Ivy getting things started," he said, his eyes closed as he faced the ceiling. "I'm going to be sore tomorrow."

I grabbed the afghan and pulled it to cover me, cold now without his body heat. Shifting to my side, I leaned close and whispered, "Sure you want me to move out of the church? I think I'm beginning to see why threesomes are so popular in the vamp circles."

Nick's eyes opened as he grunted. "You are trying to kill me, aren't you?"

Chuckling, I stood, wrapping the afghan around me. My fingers touched my neck to find the skin sore but unbroken. I wouldn't say it had been wrong to take advantage of the sensitivities Ivy set into play, but the vehement need of it had me concerned. Almost too exquisitely intense to control . . . No wonder Ivy had such a hard time.

Thoughts slow and speculative, I dug about in the bottom drawer of Nick's dresser for one of his old shirts and made my way to his shower.

Fourteen

"**H**ello." Nick's recorded voice came from my answering machine, sounding smooth and polished. "You've reached Morgan, Tamwood, and Jenks of Vampiric Charms, independent runners. They are currently unavailable. Please leave a message and let us know if you would prefer a daylight or evening return call."

I gripped the black plastic of Nick's phone tighter and waited for the beep. Having Nick leave the outgoing message on our machine had been my idea. I liked his voice, and I thought it very posh and professional for us to appear to have a man as a receptionist. 'Course, that all went out the window when they saw the church.

"Ivy?" I said, wincing at the guilt I could hear in my voice. "Pick up if you're there."

Nick walked past me from the kitchen, his hand trailing across my waist as he went into his living room.

The phone remained silent, and I rushed to fill the gap before the machine clicked off. "Hey, I'm at Nick's. Um . . . about earlier. Sorry. It was my fault." I glanced at Nick doing the "bachelor tidy shuffle" as he swooped about, shoving things out of sight under the couch and behind cushions. "Nick says he's sorry for hitting you."

"I do not," he said, and I covered the receiver thinking her vamp hearing might catch it.

"Hey, umm," I continued, "I'm going to my mom's to pick up some stuff, but I'll be back around ten. If you get home before me, why don't you pull the lasagna out and we'll have that tonight. We can eat around midnight? Make it an early dinner so I can get my homework done?" I hesitated, wanting to say more. "Well, I hope you get this," I finished lamely. "'Bye."

I clicked the phone off and turned to Nick. "What if she's still knocked out?"

His eyes tightened. "I didn't hit her that hard."

I slumped to lean against the wall. It was painted an icky brown and didn't go with anything else. Nothing in Nick's apartment went with anything else, so it kind of fit—in a warped sort of way. It wasn't that Nick didn't care about continuity, but that he looked at things differently. The time I found him wearing a blue sock with a black, he had blinked at me and said they were the same thickness.

His books, too, weren't cataloged alphabetically—his oldest tomes had no title or author—but by some ranking system I had yet to figure out. They lined an entire wall of his living room, giving me the eerie feeling of being watched whenever I was there. He had tried to get me to store them in my closet for him after his mother dumped them on his doorstep early one morning. I'd kissed him soundly and refused. They creeped me out.

Nick leaned into the kitchen and grabbed his keys. The sliding sound of metal pulled me from the wall and to the door. I glanced over my outfit before following him into the hall: blue jeans, tucked-in black cotton T, and the flip-flops I used when we swam in his apartment's pool. I had left them last month and found them washed and hung up in Nick's closet.

"I don't have my bag," I muttered as he gave the door a firm tug to lock it.

"You want to stop at the church on the way?"

His offer didn't sound genuine, and I hesitated. We'd have to cross half of the Hollows to get there. It was after sundown. The streets were getting busy, and it would take forever. There wasn't much in my bag in terms of money, and I wouldn't need my charms—I was only going to my mom's—but the thought of Ivy flat out on the floor was intolerable. "Could we?"

He took a slow breath, and with his long face twisted into a stilted expression, he nodded.

I knew he didn't want to, and the bother of that made me almost miss the step out of the apartment house and onto the dark parking lot. It was cold. There wasn't a cloud in the sky, but the stars were lost behind the city lights. My feet felt drafty in their flip-flops, and when I clutched my arms about myself, Nick handed me his coat. I shrugged into it, my anger at his reluctance to check on Ivy easing at the warmth and lingering smell of him on the thick fabric.

A faint whine came from a street lamp. My dad would have called it a thief light. Just enough illumination to let a thief know what he was doing. The sound of our feet was loud, and Nick reached for my door. "I'll get it," he said gallantly, and I smirked as he fought with the handle, grunting as he gave it a final yank and the latch released.

Nick had been working his new job for only three months but somehow managed to get a beat-up blue Ford truck already. I liked it. It was big and ugly, which was why he had gotten it so cheap. He said it was the only thing they had on the lot that didn't scrunch his legs up to his chin. The clear coat was peeling and the tailgate was rusting out, but it was transportation.

I lurched up and in, putting my feet squarely on the offensive floor mat from the previous owner as Nick slammed the door shut. The truck shook, but it was the only way to be sure the door wouldn't fly open when we went across railroad tracks.

As I waited for Nick to come around the back, a flickering shadow over the hood caught my eye. I leaned forward, squinting. Something almost smacked the window, and I jumped.

"Jenks!" I exclaimed, recognizing him. The glass between us did nothing to hide his agitation. His wings were a gossamer blur, shimmering in the street lamp as he frowned. A floppy, wide-brimmed red hat looking gray in the uncertain light was on his head, and his hands were on his hips. My guilty thoughts flashed to Ivy, and I rolled the window down, pushing it along when it got stuck halfway. He darted inside and took off his hat.

"When the hell are you two going to get a speaker phone?" he snarled. "I belong to this crappy firm as much as you, and I can't use the phone!"

He had come from the church? I didn't know he could move that fast.

"What did you do to Ivy?" he continued as Nick silently got in and shut his door. "I spend the afternoon with Glenda the Good trying to calm him down after you yelled at his dad, then I come home to find Ivy having hysterics on the bathroom floor."

"Is she all right?" I asked, then looked at Nick. "Get me home."

Nick started the truck, jerking back as Jenks landed on the gearshift. "She's fine—as much as she ever is," Jenks said, his anger shifting to worry. "Don't go back yet."

"Get off that," I said, flicking a hand under him.

Jenks flitted up, then down, staring at Nick until the man put his hands back on the wheel. "No," the pixy said. "I mean it. Give her some time. She heard your message and is calming down." Jenks flew to sit on the dash before me. "Man, what did you do to her? She was going on and on about not being able to protect you, and that Piscary was going to be angry with her, and she didn't know what she was going to do if you left." His tiny features grew worried. "Rache? Maybe you should move out. This is too weird, even for you."

I felt cold at the undead vampire's name. Maybe I hadn't pushed her too far; maybe Piscary had put her up to it. We would've been fine had she quit when I first said to. He'd probably figured out that Ivy wasn't the dominant one in our odd relationship and wanted her to rectify the situation, the little prick. It wasn't his business.

Nick put the car in gear, and the tires cracked and popped against the gravel lot. "Church?" he questioned.

I glanced at Jenks, and he shook his head. It was the wisp of fear on him that decided it for me. "No," I said. I'd wait. Give her time to collect herself.

Nick seemed as relieved as Jenks. We pulled out into traffic, headed for the bridge.

"Good," Jenks said. Eyeing my lack of earrings, he vaulted up to sit on the rearview mirror. "What the hell happened, anyway?"

I rolled my window back up, feeling the coldness of the coming night in the damp breeze. "I pushed her too far while we were working out. She tried to make me her—uh—tried to bite me. Nick knocked her out with my spell pot."

"She tried to bite you?"

I looked from the passing night to Jenks, seeing in the light from the car behind us his wings go still, then blur to nothing and go still again. Jenks looked from Nick's embarrassed face to my worried one. "Ohhh," he said, his eyes widening. "Now I get it. She wanted to bind you to her so only *she* could make your vamp scar resonate to vamp pheromones. You turned her down. My God, she must be embarrassed. No wonder she's upset."

"Jenks, shut up," I said, stifling the urge to grab him and toss him out the window. He would only catch up at the first red light.

The pixy flitted to Nick's shoulder, eyeing the lights glowing on the dash. "Nice truck."

"Thanks."

"Stock?"

Nick's gaze slid from the taillights of the car ahead to Jenks. "Modified."

Jenks's wings blurred, then steadied. "What's your top end?"

"One fifty with NOS."

"Damn!" the pixy swore admiringly as he flew back to the rearview mirror. "Check your lines. I smell a leak."

Nick's eyes darted to a grimy, obviously not factory-installed lever under the dash before returning to the road. "Thanks. I wondered." Slowly he rolled his window down a crack.

"No problem."

I opened my mouth to ask, then closed it. Must be a guy thing.

"So-o-o-o-o," Jenks drawled. "We going to your mom's?"

I nodded. "Yeah. Want to come?"

He rose an inch as we hit a pothole, hovering cross-legged. "Sure. Thanks. Her Rose of Sharon is probably still blooming. Think she'd mind if I took some of the pollen home?"

"Why don't you ask her?"

"I will." A grin came over him. "You'd better put some makeup on that love bite."

"Jenks!" I exclaimed, my hand going to cover my neck. I had forgotten. My face warmed as Jenks and Nick exchanged looks in some asinine macho thing. God help me, I felt as if I was back in the cave. *Me mark woman so Glurg keep his furry hands off her.*

"Nick," I pleaded, keenly feeling the lack of my bag. "Can I borrow some money? I have to stop at a charm shop."

But the only thing more embarrassing than buying a complexion spell is buying one with a hickey on your neck. Especially when most of the shop owners knew me. So I opted for anonymity and asked Nick to stop at a gas station. Of course, the spell rack by the register was empty, so I ended up plastering my neck with conventional makeup. Covergirl? Don't you believe it. Nick said it looked all right but Jenks laughed his wings red. He sat on Nick's shoulder and chatted about the attributes of the pixy girls he had known before meeting Matalina, his wife. The randy pixy kept it up all the way to the outskirts of Cincinnati where my mom lived while I tried to touch up my makeup in the visor's mirror.

"Left down that street," I said, wiping my fingers off on each other. "It's the third house on the right."

Nick said nothing as he pulled to the curb in front of my house. The porch light was on for us, and I swear I saw the curtain flutter. I hadn't been there for a few weeks, and the tree I'd planted with my dad's ashes was turning. The spreading maple was almost shading the garage in the twelve years it had been in the ground.

Jenks had already buzzed out Nick's open door, and as Nick leaned to get out, I reached for his arm. "Nick?" I questioned. He paused at the worried tone in my voice, easing back against the age-worn vinyl as I drew my hand away and looked at my knees. "Um, I want to apologize for my mom—before you meet her," I blurted.

He smiled, his long face going soft. He leaned across the front seat and gave me a quick kiss. "Moms are terrible, aren't they?" He got out, and I waited impatiently until he came around and jerked my door open for me.

"Nick?" I said as he took my hand and we started up the walk. "I mean it. She's a little whacked. My dad's death really threw her. She's not a psychopath or anything, but she doesn't think about what she's saying. If it comes into her head, it comes out her mouth."

His pinched expression eased. "Is that why I haven't met her yet? I thought it was me."

"You?" I questioned, then winced inside. "Oh. The human/witch thing?" I said softly, so he wouldn't have to. "No." Actually, I had forgotten about that. Suddenly nervous, I checked my hair and felt for my missing bag. My toes were cold, and the flip-flops were loud and awkward on the cement steps. Jenks was hovering beside the porch light, looking like a huge moth. I rang the bell and stood beside Nick. *Please make it one of her good days.*

"I'm glad it wasn't me," Nick said.

"Yeah," Jenks said as he landed on my shoulder. "Your mom ought to meet him. Seeing as he's bonking her daughter and all."

"Jenks!" I exclaimed, then steeled my face as the door opened.

"Rachel!" my mom cried, swooping forward and giving me a hug. I closed my eyes and returned her embrace. She was shorter than I was, and it felt odd. Hair spray caught in my throat over the faint whiff of redwood. I felt bad about not telling her the full truth about quitting the I.S. and the death threats I'd survived. I hadn't wanted to worry her.

"Hi, Mom," I said, pulling back. "This is Nick Sparagmos. And you remember Jenks?"

"Of course I do. It's good to see you again, Jenks." She stepped back into the threshold, a hand briefly going to her faded, straight red hair and then her calf-length, sweater dress. A knot of worry loosened in me. She looked good. Better than the last time. The mischievous glint was back in her eyes, and she moved quickly as she ushered us inside. "Come in, come in," she said, putting a small hand on Nick's shoulder. "Before the bugs follow you."

The hall light was on, but it did little to illuminate the shadowy green hallway. Pictures lined the narrow space, and I felt claustrophobic as she gave me another fierce hug, beaming as she pulled away. "I'm so glad you came," she said, then turned to Nick. "So you're Nick," she said, giving him a once-over, her lower lip between her teeth. She nodded sharply as she saw his scuffed dress shoes, then her lips twisted in thought as she saw my flip-flops.

"Mrs. Morgan," he said, smiling and offering his hand.

She took it, and I winced as she pulled him staggering into a hug. She was a great deal shorter than he was, and after his first startled moment, he grinned at me over her head.

"How wonderful to meet you," she said as she let him go and turned to Jenks.

The pixy had put himself at the ceiling. "Hi, Mrs. Morgan. You look nice tonight," he said warily, dipping slightly.

"Thank you." She smiled, her few wrinkles deepening. The house smelled like spaghetti sauce, and I wondered if I should have warned Mom that Nick was human. "Well, come all the way in. Can you stay for lunch? I'm making spaghetti. No problem to make a little more."

I couldn't help my sigh as she led the way to the kitchen. Slowly I started to relax. Mom seemed to be watching her mouth more than usual. We entered the kitchen, bright from the overhead light, and I breathed easier. It looked normal—human normal. My mom didn't do much spelling anymore, and only the dissolution vat of saltwater by the fridge and the copper spell pot on the stove gave anything away. She had been in high school during the Turn, and her generation was very discreet. "We just came to pick up my ley line stuff," I said, knowing my idea to get it and run was a lost cause since the copper pot was full of boiling water for pasta.

"It's no trouble," she said as she added a sheaf of spaghetti, ran her eyes down Nick, then added another. "It's after seven. You're hungry, aren't you, Nick?"

"Yes, Mrs. Morgan," he said, despite my pleading look.

She turned from the stove, content. "And you, Jenks. I don't have much in the yard, but you're welcome to what you can find. Or I can mix up some sugar water if you'd like."

Jenks brightened. "Thank you, ma'am," he said, flitting close enough to send the wisps of her red hair waving. "I'll check the yard. Would you mind if I gathered the pollen from your Rose of Sharon? It will do my youngest a world of good this late in the season."

My mother beamed. "Of course. Help yourself. Those damned fairies have just about killed everything looking for spiders." Her eyebrows arched, and I froze in a moment of panic. She had a thought. No telling what it was.

"Might you happen to have any children who would be interested in a late summer job?" she asked, and my breath escaped me in a relieved sound.

Jenks landed on her offered hand, wings glowing a satisfied pink. "Yes, ma'am. My son, Jax, would be delighted to work your yard. He and my two eldest daughters would be enough to keep the fairies out. I'll send them tomorrow before sunup if you like. By the time you have your first cup of coffee, there won't be a fairy in sight."

"Marvelous!" my mother exclaimed. "Those damn bastards have been in my yard all summer. Drove my wrens away."

Nick started at the foul word coming from such a mild-looking lady, and I shrugged.

Jenks flew an arching path from the back door to me in an unspoken request for me to open it. "If you don't mind," he said, hovering by the knob, "I'll just nip out and take a look. I don't want them running into anything unexpected. He's just a boy, and I want to be sure he knows what to watch out for."

"Excellent idea," my mother said, her heels clacking on the white linoleum. She flicked on the back light and let him out. "Well!" she said as she turned, eyeing Nick. "Sit down, please. Would you like something to drink? Water? Coffee? I think I have a beer somewhere."

"Coffee would be great, Mrs. Morgan," Nick said as he pulled a chair from under the table and lowered himself into it. I opened the fridge for the coffee, and my mom took the bag of grounds out of my hands, fussing with soft mother sounds until I sat beside Nick. The scraping of my chair was loud, and I wished she wasn't making such a fuss. Nick grinned, clearly enjoying my disquiet.

"Coffee," she said as she puttered about. "I admire a man who likes coffee with lunch. You have no idea how glad I am to meet you, Nick. It's been so long since Rachel brought a boy home. Even in high school she wasn't much for dating. I was starting to wonder if she was going to lean the other way, if you know what I mean."

"Mom!" I exclaimed, feeling my face go as red as my hair.

She blinked at me. "Not that there's anything wrong with that," she amended, scooping out the grounds and filling the filter. I couldn't look at Nick, hearing the amusement in him as he cleared his throat. I put my elbows on the table and dropped my head into my hands.

"But you know me," my mother added, her back to us as she put the coffee away. I cringed, waiting for whatever was going to come out of her mouth. "I'm of the mind that it's better to have no man than the wrong one. Your father, now, he was the right man."

Sighing, I looked up. If she was talking about Dad, she wouldn't be talking about me.

"Such a good man," she said, motions slow as she went to the stove. She stood sideways so she could see us as she took the lid off the sauce and stirred it. "You need the right man to have children with. We were lucky with Rachel," she said. "Even so, we almost lost her."

Nick sat up interested. "How so, Mrs. Morgan?"

Her face went long in an old worry, and I rose to plug the coffeemaker in, since she had forgotten. The coming story was embarrassing, but it was a known embarrassment, much better than what she might come out with, especially after having mentioned children. I sat down beside Nick as my mom started in with the usual opening line.

"Rachel was born with a rare blood disease," she said. "We had no idea it was there, just waiting for an inopportune match to show itself."

Nick turned to me, his eyebrows raised. "You never told me that."

"Well, she doesn't have it anymore," my mother said. "The nice woman at the clinic explained everything, saying that we were fortunate with Rachel's older brother, and that we had a one-out-of-four chance that my next child would be like Rachel."

"That sounds like a genetic disorder," he said. "You usually don't get better from those."

My mother nodded and turned the flame down under the boiling pasta. "Rachel responded to a course of herbal remedies and traditional medications. She's our miracle baby."

Nick didn't look convinced, so I added, "My mitochondria were kicking out this odd enzyme, and my white blood cells thought it was an infection. They were attacking healthy cells as if they were invaders, mostly the bone marrow and anything that had to do with blood production. All I know was, I was tired all the time. The herbal remedies helped, but it was when puberty kicked in that everything seemed to settle down. I'm fine now, except for being sensitive to sulfer, but it did shorten my life span by about ten years. 'Least, that's what they tell me."

Nick touched my knee under the table. "I'm sorry."

I flashed him a smile. "Hey, what's ten years? I wasn't supposed to make it to puberty." I didn't have the heart to tell him that even with ten years sliced off my life expectancy, I was still going to live decades past him. But he probably already knew that.

"Monty and I met at school, Nick," my mother said, bringing the conversation back to its original topic. I knew she didn't like talking about the first twelve years of my life. "It was so romantic. The university had just started their paranormal studies, and there was a lot of confusion about prerequisites. Anyone could take anything. I had no business being in a ley line class, and the only reason I signed up for it was because the gorgeous hunk of witch in front of me at the registrar's office was, and all my alternate classes were full."

Her spoon in the pot slowed, and steam wafted over her. "Funny how fate seems to push people together sometimes," she said softly. "I took that class to sit next to one man, but ended up falling in love with his best friend." She smiled at me. "Your father. All three of us partnered for the lab. I would have flunked if it hadn't been for Monty. I'm not a ley line witch, and since Monty couldn't stir a spell to save his life, he set all my circles for me the next two years in return for me invoking all his charms for him until he graduated."

I had never heard this one before, and as I rose to get three coffee mugs, my gaze fell upon the pot of red sauce. Brow pinching, I wondered if there was a tactful way to spill it down the garbage disposal. She was cooking in her spell pot again, too. I hoped she had remembered to wash it in saltwater, or lunch might be a bit more interesting than usual.

"How did you and Rachel meet?" my mother asked as she nudged me away from the pot and set a loaf of frozen bread to bake in the oven.

Eyes suddenly wide, I shook my head in warning at Nick. His eyes flicked from me to my mother. "Ah, a sporting event."

"The Howlers?" she questioned.

Nick looked to me for help, and I sat beside him. "We met at the rat fights, Mom," I said. "I bet on the mink, and he bet on the rat."

"Rat fights?" she said, making a face. "Nasty business, that. Who won?"

"They got away," Nick said, his eyes soft on mine. "We always imagined they escaped together and fell madly in love and are living in the city's sewers somewhere."

I choked back a laugh, but my mother let hers flow freely. My heart seemed to catch at the sound. I hadn't heard her laugh in delight in a long time.

"Yes," she said as she set her oven mitts aside. "I like that. Minks and rats. Just like Monty and me with no more children."

I blinked, wondering how she had jumped from rats and minks to her and Dad, and how that related to them not having any more children.

Nick leaned close and whispered, "Minks and rats can't procreate, either."

My mouth opened in a silent, Oh, and I thought that perhaps Nick, with his odd way of seeing the world, might understand my mother better than I did.

"Nick, dear," my mom said as she gave the sauce a quick, clockwise turn. "You don't have a cellular disease in your family, do you?"

Oh, no, I thought in panic as Nick answered evenly, "No, Mrs. Morgan."

"Call me Alice," she said. "I like you. Marry Rachel and have lots of kids."

"Mom!" I exclaimed. Nick grinned, enjoying it.

"But not right away," she continued. "Enjoy your freedom together for a while. You don't want children until you're ready. You are practicing safe sex, yes?"

"Mother!" I shouted. "Shut up!" *God, help me get through this night.*

She turned, one hand on her hip, the other holding the dripping spoon. "Rachel, if you didn't want me to bring it up, you should have spelled your hickey."

I stared at her, my mouth agape. Mortified, I rose and pulled her into the hall. "Excuse us," I managed, seeing Nick grinning.

"Mom!" I whispered in the safety of the hall. "You ought to be on medication, you know that?"

Her head drooped. "He seems like a nice man. I don't want you to drive him away like you do all your other boyfriends. I loved your father so. I just want you to be that happy."

Immediately my anger fizzled to nothing, seeing her standing alone and upset. My shoulders shifted in a sigh. *I should come over more often*, I thought. "Mom," I said. "He's human."

"Oh," she said softly. "Guess there isn't much safer sex than that, is there?"

I felt bad as the weight of that simple statement fell on her, and I wondered if that might change her opinion of Nick. There could never be any children between Nick and me. The chromosomes didn't line up right. Finding that out for sure had been the end of a long-running controversy among Inderlanders, proving that witches, unlike vamps and Weres, were a separate species from humans, as much as pixies or trolls. Vamps and Weres, whether bitten or born to their status, were only modified humans. Though witches mimicked humanity almost perfectly, we were as different as bananas from fruit flies at a cellular level. With Nick, I would be barren.

I had told Nick the first time our cuddling turned to something more intent, afraid he would notice if something didn't look quite right. I had been almost sick with the thought he would react in disgust about the different species thing. Then I almost cried when his only wide-eyed question had been, "It all looks and works the same, doesn't it?"

At the time, I honestly hadn't known. We had answered that question together.

Flushing at such thoughts in front of my mother, I gave her a weak smile. She returned it, pulling her slight body up straight. "Well," she said, "I'll go open a jar of alfredo, then."

Tension drained from me, and I gave her a hug. Her grip had a new tightness to it, and I responded in kind. I'd missed her. "Thanks, Mom," I whispered.

She patted my back, and we stepped apart. Not meeting my eyes, she turned to the kitchen. "I've an amulet in the bathroom if you want it, third drawer down." She took a breath, and with a cheerful face headed into the kitchen with quick, short steps. I listened for a moment, deciding nothing had changed as she chattered happily to Nick about the weather while packing the tomato-based sauce away. Relieved, I thumped down the shadowed hall in my flip-flops.

My mom's bathroom looked eerily like Ivy's—minus the fish in the bathtub. I found the amulet, and after washing off the Covergirl, I invoked the spell, pleased at the result. A final primp and sigh at my hair, and I hustled back to the kitchen. No telling what my mom would tell Nick if I left her alone with him too long.

Sure enough, I found them together with their heads almost touching as she pointed at the photo album. He had a cup of coffee in his hands, the steam drifting between them. "Mom," I complained. "This is why I never bring anyone over."

Jenks's wings made a harsh clatter as he rose from my mother's shoulder. "Aw, lighten up, witch. We've already got past the naked baby pictures."

I closed my eyes to gather my strength. Moving with a happy swing in her step, my mother went to stir the alfredo sauce. I took her place by Nick, pointing down. "That's my brother, Robert," I said, wishing he would return my phone calls. "And there's my dad," I said, feeling a soft emotion fill me. I smiled back at the photo, missing him.

"He looks nice," Nick said.

"He was the best." I turned the page, and Jenks landed on it, hands on his hips as he strolled over my life, carefully arranged in neat little rows and columns. "That's my favorite picture of him," I said, tapping an unlikely looking group of eleven- and twelve-year-old girls standing before a yellow bus. We were all sunburned, our hair three shades lighter than usual. Mine was cropped short and stuck out all over. My dad was standing beside me, a hand on my shoulder as he smiled at the camera. I felt a sigh slip from me.

"Those are all my friends at camp," I said, thinking my three years there had been some of my best summers. "Look," I said, pointing. "You can see the lake. It was way up in New York somewhere. I only went swimming once, since it was so cold. Made my toes cramp up."

"I never went to camp," Nick said, looking at the faces intently.

"It was one of those 'Make-a-Wish' camps," I said. "They kicked me out when they figured out I wasn't dying anymore."

"Rachel!" my mother protested. "Not everyone there was dying."

"Most were." My mood went somber as my gaze roved over the faces, and I realized I was probably the only one in the picture still alive. I tried to remember the name of the thin black-haired girl standing beside me, not liking it when I couldn't. She had been my best friend.

"Rachel was asked to not come back after she lost her temper," my mom said, "not because she was getting well. She got it into her head to punish a little boy for teasing the girls."

"Little boy," I scoffed. "He was older than everyone else there and a bully."

"What did you do?" Nick asked, a glint of amusement in his brown eyes.

I got up to put coffee in my mug. "Threw him into a tree."

Jenks snickered, and my mother rapped the spoon on the side of the sauce pot. "Don't be modest. Rachel tapped the ley line the camp was built on and threw him thirty feet up."

Jenks whistled and Nick's eyes grew wide. I poured out the coffee, embarrassed. It hadn't been a very good day. The brat had been about fifteen, and was tormenting the girl whose shoulder my arm was draped over in the picture. I had told him to leave her alone, and when he pushed me down, I lost it. I hadn't even known how to draw on a ley line; it just kind of happened. The kid landed in a tree, fell, and cut his arm. There had been so much blood, I got scared. The young vamps in the camp all had to take a special overnight trip across the lake until they could dig up the dirt he had bled on and burn it.

My dad had to fly up and sort things out. It was the first time I had used ley lines, and basically the last until I went to college since my dad had tanned my hide but good. I'd been lucky they hadn't made me leave right then and there.

I went back to the table, looking at him smiling at me from the photo. "Mom, can I have this picture? I lost mine this spring when—a misaligned spell took them out." I met Nick's eyes, the shared understanding in them reassuring me he'd say nothing about my death threats.

My mom sidled close. "That's a nice one of your father," she said, pulling the photo out and handing it to me before she went back to the stove.

I sat down in my chair and looked at the faces, searching for a name for any of them. I could recall none. It bothered me.

"Um, Rachel?" Nick said, peering down at the album.

"What?" *Amanda?* I silently asked the dark-haired girl. *Was that your name?*

Jenks's wings flashed into motion, sending my hair to dance about my face. "Holy crap!" he exclaimed.

I looked down to the picture that had been under the one now in my hand and felt my face go white. It was the same day, since the background was of the bus. But this time, instead of being surrounded by preadolescent girls, my dad was next to a man who was a dead ringer for an older Trent Kalamack.

My breath wouldn't come out. The two men were smiling, squinting against the sun. They had an arm companionably about each other's shoulders and were clearly happy.

I exchanged frightened looks with Jenks. "Mom?" I finally managed. "Who is this?"

She came close, making a small sound of surprise. "Oh, I had forgotten I had that one. That's the man who owned the camp. Your father and he were such good friends. It broke your dad's heart when he died. And so tragically, too, not six years after his wife. I think that was part of the reason your dad lost the will to fight. They died only a week apart, you know."

"No, I didn't," I whispered, staring down. It wasn't Trent, but the resemblance was eerie. It had to be his father. My dad had known Trent's father?

I put a hand to my stomach in a sudden thought. I had gone to camp with a rare blood disease and left every year feeling better. Trent dabbled in genetic research. His father might have done the same. My recovery had been called a miracle. Perhaps it had been outlawed, immoral, genetic manipulation. "God help me," I breathed.

Three summers at camp. Months of not waking until almost sundown. The unexplained soreness in my hip. The nightmares I still occasionally woke from, of a cloying vapor.

How much? I wondered. What had Trent's father taken from my dad in payment for the life of his daughter? Had he exchanged it for his own?

"Rachel?" Nick said. "Are you okay?"

"No." I concentrated on breathing, staring at the picture. "Can I have this one, too, Mom?" I asked, hearing my voice as if it weren't my own.

"Oh, I don't want it," she said, and I slipped it out, fingers trembling. "That's why it was underneath. You know I can't throw anything of your father's away."

"Thanks," I whispered.

Fifteen

I wedged one of my fuzzy pink slippers off and dismally scratched the back of my calf with my toe. It was after midnight, but the kitchen was bright, gleams of fluorescent light reflecting off my copper spell pots and hanging utensils. Standing at the stainless steel island, I ground the pestle into the mortar, pulping the wild geranium into a green paste. Jenks had found it in a vacant lot for me, trading one of his precious mushrooms for it. The pixy clan that worked the lot had gotten the better end of the deal, but I think Jenks felt sorry for them.

Nick had made us sandwiches about a half an hour ago, and the lasagna was put away into the fridge still hot. My bologna sandwich had been tasteless. I didn't think I could blame it all on the fact that Nick hadn't put ketchup on it as I asked, saying he couldn't find any in the fridge. Stupid human foible. I'd find it endearing if it didn't tick me off so much.

Ivy had yet to show, and I wouldn't eat the lasagna by myself in front of Nick. I wanted to talk to her but I'd have to wait until she was ready. She was the most private person I knew, not even telling herself what her feelings were until she found a logical reason to justify them.

Bob the fish swam in my next-to-the-largest spell pot beside me on the counter. I was going to use him as my familiar. I needed an animal, and fish were animals, right? Besides, Jenks would flip out if I so much as hinted at a kitten, and Ivy had given her owls to her sister after one narrowly escaped being torn apart when it caught Jenks's youngest daughter. Jezebel was fine. The owl might be able to fly again. Someday.

Depressed, I continued to grind the leaves to a pulp. Earth magic held more power when made between sunset and midnight, but tonight I was having difficulty concentrating, and it was already past one. My thoughts kept circling back to that photo and the Make-a-Wish camp. A heavy sigh escaped me.

Nick looked up from the opposite side of the counter, where he was perched on a bar stool finishing off the last of the bologna sandwiches. "Give it up, Rachel," he said, smiling to soften his words, clearly knowing where my thoughts lay. "I don't think you've been tampered with, and even if you were, how could anyone prove it?"

I let the pestle fall still and pushed the mortar away. "My father died because of me," I said. "If it hadn't been for me and my damned blood disease, he'd still be here. I know it."

His long face went sad. "In his mind, it was probably his fault you were sick."

That made me feel a whole lot better, and I slumped where I stood.

"Maybe they were just friends, like your mom said," Nick offered.

"And maybe Trent's father tried to blackmail my dad into something illegal and died because he wouldn't do it." *At least he had taken Trent's dad with him.*

Nick stretched his long arm out to snag the photo still on the counter where I had dropped it. "I don't know," he said, his voice soft as he gazed at it. "They look like friends to me."

I wiped my hands off on my jeans and leaned to take the picture. My eyes crinkled as I scanned my dad's face. Sealing my emotions away, I handed it back. "I didn't get well because of herbal remedies and spells. I've been tampered with."

It was the first time I had said it aloud, and my stomach tightened. "But you're alive," he offered.

I turned away and measured six cups of springwater. The tinkling as it ran into my largest copper spell pot sounded loud. "What if it got out?" I asked, unable to look at him. "They'd pack me up and put me away on some frozen island like I was a leper, afraid whatever he did to me might mutate into something and start another plague."

"Oh, Rachel . . ." Nick slipped from his stool. Anxious, I busied myself needlessly drying the measuring cup. He came up behind me, giving me a backward hug before turning me around to face him. "You're not a plague waiting to happen," he cajoled, meeting my eyes. "If Trent's father cured your blood disease, then he did. But it was just that. He fixed it. Nothing's going to happen. See? I'm still here." He smiled. "Alive and everything."

I sniffed, not liking that it bothered me so much. "I don't want to owe him anything."

"You don't. This was between your father and Trent's, and that's assuming it even happened." His hands were warm around my waist. My feet were between his, and I laced my fingers behind his back and balanced my weight against his own. "Just because your dad and Trent's father knew each other, it doesn't mean anything," he said.

Right, I thought sarcastically. We let go of each other at the same time, stepping reluctantly away. While Nick stuck his head in the pantry, I checked over my recipe for the transfer medium. The text I had for binding a familiar was in Latin, but I knew the scientific names of the plants enough to follow it. I was hoping Nick would help with the incantation.

"Thanks for keeping me company," I said, knowing that he had a half-day shift at the university tomorrow and a night shift at the museum. If he didn't leave soon, he wouldn't get any sleep before he had to go to work.

Nick glanced at the black hallway as he sat down on his stool with a bag of chips. "I was hoping to be here when Ivy came back. Why don't you spend the night at my house?"

My lips curled in a smile. "I'll be fine. She won't come home until she's calmed down. But if you're going stay for a while, how about sketching some pentagrams for me?"

The crackle of plastic stopped. Nick looked at my black paper and silver chalk stacked suspiciously on the counter, then to me. Amusement lit his eyes, and he finished rolling down the edges of the bag. "I'm not going to do your homework, Ray-ray."

"I know what they look like," I protested, putting the clippings of my hair into the spell pot and pushing them down with my ceramic spoon until they sank. "I promise I'll copy them myself later. But if I don't hand them in tomorrow, she'll flunk me and Edden will deduct the cost of tuition from my fee. It's not fair, Nick. The woman has it in for me!"

Nick ate a chip, skepticism pouring from him. "You know them?" I nodded, and he wiped his hand on his jeans before pulling my textbook closer. "All right," he challenged as he tilted the book so I couldn't see. "What does a pentagram of protection look like?"

My breath escaped me in a relieved whoosh, and I added the sanicle decoction I'd prepared earlier. "Standard graph with two braided lines in the outer circle."

"Okay . . . How about divination?"

"New moons sketched at the points, and a mobius strip in the center for balance."

The amused glint in Nick's eye turned to surprise. "Summoning?" he prompted.

I smiled and dropped the pulped wild geranium into the brew. The bits of green hung suspended as if the water were a gel. Cool. "Which one? Summoning internal power or a physical entity?"

"Both."

"Internal power has acorns and oak leaves in the midpoints, and summoning an entity uses a Celtic chain binding the points." Smug at his obvious surprise, I adjusted the flame under the pot and dug in my silverware drawer for a finger stick.

"Okay. I'm impressed." The book slipped down and he grabbed a handful of chips.

"You'll copy them for me?" I asked, delighted.

"Promise you'll do them yourself later?"

"Deal," I said cheerfully. I had already finished the short essays. Now all I had to do was make Bob my familiar and I'd be set. Piece of cake. I looked at Bob and cringed. *Yeah. Piece of cake.* "Thanks," I said softly as Nick straightened my black drawing paper by tapping the ends on the counter.

"I'll make them sloppy so she thinks you did them," he said.

I gave him a raised eyebrow look. "Thanks a lot," I amended dryly, and he grinned. Done with the brew, I jabbed my finger and massaged out three drops of blood. The scent of redwood blossomed as they plunked into the pot and the spell quickened. So far, so good.

"Earth witches don't use pentagrams," Nick said as he sharpened the chalk by rubbing it against a piece of scrap paper. "How come you know them?"

Careful to keep my bloodied finger clear, I polished my scrying mirror with a velveteen scarf borrowed from Ivy. A shudder sifted through me at the cold feel of it. I hated scrying. It gave me the willies. "From those pentagram jelly glasses," I said. Nick looked up, the lost look on his face making me feel good for some reason. "You know. Those jelly jars you can use for juice glasses when they're empty? These had pentagrams on the bottom and their uses written on the side. I lived on peanut butter and jelly sandwiches that year." My mood went soft at the memory of my dad quizzing me over toast.

Nick rolled his sleeves up and started sketching. "And I thought I was bad for digging to the bottom of my cereal box for the toy."

I was done with the prep work and ready to do some serious spelling. Time to set my circle. "In or out," I asked, and Nick looked up from my homework, blinking. Seeing his confusion, I added, "I'm ready to set my circle. Do you want to be in or out of it?"

He hesitated. "You want me to move?"

"Only if you want to be out of it."

His look turned incredulous. "You're going to enclose the entire island?"

"Is that a problem?"

"No-o-o-o." Nick scooted his bar stool closer. "Witches must be able to hold more ley line power than humans. I can't make a circle much bigger than three feet across."

I smiled. "I don't know. I'd ask Dr. Anders if she wouldn't make me feel like an idiot. I think it depends. My mom can't hold a circle bigger than three feet, either. So . . . in or out?"

"In?"

My breath slipped from me in relief. "Good. I was hoping you'd say that." Leaning over the counter, I plunked my spell book down beside him. "I need your help translating this."

"You want me to do your homework and help you bind your familiar, too?" he protested.

I winced. "The only spell I could find in my books was in Latin."

Nick looked at me in disbelief. "Rachel. I sleep at night."

I glanced at the clock above the sink. "It's only one-thirty."

Sighing, he slid the book to him. I knew he wouldn't be able to resist once he started, and sure enough, his mild annoyance shifted to hot interest before he had read more than a paragraph. "Hey, this is old Latin."

I leaned across the counter until my shadow covered the print. "I can read the plant names, and I'm sure I made the transfer medium right, as it's standard, but the incantation is iffy."

He wasn't listening anymore, his brow furrowed as he ran a long finger under the text. "Your circle needs to be modified to resolve and gather power."

"Thanks," I said, glad he was going to help. I didn't mind muddling through most things, but spelling was an exact science.

And just the idea that I needed a familiar made me uncomfortable. Most witches had them, but ley line witches needed them as a matter of safety. Dividing one's aura helped prevent a demon from pulling you into the ever-after. Poor Bob.

Nick went back to sketching pentagrams for me, glancing up as I pulled my twenty pound bag of salt from under the counter and set it thumping on top. Acutely aware of his eyes on me, I scraped a handful from the clumping mass. At Ivy's insistence, I had blown off the security deposit and etched a shallow circle in the linoleum. Ivy had helped. Actually, Ivy had done all of it, using a string and chalk contraption to be sure the circle was perfect. I'd sat on the counter and let her have at it, knowing it would tick her off if I got in her way. The result was an absolutely perfect circle. She had even taken a compass and marked true north with black nail polish to show me where to start my circle.

Now, peering down to find the black dot, I carefully sifted salt, moving clockwise around the island until I found my starting point. I added the doodads for protection and divination, put the green candles at the appropriate places, then lit them from the flame that I'd used to make the transfer medium.

Nick watched with half his attention. I liked that he accepted me as a witch. When we had met, I'd worried that since he was one of the few humans who practiced the black arts, I would eventually have to smack him up and turn him in, but Nick had taken demonology to improve his Latin and get through a language development class, not to summon demons. And the novelty of a human who accepted magic with such ease was a definite turn-on.

"Last chance to leave," I said as I turned the gas burner off and moved the media to the center island.

Nick made a noise deep in his throat, setting his perfect pentagram aside and starting on the next. Envious of his smooth, straight lines, I pushed my paraphernalia aside to make a clear spot on the counter across from him.

The memory of being punished for having unknowingly tapped into a ley line and flinging the camp bully into a tree flashed through me. I thought it stupid that my dislike of ley lines might stem from the childhood incident, but I knew it was more than that. I didn't trust ley line magic. It was too easy to lose sight of which side one's magic was on.

With earth witchcraft, it was easy. If you have to slaughter goats, it's probably a good bet it's black magic. Ley line magic required a death payment, too, but it is a more nebulous death taken from your soul, much harder to quantify and easier to dismiss—until it's too late.

The cost for white ley line witchcraft was negligible, tantamount to me pulling weeds and using them in my spelling. But the unfiltered power available through ley lines was seductive. It took a strong will to stick to self-imposed limits and remain a white ley line witch. The boundaries that looked so reasonable and prudent when set, often seemed foolish or timid when the strength of a line coursed through you. I'd seen too many friends go from the "pulling weeds" analogy to "slaughtering goats" without even realizing they'd made the jump to the black arts. And they never listened, saying I was jealous or a fool. Eventually I'd find myself hauling their asses down to the I.S. lockup when they put a black charm on the cop who pulled them over for going fifty in a thirty-five zone. Maybe that was why I couldn't keep my friends.

Those were the ones that bothered me, basically good people who had been tempted by a power greater than their will. They were pitiable, their souls slowly eaten away to pay for the black magic they played with. But it was the professional black witches who scared me, those strong enough to foster the soul-death onto someone else to pay for their magic. Eventually, though, the soul-death found its way home, probably dragging a demon along with it. All I knew was, there was screaming, and blood, and great big booms that shook the city.

And then I didn't have to worry about that particular witch anymore.

I wasn't that strong of will. I knew it, accepted it, and avoided the problem by shunning ley lines whenever I could. I hoped that taking a fish as my familiar wasn't the start of a new path but just a speed bump in my current road. Glancing at Bob, I vowed that's all it would be. All witches had familiars. And there was nothing in that binding spell that would hurt anyone.

Taking a slow breath, I closed my eyes to prepare myself for the coming disorientation of connecting to a ley line. Slowly I willed my second sight into focus. The stench of burnt amber tickled my nose. An unseen wind shifted my hair though the kitchen window was closed. It was always windy in the ever-after. I imagined the walls that surrounded me becoming transparent, and in my mind's eye they did.

My second sight strengthened, and the sensation of being outside grew until the mental scenery beyond the walls of the church became as real as the counter, unseen under my fingers. Eyes closed to block my mundane vision, I glanced over the nonexistent kitchen with my mind's eye. Nick didn't show up at all, and the memory of the church's walls had vanished to faint, silvery chalk lines. Through them, I could see the surrounding landscape.

It was parklike, with a glowing red haze reflecting off the bottom of clouds where Cincinnati would be, hiding behind the stunted trees. It was common knowledge that the demons had their own city, built on the same ley lines as Cincinnati. The trees and plants carried a similar reddish glow, and though no wind whispered through the linden tree outside the kitchen, the branches of the stunted ever-after trees tossed in the wind that lifted my hair. There were people who got off on the discrepancies between reality and the ever-after, but I thought it freaking uncomfortable. Someday, I'd go up Carew Tower and look at the broken, glowing demon city with my second sight. My stomach tightened. *Yeah, sure I would.*

My gaze was drawn to the graveyard by the stark, almost glowing white tombstones. They and the moon were the only things that seemed to exist without that red glow, unchanged in both worlds, and I stifled a shudder. The ley line made a solid-looking red smear running due north at head height above the tombstones. It was small—not even twenty yards, I guessed—but so underused that it seemed stronger than the enormous ley line the university straddled.

Conscious that Nick was probably watching with his own second sight, I stretched out my will and touched the ribbon of power. I staggered, forcing my eyes to remain shut as my grip tightened on the counter. My pulse leapt and my breath quickened. "Swell," I whispered, thinking the force surging into me seemed stronger than the last time.

I stood and did nothing as the influx continued, trying to equalize our strengths. My fingertips tingled and my toes ached as it backwashed at my theoretical extremities, which mirrored my real ones. Finally it began to balance, and a trace of energy left me to rejoin the line. It was as if I was part of a circuit, and the line's passage left a growing residue that made me feel slimy.

The link with the ley line was heady, and I was no longer able to keep my eyelids closed; they flew open. My cluttered kitchen replaced the silver outlines. Queasy with disorientation, I tried to reconcile my mind's eye with my more mundane vision, using them simultaneously. Though I couldn't see Nick with my second sight, it would cast shadows upon him through my usual vision.

Sometimes there was no difference, but I was willing to bet Nick wouldn't be one of those people. Our eyes met, and I felt my face go slack.

His aura was rimmed in black. It wasn't necessarily bad, but it pointed to an uncomfortable direction. His narrow build looked gaunt, and where his bookish mien gave him a scholarly air before, now it had undertones of danger. But what shocked me was the black circular shadow upon his left temple. It was where the demon he had saved me from had put its mark, an IOU that Nick would someday have to repay. Immediately I looked at my wrist.

My skin showed only the usual upraised scar tissue in the shape of a circle with a line running through it. That didn't mean that was all Nick could see, though. Holding my arm up, I asked him, "Is it glowing black?"

He nodded solemnly, his usual appearance starting to overshadow his threatening look as my mind's eye began to falter under the strength of my mundane sight.

"It's the demon mark, isn't it?" I said as I ran my fingers over my wrist. I didn't see any hint of black, but I couldn't see my aura, either.

"Yes," he said softly. "Did, uh, anyone tell you that you look really different while channeling a ley line?"

I nodded, my balance wavering as the two realities clashed. "Different" was better than "scary as all hell," which is what Ivy had called me once. "Do you want out of the circle? I haven't closed it yet."

"No."

Immediately I felt better. A properly closed circle couldn't be broken except by its maker. He didn't mind being trapped inside with me, and his show of trust was gratifying.

"All right, then. Here goes." Taking a steadying breath, I mentally moved the narrow rill of salt from this dimension to the ever-after. My circle made the jump with the sharpness of a snapping rubber band against my skin. I started as the salt winked out of existence, replaced with an equal ring of ever-after. The spine-tingling jolt was expected, but it got me every time.

"I hate it when it does that," I said as I glanced at Nick, but he was staring at my circle.

"Whoa," he breathed in awe. "Look at that. Did you know they were going to do that?"

I followed his gaze to the candles, and my jaw dropped. They had gone transparent. The flames still flickered, but the green wax glowed with an utterly unreal look.

Nick slid from his stool, edging carefully around the counter to avoid hitting the circle. He crouched by one of the candles, and I almost panicked when he extended a finger to touch it.

"No!" I shouted, and he jerked his hand back. "Um, I think they shifted to the ever-after with the salt. I don't know what touching them will do. Just . . . don't. Okay?"

He nodded as he stood. Looking properly cowed, he went back to his stool. He didn't pick up the chalk, though. He was going to watch. I smiled weakly at him, not liking that I was at such a disadvantage with ley line magic. But if I followed the recipe, I'd be fine.

All but the barest remnant of power I had drawn from the ley line was now running through my circle. I could feel it pressing against my skin. The molecule-thin slice of the ever-after was a red smear between me and the rest of the world, making a dome arching just over my head. Nothing could get through the bands of alternating realities. The oblong sphere was mirrored below me as well, and if it had run into any pipes or electrical lines, the circle would not have been perfect, but vulnerable to breakage at that point.

Though most of the ley line force had gone into sealing the circle, there was already a secondary buildup beginning in me. It was slower, almost insidiously so. It would continue until I broke the circle and disconnected from the ley line. Ley line witches knew how to properly store power, but I didn't, and if I remained connected to the line too long, it would drive me insane. The bare hour I'd need would come nowhere near too long.

Satisfied the circle was secure, I let my second sight die completely. The vision of Nick's aura was lost to me. "Ready for step two?" he asked, and I nodded.

Setting his pentagrams completely aside, he pulled the old book closer. His brow furrowed as he ran a finger under the text to leave a chalk mark as he read. "Next, you remove all charms and spells from yourself." He looked up. "Maybe you should have taken a salt bath."

"No. The only charms I have are amulets." I pulled the spell I had gotten from my mom off, the cord tugging at my hair. I felt my neck, giving Nick a lopsided grin at his attention on it. After a moment's hesitation, I worked my pinkie ring off and set it aside.

"I knew it!" Nick exclaimed. "I knew you had freckles. It was the ring, wasn't it?"

He was reaching out, and I handed it to him across the clutter between us. "My dad gave it to me for my thirteenth birthday," I said. "See the wood inlay? I have to renew it every year."

Nick glanced at me from under his bangs. "I like your freckles."

Embarrassed, I took my ring back and set it aside. "What do I do now?"

He glanced down. "Um . . . prepare the transfer medium."

"Done," I said, giving the spell pot a sharp tap to hear it ring. *This wasn't so bad.*

"Okay . . ." He was silent, and the ticking clock seemed to grow loud. Still reading, he said, "Now you have to stand on your scrying mirror and push your aura down into your reflection." His brown eyes pinched in worry as they met mine. "You can do that?"

"In theory. That's why I was so picky about the circle. Until I get my aura back, I'll be vulnerable to all sorts of things." He nodded, his gaze distant in thought. "Will you watch and tell me if it works? I can't see my own aura."

"Sure. It isn't going to hurt, is it?"

I shook my head as I took up the scrying mirror and set it on the floor. Looking down at its black surface, I was reminded of why I had worked so hard to avoid ley line magic. Its perfect blackness seemed to soak up the light, but at the same time was still shiny. I couldn't see myself in it, and it pegged my creepy meter.

"Barefoot," Nick added, and I kicked off my slippers. Taking a deep breath, I stepped onto the mirror. It was as cold as it was black, and I stifled a shiver, feeling I might fall through it as if it were a pothole.

"Euwie," I said, making a face at the pulling sensation from under my feet.

Nick stared, standing up and looking over the counter at my feet. "It's working," he said, his face suddenly pale.

Swallowing, I took my hands and ran them down my head as if pushing off water. An ache set my head to throb.

"Oh, yeah," Nick said, sounding sick. "That pulls it off much faster."

"It feels awful," I muttered as I continued to push my aura down to my feet. I knew it was going by the soft ache its absence left behind. There was a taste of metal on my tongue, and I glanced at the black surface, my mouth dropping as I saw my reflection in it for the first time. My red hair hung about my face, looking just as I would have expected, but my features were lost behind a smear of amber. "Is my aura brown?" I asked.

"It's bright gold," Nick answered as he dragged his stool around to my side of the counter. "Mostly. I think you got it all. Can we . . . move on?"

Hearing the unease in his voice, I met his eyes. "Please."

"Good." He sat and pulled the book onto his lap. Head bowed, he read the next passage. "Okay, put the scrying mirror into the transfer medium, being careful not to let your fingers touch the media or your aura will reattach and you'll have to start over."

I refused to look in the mirror, worried that I'd see myself trapped in it. Shoulders tense, I scuffed my slippers back on. My feet ached and my head throbbed with the beginnings of a migraine. If I didn't finish this quickly, I was going to be stuck in a dark room with a washcloth all day tomorrow. Taking up the mirror, I gingerly slipped it into the media. The specks of wild geranium flashed to nothing, dissolved by my aura. It was eerie, even by my standards, and I couldn't help an "ooooh" of appreciation. "What's next?" I asked, wanting to be done with it so I could take my aura back.

Nick's head was bent over the book. "Next, you need to anoint your familiar with the transfer medium, but you have to be careful to not touch the media yourself." He looked up. "How do you anoint a fish?"

I felt my face go slack. "I don't know. Maybe I could just slip him into the vat along with the mirror?" I reached for the book on his lap, turning the page. "Isn't there anything about making a fish your familiar?" I questioned. "Everything else is in there."

Nick pushed my hands from the pages as one tore. "No. Go put your fish in the spell pot. If it doesn't work, we'll try something else."

My mood went sour. "I don't want my aura smelling like fish," I said as I dipped a hand into Bob's bowl, and he snickered.

Bob didn't want to go in the spell pot. Trying to catch his darting shape in a round bowl was almost impossible. Getting him out of the bathtub had been easy—I simply drained it until he was beached—but now, after a frustrating moment of near misses, I was ready to dump him onto the floor. Finally I got him and, dripping water over the counter, dropped him in. I peered into the spell pot, watching his gills pump the amber liquid.

"Okay," I said, hoping he was all right. "He's anointed. What's next?"

"Just an incantation. And when the transfer medium goes clear, you can take back the aura your familiar left you."

"Incantation," I said, thinking ley line magic was stupid. Earth magic didn't need incantations. Earth magic was precise and beautiful in its simplicity. My eyes shifted to the not-there candles and I stifled a shudder.

"Here. I'll read it for you." He stood up with the book, and I made a spot for it beside Bob in the bowl. I leaned close to him over the book, thinking he smelled good, manly good. Intentionally bumping into him, I felt a warm current that was probably his aura. Too busy deciphering the text, he didn't notice. Sighing, I put my attention on the book.

Nick cleared his throat. His eyebrows bunched and his lips moved as he whispered the words, sounding dark and dangerous. I caught about one in every three words. He finished, giving me one of his half smiles. "How about that," he said. "It rhymes."

A sigh shifted my shoulder. "Do I need to say it in Latin?"

"I wouldn't think so. The only reason they made these things rhyme is so the witch can remember them. It's the intent behind the words rather than the words themselves that does the trick." He bent back over the book. "Give me a moment and I'll translate it. I think I can even make it rhyme for you. Latin is very loose in its interpretation."

"Okay." Nervous and jittery, I tucked my hair behind an ear and looked into the spell pot. Bob didn't look happy.

" 'Pars tibi, totum mihi. Vinctus vinculis, prece factis.' " Nick looked up. "Ah, 'some to you, but all to me. Bound by ties made so by plea.' "

I dutifully repeated it, feeling silly. Invocations. Could it be any more hokey? Next I'd be standing on one foot and shaking a posy of feathers at the full moon.

Nick's finger ran under the print. " 'Luna servata, lux sanata. Chaos statutum, pejus minutum.' " His brow furrowed. "Let's go with, 'Moon made safe, ancient light made sane. Chaos decreed, taken tripped if bane.' "

I echoed him, thinking ley line witches had a substantial lack of imagination.

" 'Mentem tegens, malum ferens. Semper servus, dum duret mundus.' Ah, I'd say, "Protection recalled, carrier of worth. Bound before the world's rebirth.' "

"Oh, Nick," I complained, "are you sure you're translating that right? That's dreadful."

He sighed. "Try this then." He thought for a moment. "You could also translate it as, 'lee of mind, bearer of pain. Slave until the worlds are slain.'"

That I could live with, and I said it, feeling nothing. We both peered in at Bob, waiting for the amber liquid to go clear. My head pounded, but other than that, nothing happened. "I think I did it wrong," I said, scuffing my slippers.

"Oh—shit," Nick swore, and I looked up to find him staring over my shoulder at the doorway to the kitchen. He swallowed hard, his Adam's apple bobbing.

The hair on the back of my neck pricked. My demon scar gave a pulse. Breath catching, I spun around, thinking Ivy must be home.

But it wasn't Ivy. It was a demon.

Sixteen

"**N**ick!" I cried, stumbling back. The demon grinned. It looked like an aristocratic Brit, except that I recognized it as the one who put on Ivy's face and tore out my throat that spring.

My back found the counter. I had to run. I had to get out of here! It would kill me! Flailing to put the counter between us, I hit the spell pot.

"Watch the brew!" Nick shouted, reaching out even as the bowl tipped.

I gasped, tearing my gaze from the demon long enough to see Bob's bowl spill. Aura-laced water spilled over the counter in an amber wash. Bob slid out, flopping.

"Rachel!" Nick exclaimed. "Get the fish! He has your aura. He can break the circle!"

I'm in a circle, I thought, strangling my panic. *The demon isn't. It can't hurt me.*

"Rachel!"

Nick's shout tore my eyes from the grinning demon. Nick was desperately trying to catch Bob, flopping on the counter, and keep the spilled water from reaching the edge. My face went cold. I was willing to bet just the aura-laced water would be enough to break the circle.

I lunged for the paper towels. As Nick fumbled for Bob, I made a mad dash around the counter, laying squares of white to sop up rivulets before they could make puddles on the floor that would run to the circle. My heart pounded and I frantically alternated my attention from the water to the demon standing with a bewildered, amused expression in the archway to the hall.

"Gotcha," Nick whispered, his breath exploding from him in a ragged sound as he finally gained control of the fish.

"Not the saltwater!" I warned as Nick held him over my dissolution pot. "Here." I shoved Bob's original bowl at Nick. Ordinary water sloshed out, and I blotted it up as Nick dropped Bob in. The fish shuddered, sinking to the bottom with his gills pumping.

Silence descended, framed by the heavy rasping of our breathing and the ticking of the clock above the sink. Nick's and my eyes met over the bowl. As one, we turned to the demon.

It looked pleasant enough, having taken the shape of a young man with a mustache, elegant and polished. It was dressed as an eighteenth century businessman in a suit of green velvet with lace trim and long tails. Round glasses were perched atop its thin nose. They were smoked to hide its red eyes. Though able to shift its form and shape at will—becoming everything from my roommate to a punk rocker—its eyes stayed the same unless it made the effort to take on all the abilities of whomever it was mimicking. Hence, my demon bite laced with vamp saliva. A tremor shook me as I recalled that its pupils were slitted like a goat's.

Fear tightened my stomach, and I hated being afraid. I forced my hands to unclench their grip on my elbows, pulled myself straight and tossed my head. "Ever think of updating your wardrobe?" I mocked. *I was safe in a circle. I was safe in a circle.*

My breath caught as a red mist of ever-after hazed it. The demon's clothes molded to a modern-day business suit I'd expect to see on a Fortune-twenty executive. "This is so . . . common," it said, its resonate, British-laden accent perfect for the stage. "But I wouldn't want it said that I wasn't accommodating." It took its glasses off, and my breath hissed in. I stared at the alienness of its eyes, jerking as Nick touched my arm.

Nick looked wary—not nearly scared enough to please me—and I felt a flush of embarrassment at my earlier panic. But damn it, demons scared the crap out of me. No one risked calling up demons since the Turn. Except for whoever called this one up to maul me last spring. And then there had been the one that attacked Trent Kalamack. Maybe demon summoning was more common than I wanted to admit.

I hated that Nick's respect for them stopped short of terror. They fascinated him, and I was afraid his search for knowledge would someday lead him to make a foolish decision, letting the tiger turn and eat him.

The demon smiled to show thick flat teeth as it glanced over its attire. It made a deep-in-thought sound and the wool disappeared, to become a black T-shirt tucked into leather pants with a gold chain belted around narrow hips. A black leather jacket appeared, and the demon stretched in a cloud of sensuality, showing every curve of the new, attractive muscle pulling its T-shirt tight across its chest. Blond hair cut short grew as it shook its head, and its height lengthened.

I felt myself pale. It had become Kist, pulling my old fear of him right out of my head. The demon seemed to take great delight in changing into whatever frightened me the most. I wouldn't let it shake me. I wouldn't.

"Oh, this is nice," the demon said, its accent shifting to a sultry, bad-boy drawl to match its new look. "You're afraid of the prettiest people, Rachel Mariana Morgan. I rather like being this one." Licking its lips suggestively, it sent its gaze across my neck, lingering on the scar it had given me while I was sprawled on the floor of the university library's basement, lost in a haze of vamp-saliva-induced ecstasy as it killed me.

The memory sent my heart pounding. My hand rose to cover my neck. The pressure from its gaze pushed on my skin, making it tingle. "Stop it," I demanded, frightened as it sent the scar into play and tendrils of feeling ran like molten metal from my neck to my groin. My breath hissed in through my nose. "I said stop it!"

The blue of Kist's eyes went wide and flashed to red. Seeing my resolve, the demon's outlines blurred. "You aren't afraid of this one anymore," it said, its voice shifting to become lower and laden with a proper British accent again. "Pity. I do so like to be young and testosterone laden. But I know what frightens you. Let's keep that a secret, hum? No need to let Nick Sparagmos know. Not yet. He may want to buy the information."

Nick's breathing sounded harsh beside me as the demon doffed the biker's hat—which promptly vanished in a haze of ever-after red—and shifted, returning to its previous form of British nobility in lace and green velvet. It smiled at me over its round smoked glasses. "This will do, in the meantime," it said.

I jumped as Nick touched me. "Why are you here?" he asked. "No one called you."

The demon said nothing, glancing over the kitchen with undisguised curiosity. Showing a predatorial grace, it began to circle the bright room, its shiny buckled boots silent on the linoleum. "I know you are new to all of this," it mused aloud as it tapped at

Mr. Fish's brandy snifter on the windowsill and the fish quivered, "but generally the summoner is *outside* the circle, and the summoned is on the *inside*." It turned on a heel to send its long coattails furling. "I'll give you that for free, Rachel Mariana Morgan. Because you made me laugh. I haven't laughed since the Turn. We all laughed at that."

My pulse had slowed but my knees felt watery. I wanted to sit down but didn't dare. "How can you be here?" I asked. "This is holy ground."

The vision of British grace opened my fridge. Making a tsk-tsk sound, it shuffled through the leftovers, coming out with a half-empty container of fudge frosting. "Oh yes, I *do* like this arrangement. Being on the outside is *ever* so much more interesting. I think I'll answer that query for free as well."

Oozing old world charm, it pulled the top of the frosting off. The blue plastic disappeared in a smear of ever-after, and the demon dipped the gold spoon that had taken its place into the container. "This isn't holy ground," it said as it stood in my kitchen in a gentleman's frock and ate frosting. "The kitchen was added after the sanctuary was blessed. You could have the entire grounds sanctified, but then you'd connect your bedroom to the ley line in the graveyard. Ooooh, and wouldn't *that* be delightful."

A sick feeling twisted my stomach at what that might mean. Eyebrows raised, it looked at me over its smoked glasses, its red eyes showing a shocking amount of sudden ire. "You had better have something worth hearing, or I'm going to be royally buggered."

I straightened in understanding. It thought I had summoned it with an offer of information to pay off my IOU. My pulse jackhammered back into full throttle as the container of frosting vanished from the demon's hand and it came close to the circle.

"Don't!" I blurted as it tapped the sheet of ever-after between us. The demon's face lost its amusement and, expression deadly serious, it ran its attention over the seam with the floor. I gripped Nick's arm as it mumbled about tearing summoners limb from limb, interrupted teas, and how inconsiderate it was to pull someone from their dinner or Wednesday night telly. Adrenaline shook me as the demon dissolved to a red mist and sank through the floorboards.

I clutched at Nick, my knees threatening to give way. "He's checking for pipes," I said. "There are no pipes. I looked." Fear made my shoulders hurt as I waited for the demon to rise through the floor at my feet and kill me. "I looked!" I asserted, trying to convince myself.

I knew the circle bisected rocks and roots, and the top of it went into the attic, but as long as there wasn't an open path like a phone or gas line, the circle was secure. Even a laptop could break a circle if it was connected to the net and an e-mail came in.

"Oh good. He's back," Nick breathed as the demon reappeared outside the circle, and I stifled a laugh, knowing it would sound hysterical. What kind of a life did I have when seeing a demon was a good thing?

The demon stood before us, taking a tin of what probably wasn't snuff out of a tiny vest pocket and sniffing a pinch of black powder into both nostrils. "You cast a well-built circle," it said between cultured sneezes. "As good as your father's."

My eyes widened and I stepped to the circle's edge. "What do you know of my dad?"

"Reputation, Rachel Mariana Morgan," it simpered. "Strictly reputation. He was not in my realm of expertise when he was alive. Now that he's dead, I'm interested. I specialize in secrets. As does Nick Sparagmos, it seems." It put the tin away and pulled Ivy's chair out from before her computer. "Now," it said idly as it shook the mouse and brought up the Internet, "as amusing as this is, can we get on with it? Your circle is tight. I won't be killing you now." Its red eyes went sly. "Later, perhaps."

I followed its gaze to the clock over the sink. It was one-forty. I hoped Ivy didn't walk in on this. An undead vamp might survive a demon attack, but a live one would stand as much of a chance as me.

I took a breath to tell it to go away because I didn't call it, but a thought stopped me cold. It knew Nick's last name. It had said it twice.

"It knows your last name," I said, turning to Nick. "Why does it know your name?"

Nick's mouth opened and his eyes slid to the demon. "Ah . . ."

"Why does it know your name?" I demanded, my hands on my hips. I was tired of being afraid, and Nick was a convenient outlet. "You've been calling it up, haven't you!"

"Well . . ." he said, his long face reddening.

"You idiot!" I shouted. "I told you not to call it. You promised you wouldn't!"

"No," he said, his hands taking a grip on my shoulders. "I didn't. You said I wouldn't. And it just sort of happened. I didn't even mean to call him the first time."

"The first?" I exclaimed. "How many times have there been?"

Nick scratched the bristles on his cheek. "See, I was sketching pentagrams—for practice. I wasn't going to do anything. He appeared, thinking I was trying to call him with some information to pay off my debt. Thank God I was in a circle." Nick glanced at the soggy papers with their silver chalk lines. "Just like he showed up tonight."

Together we turned to the demon, and it sent its shoulders to rise and fall in a shrug. It seemed more than willing to wait out our argument, more interested in Ivy's favorites list than us at the moment.

"It's an it, not a him," I said. "And I'm not going to let you blame this on the demon."

"How very kind of you, Rachel Mariana Morgan," the demon said, and I scowled.

Nick was starting to look angry. On sudden impulse I pushed the hair from his left temple. My breath caught as I saw two lines bisecting his demon scar instead of one. "Nick!" I wailed. "You know what happens when you get too many of those?"

He took a bothered step back, and his brown hair fell to hide it.

"It can pull you into the ever-after!" I shouted, wanting to smack him a good one. I had only one line through my demon scar, and the worry still kept me up at night.

Nick said nothing, watching me with unrepentant eyes. Damn it all to hell, he wasn't even trying to explain himself. "Talk to me!" I exclaimed.

"Rachel," he said. "Nothing is going to happen. I'm being careful."

"But you have two IOUs," I protested. "If you don't make good, you belong to it."

He smiled confidently, and I cursed his belief that the printed word held all the answers and he would be safe if he followed the rules. "It's okay," he said as he took my shoulders again. "I've only entered into a trial contract."

"Trial contract . . ." I stammered, floored. "Nick, this isn't twenty CDs for a penny with only three more to buy. It's trying to take your soul!"

The demon chuckled, and I flicked a glance at it.

"That's not going to happen," Nick soothed. "I can call on him whenever I want, same as if I gave him my soul. And at the end of three years I walk away with no ties or commitments."

"If it sounds like too good a deal, you aren't looking at the fine print."

Still he smiled, his face showing confidence instead of the terror he should have been feeling. "I read the fine print." His finger rose to touch my lips and stop my outburst. "All of it. I get minor questions answered for free, and I can put larger questions to him on credit."

My eyes closed. "Nick. Did you know your aura is rimmed in black? You look like a wraith in my mind's eye."

"So do you, love," Nick whispered, pulling me close.

Shocked, I did nothing as his arms went about me. *My aura was as tainted as his? I hadn't done anything but let it save my life.*

"He has all the answers, Rachel," Nick whispered, and I felt my hair move with his breath. "I can't help it."

The demon cleared its throat, and I pulled away from Nick.

"Nick Sparagmos is my best student since Benjamin Franklin," the demon said, its accent making it sound completely reasonable as it touched Ivy's screen to make it go blue. It didn't fool me, though. The thing couldn't be swayed by pity, guilt, or remorse. If it had found a way past my circle, it would have killed us both for the audacity of calling it from the ever-after—whether it had been intentional or not.

"Though Attila could have gone far if he had been able to look past the military applications," it continued, looking at its nails. "And it is hard to best Leonardo di ser Piero da Vinci for outright cleverness."

"Name dropper," I muttered, and the demon inclined its head graciously. It was more obvious than words that if Nick had the demon at his beck and call for three years, he would agree to anything to keep it there. Which was exactly what the demon was counting on.

"Um, Rachel," Nick said as he took my elbow. "Since he's here, you might want to arrange for a summoning name from him so he doesn't show up every time you close a circle and draw a pentagram. That's how he got my name. I gave it to him for his summoning name."

"I know your names, Rachel Mariana Morgan," the demon said. "I want a secret."

My stomach clenched. "Sure," I said tiredly, scrambling for

something. I had a few of those. My eyes fell on the photo of my dad and Trent's father, and I silently held it up to the transparent sheet of ever-after.

"Where's the secret in that?" the demon mocked. "Two men standing before a bus." Then it blinked. I watched, fascinated, as the horizontal slits went wide until its eyes were almost black. It stood, reaching out for it. A muttered curse slipped past its lips as its fingers smacked into the barrier. I smelled burnt amber.

My pulse leapt at its sudden interest. Maybe it was enough to completely pay off my debt. "Interested?" I taunted. "Clear my debt, and I'll tell you who they both are."

The demon fell back, chuckling. "Oh, you think it's that important?" it mocked. But its eyes tracked the photo as I set it on the counter behind me. Without warning, it shifted forms. The red blur of ever-after melted and flowed. I stared, appalled, as it took on my face. It even had freckles. It was like staring into a mirror, and my skin crawled as my image moved without my volition. Nick went ashen, his long face slack as he stared from me to it.

"I know who both men are," the demon said in my voice. "The one is your father, the other is Trenton Aloysius Kalamack's father. But the camp bus?" Its eyes fastened on me in a devious delight. "Rachel Mariana Morgan, you have indeed given me a secret."

It knew Trent's middle name? Then the same demon attacked us both. Someone had wanted us both dead. For an instant I was tempted to ask the demon who, then dropped my eyes. I could find that out on my own, and it wouldn't cost me my soul.

"Call us even for you having taken me through the ley lines and leave me forever," I said, and the demon laughed. I wondered if my teeth were really that big when I opened my mouth.

"Oh, you are a love," it said in my voice and its accent. "Seeing that picture is enough to buy a summoning name, perhaps, but if you want to absolve your debt, I need something more. Something that could mean your death if it was whispered into the right ear."

The thought that I might be rid of it completely filled me with a reckless daring. "What if I told you why I was there? At that camp?" Nick moved nervously beside me, but if I got rid of the demon forever, it would be worth it.

The demon snickered. "You flatter yourself. That can't be worth your soul."

"Then I'll tell you why I was there if I can summon you safely even without a circle," I blurted, thinking it didn't want to clear my debt simply so it would have a chance at me later.

At that, the demon laughed, turning my stomach as its appearance grotesquely shifted back to the British gentleman even as it roared in mirth. "A promise of safety without a circle?" it said, wiping its eyes when it could speak again. "There's nothing on this God-stinking earth that's worth that."

I swallowed hard. My secret was good—and all I wanted was to be free of it—but it wouldn't believe it was worth it unless I told it first. "I had a rare blood disease," I said before I could change my mind. "I think Trent's father fixed it with his illegal genetic therapy."

The demon chortled. "You and several thousand other brats." Coattails furling, it strode to the edge of the circle. I backpedaled to the counter, heart pounding. "You had better start taking this seriously, or I will lose my good . . ." It jerked as it caught sight of my book, open to the charm for binding a familiar. ". . . temper," it finished, the word trailing to nothing.

"Where did you—" it stammered, then it blinked, sending its goat-slitted eyes over me, then Nick. I couldn't have been more surprised when a small sound of disbelief escaped it. "Oh," it said, sounding shocked. "Damn me thrice."

Nick reached behind me, closing the book and covering it with my sheets of black paper. Suddenly I felt ten times more nervous. My gaze roved over the transparent candles and the pentagram made out of salt. What in hell was I doing?

The demon backed away with a deep-in-thought, toe-to-heel motion. White-gloved hand to its chin, it eyed me with a new intentness, giving me the sensation that it could see through me as easily as I could see through those green candles I had lit, not knowing what they were for. Its quick shift from anger to surprise to an insidious contriving went right to my core, shaking me.

"Well now, let's not be hasty," it amended, its brow furrowed as it glanced at the gadget-strewn watch that appeared on its wrist the instant it looked down. The watch was a twin to Nick's. "What to do, what to do. Kill you or keep you? Hold to tradition or bow to progress? I do believe the only thing that will stand up in court is to let you decide." It smiled, and an unstoppable shiver shook me. "And we do want this to be legal. Very, very legal."

Frightened, I slid down the counter to tuck into Nick. *When did what was legal mean anything to a demon?*

"I will not kill you if you summon me without a circle," the demon said abruptly, its heels making a sharp tap on the linoleum as it backed up, excitement showing in its jerky motions. "If I'm right, I will be giving you this anyway. We'll know soon." It grinned wickedly. "I can hardly wait. Either way, you're mine."

I jumped as Nick took my elbow. "I've never heard of a promise of safety without a circle," he whispered, his gaze pinched. "Ever."

"That's because it's only given to the walking dead, Nick Sparagmos."

The bad feeling in the pit of my stomach started working its way upward, tightening every muscle on the way. There was nothing on this God-stinking earth worth a risk-free summoning, but it gave me that instead of absolving me from my debt? *Oh, that had to be good.*

I had overlooked something. I knew it. Resolute, I pushed the feeling aside. I'd made bad deals before and survived them. "Fine," I said, my voice quavering. "I'm done with you. I want you to go directly back to the ever-after with no deviations along the way."

The demon glanced at its wrist again. "Such a harsh mistress," it said elegantly, in a grand mood as it opened the freezer and took out a frozen box of microwave fries. "But as you're in the circle and I'm out here, I'll leave when I damn well please." Its white-gloved hand was enveloped in a red smear, clearing to show the fries steaming. Opening the fridge, it frowned. "No ketchup?"

Two P.M., I thought, glancing at the clock. *Why was that important?* "Nick," I whispered, going cold. "Take the batteries out of your watch. Now."

"What?"

The clock above the sink said five minutes to two. I wasn't sure how accurate it was. "Just do it!" I shouted. "It's connected to Colorado's atomic clock. It sends out a pulse at midnight their time to reset everything. The pulse will break the circle, just like an active phone line or gas pipe."

"Oh . . . shit," Nick said, his slack face going white.

"Damn you witch!" the demon shouted, furious. "I almost had you both!"

Nick was frantically working at his watch, his long fingers prying at the back. "Do you have a coin? I need a dime to get the back off." His eyes were frightened as they jerked to the clock above the sink. His hand went into a pocket, searching.

"Give it here!" I exclaimed, snatching the watch. I threw it on the counter. Plucking the meat-tenderizing hammer from the rack above me, I swung.

"No!" Nick cried as pieces of watch went everywhere. "We had three minutes yet!"

I shrugged off his grip and beat at it. "You see!" I exclaimed, bringing the hammer down again and again. "You see how clever it is?" Adrenaline made my motions jerky as I brandished the wooden hammer at him. "It knew you had that watch. It was just waiting! That's why it agreed to giving me a safe summoning!" With a cry of frustration, I threw the hammer at the demon. It hit the unseen wall of the circle and bounced back to clatter at my feet. There wasn't much left of Nick's watch but a bent back and shards of quartz.

Nick slumped against the counter, the fingers of one hand pressing into his forehead as he bowed his head. "I thought he *wanted* to teach me," Nick whispered. "All those times, he was just trying to get me to keep him with me until the circle broke."

He jumped as I touched his shoulder, staring at me with frightened eyes. Finally he was frightened. "Do you understand now?" I said bitterly. "It's going to kill you. It's going to kill you and take your soul. Tell me you won't call it again. Please?"

Nick took a quick breath. He met my eyes, shaking his head. "I'll be more careful," he whispered.

Frustrated, I spun to the demon. "Get out of here like I told you to!" I shouted.

With an unearthly grace, the demon stood. The vision of a British gentleman took a moment to adjust the lace about its throat and then its cuffs. Motions slow and deliberate, it pushed the chair back under the table. It inclined its head to me, its red eyes watching from over its glasses. "Congratulations on binding your familiar, Rachel Mariana Morgan," it said. "Summon me with the name Algaliarept. Tell anyone my name, and you're mine by default. And don't think that because you don't have to be in a circle to summon me that you're safe. You are mine. Not even your soul is worth your freedom."

And with that it vanished in a smear of red ever-after, leaving the scent of grease and fried potatoes.

Seventeen

I sat at the lab stool and tapped my ankle against the rungs. "How much longer do you think she can drag this out?" I asked Janine as I tossed my head to Dr. Anders. The woman was at her desk before the blackboard, testing one of the students.

Janine popped her gum and twirled a finger in her enviably straight hair. Her previous fear of my demon mark had turned into a rebellious daring after I told her I got it through my past work with the I.S. Yes, it was ninety percent a lie, but I couldn't bear her distrust of me.

"Familiar evaluations take forever," the young woman agreed. The fingers of her free hand were gentling the fur between her cat's ears. The white Manx had his eyes closed, clearly enjoying the attention. My gaze slid to Bob. I had put him in one of those big peanut butter tubs with a lid to get him there. Janine had "oooohed" over him, but I knew it was a sympathy oooh. Most everyone had cats. One had a ferret. I thought that was cool, and the man to whom it belonged said they made the best familiars.

Bob and I were the only two left to be evaluated, and the room was almost empty, but Janine was waiting for Paula, the student with Dr. Anders. I nervously pulled Bob's bucket closer and glanced out the window to the lights just now flickering on over the parking lot.

I was hoping to see Ivy that night. We still hadn't crossed paths since Nick knocked her out. I knew she'd been around. There was coffee in the pot that afternoon, and the messages were cleared. She had gotten herself up and out before I woke up. That wasn't like her at all, but I knew better than to force a conversation before she was ready.

"Hey," Janine said, jerking my attention back. "Paula and I are going out to Piscary's for some lunch before the sun goes down and the place fills up with undead vamps. Do you want to come? We'll wait for you."

Her offer pleased me more than I wanted to admit, but I shook my head. "Thanks, no. I've already made plans to meet my boyfriend." Nick was working in the next building over, and as he quit today about the time my class was supposed to end, we were going to Micky-d's for his dinner and my lunch.

"Bring him along," Janine urged, her thick blue eyeliner clashing with her otherwise tasteful appearance. "Having one guy at a table of girls always brings the good-looking, single men to the table."

I couldn't help my smile. "No-o-o-o," I hedged, not wanting to tell her Piscary scared the peas out of me, set my demon scar tingling, and was my roommate's uncle, for lack of a better word. "Nick's human," I said. "It'd be kind of awkward."

"You're dating a human!" Janine whispered harshly. "Hey, is it true what they say?"

I gave her a sideways look as Paula finished with Dr. Anders and joined us. "About what?" I asked as Paula shoved her unwilling cat into a collapsible carrier amid yowls and spitting. I stared, appalled, as she zipped the door shut.

"You know . . ." Janine nudged my arm. "Do they have, uh . . . Are they really . . ."

Pulling my eyes from the shaking carrier, I grinned. "Yeah. They do. They really are."

"Yowsers!" Janine exclaimed, reaching to take Paula's arm. "You here that, Paula? I gotta charm me a human before I get too old to appreciate him."

Paula was flushed, looking especially red against her blond hair. "Stop it," she hissed, shooting a glance at Dr. Anders.

"What?" Janine said, not a bit flustered as she opened her carrier and her cat voluntarily went in, curling up and purring. "I wouldn't marry one, but what's wrong with rolling around with a human while you're looking for Mr. Right? My dad's first wife was human."

Our conversation was cut short as Dr. Anders cleared her throat. Janine grabbed her purse and slid off the lab stool. Giving the two women a thin smile, I reluctantly dragged Bob's peanut butter tub off the lab bench and made my way forward. Nick's pentagrams were tucked under my arm, and Dr. Anders didn't look up as I slid the container onto the open space of her desk.

I wanted to wrap this up and get out of here. Nick was going to drive me out to the FIB tonight after lunch so I could talk to Sara Jane. Glenn had asked her to come in so he could get an idea of Dan's daily patterns, and I wanted to ask her about Trent's whereabouts the last few days. Glenn wasn't happy about my angle of investigation, but it was my run, too, damn it.

Nervous, I forced myself to the back of the chair beside Dr. Anders's desk, wondering if Jenks was right and Sara Jane's coming to the FIB was Trent's roundabout way to get his claws into me. One thing was certain. Dr. Anders wasn't the witch hunter. She was nasty, but she wasn't a murderer.

The two women hesitated in the doorway to the hall, their cat carriers pulling them both off balance. "See you Monday, Rachel," Janine said.

I gave her a wave, and Dr. Anders made an annoyed noise deep in her throat. The uptight woman put a blank form on top of the stack of papers and printed my name in large block letters.

"Turtle?" Dr. Anders guessed as she glanced at my container.

"Fish," I said, feeling like an idiot.

"At least you know your limits," she said. "Being an earth witch, it would be difficult for you to hold enough ever-after to bind a rat to you, much less the cat I'm sure you wanted."

Her voice was just shy of patronizing, and I had to unkink my hands from their tight grip.

"You see, Ms. Morgan," Dr. Anders said as she opened the lid and took a peek, "the more power you can channel, the smarter your familiar needs to be. I have an African gray parrot as my familiar." She brought her gaze to mine. "Is that your homework?"

I stifled a surge of annoyance and handed her a pink folder full of short essays. Under it were Nick's water-spotted pentagrams, the black paper curling and warped.

Dr. Anders's lips were so tight, they were bloodless. "Thank you," she said, tossing Nick's sketches aside without even a cursory glance. "You've got a reprieve, Ms. Morgan. But you don't belong in my class, and I will remove you the first chance I get."

I kept my breathing shallow. I knew she wouldn't dare say that if anyone else was in the room.

"Well," she murmured as if tired, "let's see how much aura your fish was able to accept."

"It took a lot." My mood shifted to one of nervousness. Nick had looked over my aura before he left last night, pronouncing it to be rather thin. It would slowly replace itself, but in the interim I felt vulnerable.

Dr. Anders kept her opinion of my obvious fluster to herself. Gaze going distant, she dipped her fingers into Bob's water. The skin on the back of my neck tightened, and it seemed as if my hair drifted in the wind that always seemed to blow in the ever-after. I watched, fascinated, as a blue smear from her hands enveloped Bob. It was ley line power, having turned from red to blue as it reflected the dominant color in the woman's aura.

It was unlikely that Dr. Anders was drawing upon the university's ley line. The power had been taken earlier and stored; it made for faster spell casting. I was willing to bet having a sphere of ever-after in her gut was what made the woman so sour.

The blue haze about Bob vanished as Dr. Anders drew her fingers out of the water. "Take your fish and get out," the woman said brusquely. "Consider yourself flunked."

Floored, I could do nothing but stare. "What?" I finally managed.

Dr. Anders wiped her fingers dry on a tissue and threw it in her trash can under her desk. "This fish isn't bound to you. If it were, the ley line force I cloaked it with would have turned to the color of your aura." Her gaze went indistinct—as if she was looking through me—then her focus sharpened. "Your aura is a sickly gold. What have you been doing, Ms. Morgan, to get it soiled with such a thick haze of red and black?"

"But I followed the instructions!" I cried, not standing up as she began writing on my form. "I'm missing a good chunk of my aura. Where is it?"

"Maybe a bug got into your circle," she said irately. "Go home, call your familiar, and see what comes."

Heart pounding, I licked my lips. *How the hell do you call your familiar?*

She looked up from her writing, putting her crossed arms down upon the page. "You don't know how to call your familiar."

It wasn't a question. I lifted my left shoulder and let it fall in a shrug. What could I say?

"I'll do it," she muttered. "Give me your hand."

I started as she grabbed my wrist. Her bony grip was surprisingly strong. The metallic taste of ash coated my tongue as Dr. Anders muttered an incantation. It was like chewing tinfoil, and I pulled away as soon as her fingers slackened. Rubbing my wrist, I watched Bob, willing him to swim to the surface, or toward me, or something. He just sat on the bottom and swished his tail.

"I don't understand," I whispered, feeling betrayed by my books and the spell-casting abilities I was so confident in. "I followed the instructions to the letter."

Dr. Anders was positively smug. "You will find, Ms. Morgan, that unlike earth magic, ley line manipulation requires more than an unimaginative adherence to rules and to-do lists. It needs talent and a certain amount of freethinking and adaptability. Go home. Make a pet out of whatever shows up on your doorstep. And don't come back to my classroom."

"But I did everything right!" I protested, standing up as she made shooing motions and shuffled her papers in dismissal. "I stood on the scrying mirror and pushed my aura off. I got it into the transfer medium without touching it. I put Bob in with it—"

Dr. Anders jerked, turning her thin face up to me. "Scrying mirror?"

"I said the incantation," I continued. "Nick said it didn't matter if I couldn't say it in Latin." Frustrated, I stood before her desk and fumed. If I left, it would be over. It wasn't the money anymore. It was this woman thinking I was stupid.

"Latin?" Dr. Anders's face was slack.

"I said it," I protested, replaying the night in my head. "And then—" My breath caught and my face went cold. "And then the demon showed up," I whispered, sinking down on the chair before my knees gave way. "Oh God. Did it take my aura? Did the demon take my aura?"

"Demon?" She looked appalled. "You called a demon?"

I panicked, sitting there at the nasty woman's desk. I was scared out of my panties, and I didn't care if she knew it. Algaliarept had my aura. "It got through the circle!" I babbled, forcing myself to not clutch at her arm. "Somehow it got my aura through the circle!"

"Ms. Morgan!" Dr. Anders exclaimed. "If a demon got in your circle, you would not be sitting in front of me. You'd be in the ever-after with it, begging for your death!"

Frightened, I sat where I was with my arms clasped about me. I was a runner, not a demon killer.

The woman looked angry as she tapped her pen on the desktop. "What were you doing summoning a demon? Those things are dangerous."

"I didn't," I gushed. "You gotta believe me. It showed up on its own. See, I owe it a favor for taking me through the ley lines after it was sent to kill me. It was the only way to get back to Ivy before I bled to death. And it thought that I was trying to call it to settle my debt, what with the circle and pentagrams that Nick was copying for—uh—me."

Her eyes flicked to the water-spotted drawings. "Your boyfriend did these, did he?"

Again I nodded, unable to outright lie to her. "I was going to redo them myself later," I said. "I didn't have time to do two weeks of homework and catch a murderer both."

Dr. Anders stiffened. "I did not kill my past students."

My eyes dropped and I felt myself start to calm. "I know."

She took a breath, holding it for a moment before letting it out. I felt some kind of ley line force pass between us, and sat wide-eyed, wondering what she was doing. "You don't think I killed them," she finally said, and the feeling that I was chewing tinfoil stopped. "So why are you in my class?"

"Captain Edden of the FIB sent me to find evidence that you're the witch hunter," I said. "He won't pay me if I don't follow up on his idea. You're obnoxious, overbearing, and the meanest thing I've seen since my fourth-grade teacher, but you're not a murderer."

The older woman slumped as the tension drained from her. "Thank you," she whispered. "You don't know how good it is to hear someone say that." She pulled her head up, shocking me with a weak smile. "The not-murdering part," she added. "The adjectives I'll ignore."

Seeing a hint of humanity in her, I blurted, "I don't like ley lines, Dr. Anders. Where's the rest of my aura?"

She took a breath to say something, stopping as her gaze went over my shoulder to the door. I spun in my chair at the tentative knock on the frame. Nick peeked round the open door, and I felt my face light up. "I apologize, Dr. Anders," he said, making a show of his university work ID clipped to his shirt. "Can I interrupt for a moment?"

"I'm with a student," she said, the professional tone back in her voice. "I'll be with you in a moment if you'd like to wait in the hall. Could you shut the door, please?"

Nick winced, looking awkward as he stood in his jeans and casual shirt in the doorway. "Ah, it's Rachel I need to see. I'm really sorry for interrupting like this. I'm working in the next building over." He turned to look down the hall and back. "I wanted to see that she was all right. And possibly find out how much longer it was going to be?"

"Who are you?" Dr. Anders asked, her face blank.

"That's Nick," I said sheepishly. "My boyfriend."

Hunched in embarrassment, Nick fidgeted. "I don't know why I'm even bothering you," he said. "I'll go wait in the lounge."

A flash of what looked like horror passed over Dr. Anders. She looked from me to Nick, then surged to her feet. Heels clacking, she pulled him in and shut the door behind him.

"Stay there," she said as she left him bewildered in front of her desk. Nick's pentagrams sat before us like guilt given substance. Standing before the windows with her back to us, Dr. Anders looked at the dark parking lot. "Where did you get a familiar binding spell that was in Latin?" she asked.

Nick touched my shoulder in sympathy, and I wished I'd never gotten him into this. "Uh, out of one of my old spell books," I admitted, thinking she wanted Nick there for verification. "It was the only charm I could find on such short notice. But I know the pentagrams. I just didn't have the time to do them."

"There's a binding incantation in the appendix of your textbook," she said, sounding tired. "You were supposed to use that one." It wasn't the pentagrams she was worried about, and a cold feeling slid through me as she turned around. The wrinkles in her face looked harsh in the fluorescent light. "Tell me exactly what you did."

At Nick's encouraging nod, I said, "Uh, first I made the transfer medium. Then I closed the circle."

"Modified to summon and protect," Nick interrupted. "And I was inside it with her."

"Wait a moment," Dr. Anders said. "Just how big was your circle?"

I tucked my hair back, glad she wasn't barking at me anymore. "Maybe six feet?"

"Around?"

"Across."

She took a breath and sat down, motioning me to continue.

"Um, then I stood on my scrying mirror and pushed off my aura."

"What was that like?" she whispered, elbows on her desk as she stared out the window.

"Damn—uh—darn uncomfortable. I got the mirror into the

transfer medium without touching the surface. My aura precipitated out into the media, and then I put Bob into it."

"Into the transfer medium?"

I nodded, though she wasn't looking at me. "I figured that was the only way to anoint a fish. Then I said the incantation."

"Actually," Nick interrupted. "I said the incantation first in Latin, then translated it for her, giving her an alternate interpretation on the last part."

"That's right," I admitted. "I said it, and then the demon showed up." I glanced at Nick, but it didn't bother him as much as it bothered me. "Then I knocked over Bob's bowl. My aura was all over him. I was afraid he might break the circle if my aura touched it."

"It would have." Dr. Anders was staring at the parking lot again.

"Is that why some of my aura is missing?" I asked. "Did I throw it away with the paper towels?"

Dr. Anders brought her gaze to mine. "No. I think you made Nick your familiar."

My jaw dropped. I spun in my chair and looked up at Nick. His hand had fallen from my shoulder and he took a wide-eyed step back. "What?" I exclaimed.

"You can do that?" Nick asked.

"No. You can't," Dr. Anders said. "Sentient beings with free will can't be bound to another by incantation. But you mixed earth magic with ley line magic. I've never heard of binding a familiar like that. Where did you get that book?"

"My attic," I whispered. I looked up at Nick. "Oh, Nick," I said, embarrassed. "I'm really sorry. You must have picked up my aura when you were trying to catch Bob."

Nick looked confused. "I'm your familiar?" he whispered, his long face quizzical.

Dr. Anders made a bitter-sounding bark of laughter. "It's nothing to be proud of, Ms. Morgan. Taking a human as a familiar is heinous. It's slavery. Demonic."

"Hold up," I stammered, feeling myself go cold. "It was an accident."

The woman's eyes turned hard. "Remember what I said about a practioner's abilities being linked to his or her familiar? Demons use people as familiars. The more powerful the person is, the more power the demon can wield through him or her. That's why they are forever trying to educate the foolish in the dark arts. They teach them, gain control over their souls, then make them their familiars. You used demon magic by mixing earth and ley line witchcraft."

I put a hand to my stomach. "I'm sorry, Nick," I whispered.

He was pale, and he stood unmoving by my shoulder. "It was an accident."

Dr. Anders made a rude noise. "Accident or not, it's the foulest thing I've heard of. You have put Nick in a great deal of danger."

"How?" I fumbled for his hand. It was cold in mine, and he gave my fingers a squeeze.

"Because he's carrying some of your aura. Ley line witches give their familiars a portion of their aura to act as an anchor when they pull on a ley line. If something goes wrong, the familiar is pulled into the ever-after, not the witch. But more important, familiars insulate you from going insane from channeling too much ley line force. Ley line witches don't hold the energy they store from a line in themselves. They keep it in their familiars. Simon, my parrot, holds it for me, and I draw upon it as I need. When we're together, I'm stronger. When he's ill, my abilities decrease. If he's closer to a line than I am, I can reach it through him. If things go wrong, he dies, not me."

I gulped, cold as Dr. Anders eyed me as if I had done it on purpose.

"That's why animals are used as familiars," she said coldly. "Not people."

"Nick," I murmured. "I'm sorry." That was what, three times now I'd said it?

Dr. Anders's face wrinkled up. "Sorry? Until we get him unbound, you will not store any ley line energy. It's too dangerous."

"I don't know how to bind ley line force," I admitted. *I had made Nick my familiar?*

"Wait a moment." The woman put a thin hand to her forehead. "You don't know how to store ley line force? At all? You made a circle six feet across strong enough to keep out a demon using energy straight from the line? You didn't use any previously stored energy at all?"

I shook my head.

"You don't know how to hold even an ounce of ever-after?"

Again I shook my head.

The woman sighed. "Your father was right."

"You knew my dad?" I questioned. *Why not? Everyone else seemed to.*

"I taught one of his undergrad classes," she said. "Though I didn't know it at the time. I didn't see him again until thirteen years ago when we met to discuss you." She sat back and cocked her eyebrows. "He asked me to flunk you if you ever showed up in my class."

"Wh-Why?" I stammered.

"Apparently he knew how much strength you could pull from a line, as he wanted me to persuade you to turn to earth witchcraft instead of line magic. He said it would be safer. My class was overcrowded that year, and bending to a father's wish to protect his daughter was no skin off my nose. I had assumed he meant safer for you. In hindsight, I think he meant everyone else."

"Safer?" I whispered, feeling ill.

"Making a human your familiar isn't normal, Ms. Morgan," Dr. Anders said.

"Could you do it?" Nick asked, and I flicked a glance at him, glad he had asked, not me.

She looked affronted. "Probably. If I had the binding spell. But I wouldn't. It's demonic. The only reason I'm not calling Inderland Security is because it was an accident which we will soon rectify."

"Thanks," I breathed, numb. *I had made Nick my familiar? I had used demon magic to bind him to me?* Dizzy, I put my head between my knees, figuring it was marginally more dignified then passing out and falling to the floor. I felt Nick's hand on my back and stifled a hysterical laugh. *What had I done?*

Nick's voice came out of the blackness as I closed my eyes and struggled to keep from throwing up. "You can break the spell? I thought familiars were lifelong bonds."

"They generally are—for the familiar." She sounded tired. "But you can unbind one if your skill rises to the point where your familiar is holding you back. And then you have to supplant the old familiar with a better one. But what is better than a person, Nick?"

I pulled my head from between my knees to find Dr. Anders grimacing. "I need to see that book," she said. "There's probably something in it about how to unbind a person. Demons are notorious for taking something better when it comes along. I'd like to know how a book of demon magic ended up in your attic in the first place?"

"I live in a church," I whispered. "It was there when I moved in." I glanced out the window, my sick feeling starting to diminish. Nick had my aura. That was better than a demon having it. And we would be able to undo this—somehow. I had told Glenn I'd meet him at the FIB tonight, but Nick came first.

"I'll go get the book," I said, looking at the closed door. "Can we do this here, or does it have to be somewhere more private? We can go to my kitchen. I've a ley line in the backyard."

Dr. Anders had lost all of her ugliness. Now she looked simply tired. "I can't do anything tonight," she said, glancing apologetically at Nick. "But let me give you my address." She reached for a pen, scribbling across the folded evaluation of me and my familiar. "You can leave the book with the gateman, and I'll get to it this weekend."

"Why not tonight?" I asked as I took the paper.

"I'm busy tonight. I'll be giving a presentation tomorrow, and I have to prepare an updated success/failure statement." She flushed, which turned her years younger.

"Who for?" I asked, the cold feeling returning to the pit of my stomach.

"Mr. Kalamack."

My eyes closed in a strength-gathering blink. "Dr. Anders?" I said, hearing Nick shift from foot to foot beside me. "Trent Kalamack is the one killing the ley line witches."

The woman flashed back to her usual mien of scorn. "Don't be foolish, Ms. Morgan. Mr. Kalamack is no more a murderer than I am."

"Call me Rachel," I said, thinking we ought to be on a first-name basis. "And Kalamack is the witch hunter. I've seen the reports. He talked to every one of the victims within a month before their death."

Dr. Anders opened a lower drawer and pulled out a tasteful black purse. "I talked with him last spring at graduation and I'm still alive. He's interested in discussing my research. If I can capture his attention, he will fund me and I can do what I really want. I've been working six years to put this together, and I'm not going to lose my chance to catch a benefactor because of some fool coincidence."

I shifted to the edge of my chair, wondering how I could go from hating her to being worried so quickly. "Dr. Anders, please," I said, glancing up at Nick. "I know you think I'm a scatterbrained flop. But don't do this. I've seen the reports on the people he's killed. Every one of them died in terror. And Trent talked to all of them."

"Ah, Rachel?" Nick interrupted. "You don't know that for sure."

I spun to him. "You aren't helping!"

Dr. Anders stood with her purse. "Get me the book. I'll look at it this weekend."

"No!" I protested, seeing her tying up the ends of our conversation. "He'll kill you with no more thought than swatting a fly." My jaw gritted as she gestured to the door. "Let me come with you, then," I said as I stood up. "I've done escort service for humans into the Hollows. I know how to stay quiet and watch your back."

The woman's eyes narrowed. "I am a doctor of ley line magic. You think you can protect me better than I can protect myself?"

I took a breath to protest, then let it out. "You're right," I said, thinking it would be easier to follow her without her knowing. "Could you at least tell me when you're meeting with him? I'd feel better if I could give you a call when you're supposed to be home."

She sent one eyebrow up. "Tomorrow night at seven. We're dining at the restaurant atop Carew Tower. Is that a public enough place to please you?"

I would have to borrow some money from Ivy if I was going to follow her up there. A glass of water cost three bucks and a lousy house salad was twelve—or so I'd heard. I didn't think I had a nice enough dress, either. But I wasn't going to let her meet with Trent unwatched.

Nodding, I put the strap of my bag over my shoulder and stood by Nick. "Yes. Thank you."

Eighteen

The early afternoon sun had almost worked its way from the kitchen, a last band making a thin sliver along the sink and counter. I was sitting at Ivy's antique table, leafing through her catalogs and finishing my breakfast of coffee. I'd been up for only an hour or so, nursing my cup and waiting for Ivy. I had made a full carafe, hoping to lure her into talking to me. She still wasn't ready, having evaded me on the excuse of having to research her latest run. I wished she'd talk to me. The Turn take it, I'd be happy if she'd just listen. It didn't seem possible she would put this much weight on the incident. She had slipped before, and we had gotten past it.

Sighing, I stretched my legs out under the table. I turned the page to a collection of closet organizers, my eyes drifting aimlessly. I didn't have much to do today until Glenn, Jenks, and I went to tail Dr. Anders that night. Nick had loaned me some money, and I had a party dress that wouldn't look too cheap and would hide my splat gun.

Edden had been thrilled when I told him I was going to follow the woman—until I stupidly admitted she was meeting with Trent. We had nearly come to blows over it, shocking the officers on the floor. At this point, I didn't care if Edden threw me in jail. He'd have to wait until I did something, and by then I'd have what I needed.

Glenn wasn't happy with me, either. I'd played the daddy's-boy card to get him to keep his mouth shut and come with me tonight. I didn't care. Trent was killing people.

My eyes, roving over the catalog, fastened on an oak desk, the kind detectives had in pre-Turn movies. A sigh escaped me in an exhalation of desire. It was beautiful, with a deep luster that pressboard lacked. There were all sorts of little cubbies and a hidden compartment behind the bottom left drawer according to the sell line. It would fit nicely in the sanctuary.

A grimace pulled my face down as I thought of my pathetic furniture, some still in storage. Ivy had beautiful furniture, with smooth lines and a heavy weight. The drawers never stuck and the metal latches clicked smartly when they closed. I wanted something like that. Something permanent. Something that arrived on my doorstep fully assembled. Something that could stand a dip in saltwater if I ever got another death threat put on me.

It would never happen, I thought, pushing the catalog away. Getting nice furniture, not the death threat. My eyes slid from the shiny paper to my ley line textbook. I stared at it, thinking. *I could channel more power than most. My dad hadn't wanted me to know. Dr. Anders thought I was an idiot.* There was only one thing I could do.

Taking a breath, I pulled the book closer. I thumbed to the back and the appendices, stopping at the incantation for binding a familiar. It was all ritualistic, with notations referring to techniques I hadn't a clue on. The incantation was in English, and there were no brews or plants involved at all. It was as alien to me as geometry, and I didn't like feeling stupid.

The pages made a pleasant sound as I rifled to the front of the book looking for something I could understand. I slowed, inserting my thumb as I found an incantation for diverting objects in motion. *Cool,* I thought. It was exactly why I had wanted a wand.

Sitting straighter, I crossed my knees and leaned over the book. You were supposed to draw on stored ley line energy to manipulate small things, and connect right to a line for things with a lot of mass or that were moving quickly. The only physical thing I needed was an object to serve as a focal point.

I looked up as Jenks flitted in the open kitchen window. "Hey, Rache," he said cheerily. "Whatcha doing?"

Reaching for the furniture catalog, I slid it smoothly over the textbook. "Not much," I said as I looked down. "You're in a good mood."

"I just got back from your mom's. She's cool, you know." He flew to the center island counter, landing on it to put himself at nearly my eye level. "Jax is doing well. If your mom is cotton to the idea, I'm going to let him have a go at making a garden big enough to support him."

"Cotton?" I questioned, turning a page to some beautiful phone tables. I blanched at the price. How could something that small cost so much?

"Yeah. You know . . . cool, A-okay, keen, kosher."

"I know what it means," I said, recognizing it as one of my mother's favorite phrases and thinking it odd Jenks would have picked it up.

"Have you talked to Ivy yet?" he asked.

"No."

My frustration was obvious in the short word. Jenks hesitated, then, with a clattering of wings, he flew a swooping path to land upon my shoulder. "Sorry."

I forced a pleasant expression as I pulled my head up and tucked a curl behind my ear. "Yeah, me too."

He made an irate noise with his wings. "So-o-o, whatcha hiding under the catalog? Looking through Ivy's leather outlets?"

My jaw tightened. "It's nothing," I said softly.

"You looking to buy furniture?" he scoffed. "Give me a break."

Peeved, I waved him away. "Yeah. I want furniture, something other than pressboard—excuse me—engineered wood. Ivy's stuff makes mine look like trailer-park plastic."

Jenks laughed, the wind from his wings shifting the hair about my face. "So get yourself something nice the next time you have some money."

"Like that will ever happen," I muttered.

Jenks zipped under the table. Not trusting him, I bent to see what he was doing. "Hey! Stop it!" I cried, moving my foot as I felt a tug on my shoe. He darted away, and when I came up from retying my lace, I found he had pulled the catalog off the textbook. His hands were on his hips as he stood on it, reading. "Jenks!" I complained.

"I thought you didn't like ley lines," he said, flitting up and then right back down where he had been. "Especially now that you can't use them without endangering Nick."

"I don't," I said, wishing I hadn't told him about having accidentally made Nick my familiar. "But look. This stuff is easy."

Jenks was silent, his wings drooping as he looked at the charm. "You gonna try it?"

"No," I said quickly.

"Nick will be okay if you pull your energy right off the line. He'll never know." Jenks turned sideways so he could see me and the print both. "It says right here you don't have to use stored energy but can pull it off the line. See? Right here in black and white."

"Yeah," I said slowly, not convinced.

Jenks grinned. "You learn how to do this, and you could get back at the Howlers. You still have those tickets for next Sunday's game, don't you?"

"Yeah," I said cautiously.

Jenks strutted down the page, his wings a red blur in excitement. "You could make them pay you, and since you have Edden's paycheck coming for your rent, you could get a nice oak shoe rack or something."

"Ye-e-e-eah," I hedged.

Jenks eyed me slyly from under his blond bangs. "Unless you're afraid."

My eyes narrowed. "Anyone ever tell you you're a real prick?"

He laughed, rising up with a glittering sunbeam of pixy dust. "If I had a quarter . . ." he mused. Flitting close, he landed on my shoulder. "Is it hard?"

Leaning over the book, I swung my hair to one side so he could see, too. "No, and that's what worries me. There's an incantation, and I need a focusing object. I'll have to connect to a ley line. And there's a gesture . . ." My brow furrowed and I tapped the book. *It couldn't be this easy.*

"You gonna try it?"

The thought that Algaliarept might know I was pulling on the line flitted through me. But seeing that it was daylight and we had an agreement, I thought it was safe enough. "Yeah."

Sitting straighter, I settled myself. Reaching out with my second sight, I fumbled for the line. The sun completely overwhelmed any vision of the ever-after, but the ley line was clear enough in my mind's eye, looking like a streak of dried blood hanging above the tombstones. Thinking it was really ugly, I cautiously reached out a thought and touched it.

My breath hissed in through my nose and I stiffened.

"You okay, Rache?" Jenks questioned, launching himself off my shoulder.

Head bowed over the book, I nodded. The energy flowed through me faster than before, equalizing the strengths very quickly. It was almost as if the previous times had cleared the channels. Worried about using too much, I tried to push some of it down through me and out of my feet. It didn't do any good. The incoming force simply filled me back up again.

Resigned to the uncomfortable feeling, I mentally shook my second sight from me and looked up. Jenks was watching me in concern. I gave him an encouraging smile, and he nodded, apparently satisfied. "How about this?" Jenks said, flying to my stash of water paint balls. The red sphere was as big as his head, and clearly heavy, but he managed it all right.

"It's as good as anything," I agreed. "Toss one up, and I'll try to shift it."

Thinking this was easier than grinding plants and boiling water, I said the incantation and made a swooping loop of a figure in the air with my hand, imagining it was like writing your name with a sparkler on the Fourth of July. I said the last word as Jenks tossed the ball up.

"Ow!" I shouted as a surge of ley line force burned my left hand. I looked at Jenks in bewilderment as he laughed. "What did I do wrong?"

He flitted close with the red ball tucked under his arm, caught when it fell back to him. "You forgot your focusing object. Here. Use this."

"Ah." Embarrassed, I took the red ball as he dropped it into my hand. "Let's try it again," I said, and cradled it in my recessive hand as the book had instructed. Feeling the cool smoothness of it, I said the incantation and etched the figure in the air with my right hand.

Jenks tossed a second ball with a sharp whistle of his wings. Startled, I let loose a surge of power. This time it worked. I stifled a yelp as I felt the ley line energy dart through my hand, following my attention right to the ball. It hit it, knocking it into the wall to make a dripping smear. "Yes!" I exclaimed, meeting Jenks's grin with my own. "Look at that! It worked!"

Jenks flew to the counter to get another ball. "Try it again," he prompted, tossing it eagerly to the ceiling.

It came faster this time. I found I could do the incantation and gesture simultaneously, holding the ley line energy with my will until I wanted to release it. With that came a great deal of control, and soon I was no longer hitting them with so much force that they broke when they hit the wall. My aim was getting better, too, and the sink was littered with the balls I'd been bouncing off the screen. Mr. Fish on the sill wasn't happy.

Jenks was a willing partner, zipping about the kitchen, throwing the red balls at the ceiling. My eyes widened as he threw one at me instead. "Hey!" I cried, sending the ball through the pixy hole in the screen. "Not at me!"

"What a good idea," he said, then grinned wickedly as he made a sharp whistle. Three of his kids zipped in from the garden, all talking at once. They brought the smell of dandelions and asters with them. "Toss them at Ms. Morgan," he said, handing his sphere to the girl in pink.

"Hold it," I protested, ducking as the girl pixy threw it with as much skill and power as her father. I looked behind me to the dark splat against the yellow wall, then back to them. My mouth opened. In the instant I had looked away, they all had gotten splat balls.

"Get her!" Jenks cried.

"Jenks!" I said, laughing as I managed to divert one of the four balls. The three I missed rolled harmlessly to the floor. The smallest pixy skimmed over the linoleum, tossing them upward to where his sisters caught them. "Four against one isn't fair!" I shouted as they took aim again.

My eyes darted to the hallway as the phone rang. "Time!" I called out, lurching to escape into the living room. "Time out!" Still smiling, I reached for the phone. Jenks hovered in the archway, waiting. "Hello. Vampiric Charms. Rachel speaking," I said, ducking the ball he threw at me. I could hear pixy giggles from the kitchen and wondered what they were up to.

"Rachel?" came Nick's voice. "What the blue blazes are you doing?"

"Hi, Nick." I paused to mouth the incantation. I held the energy until Jenks lobbed a ball at me. I was getting better, almost hitting him with the diverted splat ball. "Jenks. Stop it," I protested. "I'm on the phone."

He grinned, then darted out. I flopped into one of Ivy's cushy, matching suede chairs, knowing he wouldn't risk getting water on it and have Ivy come after him.

"Hey, you're up already? You want to do something?" I asked, draping my legs over one arm and lolling my neck on the other. I shifted the red ball I was using as a focusing object between two fingers, daring it to break with the pressure I had it under.

"Um, maybe," he said. "Are you by chance pulling on a ley line?"

I waved Jenks to stop as he swooped in. "Yes!" I said, sitting up and putting my feet on the floor. "I'm sorry. I didn't think you would feel it. I'm not drawing it through you, am I?"

Jenks landed on top of a picture frame. I was sure he could hear Nick, though the pixy was on the other side of the room.

"No," Nick said, a hint of laughter in his voice, tiny through the receiver. "I'm sure I'd be able to tell. But it's odd. I'm sitting here reading, and all of a sudden it feels like you're here with me. The best way to describe it is when you're over here and I'm making dinner, watching you watch TV. You're doing your own thing, not looking for my attention, but being really noisy. It's kind of distracting."

"You watch me watch TV?" I asked, uncomfortable, and he chuckled.

"Yeah. It's a lot of fun. You jump up and down a lot."

My brow furrowed as Jenks snickered. "Sorry," I muttered, but then a faint tickle of warning pulled me straighter. Nick was up reading. He usually spent his Saturday in bed catching up on sleep. "Nick, what book are you reading?"

"Ah, yours," he admitted.

I only had one book that he'd be interested in. "Nick!" I protested as I scooted to the edge of my chair and gripped the phone tighter, "you said you'd take it to Dr. Anders." After blowing off my trip to the FIB because I was frazzled worse than my hair, Nick had taken me home. I'd thought he offered to deliver the book because of my new and healthy phobia of the literally damned tome. Obviously Nick had other plans, and it hadn't made it that far.

"She wasn't going to look at it last night," he said defensively. "And it's safer in my apartment than sitting in a guardhouse getting coffee rings. If you don't mind, I'd like to keep it one more night. There is something in it I want to ask the demon." He paused, clearly waiting for me to protest.

My face warmed. "Idiot," I said, obliging him. "You are an idiot. Dr. Anders told you what that demon is trying to do. It nearly kills both of us, and you're still pumping it for information?"

I heard Nick sigh. "I'm being careful," he said, and I made a frightened bark of laughter. "Rachel, I promise I'll take it over first thing tomorrow. She isn't going to look at it until then anyway." He hesitated, and I could almost hear him gather his resolve. "I'm going to call him. Please don't make me do this behind your back. I'd feel better if someone knew."

"Why? So I can tell your mother what killed you?" I said

sharply, then caught myself. Eyes closing, I squeezed the red ball between my fingers. He was silent, waiting. I hated that I had no right to tell him to stop. Not even as his girlfriend. Summoning demons wasn't illegal. It was just really, really stupid. "Promise you'll call me when you're done?" I asked, feeling my stomach quiver. "I'm up until about five."

"Sure," he breathed. "Thanks. I want to hear how your dinner with Trent goes."

"You bet," I echoed. "Talk to you later." *If you survive.*

I hung up, meeting Jenks's eyes. He was hovering in the middle of the room, a splat ball tucked under his arm. "You two are going to end up as dark smears on ley line circles," he said, and I flicked the splat ball I held at him. He caught it one-handed, moving several feet before stopping its momentum. He flung it back, and I dodged. It hit Ivy's chair without breaking. Thankful for small favors, I picked it up and headed for the kitchen.

"Now!" Jenks shrilled as I entered the bright room.

"Get her!" shrieked a dozen pixies.

Jerked out of my depression, I cowered as a hailstorm of splat balls hit me, breaking against my covered head. Darting to the fridge, I opened the door and hid behind it. Adrenaline made my blood seem to sing. I grinned at the sound of six or more splats against the metallic door. "You little beggars!" I shouted, peeking up to see them flitting over the far end of the kitchen like insane fireflies. My eyes widened; there must have been twenty of them!

Splat balls littered the floor, rolling slowly away from me. Thrilling in it, I said my incantation three times fast and bounced the next three missiles right back at them.

Jenks's kids shrieked in delight, their silk dresses and pants a blur of color. Pixy dust made trails of slowly falling sunshine. Jenks was standing on the ladle hanging from the rack over the center island counter. The sword he used to fight off fairies was in his grip, and he brandished it high as he shouted encouragement.

Under his noisy direction they banded together. Giggled whispers punctuated by excited shouts filled the air as they organized. Grinning, I hid behind the door with my ankles cooling in the draft from the fridge. I said the incantation over and over, feeling the ley line force swell behind my eyes. They were going to attack en masse, knowing I couldn't deflect them all.

"Now!" Jenks shouted. His tiny saber swinging, he launched himself from the ladle.

I cried out at the cheerful ferocity of his kids swarming at me.

Laughing in protest, I sent the red balls flying. Little thumps beat at me from the ones I missed. Gasping for air, I rolled under the table. They followed me, bombarding me.

I was out of incantations. "I give up!" I cried, careful not to hit any of Jenks's kids as I put my hands on the underside of the table. I was covered in spots of water, and I pushed back the damp strands of hair stuck to my face. "I give up! You win!"

They cheered, and the phone started ringing again. Proud and exuberant, Jenks bellowed out a stirring song about beating invaders from their land and coming home to seedlings. Sword held high, he made a circuit around the room, gathering his kids up in tow. All singing in glorious harmony, they flowed out the window and into the garden.

I sat in the sudden silence on the kitchen floor under the table. My entire body shifted as I took a deep breath, smiling as I exhaled. "Whew!" I puffed, still chuckling as I wiped a hand under my eye. No wonder the fairy assassins sent to kill me last year hadn't had a chance. Jenks's kids were clever, quick—and aggressive.

Still smiling, I rolled to my feet and padded into the living room to get the phone before the machine picked it up. Poor Nick. I was sure he felt that last one.

"Nick," I blurted before he could say anything. "I'm sorry. Jenks's kids had me under the kitchen table and were throwing splat balls at me. God help me, but it was funny. They're in the garden right now, making rings around the ash tree and singing about cold steel."

"Rachel?"

It was Glenn, and my mirth died at his worried tone. "What?" I said, looking at the trees through the shoulder-high windows. The spots of water covering me were suddenly cold, and I clasped an arm around myself.

"I'll be there in ten minutes," he said. "Can you be ready?"

I pushed my damp hair back. "Why? What's happened?" I asked.

I heard him cover the receiver and shout something at someone. "You got your warrant to search Kalamack's property," he said when he returned.

"How?" I questioned, not believing Edden had caved. "Not that I'm complaining!"

Glenn hesitated. He took a slow breath, and I heard excited voices in the background. "Dr. Anders called me last night," he said. "She knew you were going to follow her, so she moved her presentation to last night and asked me to go with her instead."

"The witch," I exclaimed softly, wishing I could have seen what Glenn had worn. I bet it had been sharp. But when he remained silent, the cold feeling in my stomach solidified into a sour lump.

"I'm sorry, Rachel," Glenn said softly. "Her car went off Roebling Bridge this morning, pushed over the rail by what appeared to be a huge bubble of ley line force. They just pulled her car from the river. We're still looking for the body."

Nineteen

My foot jiggled as I impatiently stood beside the stack of manuals and empty paper cups that lined the sill of Trent's gatehouse. Jenks was on my earring, muttering darkly as he watched Quen punch a button on the phone. I'd seen Quen only once before—possibly twice. The first time, he was masquerading as a gardener, actually managing to catch Jenks in a glass ball. I had a growing suspicion that Quen had been the third rider who tried to run me down on horseback the night I stole my blackmail disc from Trent. It was a feeling that solidified when Jenks told me Quen smelled just like Trent and Jonathan.

Quen reached in front of me for a pen, and I jerked back, not wanting him to touch me. Still on the phone, he smiled carefully, showing me extremely white, even teeth. *This one,* I thought, *knew what I was capable of.* This one wouldn't underestimate me as Jonathan continually did. And though it was nice being taken seriously for once, I wished Quen was as egotistical and chauvinistic as Jonathan was.

Trent had once said Quen was willing to take me on as a student—after the security officer got over his desire to kill me for infiltrating the Kalamack compound. I wondered if I would have survived having him as a teacher.

Quen looked about the age my father would be if he were still alive. He had very dark hair that curled about his ears, green eyes that always seemed to be watching me, and a dancer's grace that I knew came from a lifetime of martial arts practice. Dressed in a black security uniform with no insignia, he looked like he belonged to the night. He was a shade taller than I was in heels, and the strength in his lightly wrinkled physique had me on edge. His fingers were quick on a keyboard and his eyes were faster. The only weakness I'd noticed was a slight limp. And unlike everyone else in the room besides me, he had no weapon that I could see.

Captain Edden stood beside me, looking squat but capable in his khaki pants and white shirt. Glenn was in another of his black suits, trying to look collected despite his obvious nervousness. Edden, too, looked worried that he was going to have egg on his face if we didn't find anything.

I adjusted my bag higher onto my shoulder and fidgeted. It was full of charms to find Dr. Anders, dead or alive. I had made Glenn wait while I whipped them up, using the paper she had written her address on as the focal object. If there was a shoe box left of her, the charms would light red. With them was a lie amulet, my wire-framed glasses to see through ley line disguises, and a spell checker. I was going to take the opportunity while talking to Trent to see if he used a charm to disguise his appearance. Nobody looks that good without help.

Outside, parked in the lot beside the gatehouse, were three FIB vans. The doors were open and the officers looked hot as they waited in the heat of an unseasonably warm afternoon. The breeze from Jenks's wings sent a wisp of hair to tickle my neck. "Can you hear him?" I breathed as Quen turned away and began speaking into the phone.

"Oh, yeah," the pixy muttered. "He's talking to Jonathan. Quen is telling him he's standing in the gatehouse with you and Edden with a warrant to search the property and he bloody well just better wake him up."

"Him being Trent?" I guessed, and felt my earring swing as Jenks nodded. I looked at the clock over the door, seeing it was a little after two. Must be nice.

Edden cleared his throat as Quen hung up. Trent's security officer made no bones about letting us know he was unhappy. His light wrinkles deepened as his jaw clenched, and his green eyes were hard. "Captain Edden, Mr. Kalamack is understandably upset, and would like to speak with you while your people carry out your search."

"Of course," Edden said, and a small sound of disbelief escaped me.

"Why are you being so nice?" I muttered as Quen ushered us through the heavy glass and metal doors and back into the strong sun.

"Rachel," Edden breathed, tension carrying through his whisper, "you will be polite and gracious or you will wait in the car."

Gracious, I thought. *Since when were ex–Navy SEALs gracious?* Hard-nosed, aggressive, politically correct to the point of being anal. Ah . . . he was being politically correct.

Edden leaned close as he held the door to one of the vans for me. "And then we're going to nail his ass to a tree," he added, confirming my suspicions. "If Kalamack murdered her, we'll get him," he said, his eyes on Quen as the man swung into an estate vehicle. "But if we bull in here like storm troopers, a jury will let him go even if he confesses. It's all in the procedure. I've stopped traffic in and out. No one leaves without a search."

I squinted at him, putting a hand to my hat to keep it from blowing off. I'd much rather have screamed in with twenty cars and sirens blazing, but I'd have to be satisfied with this.

The drive up the three-mile entry road through the wood Trent maintained about his estate was quiet since Jenks had gone with Glenn in the estate car to try and figure out what kind of Inderlander Quen was. We followed Quen's security vehicle around the last turn and pulled into the empty visitor's parking lot.

I couldn't help but be impressed by Trent's main building. The three-story edifice was settled in among the surrounding vegetation as if it had been here for hundreds of years rather than forty. The white marble sent glints of sunlight to pool against the trees like a sunrise from the west. Large pillars and wide shallow steps made an inviting entry. Surrounded by trees and gardens, the office buildings had a sense of permanence those in the city lacked. Several smaller buildings sprawled from the main one, attached by covered walkways. Trent's renowned walled gardens took up much of the side and back, the acres of well-tended plants surrounded by fields of grass and then his eerie planned-out forest.

I was the first one out of the van, my gaze crossing the road to the distant low-slung buildings where Trent raised his thoroughbreds. A tour bus was just leaving, obnoxiously noisy and emblazoned with advertisements to visit Trent's gardens.

Jenks flitted up to land on my shoulder, since my current earrings were too small for him to perch on, grumbling about his inability to figure out what Quen was. I turned back to the main building and started up the stone steps, heels clicking in a steady cadence. Edden was quick behind me.

My gut tightened when I saw a familiar silhouette waiting for us by the marble pillars. "Jonathan," I whispered, my dislike for the extremely tall man swinging into a slow hatred. Just once I'd like to climb those stairs and not have his haughty eyes on me.

My lips went tight and I suddenly was glad for having worn my best suit-dress despite the unseasonable heat. Jonathan's suit was exquisite. It had to have been tailored to him since he was too tall to be able to buy anything off the rack. His dark hair was graying around the temples, and the wrinkles around his eyes were embedded as if acid had etched them in concrete. He had been a child during the Turn, seemingly marked forever by its fear in his gaunt, almost malnourished stance.

Tidy and overdressed, his manner screamed British Englishman, but his accent was as midwestern as mine. He was clean shaven, his cheeks and thin lips never stirring from a perpetual frown unless it was at someone's expense. He had grinned the entire three days I had been a mink trapped in a cage in Trent's office, his vivid blue eyes alive and eager as he tormented me.

Quen strode quickly up the stairs to pull ahead of me. My eye started to tic as the two men put their heads together. They turned, Jonathan's professional smile laced with professional irritation. Nice.

"Captain Edden," he said, extending his thin hand as Edden and I halted before them. Edden's muscular build looked almost dumpy as he shook hands with him. "I'm Jonathan, Mr. Kalamack's publicity adviser. Mr. Kalamack is waiting for you," he added, the congeniality in his voice never reaching his eyes. "He asked me to relay his desire to help any way he can."

Jenks snickered from my shoulder. "He could tell us where he stashed Dr. Anders."

He whispered it, but both Quen and Jonathan stiffened. I pretended to check the French braid I'd put my hair in—subtly threatening to smack Jenks—then put my hands behind my back to forestall a handshake with Jonathan. I wouldn't touch him. Unless it was my fist in his gut. Damn, I really missed my handcuffs.

"Thank you," Edden said, eyebrows raised at the evil glances Jonathan and I were exchanging. "We'll try to make this as quick and nonintrusive as possible."

As I stood and glowered, Edden pulled Glenn aside. "Keep the search low-key but thorough," he said as Jonathan's eyes flicked over my shoulder to the FIB officers assembling in a loose conglomeration on the wide steps. They had brought several dogs with them, all wearing blue body sleeves with FIB emblazoned on them in yellow. Their tails waved enthusiastically and they were clearly eager to get to work.

Glenn nodded, and I swung my bag around. "Here," I said, pulling out a handful of charms and dumping them into his grip. "I primed them on the way over. They're set to find Dr. Anders whether she is dead or alive. Give them to whoever will take them. They'll turn red if they get within a hundred feet of her."

"I'll make sure every team has one," Glenn said, his brown eyes startled as he tried to keep from dropping them.

"Hey, Rache," Jenks said as he flitted off my shoulder. "Glenn asked me to tag along with him. You mind? I can't do anything sitting pretty on your shoulder."

"Sure, go ahead," I said, thinking he could search the garden better than a pack of dogs.

A worried frown crossed Jonathan's long face, and I beamed sarcastically at him. Pixies and fairies weren't allowed on the grounds as a general rule, and I'd wear my panties on the outside for a week if someone would tell me what Trent was afraid Jenks might find.

Quen and Jonathan exchanged a silent look. The shorter man's lips went tight and his green eyes pinched. Looking as if he'd rather make mud pies out of crap than leave Jonathan alone to accompany us with Trent, Quen hustled after Jenks. My eyes tracked the security officer as he all but flowed down the stairs, his hurried grace mesmerizing.

Jonathan straightened as he returned his attention to us. "Mr. Kalamack is waiting for you in his front office," he said stiffly as he opened a door.

I gave him a nasty smile as I lurched into motion. "Touch me, and I'll hurt you," I threatened as I yanked open the door next to the one Jonathan held.

The main lobby was spacious and eerily empty, the hushed murmur of business silenced with everyone gone for the weekend. Not waiting for Jonathan, I went straight down the wide corridor to Trent's office. Hands fumbling in my purse, I pulled out my ungodly expensive and criminally ugly charmed ley line glasses and put them on my nose. Jonathan gave up on his show of decorum, leaving Edden behind to catch up with me.

I strode down the hallway, my fists clenched and heels thumping. I wanted to see Trent. I wanted to tell him what I thought of him and spit in his face for having tried to break my will by putting me in the city's illegal rat fights.

The frosted doors to either side of me were open, showing empty desks. Farther down was a reception desk tucked into an alcove across from Trent's door. Sara Jane's desk was as neat and organized as the woman herself. Heart pounding, I reached for the handle of Trent's door, jerking back as Jonathan caught up. Giving me a look that could rock an attacking dog back on his haunches, the tall man knocked on Trent's wooden door, waiting until his muffled voice came before opening it.

Edden came even with me, his cross look faltering in shock as he saw my glasses. On edge, I touched my hat and tugged my jacket straight. Maybe I should have asked Ivy for a loan and gotten the pretty ones. The sound of water over rocks filtered out of Trent's office, and I entered hot on Jonathan's heels.

Trent rose from behind his desk as I came in. I took a breath to give him a snide but sincere greeting. I wanted to tell him I knew he had killed Dr. Anders. I wanted to tell him he was scum. I wanted to get in his face and scream that I was better than him, that he would never break me, that he was a manipulative bastard and I was going to *bring him down.* But I did nothing, taken aback by his calm, inner core of strength. He was the most self-possessed man I had ever met, and I stood silent as his thoughts visibly shifted from other matters to focus on me. And no, he didn't use a ley line charm to make him look that good. It was all him.

Every strand of his wispy, almost transparent hair was in place. His gray, silk-lined suit was unwrinkled, accenting the narrow-waisted, wide-shouldered physique I had spent three days ogling as a mink. Standing taller than I was, he gave me his trademark smile: an enviable mix of warmth and professional interest. He adjusted his jacket with a casual slowness, his long fingers drawing my attention as he manipulated the last button. There was only a single ring on his right hand, and like me, he wore no watch at all.

Trent was supposed to be only three years older than I—making him one of the wealthiest bachelors on the freaking planet—but the suit made him look older. Even so, his nicely defined jawline as well as his smooth cheeks and small nose made him look suited more for the beach than the boardroom.

Still smiling that confident, almost pleased smile, he ducked his head, taking his wire-rimmed glasses off and tossing them to the desktop. Embarrassed, I put my own charmed spectacles away in their hard leather case. My eyes went to his right arm as he came around to the front of his desk. It had been in a cast the last time I saw him, which was probably why the gun he'd shot at me missed. There was a faint ring of lighter skin between his hand and the cuff of his jacket that the sun hadn't yet had a chance to darken.

I stiffened as his gaze drifted over me, resting briefly on the pinky ring he had stolen from me and returned to prove he could, finally settling on my neck and the almost invisible scarring from my demon attack. "Ms. Morgan, I wasn't aware you could work for the FIB," he said by way of greeting, making no move to shake my hand.

"I'm a consultant," I said, ignoring how his liquid voice had pulled my breath tight. I had forgotten his voice, all amber and honey—if color and taste could describe a sound—resonant and deep, each syllable clear and precise yet blending into the next like liquid. It was mesmerizing in a way that only ancient vampires could match. And it bothered me that I liked it.

I met his gaze, trying to show a mirror image of his confidence. Jittery, I extended my arm, forcing him to respond. His hand came out to meet mine with the barest of hesitations. A stab of satisfaction warmed me in that I had made him do something he didn't want to, even if it was something this small.

Feeling cocky, I slipped my hand into Trent's. Though his green eyes were cold with the knowledge that I'd forced him into touching me, his grip was warm and firm. I wondered how long he had been practicing it. Satisfied, I loosened my grip, but instead of doing the same, Trent's hand slipped from mine with an intimate slowness that wasn't at all professional. I would have said he had just made a pass at me but for the slight tightening of his eyes, which spoke of a wary caution.

"Mr. Kalamack," I said, refusing to wipe my hand on my skirt. "You're looking good."

"As are you." His smile was frozen in place, and his right hand was almost behind his back. "I understand you're doing reasonably well with your little investigation firm. I imagine it's difficult when you're just starting out."

Little investigation firm? My unease flashed into irritation. "Thank you," I managed.

A smile quirking the corner of his mouth, Trent turned his attention to Edden. As the two professional men made polite, politically correct and hypocritical niceties, I glanced over Trent's office. His fake window still showed a live shot of one of his yearling pastures, the artificial light shining through the video screen to make a warm patch of glowing carpet. There was a new school of black and white fish in the zoo-size fish tank, and the freestanding aquarium had been moved into a recess built into the wall behind his desk. The spot where my cage had been held a potted orange tree, and the scent-memory of food pellets made my stomach clench. The camera at the ceiling in the corner blinked its little red light at me.

"It's a pleasure to meet you, Captain Edden," Trent was saying, the smooth cadence of his voice luring my attention. "I wish it could be under better circumstances."

"Mr. Kalamack." Edden's sharp staccato sounded harsh against Trent's voice. "I apologize for any inconvenience incurred while we search your grounds."

Jonathan handed Trent the warrant, and he looked at it briefly before handing it back. "Corporal evidence leading to an arrest in the deaths known as the witch hunter murders?" he said, his eyes flicking to mine. "That's a little broad, isn't it?"

"Putting down 'dead body' looked crass," I said tightly, and Edden cleared his throat, the barest hint of worry we might find nothing staining his professional stance. I noticed Edden had fallen into a parade rest, and wondered if the ex–Navy SEAL even knew it. "You were the last person to see Dr. Anders," I added, wanting to see Trent's reaction.

"That's out of line, Ms. Morgan," Edden muttered, but I was more interested in the emotion that passed over Trent. Anger, frustration, but not shock. Trent glanced at Jonathan, who made the slightest shrug I'd ever seen. Slowly, Trent sat back on his desktop, his long, sun-tanned hands clasped in front of him. "I wasn't aware that she had died," he said.

"I never said she was dead," I said. My heart pounded as Edden gripped my arm in warning.

"She's missing?" Trent said, doing a creditable job of showing only relief. "That's good. That she is missing and not—ah—dead. I had dinner with her last night." The barest hint of worry flickered over Trent as he gestured to the two chairs behind us. "Please, sit down," he said as he went behind his desk. "I'm sure you have some questions for me—seeing as you're searching my grounds."

"Thank you, sir. I do." Edden took the seat closest to the hallway. My eyes tracked Jonathan as he closed Trent's door. He remained standing beside it, looking defensive. I eased myself down in the remaining seat in the artificial sun, forcing myself to the back of the chair. Trying for an air of nonchalance, I set my bag on my lap and felt in my jacket pocket for a finger stick. The prick of the blade zinged through me. I eased my bleeding finger into my bag, carefully searching for the charm. *Now let's see Trent lie and get away with it.*

Trent's expression froze at the clatter of my amulet. "Put your truth spell away, Ms. Morgan," he accused. "I said I would be happy to answer Captain Edden's questions, not submit to an interrogation. Your warrant is for search and seizure, not cross-examination."

"Morgan," Edden hissed, his thick hand extended. "Give me that!"

Grimacing, I wiped my fingertip clean and handed the amulet over. Edden stuffed it in a pocket. "My apologies," he said, his round face tight. "Ms. Morgan is tenacious in her desire to find the person or persons responsible for so many deaths. She has a *dangerous*"—this was directed at me—"tendency to forget she has to function within the law's parameters."

Trent's wispy hair rose in the current from the air vents. Seeing my gaze on it, he ran a hand over his head, hinting at irritation. "She means well."

How patronizing was that? Angry, I set my bag on the floor with a thump. "Dr. Anders meant well, too," I said. "Did you kill her after she turned down your offer of employment?"

Jonathan stiffened, and Edden's hands jerked as if he was trying to keep them in his lap and away from around my neck. "I'm not going to warn you again, Rachel. . . ." he growled.

Trent's smile never flickered. He was angry and trying not to show it. I was glad I could paint the walls with my feelings; it was far more satisfying. "No, it's all right," Trent said, clasping his fingers together and leaning forward to set them on his desk. "If it will ease Ms. Morgan's belief that I'm capable of such monstrous crimes, I'll be more than happy to tell you what we discussed last night." Though he was talking to Edden, his gaze didn't shift from mine. "We were discussing the possibility of my funding her research."

"Ley line research?" I questioned.

He picked up a pencil, the motion as he twirled it giving away his discomfort. He really should have broken himself of the habit. "Ley line research," he agreed. "The vein of which has little practical value. I was indulging my curiosity, nothing more."

"I think you offered her a job," I said. "And when she refused to work for you, you had her killed, just like all the other ley line witches in Cincinnati."

"Morgan!" Edden exclaimed, pulling himself upright in his chair. "Go wait in the van." He rose, giving Trent an apologetic look. "Mr. Kalamack, I'm very sorry. Ms. Morgan is entirely out of line, and is not acting under FIB authority in her accusations."

I spun in my chair to face him. "It's what he tried to do to me. Why would Dr. Anders be any different?"

Edden's face went red behind his little round glasses. I clenched my jaw, ready to argue right back. He took an angry breath, letting it out at the knock at the door. Jonathan opened it, stepping back as Glenn came in, ducking his head briefly to Trent in acknowledgment. I could tell by his hunched, furtive expression that the search wasn't going well.

He murmured something to Edden, and the captain scowled, growling something back. Trent watched the exchange with interest, his brow smoothing and the faint tension in his shoulders easing. The pencil was set aside, and he leaned back in his chair.

Jonathan went to Trent, putting a hand on his desk as he leaned to whisper in Trent's ear. My attention flicked from Jonathan's condescending smile to Edden's worried frown. Trent was going to come out of this looking like an injured citizen brutalized by the FIB. *Damn.*

Jonathan straightened and Trent's green eyes met mine, softly mocking. Edden's voice rasped at my awareness as he told Glenn to have Jenks double-check the gardens. Trent was going to get away with it. He killed those people, and he was going to get away with it!

Frustration gripped me as Glenn gave me a helpless look and left, closing the door behind him. I knew my charms were good, but they might not work if Trent was using ley line magic to hide her. My face went slack. *Ley line magic?* If he was hiding her with ley line magic, I could find her with the same.

I glanced at Trent, seeing his satisfaction falter at the sudden questioning look I knew I must be wearing. Trent held up a finger to Jonathan, keeping the tall man quiet as he focused on me, clearly trying to figure out what I was thinking.

Making a search charm using earth magic was clearly white witchcraft. It followed that one made using ley line magic would be white as well. The cost upon my karma would be negligible, far less than, say, lying about my birthday to get a free drink. And whether stemming from earth or ley line magic, a search charm was covered under the search and seizure warrant.

My heartbeat quickened, and I reached to touched my hair. I

didn't know the incantation, but Nick might have it in his books. And if Trent used ley line magic to cover his tracks, there would have to be a line close enough to use. *Interesting.*

"I need to make a call," I said, hearing my voice as if it were from outside my head.

Trent seemed at a loss for words. I liked seeing the emotion on him. "You're welcome to use my secretary's phone," he said.

"I have my own," I said, digging in my bag. "Thank you."

Edden gave me a suspicious glance and went to talk to Trent and Jonathan. By his polite stance and appeasing look, I thought he might be trying to smooth the political waves his failed FIB visit was going to cause. Tense, I rose, going to the far corner to try and stay out of the camera's view as well as their earshot.

"Be there," I whispered as I scrolled through my short list and hit the send button. "Pick up, Nicky. Please pick up. . . ." He might be getting groceries. He could be doing his laundry or taking a nap or in the shower, but I was willing to bet my nonexistent paycheck that he was still reading that damned book. My shoulders relaxed as someone picked up. He was home. I loved a predictable man.

"'Ello," he said, sounding preoccupied.

"Nick," I breathed. "Thank God."

"Rachel? What's up?" Concern laced his voice, pulling my shoulders tight again.

"I need your help," I said, glancing at Edden and Trent, trying to keep my voice soft. "I'm at Trent's with Captain Edden. We got a search warrant. Will you look in your books for a ley line charm to find—um—dead people?"

There was a long hesitation. "That's what I like about you, Ray-ray," he said as I heard the sound of a sliding book followed by a thump. "You say the sweetest things."

I waited, my stomach knotting as the sound of turning pages came faintly over the phone.

"Dead people," he murmured, not fazed at all, while the butterflies battered my stomach with jackhammers. "Dead fairies. Dead ghosts. Will an invocation for ghosts do?"

"No." I picked at my nail polish, watching Trent watch me as he talked to Edden.

"Dead kings, dead livestock . . . ah, dead people."

My pulse increased and I fumbled in my bag for a pen.

"Okay . . ." He was silent, reading it over. "It's simple enough, but I don't think you can use it during the daytime."

"Why not?"

"You know how tombstones in our world show up in the ever-after? Well, the charm makes unmarked graves in our world do the same. But you have to be able to see into the ever-after with your second sight, and you can't do that unless the sun is down."

"I can if I'm standing in a ley line," I whispered, feeling cold. I'd never seen that tidbit of information written in a book. My dad had told me when I was eight.

"Rachel," he protested after a moment's hesitation. "You can't. If that demon knows you're in a ley line, he'll try to pull you the rest of the way into the ever-after."

"It can't. It doesn't own my soul," I whispered, turning to hide my moving lips.

He was silent, and my breath sounded loud to me. "I don't like it," he finally said.

"I don't like you calling up demons. And it's an it, not a him."

The phone was silent. I glanced at Trent, then turned my back on him. I wondered how good his hearing was.

"Yes," Nick said, "but he owns two-thirds of my soul, and one-third of yours. What if—"

"Souls don't add up like numbers, Nick," I said, my voice harsh with worry. "It's an all or nothing affair. It doesn't have enough on me. It doesn't have enough on you. I'm not walking out of here without proving Trent killed that woman. What's the incantation?"

I waited, my knees going weak. "Got a pen?" he finally said, and I nodded, forgetting he couldn't see the gesture.

"Yes," I said, jiggling the phone to write on my palm like a test cheat sheet.

"Okay. It's not long. I'll translate everything but the invocation word into English, only because we don't have a word that means the glowing ashes of the dead, and I think it's important you get that part exactly right. Give me a moment, and I can make it rhyme."

"Non-rhyming is fine," I said slowly, thinking this just kept getting better and better. *Glowing ashes of the dead?* What kind of language needed its own word for that?

He cleared his throat and I readied my pen. " 'Dead unto dead, shine as the moon. Silence all but the restless.' " He hesitated. "And then the trigger word is 'favilla.' "

"Favilla," I repeated, writing it phonetically. "Any gesture?"

"No. It doesn't physically act on anything, so you don't need a gesture or focus object. Do you want me to repeat it?"

"No," I said, a little sick as I looked at my palm. *Did I really want to do this?*

"Rachel," he said, his voice sounding worried through the speaker. "Be careful."

"Yeah," I said, my pulse fast in anticipation and worry. "Thanks, Nick." I bit my lower lip in a sudden thought. "Hey, um, keep my book for me until I talk to you, okay?"

"Ray-ray?" he questioned warily.

"Ask me later," I said, flicking a glance at Edden, then Trent. I didn't have to say another word. He was a smart man.

"Wait. Don't hang up," he said, the concern in his voice giving me pause. "Keep me on the line. I can't sit here and feel those tugs on me without knowing if you're in trouble or not."

I licked my lips and forced my hand down from where it had been playing with the end of my braid. Using Nick as my familiar went against every moral fiber I had—and I'd like to think I had a lot of them—but I couldn't walk away. I wouldn't even try it if I wasn't sure Nick would be unaffected. "I'll give you to Captain Edden, okay?"

"Edden?" he said faintly, his worry taking on an edge of self-preservation.

I turned back to the three men. "Captain," I said, drawing their attention. "I'd like to try a different finding spell before we leave."

Edden's round face was pinched with frustration. "We're done here, Morgan," he said gruffly. "We've taken up more than enough of Mr. Kalamack's time."

I swallowed, trying to look like I did this every day. "This one works differently."

His breath went in and out in a rough sound. "Can I have a word with you in the hallway?" he intoned.

Hallway? I would not be pulled into the hallway like an errant child. I turned to Trent. "Mr. Kalamack won't mind. He has nothing to hide, yes?"

Trent's face was a mask of professional politeness. Jonathan stood behind him, his narrow face ugly. "As long as it falls within the parameters of your warrant," Trent said smoothly.

I felt a jolt hearing the concern he was trying to hide. He was worried. I was, too.

I made my steps slow as I crossed the office and handed Edden the phone. "It's a finding spell tuned to find unmarked graves. Nick will tell you all about it, Captain, so you can be sure it's legal. You remember him, don't you?"

Edden took the phone, the slim pink rectangle looking ridiculous in his thick hands. "If it's so simple, why didn't you tell me about it before?"

I gave him a nervous smile. "It uses ley lines."

Trent's face froze. His gaze darted to my demon-marked wrist, and he leaned back into his chair and Jonathan's protection. I arched my eyebrows though my stomach was in knots. If he protested, he would look guilty. His hands moved with a nervous quickness as he reached for his wire-rimmed glasses and tapped them on the desktop. "Please," he said as if he had any say in the matter. "Invoke your charm. I'd be interested to see how much an earth witch such as yourself knows about ley line magic."

"Me, too," Edden said dryly before he put the phone to his ear and began talking to Nick in low, intent tones, making sure what I was going to do fell within the FIB warrant, most likely.

"We'll have to move," I said almost to myself. "I need to find a ley line to stand in."

"Ah, Ms. Morgan," Trent said, clearly agitated as he sat up straight in his chair. The wire-rimmed glasses he had put back on made him look less sophisticated, giving him a softer, almost harmless look. I thought he looked a little pale, too.

Right, I thought snidely as I closed my eyes to make it easier to find a ley line with my second sight. *Like you have a ley line running through your garden.*

I reached out with my thoughts, searching for the red smear of ever-after. My breath hissed in and my eyes flashed open. I stared at Trent.

The man had a freaking ley line running right through his freaking office.

Twenty

Mouth agape, I looked across the office to Trent. His face was tight and drawn as he sat flanked by Jonathan. Neither looked happy. My pulse raced. Trent knew it was there. He could use ley lines. That meant he was either human or witch. Vamps couldn't pull on them, and humans who could and were subsequently infected with the vamp virus lost the ability. I didn't know what frightened me more, that Trent used ley lines or that he knew I knew. God help me. I was halfway to knowing Trent's most precious secret of what the hell he was.

The door to Trent's office smashed into the wall. Adrenaline surged painfully, and I fell into a defensive stance. Quen burst in. "Sa—Sir," he barked, changing his title Sa'han, mid-speech. He jerked to a stop, his eyes narrowing as he took in my tense posture in the corner and Edden sitting in his chair with my phone at his ear, carefully not moving one inch.

The man's green eyes fixed upon mine. My heart pounded. Our defensive postures eased, and I tugged my skirt down where it belonged. The door arched closed as Jenks darted in.

"Hey, Rache!" the pixy cried, his wings red in excitement. "Someone's found a ley line and it's got *someone* in an unholy snit." He stopped short, taking in the tense room. "Oh, it's you," he said, grinning. Wings clattering, he lit upon my shoulder, quickly abandoning me for Edden and the chance to overhear what Nick was saying.

Trent leaned forward to put his elbows on the desk. A bead of sweat edged his hairline. I tried to swallow, finding my mouth dry.

"Ms. Morgan is demonstrating her ley line skills for us," Trent said. "I'm very interested to see."

I'll bet you are, I thought, wondering how deep in the pile I had stepped. Ley line magic was used heavily in security, and Quen had known the moment I found it.

Uneasy, I took the opportunity to examine everyone's auras with my second sight. Jenks's was all rainbows, as most pixies' were. Edden's was a steady blue tending to yellow about his head. Quen's was a green so dark as to be almost black, shot through with vibrant orange streaks about his middle and his hands—not good. Jonathan's was green as well, much lighter and almost bland in its uniformity and shade. Trent's . . . I hesitated, faltering.

Trent's aura was sunshine yellow, streaked with a sharply defined red. The crimson slashes hinted that he had more than his share of soul-marring tragedy in his past. It was unusually close around him, rimmed in silver sparkles, like Ivy's was. They burst into existence and floated about him when he took a hand and ran it across his head to make his hair lie flat. He was looking for something—the way the sparkles embedded themselves in his main aura indicating that he had dedicated his life to this search. The money, the power, the drive, was all to serve a higher purpose. What was he looking for? I wondered.

I couldn't see my aura. Unless I was standing on a scrying mirror—which I would never do again. But I was sure Trent was looking at it, and I didn't like that he could see the demon mark on my wrist pulsating with a nasty black smear, or that my aura, too, had those same ugly red streaks, or that apart from his sparkles, our auras were almost identical.

Edden looked warily between us, knowing something was going on but not what. Brow pinching, he shifted to the edge of his chair and had a terse, hushed conversation with Nick.

"You have a ley line running through your office?" I said, light-headed.

"You have one in your backyard," Trent answered flatly. Jaw tightening, he glanced at Edden. I could almost see his wish that the FIB captain wasn't there. His expression was laced with a threatening warning. It wasn't publicized that only humans and witches could manipulate ley lines, but anyone could figure it out, and I knew he wanted me to shut up about them. I was more than willing to, knowing that having the information was like holding a cobra by the tail.

My fingers were trembling from adrenaline, and I clenched

them into fists as I turned to the three-foot-wide smear of ever-after running through Trent's office. It made an east to west swath before his desk, more accurate than any compass, and I imagined it probably ran through his back office, too. As soon as I stepped into it, I could make an educated guess.

Sweat broke out on the small of my back as I eyed the line. I'd never put myself in one before. Unless you made the effort to tap into a line, you could walk right through it and feel nothing. I took a breath, willing myself to relax. If Algaliarept did show up, all I'd have to do was step out of the line. It couldn't get out of the ever-after as long as the sun was above the horizon.

With a final, wary look at the two men standing protectively behind Trent, I closed my eyes. Stealing myself, I reached out and touched my will to the line.

Power, heady with intent, surged into me. My pulse leapt, and I think I staggered. Breath fast and shallow, I held up a hand to keep Edden from touching me. I had heard him stand. As he shot hushed questions at Nick, I hung my head and did nothing, riding the surges of power rising through me in ever stronger pulses. They backwashed at my extremities, my head throbbing in hurt as they rebounded and crashed into the continuing inflow. I felt a moment of panic as it grew, and grew, and continued to grow. Just how strong was this thing?

I felt like an overinflated balloon and it seemed I was going to burst or go insane. *This,* I thought, almost panting, *was why ley line witches have familiars.* Their animal companions filtered the raw energy, their simpler minds better able to handle the strain. I wouldn't make Nick take my risk. I had to take it all. And I had yet to actually step into the line. How much more potent it would be then was anyone's guess.

Slowly, the demanding influx ebbed, becoming almost bearable. Tingling from the inside, I took a breath that sounded suspiciously like a sob. The balance of energy finally seemed to have equalized. I could feel the wisps of my hair that had escaped my braid tickle my neck as the wind from the ever-after lifted past and through me.

"My God . . ." I heard Edden breathe, and I hoped I hadn't just lost his trust. I don't think he truly understood how different we were until that moment, seeing my hair move in the breeze that only I could feel.

"Not much of a witch," I heard Jonathan say, "staggering in a power drunk at noon."

"It would be if she were tapping it like most people," came Quen's throaty whisper, and I strained to hear him. "She's not using a familiar, Sa'han. She's channeling the entire bloody line by herself."

Jonathan's intake of alarm sent a surge of vindication through me—until he followed it up with an urgent, "Kill her. Tonight. She's not worth the risk anymore."

My eyes almost flew open, but I held them shut so they wouldn't know I had heard. My wildly pounding heart sounded loud in my ears, adding to the slow swelling of ley line force still trickling in. "Jonathan," Trent said, sounding tired. "You don't kill something because it's stronger than you. You find a way to use it."

Use me? I thought bitterly. *Over my dead body.* Hoping it wasn't a premonition, I lifted my head, crossed my fingers for luck, prayed I wasn't making a mistake, and entered the ley line.

My knees buckled as the power swelling in me vanished with a painful suddenness. It was gone. The uncomfortable influx of ever-after was gone. Not believing it, I stood, realizing I had fallen to one knee. I forced my eyes to remain shut lest I lose my second sight, slapping away Edden's hand gripping my shoulder.

The strength of the ley line swirled through me, making my skin prickle and my hair float, but the balance had become perfect. It left me shaken but no longer having to fight the strain of its power. Why had no one ever told me this? Standing in a line was a hell of a lot easier than maintaining a link to one, even if the gritty wind took getting used to.

Eyes still shut, I looked at the ever-after, thinking it was even stranger lit under the demons' sun. The walls of Trent's office were gone, and only Edden's hushed conversation with Nick kept me grounded, telling my frazzled mind that no, I hadn't crossed into the ever-after, I was standing in a trapdoor, seeing a vision of it.

Spreading in all directions was a rolling landscape of scattered groves of trees and wide, open tracts. To the east and west stretched a hazy ribbon of ley line force. I was standing two-thirds down its considerable length, and I would guess it went to Trent's back office. The sky was a washed-out yellow and the sun was intense, beating down as if trying to crush the squat, stubby trees into the ground. I felt as if it was passing right through me, bouncing up and warming the undersides of my feet. Even the coarse grass seemed stunted, barely coming to mid-calf. In the hazy distance to the west were a cluster of sharp lines and angles towering over the landscape. Eerie and strange, the demon city was clearly broken.

"Cool," I breathed, and Edden shushed Nick's demands for information.

Knowing Trent was watching, though I couldn't see him, I turned my back on him so he couldn't read my lips as I whispered the first half of the incantation. Fortunately, I recalled the short translated phrase, since I didn't want to open my eyes to read it off my palm.

As the words fell from me, a slight imbalance of ever-after energy stirred in my feet, swirling up to settle in my belly. My knees grew loose as the grass bent toward me from all sides. Ley line strength flowed into me, carrying a pleasant slurry of tingles with it. I wondered how intense the sensation would grow, not wanting to admit it felt good.

My hair lifted in a sudden swirl of power as I began the second half. With all but the word of invocation said, the energy crested, sending a swirl of prickles to push evenly through me. It hung within me for a moment, then it flashed from me in a flat pulse of yellow, to run like ripples over the contours of the land.

"Holy crap," I said, then covered my mouth, hoping I hadn't just ruined the charm. I hadn't finished it yet. Shocked, I watched with my second sight as the flat sheet of ever-after energy sped away. The pulse was the color of my aura, and I felt uneasy, reminding myself that the spell had taken only the hue of my aura, not my aura itself.

The ring continued to expand until it went faint in the distance. I didn't know whether to be pleased or alarmed that it seemed to have gone all the way to the half-seen city. The outgoing ripple didn't leave the ever-after landscape unchanged, and my awe shifted to alarm as I realized that in its wake was a smattering of glittering green smears.

Bodies. They were everywhere. Beside me I could see the small ones, some no bigger than my pinky nail. Farther out, only the larger ones could be discerned. My first gut-twisting reaction dulled as I realized the charm was picking up everything that was dead: rodents, birds, bugs, everything. A huge number of big ones lay to the west in neat and orderly rows and columns. I had a moment of panic until I realized they were right where Trent's stables lay in the real world and were probably the bodies of his past race winners.

My heart slowed, and I tried to remember the last word, the one that would sensitize the charm to show only human remains. Brow furrowed, I stood in Trent's office, my feet firmly in a gateway to the ever-after, trying to remember what it had been.

"Oh, isn't this a delight," came a richly cultured voice from behind me.

I waited for someone to tell me who had just walked into Trent's office, but no one said a word. The hair pricked on the back of my neck. Anticipating the worst, I kept my eyes closed and my second sight open, and turned. My hand rose to my mouth and I froze. It was a demon dressed in a robe and slippers.

"Rachel Mariana Morgan?" it said, then smiled wickedly. I swallowed hard. Okay—it was my demon. "What are you doing in Trenton Aloysius Kalamack's ley line?" it questioned.

My breath came faster and I waved a hand behind me, trying to find the edge of the line. "I'm working," I said, my hand throbbing as I found it. "What are you doing here?"

It shrugged, its stance lengthening as it molded into the familiar vision of a lanky, leather-clad vamp with blond hair and a torn ear. Slumping into a bad-boy swagger, it licked its pouty lips, the chain running from a back pocket to its belt loop jingling. My breath went shaky. It was getting better at picking Kisten out of my mind; it had him down perfectly.

A pair of smoked glasses with round frames appeared in its hand, and it snapped the earpieces out with a quick flick of the wrist. "I felt you, love," it said, its teeth lengthening to that of a vampire's as it put the glasses on to hide its red goat eyes. "I simply ha-a-a-ad to see if you had come for a visit. You don't mind if I be this one, do you? He's got the balls of a bull."

God, help me. I shuddered, sticking my hand out of the line despite the stabbing hurt of ever-after imbalance. "I wasn't trying to get your attention," I whispered. "Go away."

I felt a touch on my hand and I jerked away. I could smell burnt coffee, and I wished Edden would quit doing that. "Who the devil is she talking to?" the FIB captain asked softly.

"I don't know," Jenks said. "But I'm not going into that line to see."

"Leave?" the demon said, its grin widening. "No, no, no. Don't be silly. I want to see how much ever-after you can manipulate. Go on, love. Finish your little charm," it encouraged.

In the background I could hear Trent and Quen having an intense argument. I wasn't willing to open my eyes and risk losing sight of the demon, but I thought Trent was winning. Nervous, I licked my lips, hating myself when the vision of Kisten did the same with a mocking slowness. "I forgot the last word," I admitted, then stiffened as I remembered. "Favilla," I blurted in relief, and the demon clapped his hands in delight.

I jumped as a second wave of ever-after jolted through me. Clutching my arms about myself as if to keep my aura intact, I watched the flat pulse of yellow dart away, following the path of the first. Algaliarept moaned, staggering as if in pleasure as it passed through it. I watched its reaction in near horror. The demon obviously liked it, but if it could have taken my aura, it would have by now. I think.

"Spun candy," it said, closing its eyes. "Flay me and slay me. Spun candy and nectar."

Swell. I had to get out of there.

While Algaliarept ran its hand over the grass and licked from its fingers the yellow smear of ley line power my charm had left on it, I scanned the surrounding countryside. My shoulders tightened in worry. Every glittering blur marking death was gone. Algaliarept seemed content seining the grass for remnants of my spell, so I snuck a quick look behind me, my fast spin jerking to a stop.

One of the horse graves glowed a bright red. It wasn't a horse, it was a person.

Trent had killed her, I thought, my attention darting to a new shape materializing within the ley line.

It was Trent, having stepped into it to see what I was seeing. His gaze went to the flash of red, widening, but his shock was nothing compared to when the demon shifted into a mirror copy of me, sleek and dangerous in a black silk body stocking.

"Trenton Aloysius Kalamack," it said, making my voice sexier than I ever could. It suggestively licked the last of my spell off its finger, and I wondered if the demon was making me look better than I actually did. "What a dangerous direction your thoughts have taken," the demon said. "You should be more careful whom you invite to play in your ley line." It hesitated, its hip cocked as it squinted over its glasses and compared our auras. "Such a pretty pair you make, like matched horses in my stables."

And it disappeared in a sensation of tingles, leaving me to stare across the ever-after landscape at Trent.

Twenty-One

My heels clacked with more authority than I felt as I walked down the long planked porch of Trent's foaling stable ahead of Trent and Quen. The empty row of box stalls faced the south and the afternoon sun. Atop them were the vet apartments. No one was in them, seeing as it was fall. Though horses could have their foals any time of the year, most stables enforced a strict breeding program so the mares all dropped their foals at once, getting the dangerous period over with at one time.

I thought the temporarily abandoned buildings were a perfect place to hide a body.

God help me, I thought with a sudden wash of ill feeling. How could I be so cavalier? Dr. Anders was dead.

A faint baying of a beagle lifted over the hazy afternoon. My head jerked up and my heart gave a pound. Farther down the dirt road was a kennel the size of a small apartment complex. Dogs were standing against their wire runs, watching.

Trent brushed past me, the breeze of his passage smelling of fallen leaves. "They never forget their quarry," he murmured, and I tensed.

Trent and Quen had accompanied us out here, leaving Jonathan behind to supervise the FIB officers still coming in from the gardens. The two men angled for an alcove tucked dead center between the row of box stalls. The wood-walled room was completely open to the wind and sun on one side. By the rustic furniture, I guessed it was a box stall converted to an outdoor meeting place for the vets to relax during births and such. I didn't like that no one was with them, but I wasn't about to join them. Slowing, I leaned against a support post, deciding I could keep an eye on them from there.

Three FIB officers with their cadaver dogs stood by the dog van parked in the shade of a huge oak tree. The doors were open, and Glenn's authoritative voice drifted to hang over the sun-warmed pastures. Edden was with them, looking out of place on the fringes. It was obvious that Glenn was in charge, by the way Edden kept his hands in his pockets and his mouth shut.

Flitting over them was Jenks, his wings red in excitement as he got in the way and offered a steady stream of unasked for advice that was ignored. The remaining FIB officers stood under the ancient oak that shadowed the parking lot. As I watched, a crime scene van pulled in with an exaggerated slowness. Captain Edden had called it after I found a body.

I snuck a glance at Trent, deciding the businessman looked a bit bothered if anything, as he stood in the informal room with his hands behind his back. Personally, I'd be visibly upset if someone was about to find an unexplained body on my property. I was sure this was where the unmarked grave had been shining.

Cold, I stepped off the covered walkway and into the sun. Hands gripping my elbows, I came to a halt in the sawdust parking lot, surreptitiously watching Trent from around a wisp of hair that had escaped my braid. He had put on a lightweight cream-colored hat against the sun and changed his shoes to boots in deference to our trip out to his stables. Somehow the mix looked right on him. It wasn't fair he should look so calm and relaxed. But then he jerked at the sound of a car door slamming. He was wound as tight as I was; he just hid it better.

Glenn said a few last, loud words and the group broke up. Tails waving, the dogs began a methodical search: two in the nearby pastures, one through the building itself, I couldn't help but notice that the handler assigned to the stables was using his skills, too, instead of relying on the dog's nose alone, looking up into rafters and opening latched panels.

Captain Edden touched his son's shoulder and headed toward me, short arms swinging. "Rachel," he said even before he was close, and I looked up, surprised he had used my first name. "We've been over this building already."

"If it isn't this building, then it's near here. Your men may not have been using my charms properly." *Or not at all,* I finished silently, knowing the prejudice humans felt was often covered up in smiles, lies, and hypocrisy. I knew I shouldn't jump to conclusions, though. I was fairly sure Trent had used a ley line charm to cover up her whereabouts, and so my spells would have been less than useful. My attention went from the dogs to Trent as Quen leaned to speak into his ear. "Shouldn't he be under arrest, or detained, or something?" I asked.

Edden squinted from the low sun. "Keep your panties on. Murder cases are won and lost in the collection of evidence, Morgan. You ought to know that."

"I'm a runner, not a detective," I said sourly. "Most of the people I tagged were charged before I brought them in."

He grunted at that. I thought that Captain Edden's adherence to "the rules" might lead to Trent vanishing in a puff of smoke to never be seen again. Seeing me fidget, he pointed at me and then at the ground, to tell me to stay where I was before he moseyed down to Quen and Trent. The squat human's hands were in his pockets but not far from his weapon. Quen hadn't a weapon, but looking at him shifting lightly on his feet, I didn't think he needed one.

I felt better when Edden subtly moved the two men apart, snagging a passing officer and telling him to ask Quen to detail their security procedures while he talked to Trent about the upcoming FIB fund-raiser dinner. Nice.

I turned away, watching the sun shine on the dog's yellow coat. The heat soaked into me, and the smell of the stables was warm with memory. I had enjoyed my three summers at camp. The scent of sweaty horse and hay mixing with the hint of aged manure was like a balm.

My riding lessons had been to help increase my balance, improve my muscle tone, and up my red blood cell count, but I think its largest benefit had been the confidence I gained from being in control of a big beautiful animal that would do anything I asked of it. To an eleven-year-old, that feeling of power was addictive.

A smile curved over me and I closed my eyes, feeling the autumn sun soak deeper. My friend and I had snuck out of our camp house one morning to sleep in the stables with the horses. The soft sounds of their breathing had been indescribably comforting. Our cabin mother had been furious, but it was the best I had slept the entire time.

My eyes opened. It had probably been the only night I'd slept uninterrupted. Jasmin, too, had slept well at the stables. And the pale girl had desperately needed sleep. *Jasmin!* I thought, clutching at the name. That's what the dark-haired girl's name had been. Jasmin.

The sound of radio chatter pulled my gaze from the field, leaving me feeling more melancholy than I would've expected. She had possessed an inoperable brain tumor. I didn't think even Trent's father's illegal activities could have fixed that.

My attention went to Trent. His green eyes were intent on me even as he talked to Edden, and I tugged my hat straight and tucked a wisp of hair behind an ear. Refusing to let him rattle me, I stared back. His gaze flicked behind me, and I turned as Sara Jane's red car pulled up with a scattering of sawdust beside the FIB vehicles.

The small woman bolted from her car, looking like a different person in her jeans and casual blouse. Slamming the door, she stalked forward. "You!" she accused, coming to a flustered halt before me, and I took a surprised step back. "This is your doing, isn't it!" she shouted up at me.

My face went blank. "Uh."

She put herself in my face, and I took another step back. "I asked for your help in finding my boyfriend," she said shrilly, eyes flashing. "Not accuse my employer of murder! You are an *evil* witch, so evil, you could—*could fire God*!"

"Um," I stammered, glancing at Edden for help. He and Trent were on their way over, and I backed up another step, holding my bag tight against me. I hadn't thought of this.

"Sara Jane," Trent soothed even before he was close. "It's all right."

She spun to him, her blond hair catching the highlights of the sun. "Mr. Kalamack," she said, her face shifting abruptly to fear and worry. Eyes pinched, she wrung her hands. "I'm sorry. I came as soon as I heard. I didn't ask her to come here. I—I . . ." Her eyes welled, and making a small noise, she dropped her head into her hands and started crying.

My lips parted in surprise. Was she worried about her job, her boyfriend, or Trent?

Trent gave me a dark look, as if it were my fault she was upset. It melted into genuine sympathy as he put a hand upon the small woman's shaking shoulders. "Sara Jane," he soothed, ducking his head to try and meet her eyes. "Don't even think that I blame you for this. Ms. Morgan's accusations have nothing to do with you going to the FIB about Dan." His wonderful voice rose and fell like puddles of silk.

"B-But she thinks you murdered those people," she stammered, sniffing as she pulled her hands from her face and smeared her mascara into a brown blur under her eye.

Edden shifted uneasily from foot to foot. The radio chatter from the FIB vehicles rose over the crickets. I refused to feel sorry that I had made Sara Jane cry. Her boss was dirt, and the sooner she realized that, the better off she would be. Trent hadn't killed those people with his hands, but he had arranged it, making him as guilty as if he had carved them up himself. My thoughts went to the picture of the woman on the gurney, and I steeled myself.

Trent pulled Sara Jane's gaze up with a gentle encouragement. I wondered at his compassion. I wondered how it would feel to have his beautiful voice soothing me, telling me that everything was all right. Then I wondered if there was a chance in hell of Sara Jane getting away from him with her life intact.

"Don't jump to conclusions," Trent said, handing her a linen handkerchief embroidered with his initials. "No one has been accused of anything. And there's no need for you to stay here. Why don't you go back home? This ugly business will be done as soon as we find the stray dog that Ms. Morgan's charm has fixed on."

Sara Jane shot me a poisonous look. "Yes sir," she said, her voice harsh.

Stray dog? I thought, torn between my desire to take her out to lunch for a heart-to-heart and my need to slap some sense into the woman.

Edden cleared his throat. "I'd ask Ms. Gradenko and yourself to stay here until we know more, sir."

Trent's professional smile faltered. "Are we being detained?"

"No sir," he said respectfully. "Merely a request."

"Captain!" a dog handler shouted from the second floor landing. My heart pounded at the excitement in the man's voice. "Socks didn't point, but we have a locked door."

Adrenaline zinged through me. I looked at Trent. His face showed nothing.

Quen and a small man started forward, accompanied by an FIB officer. The short man was obviously a past jockey now turned manager. His face was leathered and wrinkled, and he had a wad of keys with him. They jingled as he pulled one off and handed it to Quen. Body tense with that unnerving liquid menace, Quen handed it in turn to Edden.

"Thank you," the FIB captain said. "Now go stand with the officers." He hesitated, smiling. "If you would, please." He crooked his finger at a pair of FIB officers who had just arrived, pointing at Quen. They jogged over.

Glenn left the crime scene van with its radio and headed in our direction. Jenks was with him, and the pixy circled him three times before zipping ahead. "Give me the key," Jenks said as he came to a pixy-dust-laced halt between Edden and me. "I'll take it up."

Glenn looked at the pixy in bother as he joined us. "You're not FIB. Key, please."

An unheard sigh lifted through Edden. I could tell he wanted to see what was in that room and was making a conscious effort to let his son handle it. By rights, he had no business being out here. I imagine accusing a city council member of murder gave him more justification than he might have otherwise.

Jenks's wings clattered harshly as Captain Edden handed the key to Glenn. I could smell Glenn's sweat over his cologne, his eagerness. A cluster of people had joined the dog and her handler about the door, and gripping my bag tightly, I started to the stairs right along with him.

"Rachel," Glenn said, coming to a stop and catching my elbow. "You're staying here."

"I am not!" I exclaimed, jerking out of his grip. I glanced at Captain Edden for support, and the squat man shrugged, looking put out that he hadn't been invited, either.

Glenn's face hardened as he saw the direction of my gaze. Letting go of me, he said, "Stay here. I want you to watch Kalamack. Read his emotions for me."

"That's a load of crap," I said, thinking, crap or not, it was probably a good idea. "Your d—" I bit my tongue. "Your captain can do that," I amended.

Bother pinched his brow. "All right. It's crap. But you're going to stay here. If we find Dr. Anders, I want this crime scene tighter than—"

"A straight man's butt cheeks in prison?" Jenks offered, his tiny shape starting to glow.

He landed on my shoulder, and I let him stay. "Come on, Glenn," I wheedled. "I won't touch anything. And you'll need me to tell you if there are any lethal spells."

"Jenks can do that," he said. "And he doesn't have to step on the floor to do it."

Frustrated, I cocked my hip and fumed. I could tell that under his official veneer, Glenn was worried and excited all at the same time. He had only made detective recently, and I imagined this was the biggest case he'd worked. Cops spent their entire professional lives on the job and were never assigned a case with this many potential political ramifications. All the more reason I should be there. "But I'm your Inderland consultant," I said, grasping at straws.

He put a dark hand on my shoulder, and I pushed it off. "Look," he said, the rims of his ears going red. "There are procedures to follow. I lost my first court case because of a contaminated crime scene, and I'm not going to risk losing Kalamack because you were too impatient to wait your turn. It needs to be vacuumed, photographed, dusted, analyzed, and anything else I can think of. You come in right after the psychic. Got it?"

"Psychic?" I questioned, and he frowned.

"Okay, I'm kidding about the psychic, but if you put one manicured nail over that threshold before I say, I'll throw you out of here faster than stink on snake."

Faster than stink on snake? He must have been serious if he was mixing his metaphors.

"You want an ACG suit?" he asked, his eyes shifting from mine to the dog van.

I took a slow breath at the subtle threat. Anticharm gear. The last time I tried to take Trent down, he had killed the witness right out from under me. "No," I said.

My subdued tone seemed to satisfy him. "Good," he said, turning and striding away.

Jenks hovered before me, waiting. His dragonfly wings were red in excitement and the sun caught the glitter of pixy dust. "Let me know what you find, Jenks," I said, glad at least one representative from our sorry little firm would be there.

"You bet, Rache," he said, then zipped after Glenn.

Edden silently joined me, and I felt as if we were the only two people in high school who hadn't been invited to the big pool party, standing across the road and watching. We waited with an edgy Trent, an indignant Sara Jane, and a tight-lipped Quen as Glenn knocked at the door to announce his FIB presence—as if it wasn't obvious—and unlocked it.

Jenks was the first one in. He darted out almost immediately, his flight somewhat ragged as he landed on the railing. Glenn leaned in, then out of the black rectangular opening. "Get me a mask," I heard him mutter, clear through the hush.

My breath came fast. He had found something. And it wasn't a dog.

Hand over her mouth, an FIB officer extended a surgical mask to Glenn. A foul stench came faintly over the comforting aroma of hay and manure. My nose wrinkled, and I glanced at Trent to see his face empty. The parking lot went silent. An insect shrilled and another answered it. By the upstairs door, Socks whined and pawed at her handler's legs as she looked for reassurance. I felt ill. How had they missed the smell before? I'd been right. It had to have been spelled to keep it contained in the room.

Glenn took a step into the room. For a moment his back was bright with sun, then he took another to disappear, leaving an empty black door frame. A uniformed FIB officer handed him a flashlight from the threshold, a hand over her mouth. Jenks wouldn't look at me. His back was to the door as he stood on the railing, his wings bowed and unmoving.

My heart hammered and I held my breath as the woman in the doorway backed up and Glenn came out. "It's a body," he said to a second young officer, his soft voice carrying clear down to us. "Detain Mr. Kalamack for questioning." He took a breath. "Ms. Gradenko, too."

The officer's response was subdued, and she headed down the stairs to find Trent. I triumphantly looked to Trent, then sobered as I imagined Dr. Anders dead on the floor. I superimposed the memory of watching Trent kill his leading researcher, so quick and clean with a ready alibi waiting to be implemented. I had caught him this time, having moved too fast for him to cover his butt.

Sara Jane clutched at Trent. Fear, real and full, made her eyes wide and colored her pale cheeks. Trent didn't seem to notice her grip, his face seriously blank as he looked at Quen. Knees weak, I watched Trent take a slow breath as if steadying himself.

"Mr. Kalamack?" the young officer said, gesturing for Trent to accompany him.

A flicker of emotion flickered over Trent as the FIB officer said his name. I would have said it was fear if I thought anything could shake the man. "Ms. Morgan," Trent said in parting to me as he helped Sara Jane into motion. Edden and Quen went with them, the captain's round face slack with relief. He must have put his reputation further on the line than I had thought.

Sara Jane pulled from Trent and turned to me. "You bitch," she said, fear and hatred in her high, childlike voice. "You have no idea what you've done."

Shocked, I said nothing as Trent took her elbow with what I thought might be a warning strength. My hands started shaking and my stomach clenched.

Glenn was on the stairway. There was a disposable wipe in his hands and he was running it over his fingers as he made his way to me. He pointed to the crime scene van and then the black rectangle the door made. Two men lurched into motion. With a calm tension, they wheeled a black hard-walled suitcase forward.

I was going to get Trent Kalamack arrested, I thought. *Can I survive that?*

"It's a body," Glenn said as he came to a squinting halt before me, wiping his hands with yet another wipe. "You were right." He saw my face, and I knew I must have looked anxious as he followed my gaze to Trent standing with Quen and Edden. "He's just a man."

Trent was confident and unruffled, the picture of cooperation, a sharp contrast to Sara Jane's anger and hysterics. "Is he?" I breathed.

"It's going to be a while before you can go in," he said, taking a third towel and swabbing the back of his neck. He looked a little gray. "Maybe tomorrow, even. You want a ride home?"

"I'll stay." My stomach felt light. It occurred to me that I should probably call Ivy and let her know what was going on. If she'd talk to me. "Is it bad?" I asked. By the door, the two men chatted to a third as they unpacked a vacuum from the battered suitcase and put paper sleeves on over their shoes.

Glenn didn't answer, his eyes going everywhere but to me and that black doorway. "If you're staying, you'll need this," he said as he handed me an FIB badge with the word TEMPORARY on it. People were stringing yellow crime scene tape, and it looked like they were settling in. The radio was thick with short, terse requests, and everyone but the dogs and I seemed happy. I had to get upstairs. I had to see what Trent had done to Dr. Anders.

"Thanks," I whispered, looping the badge's necklace over my head.

"Get yourself a coffee," he said, looking toward one of the vans that had come in with us. FIB officers with nothing to do were already clustered around it. I nodded, and Glenn headed back to the stairway, his long legs taking them two at a time.

I glanced only once at Trent, in the open room between the box stalls. He was talking to an officer, apparently having waived his right to counsel. To foster a perception of innocence? I wondered. Or did he think he was too smart to need one?

Numb, I joined the FIB personnel around the van. Someone handed me a soda, and after I avoided everyone's eyes, they obligingly ignored me. I didn't particularly want to make friends, and I wasn't comfortable with the lightness of the conversations. Jenks, though, proceeded to charm sips of sugar and caffeine from everyone, doing impersonations of Captain Edden that got everyone laughing.

Eventually I found myself on the outskirts listening to three conversations as the sun moved and a new chill came into the air. The vacuum cleaner was faint, the on-again, off-again sound making me jittery. Finally it quit and didn't start up. No one seemed to have noticed. My eyes rose to the upper apartments, and I pulled my jacket closer about me. Glenn had come down just moments before to vanish inside the crime scene van. My breath slid in and out of me, as easy as the day I was born. Giving myself a push, I found myself moving to the stairway.

Immediately Jenks was on my shoulder, making me wonder if he had been keeping an eye on me. "Rache," he warned. "Don't go in there."

"I have to see." I felt unreal, the rough banister under my hand still warm from the sun.

"Don't," he protested, his wings clattering. "Glenn is right. Wait your turn."

I shook my head, the swinging of my braid forcing him off my shoulder. I needed to see before the atrocity was lessened with little bags, white cards with neatly printed words, and the careful collection of data designed to give madness structure so it could be understood. "Get out of my way," I said flatly, waving at him as he hovered belligerently in front of my face. He darted back, and I jerked to a stop as I felt a fingertip flick one of his wings. *I'd hit him?*

"Hey!" he shouted. Surprise, alarm, and finally anger washed over him. "Fine!" he snapped. "Go see. I'm not your daddy." Still swearing, he flew away at head height. Heads turned in his path as a torrent of foul words spilled nonstop from him.

My legs felt heavy as I forced myself to rise up the stairs. A sharp clattering of feet drew my attention up, and I stood sideways as the first of the vacuum guys hustled past me. A rank smell of decayed flesh trailed after him, and my gore rose. Forcing it down, I continued, smiling sickly at the FIB officer standing beside the door.

The smell was worse up there. My thoughts flashed to the pictures I had seen in Glenn's office, and I almost lost it. Dr. Anders could have only been dead a few hours. How could it have gotten so bad so quickly?

"Name?" the man said, his face stiff as he tried to look unaffected by the cloying stench.

I stared for a moment, then saw the notebook in his hand. There were several names on it, the last followed by the word "photographer." The remaining man on the outside walkway snapped his suitcase shut and dragged it thumping down the stairs. By the doorway was a video camera, its sophistication somewhere between that of a news crew and the one my dad used before he died to record my and my brother's birthdays. "Oh, um, Rachel Morgan," I said faintly. "Special Inderland consultant."

"You're the witch, right?" he said, writing my name down with the time and my temporary badge number. "You want a mask with your boots and gloves?"

"Yes, thank you."

My fingers felt weak as I put the mask on first. It reeked of wintergreen, blocking the stink of decayed flesh. Thankful, I looked in at the wooden floor, shining polished and yellow under the last of the sunlight. From around the corner and out of sight came the *snick snick snick* of a camera shutter. "I'm not going to bother him, am I?" I asked, my words muffled.

The man shook his head. "Her," he said. "And no, you won't bother Gwen. Watch it, or she'll have you holding tape measures."

"Thanks," I said, resolving to not do anything of the kind. My gaze flicked to the parking lot below me as I snapped the paper covers over my shoes. The longer I stayed there, the more likely it was that Glenn would realize I wasn't where he had left me. Stealing myself, I pinched the clip of the mask tighter, jerking as the pungent fragrance hit my nose. My eyes started to water, but I wasn't going to take it off for anything. I put my gloved hands in my pockets as if I were in a black-charm shop and entered.

"Who are you?" a strong, feminine voice challenged as my shadow eclipsed the sun.

My attention jerked to a willowy woman with dark hair tied in a no-nonsense ponytail. She had a camera in hand and was dropping a roll of film into a black bag tied to her hip.

"Rachel Morgan," I said. "Edden brought me in as a—" My words cut off as my eyes fell onto the torso tied to a hard-backed chair partially hidden behind her. My hand rose to my mouth and I forced my throat closed.

It's a mannequin, I thought. It had to be a mannequin. It couldn't be Dr. Anders. But I knew it was. Yellow nylon ropes bound her to the chair, and her top-heavy upper torso sagged, sending her head forward to hide her face. Stringy hair caked with black hung to further hide her expression, and I thanked God for that. Her legs were missing below both knees, the stumps sticking out like a small child's feet at the end of a chair. The ends were raw and ugly, swollen with decay. Her arms were gone at the elbows. Old black blood covered her clothes in a fantastic rivulet pattern so thick the original color couldn't be guessed.

My eyes flicked to Gwen, shocked at her blasé expression. "Don't touch anything. I'm not done yet, okay?" she muttered as she went back to her photographing. "God bless it. Can't I have even five minutes before everyone comes traipsing in here?"

"Sorry," I breathed, surprised I could still talk. Dr. Anders's slumped body was covered in blood, but there was surprisingly little of it under the chair. I felt light-headed, but I couldn't look away. Her lower cavity had been opened at her belly button, a perfectly round patch of skin the size of my fist propped open with a silver knife to show a careful dissection of her insides. There were suspicious gaps, and the incision was entirely bloodless, as if washed—or licked—clean. Where the flesh wasn't covered in blood, it was white, like wax. My gaze went to the pristine walls and floors. The body didn't match. It had been mutilated elsewhere and moved.

"This one is a real sicko," Gwen said, camera chattering away. "Look at the window."

She pointed with her chin, and I turned. It looked like a little cityscape was arranged on the wide shadowed sill. Squatty buildings were set out in straight lines in no apparent order of size. Small lumps of gray putty held them upright like glue. They were arranged around a thick class ring, placed like a monument among the city's streets. I looked closer, horror tightening my gut. I spun to the limbless corpse and back again.

"Yup," Gwen was saying as she clicked away. "He put them there on display. The larger parts he tossed into the closet."

My gaze shot to the tiny closet, then back to the shady windowsill. They weren't buildings, they were fingers and toes. He had cut her fingers off knuckle by knuckle, arranging them like Tinkertoys. The putty was bits of her insides, the viscera keeping it all together.

I felt hot, then cold. My stomach went light and I thought I might pass out. I held my breath as I realized I was hyperventilating. I was willing to bet she'd been alive during it.

"Get out," Gwen said, casually framing another shot. "If you spew in here, Edden will have a hissy."

"Morgan!" came a faint irate shout from the parking lot. "Is that witch in there?"

The outside officer's answer was muffled. I couldn't take my eyes off the wreck of a body on the chair. The flies crawled among the city streets the mutilated digits made, climbing the buildings like monsters in a B-movie. Gwen's clicks were like my heartbeat, fast and furious. Someone grabbed my arm and I gasped.

"Rachel," Glenn said, spinning me around to him. "Get your witch ass out of here."

"Detective Glenn," the officer by the door stammered. "She signed in."

"Sign her out," he growled. "And don't let her in again."

"You're hurting me," I whispered, feeling light and unreal.

He dragged me to the door. "I told you to stay out," he muttered fiercely.

"You're hurting me," I repeated, pushing at his fingers encircling my arm as he pulled me out. I hit the setting sun. It struck me like a goad, and I took a huge breath, snapping out of my stupor. That wasn't Dr. Anders. The body was too old, and it had been a man's ring. It looked like it had the university's logo on it. I thought I'd just found Sara Jane's boyfriend.

Glenn dragged me to the stairs. "Glenn," I said as I stumbled on the first step. I would have fallen but for his hold on me. Another FIB vehicle was easing into the lot. A mobile morgue this time. Glenn, not taking any chances, was bringing everything there.

Slowly my legs lost their watery feeling as I put distance between me and what I had seen upstairs. I watched the FIB officers joking among themselves, not understanding. I was clearly not cut out for crime scene work. I was a runner, not an investigator. My father had worked in the arcane division where most of the bodies showed up. Now I knew why he never said much about his day at the dinner table.

"Glenn," I tried again as he pulled me into the open room between the stalls. Trent stood in a corner with Sara Jane and Quen, quietly answering questions. Glenn jerked to a stop as he saw them. He looked at his father, who shrugged. The FIB captain sat before a laptop resting on a bail of straw propped up on its end. Someone had run a line from the crime van, and Edden's stubby fingers skated over the keyboard as he played subordinate so he could stay.

Irritation pinched Glenn's face and he gestured to the young FIB officer with Trent.

"Glenn," I said as the officer edged his way to us. "That isn't Dr. Anders up there."

Edden's round face went questioning behind his glasses. Glenn flicked a glance at me. "I know," he said. "The body is too old. Sit down and shut up."

The FIB officer came to a halt beside us, and my eyes widened as Glenn put an aggressive arm across his shoulders. "I told you to detain them," he said softly. "What are they still doing here?"

The man went white. "You meant in one of the cruisers? I thought Mr. Kalamack would be more comfortable here."

Glenn's lips pressed together and his neck muscles tensed. "Detained for questioning means move them to the FIB offices. You don't question people at the crime scene when it's this important. Get them out of here."

"But you didn't say . . ." The man swallowed. "Yes sir." Glancing once at Edden, he headed toward Trent and Sara Jane, looking apologetic, frightened, and very young. I didn't have time to spare him any pity.

Still angry, Glenn went to stand over his father's shoulder, typing in his own password with a stiff finger. My stomach gave a lurch and settled. I pushed the top of the computer down on his hands. Glenn clenched his jaw as they both looked up at me. I turned to Trent and Sara Jane on their way out, waiting until Edden and Glenn followed my gaze to them before saying, "I can't say for sure, but I think that's Dan."

Sara Jane's face remained blank for a telling moment. Eyes widening, she clutched at Trent. Her mouth opened and closed. Burying her face in his shoulder, she began sobbing. Trent patted her shoulder gently, but his eyes on me were narrowed in anger.

Edden pursed his lips in thought, which made his graying mustache stick out as we exchanged shrewd looks. Sara Jane didn't know Dan as well as she wanted everyone to think. Why would Trent make Sara Jane come to the FIB with a phony complaint of a missing boyfriend when he knew I'd find the body on his grounds? Unless he hadn't known about it? How could he not know?

Glenn, apparently, missed everything as he grabbed my upper arm and yanked me past a hysterical Sara Jane and out into the shadows of the oak tree. "Damn it, Rachel," he hissed as Sara Jane was led sobbing to a cruiser. "I told you to shut up! You're leaving. Now. That little stunt of yours might be enough to let Kalamack walk."

Even in my heels, Glenn was taller than me, and it ticked me off. "Yeah?" I shot back. "You asked me to read Trent's emotions. Well I did. Sara Jane doesn't know Dan Smather from her mailman. Trent had him killed. And that body has been moved."

Glenn reached for me, and I stepped out of his reach. His face tightened and he took a step back, exhaling slowly. "I know. Go home," he said, extending his hand for the temporary FIB badge. "I appreciate your assistance in finding the body, but as you said, you aren't a detective. Every time you open your mouth, you're making it easier for Trent's attorney to sway a jury. Just . . . go home. I'll call you tomorrow."

Anger warmed me, the last dregs of adrenaline making me feel weak, not strong. "I found his body. You can't make me leave."

"I just did. Give me the badge."

"Glenn," I said as I ducked out of the necklace before he snapped it off my neck, "Trent murdered that witch as sure as if he had twisted the knife."

He held my badge in a tight grip, his anger slowing enough to show his frustration. "I can talk to him, even hold him for questioning, but I can't arrest him."

"But he did it!" I protested. "You've got a body. You've got a weapon. You've got probable cause."

"I have a body that's been moved," he said, his voice flat from his repressed emotions. "My probable cause is conjecture. I've got a weapon six hundred employees could have planted. There is nothing to link Trent to the murder yet. If I arrest him now, he could walk even if he confesses later. I've seen it happen. Mr. Kalamack may have done this on purpose, planted the body and made sure there was nothing to link him to it. If this one doesn't stick, it will be twice as hard to pin another corpse to him, even if he makes a mistake later."

"You're afraid to take him down," I accused, trying to goad him into arresting Trent.

"Listen to me real good, Rachel," he said, jolting me into taking a step back. "I don't give a dingo's ass if you *think* Kalamack did it. I have to *prove* it. And this is the only chance I'm going to get." Turning halfway around, he scanned the parking lot. "Someone take Ms. Morgan home!" he said loudly. Without a backward glance, he stomped to the stables, his heavy steps silent on the sawdust.

I stared, not knowing what to do. My attention went to Trent getting into a FIB cruiser, his expensive suit making it look wrong. He gave me an unfathomable look before the door shut with a metallic thump. Lights off and slow, the two cars pulled out.

My blood hummed and my head was pounding. Trent wasn't going to get away with this unscathed. Eventually I would tie each and every murder back to him. Having found Dan's body on his grounds would give Captain Edden the clout to get whatever warrant I wanted. Trent was going to fry. I could play it slow. I was a runner. I knew how to stalk prey.

I turned away, disgusted. I hated the law even as I relied on it. I'd much rather fight a coven of black witches than a courtroom any day. I understood witches' mores better than lawyers'. At least witches used theirs.

"Jenks!" I shouted as Captain Edden emerged from the stables, keys jingling in his hands. Great. Now I was going to have to listen to a lecture of wise-old-man crap all the way home. It felt good to shout, and I took another breath to yell for Jenks again when the pixy came to a short stop in front of me. He was literally glowing in excitement, the dust that had sifted from him drifting into me from his momentum.

"Yeah, Rache? Hey, I heard Glenn kicked you out. I told you not to go up there. But did you listen to me? No-o-o-o-o-o. No one listens to me. I've got thirty some kids, and the only one who listens to me is my dragonfly."

My anger hesitated for an instant as I wondered if he really had a pet dragonfly. Then I shook myself, sending my thoughts onto how to salvage something from this. "Jenks," I said, "can you get home from here all right?"

"Sure. I'll hitch with Glenn or the dogs. No problem."

"Good." I glanced at Captain Edden as he approached. "Tell me what happens, okay?"

"Gotcha. Hey, for what's it's worth, I'm sorry. You gotta learn to keep your mouth shut and your fingers to yourself. See you later."

This coming from a pixy? "I didn't touch anything," I said, peeved, but he had already flitted back to Glenn's temporary office, leaving a head-high trail of dust to slowly dissipate.

Edden spared me a single glance as he passed me. Frowning, I followed him, yanking my door open. The car started, and I got in and slammed the door shut. Belt latched, I draped my arm on the open window and stared at the empty pasture.

"What's the matter?" I said nastily. "Glenn kick you out, too?"

"No." Edden shifted the car into reverse. "I need to talk to you."

"Sure," I said, for lack of anything better. A frustrated sigh slipped from me, catching as my gaze fell upon Quen. He stood unmoving in the shade of the old oak. There was no expression on his face. He must had heard my entire conversation with Glenn concerning Trent. A chill went through me, and I wondered if I had just put myself on Quen's "special people" list.

Green eyes fixed to me with a shocking intensity, Quen reached up to a low branch and swung himself up with the ease of picking a flower, disappearing into the old oak as if he had never existed.

Twenty-Two

Edden swung the car into the church's tiny weed-choked parking lot. He hadn't said much on the way back, his white knuckles and red neck telling me what he thought of the free-flow stream of consciousness that I had been spewing forth ever since he confessed the reason why he was playing chauffeur for me.

Shortly after finding the body, word had come over the radio that I was to be "removed from the FIB payroll." Seems it got out that a witch was helping them and the I.S. called foul. I might have been able to swing it if Glenn had cared to explain that I was merely a consultant, but he hadn't said a word, apparently still sulking over me contaminating his precious crime scene. That there wouldn't even *be* a crime scene if it hadn't been for me didn't seem to mean anything.

Slamming the car into park, Edden stared out the front window and waited for me to get out. I had to give him credit. It's not easy to sit and listen while someone compares your son to squid suckers and bat guano in the same breath.

Shoulders slumping, I didn't move. If I got out, it would mean it was over, and I didn't want it to be. Besides, keeping up a tirade for twenty minutes is tiring, and I probably owed him an apology if nothing else. My arm hung out the car's open window, and I could hear a piano playing some elaborate complicated thing that composers made up to show off their dexterity rather than any artistic expression. I took a breath. "If I could just talk to Trent—"

"No."

"Can I at least listen to the tape of his interview?"

"No."

I rubbed my temples, an escaped curl tickling my cheek. "How does anyone expect me to do my job if they won't let me do it?"

"It's not your job anymore," Edden said. The hint of anger pulled my head up. I followed his gaze to the pixy children sliding down the steeple on the tiny squares of wax paper I had cut for them yesterday. Neck stiff, Edden shifted in his seat to take his wallet from a back pocket. Flipping it open, he handed me some bills. "I was told to pay you in cash. Don't claim it on your taxes," he said flatly.

My lips pressed together and I snatched it, counting the money. *Pay me in cash? Out of the captain's pocket?* Someone had fallen deep into "cover your ass" mode. My stomach tightened as I realized it was far less than what we had agreed upon. I'd been almost a week on this. "And you'll get me the rest later, right?" I asked as I shoved it into my bag.

"Management won't pay for Dr. Anders's canceled class," he said, not looking at me.

Stiffed again. Not looking forward to telling Ivy I was short with my rent, I opened the door and got out. If I didn't know better, I'd say the piano was coming from the church. "Tell you what, Edden." I slammed the door shut. "Don't call me again."

"Grow up, Rachel," he said, jerking me back around. His round face was tight as he leaned across the seat to talk to me through the window. "If it had been me, I would have arrested you and given you to the I.S. to play with. He told you to wait, and you stepped all over his authority."

Fingers pulling the strap of my bag higher up my shoulder, my scowl faltered. I hadn't thought about it like that.

"Look," he said, seeing my sudden understanding. "I don't want to break our working relationship. Maybe when things cool off, we can try this again. I'll get the rest of the money to you somehow."

"Yeah. Sure." I straightened, my beliefs in the asinine, knee-jerk reactions of upper management reinforced, but maybe I owed Glenn an apology.

"Rachel?"

Yup. I owed Glenn an apology. I turned to Edden, a depressed, frustrated sigh shifting through me. "Tell Glenn I'm sorry," I muttered. Before he could respond, I sent my heels clacking on the cracked sidewalk and up the wide stone steps. For a moment there was silence. Then the car's fan belt whined as Edden backed up and drove away. The music was coming from inside. Still upset about my missing rent, I yanked open the heavy door and went in.

Ivy must be home. My frustration with Edden died with the chance to finally talk to her. I wanted to tell her that nothing had changed and she was still my friend—if she'd have me for one. Turning down the offer to be her scion might be an insurmountable insult in the vamp world. I didn't think so, though. What little I had seen of her showed guilt, not anger.

Ivy?" I called cautiously.

The piano cut off in mid-chord. "Rachel?" Ivy responded from the sanctuary. There was a worrisome hint of alarm in her voice. Damn, she was going to run. Then my eyebrows rose. That wasn't a recording. We had a piano?

Shrugging out of my coat, I hung it up and went into the sanctuary, blinking at the sudden light. We had a piano. We had a beautiful, black, baby grand piano sitting in an amber and green sunbeam coming in through the stain-glassed windows. Its top was propped up to show its insides, the wires gleaming and the stops all velvety smooth.

"When did you get the piano?" I asked, seeing her poised and ready to run. *Double damn. If she would just slow down enough to listen.*

My shoulders eased as she took up a chamois cloth and started rubbing the gleaming wood. She was wearing jeans and a casual top, and I felt terribly overdressed in my dress suit. "Today," she said as she dusted wood that needed no dusting. Maybe if I didn't say anything about what had happened, we could get back to the way things were. Ignoring a problem was a perfectly acceptable way to deal with it, as long as both people agree to never bring it up again.

"You didn't have to stop because of me," I said, scrambling to say something before she found a reason to leave.

She edged around to polish the back as I went to hit middle C.

Ivy straightened, her eyes slipping shut and her dust cloth stopping. "Middle C," she said as peace slackened her pale oval face.

I chose another, holding the key down to listen to it echo among the rafters. It sounded wonderful in the open, hard-walled space. Especially since the exercise mats were gone.

"F-sharp," she whispered, and I hit two at a time. "C and D-sharp," she said, opening her eyes. "That's an awful combination."

I smiled, relieved when she met my gaze. "I didn't know you could play," I said, hitching my bag up higher on my shoulder.

"My mother made me take lessons."

Nodding absently, I dug the money out of my bag. My thoughts went to the discrepancy between us as I leaned through the piano and handed it to her. Ivy was buying a baby grand piano and my dresser was made of pressboard.

Head bent over the money, she counted it. "You're missing two hundred," she said.

Taking a breath, I went into the kitchen. Guilt tugged at me as I dropped my bag on Ivy's antique kitchen table and went to the fridge for the juice. "Edden shorted me," I shouted to the sanctuary, thinking she probably wouldn't leave if we were talking about money. "I'll get the rest. I'm going to talk to the baseball team again."

"Rachel . . ." Ivy said from the hall, and I spun, my heart pounding. I hadn't heard her footsteps. She took in my surprise, and a wash of inner pain flickered over her. Edden's freakin' attempt at compensation was in her hand, and I hated everything. Just everything.

"Forget it," she said, making me feel even better. "I can cover for you this month."

Again, I finished silently for her. Damn it to hell. I ought to be able to pay my own bills.

Depressed, I took off my hat and hung it on my chair. My heels were next, and I kicked them off, sending them flying out the archway to land thumping somewhere in the living room. In my stocking feet, I sat slumped at the table and nursed my juice as if it was a beer at closing time. There was an open bag of cookies on the table, and I pulled them closer. Chocolate cream would make everything better if I could get enough into me.

Ivy stretched to drop the money into the jar atop the fridge. It wasn't the safest place to keep the money we pooled to pay our bills, but who was going to steal from a Tamwood vampire? Saying nothing, she slipped into her chair across from me, the length of the table between us. The fan of her computer whirled up to speed as she jiggled the mouse. My bad mood eased. She hadn't left. She was working at her computer. I was in the same room with her. Maybe she felt safe enough that she could at least listen.

"Ivy—" I started.

"No," she said, flicking me a frightened look.

"I just want to say I'm sorry," I rushed. "Don't go. I'll drop it."

How could someone so strong and powerful be so afraid of herself? The woman was a conflicting mass of strength and vulnerability that I didn't understand.

Her eyes went everywhere but to mine. Slowly her wire-tight posture relaxed. "But it wasn't your fault," she whispered.

Then why do I feel like crap? "I'm sorry, Ivy," I said, pulling her eyes to mine for a brief moment. They were as brown as chocolate, with no hint of black rimming them. "It's just—"

"Stop," she said, her gaze going to her hand clutching the table, the nails still shiny from the clear polish she had put on to go to Piscary's. She visibly forced her grip to relax. "I . . . won't ask you to be my scion again if you don't say anything more." The last was hesitant, disquieting in her vulnerability.

It was almost as if she knew what I was going to say and couldn't bear to hear it. I would not be her scion—I couldn't. The tie that would bind us would be too tight and take from me my independence. While I knew in the vampire existence that the giving and receiving of blood was not necessarily equated with sex, to me they were the same. And I didn't want to say, "Can we just be friends?" It was trite and degrading, even if to be her friend was all I wanted. She'd take the words as the brush-off most people used them for. I liked her too much to hurt her that way. And I could tell it wasn't a lingering bitterness that prompted her promise. She wouldn't ask me to be her scion because she didn't want the pain of being rejected again.

I didn't understand vampires. But that's where Ivy and I were.

She met my eyes with a faltering sureness that strengthened as she saw my silent agreement to ignore what had happened. Her shoulders eased and she regained a wisp of her usual confidence. But as I sat in our kitchen with my feet in the sun, I went cold with the knowledge of how badly I was using her. She was freely giving me protection against the many vampires that would take advantage of my scar—in essence, she was ensuring my free will—and she was willing to overlook that I wasn't paying for it in the usual vampiric fashion. God help me, it was enough to make me hate myself. She wanted something I couldn't give her, and she was content to take my friendship in the hopes that someday I could give more.

I took a slow breath, watching her pretend not to notice my eyes on her as I let the pieces fall into place. I couldn't leave. It was more than not wanting to lose the only real friend I had had in eight years or my desire to help her win the war she fought against herself. It was the fear of being turned into a plaything by the first vampire I ran into in a moment of weakness. I was trapped by convenience, and the tiger with me was willing to lap cream and purr, betting she'd find a way to change my mind. *Great. I'd have no problem sleeping tonight.*

Ivy's eyes met mine, her breathing hesitating a bare second as she realized that I'd finally figured it out. "Where's Jenks?" she asked, turning to her screen as if nothing had happened.

I exhaled slowly, coming to grips with my new outlook. I could leave and fight off every lustful vamp I ran into, or I could stay under Ivy's mantle, trusting I'd never have to fight her off instead. As my dad was fond of saying, a known danger was far better than an unknown one.

"At Trent's helping Glenn," I said, my fingers trembling as I reached for another cookie. I'd stay. We had an understanding. Or was Nick right, in that I really did want her to bite me but couldn't accept that my "preferences" had slid a little? Surely the former. "I'm off the case. I found a body and word got out a witch was helping the FIB."

Her eyes met mine over the screen between us, her thin eyebrows high. "You found a body? At Trent's compound? You're kidding."

I nodded, slumping with my elbows on the table, unwilling to delve any deeper into my psyche right now. I was too tired. "I'm pretty sure it's Dan Smather's, but it doesn't matter. Glenn is more uptight than a pixy in a room full of frogs, but Trent's going to walk." My thoughts shifted from what I was going to do about Ivy to the memory of Dan's mutilated body strapped to the chair. "Trent is too smart to leave anything to connect him to the body," I said. "I don't understand why it was on his property to begin with."

She nodded, her attention going back to her screen. "Maybe he put it there."

A wry grimace crossed me. "That's what Glenn thinks. That Trent is the murderer but wanted us to find it, knowing we couldn't link it to him, and therefore making it twice as hard to catch him if he makes a mistake later on. It fits with Sara Jane's reaction. She doesn't know Dan Smather better than her UPS man, but something . . ." I hesitated, trying to put my feeling into words. "Something isn't right." I thought back to the picture she'd given me. It had been the same photo as the one on his TV. I should've known then that their courtship was contrived.

I was starting to doubt my own, grudge-laced belief that Trent was responsible for the murders, and that was disturbing. He was capable of murder—I'd seen that firsthand—but the mutilated, bloodless body tied to that chair and tortured was far and away from the clean, fast death he had inflicted upon his head geneticist last spring. Thinking, I reached for a cookie. Biting the head off, I got up to hunt through the fridge to decide what I was going to fix for dinner and let my subconscious work on it. Maybe I'd make something special. It had been a while since I had done more than open boxes and stir things on the stove.

I glanced at Ivy, feeling guilty and relieved all at the same time. No wonder she thought I wanted more than to be her roommate. Some of this was my fault. Most maybe.

"So what did Trent do when you found the body?" Ivy asked, mouse clicking as she checked out her chat rooms. "Any guilt?"

"Ah, no," I said, pushing my uncomfortable feelings aside even as I took a half pound of lean hamburger out of the freezer and set it clunking into the sink. "And the surprise he let slip wasn't that I found a body but that it was Dan's body. That's why I don't like the idea that he put it there to cover himself. He knows more than he's saying, though." I gazed out the window at the sunlit garden and the glimmers of pixy wings as Jenks's kids fought off a migrating hummingbird from the last of the lobelias. It had to be migrating. Jenks would have killed it before letting competition get a foothold in his garden.

As the children shouted and called, working together to drive the hapless bird away, my thoughts returned to the worry Trent had let show when I found that ley line running through his office. He had been more upset about me finding that line than finding Dan's body.

The ley line. That's where the real question lurked. My fingers tingled as I turned, wiping the frost from the hamburger off on a towel instead of my suit dress. I glanced at the window, wondering if I would draw more attention by shutting it or if I should press my luck and hope Jenks's kids were too busy to eavesdrop. Ivy pulled back from her computer screen as she saw my sudden secrecy. Jenks had a big mouth, and I didn't want him knowing of my suspicions of Trent's possible ancestry. He would blab it around, and Trent would hire a plane to "accidentally" drop Agent Orange on the entire block to stop the rumors.

Splitting the difference, I shut the curtains and stood by the window where I could see the shadow of pixy wings should any flit close enough to hear. "Trent has a ley line in his office," I said, my voice hushed.

Ivy stared at me in the blue-tinted sun. "No kidding? What are the chances of that?"

She didn't get it. "So that means he must use them," I prompted.

"And . . ." Her eyebrows rose in question.

"So who can use ley lines?" I shot back.

Her jaw dropped in sudden understanding. "He's human or a witch," she breathed. She got to her feet in a movement so quick, it set me on edge. Coming to the sink, she pushed the curtain aside and shut the window with a thump. "Does Trent know you saw it?" she asked, her eyes black in the dimmer light.

"Oh, I'd say he does." I went to get another cookie to subtly put some space between us. "Seeing as I had to use the line to find the body."

Her lips pressed together and her lanky stance went tight. "You put your head on the block again. You, me, Jenks, and his entire family. Trent will do anything to keep this quiet."

"If he was that worried about it, he wouldn't have risked putting his office on the line," I protested, hoping I was right. "Anyone looking would find it. He could still be Inderlander or human. We're safe, especially if I don't say anything about the ley line."

"Jenks might figure it out," she insisted. "You know how he'll blab it. He'd love the prestige of finding out what Trent is."

I snatched a cookie. "What am I supposed to do? If I tell him to keep his mouth shut about the line, he'll only try to figure out why."

Her fingers drummed on the counter as I ate the shortbread and cream. In an unnerving display of strength, she used one hand to lever herself up to sit atop the cabinets. Her face had come alive, her thin eyebrows creased with the chance to solve the long-running mystery. "So what do you think he is? Human or witch?"

Returning to the sink, I ran hot water over the frozen meat. "Neither." It was a flat admission. Ivy remained silent, and I turned the water off. "He's neither, Ivy. I would stake my life that he isn't a witch, and Jenks swears he's more than human."

Is this why I stayed? I wondered, seeing her eyes alight and her mind working with mine. Her logic, and my intuition. In spite of the problems, we worked well together. We always had.

Ivy shook her head, her features blurred in the blue-curtained dusk, but I could feel her tension rising. "It's the only choices we have. You eliminate everything, and whatever remains, no matter how improbable, is the answer."

It didn't surprise me she was quoting Sherlock Holmes. The anal logic and brusque nature of the fictional detective fit right in with Ivy's personality. "Well, if you want to entertain the improbable," I muttered, "you can lump demons in with the possibilities."

"Demons?" Ivy's tapping fingers stilled.

I shook my head in bother. "Trent's not a demon. I only mentioned it because demons are from the ever-after and so can manipulate ley lines, too."

"I'd forgotten that," she breathed, the soft sound sending a shiver down my spine, but she was intent on her thoughts and had no idea how creepy she was getting. "That you're related, I mean. Witches and demons." An affronted snort slipped past me, and she shrugged apologetically. "Sorry. Didn't know it was a sore spot."

"It isn't," I said tightly, though it was. There had been a flurry of controversy about a decade ago when a nosy human in the field of Inderland genealogy got hold of the few genetic maps that had survived the Turn, theorizing that because witches could manipulate ley lines, we had originated in the ever-after along with demons. Witches aren't related to demons. But much to our embarrassment, science forced us to admit aloud that we had evolved right along next to them in the ever-after.

Finding funding with that unsavory tidbit, the woman then went beyond her original theory, using the rates of RNA mutation to properly place the time of our en masse migration to this side of the ley lines about five thousand years ago. Witch mythology claimed that a demon uprising had prompted the move, leaving the elves to foolishly wage a losing battle, since they wouldn't leave their beloved fields and woods to be raped of their natural resources and polluted. It sounded like a viable theory, and the elves had lost all their history by the time they gave up and followed suit a measly two thousand years ago.

That humans had developed skill in ley line magic about that time was blamed on the elves' practice of using their magic to hybridize with humanity to stave off the extinction the demons started and the Turn finished. My thoughts turned to Nick, and I slumped. It was just as well witches were so far from humanity that even magic couldn't bridge the gap. Who knew what an uninformed witch/human hybrid skilled in ley lines might do? That the elves had brought humanity into the ley-line-using family was bad enough. The elves' dexterity with line magic had slipped into the human genome as if it belonged. It was enough to make you wonder.

Elves? I thought, going cold. It had been staring me right in the face. "Oh—my—God," I whispered.

Ivy looked up, her swinging legs stilling as she took in my expression.

"He's an elf," I whispered, the thrill of discovery bubbling up making my pulse race. "They didn't die out in the Turn. He's an elf. Trent is a freaking elf!"

"Whoa, wait a minute," Ivy warned. "They're gone. If any were alive, Jenks would know. He'd be able to smell it."

I shook my head, pacing to the hallway to look for winged eavesdroppers. "Not if the elves went underground for a pixy/fairy generation. The Turn pretty much did them in, and it wouldn't be hard to hide what survived until the last pixy who knew what they smelled like died. They only live about twenty years or so, pixies I mean." My words tumbled over themselves as I rushed to get it out. "And you saw how Trent doesn't like them or fairies. It's almost a phobia. It fits! I can't believe it! We figured it out!"

"Rachel," Ivy cajoled as she shifted atop the counter. "Don't be stupid. He's not an elf."

Arms crossed, I pressed my lips together in frustration. "He sleeps at noon and midnight," I said, "and he's most active at dawn and dusk, just like elves were. He possesses nearly vamplike reflexes. He likes his solitude but is damn good at manipulating people. My God, Ivy, the man tried to ride me down on horseback like prey under the full moon!" I tossed my arms as I gestured. "You've seen his gardens and that artificial forest of his. He's an elf! And so are Quen and Jonathan."

She shook her head. "They died. All of them. And what would they have to gain by letting even Inderland think they were gone if they weren't? You know how we throw money at endangered species. Especially intelligent ones."

"I don't know," I said, exasperated with her disbelief. "Humanity was never keen on their history of stealing human babies and substituting their own failing infants. That would be enough for me to keep my mouth shut and my head down until everyone thought we were dead."

Ivy made a noise of doubt deep in her throat, but I could see her belief shifting. "He works ley lines," I insisted. "You said it yourself. Eliminate the impossible, and what's left, no matter how

THE GOOD, THE BAD, AND THE UNDEAD • 611

improbable, is the truth. The man isn't human or witch." My eyes closed as I remembered biting both Jonathan and Trent when I had been a mink, struggling to escape. "He can't be. His blood tastes like cinnamon and wine."

"He's an elf," Ivy said, her voice shockingly flat. I opened my eyes. Her face was alive and alight. "Why didn't you tell me he tasted like cinnamon?" she said as she slipped from the counter, her black ankle boots hitting the linoleum without a sound.

Self-preservation pulled me a step from her before I knew I had moved. "I thought it might have been from the drugs he had knocked me out with," I said, not liking that the mention of blood had jerked her into motion. The brown of her irises was shrinking behind her widening pupils. I was sure it was from discovering Trent's ancestry and not me standing in her kitchen with my blood pounding and my palms sweating. But still . . . I didn't like it.

Mind whirling, I gave her a warning look and put the island counter between us. *Okay, so I knew Trent's history.* Telling him would certainly get me an audience with him, but how do you tell a serial killer you know his secret without ending up dead?

"You aren't going to tell him you know," Ivy said, giving me an apologetic look before putting her back against the counter in a blatant show of keeping her distance.

"I have to talk to Trent. He'll talk to me if I drop this on his plate and serve it up with gravy. I'll be okay. I have that blackmail on him."

"Edden will slap you with a harassment suit if you so much as call him," Ivy warned.

My eyes lit upon the bag of sandwich cookies with their little oak tree and clapboard sign. Moving slowly, I slid the bag closer, picking out a figure with all his limbs intact. Ivy's eyes dropped to the cellophane, then rose to me. I could almost see her thoughts aligning themselves to mine. She gave me one of her few honest smiles, letting slip only the barest glimmer of teeth as a wicked yet almost shy look brought her alive.

A shiver laced through me, pulling my insides tight. "I think I know how to get his attention," I said, biting the head clean off the chocolate-covered cookie and wiping the crumbs from my lips. But in the back of my head, a new question niggled, incited by Nick's constant worry. Was the thrill of anticipation I felt rising through me from my coming conversation with Trent . . . or that tiny whisper of white teeth?

Twenty-Three

The clamor of the bus's diesel engine was obnoxious as it jolted into motion and struggled to find momentum while going uphill. I stood on the weed-edged sidewalk and waited for it to pass before crossing the street. The soft whooshes of cars made a comforting background to the birds, insects, and the occasional quacking of a duck. I turned, feeling someone's eyes on me.

It was a Were, with black hair to his shoulders and a trim body that said he ran on two legs as much as he did four. His attention went from me to the park, and he sank back into the tree he was leaning against, adjusting his worn leather coat. My pace faltered as I recognized him from the university, but he looked away and pulled his hat down over his eyes, dismissing me. He wanted something, but it was obvious he knew I was busy and was willing to wait.

Loners were like that, and from his confident, set-apart look, I imagined that's what he was. He probably had a run for me and wasn't willing to knock on my door, more comfortable with waiting to catch me when I wasn't busy. It had happened before. Weres had a tendency to view anyone who lived on hallowed ground as mysterious and esoteric.

Appreciating his professionalism, I started down the sidewalk in the opposite direction of the bus, the noon sun warm on my shoulders. I liked Eden Park, especially this little used end of it. Nick worked at the art museum cleaning artifacts just down the road, and we occasionally had my lunch and his dinner alfresco at the small overlook above Cincinnati. But my favorite place was the end that looked the other way, over the river and to the Hollows.

My father had brought me here Saturday mornings, where we would eat doughnuts and feed crumbs to the ducks. My mood went somber as I recalled the one occasion when he brought me after one of his few arguments with my mother. It had been night, and we'd watched the lights of the Hollows flicker across the river, the world seeming to continue around us as we were caught in a drop of time hanging on the lip of the present, reluctant to fall and make room for the next. Sighing, I tugged my short leather jacket closer and watched my step.

Yesterday I had sent a bag of cookies to Trent by special messenger with a card that simply said "I know." The cellophane bag and sandwich cookies had been just rife with an insulting mix of elf and magic propaganda that even the enlightened times after the Turn hadn't been able to quell. Sure enough, I was awoken that morning by the phone ringing. Then ringing again when the machine clicked off. And ringing again. And again. And again.

Eight o'clock in the morning is an ungodly time for witches—I had only been asleep four hours—but Jenks couldn't answer the phone, and waking Ivy up wasn't a good idea. The long and short of it was that Trent invited me to his garden for tea. No freaking way. I told Jonathan I'd meet Trent in Eden Park at four at Twin Lakes Bridge, right after his boss's nappies.

Twin Lakes Bridge was a rather grand name for the concrete footbridge, but I knew the troll that lived under it and felt I could rely on him in a pinch. The water chattering over the artificial rapids would distort any listening spell. Better yet, on football Sunday, the park would be almost deserted, giving us enough privacy to talk, yet retain enough people to deter any stupid choices Trent might be tempted to make, like outright killing me.

I forced my gaze up from the sidewalk as I passed Glenn's unmarked FIB car parked illegally at the curb. He had probably been assigned to keep an eye on Trent. Good. That meant I wouldn't have to truss up whatever FIB officer Edden had tailing the man so Trent and I could talk uninterrupted.

I had made a point to bring no spells with me, other than my usual pinky ring. No cumbersome bag, either. Just my little used driver's license and my bus pass. The reason for the lack of personal effects was twofold. Not only could I run faster if Trent tried something, but I wouldn't give Trent the opportunity to claim I'd slipped him a charm.

The strain from my quick pace made my calves ache, and I scanned the large park, finding it as sparsely populated as I'd hoped. I had ridden past the first stop since I wanted a good look-see before getting off. Not to mention it was impossible to make a graceful entrance from a bus. Even the leather pants, matching leather jacket, and red halter top wouldn't help.

I slowed, taking in the pond water, green with copper sulfate, and the lush grass. The trees were tipped with color, not yet hurried on by frost. Trent's red blanket made a vivid splash upon the ground. He was alone, pretending to read. I wondered where Glenn was, thinking that unless he was in the few large trees or the skinny apartments across the street, he was likely lurking in the bathrooms.

Arms swinging, I waved across the park to Jonathan, standing sullen by the Gray Ghost Limo in the sun. Clearly unhappy, he raised his wrist and spoke into his watch. My stomach tightened as I imagined Quen watching me from the trees. I forced my pace to a sedate saunter as I went to the public rest rooms, my vamp-made boots silent on the walkway.

For bathrooms, they were elegant, speaking of a more gracious time, with the ivy covered stone and cedar shingles. The metal shutters and doors lent themselves to the permanence of the structure as much as the fading perennials smothering it. Sure enough, I found Glenn inside the men's room, his back to me as he stood on the toilet with a pair of binoculars, watching Trent through the broken window. The bridge was within his view, and I felt better knowing he would be watching me.

"Glenn," I said, and he spun, almost slipping off the toilet.

"God bless it!" he swore, giving me a dark look before returning his attention out the window. "What are you doing here?"

"And good morning to you, too," I said politely, wanting to smack him a good one and ask why he hadn't stuck up for me yesterday and kept me working. The room reeked of chlorine and had no partitions at all. The ladies' bathroom at least had stalls.

His neck tensed, and I gave him credit for not looking from Trent for even a moment. "Rachel," he warned. "Go home. I don't know how you found out Mr. Kalamack was here, but if you go near him, I'll give you to the I.S. myself."

"Look, I'm sorry," I said. "I made a mistake. I should have stayed put until you said I could enter that crime scene, but Trent asked me to meet him here, so you can go Turn yourself."

Glenn lowered his binoculars, his face slack as he looked at me.

"Scouts honor," I said, giving him a sarcastic salute.

His eyes went distant in thought. "This isn't your run anymore. Get out of here before I have you arrested."

"You could have at least gotten me in to Trent's FIB interview yesterday," I said, taking an aggressive step forward. "Why did you let them shut me out? This was *my run!*"

His hand rested on the two-way on his hip, right next to his weapon. His brown eyes were angry with a past incident that didn't include me. "You were ruining the case I was building against him. I told you to stay out, and you didn't."

"I said I was sorry. And there wouldn't even be a case if it wasn't for me," I exclaimed. Frustrated, I put my hand on my hip and raised my other in an angry gesture, jerking to a halt as someone came in. It was a frumpy looking man in a frumpy looking coat. He stood in shock for three heartbeats, running his eyes over Glenn in his expensive black suit standing on the can to me in my leather pants and jacket.

"Uh, I'll come back," he said, then hastened out.

I turned back to Glenn, having to tilt my head at an awkward angle to look up at him. "I can't work for the FIB anymore, thanks to you. I'm informing you of my meeting with Trent as a courtesy from one professional to another. So back off and don't interfere."

"Rachel . . ."

My eyes narrowed. "Don't mess with me, Glenn. Trent asked for this meeting."

The faint worry lines around Glenn's eyes deepened. I could see his thoughts warring among themselves. I wouldn't have bothered telling him at all except he probably would have called in everyone from his dad to the bomb squad when he saw me with Trent.

"Are we clear on this?" I asked belligerently, and he stepped off the toilet.

"If I find out you lied to me—"

"Yeah, yeah, yeah." I turned to go.

He reached for me. I felt his hand coming and jerked away, spinning. I shook my head in warning, but his eyes were wide at how fast I had moved. "You just don't get it, do you?" I said. "I am not human, this is Inderland business, and you are in way over your head." And with that thought to keep him awake at night, I strode back out into the sunlight, trusting he would keep an eye on me and not get in my way.

My arms swung as I attempted to dispel the last of the adrenaline, and my skin seemed to prickle as Jonathan's eyes fell on me. Ignoring him, I tried to spot where Quen had hidden himself as I made my way to the concrete bridge. On the other side of the twin ponds was Trent upon his blanket. He still had that book in his hand, but he knew I was here. He was going to make me wait, which was fine by me. I wasn't ready for him yet.

Deep in the shadows of the bridge ran a wide ribbon of fast water connecting the two ponds. My foot hit the bridge, and the puddle of purple amidst the current shuddered.

"Heyde-hey," I said, stopping just shy of the bridge's apex. Yeah, it was kind of stupid, but it was the traditional greeting between trolls. If I was in luck, Sharps would still have possession of this bridge.

"Heyde-ho," said the dark puddle of water, pulling itself up in a series of ripples until a dripping, craggy face showed. Algae grew on his otherwise bluish skin and his fingernails were white with the mortar he scraped from the bottom of the bridge to supplement his diet.

"Sharps," I said, truly pleased as I recognized him by his one white eye, blinded by a past fight. "How's the water flowing?"

"Officer Morgan," he said, sounding tired. "Can you wait until sundown? I promise I'll leave tonight. The sun is too bright right now."

I smiled. "It's just Rachel now. I quit the I.S. And don't move on account of me."

"You did?" The puddle of water sank back down until only a mouth and good eye showed. "That's fine. You're a nice girl. Not like the warlock they have now, coming at noon with electric prods and clangy bells."

I winced in sympathy. Trolls had extremely sensitive skin that kept them out of direct light most of the time. They tended to destroy whatever bridge they were under, which was why the I.S. continually chased them out. But it was a losing battle. As soon as one left, another took his place, and then there was a fight when the original troll wanted his home back.

"Hey, Sharps," I said. "Maybe you could help me."

"Anything I can manage." A purple-hued, skinny arm reached up to pick a grain of mortar from the underside of the bridge.

I glanced at Trent, seeing he was making motions to head my way. "Has anyone been around your bridge this morning? Maybe leaving a spell or charm behind?"

The puddle of oily water drifted to the opposite side of the bridge and into a patch of dappled shade where I lost sight of him. "Six kids kicked rocks off the bridge, one dog took a leak at the footing, three adult humans, two strollers, a Were, and five witches. Before dawn, there were two vamps. Someone got bit. I smelled the blood that hit the southwest corner."

I looked over, seeing nothing. "No one left anything, though?"

"Just the blood," he whispered, sounding like bubbles against rocks.

Trent had stood and was brushing his pants off. My pulse quickened and I pulled the strap to my shirt straight under my jacket. "Thanks, Sharps. I'll watch your bridge if you want to take a swim."

"Really?" His voice took on a hopeful, incredulous sound. "You'd do that for me, Officer Morgan? You're a damn fine woman." The smear of purple water hesitated. "You won't let anyone take my bridge?"

"No. I may have to leave quick, but I'll stay as long as I can."

"Damn fine woman," he said again. I leaned to watch a surprisingly long ribbon of purple slip out from under the bridge and flow around the rocks to the deeper pool of water in the lower basin. Trent and I would have a good measure of privacy, but a troll's territorial drive was so strong, I knew Sharps would keep an eye on me. I felt unjustifiably secure with Glenn on one side in the men's bathroom and Sharps in the water on the other.

Putting my back to the sun and Glenn's eyes, I leaned against the railing of the bridge to watch Trent stride over the grass to me. Behind him on the blanket he left an artfully arranged set of two wineglasses, a bottle packed in ice, and a bowl of out-of-season strawberries looking as if it were June, not September. His pace was measured and sure on the surface, but I could see it was fraught with nervousness beneath, giving away how young he really was.

He had covered his fair hair with a lightweight sun hat to shadow his face. It was the first time I had seen him in anything other than a business suit, and it would be easy to forget he was a murderer and a drug lord. The confidence of the boardroom was still there, but his trim waist, wide shoulders, and smooth face made him look more like an especially fit soccer dad.

His casual attire accentuated his youth instead of hiding it, as his Armani suits did. A wisp of blond hair peeked from behind the cuffs of his tasteful, button-down shirt, and I spared a thought that it was probably as soft and light as the pale hair drifting about his ears. His green eyes were pinched as he approached, squinting from the reflected sun or from worry. I was betting the latter since his hands were behind his back so I wouldn't shake with him.

Trent slowed as he stepped upon the bridge. His expressive eyebrows were slanted, and I remembered his fear when Algaliarept had turned into me. There was only one reason the demon would have done that. Trent was afraid of me, either for still falsely thinking I had set Algaliarept on him, or for having snuck into his office three times in as many weeks, or for me knowing what he was.

"None of the above," he said, his casual shoes scuffing as he came to a halt.

A wash of cold shocked through me. "I beg your pardon?" I stammered, pulling myself up and away from the railing.

"I'm not afraid of you."

I stared, his liquid voice melting itself into the chatter of water surrounding us.

"And I can't read your mind, either, just your face."

My breath came in a soft sound and I shut my mouth. *How had I lost control so fast?*

"You took care of the troll, I see," he said.

"Detective Glenn, too," I said as I touched my hair to be sure my curls hadn't escaped my braid. "He won't bother us unless you do something stupid."

His eyes tightened at the insult. He didn't move, keeping that same five feet between us. "Where's your pixy?" he asked.

Irritation pulled me straight. "His name is Jenks, and he's somewhere else. He doesn't know, and I'd just as soon keep it that way as he has a big mouth."

Trent visibly relaxed. He went to stand opposite me, the narrow width of the bridge between us. It had been hard to slip Jenks this afternoon, and Ivy finally stepped in, taking him out on a nonexistent run. I think she was actually going for doughnuts.

Sharps was playing with the ducks, pulling them under to bob to the surface and fly away quacking. Turning from the sight, Trent leaned his back against the railing and crossed one ankle against another, his position mirroring mine exactly. We were two people meeting by chance, sharing a few words and the sun. Ri-i-i-ight.

"If it gets out," he said, his eyes on the distant bathroom behind me, "I'll make the records concerning my father's little camp public. You and every one of those sorry little snots will be tracked down and treated like lepers. That is if they don't simply cremate you out of fear something will mutate and start another Turn."

My knees went loose and watery. I had been right. Trent's father had done something to me, fixed whatever had been wrong. And Trent's threat wasn't idle. The best-case scenario would involve a one-way ticket to the Antarctic. I moved my tongue around on the inside of my mouth, trying to find enough spit to swallow. "How did you know?" I asked, thinking my secret was more deadly than his.

Eyes fixed to mine, he pushed the sleeve of his shirt up to show a nicely muscled arm. The hair was bleached from the sun and his skin was well-tanned. A ragged scar marred its even smoothness. My eyes rose to his, reading an old anger.

"That was you?" I stammered. "That was you I threw into the tree?"

With motions short and abrupt, he tugged his sleeve back down, hiding the scar. "I've never forgiven you for making me cry in front of my father."

A childhood anger flared from coals I had thought long extinct. "It's your own fault. I told you to stop teasing her!" I said, not caring that my voice was louder than the surrounding water. "Jasmin was sick. She cried herself to sleep for three weeks because of you."

Trent jerked upright. "You know her name?" he exclaimed. "Write it down. Quick!"

I stared at him in disbelief. "Why do you care what her name was? She had a hard enough time without you picking on her."

"Her name!" Trent said, patting his pockets until he found a pen. "What's her name?"

Scowling, I tucked a curl behind an ear. "I'm not going to tell you," I said, embarrassed that I had forgotten it again.

Trent pressed his lips together and put the pen away. "You forgot already, didn't you?"

"Why do you care anyway? All you did was pester her."

He looked cross as he tugged his hat lower over his eyes. "I was fourteen. A very awkward fourteen, Ms. Morgan. I teased her because I liked her. Next time you recall her name, I would appreciate it if you would write it down and send it to me. There were long-term memory blockers in the camp's drinking water, and I would like to know if—"

His voice cut off, and I watched the emotion flicker behind his eyes. I was becoming good at reading them. "You want to know if she survived," I finished for him, knowing I had guessed right when his gaze went elsewhere. "Why were you there?" I asked, almost afraid he'd tell me.

"My father owned the camp. Where else would I spend my summers?"

The cadence of his voice and the slight tightening of his brow told me it had been more than that. A thrill of satisfaction warmed me; I'd found his tell for when he lied. Now all I needed was the same for when he was speaking the truth, and he'd never be able to successfully lie to me again.

"You are as filthy as your father," I said, disgusted, "blackmailing people by dangling a cure within their reach and making them your puppets. Your parents' fortune was built on the misery of hundreds, maybe thousands, Mr. Kalamack. And you're no different."

Trent's chin trembled almost imperceptibly, and I thought I saw a shimmer of sparkles about him, the memory of his aura playing tricks on me. Must be an elf thing. "I will not justify my actions to you," he said. "And you have become very adept in the art of blackmail yourself. I'm not going to waste my time bickering like children over who hurt whose feelings over a decade ago. I want to hire your services."

"Hire me?" I said, unable to keep my voice lowered as I put my hands on my hips in disbelief. "You tried to kill me in the rat fights, and you think I'm going to work for you? To help clear your name? You murdered those witches. I'm going to prove it."

He laughed, his hat shadowing his face as he bowed his head and chuckled.

"What's so funny?" I demanded, feeling foolish.

"You." His eyes were bright. "You were never in any danger in that rat pit. I was only using it to knock home your current sordid state. But I did make a few astounding contacts while I was there."

"You son of—" Lips pressed tight, I clenched my hand into a fist.

Trent's mirth vanished and his head tilted in warning as he took a step away. "I wouldn't," he threatened, raising a finger. "I really wouldn't."

I slowly rocked back, my knees shaking in the memory of the pit. The gut-twisting feeling of helplessness, of being trapped and forced to kill or be killed, washed through me. I had been Trent's toy. Him running me down on horseback was nothing compared to that. After all, I had been thieving from him at the time.

"Listen to me really good, Trent," I whispered, the thought of Quen forcing me to retreat until the concrete pressed cold into the small of my back. "I'm not working for you. I'm going to take you down. I'm going to figure out how to tie you to every one of those murders."

"Oh please," he said, and I wondered how we went so quickly from a Fortune-twenty businessman and a slick independent runner to two people squabbling over past injustices. "Are you still on that? Even Captain Edden realizes Dan Smather's body was dumped in my stables, which is why he sent his son to watch me instead of filing charges. And as for having contact with the victims, yes, I talked to them all, trying to employ them, not kill them. You have a very strong skill set, Ms. Morgan, but detective is not among them. You are far too impatient, driven by your intuitive skills, which seem to only work forward, not backward."

Affronted, I put my hands on my hips and made a sound of disbelief. *Who did he think he was, lecturing me?*

Trent reached into a shirt pocket, pulling out a white envelope and handing it to me. Leaning forward and back, I snatched it, flipping it open. My breath caught as I realized it held twenty crisp hundred-dollar bills.

"That's ten percent up front, the rest on completion," he said, and I froze, trying to look cavalier. *Twenty thousand dollars?* "I want you to identify who is responsible for the murders. I've been trying to hire a ley line witch for the last three months, and every one of them ends up dead. It's growing tiresome. All I want is a name."

"You can go to hell, Kalamack," I said, dropping the envelope when he didn't take it back. I was angry and frustrated. I had come here with information so fine, I was sure I was going to get a confession. What I got was threatened, insulted, and then bribed.

Looking unperturbed, he stooped to pick up the envelope, smacking it against his palm several times to get the grit off before tucking it away. "You do realize that with that little stunt you pulled yesterday, you are next on the killer's list? You fit the profile nicely, having shown yourself as proficient in ley line magic, and then adding our little tryst today."

Damn. I'd forgotten about that. If Trent really wasn't the murderer, than I had nothing to stop the real one from coming after me. Suddenly the sun wasn't warm enough. I felt breathless, sick that I was going to have to find the real killer before he found me.

"Now," Trent said, his voice smoother than the water. "Take the money so I can tell you what I've managed to learn."

Stomach twisting, I met his mocking gaze. I was going to do just what he wanted. He had manipulated me into helping him. Damn, damn, and double damn. Crossing to his side of the bridge, I put my elbows atop the thick railing with my back to Glenn. Sharps was deep underwater, only the lack of ducks to say he was here. Beside me stood Trent.

"Did you send Sara Jane to the FIB with the sole intention that Edden would involve me?" I asked bitterly.

Trent shifted, putting himself so near I could smell the clean scent of his aftershave. I didn't like how close he was, but if I moved, he'd know it bothered me. "Yes," he said softly.

In his voice was the sound of truth I had been waiting for, and a trickle of excitement pulled my breath tight. There it was. Now I had it. He'd never be able to lie to me again. Looking back over our past conversations in a new light, I realized that apart from the reason he'd given me for being at his father's camp, he never had. Ever.

"She doesn't know him, does she?" I asked.

"A few dates to get the picture, but no. It was a calculated certainty that he would be murdered after he agreed to work for me, though I tried to protect him. Quen is very upset," he said lightly, his gaze on Sharps's ripples. "That Mr. Smather turned up in my stables means the killer is getting cocky."

My eyes closed briefly in frustration as I scrambled to realign my thinking. Trent hadn't killed those witches. Someone else had. I could either take the money and help Trent solve his little employment problem or not take the money and he'd get it for free. I'd take the money. "You're a bastard, you know that?"

Seeing my new understanding, Trent smiled. It was all I could do to not spit in his face. His long hands hung out over the edge of the railing. The sun turned his tan a warm golden color that almost glowed against his white shirt, and his face was shadowed. Wisps of his hair moved in the breeze, almost touching my own wayward strands.

With a casual movement, he reached into his shirt pocket, and with our bodies hiding the action from Glenn, he extended the envelope. Feeling dirty, I took it, shoving it out of sight behind my jacket and into my waistband.

"Excellent," he said, warm and sincere. "I'm glad we can work together."

"Go Turn yourself, Kalamack."

"I'm reasonably confident that it's a master vampire," he said, easing away from me.

"Which one?" I asked, disgusted with myself. *Why was I doing this?*

"I don't know," he admitted, flicking a bit of mortar off the railing to land in the water. "If I did, I'd have taken care of it already."

"I just bet you would," I said sourly. "Why not take them all out? Get it over with?"

"I can't go about staking vampires at random, Ms. Morgan," he said, worrying me because he'd taken my question seriously instead of the sarcasm it was. "That's illegal, not to mention it would start a vamp war. Cincinnati might not survive it. And I know my business interests would suffer in the interim."

I snickered. "Oh, we can't let that happen, now. Can we?"

Trent sighed. "Using sarcasm to cover your fear makes you look very young."

"And twirling your pencil in your fingers makes you look nervous," I shot back. It felt good to argue with someone who wouldn't bite me if things got out of control.

His eye twitched. Lips bloodless, he turned back to the large pond before us. "I'd appreciate it if you would keep the FIB out of this. It's an Inderland matter, not human, and I'm not sure the I.S. can be trusted, either."

I found it interesting how fast he had fallen into the "them" and "us" verbiage. Apparently I wasn't the only one who knew Trent's background, and I didn't like the higher degree of intimacy it put between us.

"I'm thinking it might be a rising vamp coven trying to gain a foothold by removing me," he said. "It would be a lot less risky than taking out one of the lesser houses."

It wasn't a boast—just a tasteless fact—and my lips curled at the thought I was taking money from a man who played the underworld like a chessboard. For the first time in my life I was glad my dad was dead and couldn't ask me "Why?" The picture of our fathers standing before the camp bus intruded, and I reminded myself I couldn't trust Trent. My father had, and it killed him.

Trent sighed, the sound both regretful and tired. "Cincinnati's underground is very fluid. All of my usual contacts have gone quiet or dead. I'm losing touch with what's happening." He flicked a glance at me. "Someone is trying to keep me from increasing my reach. And without a ley line witch at my disposal, I've reached an impasse."

"Poor baby," I mocked. "Why not do the magic yourself? Bloodline too polluted with nasty human genes to manage the heavy magic anymore?"

The knuckles of his fingers whitened as he gripped the rail, then relaxed. "I will have a ley line witch. I would much rather hire someone willing than abduct them, but if every witch I talk to ends up dead, I will steal someone."

"Yes," I drawled caustically. "You elves are known for that, aren't you?"

His jaw clenched. "Be careful."

"I'm always careful," I said, knowing I wasn't a good enough witch to have to worry about him "stealing" me. I watched the rims of his ears slowly lose their red tint. I squinted, wondering if they were a little pointed or if it was my imagination. It was hard to tell with the hat he had on. "Can you narrow it down for me?" I said. *Twenty thousand dollars to sift through Cincinnati's underworld to find out who wanted to put a crimp in Mr. Kalamack's day by killing his potential employees. Yeah. That sounded like an easy run.*

"I have lots of ideas, Ms. Morgan. Lots of enemies, lots of employees."

"And no friends," I added snidely, watching Sharps make serpentlike humps like a miniature Loch Ness. My breath slipped from me in a slow sound as I imagined what Ivy was going to say when I came home and told her I was working for Trent. "If I find out you're lying, I'll come after you myself, Kalamack. And this time, the demon won't miss."

He made a scoffing bark of laughter and I turned to him. "You can drop the bluff. You didn't send that demon after me last spring."

The slight breeze was cold, and I pulled my jacket closed as I turned. "How did you . . ."

Trent gazed distantly over the lower basin. "After overhearing your conversation with your boyfriend in my office and seeing your reaction to that demon, I knew it had to have been someone else, though I'll admit seeing you beaten and blue after I freed that demon to go back to kill its summoner nearly had me convinced."

I didn't like that he had overheard me talking to Nick. Or that he had responded the exact same way as I had after gaining control over Algaliarept. Trent's shoes scuffed, and a cautious inquiry came into his eyes. "Your demon scar . . ." He hesitated, and the flicker of haunted emotion strengthened. "It was an accident?" he finished.

I watched the ripples from Sharps's disappearing humps. "It bled me so badly that—" I stopped, my lips pressing together. Why was I telling him this? "Yeah. It was."

"Good," he said, his gaze still upon the pond. "I'm glad to hear that."

Ass, I thought, thinking whoever had sent Algaliarept after us had gotten a double whammy of pain that night. "Someone sure didn't like us talking, did they," I said, then froze. My face went cold and I held my breath. What if the attacks on our lives and the recent violence were connected? Perhaps I was supposed to have been the witch hunter's first victim?

Heart pounding, I held myself still, thinking. Every single one of the victims had died in their own personal hell: the swimmer drowned, the rat caretaker ripped apart and eaten alive, two women raped, a man working with horses pressed to death. Algaliarept had been told to kill me in terror, taking the time to find out what my strongest fear was. *Damn. It was the same person.*

Trent tilted his head at my silence. "What is it?" he asked.

"Nothing." I leaned heavily into the railing. Dropping my head into my cupped hands, I willed myself to not pass out. Glenn would call someone, and that would be that.

Trent pushed away from the railing. "No," he said, and I pulled my head up. "I've seen that look on you twice before. What is it?"

I swallowed. "We were supposed to be the first victims of the witch hunter. He tried to kill both of us, giving up after we showed him we could best a demon and I made it clear I wasn't going to work for you. Only the witches who agreed to work for you were killed, yes?"

"They all agreed to work for me," he breathed, and I stifled a shudder at how the words seemed to flow over my spine. "I never thought to connect the two."

You can't accuse a demon of murder. Because there was no way to contain it if sentenced, the courts had long ago determined to treat demons as weapons, even if the comparison wasn't quite right. Free choice was involved, but as long as the payment was commensurate with the task, a demon wouldn't turn down murder. Someone, though, had summoned it. "Did the demon ever tell you who sent it to kill you?" I asked. Easiest twenty thousand I'd ever made. *God help me.*

Anger tinted in fear crossed Trent. "I was trying to stay alive, not have a conversation. You seem to have a working relationship with it, though. Why don't you ask it?"

My breath come in a jerky sound of disbelief. "Me? I already owe it one favor. You can't pay me enough to dig myself in deeper. I'll tell you what, though. I'll call it up for you, and you can ask it. I'm sure the two of you can come to some agreement about payment."

His sun-tanned face went pale. "No."

Satisfied, I looked over the small pond. "Don't call me a coward unless it's something you would do yourself. I'm reckless. Not stupid." But then I hesitated. *Nick would do it.*

A faint smile, surprising and genuine, came over Trent. "You're doing it again."

"What," I said flatly.

"You had another thought. You are such fun, Ms. Morgan. Watching you is like watching a five-year-old."

Insulted, I looked out over the water. I wondered if Nick asking who had sent it to kill me would be considered a small question or a large one, necessitating further payment. Pushing myself away from the railing, I decided I'd walk over to the museum and find out.

"So?" Trent prompted.

I shook my head. "I'll have your information after sundown," I said, and he blinked.

"You're going to call it?" His sudden, unguarded surprise caught at me, and I kept my face impassive, thinking that managing to startle him was an ego boost I badly needed. How quickly he hid it made the feeling twice as satisfying. "You just said—"

"You're paying for results, not a play-by-play. I'll let you know when I find something."

His expression shifted to what might be respect. "I've misjudged you, Ms. Morgan."

"Yeah, I'm just full of surprises," I muttered, reaching up to keep the hair out of my eyes as the wind gusted. Trent's hat threatened to blow off into the water, and I stretched to catch it before it left his head. My fingers brushed his hat, then nothing.

Trent leapt backward. I stared, blinking at where he had been. He was gone.

I found him a good four feet away, entirely off the bridge. I'd seen cats move like that. He looked frightened as he straightened, then angry that I'd seen the emotion on him. The sun glinted on his wispy hair; his hat was in the water, turning a sickly green.

I stiffened as Quen dropped out of the nearby tree to land softly before him. The man stood with his arms hanging loose, looking like a modern-day samurai in his black jeans and shirt. I didn't move as a whoosh of water came from behind me. I could smell copper sulfate and scum. I felt, more than saw, Sharps loom behind me, cold, wet, and almost as big as the bridge he lived under, having sucked in a huge amount of water to give himself more mass. A faint clatter from the nearby bathroom told me Glenn was on his way.

My heart pounded as no one moved. *I shouldn't have touched him. I should not have touched him.* Licking my lips, I tugged my jacket straight, glad Quen had the sense to know I hadn't been trying to hurt Trent. "I'll call you when I have a name," I said, my voice sounding thin. Giving Quen an apologetic look, I turned on a heel and strode quickly to the street, my heels thumping soundlessly up through my spine.

And you are afraid of me, I thought silently. *Why?*

Twenty-Four

"For the third time, Rachel. Would you like another piece of bread?"

I looked from the light glinting on the surface of my wine, finding Nick waiting with a curious, amused expression. He was holding out the plate with the bread. By his wondering expression, I guessed he'd held it there for a while. "Um, no. No, thank you," I said, glancing down to find the supper Nick had made for me almost untouched. Giving him an apologetic smile, I sent my fork under another bite of pasta and white sauce. It was his supper, my lunch, and both delicious, and even more so since I hadn't done anything but make the salad. It would likely be the last thing I ate today because Ivy had a date with Kist. That meant I'd be having dinner with Ben and Jerry in front of the TV. I thought it unusual she would go out with the living vamp, seeing as he was worse than a monkey when it came to sex and blood, but it was resolutely *not* my business.

Nick's plate was empty, and after setting the bread down, he sat back and played with the end of his knife, making it lie just so atop his napkin. "I know it's not my food," he said. "What's the matter? You've hardly said a word since you—ah—came over to the museum."

I covered my smirk with a napkin and wiped the corner of my mouth. I had caught him napping, sitting with his lanky legs up, his feet propped on his cleaning table, the eighteenth century tea towel he was supposed to be restoring draped over his eyes. If it wasn't a book, he really didn't care about it. "Is it that obvious?" I said, taking a bite.

A familiar, lopsided smile came over him. "It's not like you to be this quiet. Is it about Mr. Kalamack not being arrested after finding, er, that—body?"

I pushed the plate away in a flush of guilt. I hadn't yet told Nick I'd switched sides in the "Let's get Trent" issue. I hadn't, really, and that's what bothered me. The man was slime.

"You found a body," he said as he leaned across the table and took my hand. "The rest will follow."

I cringed, worried Nick might tell me I'd sold out. My distress must have shown because he squeezed my hand until I looked up. "What is it, Ray-ray?"

His eyes were soft with encouragement, their brown depths catching the glint from the ugly light hanging over Nick's tiny kitchen/dining room. My attention went over the short, chest-high mantel dividing it from the living room as I tried to decide how to broach the subject. I had been harping on him for months about letting sleeping demons lie, and here I was, wanting to ask him to call Algaliarept up for me. I was sure the answer was going to cost more than what Nick's "trial contract" would cover, and I didn't want to risk him paying it for me anyway. Nick had a chivalrous streak as wide as the Ohio River.

"Tell me?" he asked, ducking his head to try and see my eyes.

I licked my lips and met his gaze. "It's about Big Al." I didn't like chancing that Algaliarept would conveniently assume I was calling it every time I said its name, so I had begun referring to the demon by the somewhat insulting moniker. Nick thought it was funny; that I was worried about it showing up unsummoned, not that I called it Al.

Nick's fingers slipped from mine and he pulled away to take up his wineglass. "Don't start," he said, his eyebrows furrowed in the first signs of anger. "I know what I'm doing, and I'm going to do it whether you like it or not."

"Actually," I hedged, "I wanted to see if you might ask it something for me."

Nick's long face went slack. "Beg pardon?"

I winced. "If it won't cost you anything. If it does, forget it. I'll find another way."

He set the glass down and leaned forward. "You want me to call him?"

"See, I talked to Trent today," I said quickly, so he couldn't interrupt, "and we figure that the demon that attacked us last spring is the same one that's doing the murders—that I was supposed to be the first witch hunter victim, but because I turned Trent's job offer down, it let me go. If I can find out who sent it to kill us, then we have the murderer."

Lips parted, Nick stared at me. I could almost see his thoughts fall in place: Trent was innocent and I was working for him to find the real murderer and clear his name of suspicion. Uncomfortable, I pushed the fork around on the plate. "How much is he giving you?" Nick finally asked, his voice giving me no clue to his thoughts.

"Two thousand up front," I said, feeling it light in my pocket, since I had yet to go home. "Eighteen more when I tell him who the witch hunter is." *Hey. I'd made my rent. Whoop-de-do.*

"Twenty thousand dollars?" he said, his brown eyes large in the fluorescent light. "He's giving you twenty thousand dollars for a name? You don't have to bring him in or anything?"

I nodded, wondering if Nick thought I was selling out. I felt like I was.

Nick held himself still for three heartbeats, then rose, his chair scraping the worn linoleum. "Let's find out how much that costs," he said, halfway out of the room.

I was left blinking at his wire and plastic chair. My heart thumped. "Nick?" I stood, taking a moment to move our plates to the sink. "Doesn't it bother you I'm working for Trent? It bothers me."

"Did he kill those witches?" came his voice from the hallway to his room, and I followed it through the living room to find him moving everything out of his linen closet and stacking it on his bed with a methodical quickness.

"No. I don't think so." *God help me if I misread his tells.*

He handed me a stack of brand new, lusciously green towels. "So what's the problem?"

"The man is a biodrug lord and runs Brimstone," I said, juggling the towels to take the oversize gardener boots he handed me. I recognized them as the ones from my belfry, and I wondered why he was keeping them. "Trent is trying to take over Cincinnati's underworld, and I'm working for him. That's what's the matter."

Nick grabbed his spare sheets and edged past me to drop them on his bed. "You wouldn't be helping him unless you believed he didn't do it," he said as he returned. "And for twenty thousand dollars? Twenty thousand dollars buys a lot of therapy if you're wrong."

I grimaced, not liking Nick's "money makes everything right" philosophy. I suppose growing up watching your mother struggle for every dollar might have a lot to do with it, but I sometimes questioned Nick's priorities. But I had to find out just to save my own skin, and I'd be damned if I cleared Trent of suspicion for free.

I stood sideways in the hallway as Nick went into his room with a pile of sweaters. The closet was empty—there hadn't been much in it to start with—and after dumping everything, he took the towels and boots from my arms, adding them to the mound on the bed before returning to the closet. My eyebrows rose as he pulled a square of carpet up to reveal a circle and pentagram etched in the floor. "You summon Al into a closet?" I said in disbelief.

Nick looked up from where he was kneeling, his long face devious. "I found the circle when I moved in," he said. "Isn't it a nice one? It's lined in silver. I checked it out, and it's almost the only spot in the apartment where there are no electric or gas lines. There's another in the kitchen that you can see with a black light, but it's bigger and I can't make a circle that large that's strong enough to hold him."

I watched as he wedged the shelves off their brackets with a stiff, underhand thunk, stacking them against the wall in the hallway. Finished, he stepped into the closet and held out a hand for me to join him. I stared, surprised.

"Al said the demon was supposed to be in the circle, not the summoner," I said.

His hand dropped. "It's part of the trial membership thing. I'm not so much summoning him as asking for an audience. He can say no and not show up at all, though that hasn't happened since you gave me the idea to put myself in the circle instead of him. He shows up just to laugh now." Nick held out his hand again. "Come on. I want to make sure we both fit."

I looked to the slice of living room I could see, not wanting to get in a closet with Nick. Well, not under these circumstances, anyway. "Let's use the circle in the kitchen," I suggested. "I don't mind closing it."

"You want to risk him thinking you called him?" Nick asked, eyebrows high.

"It's an it, not a him," I said, but at his exasperated expression, I took his hand and stepped into the closet. Immediately, Nick dropped my grip and ran his gaze over where our elbows went. The closet was good-sized and deep. Right now it was okay, but add a demon trying to get in, and it would be claustrophobic. "Maybe this isn't such a good idea," I said.

"It'll be fine." Nick's motions were quick and jerky as he stepped out of the closet and reached up to the last shelf, still in place above our heads. Taking down a rattling shoe box, he opened it to show a zippy bag of gray ash and about a dozen milky green tapers already burnt. My mouth opened as I recognized them as the candles he had lit one night when we were, ah, utilizing Ivy's tub to its fullest potential. What were they doing in a box with ashes?

"Those are my candles," I said, only now realizing where they had gone.

Setting the box on his bed, he took the zippy bag and the longest candle and went into the living room. I heard a thump, and he soon reappeared, dragging the stool that I had put his obligatory housewarming plant on. Still silent, he set the candle where the peace lily had once been.

"Buy your own candles for summoning demons," I said, affronted.

He frowned as he opened the drawer under the footstool to pull out a box of matches. "They have to be lit the first time on hallowed ground or they don't work."

"Well, you've got everything figured out, don't you." I sourly wondered if the entire night had been an excuse to get those candles. How long had he been calling this demon anyway? Lips pursed, I watched him light the candle and shake the match out. But it wasn't until he took a handful of gray dust from the zippy bag that I started getting nervous. "What is that?" I asked, worried.

"You don't want to know." His voice carried a surprising amount of warning.

My face warmed as I recalled that I use to bring his kind in for grave robbing. "Yes, I do."

He looked up, his brow pinched in irritation. "It's a focus object so Algaliarept materializes outside the circle instead of in it with us. And the candle is to make sure he doesn't focus on anything but the ash on the table. I bought it, okay?"

Muttering a quick, "Sorry," I backed off. Somehow I seemed to have found the only nerve Nick had and stomped on it. I wasn't up on my demon summoning; obviously he was. "I thought all you had to do was make a circle and call them," I said, feeling nauseated. Someone had sold their grandmother's ashes so Nick could call a demon with her remains.

Nick dusted his hands together and resealed the bag. "You might be able to get away with that, but I can't. The guy at the store kept trying to sell me this outrageously expensive amulet to make a proper binding circle, not believing a human could close one of his own. He gave me ten percent off everything after I put him in a circle he couldn't break. I guess he thought I knew enough to survive to come back and buy something more."

His irritation had vanished the moment I quit barking at him. I realized that this was the first time—well, the second—he had the chance to show me his skills, something he was obviously very proud of. Humans had to work hard to manipulate ley lines as well as witches, which is why humans were known to align themselves with demons so they could keep up. Of course, they didn't last long after that, eventually making a mistake and being pulled into the ever-after. *This was so unsafe. And here I was encouraging him.*

Seeing my face, he came to me and put his hands atop my shoulders. I could feel the ash, gritty between his hands and my skin. "It's okay," he soothed, his narrow face smiling. "I've done this before."

"That's what I'm afraid of," I said, stepping back to make room for him.

As Nick tossed the zippy bag of ash to land next to the shoe box, I tried to wipe the ash off my shoulders. Nick got in the closet with me, and then, with a grunt of remembrance, wedged a piece of wood into the crack of the hinges. "He shut the door on me once," he said, shrugging.

This is not good, I thought again as the small of my back started to sweat.

"Ready?"

I glanced at the lit candle and its little mound of ash. "No."

My fingertips tingled as Nick closed his eyes and opened his second sight. An eerie feeling of my insides being rearranged started in my belly, swirling up into my throat. My eyes widened. "Whoa, whoa, whoa!" I cried as the sensation wrenched into an uncomfortable pull. "What is that?"

Nick opened his eyes. They were glazed, and I could tell he was seeing everything in that confusing mix of reality and ever-after sight. "That's what I've been telling you about," he said, his voice hollow. "It's from the binding spell. Nice, isn't it?"

I shifted from foot to foot, making sure I stayed in the circle. "It's awful," I admitted. "I'm sorry. Why didn't you tell me it was that bad?"

He shrugged, closing his eyes.

The pull through me strengthened, and I struggled to find a way to deal with it. I could feel the ever-after energy slowly building in him, paralleling what I experienced when I tapped into a ley line. The power swelled, and though it was a fraction of what I had channeled in Trent's office, it urged me to react.

With an excruciating slowness, the levels built to a usable level. My palms started to sweat and my stomach clenched. I wished he'd hurry up and close the circle. The eddies of power went deep through me, the need to do something growing.

"Can I help?" I finally asked, gripping my hands together so they wouldn't spasm.

"No."

The tingling in my palms rose to become an itch. "I'm sorry," I said. "I didn't know you could feel all this. Is this why you haven't been sleeping? Have I been waking you up?"

"No. Don't worry about it."

My heel started tapping, the jolts going up my calves feeling like fire. "We have to break the charm," I said, jittery. "How can you stand this?"

"Shut up, Rachel. I'm trying to concentrate."

"Sorry."

His breath slipped from him in a slow sound, and I wasn't surprised when he jumped, mirroring the sudden cutoff of ever-after energy I could feel running through him. Through us.

"Circle's up," he said breathlessly, and I resisted the urge to look at it. I didn't want to insult him, and having felt its construction, I knew it was good. "I'm not sure, but I think because I'm carrying some of your aura, you can break the circle, too."

"I'll be careful," I said, suddenly a lot more nervous. "So what happens now?" I questioned, looking at the candle on the footstool.

"Now I invite him over."

I stifled a shudder as Latin flowed from Nick. My lips curved down at the alienness of it. As he spoke, Nick seemed to take on a different cast, shadows under his eyes growing, to make him look ill. Even his voice changed, more resonant and somehow echoing in my head. Again there was a slow buildup of ever-after energy, rising until it was almost intolerable. I was antsy and nervous, almost relieved when Nick said Algaliarept's name with a drawn-out, careful precision.

Nick sagged, taking a clean breath. I could smell his sweat

over his deodorant in the close confines. His fingers slipped into my hand, giving me a quick squeeze before dropping it. The clock ticked from the living room, and the sound of the traffic past the window was hushed. Nothing happened.

"Is something supposed to happen?" I asked, starting to feel silly, standing in Nick's closet.

"It might take a while. Like I said, it's a trial membership, not the real thing."

I took three slow breaths, listening. "How long?"

"Since I've been putting myself in the circle instead of him? Five, ten minutes."

Nick's mood was easing, and I could feel the heat from our shoulders almost touching. An ambulance sounded faint in the distance, disappearing.

I eyed the burning candle. "What if it doesn't show?" I asked. "How long do we have to wait before we can get out of the closet?"

Nick gave me a noncommittal, stranger-in-the-elevator smile. "Uh, I wouldn't step out of the circle until sunup. Until he appears and we can banish him properly back to the ever-after, he can show up anytime between now and then."

"You mean if it doesn't show, we're stuck in this closet until morning?"

He nodded, his eyes jerking away as the smell of burnt amber came to me. "Oh, good. He's here," Nick whispered, standing straighter.

Oh, good. He's here, I repeated sarcastically in my head. God help me. My life was so screwed up.

The pile of ash at the end of the hallway was hazed with a smear of ever-after. It grew with the speed of flowing water, up and out to take a rough, animal shape. I forced myself to breathe as eyes appeared, red and orange and slit sideways like a goat's. My stomach clenched as a savage muzzle formed, saliva dripping to the rug even before it finished coalescing into the pony-size dog I remembered from the basement vault of the university library: Nick's personal fear of dogs brought to life.

Harsh panting rasped, the sound pulling an instinctive fear from the depths of my soul that I hadn't even known I had. Paws tipped with nails and powerful hindquarters appeared as it shook itself, the last of the mist forming a thick mane of yellow hair. Beside me, Nick shuddered. "You okay?" I asked, and he nodded, his face pale.

"Nicholas Gregory Sparagmos," the dog drawled, sitting on its haunches and giving us a savage doggy smile. "Already, little wizard? I was just here."

Gregory? I thought as Nick shot an unrepentant grimace at me. Nick's middle name was Gregory? And what had Nick gotten in return for telling it that?

"Or did you call me to impress Rachel Mariana Morgan?" it finished, a long red tongue lolling out as it turned its doggy smile to me.

"I've a few questions," Nick said, his voice bolder than his body language.

Nick's breath caught as the dog rose and padded into the hallway, its shoulders almost brushing the walls. I stared, horrified, as it licked the floor beside the circle, testing it. The film of everafter reality hissed as it sent its tongue over the unseen barrier. Smoke smelling like burnt amber rose, and I watched as if through a pane of glass as Algaliarept's tongue began to char and burn. Nick stiffened, and I thought I heard a whispered oath or prayer. Making an annoyed growl, the demon's outline went hazy.

My heart hammered as the dog lengthened and rose into its usual vision of a British gentleman. "Rachel Mariana Morgan," it said, hitting every accent with an elegant precession. "I must congratulate you, love, on finding that corpse. It was the sharpest bit of ley line magic I've seen in twelve years." It leaned close, and I smelled lavender. "You made quite a stir, you know," it whispered. "I was invited to all the parties. My witch's spell went to the city's square to chime the bells. Everyone got a taste, though not as much as I did." Eyes closing, the demon shuddered, its outlines wavering as its concentration lapsed.

I swallowed hard. "I'm not your witch," I said.

Nick's fingers on my elbow tightened. "Stay in that form," Nick said, his voice firm. "And stop bothering Rachel. I have questions, and I want to know the cost before I ask them."

"Your mistrust will kill you if your cheek doesn't." Algaliarept spun in a quick motion of furling coattails to return to the living room. From where I stood, I could see it open the glass-door cabinet to Nick's books. Its white-gloved fingers stretched and reached, pulling one out. "Oh, I wondered where this one had gotten to," it said, its back to us. "How splendid that you have it. We will read from this next time."

Nick glanced at me. "That's what we do, usually," he whispered. "He deciphers the Latin for me, letting all sorts of things slip."

"And you trust him?" I frowned, nervous. "Ask it."

Algaliarept had replaced the tome and taken out another, its mood lightening as it cooed and fussed as if having found an old friend.

"Algaliarept," Nick said, mouthing the word slowly, and the demon turned, the new book in its hand. "I'd like to know if you were the demon that attacked Trent Kalamack last spring."

It didn't look up from the open book cradled in his hands. I felt queasy as I realized it had lengthened its fingers to better support it. "That comes under our arrangement," it said, its voice preoccupied. "Seeing as Rachel Mariana Morgan has already guessed the answer." It looked up, its eyes over the smoked glasses orange and red. "Oh, yes, I tasted Trenton Aloysius Kalamack that night as well as you. I ought to have killed him directly, but the novelty of him was so fine, I tarried until he managed to circle me."

"Is that why I survived?" I asked. "You made a mistake?"

"Is that a question coming from you?"

I licked my lips. "No."

Algaliarept closed the book. "Your blood is common, Rachel Mariana Morgan. Tasty with subtle flavors I don't understand, but common. I didn't play with you; I tried to kill you. Had I known you could ring the tower bells, I might have handled things differently." A smile came over it, and I felt its gaze spill over me like oil. "Maybe not. I should have known you would be as your father. He rang the bells, too. Once. Before he died. Do hope it's not a premonition for you."

My stomach clenched, and Nick grabbed my arm before I could touch his circle. "You said you didn't know him," I said, anger making my voice harsh.

It simpered at me. "Another question?"

Heart pounding, I shook my head, hoping it would tell me more.

It put a finger to its nose. "Then Nicholas Gregory Sparagmos better ask another question before I'm called away by someone who is willing to pay for my services."

"You're nothing but a squealing informant, you know that?" I said, shaking.

Algaliarept's gaze resting on my neck pulled a memory of me

on the basement floor with my life spilling from me. "Only on my bad days."

Nick straightened. "I want to know who summoned you to kill Rachel, and if he or she is now summoning you to kill ley line witches."

Moving almost out of my line of sight, Algaliarept murmured, "That is a very expensive set of questions, the two together far more than our agreement." It dropped its attention back to the book in its hands and turned a page.

Worry crashed over me as Nick took a breath. "No," I said. "It isn't worth it."

"What do you want for the answers?" Nick asked, ignoring me.

"Your soul?" it said lightly.

Nick shook his head. "Come up with something reasonable, or I'll send you back right now, and you won't be able to talk to Rachel anymore."

It beamed. "You're getting cocky, little wizard. You're halfway mine." It closed the book in its hand with a sharp snap. "Give me leave to take my book back across the line, and I'll tell you who sent me to kill Rachel Mariana Morgan. If they are the same person who is summoning me to kill Trenton Aloysius Kalamack's witches? That stays with me. Your soul isn't enough for that. Rachel Mariana Morgan's, perhaps. Pity when a young man's tastes are too expensive for his means, isn't it?"

I frowned, even as I realized it had admitted it was killing the witches. It must have been luck that kept Trent and me alive when every other witch had died under it. No, not luck. It had been Quen and Nick. "And why do you even want that book?" I asked it.

"I wrote it," it said, its hard voice seeming to wedge the words into the folds of my mind.

Not good. Not good, not good, not good. "Don't give it to him, Nick."

He turned in the tight confines, bumping me. "It's just a book."

"It's your book," I agreed, "and my question. I'll find out some other way."

Algaliarept laughed, a gloved finger shifting the curtain so he could see the street. "Before I'm sent again to kill you? You're quite the topic of conversation, both sides of the ley lines. You'd best ask quick. If I'm called away suddenly, you may want to settle your affairs."

Nick's eyes went round. "Rachel! You're next?"

"No," I protested, wanting to smack Algaliarept. "It's just saying that so you'll give him the book."

"You used ley lines to find Dan's body," Nick said shortly. "And now you're working for Trent? You're on the list, Rachel. Take your book, Al. Who sent you to kill Rachel?"

"Al?" The demon brightened. "Oh, I like that. Al. Yes, you can call me Al."

"Who sent you to kill Rachel?" Nick demanded.

Algaliarept beamed. "Ptah Ammon Fineas Horton Madison Parker Piscary."

My knees threatened to give way, and I gripped Nick's arm. "Piscary?" I whispered. *Ivy's uncle was the witch hunter? And the man had seven names? Just how old was he?*

"Algaliarept, leave to not bother us again this night," Nick said suddenly.

The demon's smile sent shivers through me. "No promises," it leered, then vanished. The book in its hand hit the carpet, followed by an unseen sliding thump from the bookshelves. I listened to my heart beat, shaken. What was I going to tell Ivy? How could I protect myself from Piscary? I'd hid in a church before. I didn't like it.

"Wait," Nick said, pulling me back before I could touch the circle. I followed his gaze to the pile of ash. "He's not gone yet."

I heard Algaliarept swear, then the ash vanished.

Nick sighed, then edged his toe past the circle to break it. "Now you can leave."

Maybe Nick was better at this than I thought.

Hunched and worried looking, he went to blow the candle out and sit on the edge of his couch with his elbows on his knees and his head in his hands. "Piscary," he said to the flat carpet. "Why can't I have a normal girlfriend who only has to hide from her old prom date?"

"You're the one calling up demons," I said, my knees shaking. The night was suddenly a lot more threatening. The closet seemed bigger now that Nick wasn't in it, and I didn't want to get out. "I should go back to my church," I said, thinking I was going to set my old cot up in the sanctuary and sleep on the abandoned altar tonight. Right after I called Trent. He said he'd take care of it. *Take care of it.* I hoped that meant staking Piscary. Piscary didn't care about the law; why should I? I searched my conscience, not finding even a twinge.

I reached for my jacket and went to the door. I wanted to be in my church. I wanted to wrap myself in the ACG blanket I'd stolen from Edden and sit in the middle of my God-blessed church. "I need to make a call," I said numbly, stopping short in the middle of his living room.

"Trent?" he asked needlessly, handing me his cordless phone.

I made a fist to hid my shaking fingers after I punched in the number. I got Jonathan, sounding irate and nasty. I gave him a hard time until he agreed to let me talk to Trent directly. Finally I heard the click of an extension, and Trent's river-smooth voice came on to give me a professional "Good evening, Ms. Morgan."

"It's Piscary," I said by way of greeting. There was silence for five heartbeats, and I wondered if he had hung up.

"It told you Piscary is sending it to kill my witches?" Trent asked, the sound of his fingers snapping intruding. There followed the distinctive scratch of him writing something, and I wondered if Quen was with him. The weariness Trent had put in his voice to cover his worry didn't work.

"I asked it if it was sent to kill you last spring, and who summoned it for the task," I said, my stomach roiling as I paced. "I suggest you stay on hallowed ground after sunset. You can walk on hallowed ground, can't you?" I asked, not sure how elves handled that sort of thing.

"Don't be crass," he said. "I have a soul as much as you do. And thank you. As soon as you confirm the information, I'll send a courier with the rest of your compensation."

I jerked, my eyes meeting Nick's. "Confirmed?" I said. "What do you mean, confirmed?" I couldn't stop my hands from shaking.

"What you gave me was advice," Trent was saying. "I only pay my stockbroker for that. Get me proof, and Jonathan will cut you a check."

"I just gave you proof!" I stood up, heart pounding. "I just talked to that damned demon and it said it's killing your witches. How much more proof do you need?"

"More than one person can summon a demon, Ms. Morgan. If you didn't ask it if Piscary summoned it to murder those witches, you have only speculation."

My breath caught, and I turned my back to Nick. "That was too expensive," I said, lowering my voice and running a hand over my braid. "But it attacked us both under Piscary's binding, and it admitted to killing the witches."

"Not good enough. I need proof before I go about staking a master vampire. I suggest you get it quickly."

"You're going to stiff me!" I shouted, spinning to the curtained window as my fear shifted to frustration. "Why not?" I cried sarcastically. "The Howlers are. The FIB is. Why should you be any different?"

"I'm not stiffing you," he said, anger making the gray of his voice turn from silk to cold iron. "But I won't pay for shoddy work. As you said, I'm paying you for results, not a play-by-play—or speculation."

"Sounds to me you aren't paying me anything! I'm telling you it was Piscary, and a lousy twenty thousand isn't enough to get me to waltz into a four-hundred-year-old-plus vampire's lair and ask him if he has been sending his demon to kill citizens of Cincinnati."

"If you don't want the job, then I expect you to return my retaining fee."

I hung up on him.

The phone was hot in my grip, and I set it gently on the mantel between Nick's kitchen and living room before I threw it at something. "Get me home, please?" I asked tightly.

Nick was staring at his bookshelf, running his fingers over the titles.

"Nick," I said louder, angry and frustrated. "I really want to get home."

"Just a minute," he mumbled, intent on his books.

"Nick!" I exclaimed, gripping my elbows. "You can pick out your bedtime story later. I really want to get home!"

He turned, a sick look on his long face. "He took it."

"Took what?"

"I thought he was talking about the book in his hand. But he took the one that you used to make me your familiar."

My lip curled. "Al wrote the book on how to make humans into familiars? He can have it."

"No," he said, his expression drawn and pale. "If he's got it, how are we going to break the spell?"

My face went slack. "Oh." *I hadn't thought of that.*

Twenty-Five

T he low *lub-lub-lub-lub* of a bike pulled my eyes up from my book. Recognizing the cadence of Kist's motorbike, I pulled my knees to my chin, tugged my covers farther up, and clicked off my bedside lamp. The sliver of black beyond my propped-open stained-glass window showed a lighter gray. Ivy was home. If Kist came in, I was going to pretend to be asleep until he left. But his bike hardly paused before it idled back up the street. My eyes went to the glowing green numbers of my clock. Four in the morning. She was early.

Closing the book upon my finger to mark the page, I listened for her footsteps on the walk. The cold, predawn September air had pooled in my room. If I were smart, I'd get up and close my window; Ivy would probably turn the heat on when she came in.

I thanked all that was holy that my bedroom was part of the original church and fell under the sacred-ground clause: guaranteed to keep out undead vamps, demons, and mothers-in-law. I was safe in my bed until the sun came up. I still had to worry about Kist. But he wouldn't touch me while Ivy breathed. He wouldn't touch me if she were dead, either.

A stirring of unease pulled my finger out of the book, and I set it on the cloth-covered box I was using as a table. Ivy hadn't come in yet. It *had* been Kist's bike I heard driving away.

I listened to my heartbeat, waiting for Ivy's soft steps or the closing of the church's door. But what met me was the sound of someone retching, faint through the cold-silenced night.

"Ivy," I whispered, throwing off my covers. Chilled, I lurched from my bed, snatched my robe, jammed my feet into my fuzzy pink slippers, and went into the hall. Skittering to a halt, I retraced my steps. Standing before my pressboard chest of drawers, I sent my fingers over the shadowed bumps of my perfumes.

Choosing the new one I had found among the rest just yesterday, I impatiently dumped a splash on me. Citrus blossomed, clean and sharp, and I set the bottle down, knocking over half of what remained with a harsh clatter. Feeling unreal and disoriented, I almost ran through the empty church, tugging my robe on as I went. I hoped this one worked better than the last.

A sharp clattering of wings was my only warning as Jenks dropped from the ceiling. I jerked to a stop as he hovered before me. He was glowing black. I blinked in shock. He was freaking glowing black.

"Don't go out there," he said, fear thick in his high voice. "Go out the back. Get on a bus. Go to Nick's."

My gaze shot past him to the door as I heard Ivy vomiting again, the ugly sounding gags mixing with heavy sobs. "What happened?" I asked, frightened.

"Ivy fell off the wagon."

I stood there, not understanding. "What?"

"She fell off the wagon," he repeated. "She's sipping the B-juice. She's sampling the wine. She's practicing again, Rachel. And she's off her rocker. Go. My family is waiting for you by the far wall. Get them to Nick's for me. I'll stay here and keep an eye on her. To make sure she—" He glanced at the door. "I'll make sure she isn't going to come after you."

The sound of Ivy vomiting stopped. I stood in my nightgown and robe in the middle of the sanctuary, listening. Fear soaked in with the stillness, settling in my gut. I heard a small noise that grew into a steady, soft crying.

"Excuse me," I whispered, moving around Jenks. My heart was pounding and my knees were weak as I pushed open one side of the heavy door.

The glow from the streetlight was enough to see. Deep in the shadows cast by the oaks, Ivy was sprawled in her biker leather, half lying across the church's two lowest steps, dumped and left to fend for herself. A gelatinous dark vomit spread over the steps, dripping to the sidewalk in ugly syrupy clumps. The cloying smell of blood was thick, overpowering my citrus scent.

Gathering the hem of my robe, I went down the steps with a calm born in fear.

"Rachel!" Jenks shouted, his wings a harsh clatter. "You can't help her. Leave!"

I faltered as I stood over Ivy, her long legs askew and her hair sticking to the black vomit. Her sobs had turned silent, shaking her shoulders. *God, help me through this.*

Breath held, I reached from behind, gripping under her arms to try to get her to her feet. She flinched at my touch. Coherency flickered over her. Focus wavering, she angled her feet under her to help. "I told him no," she said, her voice cracking. "I said no."

My stomach clenched at the sound of her voice, bewildered and confused. The acidic smell of vomit caught in my throat. Under it was a rich scent of well-turned earth, mixing with her burnt ash smell.

Jenks flitted around us as I got her to her feet. Pixy dust sifted from him to make a glowing cloud. "Careful," he whispered, first on my left side, then my right. "Be careful. I can't stop her if she attacks you."

"She's not going to attack me," I said, anger joining my fear to make a nauseating mix. "She didn't fall off the wagon. Listen to her. Someone pushed her."

Ivy shuddered as we reached the top step. Her hand touched the door for support, and she jerked as if burned. Like an animal, she clawed her way from me. Gasping, I fell back, wide-eyed. Her crucifix was gone.

She stood before me on the church's landing, tension pulling her tall. Her gaze took me in, and I went cold. There was nothing in Ivy's black eyes. Then they flashed into a ravenous hunger, and she lunged.

I had not a chance.

Ivy grabbed me by my neck, pinning me to the door of the church. Adrenaline surged, flashed through me in a pained assault. Her hand was like warm stone under my chin. My last breath made an ugly sound. Toes brushing the stone landing, I hung. Terrified, I tried to kick out, but she pressed into me, heat going through my robe. Eyes bulging, I pried at her fingers about my throat.

Struggling to breathe, I watched her eyes. They were utterly black in the streetlight. Fear, despair, hunger all mixed. Nothing there was her. Nothing at all.

"He told me to do it," she said, her feather-light voice a shocking contrast to her twisted face, terrifying in its absolute hunger. "I told him I wouldn't."

"Ivy," I rasped, managing a breath. "Put me down." Again I made that ugly noise as her grip tightened.

"Not this way!" Jenks shrilled. "Ivy! It's not what you want!"

The fingers on my neck clenched. My lungs struggled, a fire burning as they tried to fill. The black of Ivy's eyes grew as my body started to shut down. Panicking, I stretched for my ley line. The disorientation of connection flashed through the chaos almost unnoticed. Reeling from the lack of oxygen, I let the surge of power explode from me, uncontrolled.

Ivy was flung back. I fell to my knees, drawn forward even as her grip around my neck pulled away. My breath came in a ragged gasp. Pain went all the way to my skull as my knees hit the stone landing. I coughed, feeling my throat. I took a breath, then another. Jenks was a blur of green and black. The black spots dancing before me shrank and vanished.

I looked up to find Ivy curled in a fetal position against the closed doors, her arms over her head as if she had been beaten, rocking herself. "I said no. I said no. I said no."

"Jenks," I rasped, watching her around the strands of my hair. "Go get Nick."

The pixy hovered before me as I staggered to my feet. "I'm not leaving."

I felt my neck as I swallowed. "Go get him, if he's not already on his way here. He must have felt me pull on that line."

Jenks's face was set. "You should run. Run while you can."

Shaking my head, I watched Ivy, her confident self-assurance shattered into nothing as she rocked herself and cried. I couldn't go. I couldn't walk away because it would be safer. She needed help, and I was the only one who stood a chance of surviving her.

"Damn it all to hell!" Jenks shouted. "She's going to kill you!"

"We'll be okay," I said as I lurched to her. "Go get Nick. Please. I need him to get through this."

The pitch of his wings rose and fell in tandem with his visible indecision. Finally he nodded and left. The silence his absence made reminded me of the quiet left in a cruddy little hospital room when two faltered to one. Swallowing, I tightened my robe tie. "Ivy," I whispered. "Come on, Ivy. I'm going to get you inside." Stealing myself, I reached out and put a shaking hand on her shoulder, jerking away as she shuddered.

"Run away," she whispered as she stopped rocking, falling into a wire-tight stillness.

My heart pounded as she looked up at me, her eyes empty and her hair wild.

"Run away," she repeated. "If you run, I'll know what to do."

Trembling, I forced myself to remain still, not wanting to trigger her instincts.

Her face went slack, and with a sudden creasing of her brow, a ring of brown showed in her eyes. "Oh God. Help me, Rachel," she whimpered.

It scared the crap out of me.

My legs trembled. I wanted to run. I wanted to leave her on the steps of the church and go. No one would say anything if I did. But instead I reached out and put my hands under her shoulders and lifted. "Come on," I whispered as I pulled her to her feet. All my instincts screamed to drop her as her hot skin touched mine. "Let's get you inside."

She hung slack in my grip. "I said no," she said, her words starting to slur. "I said no."

Ivy was taller than I, but my shoulder fit nicely under hers, and supporting most of her weight, I wedged the door open.

"He didn't listen," Ivy said, all but incoherent as I dragged her inside and shut the door behind us, shutting out the vomit and blood on the steps outside.

The black of the foyer was smothering. I staggered into motion, the light brightening as we entered the sanctuary. Ivy doubled over, panting around a moan. There was a dark smear of new blood on my robe, and I looked closer. "Ivy," I said. "You're bleeding."

I went cold as her new mantra of "He said it was all right" turned into a giggle. It was a deep, skin crawling giggle, and my mouth went dry.

"Yes," she said, the word sliding from her with a sultry heat. "I'm bleeding. Want a taste?" Horror settled into me as her giggle slipped into a sobbing moan. "Everyone should have a taste," she whimpered. "It doesn't matter anymore."

My jaw clenched and I tightened my grip on her shoulders. Anger mixed with my fear. Someone had used her. Someone had forced her to take blood against her will. She was out of her mind, an addict coming off a high.

"Rachel?" she quavered, her steps slowing. "I think I'm going to be sick. . . ."

"We're almost there," I said grimly. "Hold on. Just hold on."

We barely made it, and I held Ivy's vomit-strewn hair out of the way as she gagged and retched into her black porcelain toilet. I looked once in the glow of the seashell night-light, then closed my eyes as she vomited thick, black blood over and over. Sobs shook her shoulders, and when she finished, I flushed the toilet, wanting to get rid of what ugliness I could.

I stretched to flick the light on, and a rosy glow filled her bathroom. Ivy sat on the floor with her forehead on the toilet, crying. Her leather pants were shiny with blood down to her knees. Under her jacket, her silk blouse was torn. It clung to her, sticky with blood coming from her neck. Ignoring the warning coursing through me, I carefully gathered her hair to see.

My stomach knotted. Ivy's perfect neck had been ravaged, one long low tear marking the austere whiteness of her skin. It was still bleeding, and I tried not to breathe on it lest the lingering vamp saliva might set it into play.

Frightened, I let her hair fall and backed away. In vampire terms, she had been raped.

"I told him no," she said, her sobs slowing as she realized I wasn't standing over her anymore. "I told him no."

The image of me in the mirror looked white and scared. I took a breath to steady myself. I wanted it to go away. I wanted it all to just go away. But I had to get the blood off her. I had to get her in bed with a pillow to cry on. I had to get her a cup of cocoa and a really good shrink. Did they have shrinks for abused vampires? I wondered as I put a hand on her shoulder.

"Ivy," I coaxed. "It's time to get cleaned up." I looked at her bathtub where that stupid fish still swam. She needed a shower, not a bath where she would be sitting in the filth she had to get off her. "Let's go, Ivy," I encouraged. "A quick shower in my bathroom. I'll get your nightgown. Come on . . ."

"No," she protested, eyes not focused and unable to help as I lugged her upright. "I couldn't stop. I told him no. Why didn't he stop?"

"I don't know," I murmured, my anger growing. I supported her across the hall and into my bathroom. Hitting the light switch with my elbow, I left her slumped upright against the washer and dryer and went to start the shower.

The sound of the water seemed to revive her. "I smell," she whispered vacantly, looking down at herself.

She wouldn't look at me. "Can you take your shower by yourself?" I asked, hoping to spark some motion.

Face empty and slack, she looked down at herself, seeing she was covered in coagulated, vomited blood. My stomach clenched as she touched the shiny blood with a careful finger and licked it. Tension tightened my shoulders until they hurt.

Ivy started to cry. "Three years," she said in a soft exhalation, tears running down her oval face until she ran the back of her hand under her chin to leave a smear of blood. "Three years . . ."

Head bowed, she reached for the side zipper on her pants, and I lurched to the door. "I'll make you a cup of cocoa," I said, feeling entirely inadequate. I hesitated. "Will you be all right for a few minutes?"

"Yeah," she breathed, and I shut the door softly behind me.

Feeling weightless and unreal, I went into the kitchen. I flicked on the light, gripping my arms around myself, hearing the emptiness of the room. Her makeshift desk with its silver technology smelling faintly of ozone looked oddly right beside my shiny copper pots, ceramic spoons, and herbs hanging from a sweater rack. The kitchen was full of us, carefully separated by space but contained by the same walls. I wanted to call someone, to rage, to rant, to ask for help. But everyone would tell me to leave her and get out.

My fingers shook as I methodically got the milk and cocoa out and started to make Ivy a drink. *Hot cocoa,* I thought bitterly. Someone had raped Ivy, and all I could do was make her a damned cup of cocoa.

It had to be Piscary. Only Piscary was strong or bold enough to rape her. And it had been rape. She told him to stop. He took her against her will. It had been rape.

The timer on the microwave dinged, and I tightened the tie on my robe. My face went cold as I saw the blood on it and my slippers, some of it black and coagulated, some fresh and red from her neck. The former was smoldering. It was undead vampire blood. No wonder Ivy was retching. It must be burning inside her.

Ignoring the rank smell of cauterized blood, I resolutely finished making Ivy's cocoa, taking it to her room as the shower was still running.

The light from her bedside table filled the pink and white room with a soft glow. Ivy's bedroom was as far from a vampire's lair as her bathroom was. The leather curtains to keep out the morning light were hidden behind white curtains. Gunmetal-framed pictures of her, her mother, father, sister, and their lives took up an entire wall, looking like a shrine.

There were grainy photos taken before Christmas trees with

robes, smiles, and uncombed hair. Vacations in front of roller coasters, with sunburned noses and wide-brimmed hats. A sunrise on the beach, her father's arms about Ivy and her sister, protecting them from the cold. The newer pictures were in focus and in vibrant color, but I thought them less beautiful. The smiles had become mechanical. Her father looked tired. A new distance existed between Ivy and her mother. The most recent photos didn't have her mother in them at all.

Turning away, I pulled Ivy's soft coverlet down to expose the black satin smelling of wood ash. The book on the nightstand concerned deep meditation and the practice of reaching altered states of consciousness. My anger swelled. She had been trying so hard, and now she was back to square one. Why? What had it all been for?

Leaving the cocoa beside the book, I went across the hall to get rid of my bloodied robe. Motions quick with spent adrenaline, I brushed through my hair and threw on a pair of jeans and my black halter top, the warmest clean thing I had since I hadn't gotten my winter stuff out of storage yet. Leaving my robe and smoldering slippers in an ugly pile on the floor, I padded barefoot through the church, getting her nightgown from the back of her bathroom door.

"Ivy?" I called, knocking hesitantly on my bathroom door, hearing only the water running. There was no answer, and so knocking again, I pushed the door open. A heavy mist blurred everything, filling my lungs and making them seem heavy. "Ivy?" I called again, worry striking through me. "Ivy, are you all right?"

I found her on the floor of the shower stall, crumpled in a huddle of long legs and arms. The water flowed over her bowed head, blood making a thin rivulet to the drain from her neck. A shimmer of lighter red colored the bottom of the stall, coming from her legs. I stared, unable to look away. Her inner thighs were marred with deep scratches. Maybe it had been rape in the traditional sense as well.

I thought I was going to be sick. Ivy's hair was plastered to her. Her skin was white and her arms and legs were askew. The black of the twin ankle bracelets showed dark against the white of her skin, looking like shackles. She was shivering though the water was scalding, her eyes closed and her face twisted in a memory that would haunt her the rest of her life and into her death. Who said vampirism was glamorous? It was a lie, an illusion to cover the ugly reality.

I took a breath. "Ivy?"

Her eyes flashed open, and I jerked back.

"I don't want to think anymore," she said softly, unblinking though the water flowed over her face. "If I kill you, I won't have to."

I tried to swallow. "Should I leave?" I whispered, but I knew she could hear me.

Her eyes closed and her face scrunched up. Drawing her knees to her chin to cover herself, she wrapped her arms around her legs and started to cry again. "Yes."

Shaking inside, I stretched over her and turned off the water. The cotton towel was rough on my fingertips as I grabbed it and hesitated. "Ivy?" I said, frightened. "I don't want to touch you. Please get up."

Tears silently mixing with the water, she rose and took the towel. After she promised she would get herself dried off and dressed, I took her blood-soaked clothes along with my slippers and robe through the church to drop them on the back porch. The smell of burning blood turned my stomach like bad incense. I'd bury them in the cemetery later.

I found her huddled in her bed when I came back, her damp hair soaking her pillow and her untouched cocoa on the nightstand. Her face was to the wall and she wasn't moving. I pulled the afghan from the foot of the bed over her, and she trembled. "Ivy?" I said, then hesitated, not knowing what to do.

"I told him no," she said, her voice a whisper, torn gray silk drifting to rest atop snow.

I sat down on the cloth-draped trunk against the wall. *Piscary.* But I wouldn't say his name for fear of triggering something.

"Kist took me to him," she said, her words having the cadence of repeated memory. She had crossed her arms over her chest, only her fingers showing as they clutched her shoulders. I blanched as I saw what must be flesh under her nails, and I tugged the afghan up to hide it.

"Kisten took me to see him," she repeated, her words slow and deliberate. "He was angry. He said you were causing trouble. I told him you weren't going to hurt him, but he was angry. He was so angry with me."

I leaned closer, not liking this.

"He said," Ivy whispered, her voice almost unheard, "that if I couldn't curb you, that he would. I told him I'd make you my scion, that you would behave and he wouldn't have to kill you, but

I couldn't do it." Her voice got higher, almost frantic. "You didn't want it, and it's supposed to be a gift. I'm sorry. I'm so sorry. I tried to tell you," she said to the wall. "I tried to keep you alive, but he wants to see you now. He wants to talk to you. Unless . . ." Her trembling ceased. "Rachel? Yesterday . . . when you said you were sorry, was it because you thought you'd pushed me too far, or that you said no?"

I took a breath to answer, shocked when my words got stuck in my throat.

"Do you want to be my scion?" she breathed, softer than a guilty prayer.

"No," I whispered, frightened out of my mind.

She started shaking, and I realized she was crying again. "I said no, too," she said around her gulps for air. "I said no, but he did anyway. I think I'm dead, Rachel. Am I dead?" she questioned, her tears cutting off in her sudden fear.

My mouth was dry and I clutched my arms around myself. "What happened?"

Her breath came in a quick sound, and she held it for a moment. "He was angry. He said I had failed him. But he said it was all right. That I was the child of his heart, and that he loved me, that he forgave me. He told me he understood about pets. That he once kept them himself but that they always turned on him and he had to kill them. It hurt him, when they betrayed him time and again. He said if I couldn't bring myself to make you safe, that he'd do it for me. I said I'd do it, but he knew I was lying." A frightening moan came from her. "He knew I was lying."

I was a pet. I was a dangerous pet to be tamed. That's what Piscary thought I was.

"He said he understood my want for a friend instead of a pet, but that it wasn't safe to let you stay as you were. He said I had lost control and people were talking. I started to cry then, because he was so kind and I had disappointed him." Her words came in short bursts as she struggled to get the words out. "And he made me sit beside him, holding me as he whispered how proud he was of me and that he loved my great-grandmother almost as much as he loved me. That was all I ever wanted," she said. "Him to be proud of me."

She made a short gasp of pained laugher. "He said he understood about wanting a friend," she said to the wall, her face hidden behind her hair. "He told me he had been looking for centuries for someone strong enough to survive with him, that my mother, grandmother, and great-grandmother were all too weak but that I had the will to survive. I told him I didn't want to live forever, and he shushed me, telling me I was his chosen, that I would stay with him forever."

Her shoulders shook under the coverlet. "He held me, soothing my fears of the future. He said he loved me and was proud of me. And then he took my finger and drew blood from himself."

Stomach acid bubbled up, and I swallowed it down.

Her voice had gone wispy, her hunger and need a hidden ribbon of steel. "Oh God, Rachel. He's so old. It was like liquid electricity, welling up from him. I tried to leave. I wanted it, and I tried to leave, but he wouldn't let me. I said no, and then I ran. But he caught me. I tried to fight, but it didn't matter. Then I begged him no, but he held me and forced me to taste him."

Her voice was husky and her body shook. I moved to sit on the edge of the bed, horrified. Ivy went still, and I waited, unable to see her face, afraid to.

"And then I didn't have to think anymore," she said, the flat sound of her voice shocking. "I think I passed out for a moment. I wanted it. The power, the passion. He's so old. I pulled him to the floor and straddled him. I took everything he had as he clutched me to him, urging me to go deeper, to draw more. And I took it, Rachel. I took more than I should have. He should have stopped me, but he let me take it all."

I couldn't move, riveted by the terror of it.

"Kist tried to stop us. He tried to get between us, to stop Piscary from letting me take too much, but with every swallow, I lost more of myself. I think I—hurt Kist. I think I broke him. All I know is he went away, and Piscary . . ." A soft, pleasure-filled sound escaped her as she said his name again. ". . . Piscary drew me back." She moved languorously beneath the black sheets, suggestively. "He gentled my head against him and pressed me closer until I was sure he wanted me and I found he had more to give."

A harsh breath shook her, and she clenched into a huddled knot, the sated lover flashing into a beaten child. "I took everything. He let me take everything. I knew why he let me, and I did it anyway."

She was silent, but I knew she wasn't done yet. I didn't want to hear anymore, but she had to say it or she would drive herself slowly insane.

"With every pull, I could feel his hunger growing," she said, whispering. "With my every swallow his need swelled. I knew what would happen if I didn't stop, but he said it was all right, and it had been so long," she almost moaned. "I didn't want to stop. I knew what would happen, and I didn't want to stop. It was my fault. My fault."

I recognized the phrase from rape victims. "It wasn't your fault," I said, resting my hand upon her covered shoulder.

"It was," she said, and I pulled away as her voice became low and sultry. "I knew what would happen. And when I had everything he was, he asked for his blood back—like I knew he would. And I gave it to him. I wanted to, and I did. And it was fantastic."

I forced myself to breathe.

"God help me," she whispered. "I was alive. I hadn't been alive for three years. I was a goddess. I could give life. I could take it away. I saw him for what he was, and I wanted to be like him. And with his blood burning in me as if it was mine, his strength wholly mine, and his power wholly mine, burning into me the ugly, beautiful truth of his existence, he asked me to be his scion. He asked me to take Kisten's place, that he had been waiting for me to understand what it meant before he offered it to me. And that when I died, I would be his equal."

I kept my hand moving over her head in a soothing motion as her eyes closed and her shaking stopped. She was getting drowsy, her face going slack as her mind unwound her nightmare, finding a way to deal with it. I wondered if it had anything to do with the sky past her curtains brightening with the coming dawn.

"I went to him, Rachel," she whispered, color starting to come back into her lips. "I went to him, and he tore into me like a beast. I welcomed the pain. His teeth were God's truth, cutting clean into my soul. He savaged me, out of control from the joy of getting his power back after giving it to me so freely. And I gloried in it even as he bruised my arms and tore my neck open."

I forced my hand to keep moving.

"It hurt," she whispered, sounding like a child as her eyelids fluttered. "No one has enough vamp saliva in them to transmute that much pain, and he lapped up my misery and anguish along with my blood. I wanted to give him more, prove my loyalty to him, prove that though I failed by not taming you, that I would be his scion. Blood tastes better during sex," she said faintly. "The hormones make it sweet, so I opened myself to him. He said no, even as he moaned for it, that he might kill me by mistake. But I worked him until he couldn't stop himself. I wanted it. I wanted it even as he hurt me. He took it all, bringing us to climax even as he killed me." She shuddered, her eyes closed. "Oh God, Rachel. I think he killed me."

"You aren't dead," I whispered, frightened because I wasn't sure. She couldn't be in a church if she was dead, yes? Unless she was still in transition. The space of time when the chemistry shifted over had no hard and fast rules. What the hell was I doing?

"I think he killed me," she said again, her voice starting to slur as she fell asleep. "I think I killed myself." Her voice grew childlike. Her eyelids fluttered. "Am I dead, Rachel? Will you watch over me? Make sure the sun doesn't burn me while I sleep? Will you keep me safe?"

"Shhhh," I whispered, scared. "Go to sleep, Ivy."

"I don't want to be dead," she mumbled. "I made a mistake. I don't want to be Piscary's scion. I want to stay here with you. Can I stay here with you? Will you watch over me?"

"Hush," I murmured, running a hand over her hair. "Go to sleep."

"You smell good . . . like oranges," she whispered, setting my pulse pounding, but at least I didn't smell like her. I kept my hand moving until her breathing slowed and grew deep. I wondered if, when she fell asleep, it would stop. I wasn't sure Ivy was alive anymore.

My gaze went to the stained-glass window, the hint of dawn leaking around the edges. The sun would be up soon, and I didn't know anything about vampires crossing over except they had to be six feet under or in a light-tight room. That, and that they woke hungry the next sunset. *Oh God. What if Ivy was dead?*

I looked at the jewelry box on her mahogany dresser that held her "in case of death" bracelet that she refused to wear. Ivy had good insurance. If I called the number engraved on the silver band, an ambulance would be there in a guaranteed five minutes, whisking her away to a nice dark hole in the ground to emerge when darkness fell as a beautiful reborn undead.

My stomach churned and I rose to go to my room for my tiny cross. If she was dead, there would be some reaction, even if she was in transition. Passing out in a church is one thing; having a consecrated cross touch your skin is another.

Nauseated, I returned. Charms jingling, I held my breath and dangled my bracelet over Ivy. There was no response. I brought the cross close to her neck behind her ear, breathing easier when again there was no reaction. Silently asking for her forgiveness if I was wrong, I touched the cross to her skin. She didn't move, her pulse at her neck staying slow and sedate. Her skin, when I pulled the cross away, was white and unblemished.

I straightened, saying a silent prayer. I didn't think she was dead.

Slowly I crept from Ivy's room, shutting the door behind me. Piscary had raped Ivy for one reason. He knew I had figured it out. Ivy said he wanted to talk to me. If I stayed in my church, he would go for my mother next, then Nick, and then probably track down my brother.

My thoughts returned to Ivy, huddled under her covers in a shock-induced sleep. My mother would be next. And she would die not even knowing why she was being tortured.

Shaking inside, I went into the living room for the phone. My fingers were trembling so badly, I had to dial it twice. It took a precious three minutes of arguing to get to Rose.

"I'm sorry, Ms. Morgan," the woman said, her voice so politically correct I could freeze an egg on it. "Captain Edden is not available, and Detective Glenn left word that he is not to be disturbed."

"Not to be—" I stammered. "Listen. I know who murdered them. We have to go out there now. Before he sends someone after my mother!"

"I'm sorry, Ms. Morgan," the woman said politely. "You are no longer a consultant. If you have a complaint or death threat, please hold and I'll transfer you back to the front desk."

"No! Wait!" I pleaded. "You don't understand. Just let me talk to Glenn!"

"No, Morgan." Rose's calm, reasonable voice was suddenly thick with an unexpected anger. "You don't understand. No one here wants to talk to you."

"But I know who the witch hunter is!" I exclaimed, and the connection clicked off.

"You sorry-assed *idiots!*" I shouted, throwing the phone across the room. It hit the wall, the back coming off and the batteries rolling over the floor. Frustrated, I stomped into the kitchen, spilling Ivy's pens over the table as I reached for one. Heart pounding, I scratched a note to thumbtack to the door of the church.

Nick was coming. Glenn would talk to Nick. He could convince them I was right, tell them where I'd gone. They'd have to come out, if only to arrest me for interfering. I would have told him to call the I.S., but Piscary probably owned them. And though humans had as much chance of besting a master vampire as I did, perhaps just the interruption might be enough to save my butt.

Spinning, I reached for the cupboard, pulling amulets from hooks and jamming them into my bag. I yanked open a bottom drawer and grabbed three wooden stakes. I added the big butcher cleaver from the knife block. My splat gun was next, loaded with the strongest spell a white witch would have: sleepy-time charms. From the island counter I took a bottle of holy water. Thinking for a moment, I pulled up the valve top, took a swallow, recapped it, then shoved it in with the rest. Holy water wasn't much good unless it was all you'd been drinking for the last three days, but I'd take all the deterrent I could scrape together.

Not slowing, I strode into the hall for my boots. I slipped them on and headed for the front door, laces flapping. Jerking to a halt in the hallway, I spun, returning to the kitchen. Grabbing a handful of change for the bus, I left.

Piscary wanted to talk to me? Good. I wanted to talk to him.

Twenty-Six

The bus was crowded at five in the morning. Living vamps, mostly, and vamp wannabes on their way home to take stock of their sorry existence. They gave me a wide birth. It could have been that I stank of holy water. It could have been that I looked like hell warmed over in my ugly, heavy winter coat with the fake fur around the collar that I had worn so the driver wouldn't recognize me and would pick me up. But I was betting it was the stakes.

Face tight, I got off the bus at Piscary's restaurant. I stood where my feet hit the pavement and waited while the door shut and the bus drove away. Slowly the noise faltered until it melted into the background hum of swelling morning traffic. My eyes pinched as I looked straight up at the brightening sky. The mist from my breath obscured the fragile-looking, pale blue. I wondered if it was going to be the last sky I'd ever see. It would be dawn soon. If I were smart, I would wait until the sun was up before I went in.

I pushed myself into motion. Piscary's was two stories tall, and all the windows were dark. The yacht was still tied to the quay, and the water lapped softly. There were only a few cars in the lot at the outskirts. Employees, probably. As I walked, I swung my bag around. Pulling out the stakes, I flung them away. Their harsh clatters on the asphalt shocked my ears. Bringing them had been stupid. Like I could stake an undead vampire. The splat gun at the small of my back was probably a futile gesture, too, since I was sure I would be searched before they took me to Piscary. The master vampire said he wanted to talk, but I'd be a fool to think it would stop there. If I wanted to meet him with all my spells and charms, I'd have to fight my way to him. If I let them take away everything I had, I'd get to him unscathed but pretty much helpless.

I opened the bottle of holy water and chugged it, spilling the last drops into my hands and patting my neck. The empty bottle clattered after the stakes. I strode forward in my soundless boots, my fear for my mother and my anger at what he had done to Ivy keeping my feet moving. If there were too many of them, I'd go in charmless. Nick and the FIB were my ace in the hole.

My stomach knotted as I pushed open the heavy door. The faint hope that there might be no one died as half a dozen people looked up from their scattered work, all of them living vamps. The human staff was gone. I'd be willing to bet that the pretty, scarred, adoring humans had gone home with favorite customers.

The lights were up high while the wait staff cleaned, and where the large room with its log-cabin walls had looked mysterious and exciting, now it looked dirty and tired. Kind of like me. The shoulder-high wall of stained glass that divided the room was broken. A petite woman with hair to her waist was sweeping the shards of green and gold toward the wall. She stopped to lean on the broom as I came in. There was an odd smell at the back of my throat, rich and cloying. My feet faltered as I realized the vamp pheromones were so thick I could taste them.

At least Ivy had put up a fight, I thought, realizing most of the vamps were sporting a bandage or bruise, and all of them, with the exception of the vamp sitting at the bar, were in a bad mood. One had been bit, his neck torn and his uniform ripped at the collar. In the bright light of morning, their glamour and sexual tension had been wiped away, to leave only a tired ugliness. My lip curled in distaste. Seeing them like this, they were repellant. And yet my scar on my neck started to tingle.

"Well, look who showed," the vamp sitting at the bar drawled. His uniform was more elaborate than the rest, and he took his name tag off as he saw my eyes on it. It read SAMUEL, the vampire that had let Tarra upstairs the night we were there. Samuel got up, leaning to flick a switch behind the counter. The open sign behind me in the window went out. "You're Rachel Morgan?" he asked, his vamp-confident voice slow and patronizing.

Clutching my bag, I boldly walked past the WAIT HERE FOR HOST sign. Yeah, I was a bad girl. "That's me," I said, wishing there were fewer tables. My feet slowed as caution finally worked its way past my anger. I had broken rule number one: going in mad. I would have been okay if I hadn't also broken the more important rule number two: confronting an undead vamp on his own turf.

The wait staff was watching, and my pulse quickened as Samuel went to the door and locked it. Turning, he casually threw the wad of keys clear across the room. A figure by the unused fireplace raised his arm, and I recognized Kisten, unseen in the shadows until he moved. The keys hit Kist's palm with a jingle and disappeared. I didn't know if I should be angry with him or not. He had dumped Ivy and driven off, but he had tried to stop them, too.

"This is what Piscary is worried about?" Samuel said, his beautiful face sneering. "Skinny little thing. Not much on top." He leered. "Or bottom. I thought you'd be taller."

He reached for me. Jerking into motion, I stiff-armed him, feeling my fist pop into his open palm. I twisted my wrist, grabbing his. I yanked him forward into my upraised foot. His breath whooshed out as it hit his stomach, knocking him backward. I followed him down, giving him a jab at his crotch before I got to my feet. "And I thought you'd be smarter," I said, backing away as he writhed on the floor, gasping.

It probably hadn't been the smartest thing to do.

Dropping their rags and brooms, the wait staff converged on me with an unnerving, unhurried pace. My breath came fast, and I shimmied out of my coat, shoving one of the tables away with my foot to make room to move. Seven spells in my gun. Nine vamps. I'd never get them all. My face went cold and I shivered in the draft on my bare shoulders.

"No," Kist said from his corner, and they hesitated. "I said no!" he shouted as he got to his feet and started over, his fast pace jerking into a slower one to hide a new limp.

Their faces twisting to an ugly promise, they stopped, making a ring about me a good eight feet back. *Eight feet,* I thought, feeling ill as I remembered my and Ivy's workouts. That was a living vamp's reach.

Crotch-boy got to his feet, his shoulders hunched and his face pained. Kist pushed through the circle to stand opposite him, hands on his hips and feet spread wide. His dark silk shirt and dress pants gave him more sophistication than his usual leather. A bruise spread upward across his lightly stubbled cheek to just miss his eye. By the way he held himself, I guessed his ribs were hurting, but I thought the real damage was to his pride. He had lost his scion status to Ivy.

"He said bring her down, not rough her up," Kist said, his lips going bloodless as my gaze lingered on the fingernail gouge behind his bangs.

Though Samuel was bigger, Kist's demand for obedience was unmistakable. A hard, bad temper had replaced his usual mien of casual flirtation, giving him a rough edge that I'd always found attractive in men. Like every manager, Kist had problems with his employees, and somehow the fact that he had to deal with crap just like everyone else made him more appealing. My gaze roved over him, my thoughts following my eyes. *Damn vamp pheromones.*

Still panting, the larger vamp darted his eyes to me and back to Kist. "She needs to be searched." He licked his lips, looking at me to make my pulse race. "I'll do it."

I stiffened, my thoughts going to my splat gun. There were too many of them.

"I'm doing it," Kist said, his blue eyes starting to vanish behind a swelling circle of black.

Swell.

Samuel sullenly backed off, and Kist held out his hand for my bag. I hesitated, then seeing him arch his eyebrow as if to say, "Just give me a reason," I extended it. He took it, roughly setting it on a nearby table. "Give me what you have on you," he said softly.

Eyes on his, I slowly reached behind me and handed him my splat gun. There wasn't a sound from the surrounding vampires. Perhaps some respect for my little red paint-ball gun? They didn't know what it was loaded with. I had known the moment I tucked it behind my waistband I'd never get to use it, and I frowned at lost chances that never really existed.

"The cross?" he asked, and I worked the clasp of my charm bracelet, dropping it into his waiting hand. Saying nothing, he set it and my gun on the table behind him. Stepping forward, he put his arms out wide. I obediently mimicked him, and he came close to pat me down.

Jaw gritted, I felt his hands run over me. Where he touched, a warm tingling started, working its way to my middle. *Not the scar, not the scar,* I thought desperately, knowing what would happen if he touched it. The vamp pheromones were almost thick enough to see, and just the breeze from the fan was making a pleasant sensation run from my neck to my groin.

I shook in relief when his hands fell away. "The charm on your pinky," he demanded, and I took it off, slapping it in his palm. He dropped it beside my gun. A tight look came into his eye as he stood before me. "If you move, you die," he said.

I stared at him, not understanding.

Kist eased close, and my breath hissed. I could smell his tension, his wire-tight reactions balancing on the possibility of my next move. He sent his breath against my collarbone, and my thoughts jerked back to his lips brushing my ear four days ago. Head tilted, he looked down at me, hesitating, an empty look in his blue eyes, his hunger well-hidden.

Reaching up, he ran a finger from my ear, across my neck and the bumps of my scar.

My knees buckled. Sucking in air, I pulled myself upright, and with waves of need demanding to be met, I backhanded him. He caught my wrist before it landed, yanking me into him. Twisting, I swung my foot up. He caught it.

Kist jerked me off my feet and let go.

I fell on my can, the wooden floor bruising. I stared up at him as the vamps laughed. Kist's face, though, was empty. No anger, no speculation. Nothing.

"You smell like Ivy," he said as I got to my feet, my heart hammering. "You aren't bound to her, though." A sliver of satisfaction marred his stoic expression. "She couldn't do it."

"What are you talking about?" I snarled, embarrassed and angry as I brushed myself off.

His eyes narrowed. "It felt good, didn't it? Me touching your scar? Once a vamp binds you by blood, only they can elicit that kind of a response. Who bit you and didn't bother to claim you?" His face went thoughtful, and I thought I saw a glimmer of lust. "Or did you kill your attacker afterward to prevent being bound? You're a bad little girl."

I said nothing, letting him believe what he wanted, and he shrugged. "Since you aren't tied to anyone, any vamp can entice that kind of reaction." His eyebrows rose. "Any vamp," he repeated, and a chill went through me at the thought of Piscary waiting for me. "You should have an interesting morning," he added.

Vision clearing, he reached behind him and dragged my bag from the table. The vamps had begun to talk among themselves, making casual, unnerving speculations as to how long I would last. Kist pulled out the butcher knife first, and hooting laughter rippled over them. My gaze went over the destruction of Piscary's as Kist set a handful of charms clattering on the table.

"Did Ivy do this?" I asked, trying to find a sliver of my confidence. The longer I kept them talking, the better the chance that Nick would get the FIB out there in time.

The vamp I had crotch-punched sneered. "In a manner of speaking." He looked at Kist, and I thought I saw the blond vamp's jaw clench. "Your roommate's a good lay," Samuel said, going smug as Kist's breath quickened and his fingers digging through my bag became rough.

"Yeah," Samuel continued in a good-old-boy's drawl. "She and Piscary got the entire restaurant hopped-up on vamp pheromones. Ended up with three fights, a couple of bites." He leaned against a table, crossed his arms and smirked. "Someone died and got carted off to the city's temporary vaults. See? He got his picture on the wall and a coupon for a free dinner. We were damned lucky we figured out what was going on and got everyone not a vamp outta here before all hell broke loose. God help us if Piscary lost his MPL and had to reapply. Took him almost a year last time." Samuel took a peanut from a bowl and threw it into the air, catching it with his mouth and grinning as he chewed.

Kist's face was red with anger. "Shut up," he said, pulling the ties to my bag closed.

"Whatsa matter?" Samuel mocked. "Just 'cause you never got Piscary that worked up doesn't mean he's gonna make her his scion."

Kist stiffened. He hadn't told anyone that Piscary already did. My eyes darted to him, his anger keeping my mouth shut.

"I said shut up," Kist warned, the heat from him almost visible.

The surrounding vamps were casually shifting back. Samuel laughed, clearly wanting to push Kist as far as he could. "Kist is jealous," he said to me with the sole intent to irritate him. "The most that ever happened when he and Piscary were going at it was a bar fight." His full lips split into a nasty grin, and he glanced cockily at the surrounding vamps. "Don't worry, old man," he directed to Kist. "Piscary will get tired of her as soon as she dies, and you'll be back on top—or bottom—or somewhere in between if you're lucky. Maybe they'll let you sit in and Ivy can teach you a thing or two."

Kist's fingers trembled. In the space between one heartbeat and the next, he moved. Too fast to follow, he crossed the circle, grabbed Samuel by the shirtfront, and shoved him up against a thick support post. The timber groaned, and I heard something snap in Samuel's chest. The bigger man's face showed a surprised shock, his eyes wide and his mouth open in pain he hadn't had time to feel.

"Shut up," Kist said softly. His jaw clenched and his eye twitched. Dropping him, Kist gave Samuel a shove, twisting his arm at an unnatural angle as the larger man fell to his knees. My breath caught at the audible pop of his shoulder dislocating.

Samuel's eyes bulged. Mouth open in a silent scream, he knelt, his arm still bent behind him, since Kist had never let go of his wrist. Kist dropped it, and Samuel gasped for air.

I stood—unable to move—frightened at how fast it had been.

Kist was suddenly before to me, and I jerked. "Here's your bag," he said, handing it to me. I snatched it, and Kist gestured that I should go before him. An opening parted in the circle. The surrounding vamps looked properly cowed. No one had gone to help Samuel, and his ragged pants for air as he lay unmoving struck me to my core.

"Don't touch me," I said as I passed Kist. "And none of you had better mess with my things while I'm gone," I added, shaking inside. My pace faltered as I took a last look at my charms and realized only about half of what I had brought was on the table.

Kist took my elbow and pulled me into motion. "Let me go," I said, the memory of him dislocating Samuel's arm keeping me from pulling away.

"Shut up," he said, the tension in his voice giving me pause.

Mind whirling, I followed his not-so-subtle direction, weaving through the tables to pass through a set of swinging doors and into the kitchen. Behind us the wait staff went back to their work, the speculations flying as they ignored Samuel.

I couldn't help notice that though smaller, my kitchen was nicer than Piscary's. Kist led me to a metal institutional-looking fire door. He opened it and flicked on a light to show a small white room floored in oak. The silver doors of an elevator were tucked out of the way. A wide-mouthed, spiral stairway leading downward took up much of one wall. The stairway was elegant, the modest chandelier above it clinking faintly in the upwelling draft. A wooden clock the size of a table hung on the wall opposite the stairway, ticking loudly.

"Down?" I said, trying to keep from looking scared. If Nick didn't find my note, there was no chance I'd be coming back up those stairs.

The fire door snicked shut behind him, and I felt the air pressure change. The draft smelled like nothing, almost a void in itself. "Let's take the elevator," Kist said, his voice unexpectedly soft. His entire posture changed as he focused on an unknown thought. *He had left me some of my charms. . . .*

The elevator doors opened immediately when he pushed the button, and I got in. Kist was tight behind me, and we faced the doors as they closed. With a soft pull at my stomach, the elevator started down. Immediately I swung my bag around and opened it.

"Idiot!" Kist hissed.

A tiny shriek escaped me as he slid, pinning me into a corner. The room shifted under me and I froze, poised to act. His teeth were inches from me. My demon scar pulsed and I held my breath. The pheromones were less in here, but it didn't seem to matter. If there was elevator music, I was going to scream.

"Don't be stupid. You don't think he's got cameras in here?" My breath came in a soft pant. "Get away from me."

"Don't think so, love," he whispered, his breath sending tingling jolts from my neck and making my blood pound. "I'm going to see just how far that scar on your neck can take you . . . and when I'm done, you're going to find a vial in your purse."

I stiffened as he pressed closer. The scent of leather and silk was a pleasing assault. I couldn't breathe as he nuzzled my hair out of the way. "It's Egyptian embalming fluid," he said, and I tensed as his lips shifted against my neck with his words. I didn't dare move, and if I was honest, I'd admit that I didn't want to as tingling ribbons of promise flowed from my scar. "Get it in his eyes, and it will knock him unconscious."

I couldn't help it. My body demanded I do something. Shoulders easing, I closed my eyes and ran my hands up the smooth expanse of his back. He paused in surprise, then his hands slid down my sides to grasp my waist. The muscles under his silk shirt bunched beneath my fingers. Reaching upward, my nails played with the hair at the nape of his neck. The soft strands had a uniform color that you can only find in a box, and I realized he dyed his hair.

"Why are you helping me?" I breathed, fingering the black chain about his neck. The body-warm links were the same pattern as the bracelets about Ivy's ankle.

I felt his muscles shift, tightening with pain instead of desire. "He said I was his scion," he said as he hid his face in my hair to hide his moving lips from the unseen camera—at least, that's what I told myself. "He said I would be with him forever, and he betrayed me for Ivy. She doesn't deserve him." Hurt stained his voice. "She doesn't even love him."

My eyes closed. I would never understand vampires. Not knowing why I did, I sent my fingers gently through his hair, soothing him as his breath caressed my demon scar into mounting surges demanding to be met. Common sense told me to stop, but he was hurt, and I'd been betrayed like that, too.

Kist's breath faltered as I sent the hint of my fingernails under his ear. Making a low guttural sound, he pressed closer, his heat obvious through the thin material of my shirt. His tension became deeper, more dangerous. "My God," he whispered, his voice a husky thread. "Ivy was right. Leaving you unbound and free of compulsion would be like fucking a tiger."

"Watch your mouth," I said breathily, his hair tickling my face. "I don't like that kind of language." *I was already dead. Why not enjoy my last few moments?*

"Yes, ma'am," he said obediently, his voice shocking in its submissiveness even as he forced his lips to mine. My head hit the back of the elevator with the force of his kiss. I pushed back, unafraid.

"Don't call me that," I mumbled around his mouth, remembering what Ivy had said about him playing the subordinate. Maybe I could survive a submissive vampire.

His weight pressing harder into me, he pulled his lips from mine. I met his eyes—his faultless blue eyes—studying them with the breathless understanding that I didn't know what was going to happen next, but praying that whatever it was, it would happen.

"Let me do this," he said, his rumbling voice just shy of a growl. His hands were free, and he took my chin and held my head unmoving. I caught a glint of tooth, then he was too close to see anything. Not a shimmer of fear struck me as he kissed me again, pushed out by a sudden realization.

He wasn't after blood. Ivy wanted blood; Kist wanted sex. And the risk that his desire might turn to blood catapulted me past my sensibilities and into a reckless daring.

His lips were soft with a moist warmth. His blond stubble was a striking contrast, adding to my fervor. Heart pounding, I hooked a foot behind his leg and pulled him closer. Feeling it, his breath came and went in a pant. A soft sound of real bliss escaped me. My tongue found the smoothness of his teeth, and his muscles under my hands tensed. I pulled my tongue away, teasing.

Our mouths parted. Heat was in his eyes, black and full of a fervent, unashamed desire. And still there was no fear. "Give this to me. . . ." he breathed. "I won't break your skin if . . ." He took a breath. ". . . you give this to me."

"Shut up, Kisten," I whispered, closing my eyes to block what I could of the confusing swirl of rising tensions.

"Yes, Ms. Morgan."

It was the softest whisper. I wasn't even sure I had heard it. The need in me swelled, compelling beyond sanity. I knew I shouldn't, but heart quickening, I ran my nails down his neck to leave red pressure trails. Kisten shuddered, his hands falling to find the small of my back, firm and questing. Liquid fire raced from my neck as he angled his head and found my scar. His breath came in strong surges, sending wave after delicious wave through me from his lips alone.

"I will not—I will not," he panted, and I realized he was balanced on the brink of something more. A tremor passed through me as he traced a path across my neck with his gentle teeth. A whisper of words unrecognized pattered through my thoughts, pinging my sensibilities. "Say yes . . ." he urged, a wisp of urgent promise in his low, coaxing voice. "Say it, love. Please . . . give me this, too."

My knees trembled as the coolness of his teeth grazed over my skin again, testing, luring. His hands on my shoulders held me firm. *Did I want this?* Eyes warming with unshed tears, I admitted I didn't know anymore. Where Ivy couldn't move me, Kisten did. I prayed Kisten didn't feel it in my fingers gripping his arms as if he was the only thing keeping me sane at this brink of time.

"You need to hear me say yes?" I breathed, recognizing the passion in my voice. I would rather die here with Kisten then in fear with Piscary.

The ding of the elevator intruded and the doors opened.

A flush of cool air drifted about my ankles. Reality flashed back in a painful rush. It was too late. I had tarried too long. "Do I have the vial?" I questioned, breathless as my fingers twined among the short hair at the nape of his neck. His weight was heavy against me, and the scent of leather and silk would forever mean Kisten to me. I didn't want to move. I didn't want to get out of this elevator.

I felt Kist's heartbeat and heard him swallow. "It's in your purse," he breathed.

"Good." My jaw clenched and my grip in his hair tightened. Yanking his head back, I brought my knee up.

Kist flung himself away from me. The elevator shook as he hit the opposite wall. I'd missed him. Damn.

Breathless and disheveled, he pulled himself straight and felt his ribs. "You have to move faster than that, witch." Flipping the hair from his eyes, he gestured for me to go out before him.

Knees watery and loose, I gathered myself and walked out of the elevator.

Twenty-Seven

Piscary's daytime quarters were not what I had expected. I walked out of the elevator, my head swinging from side to side, taking it all in. The ceilings were high—I guessed ten feet— and were painted white where they weren't covered with warm, primary-colored sheets of fabric draped into soothing folds. Large archways hinted at equally spacious rooms farther in. It had the soft comfort of a playboy mansion mixed with the air of a museum. I spared a moment to try to find a ley line, not surprised to find I was too deep underground.

My boots trod upon a plush off-white carpet. The furniture was tasteful, and there was occasional artwork under spotlights. Floor-to-ceiling curtains at regular intervals gave the illusion of windows behind them. Bookshelves behind glass were between them, every tome looking older than the Turn. Nick would have loved it, and I spared a thought, desperately hoping he had found my note. The first hints of possible success made me walk with more confidence than I deserved. Between Kisten's vial and Nick's note, maybe I could escape with my life.

The doors to the elevator shut. I turned, noticing there was no button to push to make them open up again. The stairway, too, was missing. It must come out somewhere else. My heart gave a pound and settled. Escape with my life? *Maybe.*

"Take off your boots," Kist said.

I cocked my head in disbelief. "Excuse me?"

"They're dirty." His attention was on my feet. He was still flushed. "Take them off."

I looked at the expanse of white carpet. *He wanted me to kill*

Piscary, and he was worried about my boots on the carpet? Grimacing, I slipped them off and left them askew by the elevator. I did not believe this. I was going to die in my bare feet.

But the carpet felt nice on my arches as I followed Kisten, forcing myself to not feel the outside of my bag for the vial he had promised was there. He was tense again, his jaw tight and his manner sullen, far from the domineering vampire that had driven me to the brink of capitulation. He looked jealous and wronged. Just what I would expect from a betrayed lover.

Give me this. . . . echoed in my memory, pulling an unstoppable shudder through me. I wondered if he begged Piscary like that, knowing that he had been asking for blood. And I wondered if, to Kisten, the taking of blood was a casual commitment or something more.

The sound of muted traffic drew my attention from the picture of what looked like Piscary and Lindburgh sharing a pint in a British pub. Steps slow to hid his limp, Kisten led me into a sunken living room. At the end of it was a tiled breakfast nook before what looked like, for all the world, a window overlooking the river from the second story. Piscary was lounging at a small metal-weave table dead center of the circular tiled space, surrounded by carpet. I knew I was underground and that it was only a live video feed, but it sure looked like a window to me.

The sky was brightening with the coming dawn, giving the gray river a soft sheen. Cincinnati's taller buildings were dark silhouettes against the lighter sky. Smoke came from the paddleboats as they stoked their boilers, readying themselves for the first wave of tourists. Sunday traffic was light, and the individual whooshes of cars were lost behind the thousands of clatters, clanks, and unseen calls that make up the background of a city. I watched the water ripple under the breeze, and my hair lifted in a gust in time with a soft hush of wind. Taken aback at the detail, I searched the ceiling and floor until I found a vent. A horn blew in the distance.

"Enjoy yourself, Kist?" Piscary said, pulling my attention away from the jogger and his dog running the footpath beside the river.

Kist's neck went red and he ducked his head. "I wanted to know what Ivy was talking about," he mumbled, looking like a child caught kissing the neighbor girl.

Piscary smiled. "Exciting, isn't it? Leaving her unbound like that is loads of fun until she tries to kill you. But then, that's where the thrill comes from, yes?"

My tension flowed back. Piscary looked relaxed, sitting at one of the table's two wireweave chairs in a lightweight, midnight-blue silk robe. The morning paper sat folded by his hand. The deep color of his robe went nicely with his amber skin. His bare feet were visible through the table. They were long and skinny, the same honey hue as his bare scalp. My anxiety strengthened at his bedroom-casual appearance. *Great. This is just what I needed.*

"Nice window," I said, thinking it was better than Trent's, the toad. He could have taken care of all of this had he acted when I told him Piscary was the murderer. Men were all alike: take what they can get without paying for it, lie about the rest.

Piscary shifted in his chair, and his robe parted to show his knee. I quickly looked away. "Thank you," he said. "I hated sunrises when I was alive. Now it's my favorite part of the day." I sneered, and he gestured to the table. "Would you like a cup of coffee?"

"Coffee?" I said. "I would have thought it was against the gangster code to have coffee with someone before killing them."

His thin black eyebrows rose. I realized he must want something from me, otherwise he would have just sent Algaliarept to kill me on the bus.

"Black," I said. "No sugar."

Piscary gave Kisten a directive nod, and he slipped soundlessly away. I pulled out the second chair across from Piscary, flopping down with my bag on my lap. I glanced out the fake window in the silence. "I like your lair," I said sarcastically.

Piscary raised one eyebrow. I wished I could do that. Too late to learn how now. "It was originally part of the underground railroad," he said. "A foul hole in the ground under someone's shipping dock. Ironic, isn't it?" I said nothing, and he added, "This used to be the gateway to the free world. It still is, occasionally. There's nothing like death to free a person."

A small sigh slipped from me, and I turned to the window, wondering how much wise-old-man-crap he was going to make me listen to before killing me. Piscary cleared his throat, and I looked back. A wisp of black hair showed behind the V of his robe, and his calves visible through the wire mesh of the table were hard with muscle. I recalled my lust rising hot and fast in the elevator with Kisten, knowing it had mostly been vamp pheromones. *Liar.* That Piscary could to that to me and more with nothing more than a sound turned my stomach.

Unable to stop myself, I sent my hand over my neck as if to

brush my hair from my eyes. I wanted to hide my scar, though Piscary was probably more aware of it than the nose on my face. "You didn't have to rape her to get me to come see you," I said, deciding to be angry instead of afraid. "A dead horse head in my bed would have done it."

"I wanted to," he said, his low voice carrying the strength of the wind. "Much as you'd like to think otherwise, this isn't all about you, Rachel. Some of it, but not all."

"My name is Ms. Morgan."

He acknowledged this with a three-second, mocking silence. "I have been spoiling Ivy. People are beginning to talk. It was time to bring her back into the fold. And it was a pleasure—for both of us." A smile of remembrance came over him, a glint of fang and a soft, almost subliminal, guttural sigh. "She surprised me, going far past my intended purpose. I haven't lost control like that for at least three hundred years."

My stomach quivered as a surge of his vamp-induced desire flashed through me and was gone. Its potency took my breath away, and I found myself reaching out to catch it. "Bastard," I said, wide-eyed as my blood pounded in me.

"Flatterer," he said back, his eyebrows high.

"She changed her mind," I said, as the last of his need died in me. "She doesn't want to be your scion. Leave her alone."

"It's too late. And she does want it. I put no compulsion on her when she made her decision. I didn't need to. She had been bred and raised for the position, and when she dies, she will have the complexity to be a suitable companion, varied and sophisticated enough in her thoughts so that I don't become bored with her and she with me. You see, Rachel, it's not honest to say that the lack of blood is what causes a vampire to go insane and walk out into the sun. It's the boredom that brings on a lack of appetite that leads to insanity. Working to bring Ivy about has helped me stave that off. Now that she is poised upon her potential, she's going to keep me from going insane." He inclined his head graciously. "And I'll do the same for her."

His attention went over my shoulder, and the hair on the back of my neck pricked. It was Kisten. The whisper of his passage brushed against me, and I stifled a shudder. The bruised and beaten vamp silently set a cup of coffee on a saucer before me and left. He never met my eyes, his manner holding a subdued pain. The steam from the porcelain rose three inches before the artificial wind caught it and blew it away. I didn't reach for the cup. Fatigue pulled at me and adrenaline made me feel ill. I thought of the charms in my bag. Why was Piscary waiting?

"Kist?" the undead vampire said softly, and Kisten turned. "Give it to me."

Piscary held out his hand, and Kisten dropped a crumpled paper in his palm. My face went slack in panic. It was my note to Nick.

"Did she call anyone?" Piscary asked Kist, and the young vampire ducked his head.

"She called the FIB. They hung up on her."

Shocked, I looked at Kisten. He had watched the entire thing. He had hidden in the shadows while I held Ivy's hair as she vomited, watched as I made her cocoa, and listened as I sat beside Ivy while she relived her nightmare. While I had been taking forever on the bus, Kisten had ripped my salvation from the door. No one was coming. No one at all.

Not meeting my eyes, he walked away. There was the distant sound of a door closing. My gaze flicked to Piscary's and my breath froze. His eyes were entirely black. *Shit.*

The unblinking obsidian orbs made my palms sweat. With the coiled tension of a predator, he reclined before me in his midnight-blue robe with that fake wind moving the wisps of hair on his bare arms, tan and healthy looking. The hem of his robe shifted with his subtle movements. His chest moved as he breathed in an effort to ease my subconscious. And as I sat before him, the enormity of what was going to happen fell on me.

My breath came and went, and I held it. Seeing me recognize my death, he blinked slowly and smiled with a knowing glint. *Not yet, but soon. When he could wait no longer.*

"It's amusing you care for her so deeply," he said, the power seeping from his voice to clench about my heart. "She betrayed you so utterly. My beautiful, dangerous *filiola custos.* I sent her to watch you four years ago, and she joined the I.S. I bought a church and told her to move into it; she did. I asked her to put in a witch's kitchen and stock it with appropriate books; she went beyond to arrange for a garden that would be irresistible."

My face was cold and my legs trembled. *Her friendship had been a lie? A sham to keep tabs on me?* I couldn't believe it. Remembering the lost sound of her voice as she asked me to keep the sun from killing her, I couldn't believe her friendship had been a lie.

"I told her to follow you when you quit," Piscary said, the

blackness in his eyes taking on the tension of a remembered passion. "It was our first argument, and I thought that I had found the point where I could make her my scion, where she would show her strength and prove she could hold her own against me. But she capitulated. For a time I thought I might have made a mistake and she lacked the strength of will to survive infinity with me and I'd have to wait yet another generation and try with a daughter born of her and Kisten. I was so disappointed. Imagine my delight when I realized she had her own agenda and was using me."

He smiled, the slip of teeth a little bigger, showing a little longer. "She had fastened upon you as her way out of the future I saw for her. She thought you could find a way to keep her from losing her soul when she dies." He shook his head in a controlled motion, the light glinting across his smooth scalp. "Can't be done, but she won't believe."

I swallowed, making fists as my feelings of betrayal faltered. She had been using him, not following his direction. "Does she know you murdered those witches?" I whispered, sick at heart that she might have known and never told me.

"No," Piscary said. "I'm sure she suspects, but my interest in you stems from an older reason, having nothing to do with Kalamack's current holy grail of a ley line witch."

I kept my eyes from my hands gripped tightly in my lap above the opening of my bag. I couldn't reach for the vial. *If it wasn't for that, why did Piscary want me dead?*

"It must have cost her pride dearly to come to me, begging for clemency when you survived your demon attack. She was so upset. It's hard to be young. I understood more than she knows what it is to want an equal. And I was inclined to spoil her more once I realized she had used me without my knowing. So I let you live, provided she break her fast and take you completely. You being her shadow had an ironic twist I liked. She promised she would, but I knew she was lying. Even so, I didn't mind as long as she kept you and Kalamack apart."

"But I'm not a ley line witch," I said, keeping my voice soft so it wouldn't shake. I could have breathed the words and he would have heard. "Why?"

He hadn't taken a breath since he stopped talking. The balls of his feet were pressed to the floor. His calves were tense. *Almost,* I thought, moving my fingers to the opening of my bag. *He was almost ready. What was he waiting for?*

"You are your father's daughter," he said, the skin around his eyes tightening. "Trent is his father's son. Apart you are annoying. Together . . . you have the potential to be a problem."

My gaze went distant then sharpened as I met his eyes, knowing my face had taken on a horrified expression. The picture of my father and Trent's outside a yellow camp bus. Piscary had killed them. It had been Piscary.

Hard and strong, my blood pounded in my temples. My body demanded I do something, but I sat, knowing if I moved, he would move.

He shrugged, a calculated motion that pulled my eyes to a flash of amber skin beneath his robe. "They were getting too close to solving the elven riddle," he said, watching my reaction.

I kept my face impassive as he said Trent's most precious secret, telling him I, too, knew. Apparently it was the right thing to do.

"I'm not going to let you two pick up where they left off," he added, prodding.

I said nothing, stomach roiling. Piscary had killed them. Trent's father and my dad had been friends. They had been working together. They had been working together against Piscary.

Piscary went very still. "Has he sent you into the ever-after yet?"

My gaze shot to his, fear in my gut. There it was. The question he wanted answered, the one he hid among others so I wouldn't know. As soon as I answered it, I'd be dead.

"I'm not in the habit of breaking my client confidentiality," I said, my mouth dry.

His cool dispassion cracked as he took a breath. It was subtle, but there it was. "He has. Did you find one?" he asked, catching himself before he could lean forward over the table. "Was it sound enough to read?"

One? Read what? I said nothing, desperately wanting to hide my pulse pounding in my neck, but though his eyes were black, he wasn't interested in my blood. That was almost too frightening to believe. I didn't know how to answer. Would yes save my life or damn it?

Frowning, he studied me a long moment while I listened to my heart pound and sweat broke out on my arms. "I can't interpret your silence," he said, seeming irritated.

I took a breath.

Piscary moved.

The adrenaline hurt. I pushed myself from the table in a blind panic. My chair tipped over backward, with me still in it.

Piscary flung the table out of the way. It crashed aside, my untouched coffee making a fantastic pattern on the white carpet.

I scrabbled backward, my bare feet squeaking against the circle of tile. My fingers found the carpet and I clutched at it, rolling over and pulling myself forward.

A shriek escaped me as he yanked me up by my wrist. I clawed at him in panic. He took it all. Face dispassionate, he drew a fingernail across my right arm, follow the blue of a vein. Fire traced his nail as he opened my skin, then bliss. Silently, savagely, I fought to get free as he held me by my wrist, unmoving as a tree. My blood welled and I felt the bubble of insanity swell in me. *Not again. I couldn't be ravaged by a vampire again!*

He looked at my blood, then my eyes. Taking his free hand, he swiped it across my arm.

"No!" I screamed.

He let go of my wrist, and I fell to the carpet. Breath a harsh pant, I scrabbled backward. I found my feet, adrenaline pounding through me as I headed for the elevator.

Piscary jerked me back.

"You son of a bitch!" I screamed. "Leave me alone!"

He gave my head a smack to make me see stars.

I crumpled. Panting, I lay at his feet as he stood above me, an amulet in his hand. He smeared my blood across it, and it glowed red. His hand was enveloped in a red haze as he nudged my fallen chair farther onto the surrounding carpet. I pulled my head up, seeing past my hair that the pattern on the tiled floor before us made a perfect circle. The circle of blue tile around the white stone was one piece of marble. It was a summoning circle.

"God help me," I whispered, knowing what was going to happen when Piscary tossed the amulet to land dead center of the circle. I watched the ball of ever-after energy expand to form a protective bubble. My skin hummed with the power from another witch, kindled to life with my blood as Piscary prepared to call his demon.

Twenty-Eight

Piscary brought his hand to his mouth to lick away my remaining blood, recoiling. "Holy water?" he said, his dispassionate face showing a glimmer of distaste. Taking his robe hem, he wiped my blood from him, leaving his palm showing only a mild redness. "You need more than that to do more than annoy me. And don't flatter yourself. I wasn't going to bite you. I don't even like you, but you'd enjoy it. Instead, you will be dying slowly and in pain."

"Bring it on . . ." I panted, slumped at his feet as my eyes remembered how to focus.

He moved that hated eight feet away, staying between the elevator and me. Carefully pronounced Latin came from him. I recognized some of the words from Nick's summoning. My pulse quickened and I looked frantically over the plush, spacious white room for anything. I was too far underground to tap into a ley line. Algaliarept was coming. Piscary was going to give me to it.

I froze as Piscary said its name. The taste of burnt amber coated my tongue, and a haze of ever-after red melted into existence within the summoning circle. "Oh, look. A demon," I whispered, dragging myself to the fallen table and pulling myself up. "This just keeps getting better and better."

Swaying, I watched as it swelled to grow into a six-foot-high figure. The ever-after red soaked inward, coalescing as an athletic, amber-skinned body dressed in a loincloth decorated with stones and colored ribbons. Algaliarept had bare muscular legs, an impossibly thin waist, and a magnificently sculptured chest that would make Schwarzenegger weep. And atop it was a jackal head, alive with pointing ears and a long savage muzzle.

My mouth dropped open and I looked from the vision of the Egyptian god of death to Piscary, seeing the vampire's features with new meaning. Piscary was Egyptian?

Piscary stiffened. "I told you not to appear before me like that," he said tightly.

The death mask grinned, fascinating in that it was alive and part of him. "I forgot," it drawled in an incredibly deep voice that seemed to set my insides resonating. A thin red tongue slipped past the jackal teeth to caress its muzzle. There was the clopping sound of teeth and lips.

My heart pounded, and as if hearing it, Algaliarept slowly turned to me. "Rachel Mariana Morgan," it said, its ears pricked. "You are the little gadabout."

"Shut up," Piscary said, and Algaliarept's eyes narrowed to slits. "What do you want for making her tell me what she knows about Kalamack's progress?"

"Six seconds with you outside your circle." The sheer desire to kill Piscary in its voice was like ice down my back.

Piscary shook his head, his cool compassion unshaken. "I'll give you her. I don't care what you do with her as long as she doesn't walk this side of the ley lines ever again. In return, you will make her tell me how far Trent Kalamack is in his research. Before you take her. Agreed?"

Not the ever-after. Not with Algaliarept.

Algaliarept's canine grin was pleased. "Rachel Mariana Morgan as payment? Mmmm, I agree." The Egyptian god clenched its hands and took a step forward, halting at the edge of the circle. Its jackal ears pricked and its doggy eyebrows rose.

"You can't do that!" I protested, heart pounding. I looked at Piscary. "You can't do that. I don't agree." I turned to Algaliarept. "He doesn't own my soul. He can't give it to you!"

The demon spared me a glance. "He has your body. Control the body, control the soul."

"That's not fair!" I shouted, ignored.

Piscary came close to the circle. He put his hands upon his hips, taking an aggressive stance. "You will," he intoned, "not attempt to kill or touch me in any fashion. And when I say, you will leave and return directly to the ever-after."

"Agreed," the jackal head said. A drop of saliva fell from a fang, hissing as it flowed down the ever-after between them.

Never dropping the demon's gaze, Piscary rubbed his big toe over the circle to break it.

Algaliarept lunged out of the circle.

Gasping, I backpedaled. A powerful hand reached out and grasped my throat.

"Stop!" Piscary shouted.

My breath choked and I pried at the golden fingers. It had three rings with blue stones, all pinching my skin. I swung to kick it, and Algaliarept shifted me higher to avoid my strike. A wet sound escaped me.

"Drop her!" Piscary demanded. "You can't have her until I get what I want!"

"I'll get your information some other way," the jackal said, the rumble of its words joining the rushing sound of my blood. My head felt as if it was going to explode.

"I called you to get information from *her*," Piscary said. "If you kill her now, you violate your summoning. I want it now, not next week or next year."

The fingers around my throat dissolved. I dropped to the carpet, gasping. Its sandals were made of leather and thick ribbons. Slowly I pulled my head up, feeling my throat.

"A reprieve only, Rachel Mariana Morgan," the jackal head said, its tongue moving in fantastic patterns as it spoke. "You will be warming my bed tonight."

I knelt before it, sucking in air as I tried not to figure out how I could be warming its bed if I was dead. "You know," I wheezed, "I'm really getting tired of this." Heart pounding, I got to my feet. It had agreed to a task. It was susceptible to being summoned again. "Algaliarept," I said clearly. "I call you, you dog-faced, murdering son of a bitch."

Piscary's face went slack in surprise, and I swear Algaliarept winked at me. "Oh, let me be the one in leather?" the jackal head said. "Be afraid of him. I like being him."

"Sure, whatever," I said, knees shaking.

Black leather driving gloves slid into existence over the amber-skinned hands, and the jackal-headed Egyptian god's stance melted from a ramrod stiffness into a confidant slouch. Kisten took shape, wearing head-to-toe leather and thick-heeled black boots. There was a jingle of chain and a whiff of gasoline. "This is good," the demon said, showing a glint of fang as it slicked its blond hair back, its passing hand leaving it shower-wet and smelling of shampoo.

I thought it looked good, too. Unfortunately.

Exhaling slowly, the image of Kist bit its lower lip to make it redden, a tongue slipping out to leave it with a wet shine. A shudder went through me as I recalled how soft Kist's lips were. As if reading my mind, the demon sighed, strong fingers reaching down its leather pants to draw my eyes to it. A scratch melted into existence over its eye, mirroring Kist's new wound.

"Damn vamp pheromones," I whispered, pushing the memory of the elevator away.

"Not this time," Algaliarept said, smirking.

Piscary was staring in confusion. "I summoned you. You do what I say!"

The image of Kisten turned to Piscary, belligerently flipping him off. "And Rachel Mariana Morgan summoned me, too. The witch and I have a preexisting debt to settle. And if she has enough guile to win a circleless summoning from me, then I will hold to it."

Piscary's teeth ground together. He lunged at us.

I gasped, lurching back. There was a wrenching sensation, and I stared as Piscary slammed into a wall of ever-after, falling in a shocked tangle of arms and legs. I went cold as I realized Algaliarept had put us in a circle of its own construction.

The thick haze of red pulsed and hummed, pressing down against my skin though I was two feet away. As Piscary got to his feet and adjusted his robe, I extended a finger and touched the barrier. A sliver of ice shivered through me as the surface rippled. It was the strongest, thickest sheet of ever-after I'd ever witnessed. Feeling Algaliarept's eyes on me, I pulled my hand back and wiped it on my jeans.

"I didn't know you could do that," I said, and it chuckled. In hindsight it made sense. It was a demon. It existed in the ever-after. Of course it would know how.

"And I'm willing to teach you how to survive manipulating as much ever-after, too, Rachel Mariana Morgan," it said as if reading my mind. "For a price."

I shook my head.

"Later, perhaps?"

With a cry of frustrated rage, Piscary took a wire-weave chair and slammed it against the barrier. I jumped, my mouth going dry.

Algaliarept gave the incensed vampire a sideways glance as Piscary ripped the leg off the chair and tried to pierce the barrier like a sword. The demon took a belligerent stance at the edge of the circle, showing me its tight butt in leather pants. "Bugger off, old man," it mocked in Kist's fake accent, infuriating Piscary all the more. "The sun will be up soon. You'll have another chance at her in about three minutes."

My head came up. *Three minutes? Was the sun that close to rising?*

Furious, Piscary threw the bar, which skittered and rolled across the carpet. His eyes black pits, he began to make slow, sedate circles about us in anticipation.

But for the moment I was safe in Algaliarept's circle. *What's wrong with this picture?*

Forcing my arms down from the tight grip around myself, I glanced at Piscary's fake window, seeing the glint of sun on the highest buildings. Three minutes. I pushed my fingertips into my forehead. "If I ask you to kill Piscary, will you call us even?" I asked as I looked up.

It struck a sideways pose. "No. Even though killing Ptah Ammon Fineas Horton Madison Parker Piscary is on my to-do list, it is still a request and would cost you, not absolve your debt. Besides, if you send me after him, he will likely summon me again as you did and you'd be right back where you started. The only reason he can't summon me now is because we haven't agreed on anything and we're in summoning limbo, so to speak."

It grinned, and I looked away. Piscary stood and listened, clearly thinking.

"Can you get me out of here?" I asked, thinking of escape.

"Through a ley line, yes. But this time, it will cost you your soul." It licked its lips. "And then, you're mine."

Happy, happy choices. "Can you give me something to protect myself from him?" I pleaded, getting desperate.

"Just as expensive . . ." It tugged its gloves tighter to its fingers. "And you already have what you need. Tick-tock, Rachel Mariana Morgan. Anything that will save your life will require your soul."

Piscary was grinning, and my stomach turned as he came to a standstill eight feet away. My eyes darted to my bag with the vial Kist had given me. It was out of reach on the wrong side of the barrier. "What should I ask for?" I cried desperately.

"If I answer that, you won't have enough left to pay for it, love," it breathed, bending close and sending my curls drifting. I jerked back as I smelled Brimstone. "And you're a resourceful witch," it added. "Anyone who can ring the city's bells can survive a vampire. Even one as old as Ptah Ammon Fineas Horton Madison Parker Piscary."

"But I'm three stories down!" I protested. "I can't reach a ley line through that."

Leather creaked as it circled me, hands laced behind its back. "What *will* you do?"

I swore under my breath. Past our circle, Piscary waited. Even if I managed to escape, Piscary would walk. It wasn't as if I could ask Algaliarept to testify.

Eyes widening, I looked up. "Time?" I asked.

The vision of Kist looked at its wrist, and a watch twin to the one I had smashed with my meat tenderizer appeared about it. "One minute, thirty."

My face went cold. "What do you want for you to testify in an I.S. or FIB courtroom that Piscary is the witch serial killer?"

Algaliarept grinned. "I like the way you think, Rachel Mariana Morgan."

"How much?" I shouted, looking at the sun creeping down the side of the buildings.

"My price hasn't changed. I need a new familiar, and it's taking too long to get Nicholas Gregory Sparagmos's soul."

My soul. I couldn't do it, even if it would satisfy Algaliarept and ultimately save Nick from losing his soul and being pulled into the ever-after to be the demon's familiar. My face went slack and I stared at Algaliarept so intently that it blinked in surprise. I had an idea. It was foolish and risky, but maybe it was crazy enough to work.

"I'll voluntarily be your familiar," I whispered, not knowing if I could survive the energy it might pull through me or force me to hold for it. "I'll freely be your familiar, but I get to keep my soul." Maybe if I retained my soul, it couldn't pull me into the ever-after. I could stay on this side of the ley lines. It could use me only when the sun was down. Maybe. The question was, would Algaliarept take the time to think it through? "And I want you to testify before my end of the agreement becomes enforceable," I added in case I managed to survive.

"Voluntarily?" it said, its form blurring at the edges. Even Piscary looked shocked. "That's not how it works. No one has ever willingly been a familiar before. I don't know what that means."

"It means I'm your damn familiar!" I shouted, knowing that if it thought about it, it would realize it was only getting half of me. "You say yes now, or in thirty seconds either I or Piscary is going to be dead, and you will have nothing. Nothing! Do we have a deal or not?"

The vision of Kist leaned forward and I shirked away. It looked at its watch. "Voluntarily?" Its eyes were wide in wonder and avarice.

In a wash of panic, I nodded. I'd worry about it later. If I had a later.

"Done," it said, so quickly I thought for sure I'd made a mistake. Relief filled me, then reality hit with a soul-shaking slap. *God help me. I was going to be a demon's familiar.*

I jerked back as it reached for my wrist.

"We agreed," it said, snatching my arm with a vamp quickness.

I kicked it square in the stomach. It did nothing, rocking back with the transfer of momentum but otherwise unmoved. A gasp slipped from me as it scratched a line across my demon mark. Blood flowed. I jerked back, and making shushing noises, the demon bent its head over my wrist and blew on it.

I tried to pull away, but it was stronger than me. I was sick of the blood, of everything. It let me go and I fell back, sliding down the arch of its barrier, feeling my back tingle. Immediately I looked at my wrist. There were two lines where one had once been. The new one looked as old as the first. "It didn't hurt this time," I said, too strung-out to be shocked.

"It wouldn't have hurt the first time had you not tried to stitch it up. What you felt was the fiber burning away. I'm a demon, not a sadist."

"Algaliarept!" Piscary shouted as our agreement was sealed.

"Too late," the grinning demon said, and disappeared.

I fell backward as its barrier vanished from behind me, shrieking as Piscary lunged. Bracing myself against the floor, I brought my legs up into him, flipping him over me. I scrambled for my bag and the vial. My hand dove into my bag, and Piscary jerked me back.

"Witch," he hissed, gripping my shoulder. "I'll have what I want. And then you'll die."

"Go to hell, Piscary," I snarled, thumbing the vial open with a soft pop and throwing it into his face.

Crying out, Piscary violently pushed away from me. From the floor, I watched him lurch away, wiping at his face with frantic motions.

Heart in my throat, I waited for him to fall, waited for him to pass out. He did neither.

My gut tightened in fear as Piscary wiped his face, bringing his fingers to his nose. "Kisten," he said, his disgust melting into a weary disappointment. "Oh, Kisten. Not you?"

I swallowed hard. "It's harmless, isn't it."

He met my eyes. "You don't think I survived this long by telling my children what can really kill me, do you?"

I had nothing left. For three heartbeats I stared. His lips curved into an eager smile.

I jerked into motion. Piscary casually reached out and grabbed my ankle as I tried to rise. I fell, kicking out, managing to hit his face twice before he pulled me to him and immobilized me under his weight.

The scar on my neck gave a pulse, and fear surged through it, making a nauseating mix.

"No," Piscary said softly, pinning me to the carpet. "You will be in pain for this."

His fangs were bared. Saliva dripped from them.

I struggled for air, trying to get out from under him. He shifted, holding my left arm over my head. My right arm was free. Teeth gritted, I went for his eyes.

Piscary jerked back. With a vamp strength, he grasped my right arm and snapped it.

My scream echoed against the high ceilings. My back arched and I gasped for air.

Piscary's eyes flashed black. "Tell me if Kalamack has a viable sample," he demanded.

Lungs heaving, I tried to breathe. The wave of misery thrummed from my arm and echoed in my head. "Go to hell . . ." I rasped.

Still pinning me to the carpet, he squeezed my broken arm.

I writhed as agony sang through me. Every nerve ending pulsed into a burn. A guttural sound escaped me, pain and determination. I wouldn't tell him. I didn't even know the answer.

He leaned his weight onto my arm, and I screamed again so I wouldn't go insane. Fear made my skull hurt as Piscary's eyes flashed into hunger. His instinctive need had risen high, triggered by my struggles. The black of his eyes swelled. I heard my sounds of pain as if outside my head. Silver sparkles from shock started between me and Piscary's eyes, and my cries turned to relief. I was going to pass out. *Thank you, God.*

Piscary saw it, too. "No," he whispered, his tongue making a quick pass over his teeth to catch the saliva before it fell. "I'm better than that." He took his weight from my arm. A groan came from me as the agony dulled to a throb.

He leaned to put his face inches from mine, watching my pupils with a cool detachment as the sparkles disappeared and my focus returned. Under his impassivity was a growing excitement. If he hadn't already sated his hunger with Ivy, he wouldn't have been able to keep from draining me. He knew the instant my will returned, smiling in anticipation.

Taking a breath, I spit in his face, tears mixing with my saliva.

Piscary closed his eyes, his expression showing a tired irritation. He let go of my left wrist to wipe his face.

I swung the heel of my hand up to smash it into his nose.

He caught my wrist before it hit. Fangs glinting, he held my arm. My eyes traveled down the scratch he had cut in me to invoke the amulet. My heart gave a hard pound. A ribbon of blood trailed slowly to my elbow. A drop of red swelled, quivered, and fell to land upon my chest, warm and soft.

My breath was shaking. I stared, waiting. His tension rose, his muscles tightening as he lay atop me. His gaze was fixed to my wrist. Another drop fell, feeling heavy against me.

"No!" I shrieked as a carnal groan slipped from him.

"I see now," he said, his voice terrifyingly soft, harnessed need pulsing under it. "No wonder Algaliarept took so long finding out what frightens you." Pinning my arm to the floor, he leaned closer until our noses lay side by side. I couldn't move. I couldn't breathe. "You're afraid of desire," he whispered. "Tell me, little witch, what I want to know or I will slice you open, filling your veins with me, making you my plaything. But I will let you remember your freedom—mine forever."

"Go to hell. . . ." I said, terrified.

He eased back to see my face. It was hot where his robe had shifted and his skin touched mine. "I will start here," he said, pulling my dripping arm to where I could see it.

"No . . ." I protested. My voice was soft and frightened. I couldn't help it. I tried to bring my arm closer, but Piscary had it tight. He pulled my arm in a slow controlled motion as I fought to keep it unmoving. My broken arm sent surges of nausea through me as I tried to use it, pushing at him with the strength of a kitten.

"God no, God no!" I screamed, redoubling my struggles as he tilted his head and sent his tongue across my elbow, moaning as he cleaned it, his tongue moving slowly to where the blood flowed freely. If his saliva reached my veins, I would be his. Forever.

I wiggled. I thrashed. The warm wetness of his tongue was replaced with the cool sharpness of teeth, grazing but not piercing.

"Tell me," he whispered, tilting his head so he could see my eyes, "and I'll kill you now instead of in a hundred years."

Nausea bubbled up, mixing with the darkness of insanity. I bucked under him. The fingers of my broken arm found his ear. I tore at them, reaching for his eyes. I fought like an animal, instinct a hazy mist between me and madness.

Piscary's breath came in a harsh pant as my struggles and pain whipped him into a frenzy of restraint I'd seen in Ivy far too often. "Oh, the hell with it," he said, his flowing voice cutting through me. "I'm going to drain you. I can find out some other way. I may be dead, but I'm still a man."

"No!" I shrieked. But it was too late.

Piscary's lips pulled back. Forcing my bleeding arm to the floor, his head tilted to reach my neck. The haze of pain swelled into ecstasy as he ground his fingers into my broken arm. I screamed into his moan of anticipation.

A distant boom of sound struck through me, and the floor trembled. I spasmed, the warm rapture of my arm shocking into a breathless feeling of pain. The sound of men shouting filtered in through the haze of nausea.

"They won't reach us in time," Piscary murmured. "They're too late for you."

Not like this, I thought, out of my mind in fear and cursing the stupidity of it all. I didn't want to die like this. He bent to me, his face savage with hunger. I took a last breath.

It exploded from me as a green ball of ever-after smashed into Piscary.

I wiggled in the minuscule shifting of weight. Still on me, Piscary snarled and looked up.

My arm was free, and I wedged my knees between us. Tears blurred my vision as I fought with renewed desperation. Someone was there. Someone was there to help me.

Another blast of green smashed into Piscary. He rocked back. I got a leg under me and levered us up, flipping Piscary off me.

Scrabbling to my feet, I grabbed a chair and swung. It hit him, the shock echoing up my arm.

Piscary turned, his face savage. He tensed, gathering himself to leap at me.

I backpedaled, my broken arm clutched tight to me.

A third blast of green ever-after hissed past me, hitting Piscary and sending him flying backward into a wall.

I spun to the distant elevator.

Quen.

The man stood beside a huge hole in the wall beside the elevator in a cloud of dust, a growing ball of ever-after in his hand, still red but taking on the tinges of his aura. He must have had the energy stored in his chi, since we were too deep underground to reach a line. A black satchel sat beside his feet, several wooden swordlike stakes extending out from the open zipper. Beyond the hole was the stairway. "It's about time you got here," I panted, staggering.

"I got caught behind a train," he said, his hands moving in ley line magic. "Bringing the FIB into this was a mistake."

"I wouldn't have had to if your boss wasn't such a prick!" I shouted, then took a shallow breath, trying not to cough at the dust. Kisten had taken my note. How did the FIB get there if Quen didn't bring them?

Piscary had regained his feet. He took us in, showing his fangs in a wide smile. "And now elf blood? I haven't fed this well since the Turn."

With a vamp's speed, he raced across the large room to Quen, backhanding me in passing. I was flung backward. My back hit the wall and I slumped to the floor. Dazed and hovering on the edge of unconsciousness, I watched Quen evade Piscary, looking like a shadow in his black bodysuit. He had a wooden stake the length of my arm in one hand, a growing ball of ever-after in the other. The Latin spilled from him, the words of the black charm burning themselves into my mind.

The back of my head throbbed. Nausea flooded me as I touched a spot of agony, but I found no blood. The black spots before me cleared as I got to my feet. Dazed, I looked for my bag of charms through the haze of wall-dust.

A masculine cry of agony jerked my attention to Quen. My heart seemed to stop.

Piscary had caught him. Holding him like a lover, Piscary was fastened to his neck, supporting both their weights. Quen went slack and the wooden sword fell to the floor. His shriek of pain swelled into a moan of ecstasy.

Using the wall for support, I got to my feet. "Piscary!" I shouted, and he turned, his mouth red with Quen's blood.

"Wait your turn," he snarled, showing me his red-smeared teeth.

"I *was* here first," I said.

Angry, he dropped Quen. If he had been hungry, nothing would have moved him from downed prey. Quen's arm lifted weakly. He didn't get up. I knew why. It felt too good.

"You don't know when to leave well enough alone," Piscary said, coming at me.

Latin fell from me, burned into my mind from Quen's attack. My hands moved, etching black magic. My tongue swelled at the taste of tinfoil. I stretched for a ley line, not finding it.

Piscary slammed into me. I gasped, unable to breathe. He was on me again, reaching.

In the fear, something broke. A flood of ever-after flowed into me. I heard my scream at the shock of the unexpected influx of power. Gold laced with black and red burst from my hands. Piscary lifted from me. He crashed into a wall, shaking the lights.

I pulled myself up as he slumped on the floor, realizing where the energy had come from. "Nick!" I cried in fear. "Oh God. Nick! I'm sorry!"

I had pulled on a line through him. I had pulled the energy through him as if he had been a familiar. It had raced through him as it had me. I had pulled more than he could handle. *What had I done?*

Piscary was slumped where the wall met the floor. His foot shifted and he swung his head up. His eyes weren't focused, but they were black with hatred. I couldn't let him get up.

Racked in pain, I grabbed the leg of the chair Piscary had torn free and staggered across the room.

He lurched to his feet, supporting himself with a hand against the wall. His robe was almost undone. His eyes suddenly focused.

I gripped the metal rod in one hand like a bat, pulling it back even as I ran. "This is for trying to kill me," I said, swinging.

The bar of metal hit him behind the ear with a sodden smack. Piscary staggered, but didn't go down.

My breath came in an angry sound. "This is for raping Ivy!" I shouted, my anger at him for hurting something so strong and vulnerable giving me strength. I swung, grunting in effort.

The metal rod met the back of his skull with the sound of a melon.

I stumbled, catching my balance. Piscary fell to his knees. Blood seeped from his scalp.

"And this," I said, feeling my eyes grow hot and my vision blur from tears, "is for killing my dad," I whispered.

With a cry of anguish, I swung a third time. It smacked into Piscary's head. Spinning from the momentum, I fell to my knees. My hands stung and the rod slipped from my senseless grip. Piscary's eyes rolled up and he dropped.

Breath sounding like sobs, I looked at him and wiped the back of my hand across my cheek. He wasn't moving. I looked past my hair at the fake window. The sun was up, shining on the buildings. He would probably stay down until nightfall. Probably.

"Kill him," Quen croaked.

I pulled my head up, I'd forgotten he was there.

Quen had risen, a hand against his neck. The blood seeping through his fingers made an ugly pattern on the white carpet. He threw a second wooden sword at me. "Kill him now."

I caught it as if I had been catching swords my entire life. Trembling, I turned its point into the carpet and used it to get up. Shouts and calls were coming from the hole in the wall. The FIB had arrived. Late as usual. "I'm a runner," I said, my throat sore and my words rough. "I don't kill my marks. I bring them in alive."

"Then you're a fool."

I lurched to an overstuffed chair before I fell down. Dropping the sword, I put my head between my knees and stared at the carpet. "You kill him, then," I whispered, knowing he could hear me.

Quen moved unsteadily to his satchel by the ragged hole in the wall. "I can't. I'm not here."

The puff of air that escaped me hurt. I looked up as he crossed the room to me, his steps slow and careful. He took the sword from the floor, jamming it into in his duffle bag with a bloody hand. I thought I saw a gray square of explosive in there, too, telling me how he had blown a hole in the wall.

He looked tired, his lanky stature hunched in pain. His neck didn't look bad, but I'd rather be in traction for six months than have one saliva-laced bite from Piscary. Quen was an Inderlander and so couldn't be turned vampire, but by the look of fear edging his veneer of confidence, he knew he might be tied to Piscary. With a vampire that old, the bond might last a lifetime. Time would tell how much binding saliva, if any, Piscary had laced the bite with.

"Sa'han is wrong about you," he said wearily. "If you can't survive a vampire without help, your value is questionable. And your unpredictability makes you unreliable and therefore unsafe." Quen gave me a nod before he turned and headed for the stairway. I watched him go, my mouth hanging open.

Sa'han is wrong about me, I thought sarcastically. *Well goodie for Trent.*

My hands hurt, the palms red with what looked like first-degree burns. Edden's voice in the stairway was loud. The FIB could take care of Piscary. I could go home. . . .

Home to Ivy, I thought, closing my eyes briefly. *How did my life get this ugly?*

Tired beyond belief, I got to my feet as Edden and a string of FIB officers exploded out of the hole Quen had made.

"It's me!" I croaked, putting my good hand in the air since there was a frightening clatter of safeties going off. "Don't shoot me!"

"Morgan!" Edden peered through the sifting dust and lowered his weapon. Only half the FIB officers did the same. It was a better than average number. "You're alive?"

He sounded surprised. Bent in pain, I looked down at myself, my broken arm clutched close. "Yeah. I think so." I started shivering, cold.

Someone snickered, and the remaining weapons were lowered. Edden made a motion, and the officers fanned out. "Piscary is over there," I said, looking that way. "He's down until sunset. I think."

Coming closer, Edden eyed Piscary, his robe fallen open to show a good portion of muscular thigh. "What was he trying to do, seduce you?"

"No," I whispered, so my throat wouldn't hurt so much. "He was trying to kill me." I met his eyes and added, "There is a living vamp named Kisten around somewhere. He's blond and angry. Please don't shoot him. Other than him and Quen, I haven't seen anyone but the eight living vamps upstairs. You can shoot them if you want."

"Mr. Kalamack's security officer?" Edden's gaze roved over me, cataloging my hurts. "He came with you?" He put a hand on my shoulder to steady me. "It looks like your arm is broken."

"It is," I said, jerking back as he reached for it. *Why do people do that?* "And yeah, he came out here. Why didn't you?" Suddenly angry, I poked him in the chest. "You ever refuse to take my call again, and I swear I'll have Jenks pix you every night for a month."

Arrogance crossed Edden's face and he flicked a glance at the

FIB officers warily circling Piscary. Someone called for an I.S. ambulance. "I didn't refuse your call. I was asleep. Being woken up by a frantic pixy and a panicking boyfriend telling me you went out to stake one of Cincinnati's master vampires is not my favorite way to wake up. And who gave you my unlisted number?"

Oh God, Nick. The remembered burst of ley line energy I'd pulled through him made my face go cold. "Nick," I stammered. "I have to call Nick." But as I looked over the room for my bag and the phone in it, I hesitated. Quen's blood was gone. All of it. I guess Quen was serious about not wanting any evidence that he was here. How had he done that? *A little elven magic, perhaps?*

"Mr. Sparagmos is in the parking lot," Edden said. Peering at me and my cold face, he snagged a passing officer. "Get me a blanket. She's going shocky."

Numb, I let him help me across the room and the hole in the wall. "Poor guy passed out, he was so worried about you. I wouldn't let him or Jenks out of the car." Eyes alight in a sudden thought, he reached for the radio on his belt. "Tell Mr. Sparagmos and Jenks that we found her and she's all right," he said into it, getting a garbled answer back. Taking my elbow, he muttered, "Please tell me you didn't really leave a note on your door saying you were going to stake Piscary?"

My eyes were fixed upon my bag with its pain amulet clear across the room, but my head snapped up at his words. "No!" I protested as my vision swam at the quick movement. "I said I was going to talk to him and that he was the witch hunter. Kisten must have done that, because my note is here somewhere. I saw it!" *Kisten had replaced my note?*

I stumbled in confusion as Edden pulled me forward. Kisten had replaced my note, giving Nick the only number that would bring the FIB out here. Why? Had it been to help me, or simply to cover his betrayal of Piscary?

"Kisten?" Edden questioned. "That's the living vamp you don't want me to shoot, right?" He took the blue FIB blanket someone held out and draped it over my shoulders. "Come on. I want to get you upstairs. We can figure this out later."

Leaning heavily on him, I tugged the blanket closer, wincing as the rough wool hurt my hands. I wouldn't look at them, thinking they were nothing compared to the smut on my soul for having invoked that black charm Quen had taught me. I took a slow breath. *What did it matter if I knew black charms? I was going to be a demon's familiar.*

"My God, Morgan," Edden said as he put the two-way back on his belt. "Did you have to blow a hole in his wall?"

"I didn't," I said, focusing on the carpet three feet in front of me. "It was Quen."

More officers clattered down the stairs and into the room, a hoard of official presences suddenly making me feel like an alien. "Rachel, Quen isn't here."

"Yeah," I said, shivering violently as I looked over my shoulder at the pristine carpet. "I probably imagined it all." The adrenaline was gone, and fatigue and nausea pulled at me. People were moving quickly around us, making me dizzy. My arm was a solid ache. I wanted my bag and the pain amulet in it, but we were moving in the wrong direction, and it looked as if someone had dropped an evidence card by it. Swell.

My mood darkened even further when a woman in an FIB uniform stopped us short by dangling my gun in front of Edden. It was in an evidence bag, and I couldn't stop my hand from reaching out. "Hey, my splat gun," I said, and Edden sighed, not sounding at all happy.

"Tag it," he said, his voice laced with guilt. "Put Ms. Morgan as a positive ID."

The woman looked almost frightened as she nodded and turned away.

"Hey," I protested again, and Edden kept me from following her.

"Sorry, Rachel. It's evidence." He ran a quick look over the surrounding officers before whispering, "But thanks for leaving it where we could find it. Glenn couldn't have downed those living vamps without it."

"But . . ." I stammered, seeing the woman disappear upstairs with my splat gun. The dust was worse here, and I swallowed hard so I wouldn't cough and make myself pass out.

"Let's go," Edden said, sounding tired as he tried to pull me forward. "I hate to do this, but I should get a statement from you before Piscary wakes up and presses charges."

"Presses charges? For what?" I jerked out of his grip, refusing to move. What in hell was going on? I had just tagged the witch hunter, and I was the one being arrested?

The nearby officers were carefully listening, and Edden's round face went even more guilty. "For assault and battery, slander, trespassing, illegal entry, malicious destruction of private property, and whatever else his pre-Turn lawyer can come up with. What did you think you were doing, coming down here and trying to kill him?"

I struggled to speak, affronted. "I didn't kill him, though he by God deserves it. He raped Ivy to get me to come here so he could kill me because I found out he was the witch hunter!" I reached up with my good hand as if it could sooth the raw ache of my throat from the outside. "And I have a witness willing to testify that Piscary contracted it to kill the victims. Is that enough for you?"

Edden's brow rose. "It?" He turned to look at Piscary, surrounded by nervous FIB officers until the I.S. ambulance got there. "Which *it* would that be?"

"You don't want to know." I closed my eyes. I was going to be a demon's familiar. But I was alive. I hadn't lost my soul. Focus on the positive.

"Can I go?" I asked as I saw the first of the stairs past the hole in the wall. I had no idea how I was going to make it up all of them. Maybe if I let Edden arrest me, they would carry me up. Not waiting for his permission, I pulled away and held my arm close as I limped to the ragged hole in the wall. I had just tagged Cincinnati's most powerful vampire as a serial murderer, and all I wanted to do was throw up.

Edden took a step to catch up, still not having answered me. "Can I at least have my boots?" I asked as I saw Gwen taking pictures of them, carefully making her way through the room, her video camera recording everything.

The FIB captain started, looking down at my feet. "You always tag master vampires in your bare feet?"

"Only when they're in their pj's." I clutched the blanket around myself miserably. "Want to keep it sporting, you know."

Edden's round face broke into a grin. "Hey, Gwen! Knock it off," he said loudly as he took my elbow and helped me wobble to the stairs. "This isn't a crime scene. It's an arrest."

Twenty-Nine

"**H**ey! Here!" I shouted, sitting straighter on the hard ballpark seat and waving to get the attention of the wandering vendor. It was almost a good forty minutes before the game was scheduled to start, and though the stands were starting to fill, the vendors weren't very attentive.

I squinted and held up four fingers as he turned, and he held up eight in return. I winced. *Eight bucks for four hot dogs?* I thought, passing my money down. Oh well. It wasn't as if I had bought the tickets.

"Thanks, Rachel," Glenn said from beside me as the paper-wrapped package hit his hand, thrown by the vendor. He set it on his lap and caught the rest since my arm was in a sling and obviously not working. He handed one to his dad and Jenks on his left. The next he gave to me, and I passed it to Nick on my other side. Nick flashed me a thin smile, immediately looking down to where the Howlers were warming up.

My shoulders slumped, and Glenn leaned closer under the excuse of unwrapping my hot dog and handing it to me. "Give him some time."

I said nothing, my gaze riveted to the highly manicured ballpark. Though Nick wouldn't admit it, a new ribbon of fear had slid between us. We'd had a painful discussion last week where I had apologized profusely for having pulled such a massive amount of ley line energy through him and told him it had been an accident. He insisted that it was all right, that he understood, that he was glad I had done it since it saved my life. His words were earnest and heartfelt, and I knew to the depths of my soul he believed them. But he would only rarely meet my eyes anymore, and he worked hard to keep from touching me.

As if to prove nothing had changed, he had insisted on our usual weekend sleepover last night. It had been a mistake. The dinner conversation was stilted at best: *How was your day, dear? Fine, thank you; how was yours?* We followed that with several hours of TV where I sat on the couch and he sat on the chair across the room. I had hoped for some improvement after retiring at an ungodly early one o'clock in the morning, but he pretended to fall asleep right away, setting me almost to tears when he moved away from the touch of my foot.

The night was brilliantly capped off at four in the morning when he woke from a sound sleep in a nightmare. He all but panicked when he found me in bed with him.

I had quietly excused myself and took the bus home, saying that as long as I was up, I should make sure Ivy got home all right and that I'd see him later. He hadn't stopped me. He sat on the edge of his bed with his head in his hands and hadn't stopped me.

I squinted into the bright afternoon sun, sniffing back any hint of tears. It was the sun. That's all. I took a bite of hot dog. It seemed to take a lot of effort to chew, and it sat heavy in my middle when I finally swallowed. Below, the Howlers called and threw the ball about.

Setting the hot dog down on the paper wrapping across my lap, I took up a baseball in my injured hand. My lips moved in unvoiced Latin as I quietly sketched a complex figure with my good left hand. The fingers about the ball tingled as I said the last word of the charm. A melancholy satisfaction stirred me as the pitcher's throw went wild. The catcher stood to reach it, hesitating in question before he returned to his crouch.

Jenks rubbed his wings together to get my attention, giving me a merry thumbs-up for the bit of ley line magic. I returned his grin with a weak smile. The pixy was sitting on Captain Edden's shoulder so he could see better. The two had mended their fences over a conversation about country western singers and a night out at a karaoke bar. I didn't want to know. Really.

Edden followed Jenks's attention to me, his eyes behind his round-framed glasses suddenly suspicious. Jenks distracted him by loudly extolling the features of a trio of women headed up the concrete steps. The squat man's face reddened but the smile remained.

Grateful, I turned to Glenn, finding he had already finished his hot dog. I should have gotten him two. "How's Piscary's court case shaping up?" I asked.

The tall man shifted in his seat with a bound excitement as he wiped his fingers off on his jeans. Out of his suit and tie, he looked like another person, the sweatshirt emblazoned with the Howlers' logo making him appear comfortable and safe. "With your demon's testimony, I think it's reasonably secure," he said. "I've been waiting for a surge in violent crimes, but they've dropped." He glanced at his dad. "I'm thinking the lesser houses are waiting until Piscary is officially incarcerated before they start vying for his territory."

"They won't." My fingers and words sent another ball clean out of the park with a boost of ever-after energy. It was harder to gather the power from the nearby line. The park's safeguards were kicking in. "Kisten is handling Piscary's affairs," I said sourly. "It's business as usual."

"Kisten?" He leaned closer. "He's not a master vamp. Won't that cause problems?"

Nodding, I sent a pop fly to bounce wrong. The players became slow with tension as it hit the wall and rolled in an odd direction. Glenn had no idea how much trouble it was going to be. Ivy was Piscary's scion. By unwritten vamp law, she was in charge whether she wanted to be or not. It put the retired I.S. runner in a huge moral dilemma, caught between her vampire responsibilities and her need to be true to herself. She was ignoring Piscary's summons to his jail cell, along with a lot of other things that were quietly building.

Hiding behind the excuse that everyone thought Kist was still Piscary's scion, she did nothing, claiming that Kisten had the clout, if not the physical presence, to hold everything together. It didn't look good, but I wasn't about to advise her to start handling Piscary's affairs. Not only had she devoted her life to bringing in those who broke the law, but she'd snap while trying to best the pull of blood and domination such a position would magnify.

Seeing no more comments forthcoming, Glenn crumbled his paper and dropped it into a coat pocket. "So, Rachel," he said, glancing at the empty seat beside Nick. "How is your roommate? Better?"

I took another bite. "She's handling it," I said around my full mouth. "She would have come today but the sun really bothers her—lately."

Lots of things bothered her since having glutted herself on Piscary's blood: the sun, too much noise, not enough noise, the lack of speed of her computer, the pulp in her orange juice, the fish in her bathtub until Jenks took it out back and had a fish fry to boost his kids' protein levels before fall hibernation. She had been violently ill after returning from midnight church services this morning, but she wouldn't stop going. She told me it would help keep space between her and Piscary. Mental space, apparently. Time and distance were enough to break the bond a lesser vamp could put on another with a bite, but Piscary was a master vampire. The bond would last until Piscary wanted it ended.

Slowly Ivy and I were finding a new balance. When the sun was high and bright, she was Ivy, my friend and partner, cheerful with her dry, sarcastic humor as we thought up practical jokes to play on Jenks or discussed possible improvements to the church to make it more livable. After sunset, she left so I wouldn't see what the night did to her now. She was strong in the sunlight, a cruel goddess after sunset, balanced on the edge of helplessness in the battle she fought against herself.

Uncomfortable with my thoughts, I pulled on the ley line and sent a pitched ball wild, to smack into the wall behind the catcher.

"Rachel?" Captain Edden said, his eyes behind his glasses taking on a hard look as he leaned past his son to see me. "Let me know if she wants to talk to Piscary. I'd be glad to look the other way if she wants to smack him around."

He eased back as I gave him a wan smile. Piscary had been extradited to I.S. custody, safe and sound in a vamp jail cell. The preliminary hearing had gone well, the sensationalism of the situation prompting an unexpected opening in the court docket. Algaliarept showed up to prove he was a reliable witness. The demon made all the papers, morphing into all sorts of figures to scare the pants off everyone in the courtroom. What disturbed me most was that the judge was afraid of a little towheaded girl with a lisp and a limp. I think the demon enjoyed it.

I adjusted my red Howlers' hat against the sun as a batter came to the mound to pop a few into the infield. Hot dog in my lap, I shifted my fingers and mouthed the incantation. The park's safeguards had risen higher, and I had to punch a hole through them to reach the line. A sudden influx of ever-after coursed through me, and Nick stiffened. Excusing himself, he slid past me, muttering about the bathroom. His lanky form hastened down the steps and vanished.

Unhappy, I sent the ever-after energy into the pitcher's throw. There was a sharp crack as the bat broke. The batter dropped the shattered ash, swearing loud enough that I could hear him. He turned to look at the stands in accusation. The pitcher put his mitt on his hip. The catcher stood. My eyes narrowed in satisfaction as the coach whistled, pulling everyone in.

"Nice one, Rache," Jenks said, and Captain Edden started, giving me a questioning look.

"That you?" he asked, and I shrugged. "You're going to get yourself banned."

"Maybe they should have paid me." I was being careful. No one was getting hurt. I could make their runners twist their ankles and the wild throws hit players if I wanted. I wasn't. I was just messing with their warm-up. I poked about in the napkin the hot dog had been wrapped in. *Where was my ketchup packet? This hot dog was utterly tasteless.*

The FIB captain moved uneasily. "Ah, about your compensation, Morgan . . ."

"Forget it," I offered quickly. "I figure I still owe you for paying off my I.S. contract."

"No," he said. "We had an agreement. It's not your fault the class was canceled—"

"Glenn, can I have your ketchup?" I said brusquely, cutting Edden off. "I don't know how you people can eat hot dogs without it. Why the Turn didn't that guy give me any ketchup?"

Edden leaned back, a heavy sigh slipping from him. Glenn obediently shuffled about his wad of paper until he came up with a white plastic packet. Face drawn, he looked at my broken arm and hesitated. "I'll—uh—open it for you," he offered.

"Thanks," I muttered, not liking being helpless. Trying not to scowl, I watched the detective carefully tear open the packet. He handed it to me, and with the hot dog balanced on my lap, I awkwardly squeezed the ketchup out. So intent was I on getting it on the right spot, I almost missed Glenn raising his hand and surreptitiously licking a red smear off his fingers.

Glenn? I thought. My face went slack as I remembered our missing ketchup and the pieces fell into place. "You . . ." I sputtered. *Glenn had stolen our ketchup?*

The man's face went panicked, and he reached out, almost covering my mouth before he drew back. "No," he pleaded, leaning close. "Don't say anything."

"You took our ketchup!" I breathed, shocked. Beyond Glenn I

could see Jenks rocking in mirth on Edden's shoulder, able to hear our whispers and keep up a running conversation to distract the FIB captain at the same time.

Glenn shot a guilty look at his dad. "I'll pay you for it," he begged. "Anything you want. Just don't tell my dad. Oh God, Rachel. It would kill him."

For a moment I could only stare. *He had taken our ketchup. Right off our table.* "I want your handcuffs," I said suddenly. "I can't find anything real without fake purple fur glued to it."

His panicked look eased and he shifted back. "Monday."

"Soon enough for me." My words were calm, but inside I was singing. *I was going to get my cuffs back!* It was going to be a good day.

He darted a guilty look toward his dad. "Will you—get me a bottle of spicy?"

My eyes jerked to his.

"Maybe some barbecue sauce?"

I closed my mouth before a bug flew into it. "Sure." I did not believe this. I was pimping ketchup to the son of the FIB's captain.

I looked up to see a park official wearing a red polyester vest loping up the stairs toward us, scanning the faces. A smile curved over me as he met my eyes. He worked his way down the relatively empty aisle in front of us as I wrapped up what was left of my hot dog and set it on Nick's seat, then dropped the baseball into my bag out of sight. It had been fun while it lasted. I wasn't going to interfere with the game, but they didn't know that.

Jenks flitted from Captain Edden to me. He was wearing all red and white in honor of the team, the brightness hurting my eyes. "Oooooh," he mocked. "You're in trouble now." Edden gave me one last warning look before putting his attention on the field, clearly trying to divorce himself from me lest they kick him out, too.

"Ms. Rachel Morgan?" the young man in the red vest questioned as he reached us.

I stood with my bag. "Yes."

"I'm Matt Ingle. Park ley line security? Could you come with me, please?"

Glenn got to his feet, standing with his feet spread wide and his hands on his hips. "Is there a problem?" he asked, turning the angry-young-black-man mien on high. I was too thrown by him liking ketchup to get angry at him wanting to protect me.

Matt shook his head, not cowed at all. "No sir. The Howlers' owner heard about Ms. Morgan's efforts to retrieve their mascot and would like to speak with her."

"I'd be happy to talk to her," I said as Jenks chortled, his wings turning a bright red. Despite Captain Edden keeping my name out of the paper, the entirety of Cincinnati and the Hollows knew who had solved the witch hunter murders, made the tag, and summoned the demon into the courtroom. My phone was ringing off the hook with requests for help. Overnight, I had gone from struggling entrepreneur to bad-ass runner. What did I have to fear from the owner of the Howlers?

"I'm coming with you," Glenn said.

"I can handle this," I said, mildly affronted.

"I know, but I want to talk to you, and I think they're going to kick you out of the park."

Edden chuckled, shifting his squat bulk deeper into the hard seat. Taking a key chain from his front pocket, he handed it to Glenn.

"You think?" I said, waving 'bye to Jenks and telling him with a finger motion and a nod that I'd see him back at the church. The pixy nodded, settling himself back on Captain Edden's shoulder, hooting and hollering, having too much fun to leave.

Glenn and I followed the ley line security guy to a waiting golf cart, and he drove us deeper into the stadium. It grew cool and quiet, the thrum of the unseen thousands around us a low, almost subliminal thunder. Far into the authorized personnel areas and amid black suits and champagne, Matt stopped the cart. Glenn helped me out, and I took my cap off, handing it to him as I fluffed my hair. I was dressed nice in jeans and white sweater, but everyone I'd seen in the last two minutes was wearing a tie or diamond earrings. Some had both.

Matt looked nervous as he took us up an elevator and left us in a long plush room that overlooked the field. It was comfortably full of talk and nicely dressed people. The faint smell of musk tickled my nose. Glenn tried to give me my hat back, and I motioned for him to keep it.

"Ms. Morgan," a small woman said, excusing herself from a group of men. "I am so glad to meet you. I'm Mrs. Sarong," she said as she approached, her hands extended.

She was shorter than me, and clearly a Were. Her dark hair was graying in wispy streaks that looked good on her, and her hands were small and powerful. She moved with a predatory grace that drew attention, her eyes seeing everything. Were men had to work hard to hide their rough edges. Were women got more dangerous-looking.

"I'm pleased to meet you," I said as she briefly touched my shoulder in greeting since my right arm was in a sling. "This is Detective Glenn, of the FIB."

"Ma'am," he said shortly, and the small woman smiled to show flat, even teeth.

"Delighted," she said pleasantly. "If you would excuse us, Detective? Ms. Morgan and I have a need to chat before the game begins."

Glenn bobbed his head. "Yes ma'am. I'll get you both a drink if I might."

"That would be lovely."

I rolled my eyes at the political niceties, relieved when Mrs. Sarong put a light hand on my shoulder and led me away. She smelled like ferns and moss. Every man watched us as we moved together to stand by a window with an excellent view of the field. It was a long way down, making me slightly queasy.

"Ms. Morgan," she said, her eyes not at all apologetic, "it has just come to my attention that you were contracted to retrieve our mascot. A mascot that was never missing."

"Yes ma'am," I said, surprised how the title of respect just seemed to flow out of me. "When I was told, my time and energies were given no consideration."

She exhaled slowly. "I detest digging out prey. Have you been magicking the field?"

Pleased at her frankness, I decided to be the same. "I spent three days planning how to break into Mr. Ray's office when I could have been working on other cases," I said. "And while I admit that isn't your fault, someone should have called me."

"Perhaps, but it remains that the fish was not missing. I am not in the habit of paying out blackmail. You will stop."

"And I'm not in the habit of offering it," I said, having no trouble keeping my temper as her pack surrounded me. "But I'd be remiss if I didn't make you aware of my feelings in the matter. I give my word I won't interfere with the game. I don't need to. Until I get paid, every time a ball goes foul or a bat cracks, your players will wonder if it's me." I smiled without showing my teeth. "Five hundred dollars is a small price for your players' peace of mind." *Lousy five hundred dollars. It should have been ten-times that. Why Ray's henchmen wasted bullets on me for a lousy stinking fish was still beyond me.*

Her lips parted and I swear I heard a small growl in her sigh. Athletes were notorious for being superstitious. She'd pay.

"It's not the money, Mrs. Sarong," I said, though at first it had been. "But if I let one pack treat me like a cur, then that's what I'll be. And I'm not a cur."

She brought her gaze up from the field. "Not a cur," she agreed. "You are a lone wolf." With a graceful motion, she motioned to a nearby Were, one that looked oddly familiar, in fact. He hastened forward with a leather-bound checkbook the size of a Bible, which took two hands to handle. "It's the lone wolf that is the most dangerous," she said as she wrote. "They also have extremely short life spans. Get yourself a pack, Ms. Morgan."

The rip of the check was loud. I wasn't sure if she was giving me advice or a threat. "Thank you, I have one," I said, not looking at the amount as I tucked it in my bag. The smooth shape of the baseball touched my knuckles and I pulled it out. I set it into her waiting hand. "I'll leave before the game starts," I said, knowing there was no way they would let me back in the stands. "How long am I banned for?"

"Life," she said, smiling like the devil herself. "I, too, am not a cur."

I smiled back, genuinely liking the older woman. Glenn drifted closer. I took the champagne he handed me and set it on the windowsill. "Good-bye, Mrs. Sarong."

She inclined her head as way of dismissal, the second flute of champagne Glenn had brought resting easy in her grip. Three young men lurked behind her, sulky and well-groomed. I was glad I didn't have her job, though it looked as if the perks were great.

Glenn's shoes sounded loud on the concrete as we made our way back to the front gate without the help of Matt and his golf cart. "You'll tell everyone good-bye for me?" I asked, meaning Nick.

"Sure." His eyes were on the huge signs with their letters and arrows pointing to the exits. The sun was warm when we found it, and I relaxed as I went to stand at the bus stop. Glenn came to a halt beside me and handed me my hat. "About your fee—" he started.

"Glenn," I said as I put it on, "like I told your dad, don't worry about it. I'm grateful for them paying off my I.S. contract, and with the two thousand Trent gave me, I've enough to see me through until my arm heals."

"Would you shut up?" he said, digging in his pocket. "We worked something out."

I turned, my gaze dropping to the key in his hands and then rising to his eyes.

"We couldn't get approval to reimburse you for the canceled class, but there was this car in impound. The insurance agency salvaged the title, so we couldn't put it up for auction."

A car? Edden was going to give me a car?

Glenn's brown eyes were bright. "We got the clutch and the transmission repaired. There was something wrong with the electrical system, too, but the FIB garage guys fixed it, no charge. We would have gotten it to you sooner," he said, "but the DMV office didn't understand what I was trying to do so it took three trips down there to get it transferred to your name."

"You guys bought me a car?" I said, excitement bubbling up into my voice.

Glenn grinned and handed me a zebra-striped key on a purple rabbit's foot key chain. "The money the FIB put into it just about equals what we owed you. I'll drive you home. It's a stick, and I don't think you can handle shifting gears yet with your arm."

Heart suddenly pounding, I fell into step beside him, scanning the lot. "Which one?"

Glenn pointed, and the sound of my heels on the pavement faltered as I saw the red convertible, recognizing it. "That's Francis's car," I said, not sure what I was feeling.

"That's okay, isn't it?" Glenn asked, suddenly concerned. "It was going to be scrapped. You aren't superstitious, are you?"

"Um . . ." I stammered, drawn forward by the shiny red paint. I touched it, feeling the clean smoothness. The top was down, and I turned, smiling. Glenn's worried frown eased into relief. "Thank you," I whispered, not believing it was really mine. *It was mine?*

Steps light, I walked to the front, then the back. It had a new vanity plate: RUNNIN'. It was perfect. "It's mine?" I said, heart racing.

"Go on, get in," Glenn said, his face transformed by his pleased enthusiasm.

"It's wonderful," I said, refusing to cry. *No more expired bus passes. No more standing in the cold. No more disguise charms just so they would pick me up.*

I opened the door. The leather seat was warm from the afternoon sun and as smooth as chocolate milk. The cheerful dinging of the door being opened was heaven. I put in the key, checked that it was in neutral, pushed in the clutch, and started it up. The thrum of the engine was freedom itself. I shut the door and beamed at Glenn. "Really?" I asked, voice cracking.

He nodded, beaming.

I was delighted. With my broken arm, I couldn't safely manage the gearshift, but I could try all the buttons. I turned on the radio, thinking it must be an omen when Madonna thundered out. I turned "Material Girl" down and opened the glove box just to see my name on the registration. A thick yellow business-size envelope slid out, and I picked it up off the floor.

"I didn't put that there," Glenn said, his voice carrying a new concern.

I brought it to my nose, my face going slack as I recognized the clean scent of pine. "It's from Trent."

Glenn straightened. "Get out of the car," he said in a hard staccato, every syllable laced with authority.

"Don't be stupid," I said. "If he wanted me dead, he wouldn't have had Quen bail me out."

Jaw tight, Glenn opened the door. My car started chiming. "Get out. I'll have it looked at and bring it over tomorrow."

"Glenn . . ." I cajoled as I opened the envelope and my protests wavered. "Um," I stammered. "He's not trying to kill me, he's paying me."

Glenn leaned to see, and I tilted the envelope to him. A muttered oath came from him. "How much is that, you think?" he asked as I closed it and shoved it in my bag.

"I'm guessing eighteen thousand." I tried to be cavalier, ruining it with my trembling fingers. "It was what he offered me to clear his name." Brushing the hair from my eyes, I looked up. My breath caught. Visible in the rearview mirror was Trent's Gray Ghost limo sitting in the fire lane. It hadn't been there a moment ago. At least, I hadn't seen it. Trent and Jonathan were standing beside it. Glenn saw where my attention was and turned.

"Oh," he said, then a concerned wariness tightened the corners of his eyes. "Rachel, I'm going to go over to the ticket booth right over there . . ." He pointed. ". . . and talk to the lady about possibly buying a block of seats for the FIB's company picnic next year." He hesitated, shutting my door with a solid thump. His dark fingers stood out against the bright red paint. "You going to be all right?"

"Yeah." I pulled my eyes from Trent. "Thanks, Glenn. If he kills me, tell your dad I loved the car."

A trace of a smile crossed him, and he turned away.

My eyes were fixed to my rearview mirror as his steps grew faint. Behind me came a roar of fans as the game began. I watched Trent have an intent conversation with Jonathan. He left the angry tall man and ambled slowly to me. His hands were in his pockets and he looked good. Better than good, really, dressed in casual slacks, comfortable shoes, and a cable-knit sweater against the slight chill in the air. The collar of a silk shirt the color of midnight showed behind it, contrasting wonderfully with his tan. A tweed cap shaded his green eyes and kept his fine hair under control.

He came to a slow halt beside me, his eyes never leaving mine to touch upon the car even once. Feet scuffing, he half turned to look at Jonathan. It stuck in my craw that I had helped clear his name. He had murdered at least two people in less than six months—one of them Francis. And here I was, sitting in the dead witch's car.

I said nothing, gripping the wheel with my one good hand, my broken arm sitting in my lap, reminding myself that Trent was afraid of me. From the radio, a fast-talking announcer took over, and I turned the radio almost off. "I found the money," I said as way of greeting.

He squinted at me, then shifted to stand by the side mirror to put his face in shadow. "You're welcome."

I peered up at him. "I never said thank you."

"You're welcome anyway."

My lips pressed together. *Ass.*

Trent's eyes dropped to my arm. "How long until it heals?"

Surprised, I blinked. "Not long. It was a clean break." I touched the pain amulet about my neck. "There was some muscle damage, though, which is why I can't use it well yet, but they say I don't need any therapy. I'll be back on the streets in six weeks."

"Good. That's good."

It had been a quick comment—and it was followed by a long silence. I sat in my car, wondering what he wanted. There was a jittery cast to him, his eyebrows a shade too high. He wasn't afraid, and he wasn't worried. I couldn't tell what he wanted. "Piscary said our fathers worked together," I said. "Was he lying?"

The sun glinted on Trent's white hair as he shook his head. "No."

A sliver of ice dropped down my spine. I licked my lips and brushed a spot of dust from the steering wheel. "Doing what?" I asked casually.

"Come work for me, and I'll tell you."

My eyes went to his. "You are a thief, a cheat, a murderer, and a not-nice-man," I said calmly. "I don't like you."

He shrugged, the motion making him look utterly harmless. "I'm not a thief," he said. "And I don't mind manipulating you into working for me when I need it." He smiled, showing me perfect teeth. "I enjoy it, actually."

I felt my face warm. "You are so full of yourself, Trent," I said, wishing I could shift the car into reverse and drive over his foot.

His smile widened.

"What?" I demanded.

"You called me by my first name. I like that."

I opened my mouth, then closed it. "So throw a party and invite the Pope. My dad may have worked for your dad, but you are scum, and the only reason I'm not throwing your money back in your face is a, I earned it, and b, I need something to live on while I recover from injuries gained from keeping your ass out of prison!"

His eyes were glinting in amusement, and it made me furious. "Thank you for clearing my name," he said. He went to touch my car, stopping as I made an ugly noise in warning. He turned the motion into seeing if Jonathan had moved. He hadn't. Glenn, too, was watching us.

"Just forget it, okay?" I said. "I went after Piscary to save my mom's life, not yours."

"Thank you anyway. If it means anything, I'm sorry now for putting you in that rat pit."

I tilted my head to see him, holding the hair out of my face as the wind gusted. "And you think that means anything to me?" I said tightly. Then I squinted. He was almost jiggling where he stood. What was up with him?

"Scoot over," he finally said, looking at the empty seat beside me.

I stared at him. "What?"

He looked past me to Jonathan and back. "I want to drive your car. Scoot over. Jon never lets me drive. He says it's beneath me." He looked over at Glenn skulking beside a pillar. "Unless you would rather have an FIB detective drive you home at the posted speed limit?"

Surprise kept the anger out of my voice. "You can drive a stick?"

"Better than you."

I looked at Glenn, then back to Trent. I slowly sank back into the seat. "Tell you what," I said, my eyebrows rising. "You can drive me home if we keep to one topic on the way."

"Your father?" he guessed, and I nodded. I was getting used to this deal-with-a-demon business.

Trent put his hands back in his pockets and rocked back and forth once on his heels in thought. Bringing his attention from the blue sky, he nodded.

"I do not believe I'm doing this," I muttered as I threw my bag in the back and awkwardly shifted over the gear stick to the other seat. Taking my red Howlers cap off, I wound my hair up into a bun and jammed the hat back on against the coming wind.

Glenn had started forward, slowing as I waved good-bye to him. Shaking his head as if in disbelief, he turned and went back inside the ballpark.

I buckled my belt as Trent opened the door and slid into the front. He adjusted the mirrors, then revved the engine twice before pushing in the clutch and shifting it into first. I braced myself against the dash, but he eased forward as smoothly as if he parked cars for a living.

While Jonathan hurriedly got into the limo, I snuck a glance at Trent. My eyes narrowed as he took it upon himself to fiddle with the radio while at a stoplight, not moving even when it turned green. I was ready to smack him for messing with my radio when he found a station playing Takata and turned it up. Peeved, I hit the set button.

The traffic signal changed from green to yellow, and he sent the car leaping through the intersection, slipping ahead of oncoming traffic amid squealing tires and horns. Teeth gritted, I swore if he wrecked my car before I had a chance to, I'd sue his ass.

"I won't work for you again," I said as he gave the irate drivers behind him a friendly wave and merged onto expressway traffic. My anger hesitated as I realized he had intentionally sat through the green light so that Jonathan would be forced to wait until it changed again.

I looked at Trent in disbelief. Seeing my understanding, he floored it. A shiver of excitement struck me as he shot me a quick smile, the wind pulling his short hair to hide the green of his eyes. "If that helps you sleep, Ms. Morgan, please, continue to believe so."

The wind tugged at me, and I closed my eyes against the sun, feeling the pavement hum all the way to my bones. Tomorrow I'd start thinking about how I was going to get out of my agreement with Algaliarept, remove the demon mark, get Nick unbound as my familiar, and live with a vampire who was trying to hide that she was practicing again. Right now I was riding shotgun to Cincinnati's most powerful bachelor with eighteen thousand six dollars and fifty-seven cents in my pocket. And no one was going to stop us from speeding.

Not a bad week's work, all things considered.